THE MYTHOLOGY CLASS

Where Philippine Legends Become Reality

A graphic novel by
ARNOLD ARRE

TUTTLE Publishing

Tokyo | Rutland, Vermont | Singapore

For my family, dearest friends,
and all of you who have supported
my work through the years.
And for Cynthia, my miracle.

"This is a book of wonder. Arnold Arre conjures up the kind of spell that needs nothing but the alchemy of words and images to create a story for an entire world to fit in. A classic that can be read and reread with growing delight."

– **ERWIN ROMULO**, Esquire Philippines Editor-in-Chief

"A modern Filipino literary classic. Arnold is a true inspiration to his fellow comic creators and fans."

– **LEINIL FRANCIS YU**, Marvel Comics Artist of "Avengers" and "Secret Invasion"

"It's been almost a decade since I last read 'The Mythology Class,' and upon rereading it I found myself once again laughing at Bob and Gio's antics, getting crushes on Lisa and Lane, feeling sorry for Gina, being kilig about Kubin and Nicole, and yes, even learning to love Misha and Rey. I always knew Arnold was amazing at crafting an epic tale that deserves its place among our legends, but I'd forgotten just how great he was at making characters you feel for, love, and actually miss.

I think it's high time for a sequel, Mr. Arre."

– **QUARK HENARES**, Director of "Rakenrol" and "Keka"

"I could not put down this book the first time I read it. Even though it was gift given me, it felt like a surprise, a real find. My very own treasure!

You have to read 'The Mythology Class" and discover that the supernatural stories which you heard as a kid and dreamt and wondered about are alive and kicking butt in Arnold Arre's storytelling."

– **BUDDY ZABALA**, Bassist of The Dawn and Eraserheads

"It's startling to realize how fully-formed a cartoonist Arnold Arre already was when he was doing 'The Mythology Class'. Though he has continued to refine his technique and storytelling skills since, the hallmarks of his work are already present: the ambitious scope, the humor and warmth of the characters, and the sheer imagination on display with his expressive line art. An inspiring work, filled to overflowing with ideas."

– Writer/Editor **RAMON DE VEYRA** ("Ang Nawawala")

"Arre's imagination and creativity soar to dizzying heights. More than a decade since its first publication, 'The Mythology Class' remains potent and exhilarating. Beyond the narrative, it is a valiant attempt to reconnect the modern Filipino with his or her ancient roots. These are our heroes and myths raging against the dying of the light—and, boy, what a battle to behold."

– **JERROLD TAROG**, Director of "Sana Dati" and "Senior Year"

“Noong nabasa ko ang ‘The Mythology Class’ ni Arnold Arre, nakita ko talaga ang kapangyarihan ng komiks, at ang kapangyarihan ng napakagandang kwento na naikwento sa napakagandang paraan.

Isa ito sa mga librong pinakamamahal ko, nakapagbigay inspirasyon; isang libro na maiisip mong napakaswerte mo at nabasa mo ito.

Hindi lang siya kasi kwentong pagkatapos mo mabasa, okay ka na; ito yung tipong mapapaisip ka, na ang sarap maging Pilipino, ang sarap maging tao, ang sarap makadama, ang sarap malaman na marami pa tayong makakalap at maipapamahagi sa sangkalawakan.”

– **MANIX ABRERA**,
Creator of “Kikomachine Komix,” and “12” & “14” silent comics

“‘The Mythology Class’ is better than any textbook I read in school about myths and demons. It’s like a college-level ‘Monster Squad.’ The fact that Arre can enlighten and entertain while both deconstructing and reinventing these fables is a magical talent. I need to see this series as a bunch of movies, STAT.”

– **MARIE JAMORA**,
Director of “Ang Nawawala”

“The tragedy of the Philippines is that more money is invested in politics than literature. Arnold Arre’s ‘The Mythology Class’ can and will shape a future generation more than any city ordinance can–if only more will encounter this book. What a stroke of luck! You have in your hands a re-print. Buy ten more and give it to random kids you see. Make this your mission and chalk it under ‘nation building.’”

– **GANG BADOY**,
Founder of Rock Ed Philippines

“Arnold Arre is one of the most imaginative storytellers today. You get a sense of his vast creativity in ‘The Mythology Class,’ his first graphic novel, one that captures the Filipino fascination of friends discovering the spirit world together that still rings true today. Arnold went on to write more graphic novels, make animated films (and win awards for both), and inspire people.

What makes his work so compelling is his knack for laying out the little dramas of real life amidst the most fantastic of settings. His work reminds us to be kind, to love and fight for what you hold dear, to forgive yourself and others, because we’re all human.

The reason ‘The Mythology Class’ still resonates today is because we all have friends, and no matter how old we are, we are still discovering that the world is a beautiful and mysterious place, and more than enkantos and tikbalangs and what-have-yous, it’s the time we spend with our barkada that makes life exciting.”

– **YVETTE TAN**, Author of “Waking the Dead” and “Kaba”

WHAT IS
THE MYTHOLOGY CLASS?

It's not just a thoroughly enchanting, uniquely Filipino graphic novel. This is what happens when an artist says, "To heck with what everyone says about what should or shouldn't be done, or how big or how small one can dream... I am doing my thing, my way." And well, somehow, he did it.

"The Mythology Class" was a work plainly done with no compromises, no limits and no details spared. Arnold is a storyteller who never dreams small. He dreams worlds first, then focuses inward to find the stories mingling in the crowds. That's how epic yet how personal this book is.

And this is a work that impresses from every angle. From the meticulous panels of hand-drawn art and hand-lettered dialogue, to pages crammed with detail, emotion and movement to full-page visions of whimsical fantasy, you can feel the creator's exuberance and energy as he tells his tale. A tale told so earnestly, so vividly and purely, I could practically feel the night wind in my face as we chased a fantastic beast of legend down a highway, or smell the stench of demon breath as beings of primal darkness reveled under a murky, rain-drenched sky.

In this book is a Manila fused with Old Magic, with as much wonder and discovery as there is danger and daring-do. So grab on tight and get ready for a ride.

So many years after it was first cast, the magic is still there and just as strong as ever.

MARCO DIMAANO
Quezon City, Octoaber 24, 2014

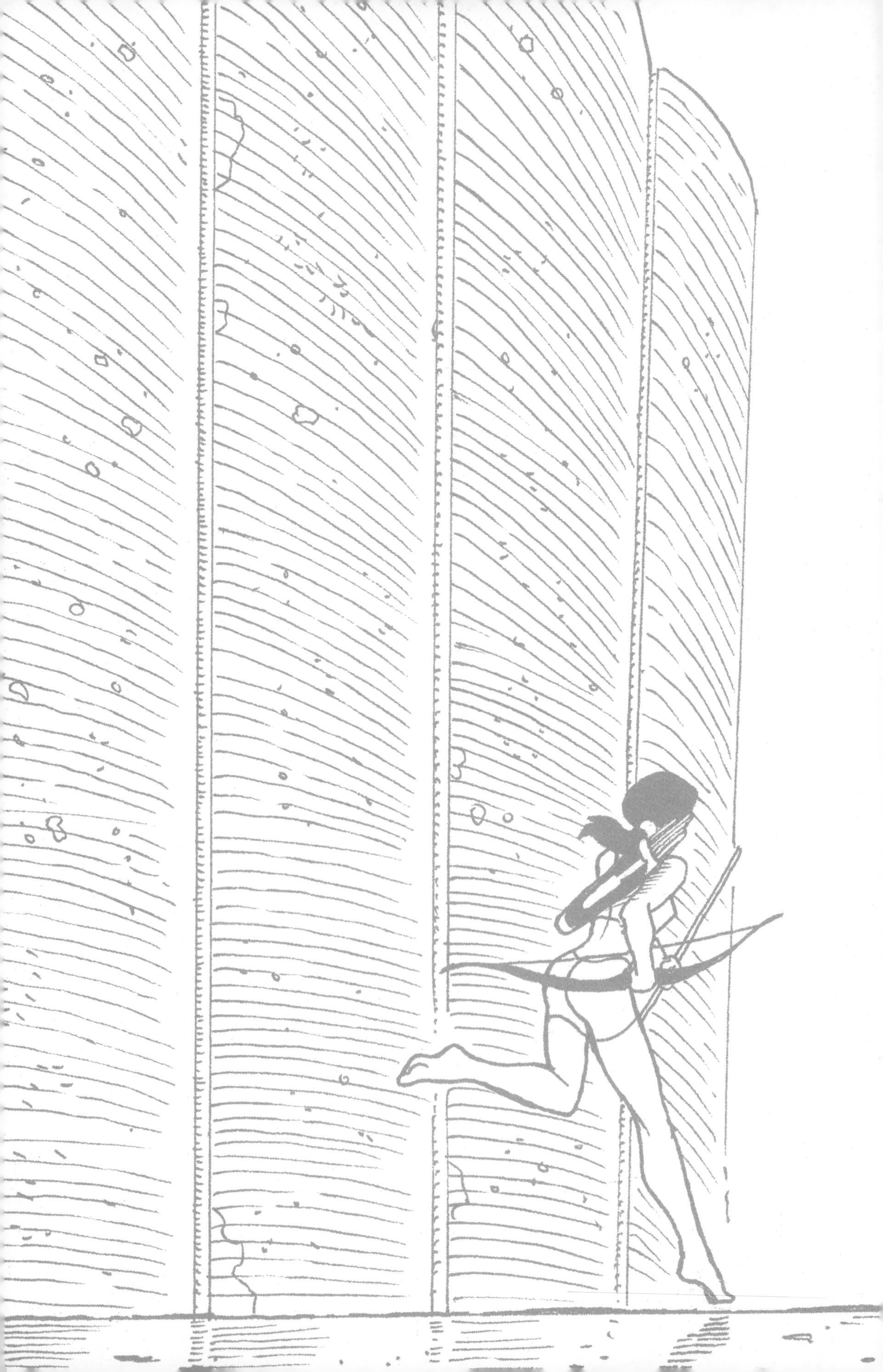

INTRODUCTION

I met Arnold Arre almost twenty years ago. He was either drawing or playing games of "what if"—coming up with scenarios in his head of different worlds, parallel universes, regular folks like you and me suddenly finding themselves on unusual paths.

I distinctly remember one night along J. Nakpil Street in Malate, Arnold was drawing caricatures for some cause or event—I forgot. What I did remember was that it cost P50.00 for one and my dearest friend Tricia told me, "I'm holding on to mine. This is going to be worth something in the future." (Or something like that.) I remembered that because she was so certain Arnold would just continue to amaze and fly with his craft.

A few years later, in 1999, Arnold came out with the first issue of "The Mythology Class." In 2005, he released the collected edition of all four issues. Arnold has done other comic book / graphic novel titles, animated shorts and album covers. A ton of which have won awards.

I am only too happy to be writing the introduction to the 2014 re-release of the "The Mythology Class" omnibus. "The Mythology Class" is a book that celebrates youth, friendship, Philippine myths, legends and folklore, magic, imagination and dreaming.

It has a few hints in it of "Alice in Wonderland," "The Phantom Tollbooth" and "The Lord of the Rings." A bunch of college students are thrown into a fantastic quest and they're just not the same again after they return to the "real world."

However, there is always a little magic to be found in the "real world"—in certain people we meet, in nooks and crannies hidden beneath the noise, traffic and "technological advancement" of the world we live in.

Arnold Arre seems to think so.

KAREN KUNAWICZ
Manila, October 21, 2014

FOREWORD

It was 15 years ago when I first held a copy of "The Mythology Class." Back then it came out as four oversized volumes. It was quite unlike anything local komiks creators were coming out with at the time. In 1999, the new Pinoy comics industry of self-publishers was just 5 years old. All of us creators were still honing our skills, learning the craft, coming out with comic books that we thought were good. Then Arnold Arre released "The Mythology Class" and it was like a gigantic leap forward, and showed us all the true meaning of "good".

I knew Arnold was a talented dude when I first met him. He wasn't detail-obsessed like me and other artists. Detail, of course, was what we excelled in because it was a crutch. We tried to hide our errors of drawing in a mass of cross-hatching hoping nobody would notice. But even back then Arnold concentrated on drawing things right with just the right amount of detail. That spoke of an artistic maturity that many of us were yet to achieve.

Now in 2014 comes a brand new collected edition of "The Mythology Class.." And it comes at a perfect time. It's time to show a new generation of comic book creators what a good comic book is. Look at the art. Read the story. Look at how Arnold manipulates both words and pictures, how he bends and twists and breaks apart every element to create a unique reading experience.

"The Mythology Class" demonstrates that Arnold is more than just a talented artist–he is also an excellent and intelligent writer who knows fully well how to coalesce his ideas into one complete graphic novel.

With this book, Arnold proves himself as a true major comics creator. It has everything there is for a good comics story. One, it must be something you just can't put down. I read the four individual volumes again over the last day and it completely engrossed me from beginning to end, furiously turning the pages wanting to know what happens next. Two,

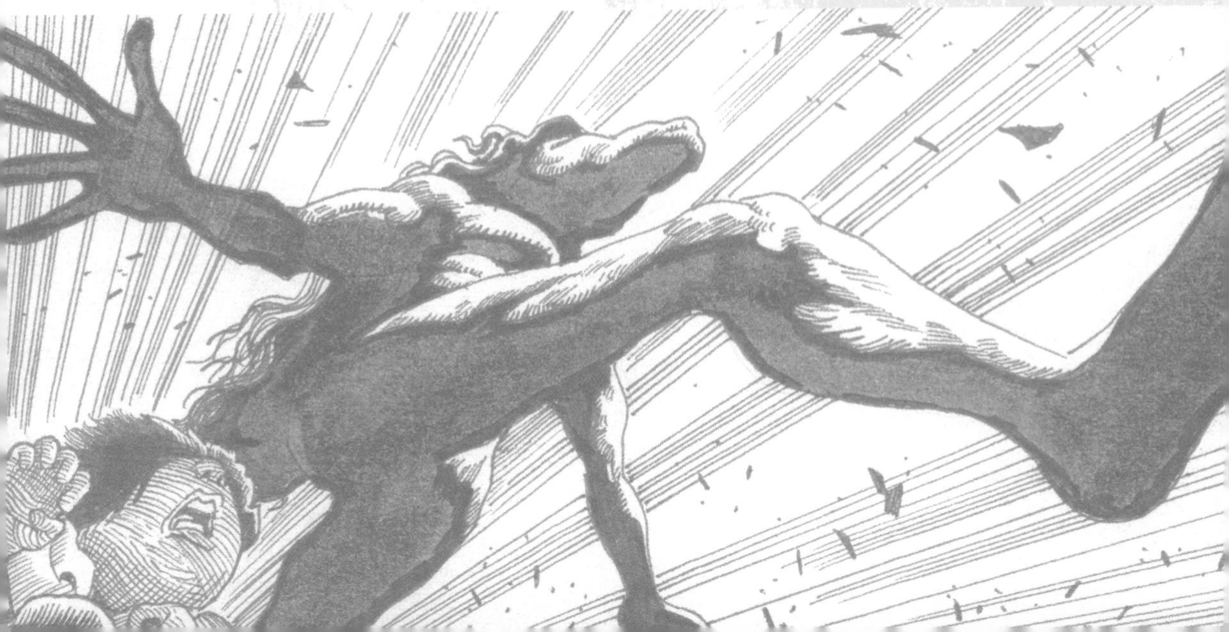

it must have characters that come alive with their own unique voices. During the time I was reading it, Tala, Nicole, Rey, Misha, Kubin, Gina and the rest of the gang became living beings in my mind. I felt convinced that somewhere, somehow, these characters were real, living and breathing. When the book ended, I felt utterly sad that I won't ever see these characters again.

Arnold also knows how to visually present a story in a compelling and exciting way. There's a chase scene here which is probably the best chase scene ever in the history of Pinoy komiks. There are pages in this book that build up to splash pages that simply takes your breath away. There are euphoric moments, moments of visual triumph that seem much larger than the printed page. I won't be specific, but there is a scene that happens after this little bit with a helicopter which demonstrates such a moment. As I read it, I felt my heart soar and I felt little tears forming around my eyes. It's an intense and beautiful scene. In my mind I was throwing curse words at Arnold for making me feel this way like no local comics creator ever had.

You have no idea how lucky you are, if you are reading this book for the first time. You are in for a reading experience quite unlike you've ever had before. Even though this is a fifteen year old story, it still remains as fresh and as exciting as it did in 1999.

I'm very excited to see "The Mythology Class" back in circulation after having been out of print for so many years. Many Filipino comics readers today may no longer be familiar with it, completely unaware of how good it is, and how much of a juggernaut Arnold is as a comics creator. It's time to show that Arnold stands among the very best this country has to offer.

I hope this book stays in print this time!

GERRY ALANGUILAN
San Pablo City, October 26, 2014

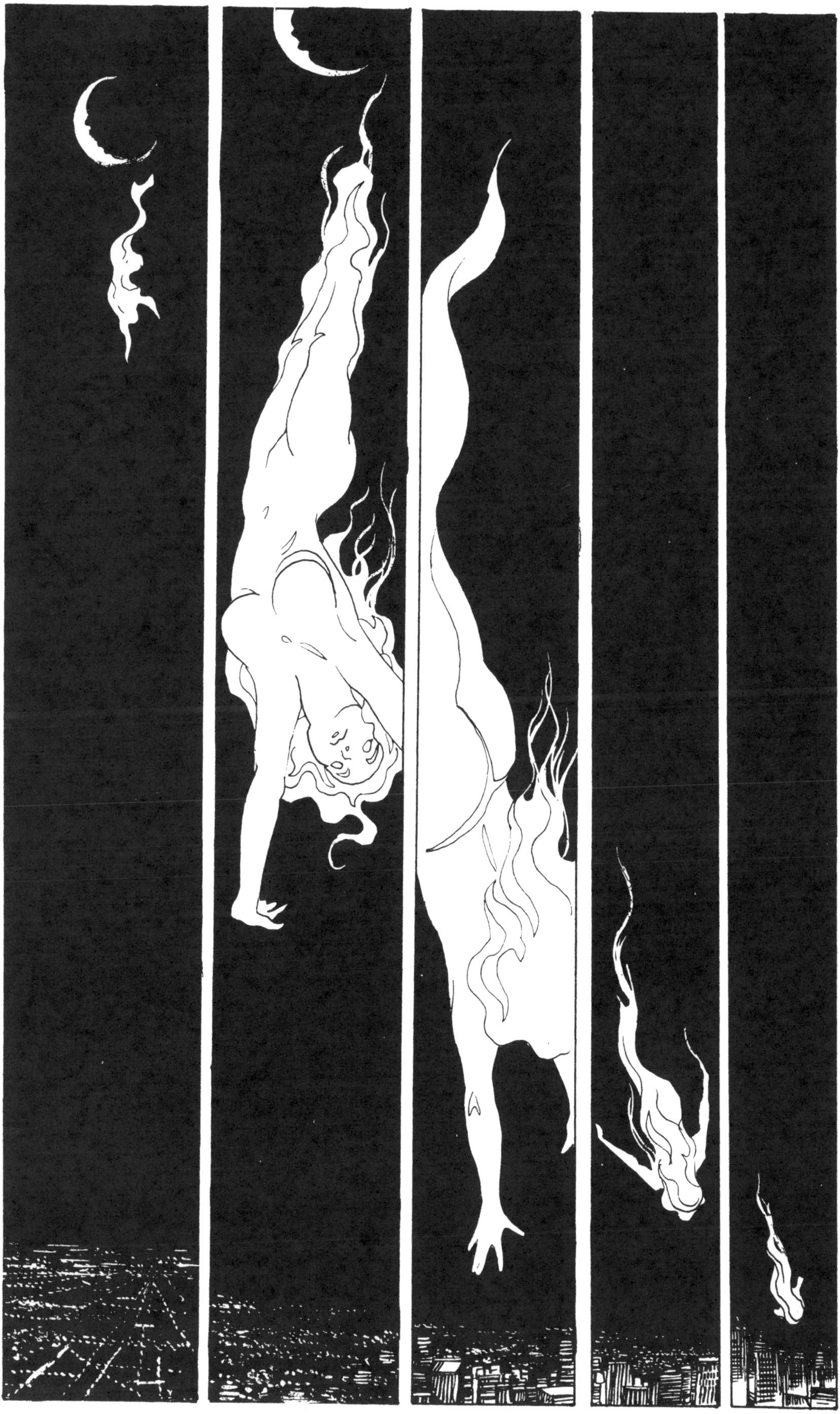

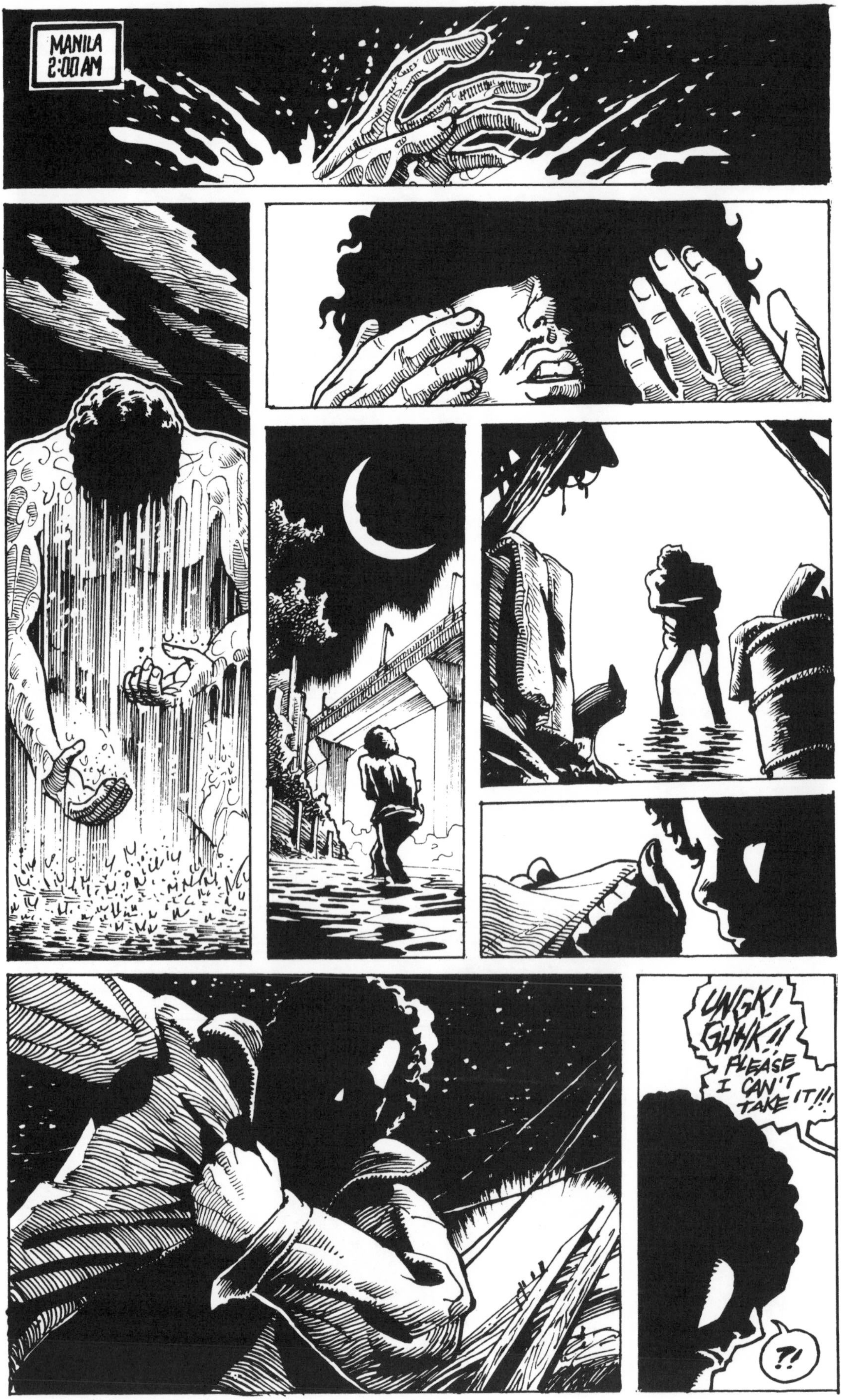
MANILA
2:00 AM
UNGK! GHHK!! PLEASE I CAN'T TAKE IT!!!
?!

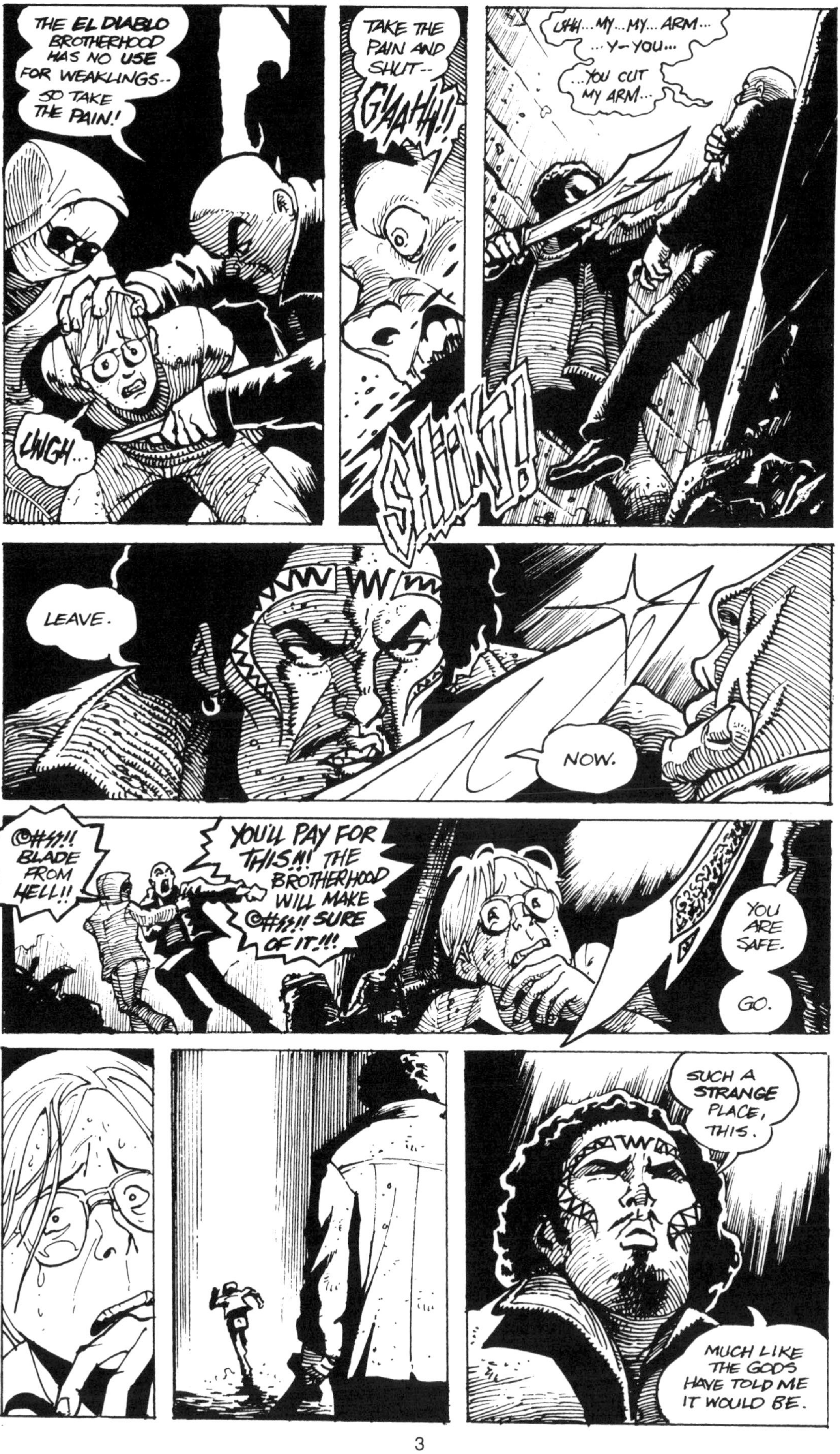
THE EL DIABLO BROTHERHOOD HAS NO USE FOR WEAKLINGS-- SO TAKE THE PAIN!
UNGH...
TAKE THE PAIN AND SHUT--
GYAAHH!!
SHIKT!
UHH... MY... MY... ARM... ...Y-YOU... ...YOU CUT MY ARM...
LEAVE.
NOW.
@#$$!! BLADE FROM HELL!!
YOU'LL PAY FOR THIS!! THE BROTHERHOOD WILL MAKE @#$$!! SURE OF IT!!!
YOU ARE SAFE.
GO.
SUCH A STRANGE PLACE, THIS.
MUCH LIKE THE GODS HAVE TOLD ME IT WOULD BE.

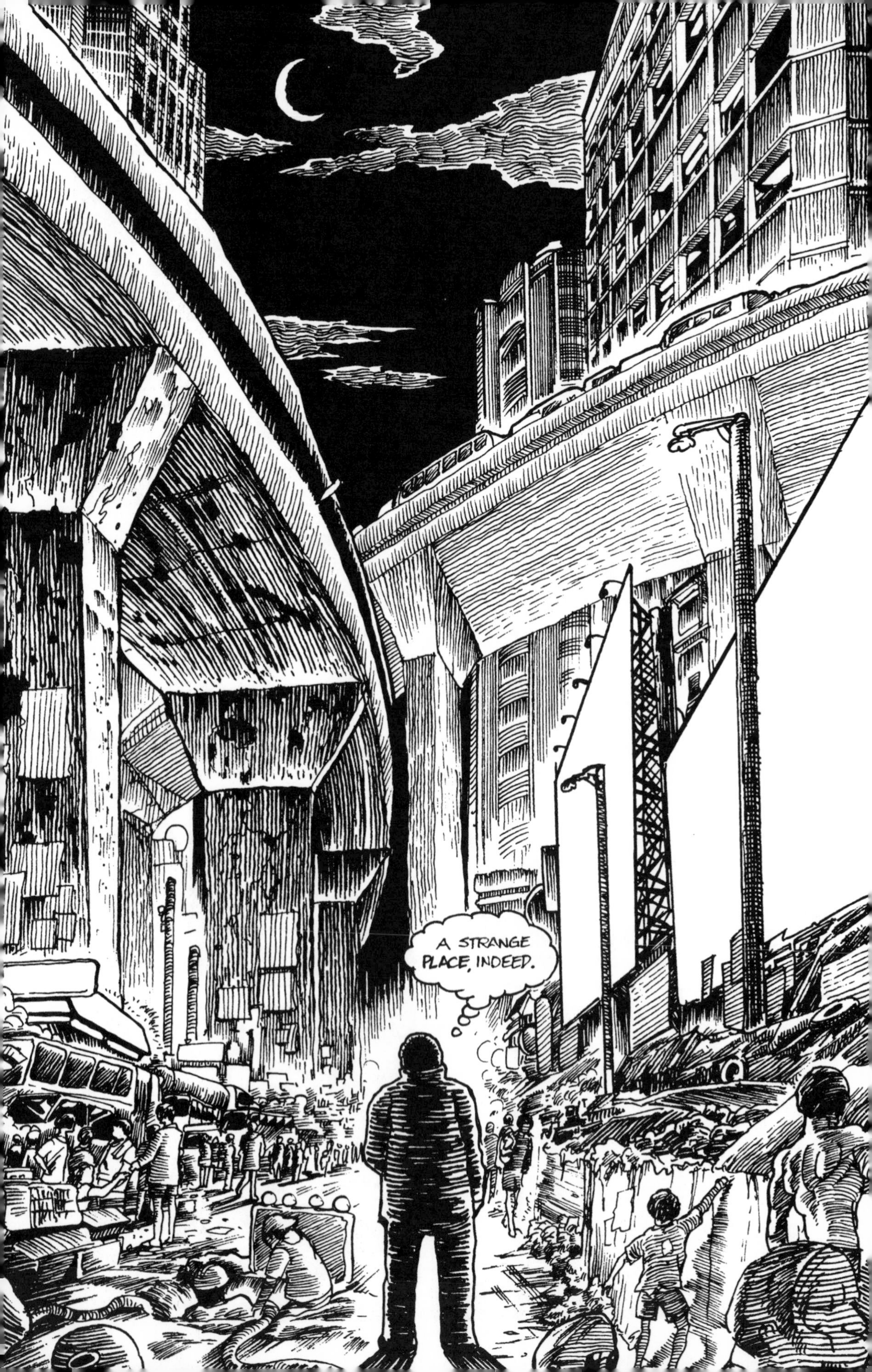
A STRANGE PLACE, INDEED.

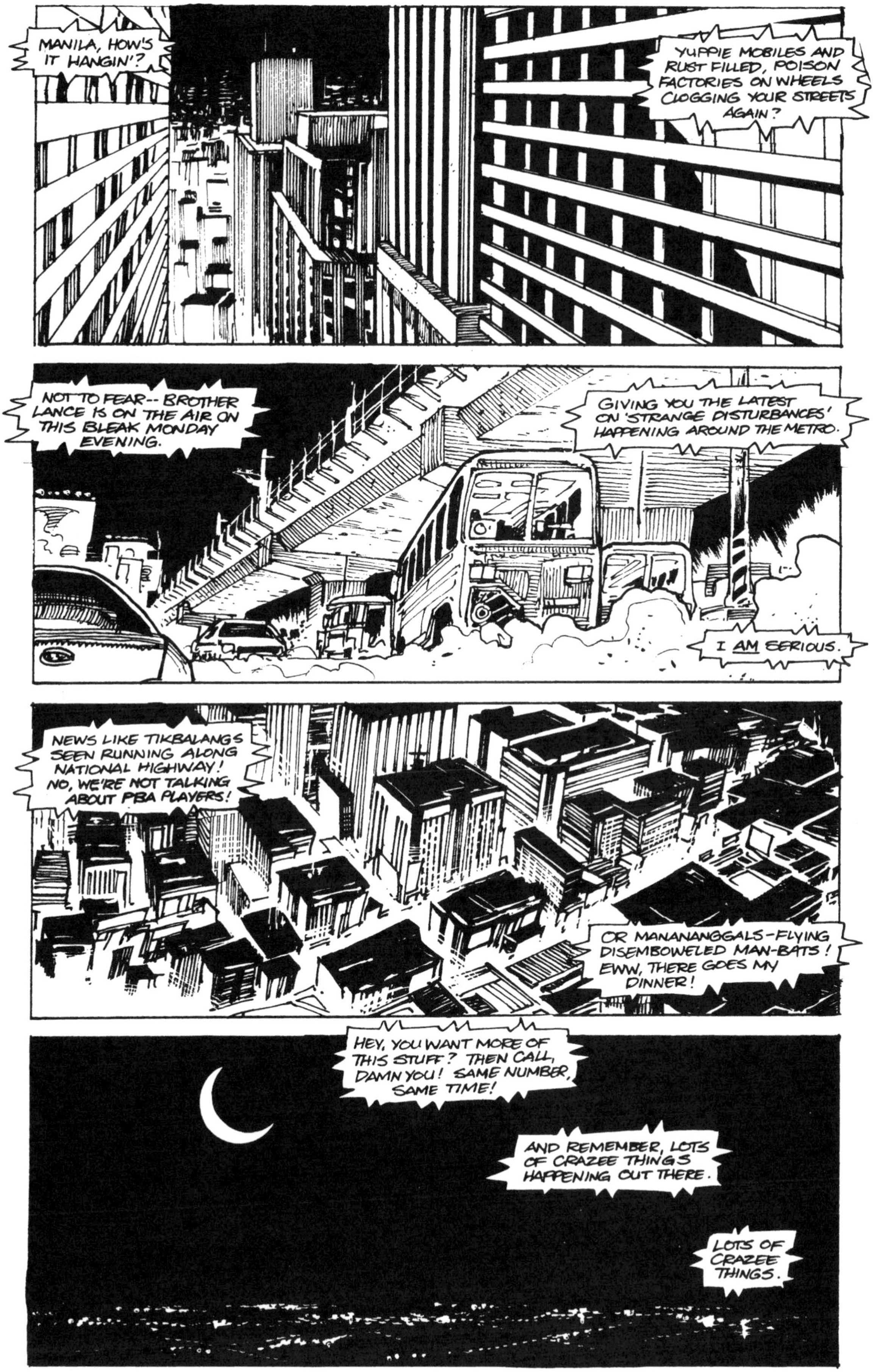
MANILA, HOW'S IT HANGIN'?
YUPPIE MOBILES AND RUST FILLED, POISON FACTORIES ON WHEELS CLOGGING YOUR STREETS AGAIN?
NOT TO FEAR-- BROTHER LANCE IS ON THE AIR ON THIS BLEAK MONDAY EVENING.
GIVING YOU THE LATEST ON 'STRANGE DISTURBANCES' HAPPENING AROUND THE METRO.
I AM SERIOUS.
NEWS LIKE TIKBALANGS SEEN RUNNING ALONG NATIONAL HIGHWAY! NO, WE'RE NOT TALKING ABOUT PBA PLAYERS!
OR MANANANGGALS-FLYING DISEMBOWELED MAN-BATS! EWW, THERE GOES MY DINNER!
HEY, YOU WANT MORE OF THIS STUFF? THEN CALL, DAMN YOU! SAME NUMBER, SAME TIME!
AND REMEMBER, LOTS OF CRAZEE THINGS HAPPENING OUT THERE.
LOTS OF CRAZEE THINGS.

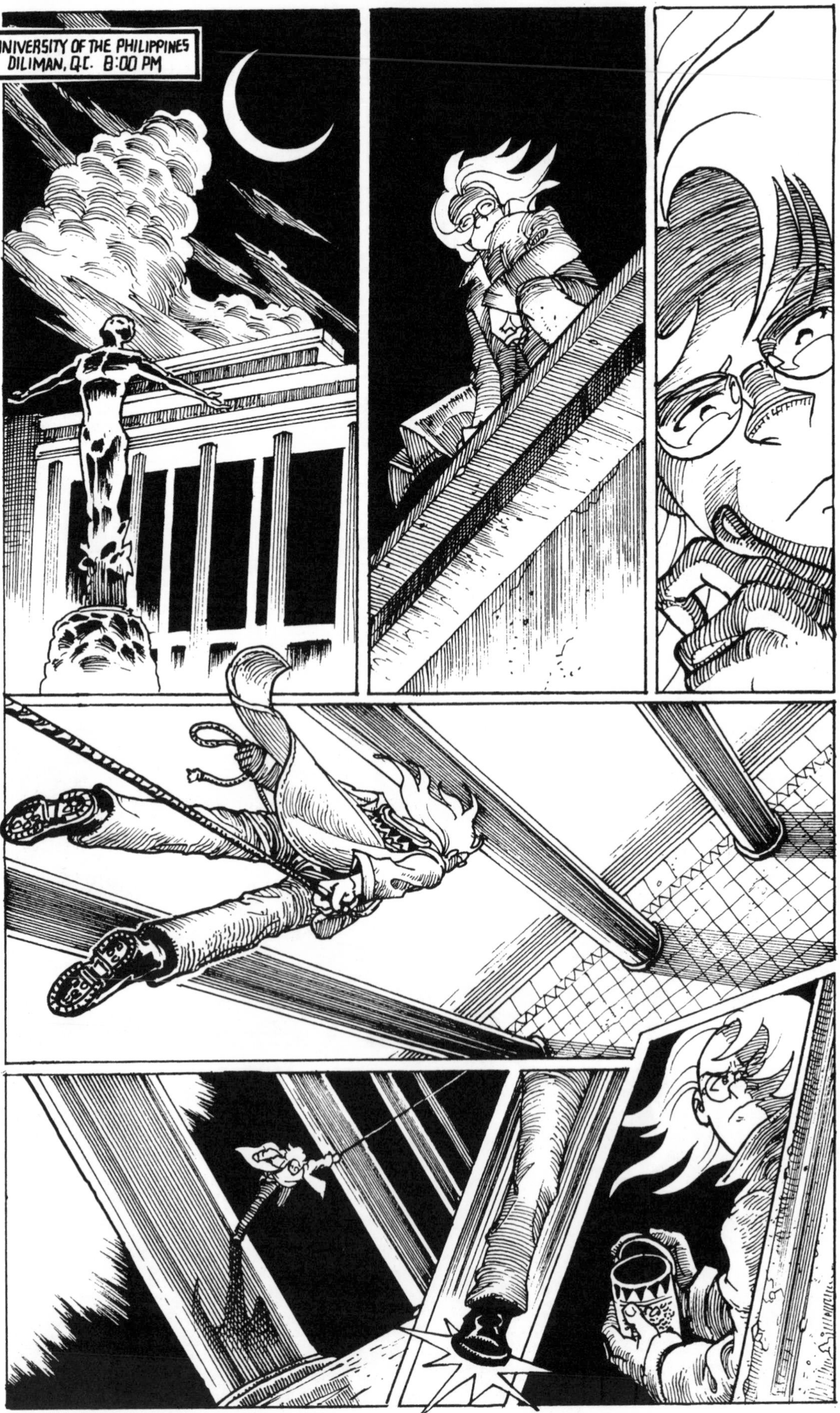
UNIVERSITY OF THE PHILIPPINES
DILIMAN, Q.C. 8:00 PM

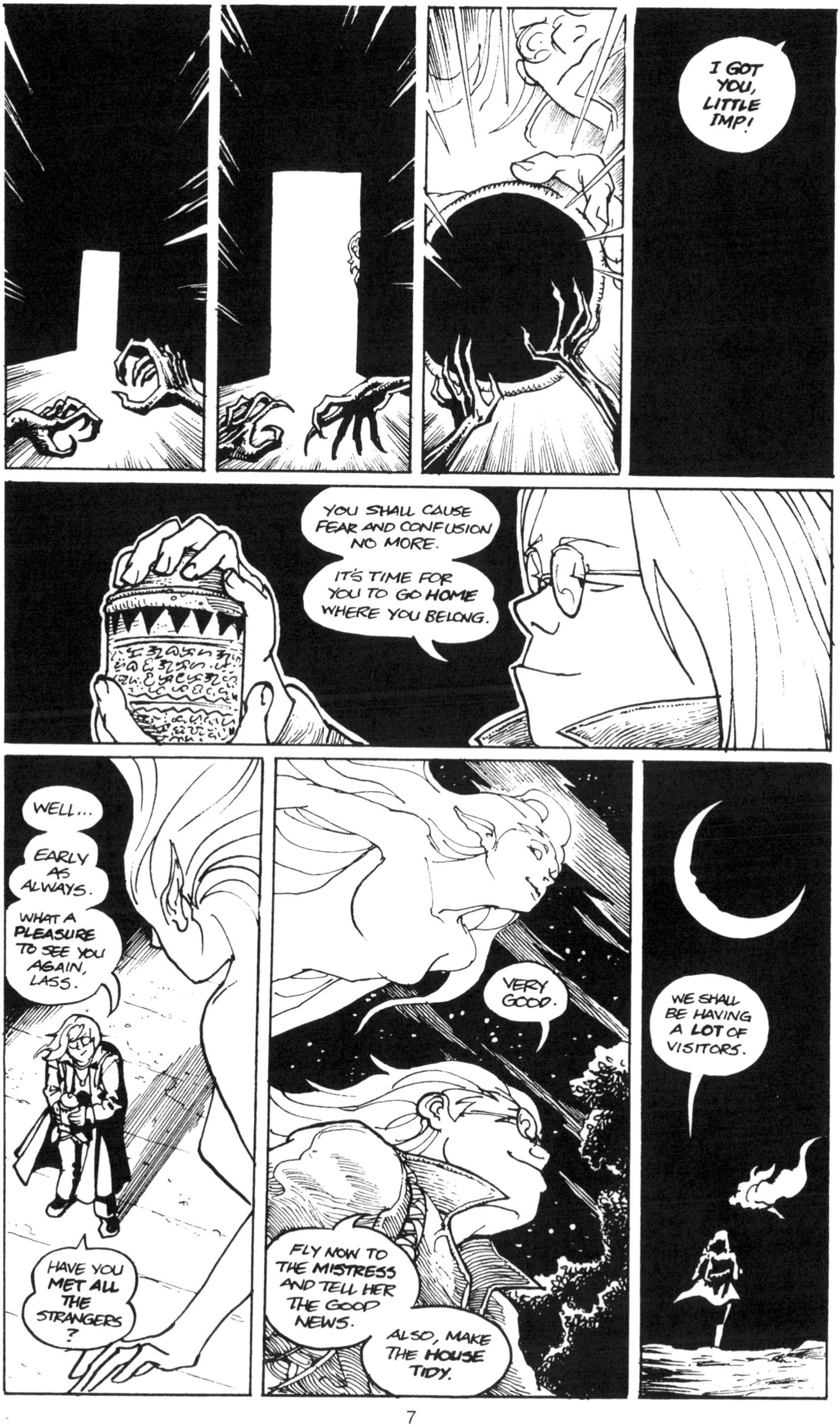
I GOT YOU, LITTLE IMP!
YOU SHALL CAUSE FEAR AND CONFUSION NO MORE.
IT'S TIME FOR YOU TO GO HOME WHERE YOU BELONG.
WELL...
EARLY AS ALWAYS.
WHAT A PLEASURE TO SEE YOU AGAIN, LASS.
HAVE YOU MET ALL THE STRANGERS ?
VERY GOOD.
FLY NOW TO THE MISTRESS AND TELL HER THE GOOD NEWS.
ALSO, MAKE THE HOUSE TIDY.
WE SHALL BE HAVING A LOT OF VISITORS.

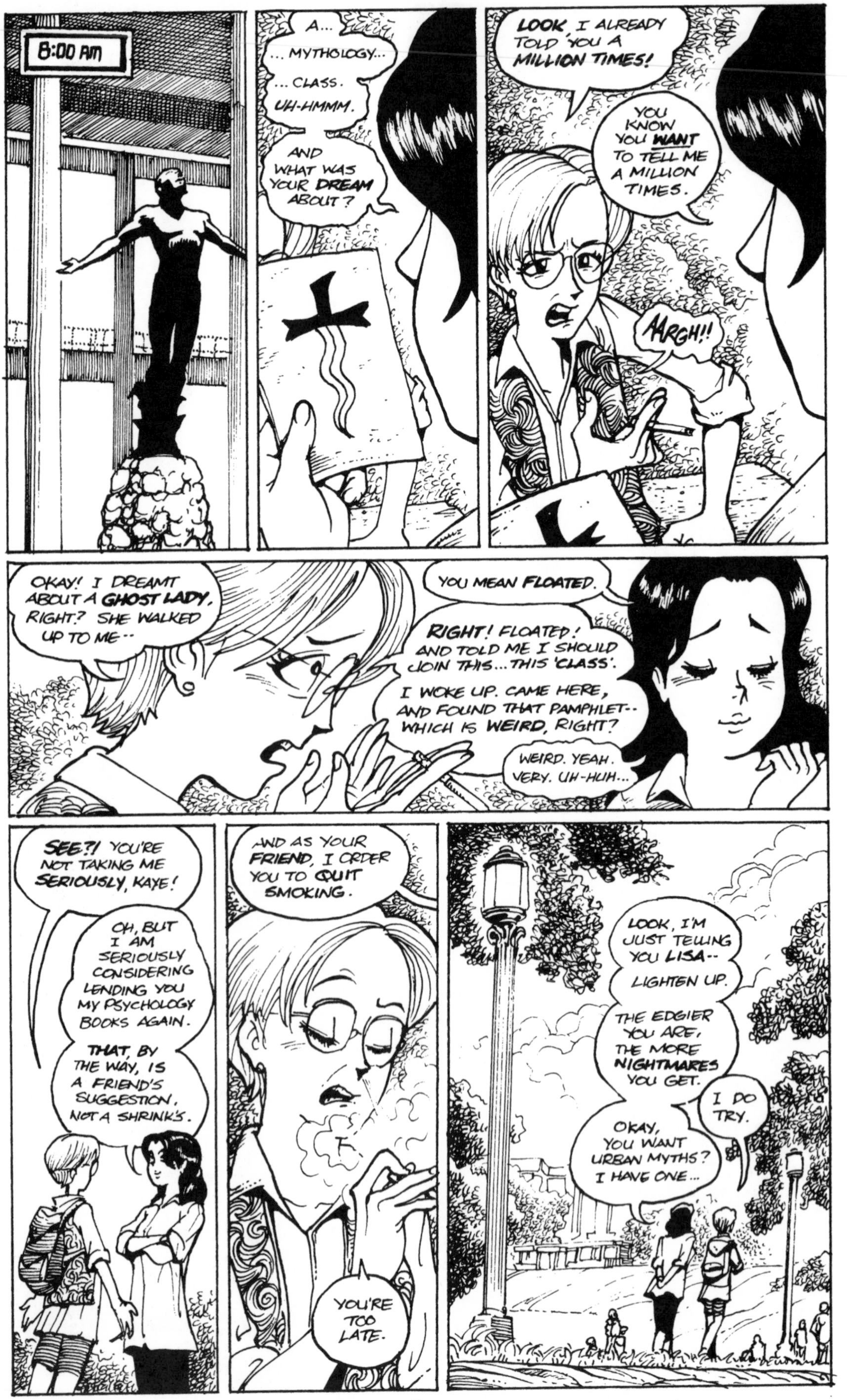
8:00 AM
A...
... MYTHOLOGY...
... CLASS.
UH-HMMM.
AND WHAT WAS YOUR DREAM ABOUT?
LOOK, I ALREADY TOLD YOU A MILLION TIMES!
YOU KNOW YOU WANT TO TELL ME A MILLION TIMES.
AARGH!!
OKAY! I DREAMT ABOUT A GHOST LADY. RIGHT? SHE WALKED UP TO ME--
YOU MEAN FLOATED.
RIGHT! FLOATED! AND TOLD ME I SHOULD JOIN THIS... THIS 'CLASS'.
I WOKE UP. CAME HERE, AND FOUND THAT PAMPHLET-- WHICH IS WEIRD, RIGHT?
WEIRD. YEAH. VERY. UH-HUH...
SEE?! YOU'RE NOT TAKING ME SERIOUSLY, KAYE!
OH, BUT I AM SERIOUSLY CONSIDERING LENDING YOU MY PSYCHOLOGY BOOKS AGAIN.
THAT, BY THE WAY, IS A FRIEND'S SUGGESTION, NOT A SHRINK'S.
AND AS YOUR FRIEND, I ORDER YOU TO QUIT SMOKING.
YOU'RE TOO LATE.
LOOK, I'M JUST TELLING YOU LISA--
LIGHTEN UP.
THE EDGIER YOU ARE, THE MORE NIGHTMARES YOU GET.
I DO TRY.
OKAY, YOU WANT URBAN MYTHS? I HAVE ONE...

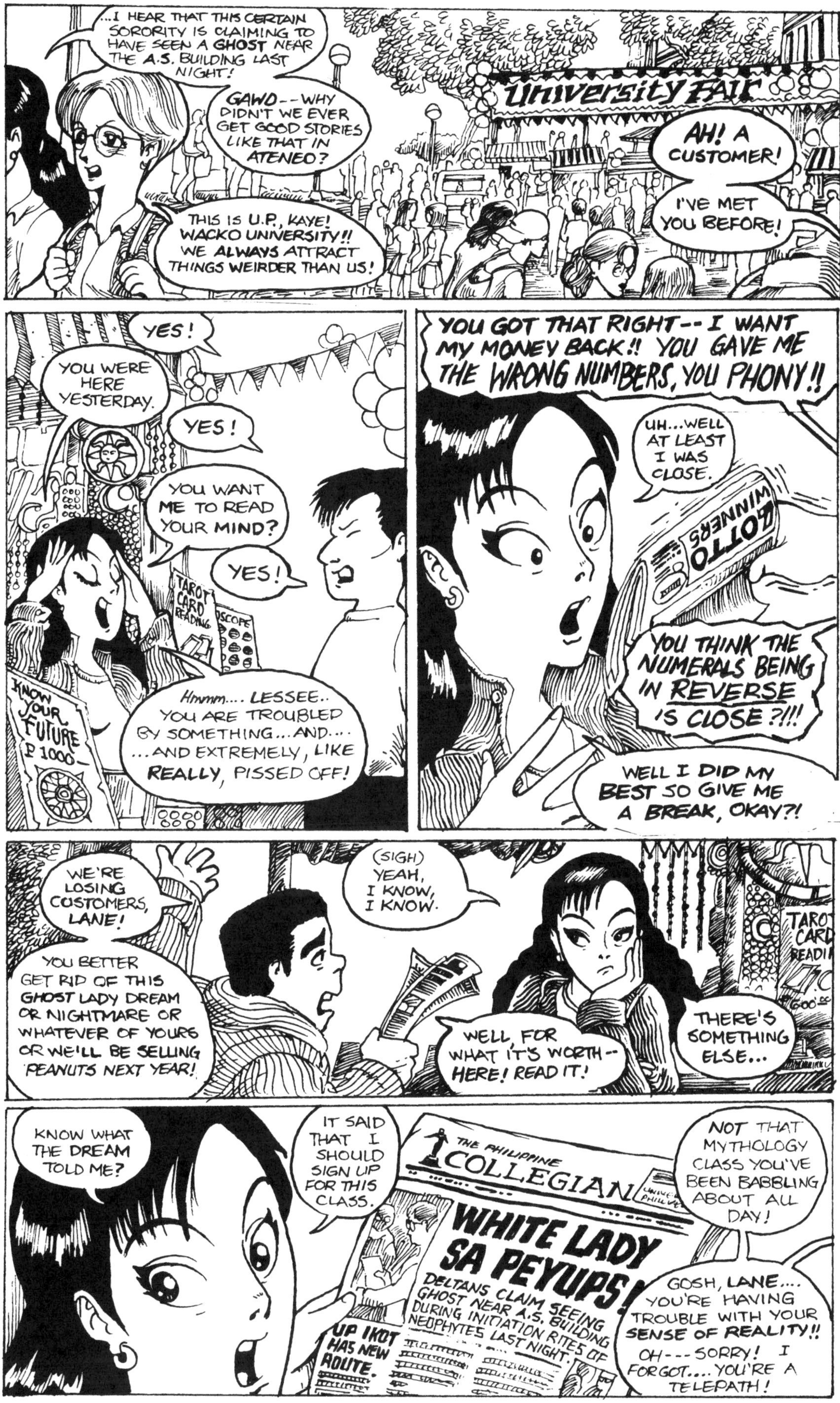
...I HEAR THAT THIS CERTAIN SORORITY IS CLAIMING TO HAVE SEEN A GHOST NEAR THE A.S. BUILDING LAST NIGHT!
GAWD--WHY DIDN'T WE EVER GET GOOD STORIES LIKE THAT IN ATENEO?
THIS IS U.P., KAYE! WACKO UNIVERSITY!! WE ALWAYS ATTRACT THINGS WEIRDER THAN US!
University FAIR
AH! A CUSTOMER!
I'VE MET YOU BEFORE!
YES!
YOU WERE HERE YESTERDAY.
YES!
YOU WANT ME TO READ YOUR MIND?
YES!
TAROT CARD READING
KNOW YOUR FUTURE ₱1000
Hmmm.... LESSEE.. YOU ARE TROUBLED BY SOMETHING...AND.... ...AND EXTREMELY, LIKE REALLY, PISSED OFF!
YOU GOT THAT RIGHT-- I WANT MY MONEY BACK!! YOU GAVE ME THE WRONG NUMBERS, YOU PHONY!!
UH...WELL AT LEAST I WAS CLOSE.
LOTTO WINNERS
YOU THINK THE NUMERALS BEING IN REVERSE IS CLOSE?!!!
WELL I DID MY BEST SO GIVE ME A BREAK, OKAY?!
WE'RE LOSING CUSTOMERS, LANE!
(SIGH) YEAH, I KNOW, I KNOW.
YOU BETTER GET RID OF THIS GHOST LADY DREAM OR NIGHTMARE OR WHATEVER OF YOURS OR WE'LL BE SELLING PEANUTS NEXT YEAR!
WELL, FOR WHAT IT'S WORTH-- HERE! READ IT!
THERE'S SOMETHING ELSE...
KNOW WHAT THE DREAM TOLD ME?
IT SAID THAT I SHOULD SIGN UP FOR THIS CLASS.
THE PHILIPPINE COLLEGIAN
WHITE LADY SA PEYUPS!
DELTANS CLAIM SEEING GHOST NEAR A.S. BUILDING DURING INITIATION RITES OF NEOPHYTES LAST NIGHT.
UP IKOT HAS NEW ROUTE.
NOT THAT MYTHOLOGY CLASS YOU'VE BEEN BABBLING ABOUT ALL DAY!
GOSH, LANE.... YOU'RE HAVING TROUBLE WITH YOUR SENSE OF REALITY!!
OH---SORRY! I FORGOT.... YOU'RE A TELEPATH!

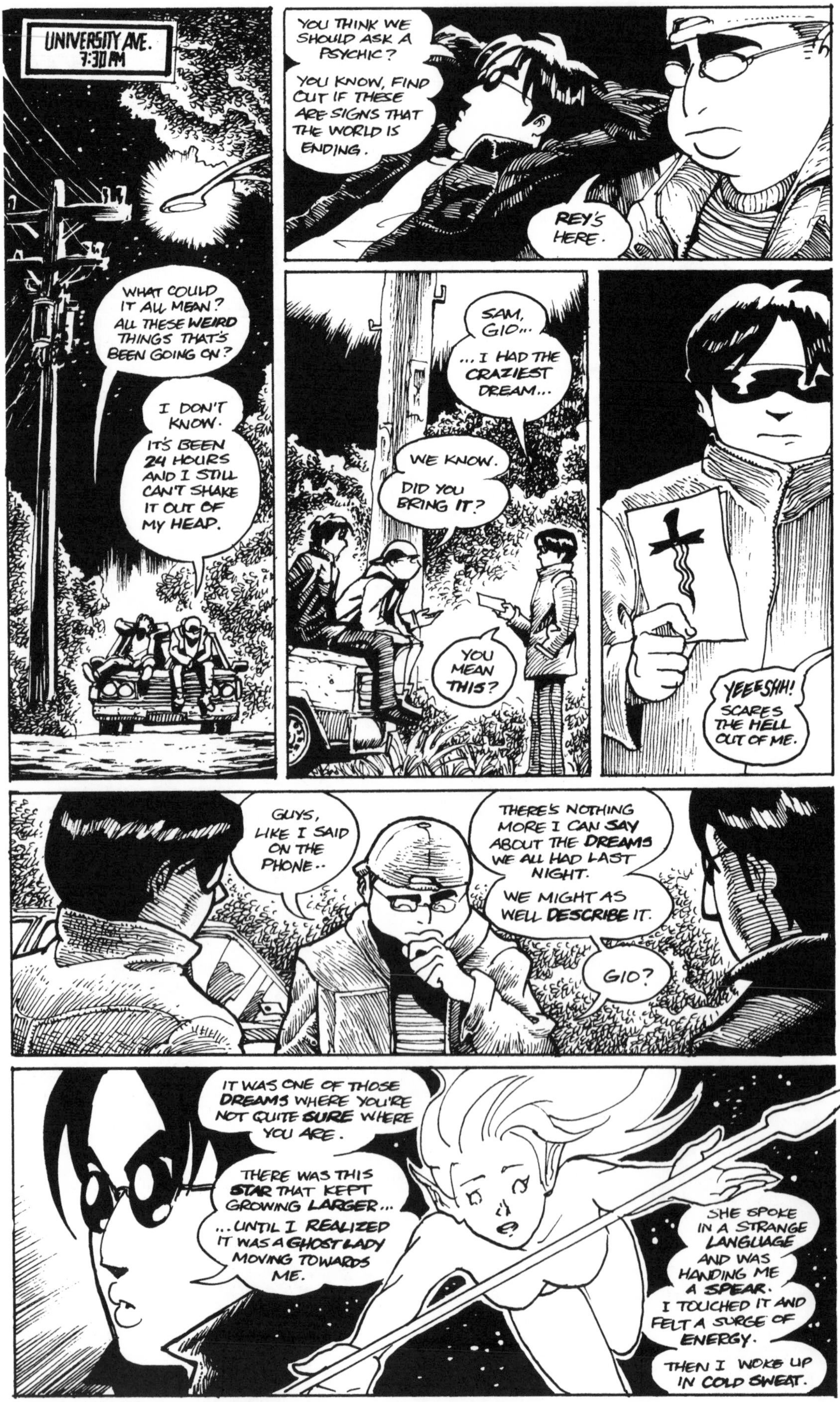
UNIVERSITY AVE. 7:30 PM
WHAT COULD IT ALL MEAN? ALL THESE WEIRD THINGS THAT'S BEEN GOING ON?
I DON'T KNOW.
IT'S BEEN 24 HOURS AND I STILL CAN'T SHAKE IT OUT OF MY HEAD.
YOU THINK WE SHOULD ASK A PSYCHIC?
YOU KNOW, FIND OUT IF THESE ARE SIGNS THAT THE WORLD IS ENDING.
REY'S HERE.
SAM, GIO...
...I HAD THE CRAZIEST DREAM...
WE KNOW.
DID YOU BRING IT?
YOU MEAN THIS?
YEEESHH! SCARES THE HELL OUT OF ME.
GUYS, LIKE I SAID ON THE PHONE..
THERE'S NOTHING MORE I CAN SAY ABOUT THE DREAMS WE ALL HAD LAST NIGHT.
WE MIGHT AS WELL DESCRIBE IT.
GIO?
IT WAS ONE OF THOSE DREAMS WHERE YOU'RE NOT QUITE SURE WHERE YOU ARE.
THERE WAS THIS STAR THAT KEPT GROWING LARGER...
...UNTIL I REALIZED IT WAS A GHOST LADY MOVING TOWARDS ME.
SHE SPOKE IN A STRANGE LANGUAGE AND WAS HANDING ME A SPEAR.
I TOUCHED IT AND FELT A SURGE OF ENERGY.
THEN I WOKE UP IN COLD SWEAT.

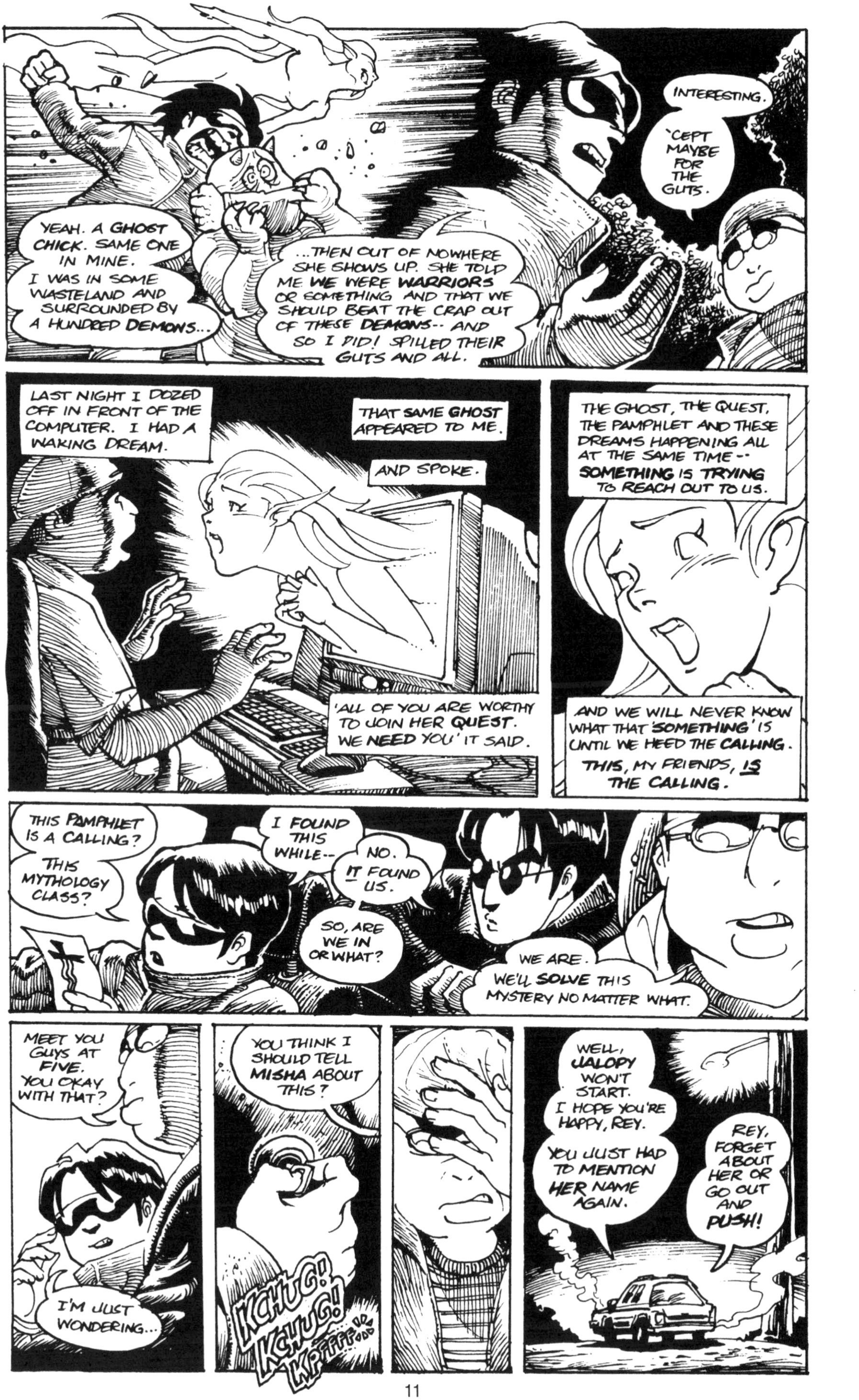
YEAH. A GHOST CHICK. SAME ONE IN MINE.
I WAS IN SOME WASTELAND AND SURROUNDED BY A HUNDRED DEMONS...
...THEN OUT OF NOWHERE SHE SHOWS UP. SHE TOLD ME WE WERE WARRIORS OR SOMETHING AND THAT WE SHOULD BEAT THE CRAP OUT OF THESE DEMONS-- AND SO I DID! SPILLED THEIR GUTS AND ALL.
INTERESTING.
'CEPT MAYBE FOR THE GUTS.
LAST NIGHT I DOZED OFF IN FRONT OF THE COMPUTER. I HAD A WAKING DREAM.
THAT SAME GHOST APPEARED TO ME.
AND SPOKE.
'ALL OF YOU ARE WORTHY TO JOIN HER QUEST. WE NEED YOU' IT SAID.
THE GHOST, THE QUEST, THE PAMPHLET AND THESE DREAMS HAPPENING ALL AT THE SAME TIME-- SOMETHING IS TRYING TO REACH OUT TO US.
AND WE WILL NEVER KNOW WHAT THAT 'SOMETHING' IS UNTIL WE HEED THE CALLING.
THIS, MY FRIENDS, IS THE CALLING.
THIS PAMPHLET IS A CALLING?
THIS MYTHOLOGY CLASS?
I FOUND THIS WHILE--
NO. IT FOUND US.
SO, ARE WE IN OR WHAT?
WE ARE.
WE'LL SOLVE THIS MYSTERY NO MATTER WHAT.
MEET YOU GUYS AT FIVE. YOU OKAY WITH THAT?
I'M JUST WONDERING...
YOU THINK I SHOULD TELL MISHA ABOUT THIS?
KCHUG! KCHUG! KPFFFT
WELL, JALOPY WON'T START.
I HOPE YOU'RE HAPPY, REY.
YOU JUST HAD TO MENTION HER NAME AGAIN.
REY, FORGET ABOUT HER OR GO OUT AND PUSH!

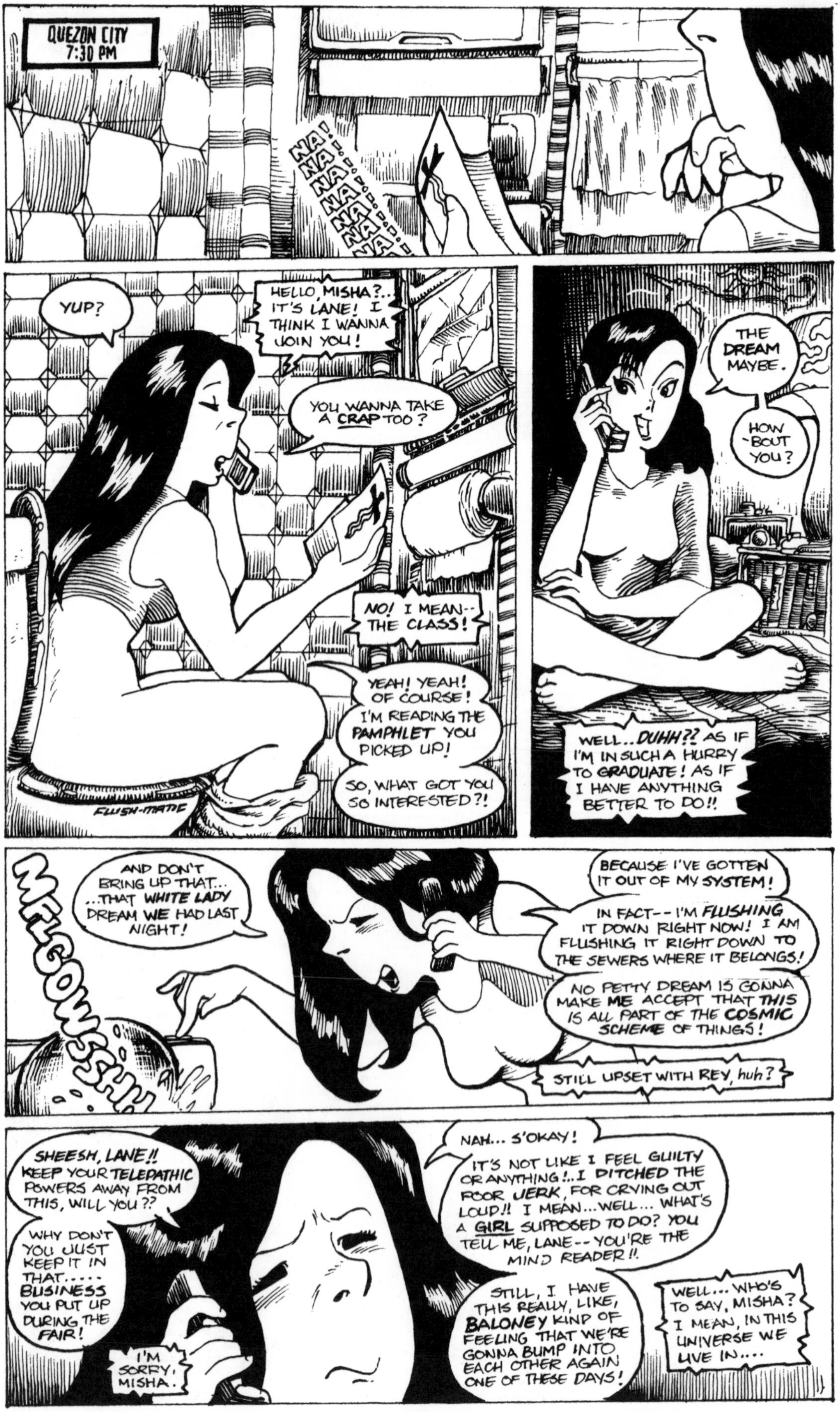
QUEZON CITY 7:30 PM
NA! NA! NA! NA! NA! NA!
YUP?
HELLO, MISHA?.. IT'S LANE! I THINK I WANNA JOIN YOU!
YOU WANNA TAKE A CRAP TOO?
NO! I MEAN-- THE CLASS!
YEAH! YEAH! OF COURSE! I'M READING THE PAMPHLET YOU PICKED UP!
SO, WHAT GOT YOU SO INTERESTED?!
FLUSH-MATIC
THE DREAM MAYBE.
HOW-BOUT YOU?
WELL.. DUHH?? AS IF I'M IN SUCH A HURRY TO GRADUATE! AS IF I HAVE ANYTHING BETTER TO DO!!
AND DON'T BRING UP THAT... ...THAT WHITE LADY DREAM WE HAD LAST NIGHT!
BECAUSE I'VE GOTTEN IT OUT OF MY SYSTEM!
IN FACT-- I'M FLUSHING IT DOWN RIGHT NOW! I AM FLUSHING IT RIGHT DOWN TO THE SEWERS WHERE IT BELONGS!
NO PETTY DREAM IS GONNA MAKE ME ACCEPT THAT THIS IS ALL PART OF THE COSMIC SCHEME OF THINGS!
MFLGOWSSHH!
STILL UPSET WITH REY, huh?
SHEESH, LANE!! KEEP YOUR TELEPATHIC POWERS AWAY FROM THIS, WILL YOU??
WHY DON'T YOU JUST KEEP IT IN THAT..... BUSINESS YOU PUT UP DURING THE FAIR!
I'M SORRY, MISHA.
NAH... S'OKAY!
IT'S NOT LIKE I FEEL GUILTY OR ANYTHING!..I DITCHED THE POOR JERK, FOR CRYING OUT LOUD!! I MEAN...WELL... WHAT'S A GIRL SUPPOSED TO DO? YOU TELL ME, LANE-- YOU'RE THE MIND READER!!
STILL, I HAVE THIS REALLY, LIKE, BALONEY KIND OF FEELING THAT WE'RE GONNA BUMP INTO EACH OTHER AGAIN ONE OF THESE DAYS!
WELL... WHO'S TO SAY, MISHA? I MEAN, IN THIS UNIVERSE WE LIVE IN....

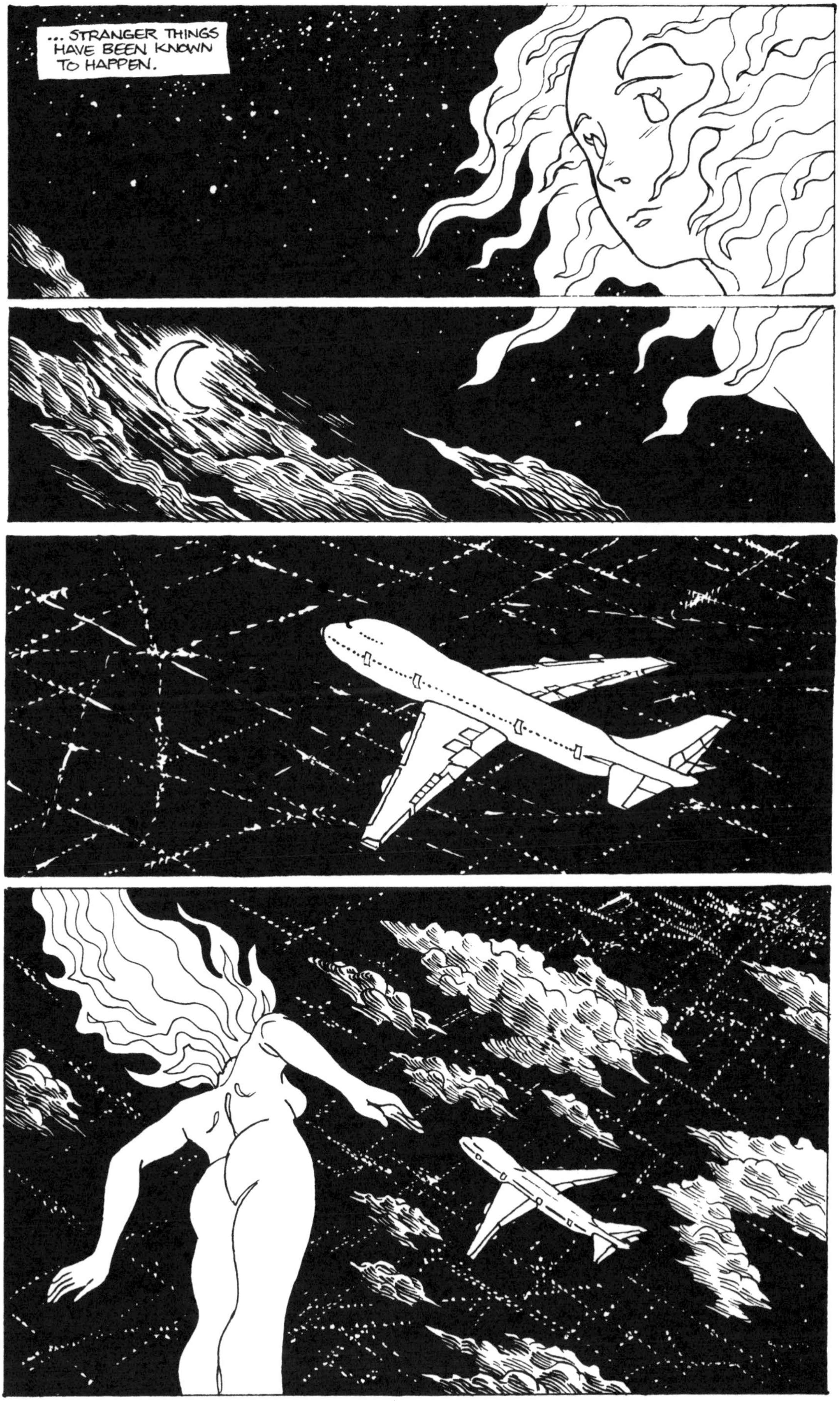
... STRANGER THINGS HAVE BEEN KNOWN TO HAPPEN.

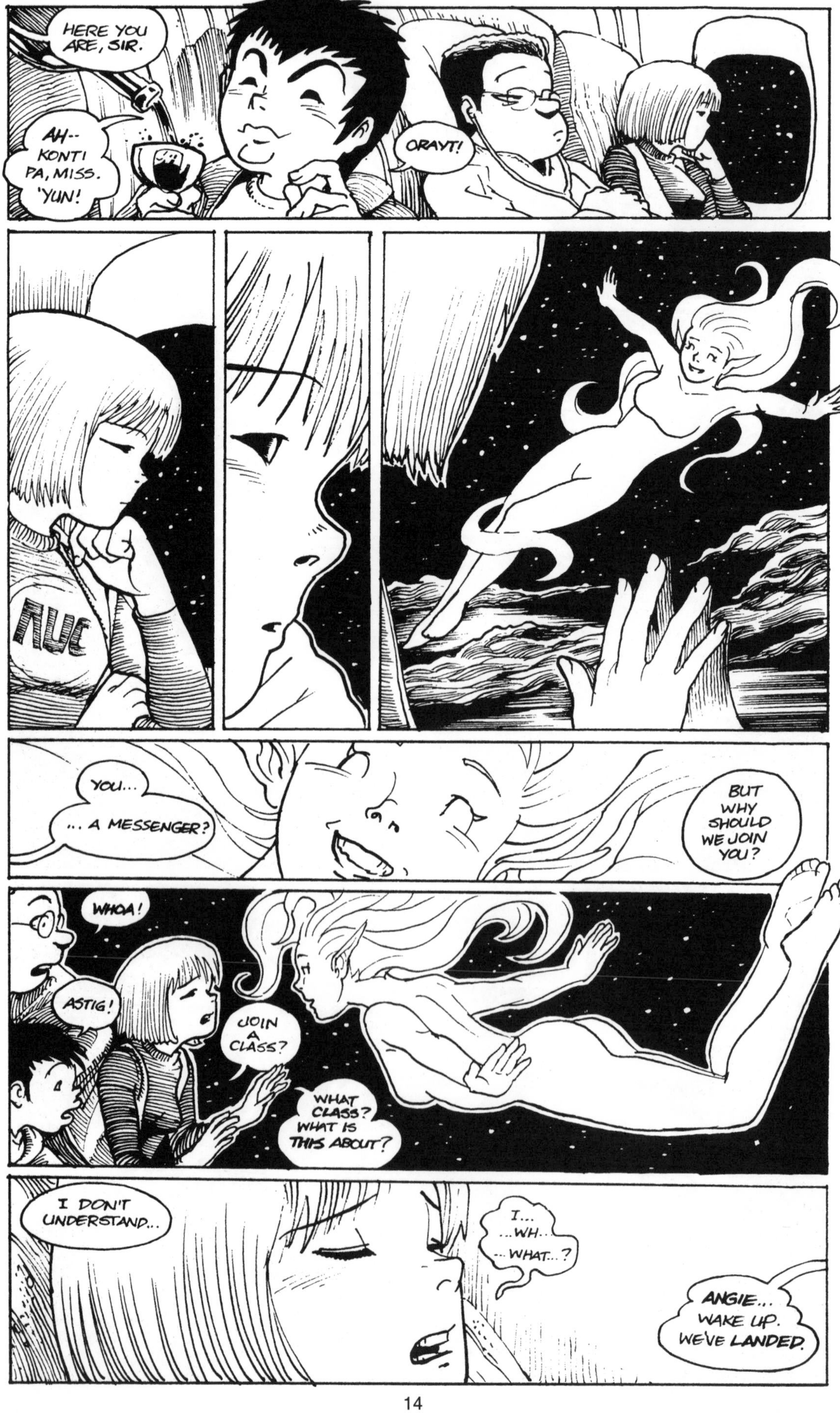
HERE YOU ARE, SIR.
AH-- KONTI PA, MISS. 'YUN!
ORAYT!
AUC
YOU...
... A MESSENGER?
BUT WHY SHOULD WE JOIN YOU?
WHOA!
ASTIG!
JOIN A CLASS?
WHAT CLASS? WHAT IS THIS ABOUT?
I DON'T UNDERSTAND...
I... ...WH... ...WHAT...?
ANGIE... WAKE UP. WE'VE LANDED.

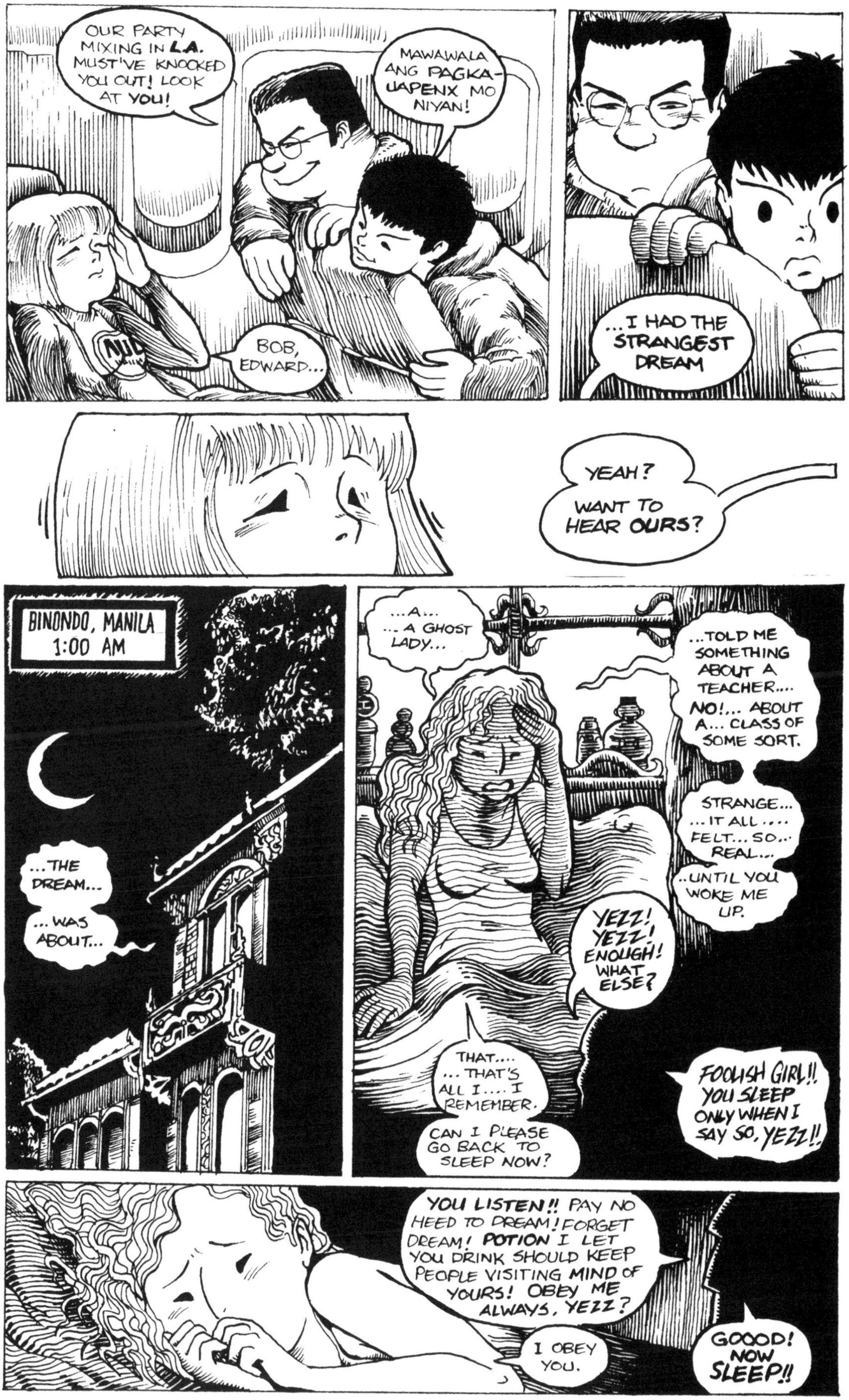
OUR PARTY MIXING IN L.A. MUST'VE KNOCKED YOU OUT! LOOK AT YOU!
MAWAWALA ANG PAGKA-JAPENX MO NIYAN!
BOB, EDWARD...
...I HAD THE STRANGEST DREAM
YEAH? WANT TO HEAR OURS?
BINONDO, MANILA 1:00 AM
...THE DREAM...
...WAS ABOUT...
...A... ...A GHOST LADY...
...TOLD ME SOMETHING ABOUT A TEACHER.... NO!... ABOUT A... CLASS OF SOME SORT.
STRANGE... ...IT ALL.... FELT... SO... REAL...
...UNTIL YOU WOKE ME UP.
YEZZ! YEZZ! ENOUGH! WHAT ELSE?
THAT.... ...THAT'S ALL I.... I REMEMBER.
CAN I PLEASE GO BACK TO SLEEP NOW?
FOOLISH GIRL!! YOU SLEEP ONLY WHEN I SAY SO, YEZZ!!
YOU LISTEN!! PAY NO HEED TO DREAM! FORGET DREAM! POTION I LET YOU DRINK SHOULD KEEP PEOPLE VISITING MIND OF YOURS! OBEY ME ALWAYS, YEZZ?
I OBEY YOU.
GOOOD! NOW SLEEP!!

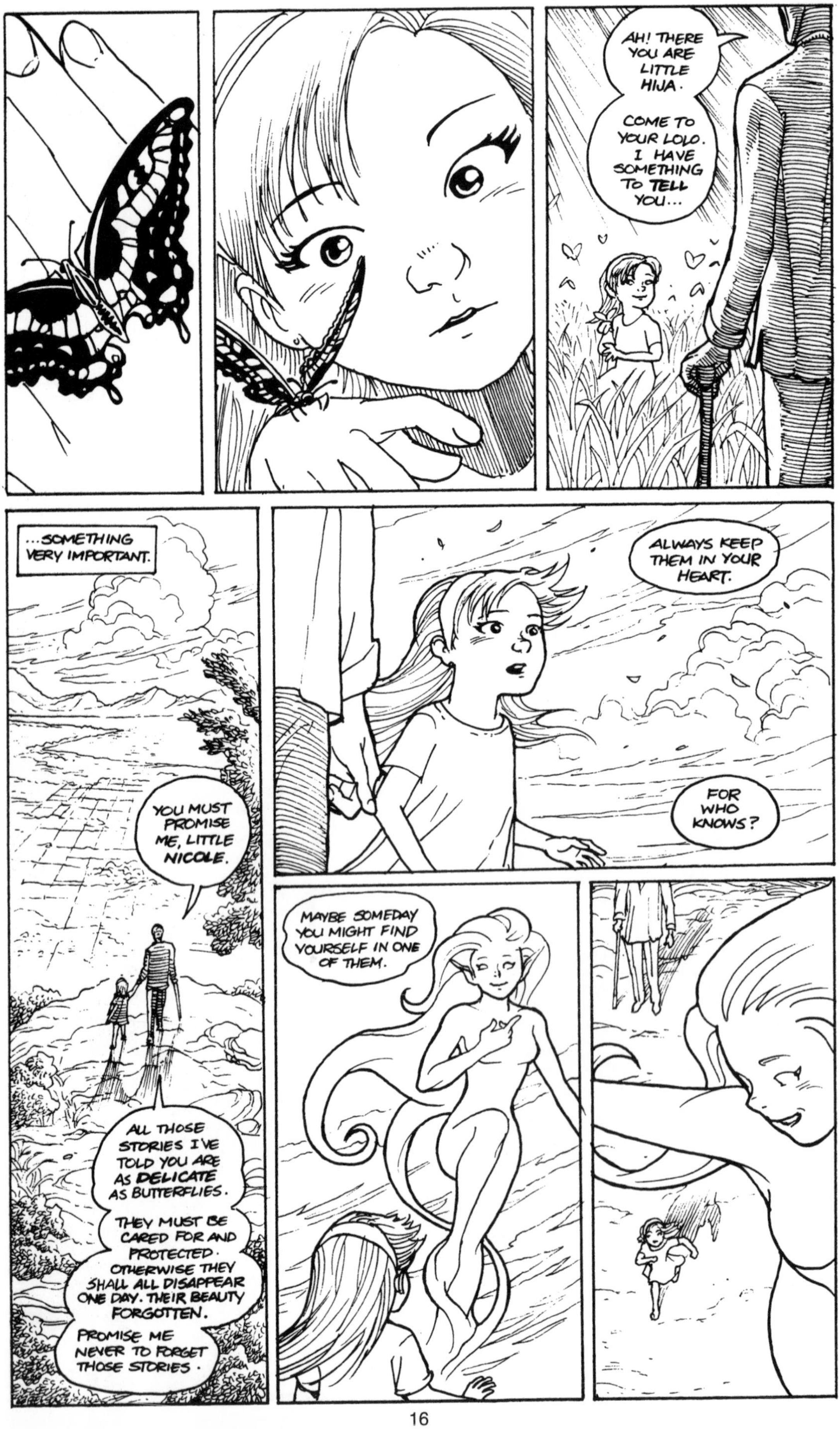
AH! THERE YOU ARE LITTLE HIJA.
COME TO YOUR LOLO. I HAVE SOMETHING TO TELL YOU...
...SOMETHING VERY IMPORTANT.
YOU MUST PROMISE ME, LITTLE NICOLE.
ALL THOSE STORIES I'VE TOLD YOU ARE AS DELICATE AS BUTTERFLIES.
THEY MUST BE CARED FOR AND PROTECTED. OTHERWISE THEY SHALL ALL DISAPPEAR ONE DAY. THEIR BEAUTY FORGOTTEN.
PROMISE ME NEVER TO FORGET THOSE STORIES.
ALWAYS KEEP THEM IN YOUR HEART.
FOR WHO KNOWS?
MAYBE SOMEDAY YOU MIGHT FIND YOURSELF IN ONE OF THEM.

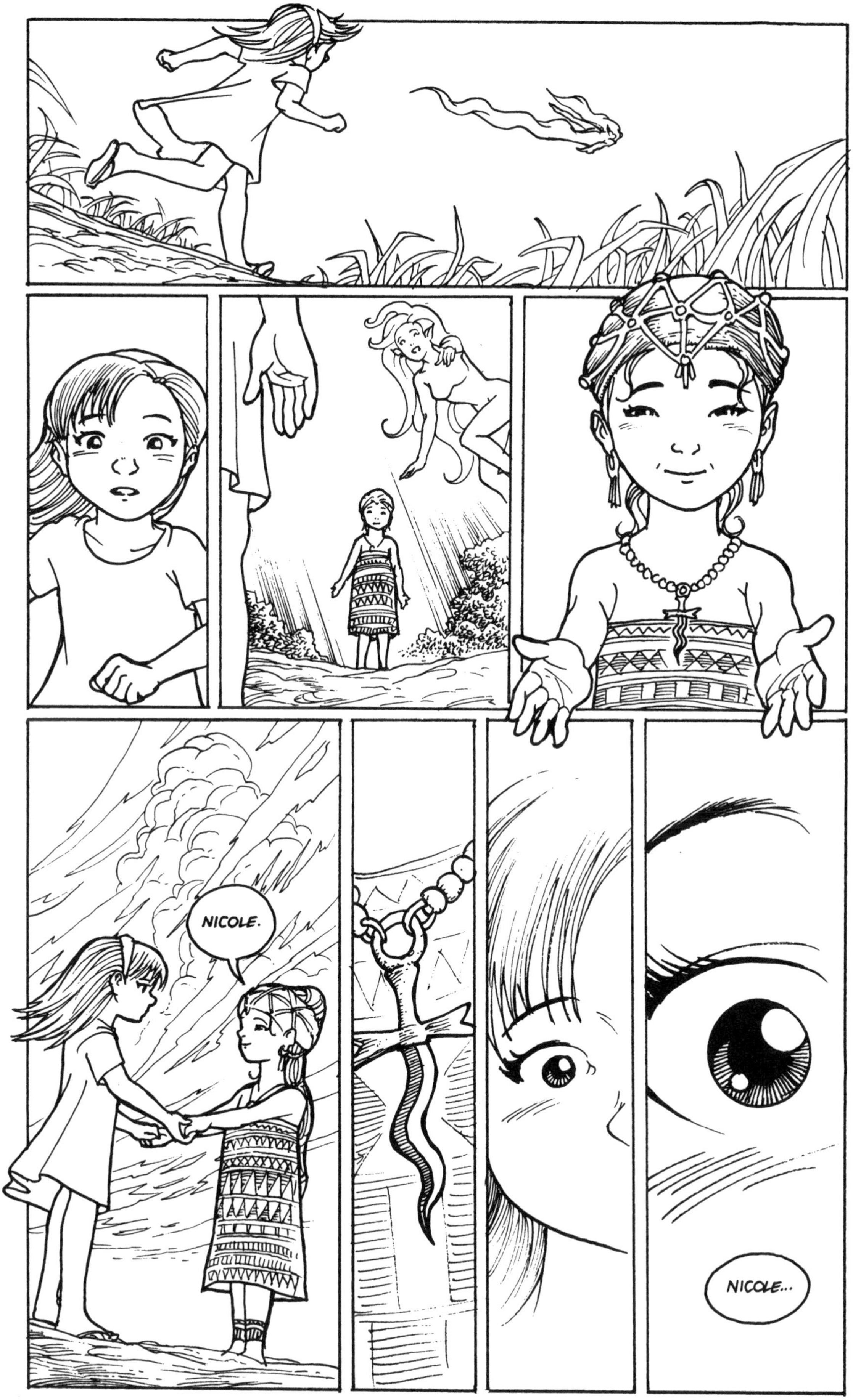
NICOLE.
NICOLE...

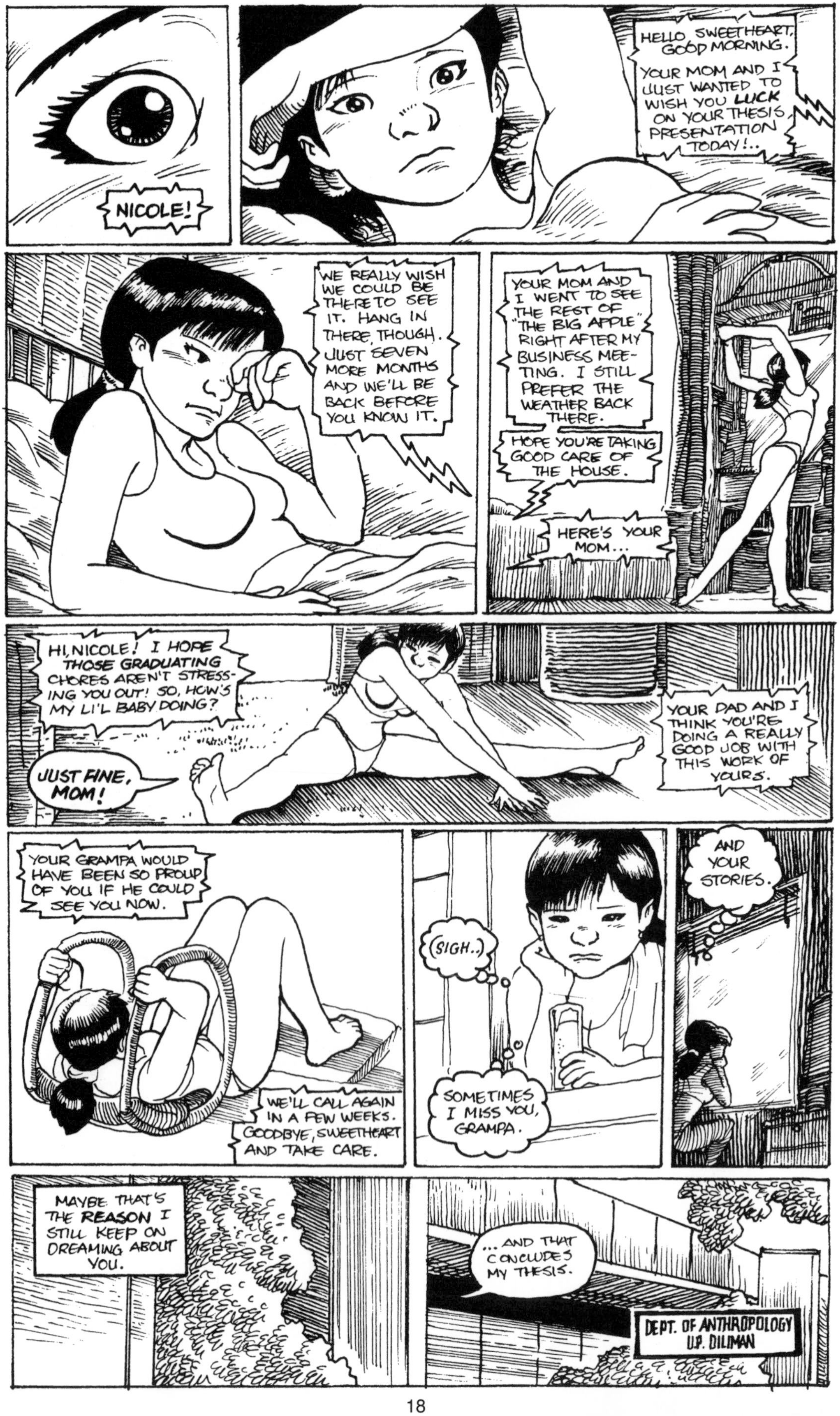
NICOLE!
HELLO, SWEETHEART, GOOD MORNING.
YOUR MOM AND I JUST WANTED TO WISH YOU LUCK ON YOUR THESIS PRESENTATION TODAY!..
WE REALLY WISH WE COULD BE THERE TO SEE IT. HANG IN THERE, THOUGH. JUST SEVEN MORE MONTHS AND WE'LL BE BACK BEFORE YOU KNOW IT.
YOUR MOM AND I WENT TO SEE THE REST OF "THE BIG APPLE" RIGHT AFTER MY BUSINESS MEETING. I STILL PREFER THE WEATHER BACK THERE.
HOPE YOU'RE TAKING GOOD CARE OF THE HOUSE.
HERE'S YOUR MOM...
HI, NICOLE! I HOPE THOSE GRADUATING CHORES AREN'T STRESSING YOU OUT! SO, HOW'S MY LI'L BABY DOING?
JUST FINE, MOM!
YOUR DAD AND I THINK YOU'RE DOING A REALLY GOOD JOB WITH THIS WORK OF YOURS.
YOUR GRAMPA WOULD HAVE BEEN SO PROUD OF YOU IF HE COULD SEE YOU NOW.
WE'LL CALL AGAIN IN A FEW WEEKS. GOODBYE, SWEETHEART AND TAKE CARE.
(SIGH..)
SOMETIMES I MISS YOU, GRAMPA.
AND YOUR STORIES.
MAYBE THAT'S THE REASON I STILL KEEP ON DREAMING ABOUT YOU.
...AND THAT CONCLUDES MY THESIS.
DEPT. OF ANTHROPOLOGY
U.P. DILIMAN

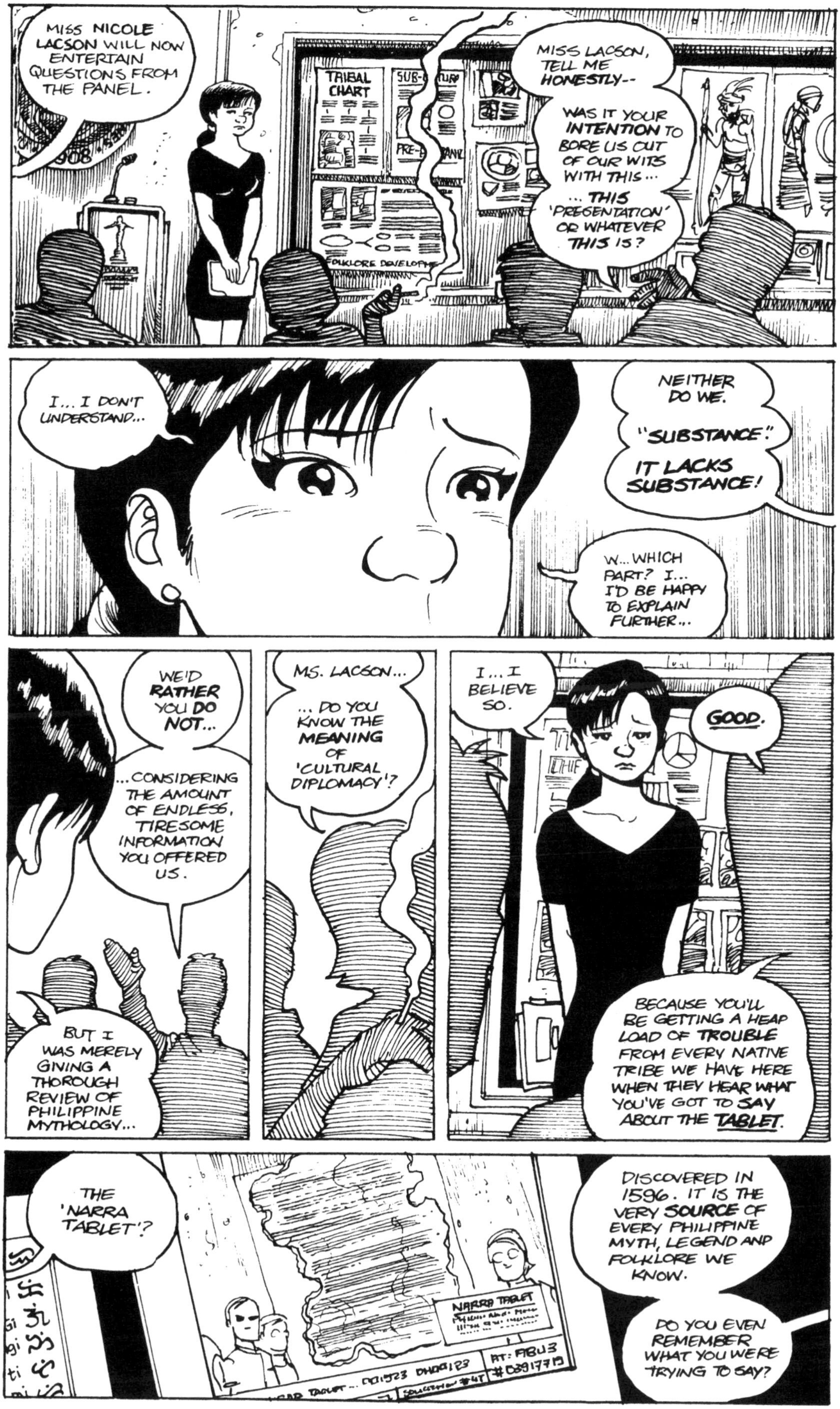
MISS NICOLE LACSON WILL NOW ENTERTAIN QUESTIONS FROM THE PANEL.
TRIBAL CHART
FOLKLORE DEVELOPM
MISS LACSON, TELL ME HONESTLY--
WAS IT YOUR INTENTION TO BORE US OUT OF OUR WITS WITH THIS...
...THIS 'PRESENTATION' OR WHATEVER THIS IS?
I... I DON'T UNDERSTAND...
NEITHER DO WE.
"SUBSTANCE."
IT LACKS SUBSTANCE!
W...WHICH PART? I... I'D BE HAPPY TO EXPLAIN FURTHER...
WE'D RATHER YOU DO NOT...
...CONSIDERING THE AMOUNT OF ENDLESS, TIRESOME INFORMATION YOU OFFERED US.
BUT I WAS MERELY GIVING A THOROUGH REVIEW OF PHILIPPINE MYTHOLOGY...
MS. LACSON...
...DO YOU KNOW THE MEANING OF 'CULTURAL DIPLOMACY'?
I... I BELIEVE SO.
GOOD.
BECAUSE YOU'LL BE GETTING A HEAP LOAD OF TROUBLE FROM EVERY NATIVE TRIBE WE HAVE HERE WHEN THEY HEAR WHAT YOU'VE GOT TO SAY ABOUT THE TABLET.
THE 'NARRA TABLET'?
NARRA TABLET
DISCOVERED IN 1596. IT IS THE VERY SOURCE OF EVERY PHILIPPINE MYTH, LEGEND AND FOLKLORE WE KNOW.
DO YOU EVEN REMEMBER WHAT YOU WERE TRYING TO SAY?

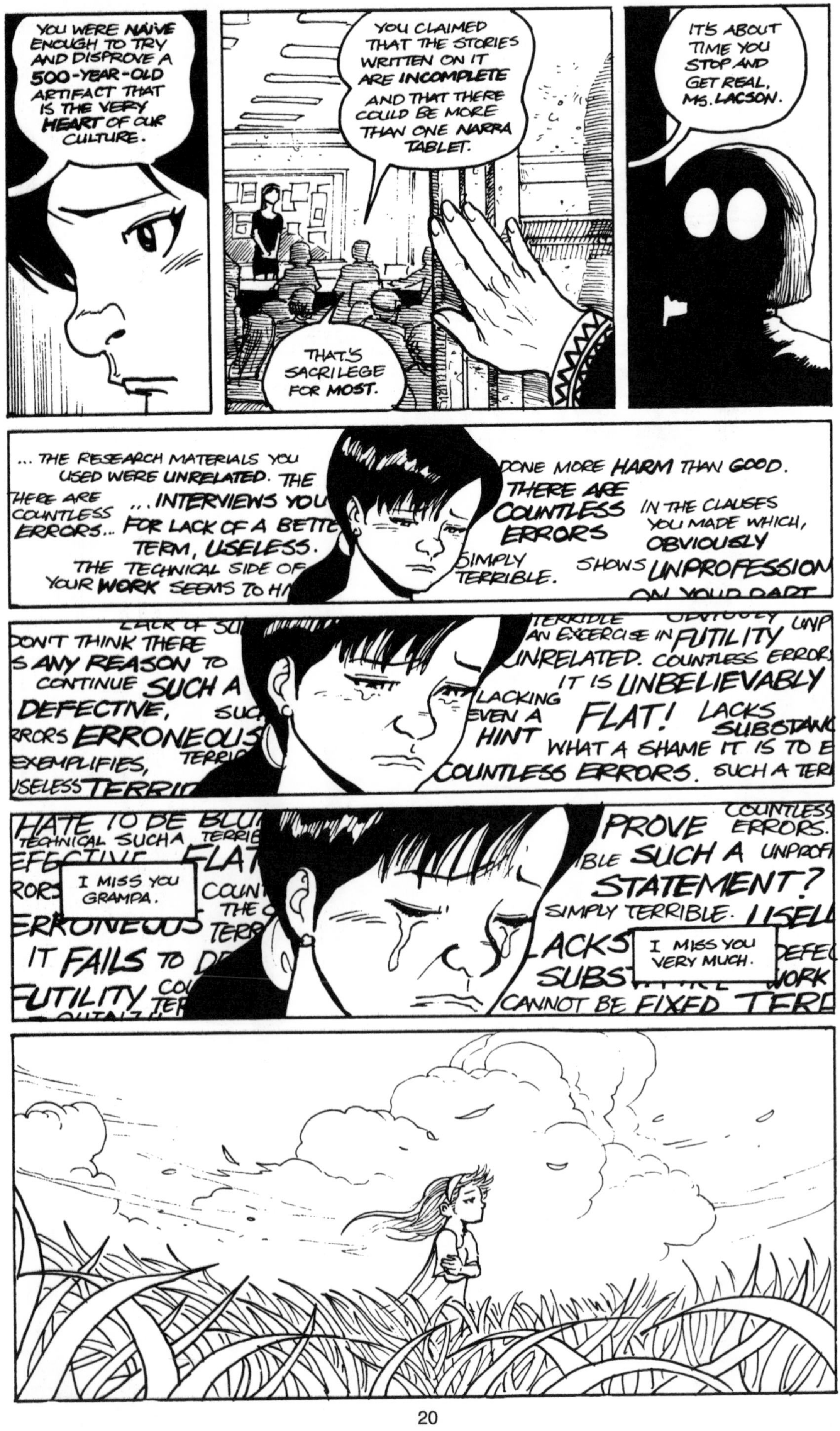
YOU WERE NAÏVE ENOUGH TO TRY AND DISPROVE A 500-YEAR-OLD ARTIFACT THAT IS THE VERY HEART OF OUR CULTURE.
YOU CLAIMED THAT THE STORIES WRITTEN ON IT ARE INCOMPLETE AND THAT THERE COULD BE MORE THAN ONE NARRA TABLET.
THAT'S SACRILEGE FOR MOST.
IT'S ABOUT TIME YOU STOP AND GET REAL, MS. LACSON.
... THE RESEARCH MATERIALS YOU USED WERE UNRELATED.
... INTERVIEWS
FOR LACK OF A
TERM, USELESS.
THE TECHNICAL SIDE OF YOUR WORK SEEMS TO
DONE MORE HARM THAN GOOD.
THERE ARE COUNTLESS ERRORS
IN THE CLAUSES YOU MADE WHICH, OBVIOUSLY
SIMPLY TERRIBLE.
SHOWS
AN EXCERCISE IN FUTILITY
ANY REASON TO CONTINUE SUCH A
DEFECTIVE,
UNRELATED.
IT IS UNBELIEVABLY
LACKING EVEN A HINT
FLAT! LACKS
WHAT A SHAME IT IS TO
COUNTLESS ERRORS.
PROVE SUCH A STATEMENT?
COUNTLESS ERRORS.
I MISS YOU GRAMPA.
SIMPLY TERRIBLE.
IT FAILS TO
I MISS YOU VERY MUCH.
CANNOT BE FIXED

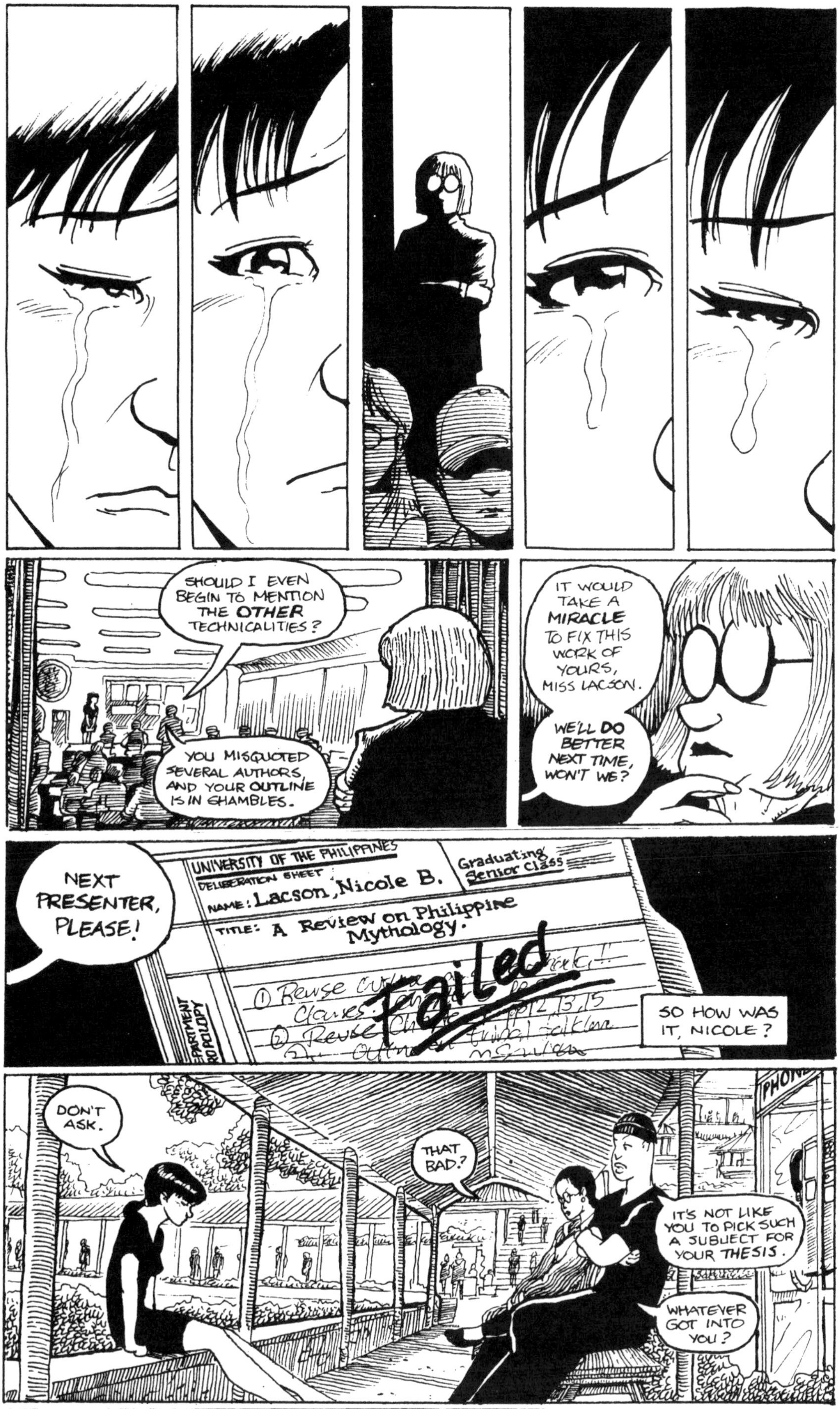
SHOULD I EVEN BEGIN TO MENTION THE OTHER TECHNICALITIES?
YOU MISQUOTED SEVERAL AUTHORS, AND YOUR OUTLINE IS IN SHAMBLES.
IT WOULD TAKE A MIRACLE TO FIX THIS WORK OF YOURS, MISS LACSON.
WE'LL DO BETTER NEXT TIME, WON'T WE?
NEXT PRESENTER, PLEASE!
UNIVERSITY OF THE PHILIPPINES
DELIBERATION SHEET
NAME: Lacson, Nicole B.
Graduating Senior Class
TITLE: A Review on Philippine Mythology.
Failed
SO HOW WAS IT, NICOLE?
DON'T ASK.
THAT BAD?
IT'S NOT LIKE YOU TO PICK SUCH A SUBJECT FOR YOUR THESIS.
WHATEVER GOT INTO YOU?

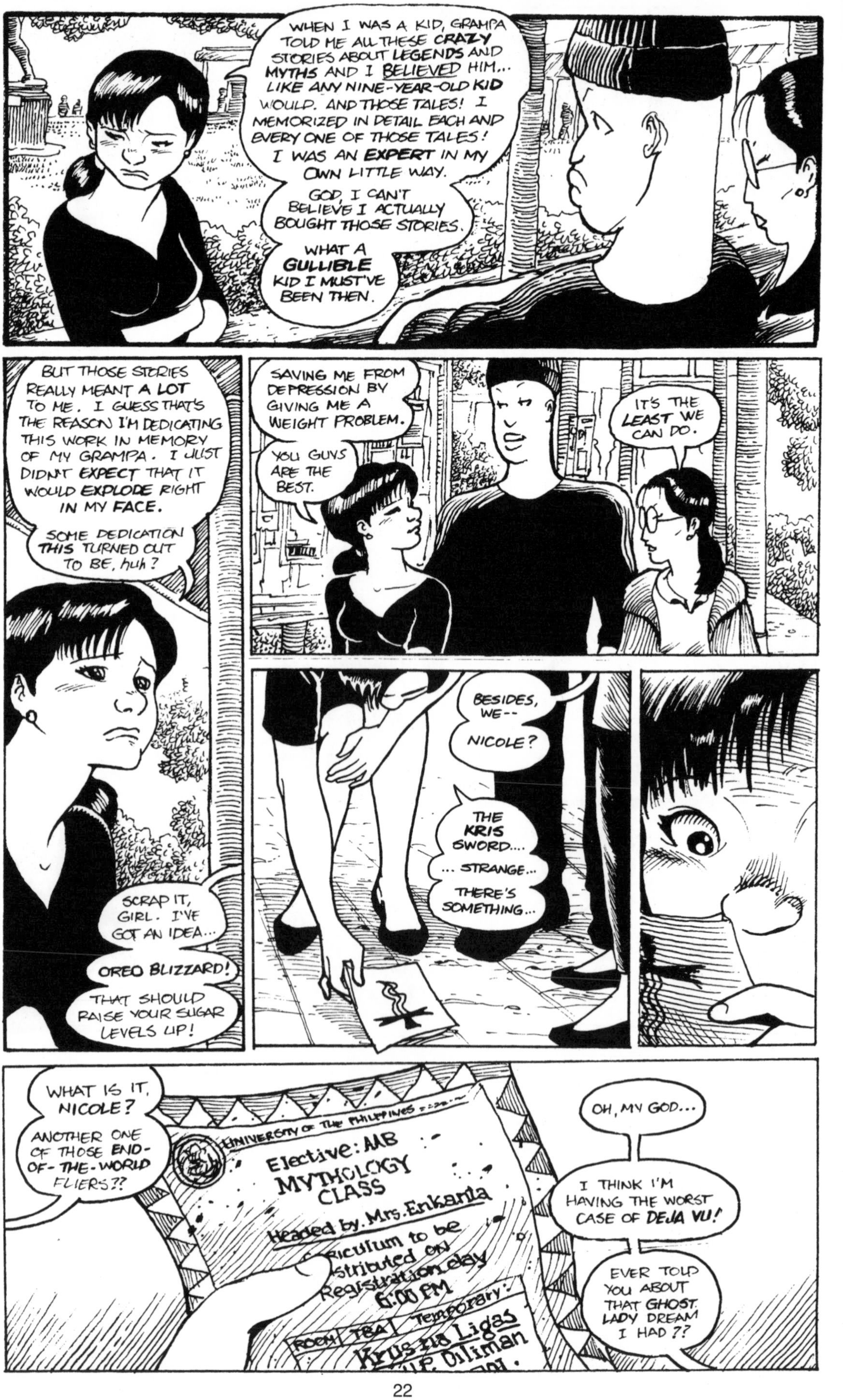
WHEN I WAS A KID, GRAMPA TOLD ME ALL THESE CRAZY STORIES ABOUT LEGENDS AND MYTHS AND I BELIEVED HIM... LIKE ANY NINE-YEAR-OLD KID WOULD. AND THOSE TALES! I MEMORIZED IN DETAIL EACH AND EVERY ONE OF THOSE TALES! I WAS AN EXPERT IN MY OWN LITTLE WAY.
GOD, I CAN'T BELIEVE I ACTUALLY BOUGHT THOSE STORIES.
WHAT A GULLIBLE KID I MUST'VE BEEN THEN.
BUT THOSE STORIES REALLY MEANT A LOT TO ME. I GUESS THAT'S THE REASON I'M DEDICATING THIS WORK IN MEMORY OF MY GRAMPA. I JUST DIDN'T EXPECT THAT IT WOULD EXPLODE RIGHT IN MY FACE.
SOME DEDICATION THIS TURNED OUT TO BE, huh?
SCRAP IT, GIRL. I'VE GOT AN IDEA...
OREO BLIZZARD!
THAT SHOULD RAISE YOUR SUGAR LEVELS UP!
SAVING ME FROM DEPRESSION BY GIVING ME A WEIGHT PROBLEM.
YOU GUYS ARE THE BEST.
IT'S THE LEAST WE CAN DO.
BESIDES, WE--
NICOLE?
THE KRIS SWORD...
...STRANGE...
THERE'S SOMETHING...
WHAT IS IT, NICOLE?
ANOTHER ONE OF THOSE END-OF-THE-WORLD FLIERS??
UNIVERSITY OF THE PHILIPPINES
Elective: AAB
MYTHOLOGY CLASS
Headed by. Mrs. Enkanta
Curriculum to be distributed on Registration day
6:00 PM
ROOM TBA Temporary
Krus na Ligas
U.P. Diliman
OH, MY GOD...
I THINK I'M HAVING THE WORST CASE OF DEJA VU!
EVER TOLD YOU ABOUT THAT GHOST LADY DREAM I HAD??

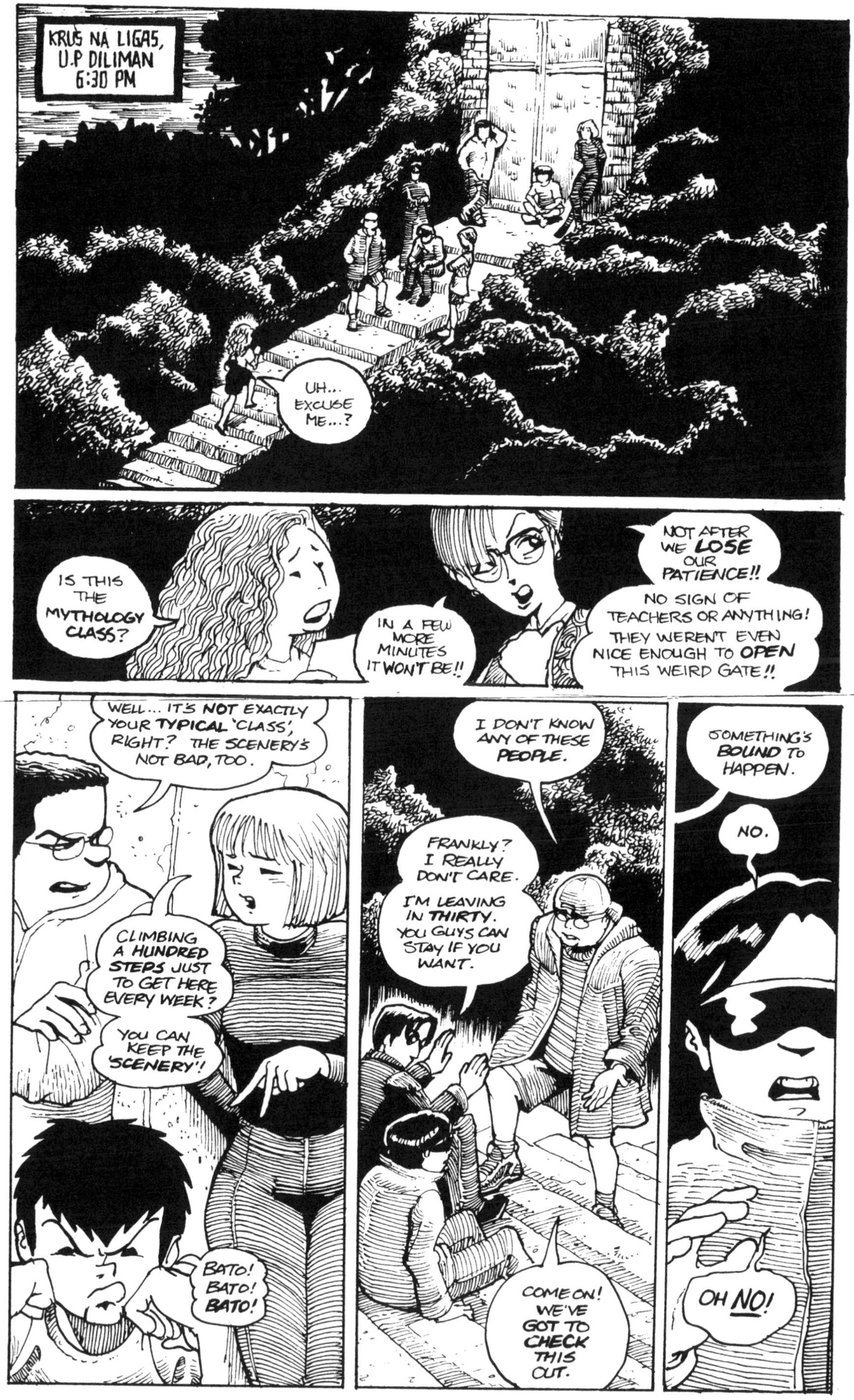
KRUS NA LIGAS, U.P DILIMAN 6:30 PM
UH... EXCUSE ME...?
IS THIS THE MYTHOLOGY CLASS?
IN A FEW MORE MINUTES IT WON'T BE!!
NOT AFTER WE LOSE OUR PATIENCE!!
NO SIGN OF TEACHERS OR ANYTHING! THEY WEREN'T EVEN NICE ENOUGH TO OPEN THIS WEIRD GATE!!
WELL... IT'S NOT EXACTLY YOUR TYPICAL 'CLASS', RIGHT? THE SCENERY'S NOT BAD, TOO.
CLIMBING A HUNDRED STEPS JUST TO GET HERE EVERY WEEK?
YOU CAN KEEP THE 'SCENERY'!
BATO! BATO! BATO!
I DON'T KNOW ANY OF THESE PEOPLE.
FRANKLY? I REALLY DON'T CARE.
I'M LEAVING IN THIRTY. YOU GUYS CAN STAY IF YOU WANT.
COME ON! WE'VE GOT TO CHECK THIS OUT.
SOMETHING'S BOUND TO HAPPEN.
NO.
OH NO!

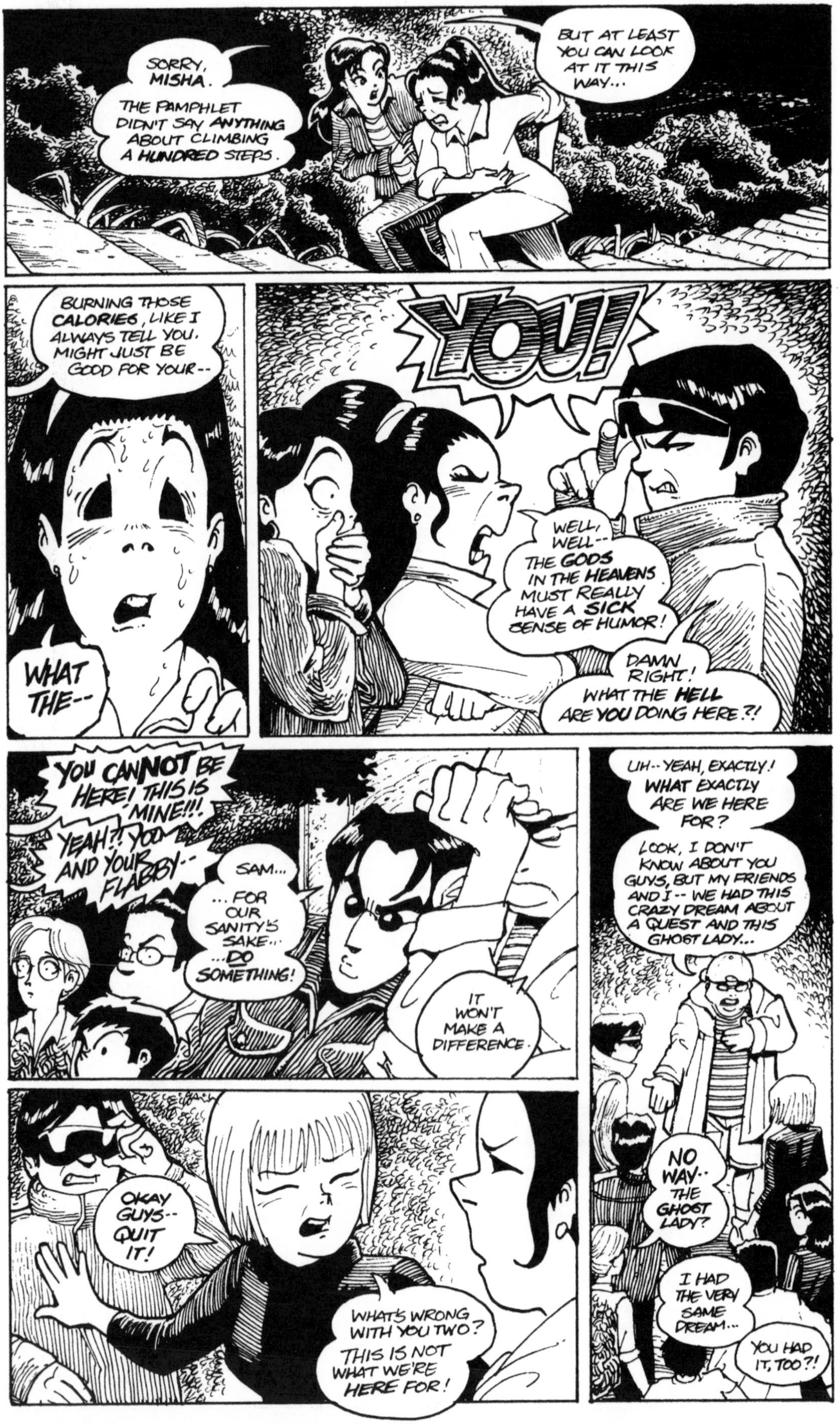
SORRY, MISHA.
THE PAMPHLET DIDN'T SAY ANYTHING ABOUT CLIMBING A HUNDRED STEPS.
BUT AT LEAST YOU CAN LOOK AT IT THIS WAY...
BURNING THOSE CALORIES, LIKE I ALWAYS TELL YOU. MIGHT JUST BE GOOD FOR YOUR--
WHAT THE--
YOU!
WELL, WELL-- THE GODS IN THE HEAVENS MUST REALLY HAVE A SICK SENSE OF HUMOR!
DAMN RIGHT! WHAT THE HELL ARE YOU DOING HERE?!
YOU CANNOT BE HERE! THIS IS MINE!!!
YEAH?! YOU AND YOUR FLABBY--
SAM...
...FOR OUR SANITY'S SAKE... ...DO SOMETHING!
IT WON'T MAKE A DIFFERENCE.
UH-- YEAH, EXACTLY! WHAT EXACTLY ARE WE HERE FOR?
LOOK, I DON'T KNOW ABOUT YOU GUYS, BUT MY FRIENDS AND I-- WE HAD THIS CRAZY DREAM ABOUT A QUEST AND THIS GHOST LADY...
OKAY GUYS-- QUIT IT!
WHAT'S WRONG WITH YOU TWO?
THIS IS NOT WHAT WE'RE HERE FOR!
NO WAY.. THE GHOST LADY?
I HAD THE VERY SAME DREAM...
YOU HAD IT, TOO?!

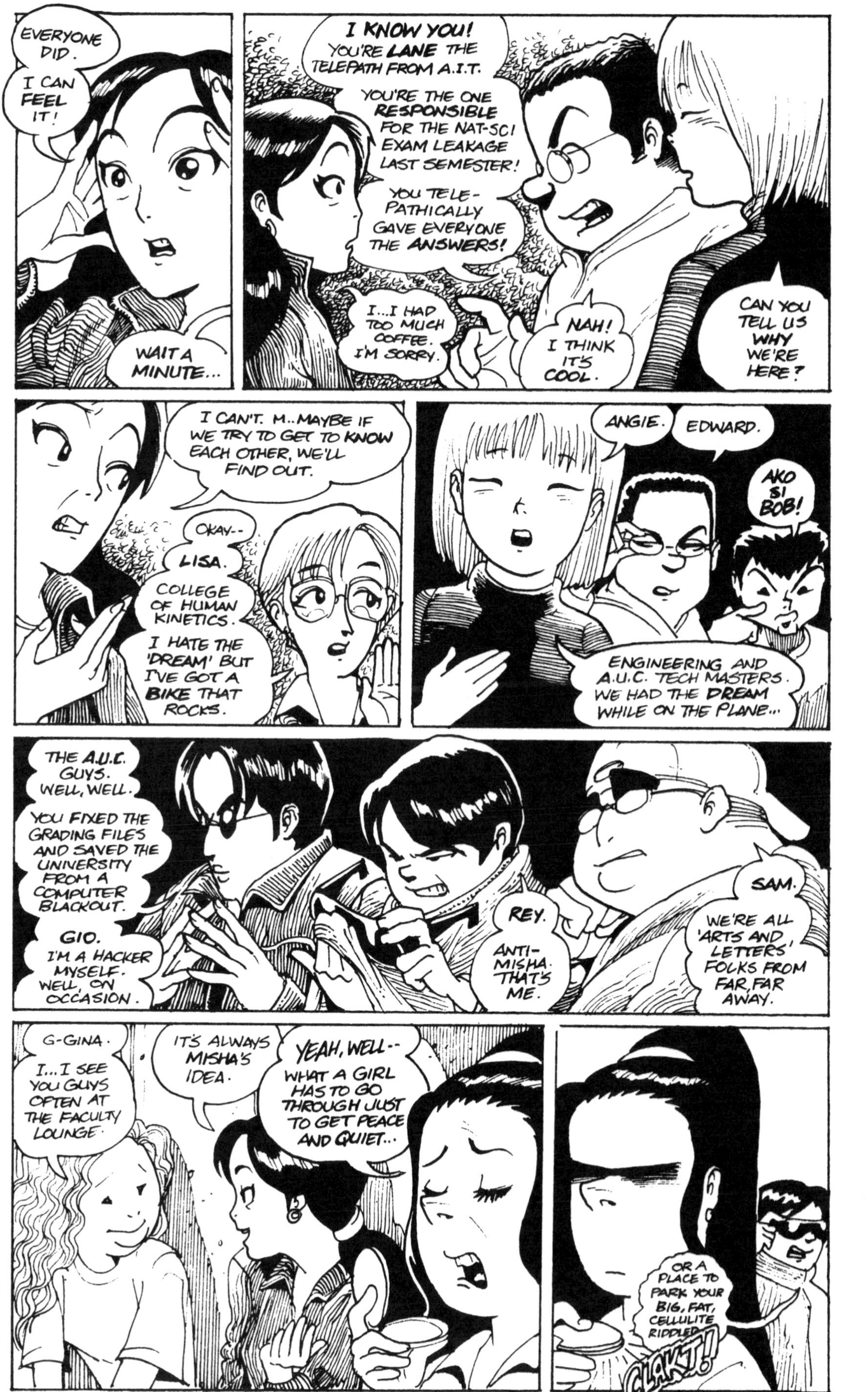
EVERYONE DID.
I CAN FEEL IT!
WAIT A MINUTE...
I KNOW YOU! YOU'RE LANE THE TELEPATH FROM A.I.T.
YOU'RE THE ONE RESPONSIBLE FOR THE NAT-SCI EXAM LEAKAGE LAST SEMESTER!
YOU TELE-PATHICALLY GAVE EVERYONE THE ANSWERS!
I...I HAD TOO MUCH COFFEE. I'M SORRY.
NAH! I THINK IT'S COOL.
CAN YOU TELL US WHY WE'RE HERE?
I CAN'T. M...MAYBE IF WE TRY TO GET TO KNOW EACH OTHER, WE'LL FIND OUT.
OKAY--
LISA.
COLLEGE OF HUMAN KINETICS.
I HATE THE 'DREAM' BUT I'VE GOT A BIKE THAT ROCKS.
ANGIE.
EDWARD.
AKO SI BOB!
ENGINEERING AND A.U.C. TECH MASTERS. WE HAD THE DREAM WHILE ON THE PLANE...
THE A.U.C. GUYS. WELL, WELL.
YOU FIXED THE GRADING FILES AND SAVED THE UNIVERSITY FROM A COMPUTER BLACKOUT.
GIO.
I'M A HACKER MYSELF. WELL, ON OCCASION.
REY.
ANTI-MISHA. THAT'S ME.
SAM.
WE'RE ALL 'ARTS AND LETTERS' FOLKS FROM FAR, FAR AWAY.
G-GINA.
I...I SEE YOU GUYS OFTEN AT THE FACULTY LOUNGE.
IT'S ALWAYS MISHA'S IDEA.
YEAH, WELL--
WHAT A GIRL HAS TO GO THROUGH JUST TO GET PEACE AND QUIET...
OR A PLACE TO PARK YOUR BIG, FAT, CELLULITE RIDDLED
CLAKT!

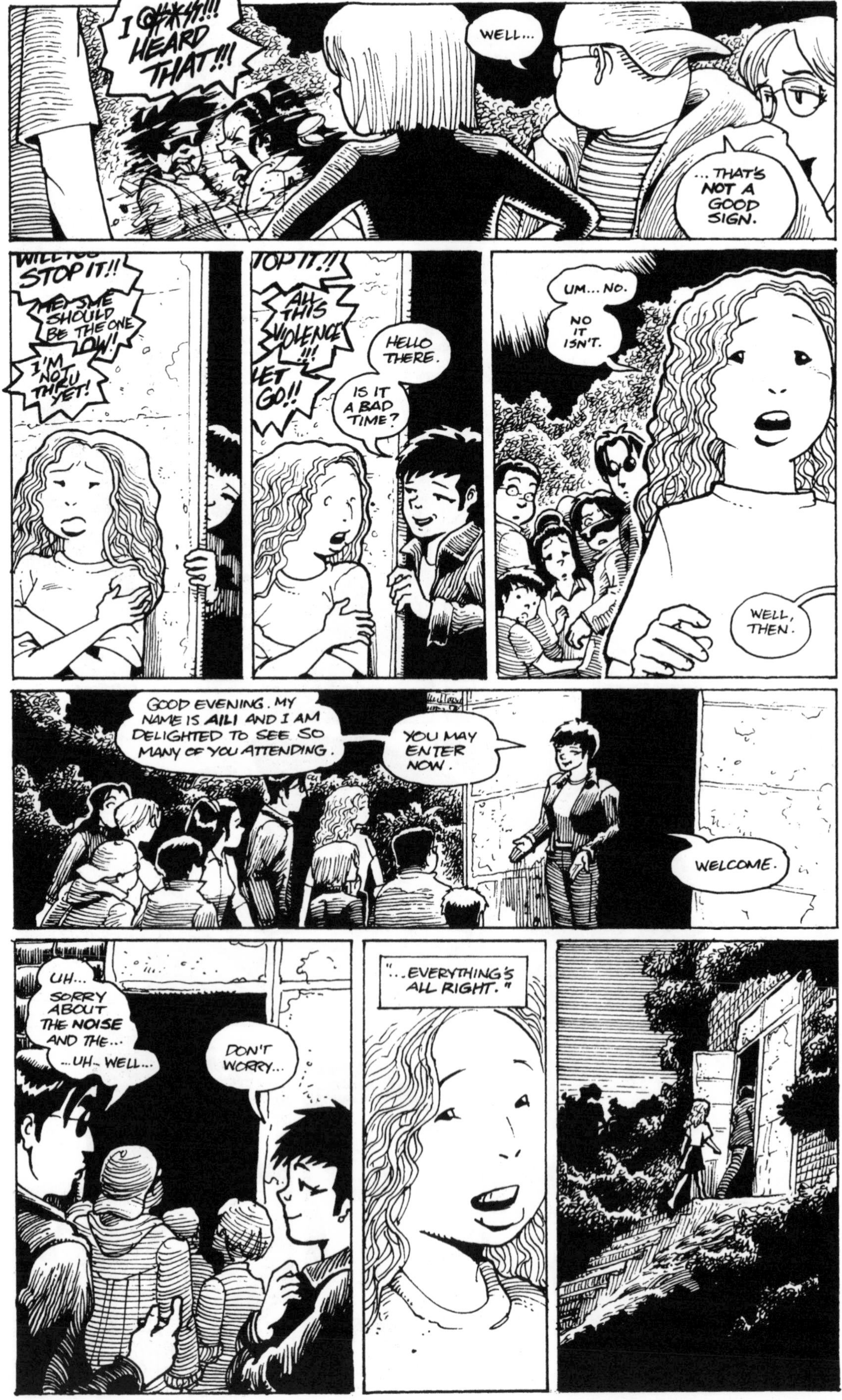
I @#*$!!! HEARD THAT!!!
WELL...
...THAT'S NOT A GOOD SIGN.
STOP IT!!
SHOULD BE THE ONE
I'M NOT THRU YET!
ALL THIS VIOLENCE!!!
GO!!
HELLO THERE.
IS IT A BAD TIME?
UM... NO.
NO IT ISN'T.
WELL, THEN.
GOOD EVENING. MY NAME IS AILI AND I AM DELIGHTED TO SEE SO MANY OF YOU ATTENDING.
YOU MAY ENTER NOW.
WELCOME.
UH... SORRY ABOUT THE NOISE AND THE... ...UH.. WELL...
DON'T WORRY...
"...EVERYTHING'S ALL RIGHT."

MANILA
7:30 PM

STRANGE OBJECT.

HELP THE AETAS FIND A HOME

ᜅᜒᜆ᜔ᜎᜓᜬ ᜀᜆ᜔ᜎᜓᜬ!!

ᜅᜒᜆ᜔ᜎᜓᜬ ᜀᜆ᜔ᜎᜓᜬ ᜃᜓ!

YES, THE LEGEND IS TRUE, FOR I AM HE. BROTHER OF YOUR ANCESTORS, SENT BY THE GODS ON AN IMPORTANT MISSION.

BUT... SO MANY OF YOU HERE.

BATHALA WOULD FIND IT UPSETTING THAT YOU LEFT THE LAND HE GAVE YOUR PEOPLE.

I SEEK AN ITEM.

WILL YOU HELP ME?

ᜀᜆ᜔ᜎᜓ ᜃᜓ᜔

YOU KNOW OF IT?

YOU SAW THE ONE WHO TOOK IT?

ᜊᜒᜆ᜔ᜎᜓᜬ᜔

SHARE WITH ME YOUR THOUGHTS.

27

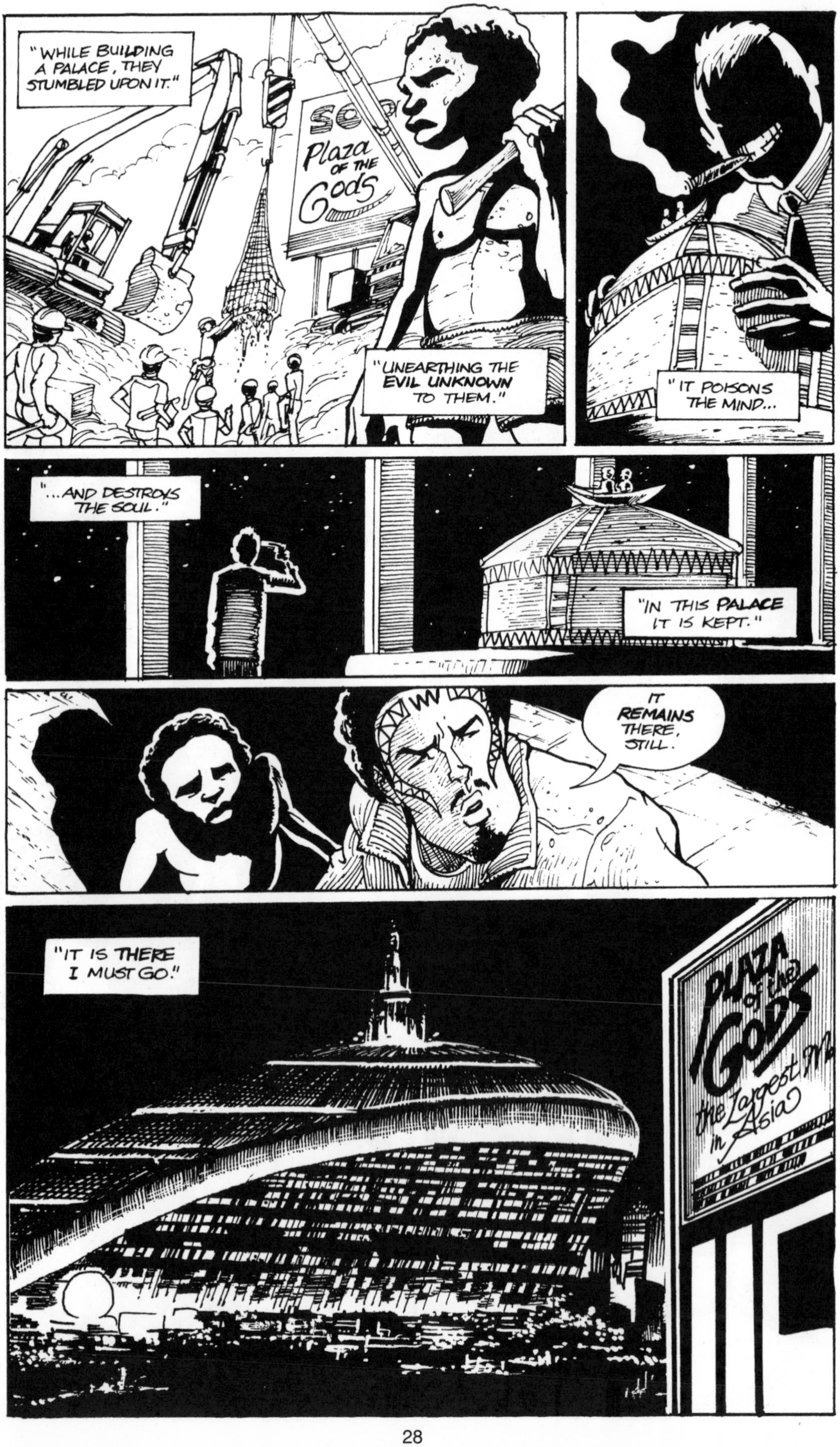
"WHILE BUILDING A PALACE, THEY STUMBLED UPON IT."
SOGO
Plaza OF THE Gods
"UNEARTHING THE EVIL UNKNOWN TO THEM."
"IT POISONS THE MIND...
"...AND DESTROYS THE SOUL."
"IN THIS PALACE IT IS KEPT."
IT REMAINS THERE, STILL.
"IT IS THERE I MUST GO."
PLAZA OF THE GODS
the Largest

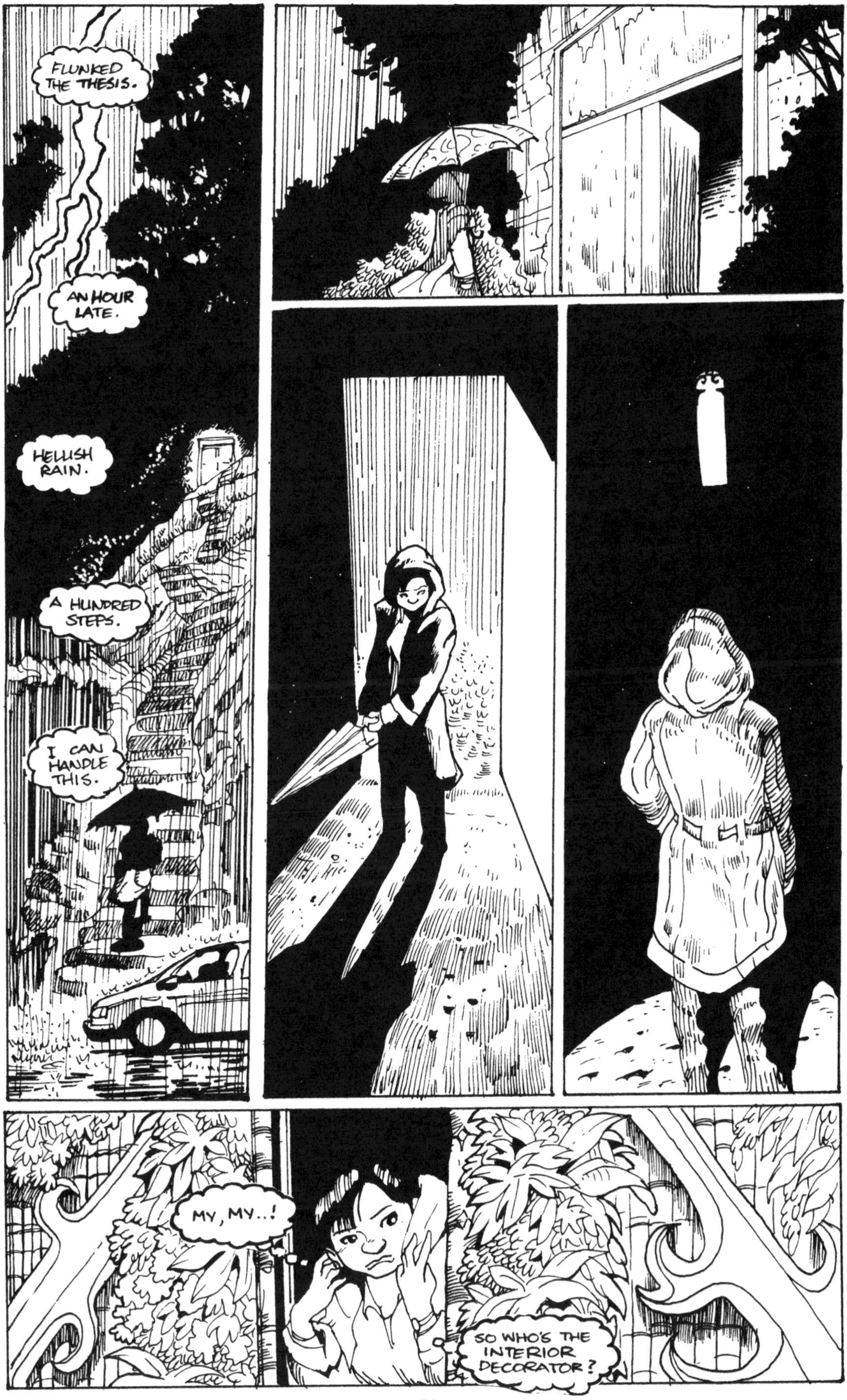
FLUNKED THE THESIS.
AN HOUR LATE.
HELLISH RAIN.
A HUNDRED STEPS.
I CAN HANDLE THIS.
MY, MY...!
SO WHO'S THE INTERIOR DECORATOR?

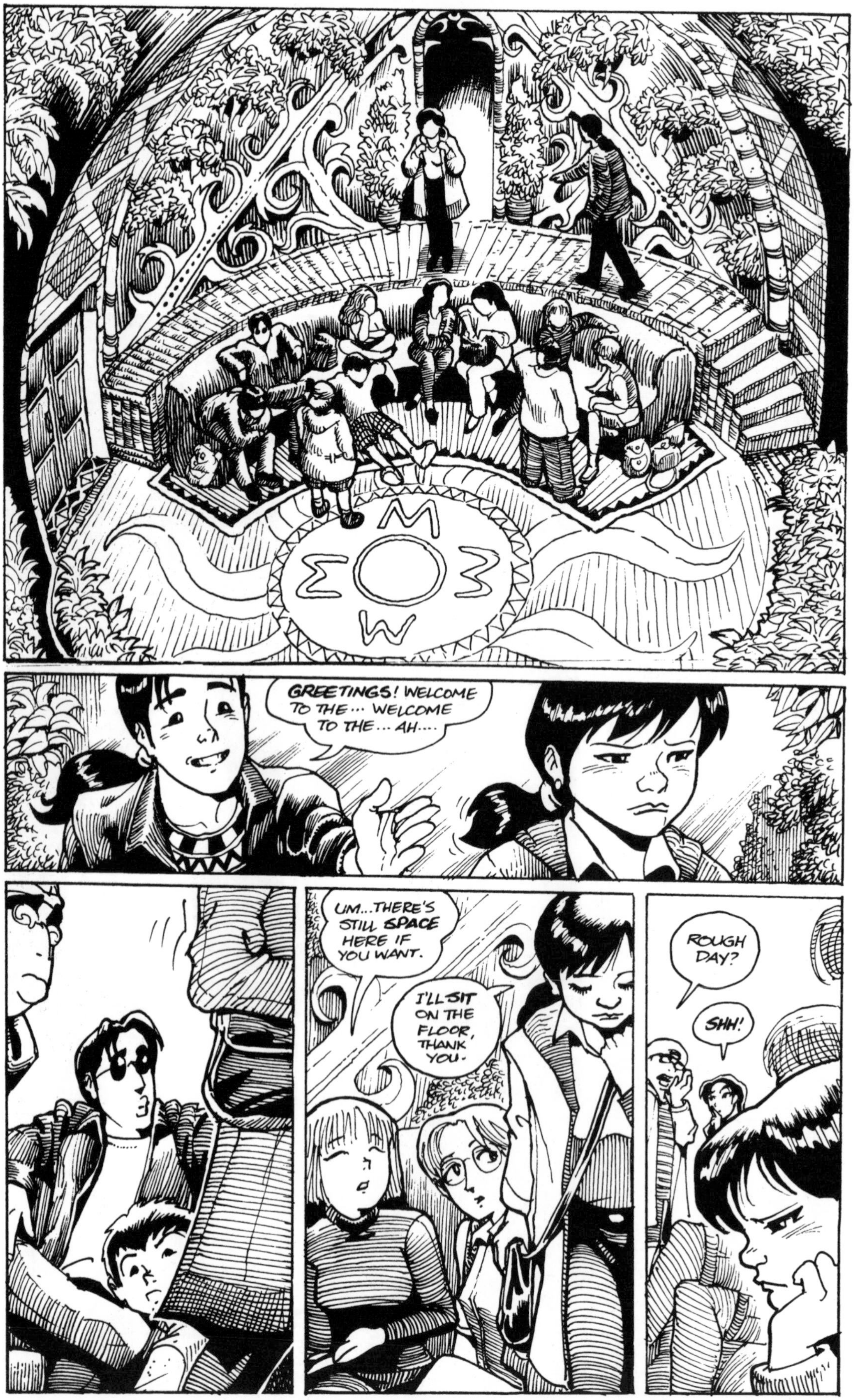
GREETINGS! WELCOME TO THE... WELCOME TO THE... AH....
UM...THERE'S STILL SPACE HERE IF YOU WANT.
I'LL SIT ON THE FLOOR, THANK YOU.
ROUGH DAY?
SHH!

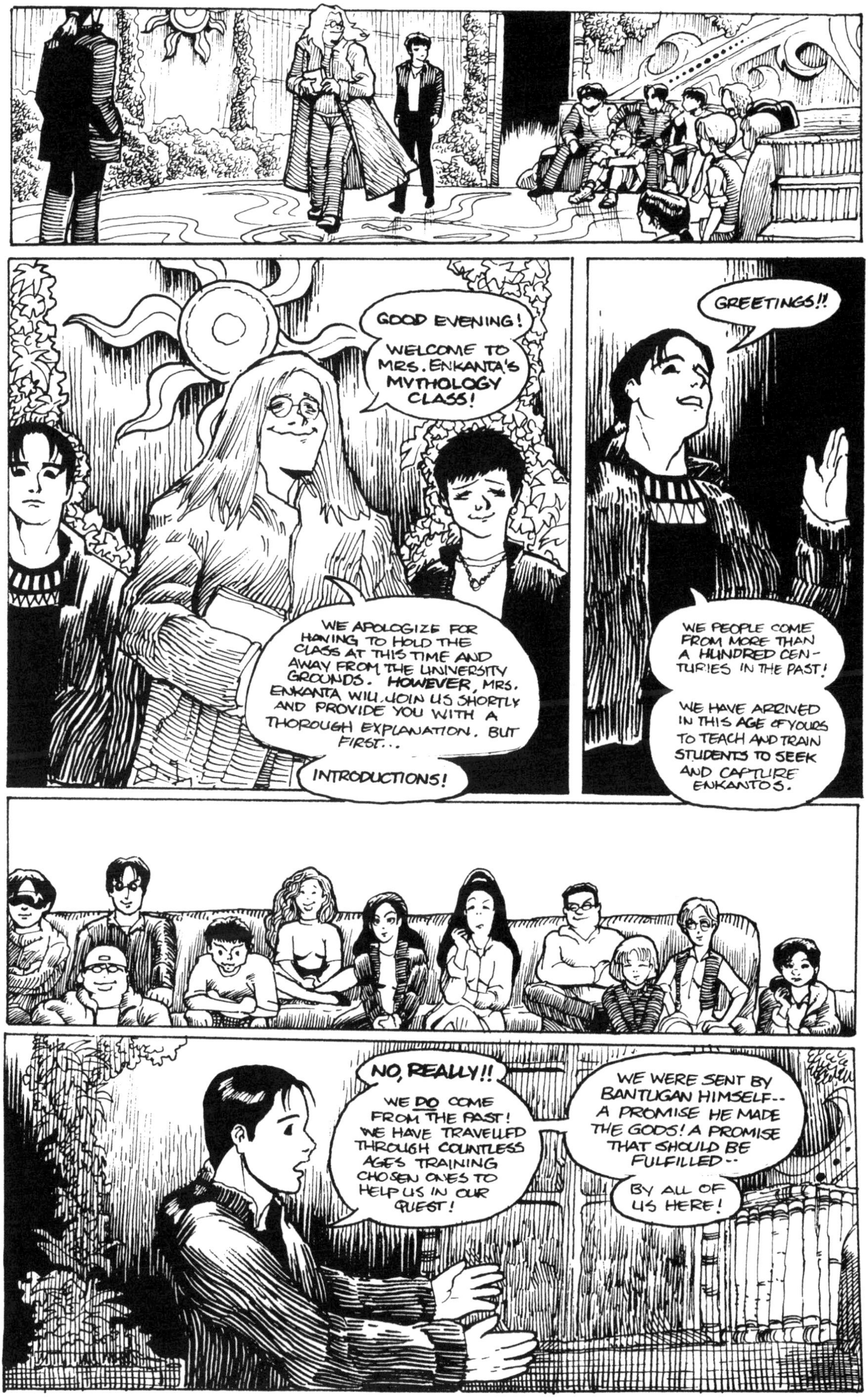
GOOD EVENING!
WELCOME TO MRS. ENKANTA'S MYTHOLOGY CLASS!
WE APOLOGIZE FOR HAVING TO HOLD THE CLASS AT THIS TIME AND AWAY FROM THE UNIVERSITY GROUNDS. HOWEVER, MRS. ENKANTA WILL JOIN US SHORTLY AND PROVIDE YOU WITH A THOROUGH EXPLANATION. BUT FIRST...
INTRODUCTIONS!
GREETINGS!!
WE PEOPLE COME FROM MORE THAN A HUNDRED CENTURIES IN THE PAST!
WE HAVE ARRIVED IN THIS AGE OF YOURS TO TEACH AND TRAIN STUDENTS TO SEEK AND CAPTURE ENKANTOS.
NO, REALLY!!
WE DO COME FROM THE PAST! WE HAVE TRAVELLED THROUGH COUNTLESS AGES TRAINING CHOSEN ONES TO HELP US IN OUR QUEST!
WE WERE SENT BY BANTUGAN HIMSELF-- A PROMISE HE MADE THE GODS! A PROMISE THAT SHOULD BE FULFILLED--
BY ALL OF US HERE!

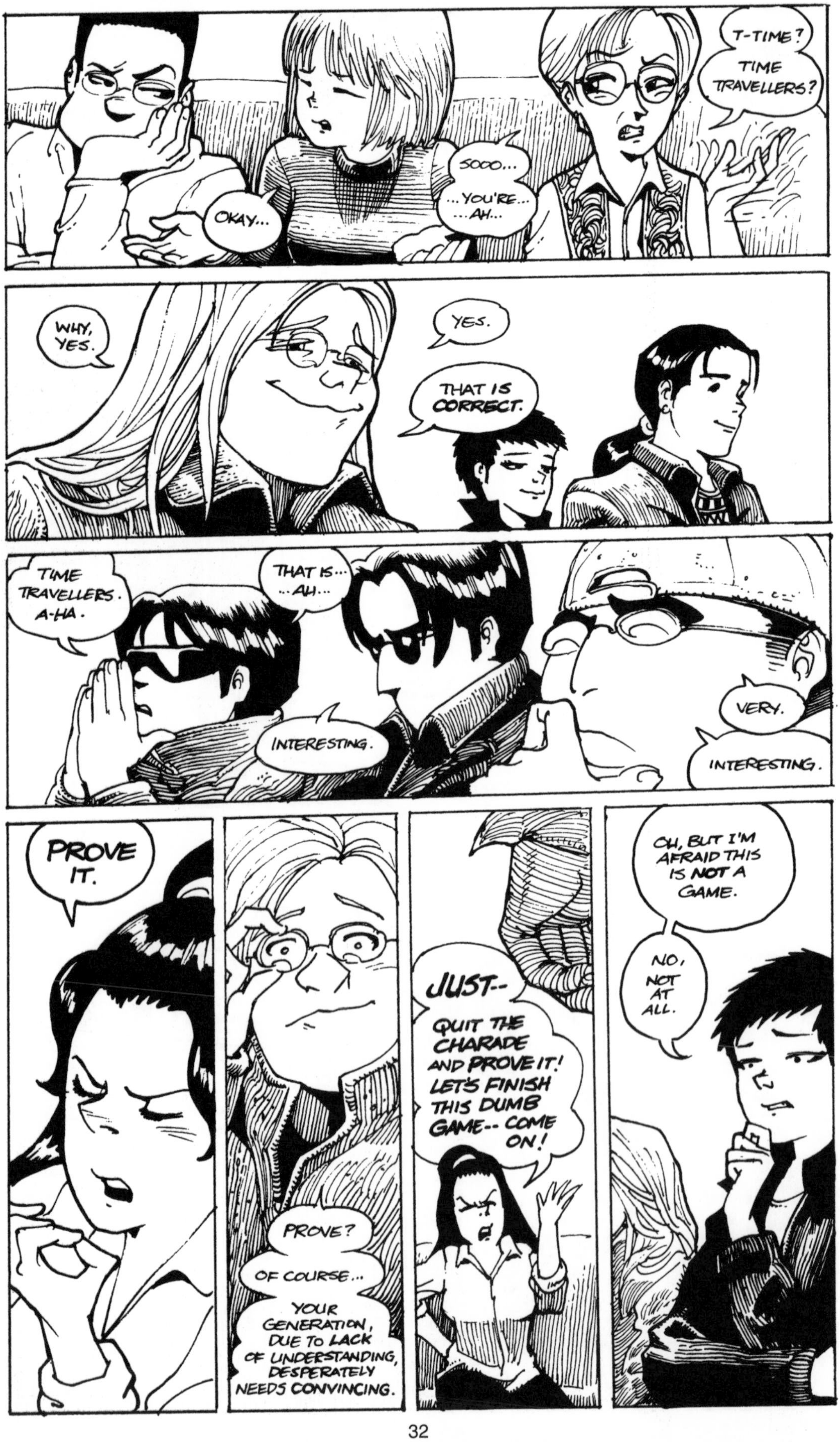
T-TIME?
TIME TRAVELLERS?
OKAY...
SOOO...
...YOU'RE... ...AH...
WHY, YES.
YES.
THAT IS CORRECT.
TIME TRAVELLERS. A-HA.
THAT IS... ...AH...
INTERESTING.
VERY.
INTERESTING.
PROVE IT.
PROVE?
OF COURSE...
YOUR GENERATION, DUE TO LACK OF UNDERSTANDING, DESPERATELY NEEDS CONVINCING.
JUST--
QUIT THE CHARADE AND PROVE IT! LET'S FINISH THIS DUMB GAME-- COME ON!
OH, BUT I'M AFRAID THIS IS NOT A GAME.
NO, NOT AT ALL.

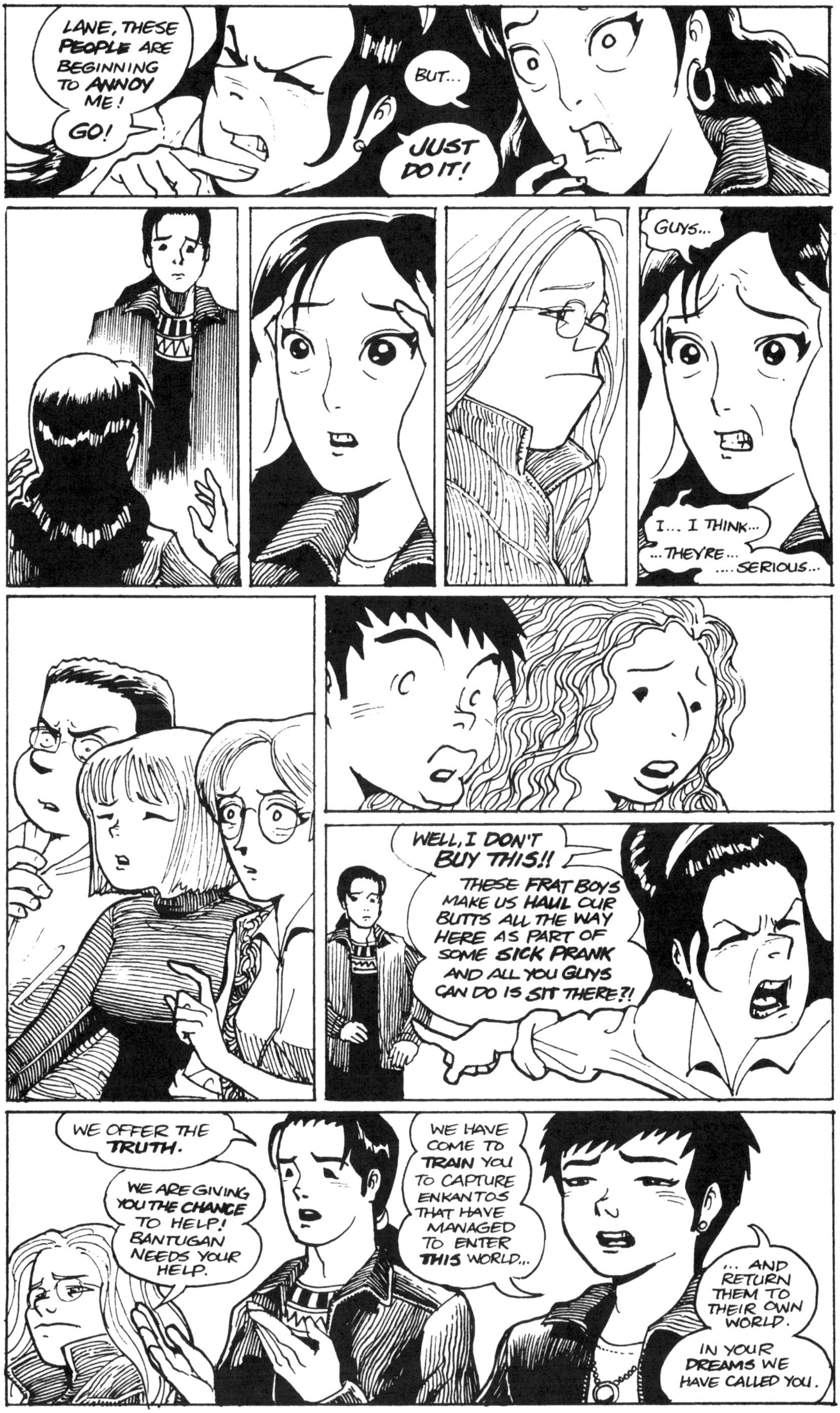
LANE, THESE PEOPLE ARE BEGINNING TO ANNOY ME!
GO!
BUT...
JUST DO IT!
GUYS...
I... I THINK...
...THEY'RE...
....SERIOUS...
WELL, I DON'T BUY THIS!!
THESE FRAT BOYS MAKE US HAUL OUR BUTTS ALL THE WAY HERE AS PART OF SOME SICK PRANK AND ALL YOU GUYS CAN DO IS SIT THERE?!
WE OFFER THE TRUTH.
WE ARE GIVING YOU THE CHANCE TO HELP! BANTUGAN NEEDS YOUR HELP.
WE HAVE COME TO TRAIN YOU TO CAPTURE ENKANTOS THAT HAVE MANAGED TO ENTER THIS WORLD...
... AND RETURN THEM TO THEIR OWN WORLD.
IN YOUR DREAMS WE HAVE CALLED YOU.

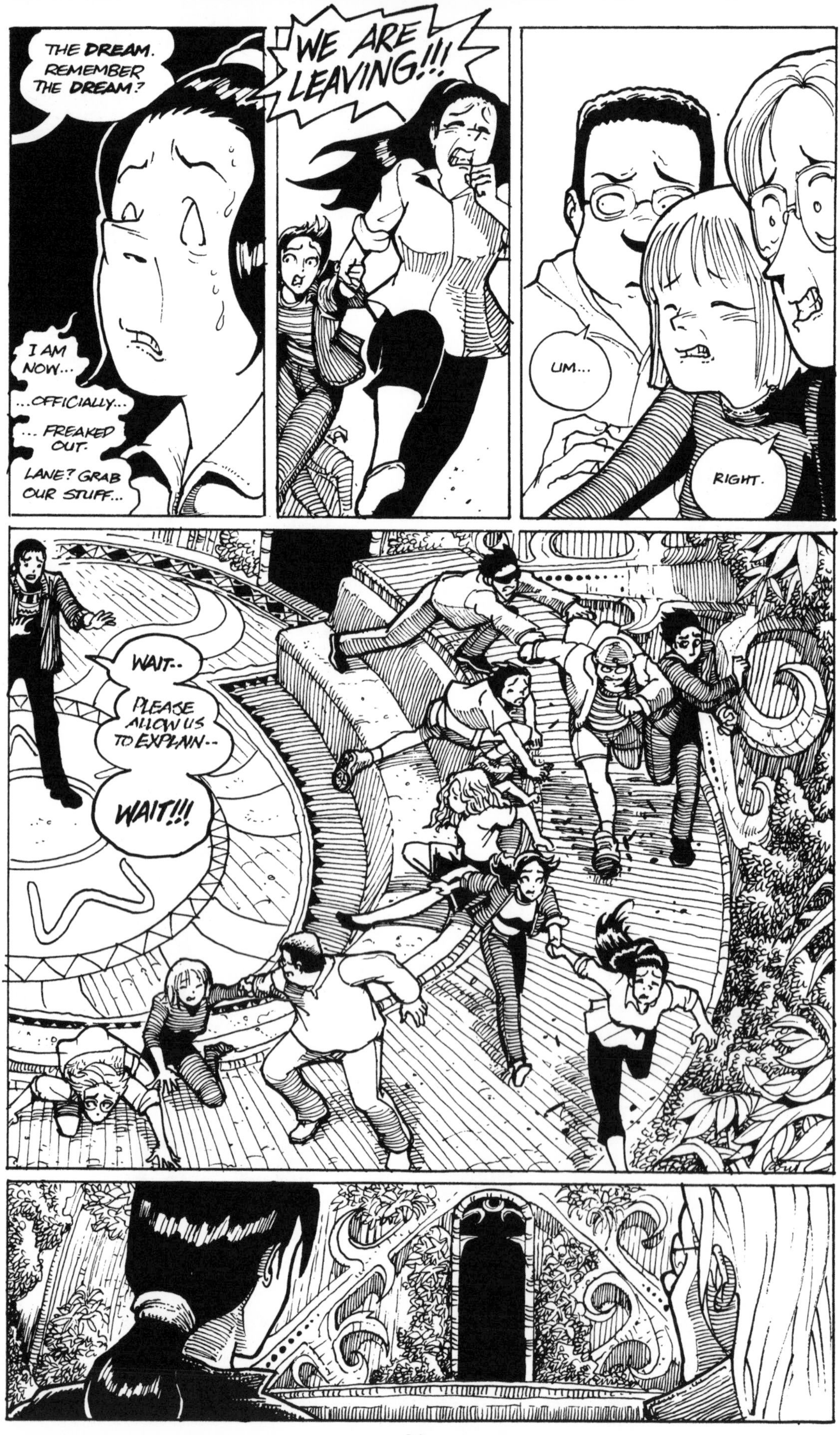
THE DREAM. REMEMBER THE DREAM?
I AM NOW...
...OFFICIALLY...
...FREAKED OUT.
LANE? GRAB OUR STUFF...
WE ARE LEAVING!!!
UM...
RIGHT.
WAIT--
PLEASE ALLOW US TO EXPLAIN--
WAIT!!!

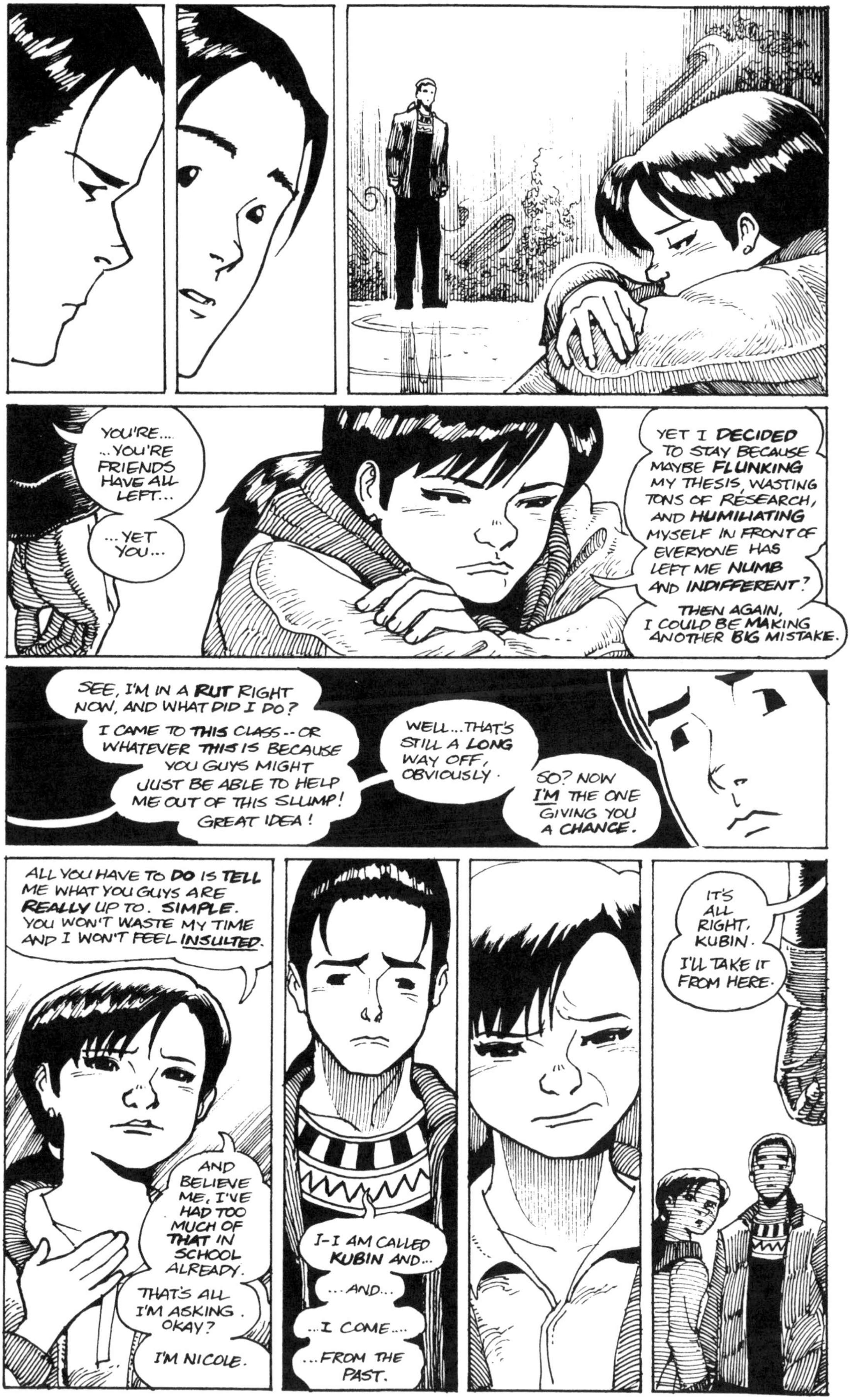
YOU'RE.... ...YOU'RE FRIENDS HAVE ALL LEFT...
...YET YOU...
YET I DECIDED TO STAY BECAUSE MAYBE FLUNKING MY THESIS, WASTING TONS OF RESEARCH, AND HUMILIATING MYSELF IN FRONT OF EVERYONE HAS LEFT ME NUMB AND INDIFFERENT?
THEN AGAIN, I COULD BE MAKING ANOTHER BIG MISTAKE.
SEE, I'M IN A RUT RIGHT NOW, AND WHAT DID I DO?
I CAME TO THIS CLASS -- OR WHATEVER THIS IS BECAUSE YOU GUYS MIGHT JUST BE ABLE TO HELP ME OUT OF THIS SLUMP! GREAT IDEA!
WELL... THAT'S STILL A LONG WAY OFF, OBVIOUSLY.
SO? NOW I'M THE ONE GIVING YOU A CHANCE.
ALL YOU HAVE TO DO IS TELL ME WHAT YOU GUYS ARE REALLY UP TO. SIMPLE. YOU WON'T WASTE MY TIME AND I WON'T FEEL INSULTED.
AND BELIEVE ME, I'VE HAD TOO MUCH OF THAT IN SCHOOL ALREADY.
THAT'S ALL I'M ASKING. OKAY?
I'M NICOLE.
I-I AM CALLED KUBIN AND...
...AND...
...I COME....
...FROM THE PAST.
IT'S ALL RIGHT, KUBIN.
I'LL TAKE IT FROM HERE.

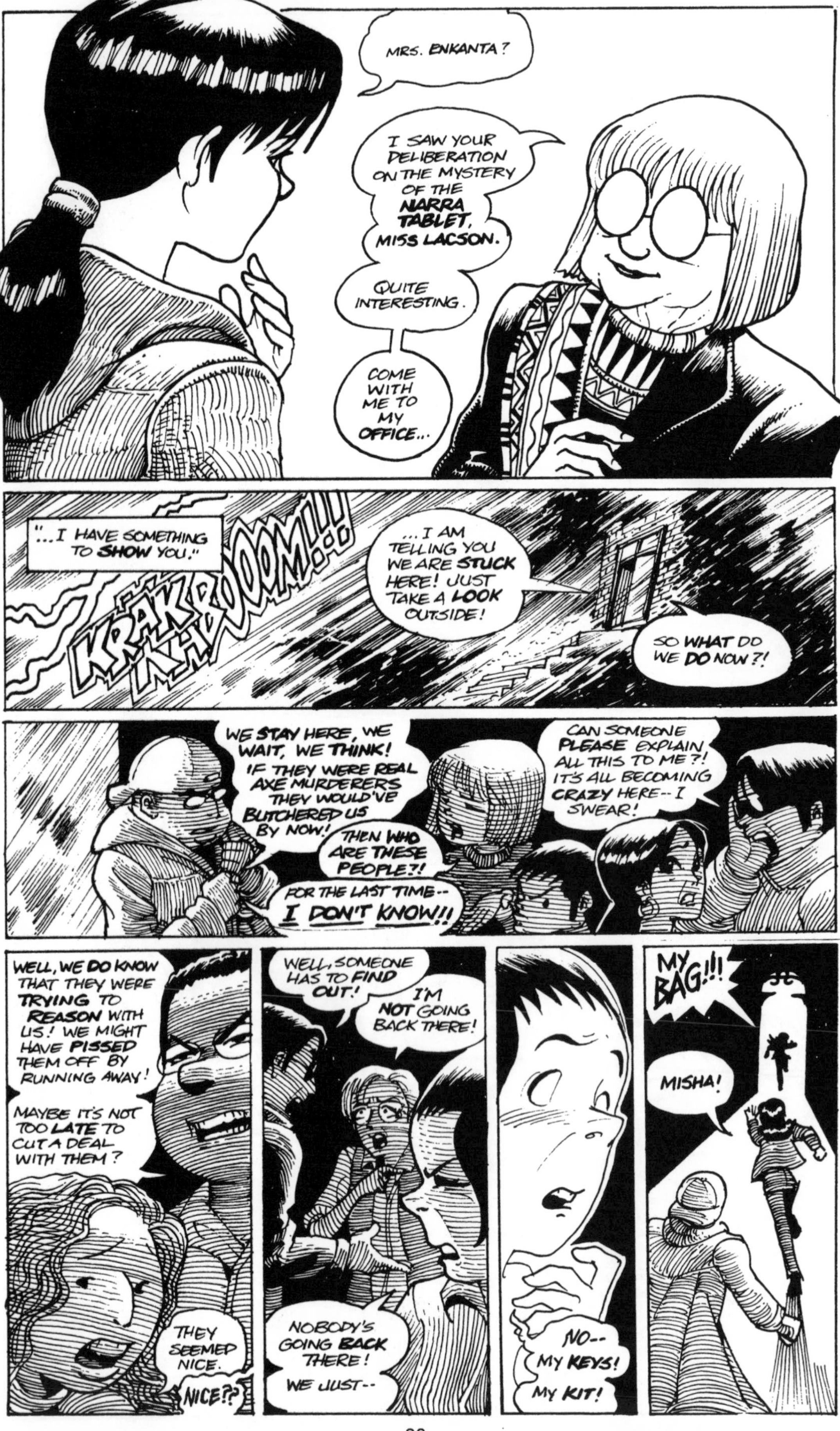
MRS. ENKANTA?
I SAW YOUR DELIBERATION ON THE MYSTERY OF THE NARRA TABLET, MISS LACSON.
QUITE INTERESTING.
COME WITH ME TO MY OFFICE...
"...I HAVE SOMETHING TO SHOW YOU."
KRAKKABOOM!!!
...I AM TELLING YOU WE ARE STUCK HERE! JUST TAKE A LOOK OUTSIDE!
SO WHAT DO WE DO NOW?!
WE STAY HERE, WE WAIT, WE THINK! IF THEY WERE REAL AXE MURDERERS THEY WOULD'VE BUTCHERED US BY NOW!
CAN SOMEONE PLEASE EXPLAIN ALL THIS TO ME?! IT'S ALL BECOMING CRAZY HERE-- I SWEAR!
THEN WHO ARE THESE PEOPLE?!
FOR THE LAST TIME-- I DON'T KNOW!!
WELL, WE DO KNOW THAT THEY WERE TRYING TO REASON WITH US! WE MIGHT HAVE PISSED THEM OFF BY RUNNING AWAY!
MAYBE IT'S NOT TOO LATE TO CUT A DEAL WITH THEM?
THEY SEEMED NICE.
NICE??
WELL, SOMEONE HAS TO FIND OUT!
I'M NOT GOING BACK THERE!
NOBODY'S GOING BACK THERE!
WE JUST--
NO-- MY KEYS!
MY KIT!
MY BAG!!!
MISHA!

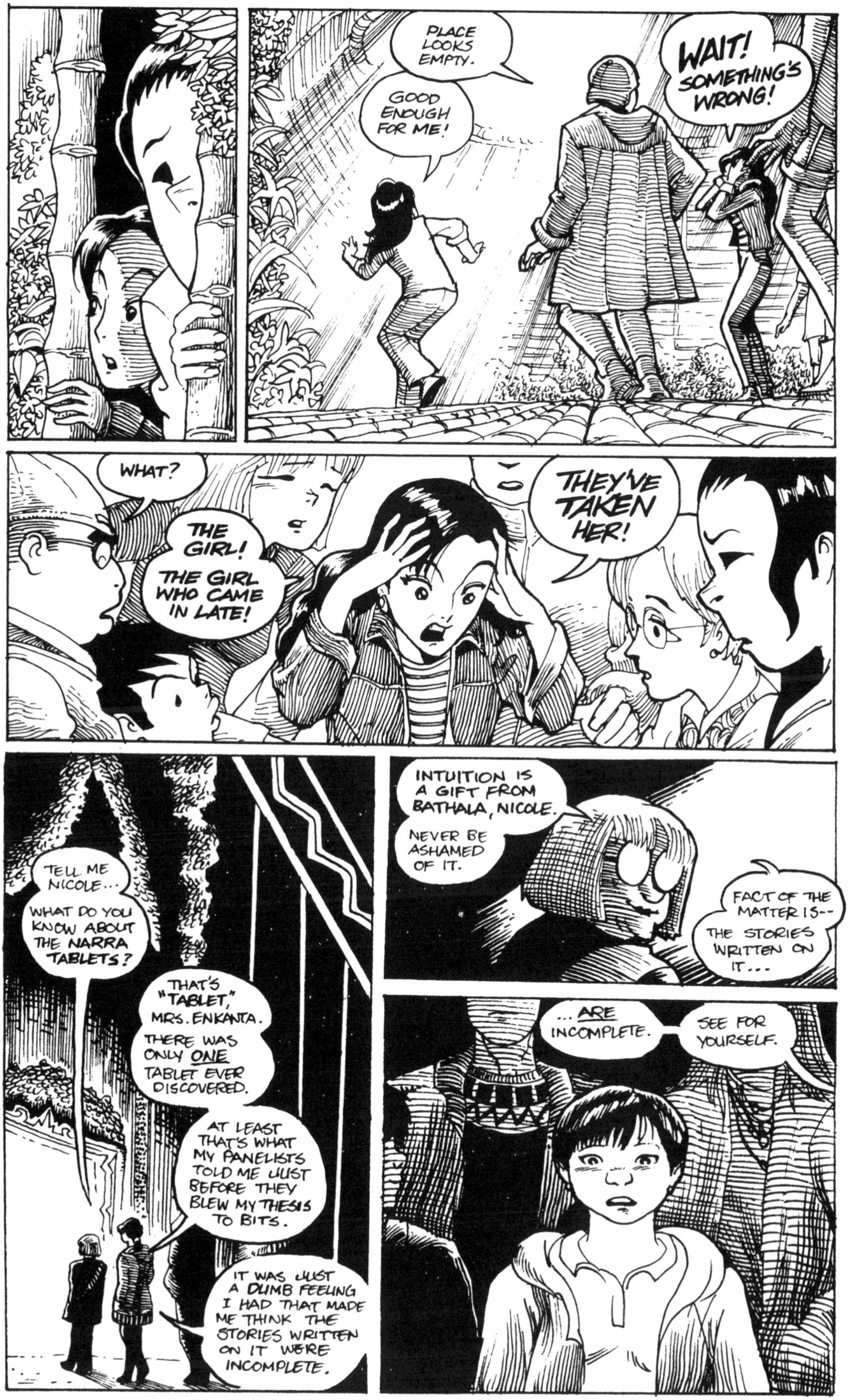
PLACE LOOKS EMPTY.
GOOD ENOUGH FOR ME!
WAIT! SOMETHING'S WRONG!
WHAT?
THE GIRL!
THE GIRL WHO CAME IN LATE!
THEY'VE TAKEN HER!
TELL ME NICOLE...
WHAT DO YOU KNOW ABOUT THE NARRA TABLETS?
THAT'S "TABLET," MRS. ENKANTA.
THERE WAS ONLY ONE TABLET EVER DISCOVERED.
AT LEAST THAT'S WHAT MY PANELISTS TOLD ME JUST BEFORE THEY BLEW MY THESIS TO BITS.
IT WAS JUST A DUMB FEELING I HAD THAT MADE ME THINK THE STORIES WRITTEN ON IT WERE INCOMPLETE.
INTUITION IS A GIFT FROM BATHALA, NICOLE.
NEVER BE ASHAMED OF IT.
FACT OF THE MATTER IS--
THE STORIES WRITTEN ON IT...
...ARE INCOMPLETE.
SEE FOR YOURSELF.

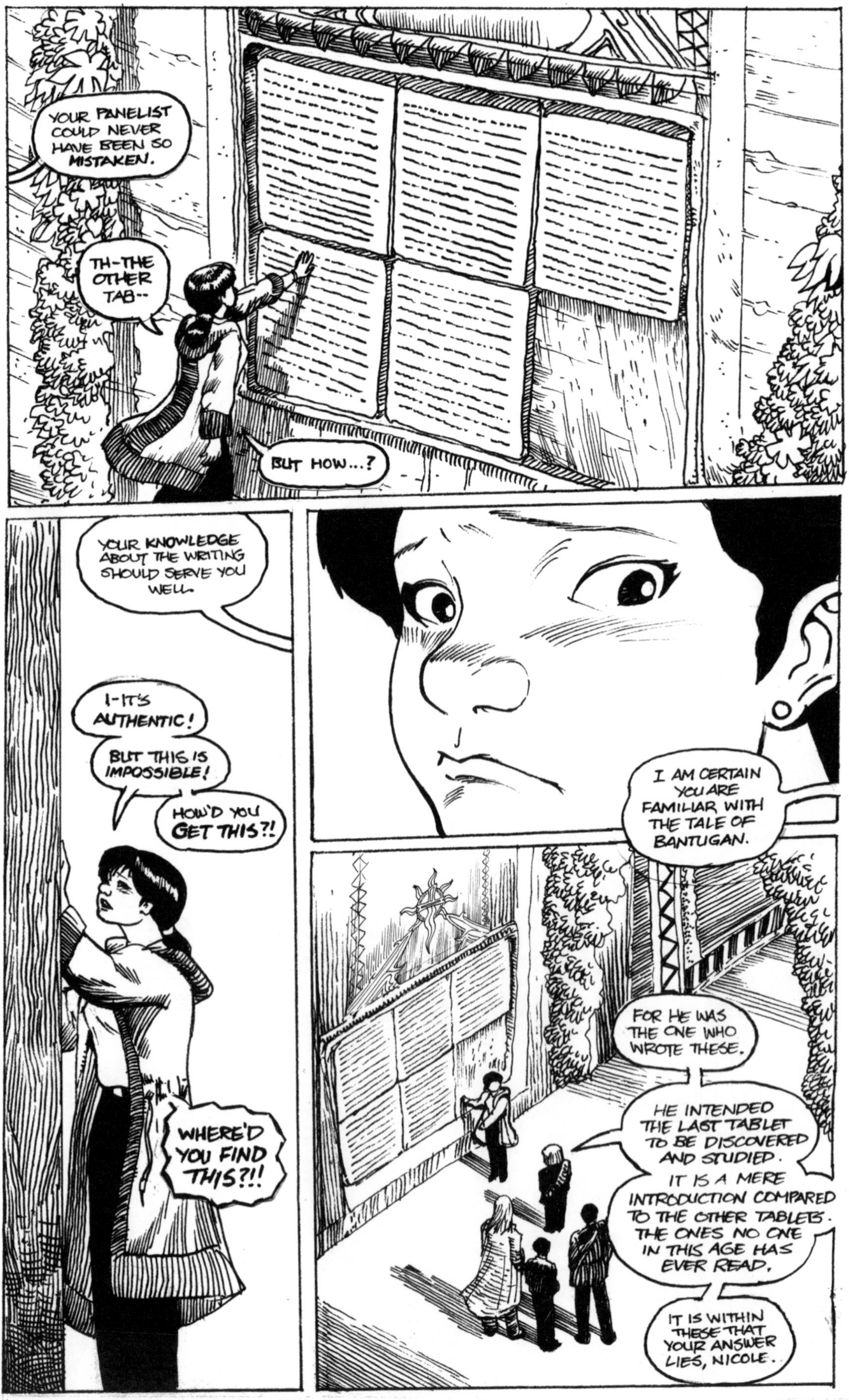
YOUR PANELIST COULD NEVER HAVE BEEN SO MISTAKEN.
TH-THE OTHER TAB--
BUT HOW...?
YOUR KNOWLEDGE ABOUT THE WRITING SHOULD SERVE YOU WELL.
I-IT'S AUTHENTIC!
BUT THIS IS IMPOSSIBLE!
HOW'D YOU GET THIS?!
WHERE'D YOU FIND THIS?!!
I AM CERTAIN YOU ARE FAMILIAR WITH THE TALE OF BANTUGAN.
FOR HE WAS THE ONE WHO WROTE THESE.
HE INTENDED THE LAST TABLET TO BE DISCOVERED AND STUDIED.
IT IS A MERE INTRODUCTION COMPARED TO THE OTHER TABLETS. THE ONES NO ONE IN THIS AGE HAS EVER READ.
IT IS WITHIN THESE THAT YOUR ANSWER LIES, NICOLE.

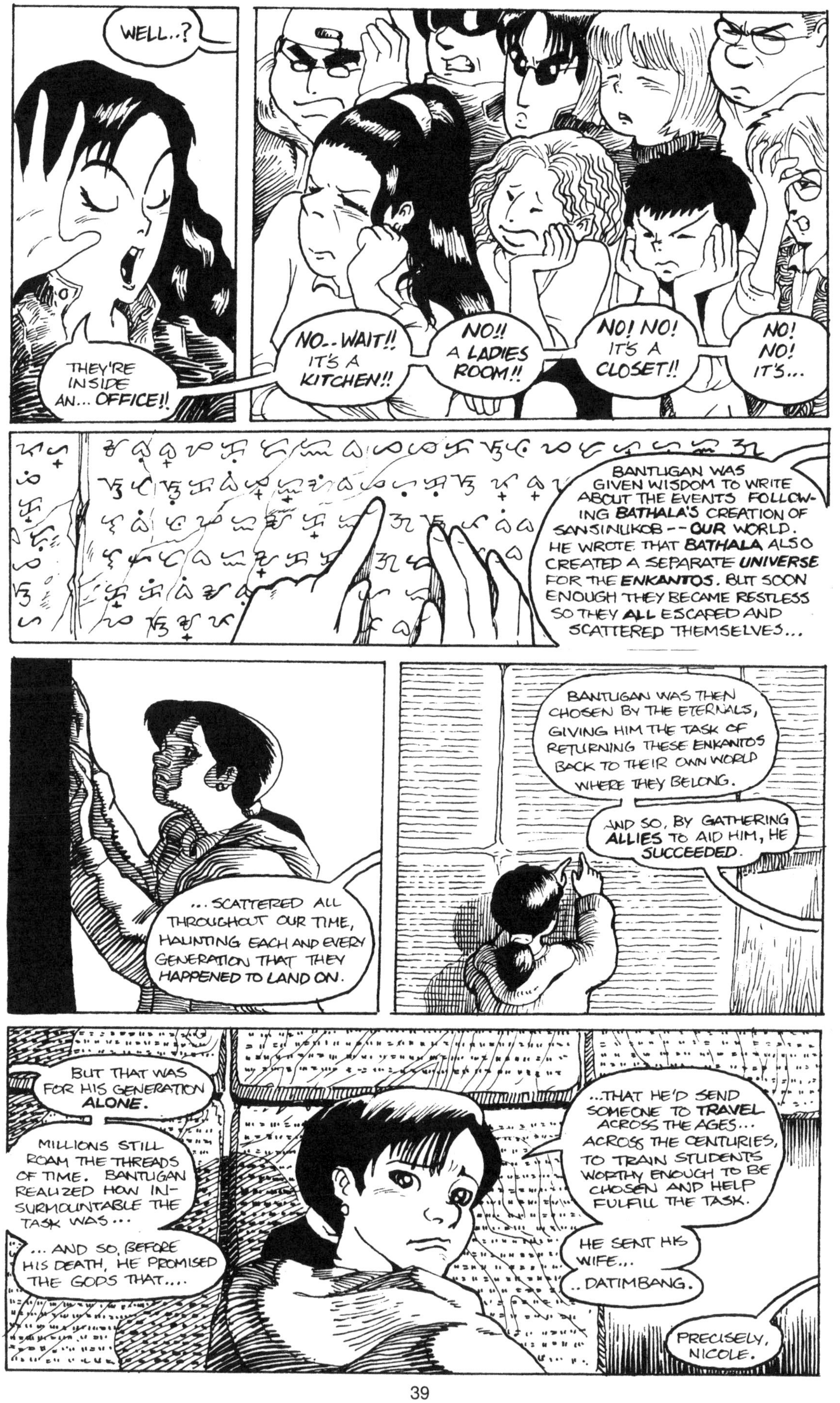
WELL..?
THEY'RE INSIDE AN... OFFICE!!
NO-- WAIT!! IT'S A KITCHEN!!
NO!! A LADIES ROOM!!
NO! NO! IT'S A CLOSET!!
NO! NO! IT'S...
BANTUGAN WAS GIVEN WISDOM TO WRITE ABOUT THE EVENTS FOLLOWING BATHALA'S CREATION OF SANSINUKOB -- OUR WORLD. HE WROTE THAT BATHALA ALSO CREATED A SEPARATE UNIVERSE FOR THE ENKANTOS. BUT SOON ENOUGH THEY BECAME RESTLESS SO THEY ALL ESCAPED AND SCATTERED THEMSELVES...
...SCATTERED ALL THROUGHOUT OUR TIME, HAUNTING EACH AND EVERY GENERATION THAT THEY HAPPENED TO LAND ON.
BANTUGAN WAS THEN CHOSEN BY THE ETERNALS, GIVING HIM THE TASK OF RETURNING THESE ENKANTOS BACK TO THEIR OWN WORLD WHERE THEY BELONG.
AND SO, BY GATHERING ALLIES TO AID HIM, HE SUCCEEDED.
BUT THAT WAS FOR HIS GENERATION ALONE.
MILLIONS STILL ROAM THE THREADS OF TIME. BANTUGAN REALIZED HOW INSURMOUNTABLE THE TASK WAS...
...AND SO, BEFORE HIS DEATH, HE PROMISED THE GODS THAT....
...THAT HE'D SEND SOMEONE TO TRAVEL ACROSS THE AGES... ACROSS THE CENTURIES, TO TRAIN STUDENTS WORTHY ENOUGH TO BE CHOSEN AND HELP FULFILL THE TASK.
HE SENT HIS WIFE...
..DATIMBANG.
PRECISELY, NICOLE.

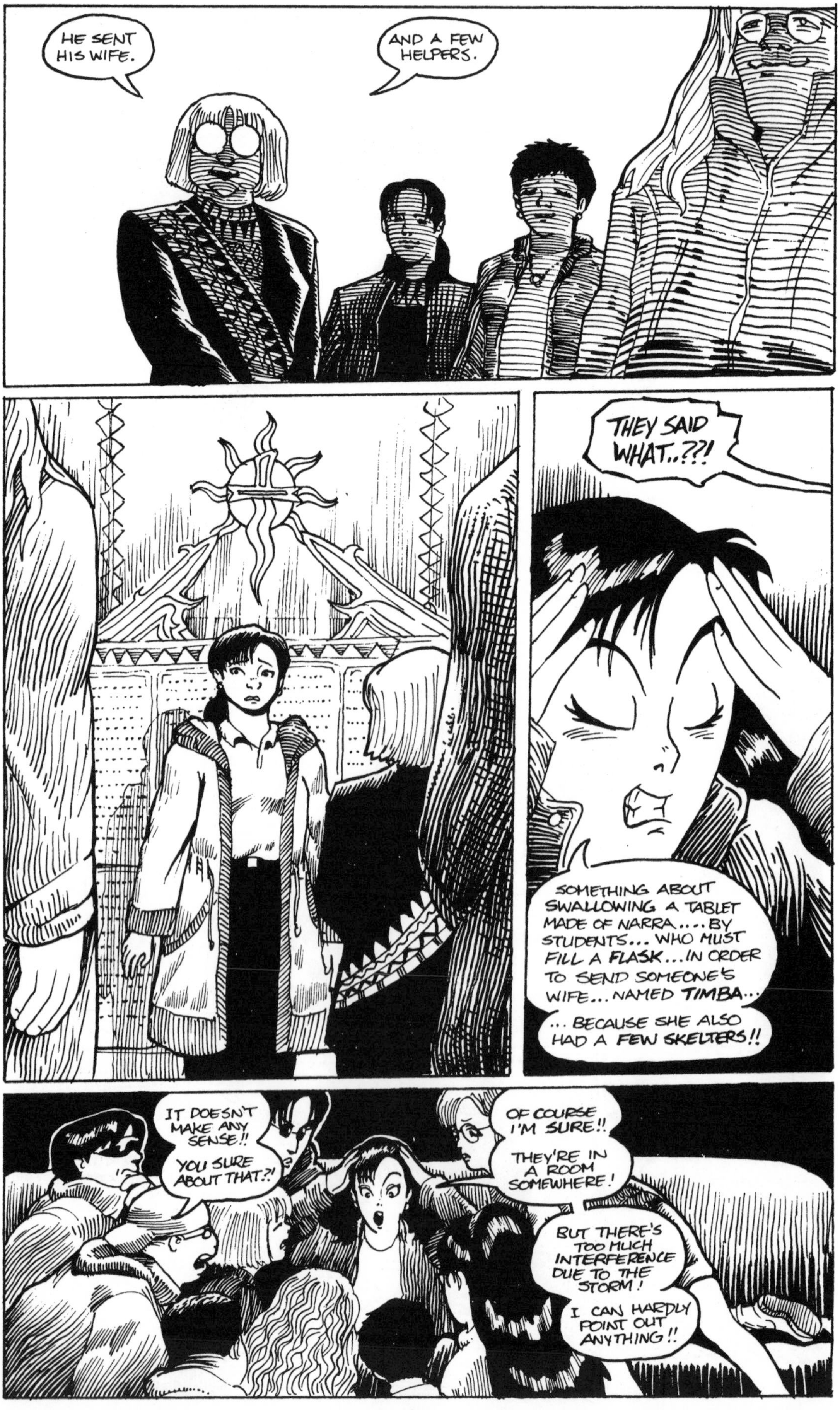
HE SENT HIS WIFE.
AND A FEW HELPERS.
THEY SAID WHAT..??!
SOMETHING ABOUT SWALLOWING A TABLET MADE OF NARRA....BY STUDENTS... WHO MUST FILL A FLASK...IN ORDER TO SEND SOMEONE'S WIFE...NAMED TIMBA...
...BECAUSE SHE ALSO HAD A FEW SKELTERS!!
IT DOESN'T MAKE ANY SENSE!!
YOU SURE ABOUT THAT?!
OF COURSE I'M SURE!!
THEY'RE IN A ROOM SOMEWHERE!
BUT THERE'S TOO MUCH INTERFERENCE DUE TO THE STORM!
I CAN HARDLY POINT OUT ANYTHING!!

I'M GOING WITH YOU.

THAT'S IT!! I'M GONNA CHECK WHAT'S GOING ON IN *THERE!!!*

JUST WHEN I THOUGHT THINGS WON'T GET ANY CRAZIER...

YOU THINK THIS IS WISE?

I DON'T KNOW ANYMORE!

WE WERE TOLD THAT YOUR GENERATION... THE PEOPLE OF THIS AGE... ARE THE HARDEST TO CONVINCE.

AND I DON'T BLAME YOU.

STORIES ABOUT US HAVE BEEN PASSED ON FOR CENTURIES!

SAD TO SAY, THOUGH, THAT WE ENDED UP MERELY *AS* STORIES.

THAT'S WHY WE THINK IT IS ONLY *JUST* THAT WE SHOW YOU PROOF.

WHAT IS *WRONG* WITH THESE PEOPLE?

JUST GO WITH THE *CROWD,* MAN.

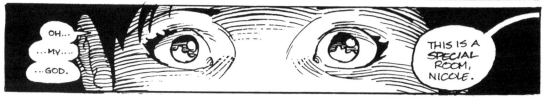

OH... ...MY... ...GOD.

THIS IS A *SPECIAL* ROOM, NICOLE.

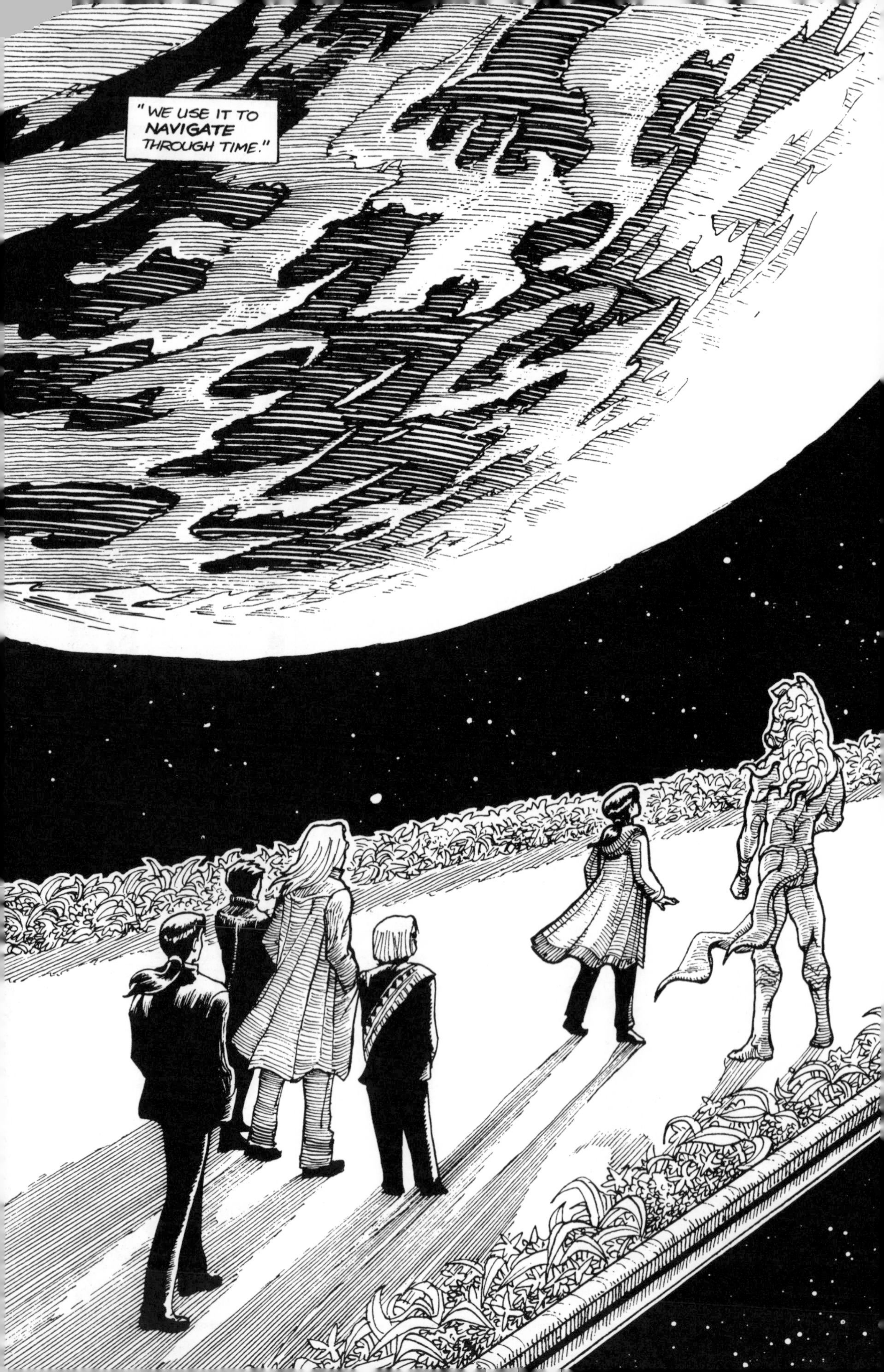
"WE USE IT TO NAVIGATE THROUGH TIME."

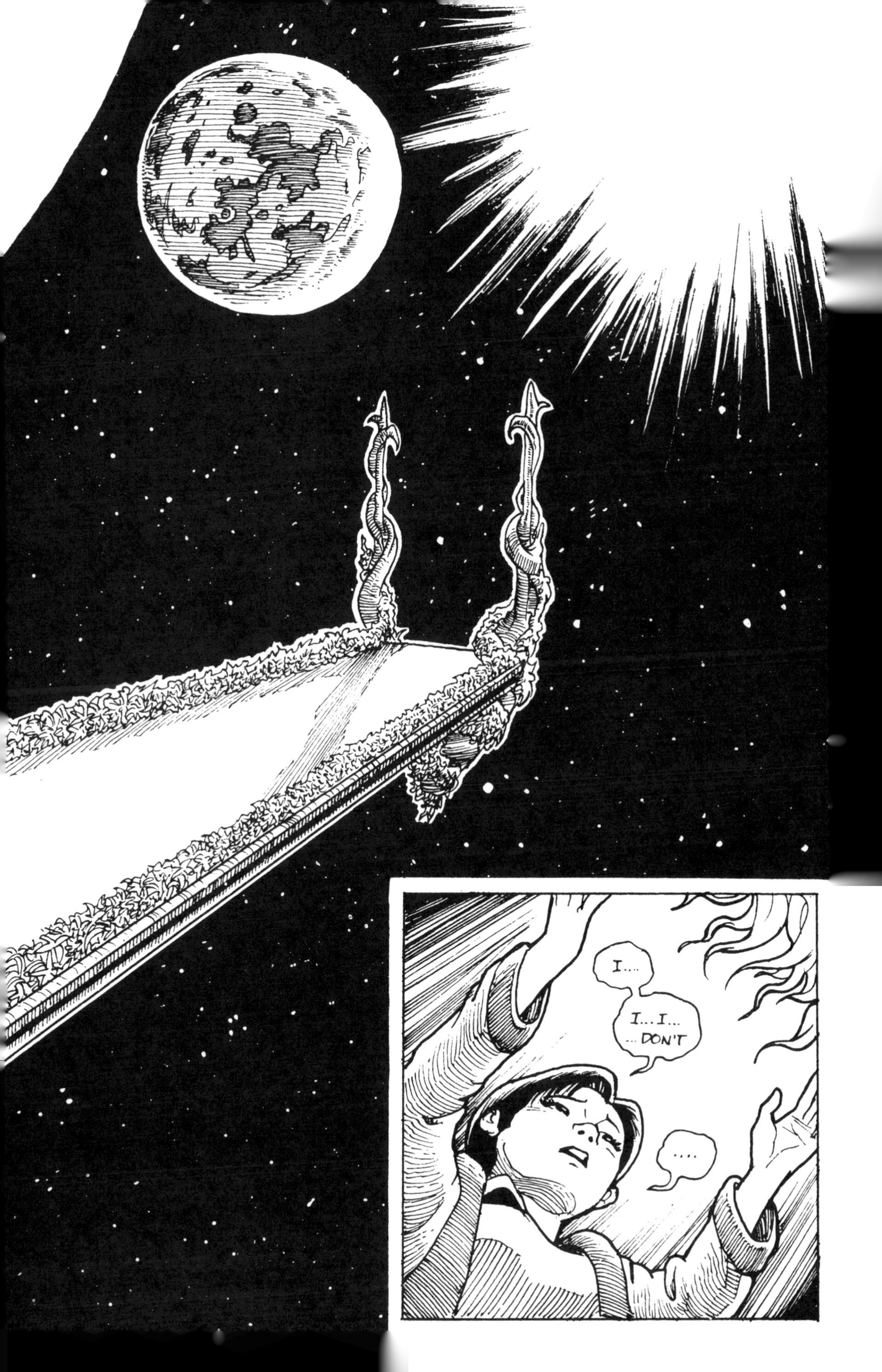
I....
I... I...
... DON'T
....

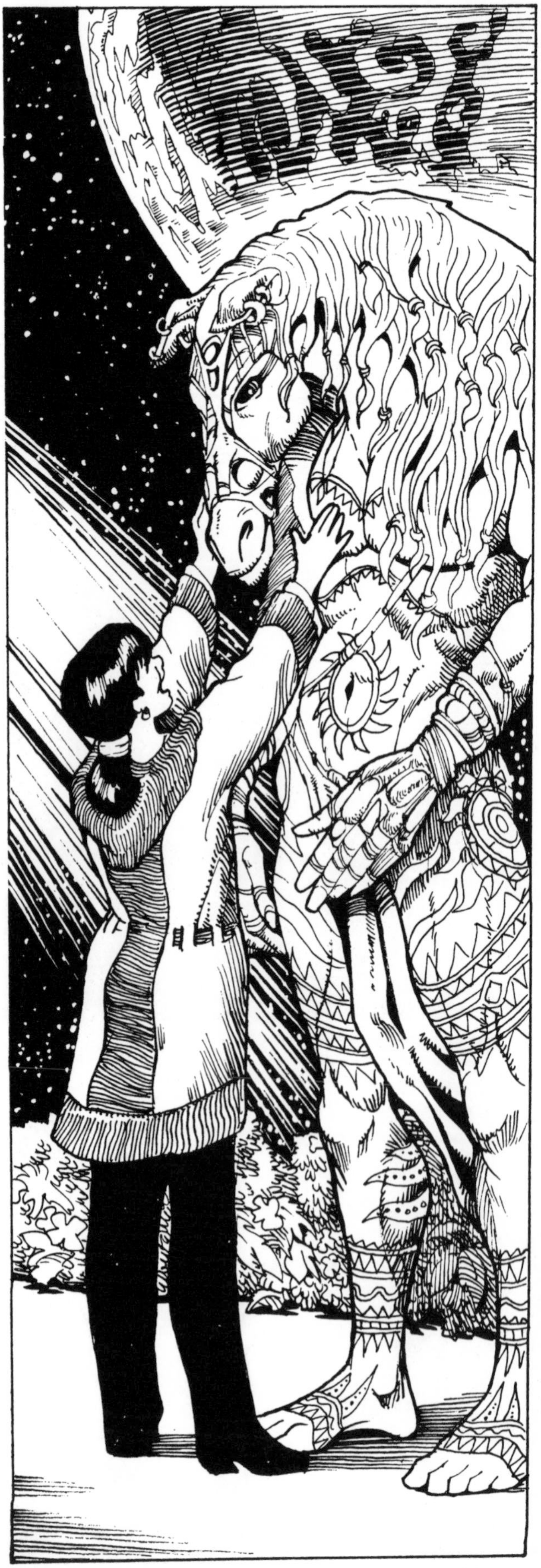

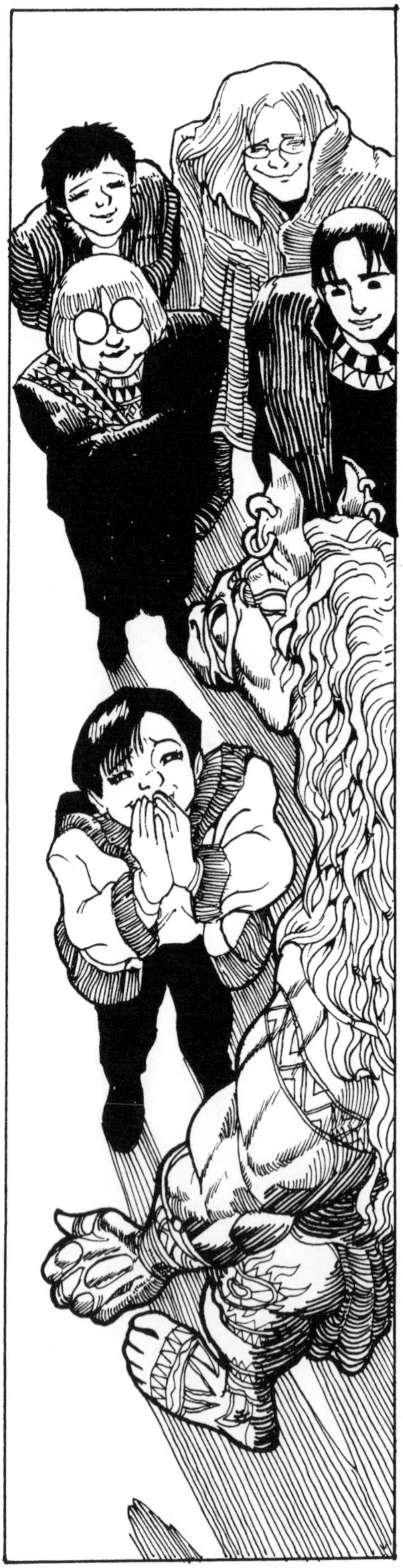

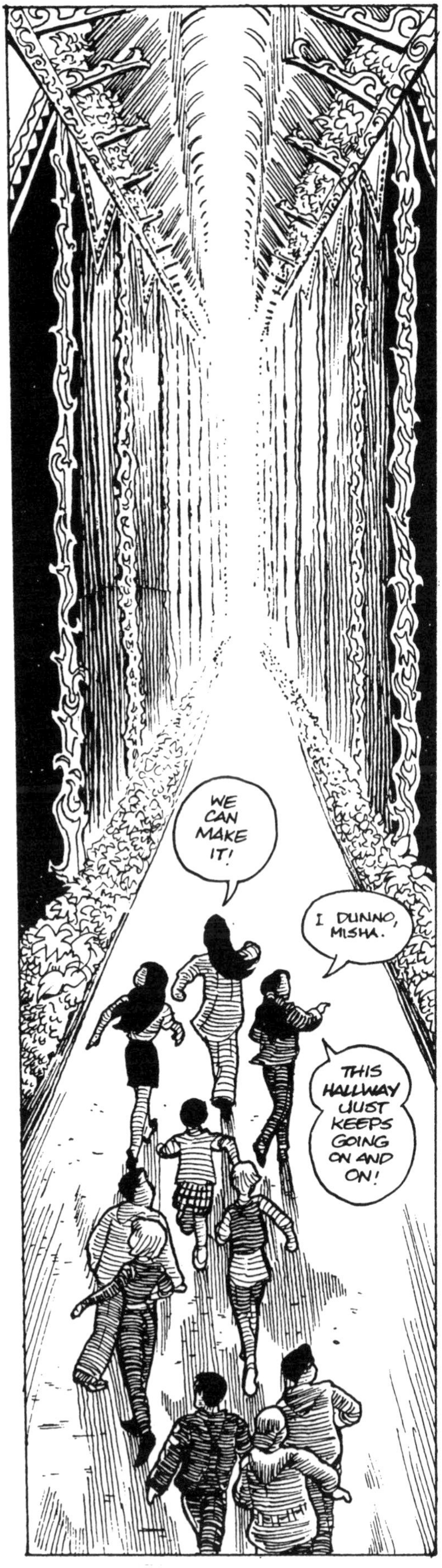
WE CAN MAKE IT!
I DUNNO, MISHA.
THIS HALLWAY JUST KEEPS GOING ON AND ON!

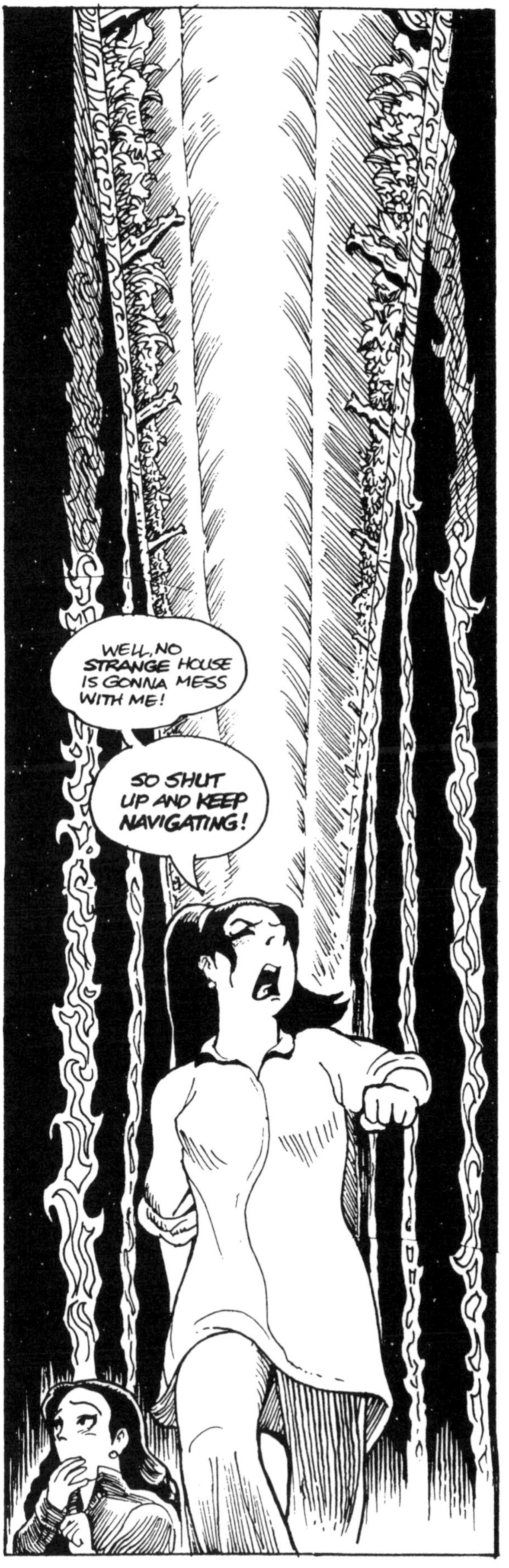
WELL, NO STRANGE HOUSE IS GONNA MESS WITH ME!
SO SHUT UP AND KEEP NAVIGATING!

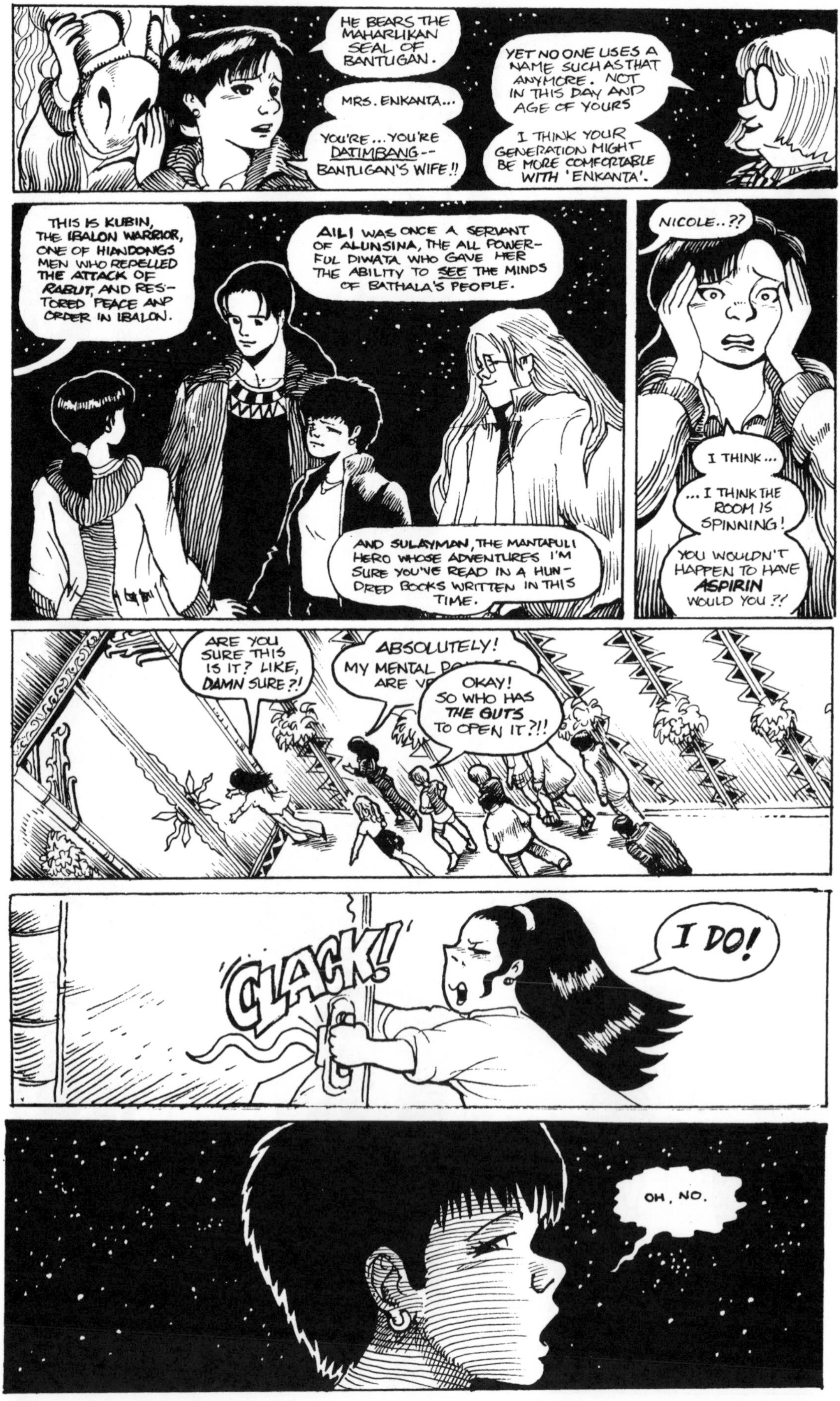
HE BEARS THE MAHARLIKAN SEAL OF BANTUGAN.
MRS. ENKANTA...
YOU'RE... YOU'RE DATIMBANG-- BANTUGAN'S WIFE!!
YET NO ONE USES A NAME SUCH AS THAT ANYMORE. NOT IN THIS DAY AND AGE OF YOURS
I THINK YOUR GENERATION MIGHT BE MORE COMFORTABLE WITH 'ENKANTA'.
THIS IS KUBIN, THE IBALON WARRIOR, ONE OF HIANDONG'S MEN WHO REPELLED THE ATTACK OF RABUT, AND RESTORED PEACE AND ORDER IN IBALON.
AILI WAS ONCE A SERVANT OF ALUNSINA, THE ALL POWERFUL DIWATA WHO GAVE HER THE ABILITY TO SEE THE MINDS OF BATHALA'S PEOPLE.
AND SULAYMAN, THE MANTAPULI HERO WHOSE ADVENTURES I'M SURE YOU'VE READ IN A HUNDRED BOOKS WRITTEN IN THIS TIME.
NICOLE..??
I THINK...
...I THINK THE ROOM IS SPINNING!
YOU WOULDN'T HAPPEN TO HAVE ASPIRIN WOULD YOU?!
ARE YOU SURE THIS IS IT? LIKE, DAMN SURE?!
ABSOLUTELY! MY MENTAL PO
OKAY! SO WHO HAS THE GUTS TO OPEN IT?!!
CLACK!
I DO!
OH, NO.

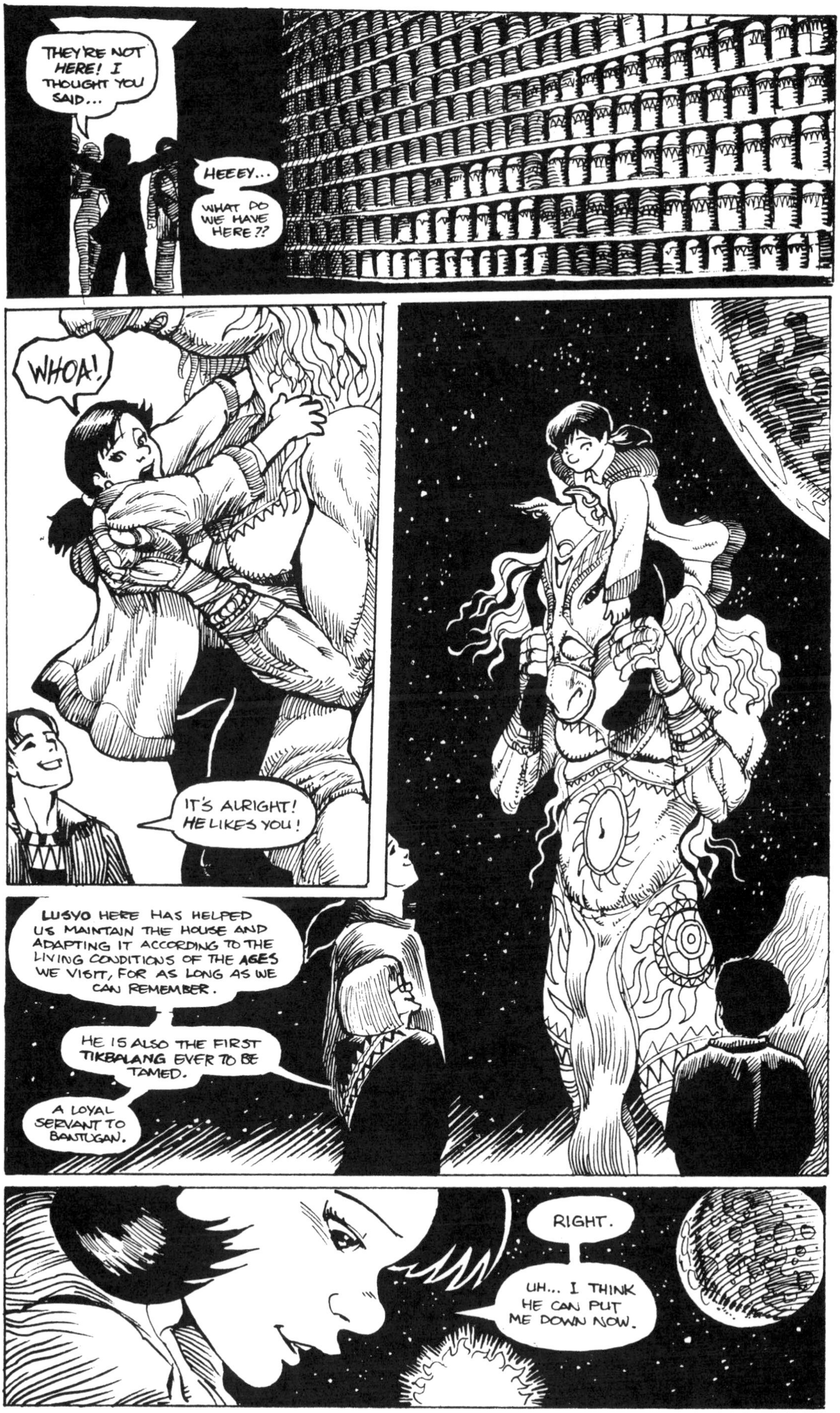

THEY'RE NOT HERE! I THOUGHT YOU SAID...
HEEEY...
WHAT DO WE HAVE HERE??
WHOA!
IT'S ALRIGHT! HE LIKES YOU!
LUSYO HERE HAS HELPED US MAINTAIN THE HOUSE AND ADAPTING IT ACCORDING TO THE LIVING CONDITIONS OF THE AGES WE VISIT, FOR AS LONG AS WE CAN REMEMBER.
HE IS ALSO THE FIRST TIKBALANG EVER TO BE TAMED.
A LOYAL SERVANT TO BANTUGAN.
RIGHT.
UH... I THINK HE CAN PUT ME DOWN NOW.

UM....WE'RE GOING TO HAVE TROUBLE IN THE STORAGE ROOM.

FK! FK! FK! FK! FK!

LESSEE....

IT'S *UNBELIEVABLE!!* IT WASN'T JUST A TALE, WAS IT? IT'S TRUE! *IT'S ALL REAL!!*

BACK OFF!! THIS IS MINE!!!

THE OTHERS-- THEY HAVE TO KNOW! THEY HAVE TO FIND OUT!

I THINK THEY ALREADY HAVE.

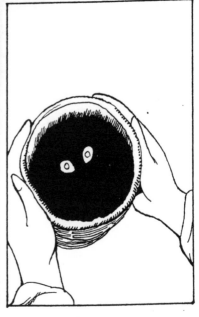

48

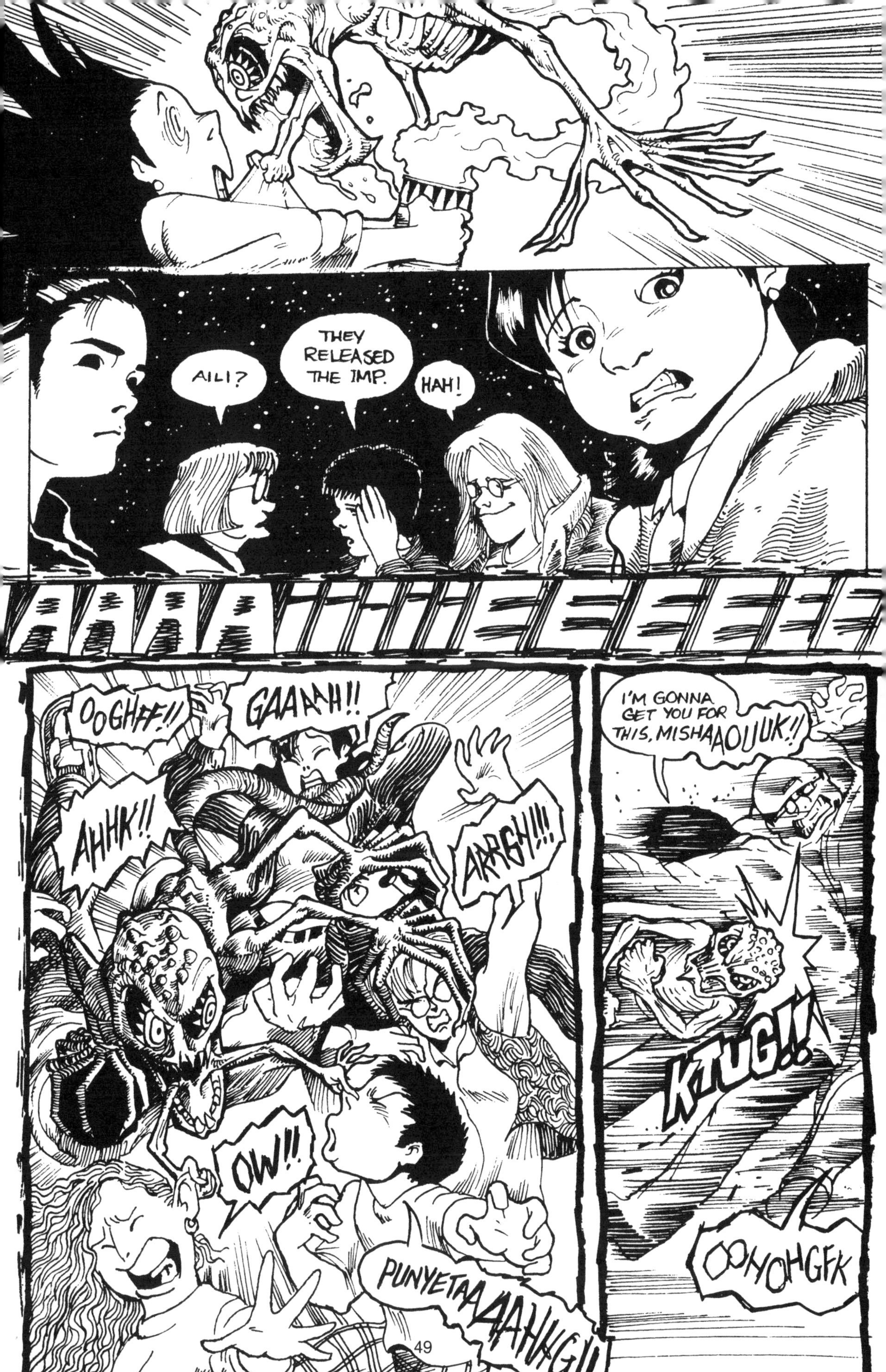
AILI?
THEY RELEASED THE IMP.
HAH!
AAAAIIIIEEEEEEE
OOGHFF!!
GAAAAH!!
AHHK!!
ARRGH!!!
OW!!
PUNYETAAAAAHHGII
I'M GONNA GET YOU FOR THIS, MISHAAOUUK!!
KTUG!!
OOHOHGFK

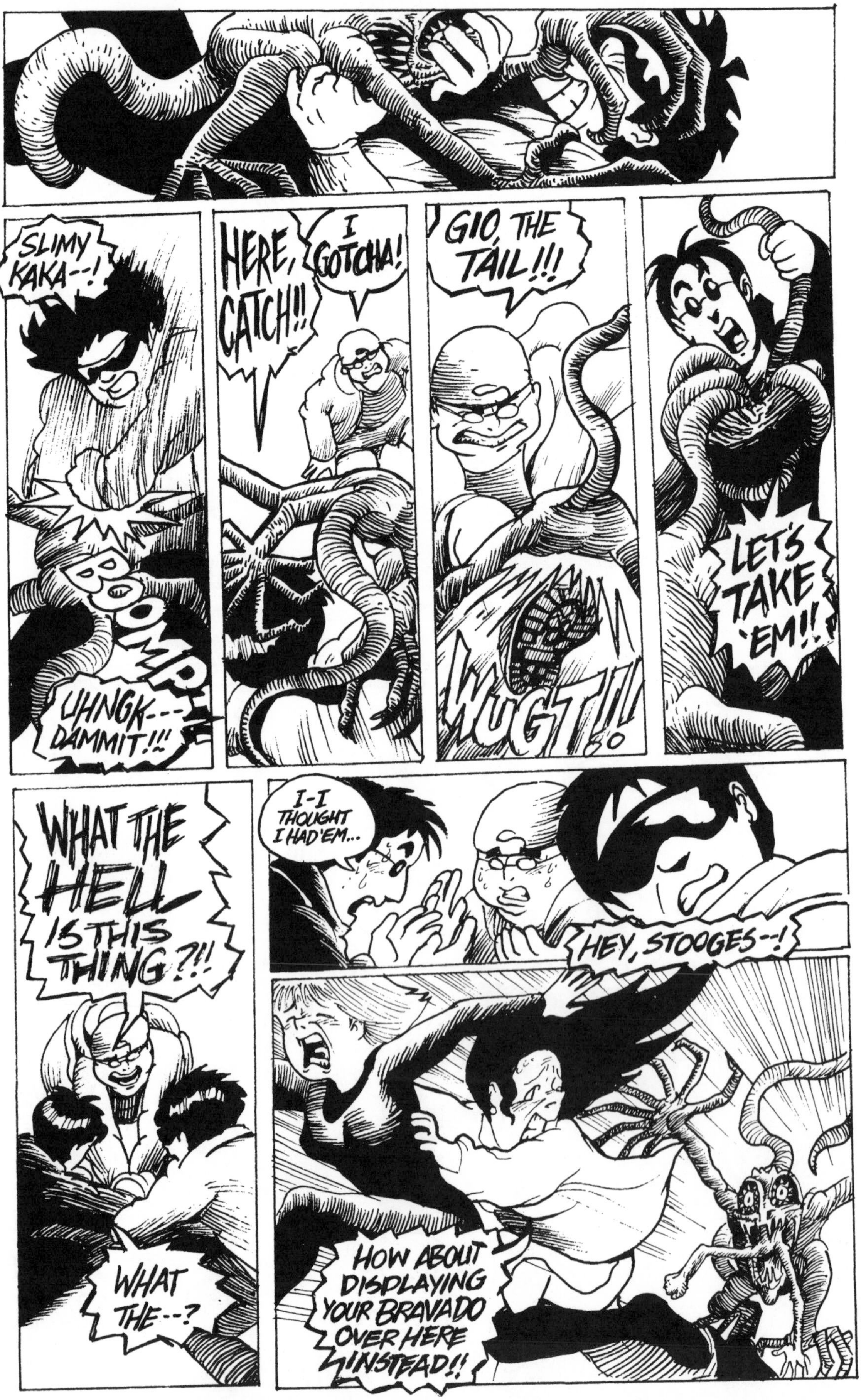
SLIMY KAKA--!
BOOMP!!
UHNGK--- DAMMIT!!!
HERE, CATCH!!
I GOTCHA!
GIO, THE TAIL!!!
WUGT!!
LET'S TAKE 'EM!!
WHAT THE HELL IS THIS THING?!!
WHAT THE--?
I-I THOUGHT I HAD'EM...
HEY, STOOGES--!
HOW ABOUT DISPLAYING YOUR BRAVADO OVER HERE INSTEAD!!

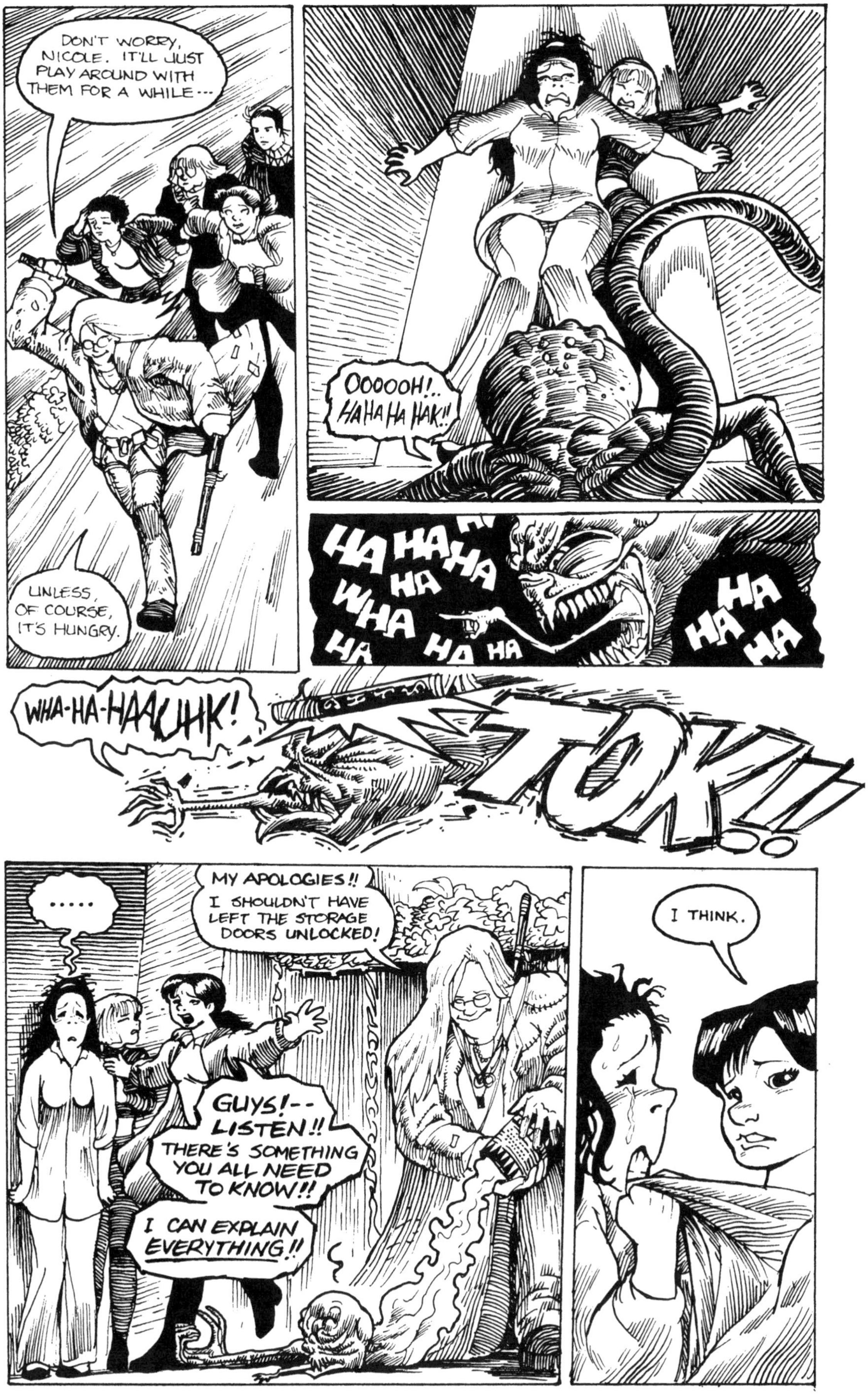
DON'T WORRY, NICOLE. IT'LL JUST PLAY AROUND WITH THEM FOR A WHILE---
UNLESS, OF COURSE, IT'S HUNGRY.
OOOOOH!.. HAHAHA HAK!!
HA HA HA HA HA
WHA
HA HA HA
HA HA HA HA
WHA-HA-HAAUHK!
TOK!!
.....
MY APOLOGIES!! I SHOULDN'T HAVE LEFT THE STORAGE DOORS UNLOCKED!
GUYS!-- LISTEN!! THERE'S SOMETHING YOU ALL NEED TO KNOW!!
I CAN EXPLAIN EVERYTHING!!
I THINK.

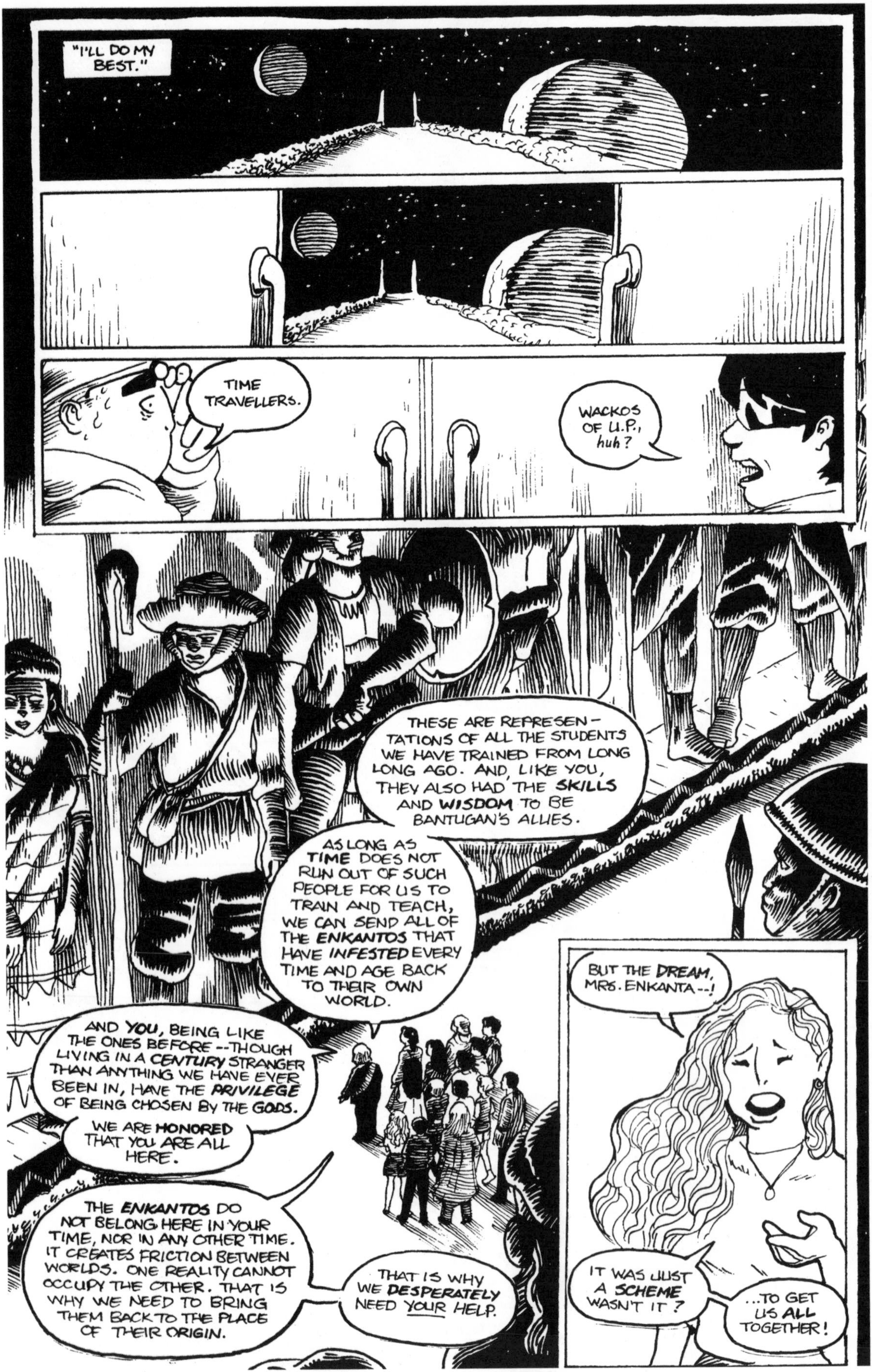
"I'LL DO MY BEST."
TIME TRAVELLERS.
WACKOS OF U.P., huh?
THESE ARE REPRESENTATIONS OF ALL THE STUDENTS WE HAVE TRAINED FROM LONG LONG AGO. AND, LIKE YOU, THEY ALSO HAD THE SKILLS AND WISDOM TO BE BANTUGAN'S ALLIES.
AS LONG AS TIME DOES NOT RUN OUT OF SUCH PEOPLE FOR US TO TRAIN AND TEACH, WE CAN SEND ALL OF THE ENKANTOS THAT HAVE INFESTED EVERY TIME AND AGE BACK TO THEIR OWN WORLD.
AND YOU, BEING LIKE THE ONES BEFORE --THOUGH LIVING IN A CENTURY STRANGER THAN ANYTHING WE HAVE EVER BEEN IN, HAVE THE PRIVILEGE OF BEING CHOSEN BY THE GODS.
WE ARE HONORED THAT YOU ARE ALL HERE.
THE ENKANTOS DO NOT BELONG HERE IN YOUR TIME, NOR IN ANY OTHER TIME. IT CREATES FRICTION BETWEEN WORLDS. ONE REALITY CANNOT OCCUPY THE OTHER. THAT IS WHY WE NEED TO BRING THEM BACK TO THE PLACE OF THEIR ORIGIN.
THAT IS WHY WE DESPERATELY NEED YOUR HELP.
BUT THE DREAM, MRS. ENKANTA--!
IT WAS JUST A SCHEME WASN'T IT?
...TO GET US ALL TOGETHER!

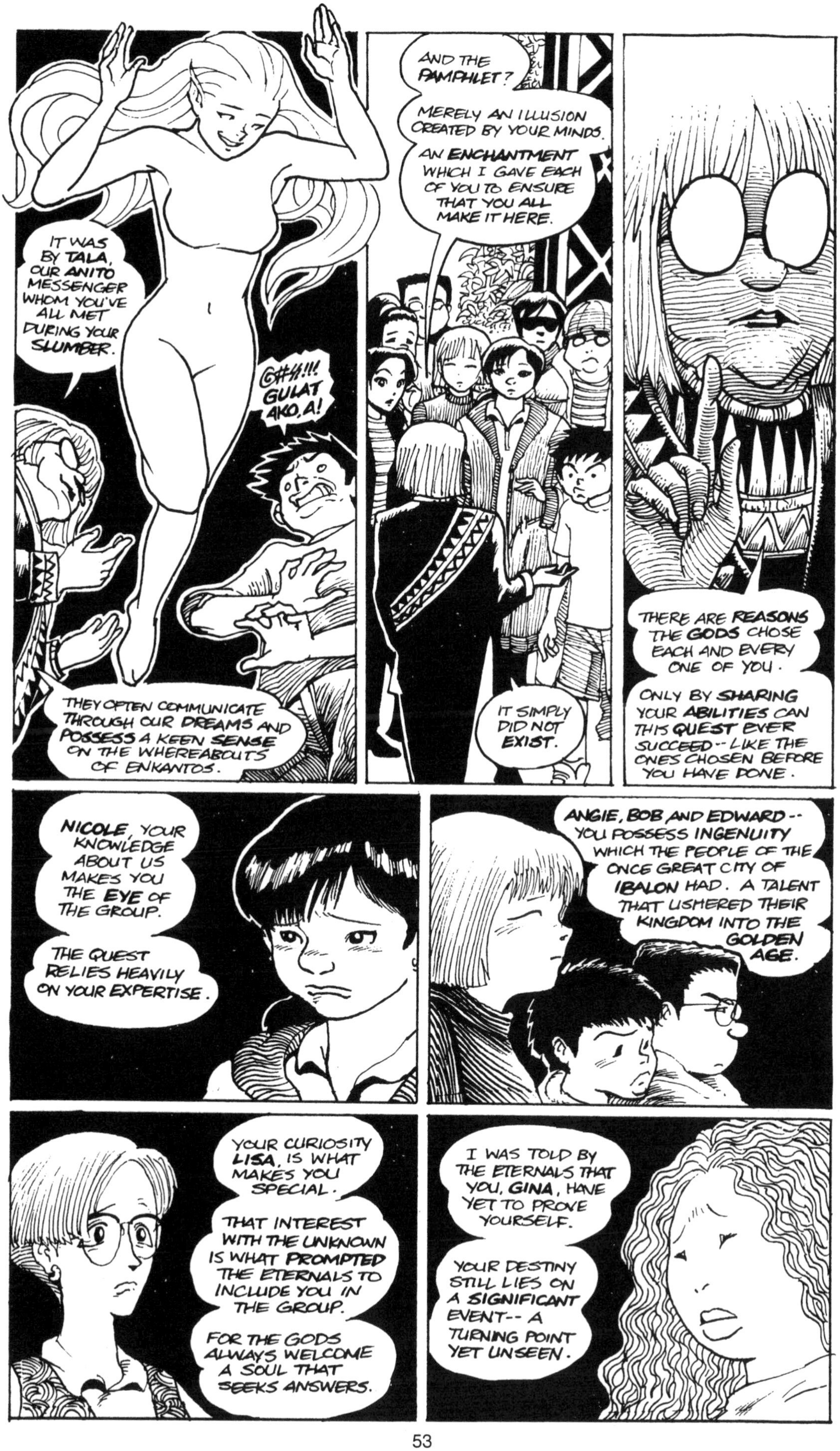
IT WAS BY TALA, OUR ANITO MESSENGER WHOM YOU'VE ALL MET DURING YOUR SLUMBER.
G#%!!! GULAT AKO, A!
THEY OFTEN COMMUNICATE THROUGH OUR DREAMS AND POSSESS A KEEN SENSE ON THE WHEREABOUTS OF ENKANTOS.
AND THE PAMPHLET?
MERELY AN ILLUSION CREATED BY YOUR MINDS.
AN ENCHANTMENT WHICH I GAVE EACH OF YOU TO ENSURE THAT YOU ALL MAKE IT HERE.
IT SIMPLY DID NOT EXIST.
THERE ARE REASONS THE GODS CHOSE EACH AND EVERY ONE OF YOU.
ONLY BY SHARING YOUR ABILITIES CAN THIS QUEST EVER SUCCEED-- LIKE THE ONES CHOSEN BEFORE YOU HAVE DONE.
NICOLE, YOUR KNOWLEDGE ABOUT US MAKES YOU THE EYE OF THE GROUP.
THE QUEST RELIES HEAVILY ON YOUR EXPERTISE.
ANGIE, BOB AND EDWARD-- YOU POSSESS INGENUITY WHICH THE PEOPLE OF THE ONCE GREAT CITY OF IBALON HAD. A TALENT THAT USHERED THEIR KINGDOM INTO THE GOLDEN AGE.
YOUR CURIOSITY LISA, IS WHAT MAKES YOU SPECIAL.
THAT INTEREST WITH THE UNKNOWN IS WHAT PROMPTED THE ETERNALS TO INCLUDE YOU IN THE GROUP.
FOR THE GODS ALWAYS WELCOME A SOUL THAT SEEKS ANSWERS.
I WAS TOLD BY THE ETERNALS THAT YOU, GINA, HAVE YET TO PROVE YOURSELF.
YOUR DESTINY STILL LIES ON A SIGNIFICANT EVENT-- A TURNING POINT YET UNSEEN.

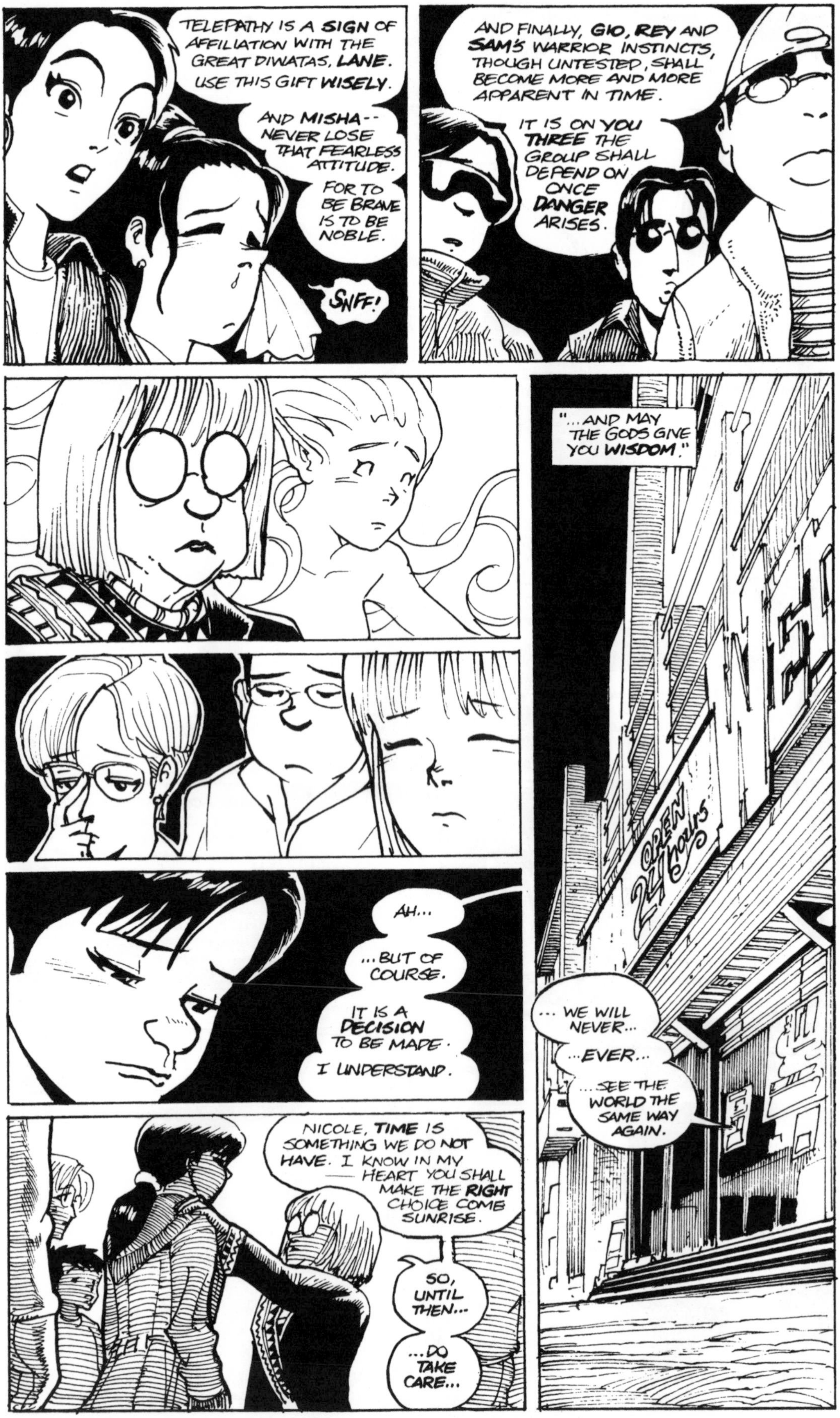
TELEPATHY IS A SIGN OF AFFILIATION WITH THE GREAT DIWATAS, LANE. USE THIS GIFT WISELY.
AND MISHA-- NEVER LOSE THAT FEARLESS ATTITUDE.
FOR TO BE BRAVE IS TO BE NOBLE.
SNFF!
AND FINALLY, GIO, REY AND SAM'S WARRIOR INSTINCTS, THOUGH UNTESTED, SHALL BECOME MORE AND MORE APPARENT IN TIME.
IT IS ON YOU THREE THE GROUP SHALL DEPEND ON ONCE DANGER ARISES.
"...AND MAY THE GODS GIVE YOU WISDOM."
AH...
...BUT OF COURSE.
IT IS A DECISION TO BE MADE.
I UNDERSTAND.
NICOLE, TIME IS SOMETHING WE DO NOT HAVE. I KNOW IN MY HEART YOU SHALL MAKE THE RIGHT CHOICE COME SUNRISE.
SO, UNTIL THEN...
...DO TAKE CARE...
OPEN 24 hours
... WE WILL NEVER...
...EVER...
...SEE THE WORLD THE SAME WAY AGAIN.

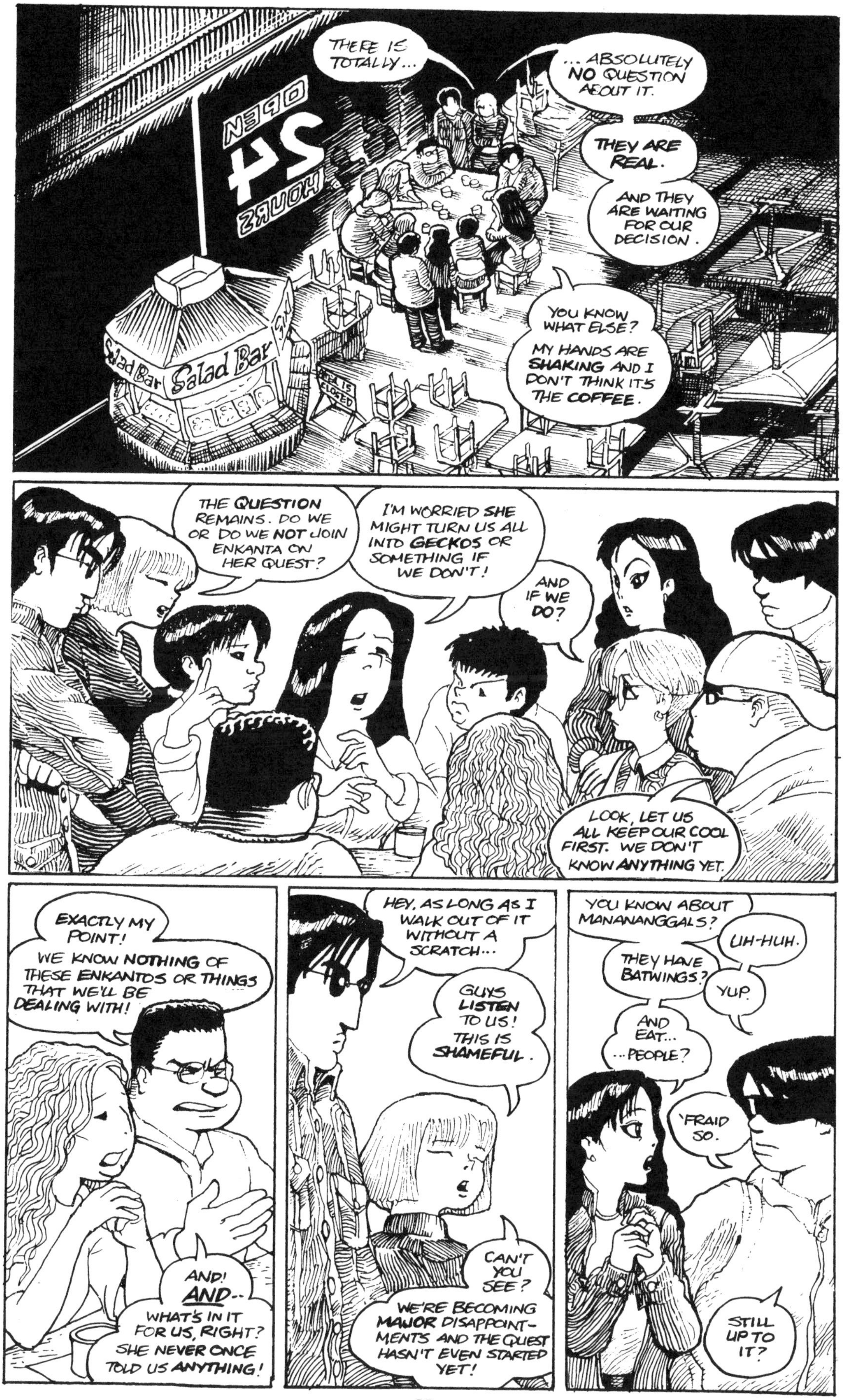

OPEN 24 HOURS
Salad Bar
Salad Bar
THERE IS TOTALLY...
...ABSOLUTELY NO QUESTION ABOUT IT.
THEY ARE REAL.
AND THEY ARE WAITING FOR OUR DECISION.
YOU KNOW WHAT ELSE?
MY HANDS ARE SHAKING AND I DON'T THINK IT'S THE COFFEE.
THE QUESTION REMAINS. DO WE OR DO WE NOT JOIN ENKANTA ON HER QUEST?
I'M WORRIED SHE MIGHT TURN US ALL INTO GECKOS OR SOMETHING IF WE DON'T!
AND IF WE DO?
LOOK, LET US ALL KEEP OUR COOL FIRST. WE DON'T KNOW ANYTHING YET.
EXACTLY MY POINT!
WE KNOW NOTHING OF THESE ENKANTOS OR THINGS THAT WE'LL BE DEALING WITH!
AND! AND--
WHAT'S IN IT FOR US, RIGHT? SHE NEVER ONCE TOLD US ANYTHING!
HEY, AS LONG AS I WALK OUT OF IT WITHOUT A SCRATCH...
GUYS LISTEN TO US! THIS IS SHAMEFUL.
CAN'T YOU SEE?
WE'RE BECOMING MAJOR DISAPPOINT-MENTS AND THE QUEST HASN'T EVEN STARTED YET!
YOU KNOW ABOUT MANANANGGALS?
UH-HUH.
THEY HAVE BATWINGS?
YUP.
AND EAT... ...PEOPLE?
'FRAID SO.
STILL UP TO IT?

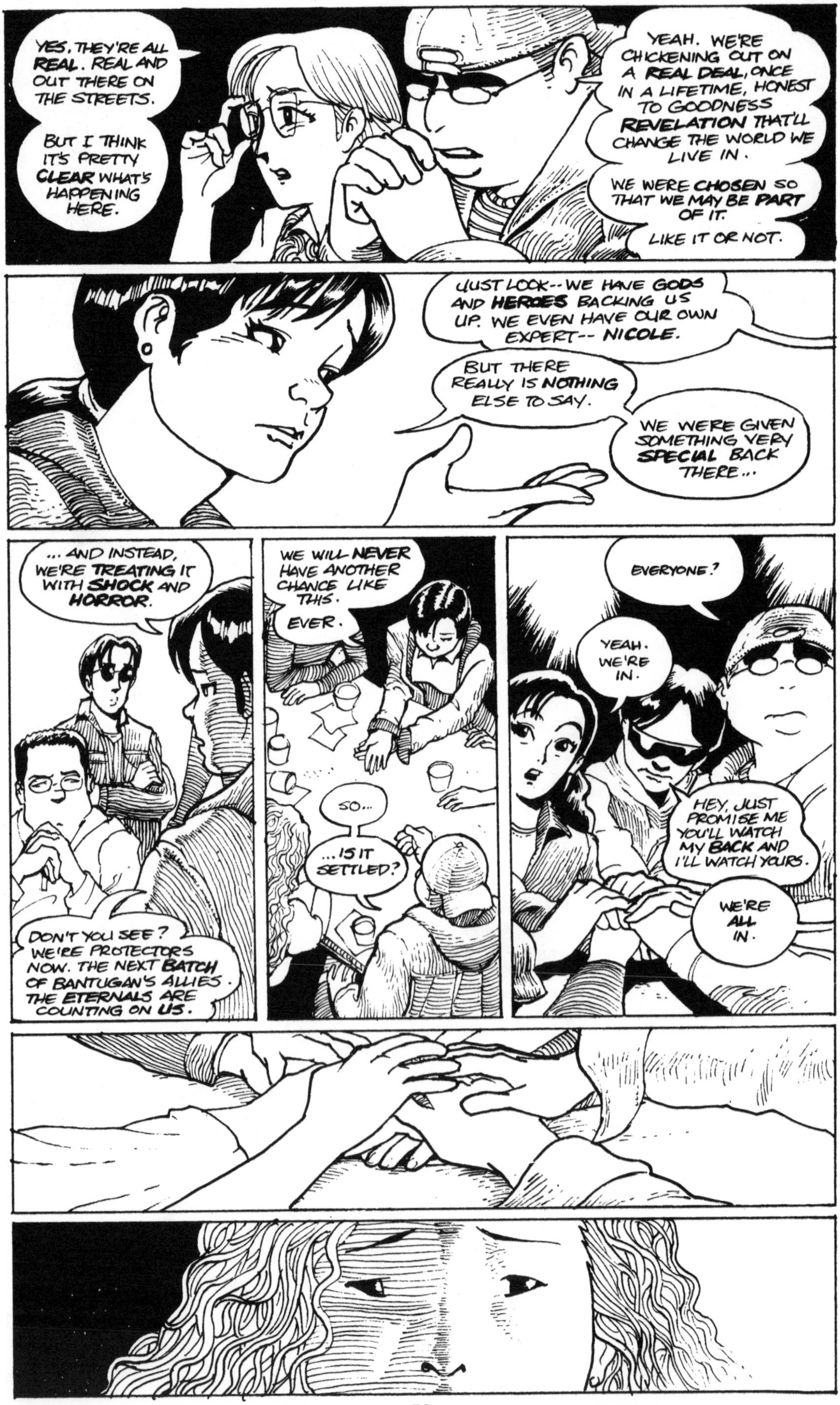
YES, THEY'RE ALL REAL. REAL AND OUT THERE ON THE STREETS.
BUT I THINK IT'S PRETTY CLEAR WHAT'S HAPPENING HERE.
YEAH. WE'RE CHICKENING OUT ON A REAL DEAL, ONCE IN A LIFETIME, HONEST TO GOODNESS REVELATION THAT'LL CHANGE THE WORLD WE LIVE IN.
WE WERE CHOSEN SO THAT WE MAY BE PART OF IT.
LIKE IT OR NOT.
JUST LOOK-- WE HAVE GODS AND HEROES BACKING US UP. WE EVEN HAVE OUR OWN EXPERT-- NICOLE.
BUT THERE REALLY IS NOTHING ELSE TO SAY.
WE WERE GIVEN SOMETHING VERY SPECIAL BACK THERE...
... AND INSTEAD, WE'RE TREATING IT WITH SHOCK AND HORROR.
DON'T YOU SEE? WE'RE PROTECTORS NOW. THE NEXT BATCH OF BANTUGAN'S ALLIES. THE ETERNALS ARE COUNTING ON US.
WE WILL NEVER HAVE ANOTHER CHANCE LIKE THIS.
EVER.
SO...
... IS IT SETTLED?
EVERYONE?
YEAH. WE'RE IN.
HEY, JUST PROMISE ME YOU'LL WATCH MY BACK AND I'LL WATCH YOURS.
WE'RE ALL IN.

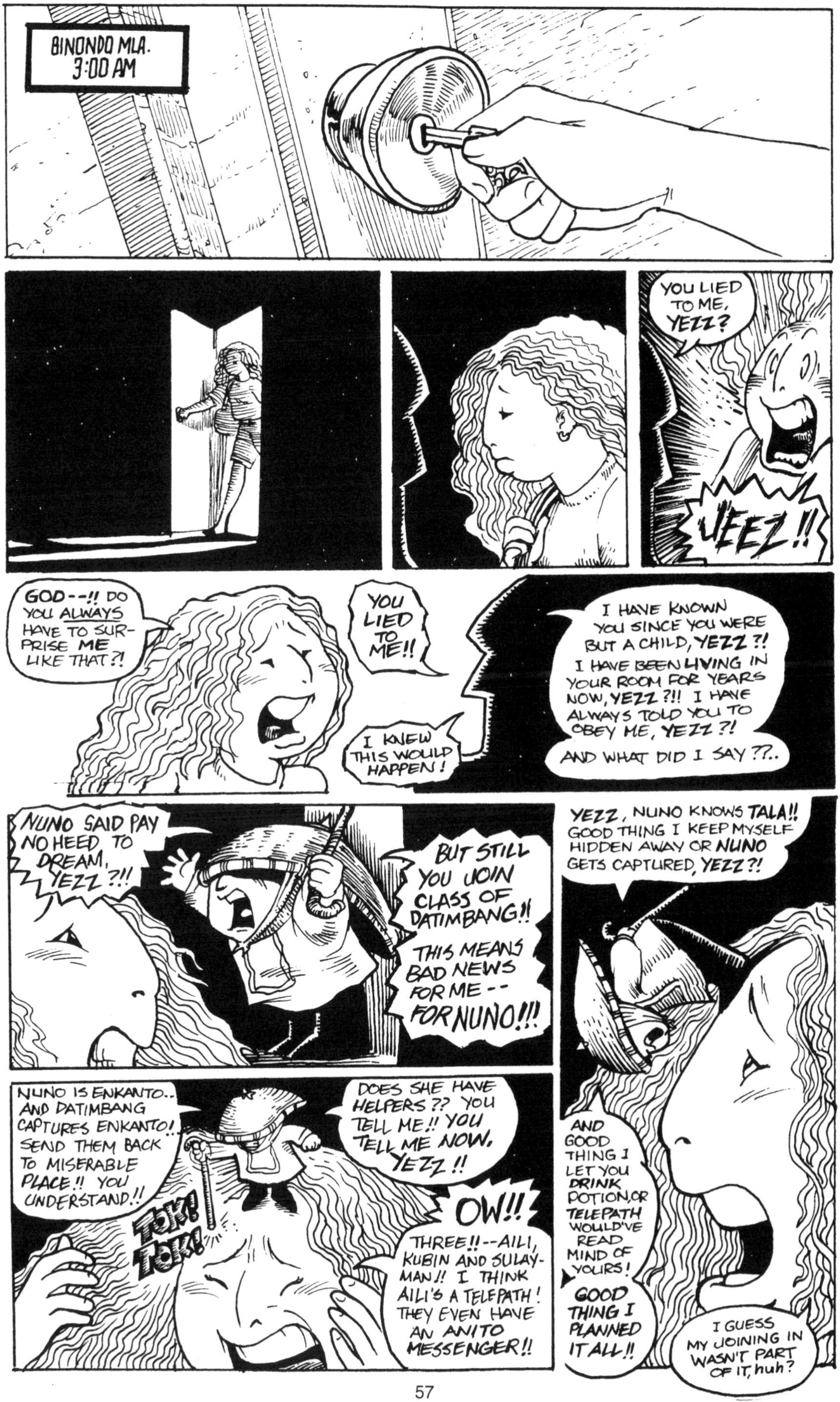
BINONDO MLA.
3:00 AM
YOU LIED TO ME, YEZZ?
YEEZ!!
GOD--!! DO YOU ALWAYS HAVE TO SURPRISE ME LIKE THAT?!
YOU LIED TO ME!!
I KNEW THIS WOULD HAPPEN!
I HAVE KNOWN YOU SINCE YOU WERE BUT A CHILD, YEZZ?! I HAVE BEEN LIVING IN YOUR ROOM FOR YEARS NOW, YEZZ?!! I HAVE ALWAYS TOLD YOU TO OBEY ME, YEZZ?!
AND WHAT DID I SAY??..
NUNO SAID PAY NO HEED TO DREAM, YEZZ?!!
BUT STILL YOU JOIN CLASS OF DATIMBANG!!
THIS MEANS BAD NEWS FOR ME--FOR NUNO!!!
YEZZ, NUNO KNOWS TALA!! GOOD THING I KEEP MYSELF HIDDEN AWAY OR NUNO GETS CAPTURED, YEZZ?!
NUNO IS ENKANTO.. AND DATIMBANG CAPTURES ENKANTO!.. SEND THEM BACK TO MISERABLE PLACE!! YOU UNDERSTAND!!
TOK! TOK!
DOES SHE HAVE HELPERS?? YOU TELL ME!! YOU TELL ME NOW, YEZZ!!
OW!!
THREE!!--AILI, KUBIN AND SULAYMAN!! I THINK AILI'S A TELEPATH! THEY EVEN HAVE AN ANITO MESSENGER!!
AND GOOD THING I LET YOU DRINK POTION, OR TELEPATH WOULD'VE READ MIND OF YOURS!
GOOD THING I PLANNED IT ALL!!
I GUESS MY JOINING IN WASN'T PART OF IT, huh?

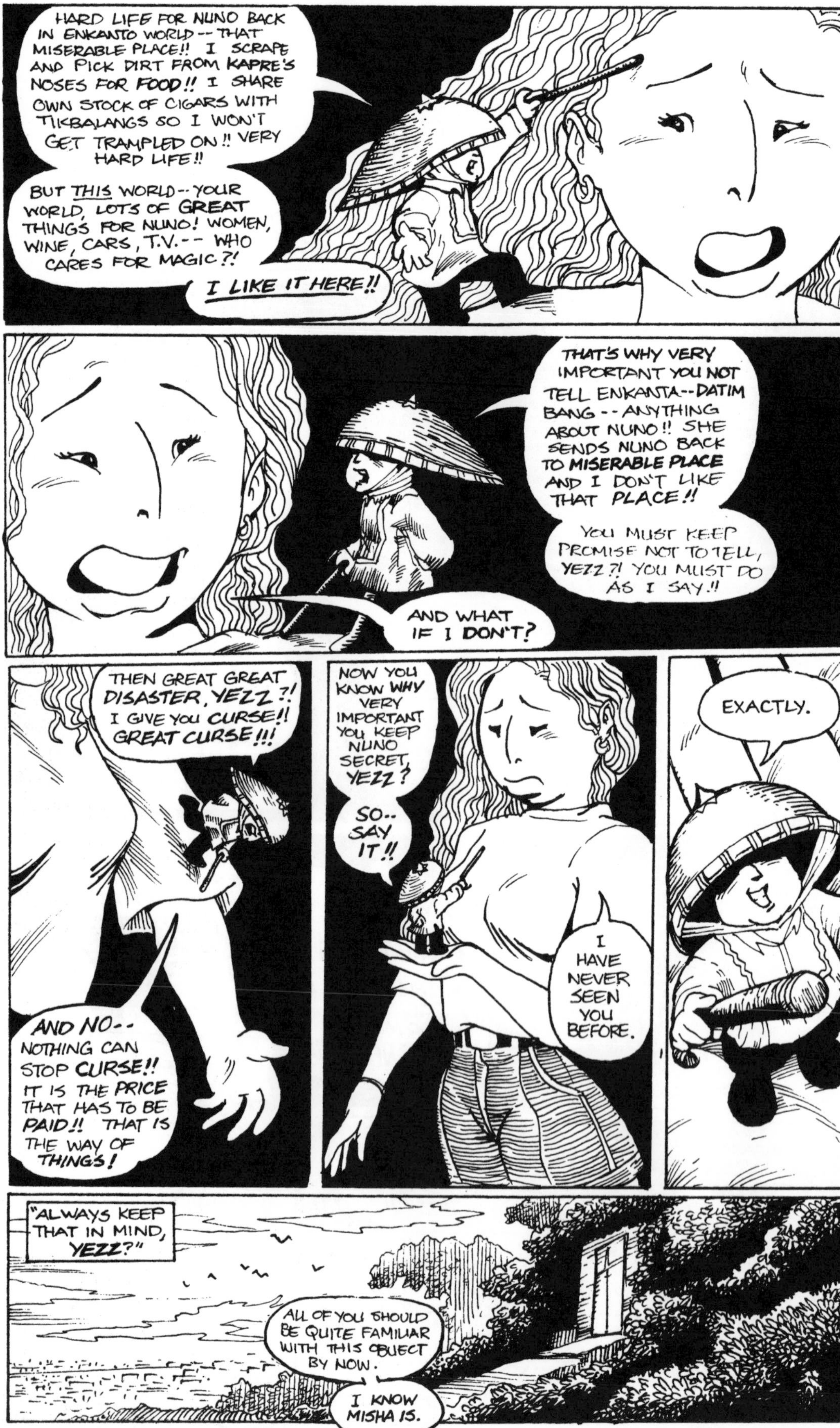
HARD LIFE FOR NUNO BACK IN ENKANTO WORLD -- THAT MISERABLE PLACE!! I SCRAPE AND PICK DIRT FROM KAPRE'S NOSES FOR FOOD!! I SHARE OWN STOCK OF CIGARS WITH TIKBALANGS SO I WON'T GET TRAMPLED ON!! VERY HARD LIFE!!
BUT THIS WORLD-- YOUR WORLD, LOTS OF GREAT THINGS FOR NUNO! WOMEN, WINE, CARS, T.V.-- WHO CARES FOR MAGIC?!
I LIKE IT HERE!!
THAT'S WHY VERY IMPORTANT YOU NOT TELL ENKANTA--DATIM BANG -- ANYTHING ABOUT NUNO!! SHE SENDS NUNO BACK TO MISERABLE PLACE AND I DON'T LIKE THAT PLACE!!
YOU MUST KEEP PROMISE NOT TO TELL, YEZZ?! YOU MUST DO AS I SAY!!
AND WHAT IF I DON'T?
THEN GREAT GREAT DISASTER, YEZZ?! I GIVE YOU CURSE!! GREAT CURSE!!!
AND NO-- NOTHING CAN STOP CURSE!! IT IS THE PRICE THAT HAS TO BE PAID!! THAT IS THE WAY OF THINGS!
NOW YOU KNOW WHY VERY IMPORTANT YOU KEEP NUNO SECRET, YEZZ?
SO.. SAY IT!!
I HAVE NEVER SEEN YOU BEFORE.
EXACTLY.
"ALWAYS KEEP THAT IN MIND, YEZZ?"
ALL OF YOU SHOULD BE QUITE FAMILIAR WITH THIS OBJECT BY NOW.
I KNOW MISHA IS.

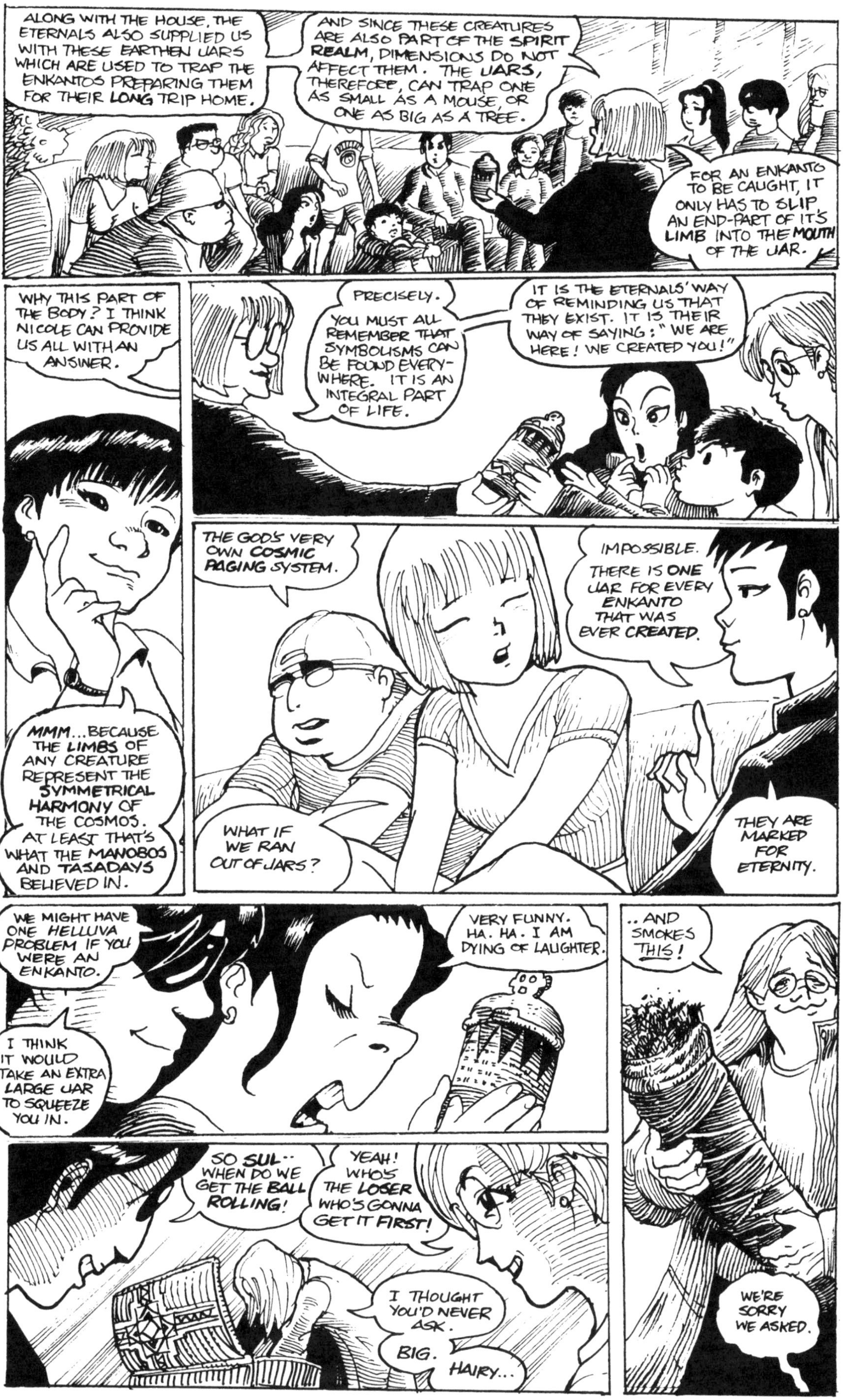
ALONG WITH THE HOUSE, THE ETERNALS ALSO SUPPLIED US WITH THESE EARTHEN JARS WHICH ARE USED TO TRAP THE ENKANTOS PREPARING THEM FOR THEIR LONG TRIP HOME.
AND SINCE THESE CREATURES ARE ALSO PART OF THE SPIRIT REALM, DIMENSIONS DO NOT AFFECT THEM. THE JARS, THEREFORE, CAN TRAP ONE AS SMALL AS A MOUSE, OR ONE AS BIG AS A TREE.
FOR AN ENKANTO TO BE CAUGHT, IT ONLY HAS TO SLIP AN END-PART OF IT'S LIMB INTO THE MOUTH OF THE JAR.
WHY THIS PART OF THE BODY? I THINK NICOLE CAN PROVIDE US ALL WITH AN ANSWER.
MMM... BECAUSE THE LIMBS OF ANY CREATURE REPRESENT THE SYMMETRICAL HARMONY OF THE COSMOS. AT LEAST THAT'S WHAT THE MANOBOS AND TASADAYS BELIEVED IN.
PRECISELY.
YOU MUST ALL REMEMBER THAT SYMBOLISMS CAN BE FOUND EVERYWHERE. IT IS AN INTEGRAL PART OF LIFE.
IT IS THE ETERNALS' WAY OF REMINDING US THAT THEY EXIST. IT IS THEIR WAY OF SAYING: "WE ARE HERE! WE CREATED YOU!"
THE GOD'S VERY OWN COSMIC PAGING SYSTEM.
WHAT IF WE RAN OUT OF JARS?
IMPOSSIBLE.
THERE IS ONE JAR FOR EVERY ENKANTO THAT WAS EVER CREATED.
THEY ARE MARKED FOR ETERNITY.
WE MIGHT HAVE ONE HELLUVA PROBLEM IF YOU WERE AN ENKANTO.
I THINK IT WOULD TAKE AN EXTRA LARGE JAR TO SQUEEZE YOU IN.
VERY FUNNY. HA. HA. I AM DYING OF LAUGHTER.
.. AND SMOKES THIS!
SO SUL.. WHEN DO WE GET THE BALL ROLLING!
YEAH! WHO'S THE LOSER WHO'S GONNA GET IT FIRST!
I THOUGHT YOU'D NEVER ASK.
BIG.
HAIRY...
WE'RE SORRY WE ASKED.

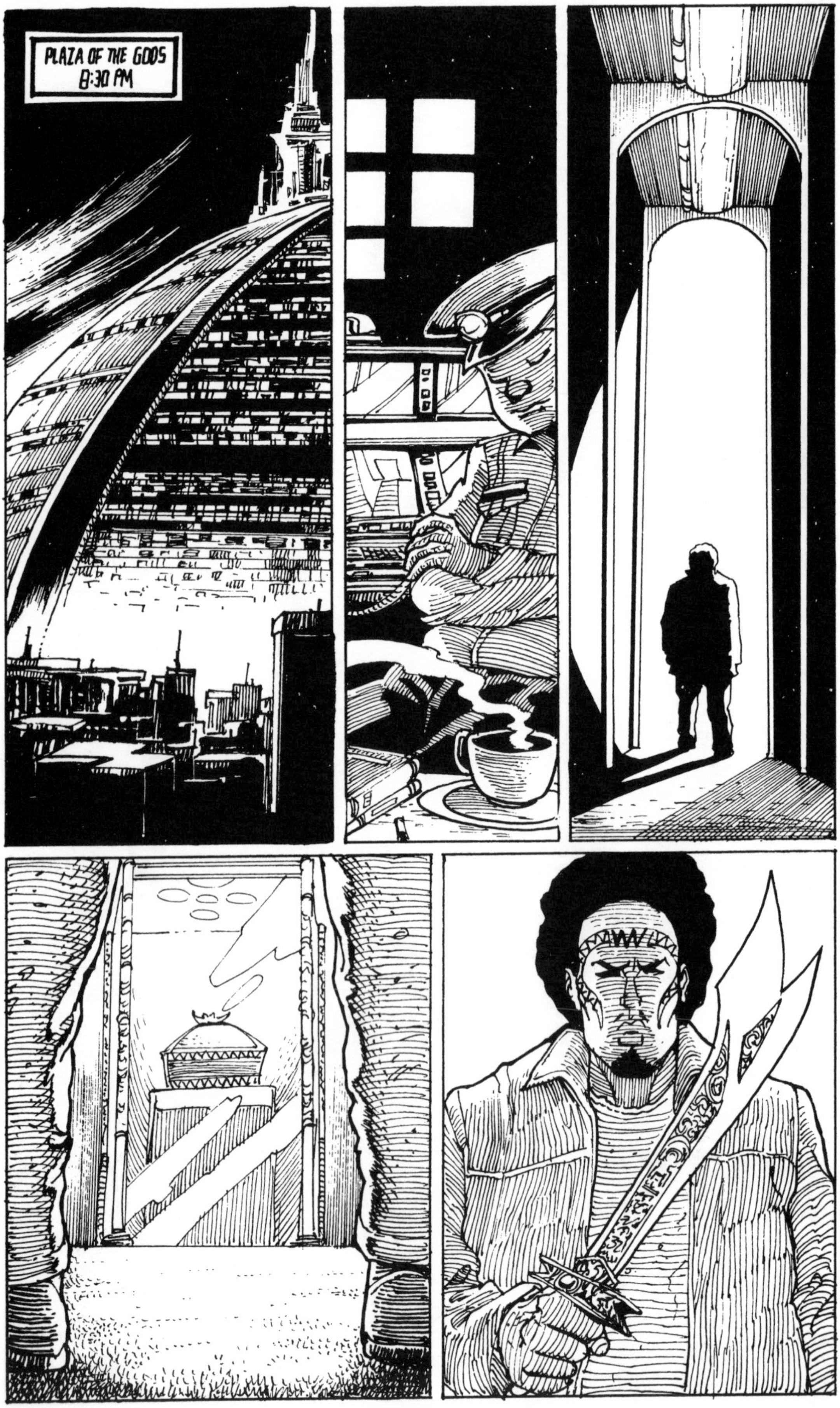
PLAZA OF THE GODS
8:30 PM

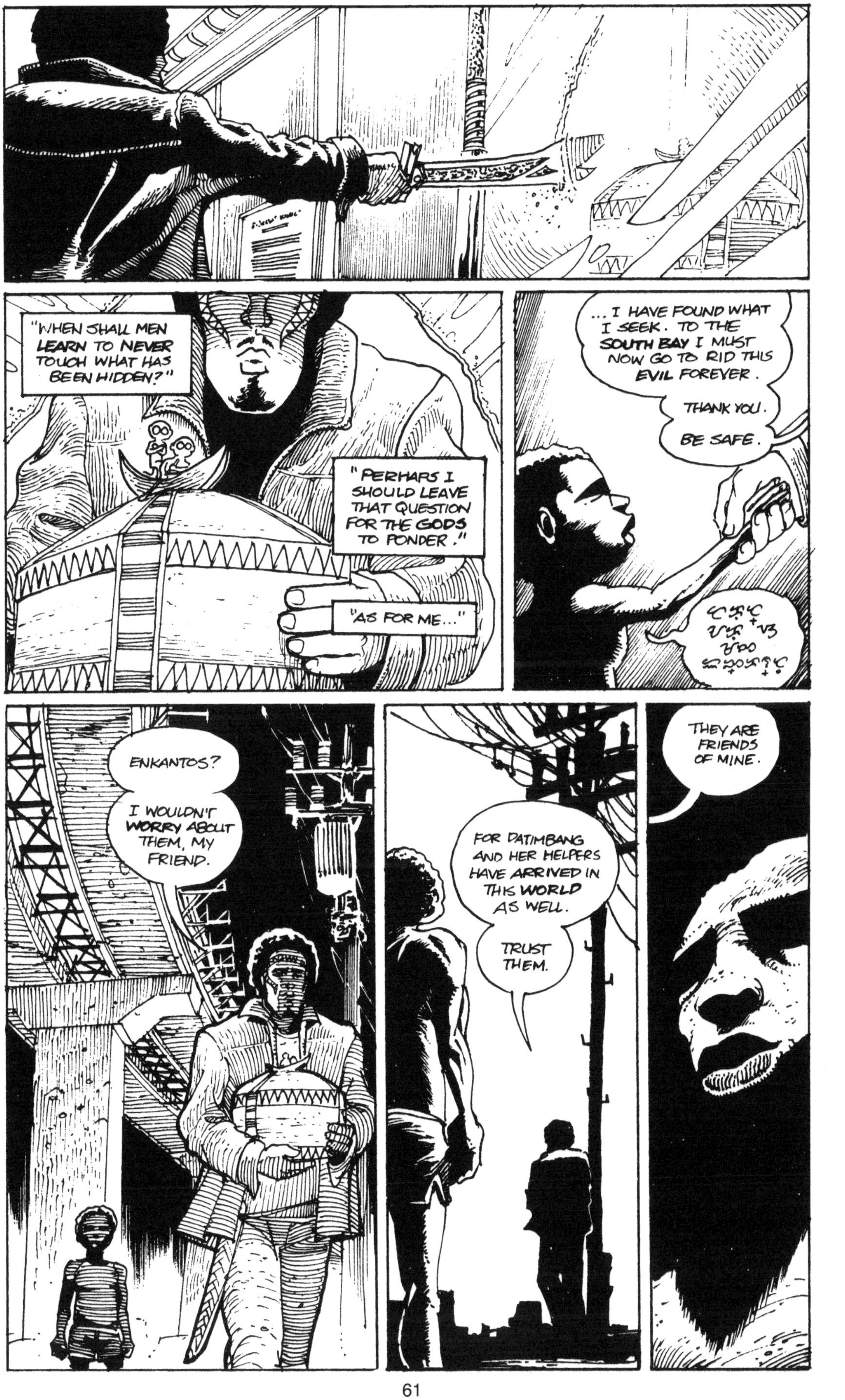
"WHEN SHALL MEN LEARN TO NEVER TOUCH WHAT HAS BEEN HIDDEN?"
"PERHAPS I SHOULD LEAVE THAT QUESTION FOR THE GODS TO PONDER."
"AS FOR ME..."
...I HAVE FOUND WHAT I SEEK. TO THE SOUTH BAY I MUST NOW GO TO RID THIS EVIL FOREVER.
THANK YOU.
BE SAFE.
ENKANTOS?
I WOULDN'T WORRY ABOUT THEM, MY FRIEND.
FOR DATIMBANG AND HER HELPERS HAVE ARRIVED IN THIS WORLD AS WELL.
TRUST THEM.
THEY ARE FRIENDS OF MINE.

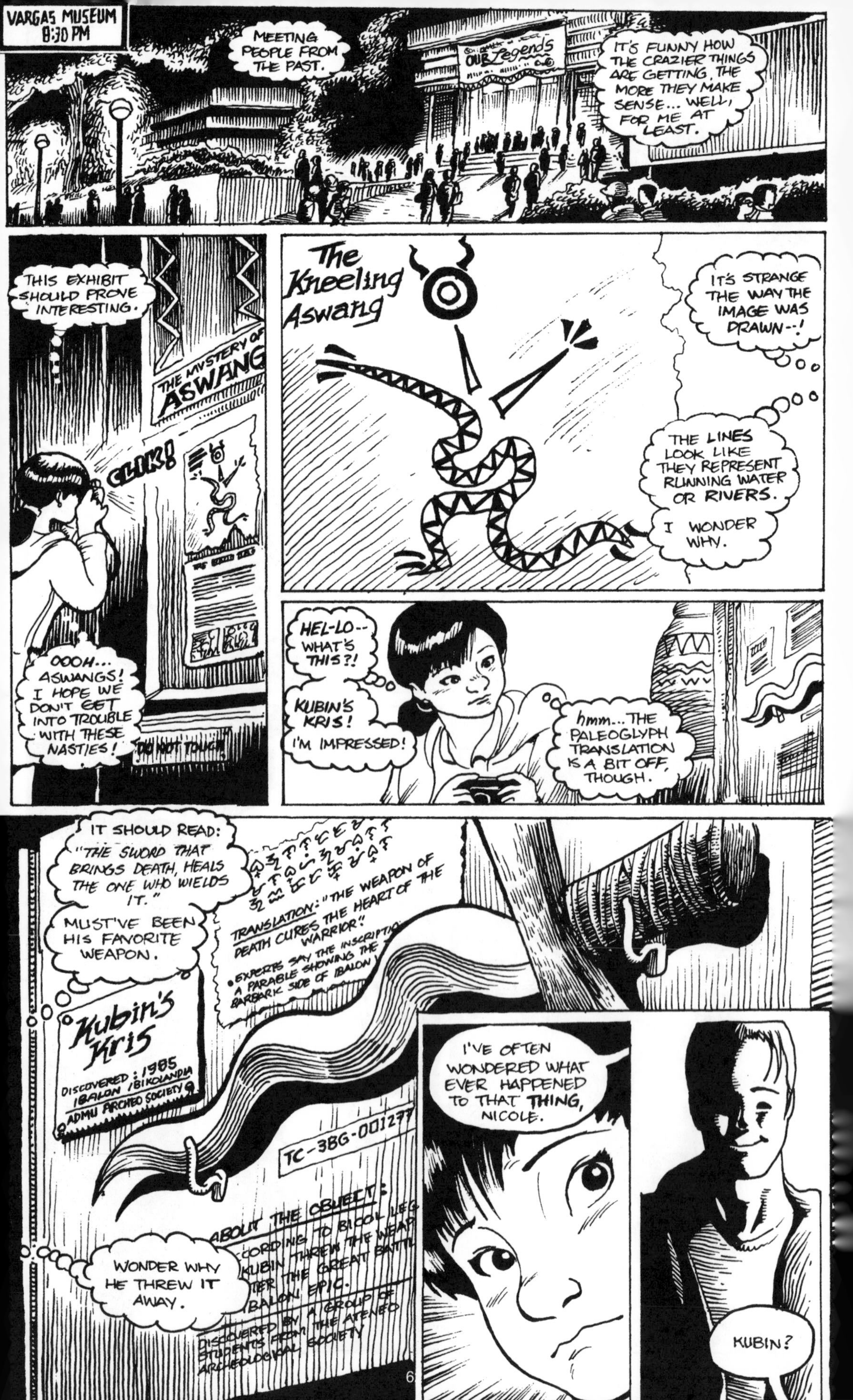

VARGAS MUSEUM 8:30 PM
OUR Legends
MEETING PEOPLE FROM THE PAST.
IT'S FUNNY HOW THE CRAZIER THINGS ARE GETTING, THE MORE THEY MAKE SENSE... WELL, FOR ME AT LEAST.
THIS EXHIBIT SHOULD PROVE INTERESTING.
THE MYSTERY OF ASWANG
CLIK!
OOOH... ASWANGS! I HOPE WE DON'T GET INTO TROUBLE WITH THESE NASTIES!
DO NOT TOUCH
The Kneeling Aswang
IT'S STRANGE THE WAY THE IMAGE WAS DRAWN--!
THE LINES LOOK LIKE THEY REPRESENT RUNNING WATER OR RIVERS.
I WONDER WHY.
HEL-LO-- WHAT'S THIS?!
KUBIN'S KRIS! I'M IMPRESSED!
hmm... THE PALEOGLYPH TRANSLATION IS A BIT OFF, THOUGH.
IT SHOULD READ: "THE SWORD THAT BRINGS DEATH, HEALS THE ONE WHO WIELDS IT."
MUST'VE BEEN HIS FAVORITE WEAPON.
TRANSLATION: "THE WEAPON OF DEATH CURES THE HEART OF THE WARRIOR"
• EXPERTS SAY THE INSCRIPTIO A PARABLE SHOWING THE BARBARIC SIDE OF IBALON
Kubin's Kris
DISCOVERED: 1985 IBALON / BIKOLANDIA ADMU ARCHEO SOCIETY
TC-3BG-001277
ABOUT THE OBJECT:
WONDER WHY HE THREW IT AWAY.
I'VE OFTEN WONDERED WHAT EVER HAPPENED TO THAT THING, NICOLE.
KUBIN?

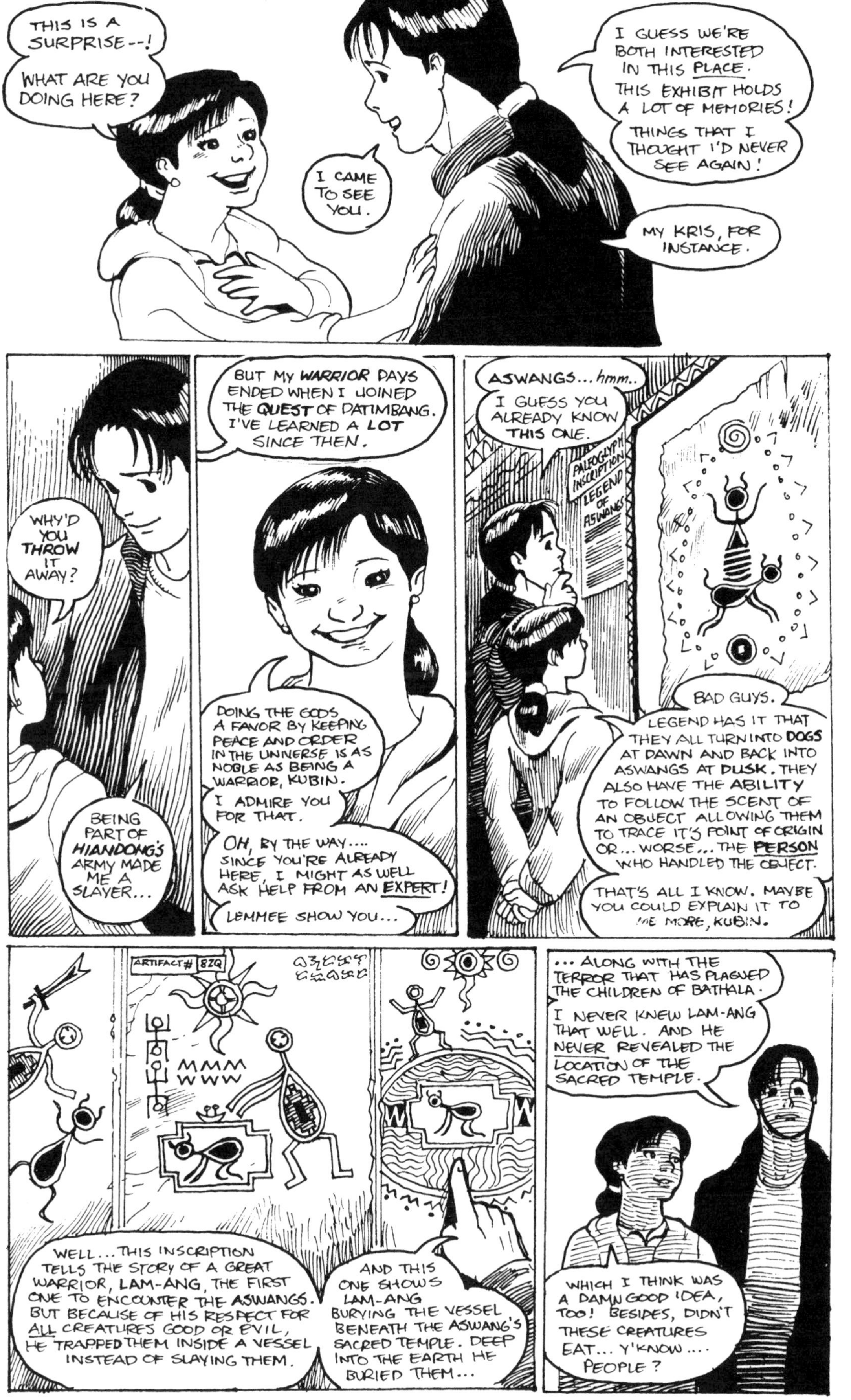
THIS IS A SURPRISE--!
WHAT ARE YOU DOING HERE?
I CAME TO SEE YOU.
I GUESS WE'RE BOTH INTERESTED IN THIS PLACE.
THIS EXHIBIT HOLDS A LOT OF MEMORIES!
THINGS THAT I THOUGHT I'D NEVER SEE AGAIN!
MY KRIS, FOR INSTANCE.
WHY'D YOU THROW IT AWAY?
BEING PART OF HIANDONG'S ARMY MADE ME A SLAYER...
BUT MY WARRIOR DAYS ENDED WHEN I JOINED THE QUEST OF PATIMBANG. I'VE LEARNED A LOT SINCE THEN.
DOING THE GODS A FAVOR BY KEEPING PEACE AND ORDER IN THE UNIVERSE IS AS NOBLE AS BEING A WARRIOR, KUBIN.
I ADMIRE YOU FOR THAT.
OH, BY THE WAY.... SINCE YOU'RE ALREADY HERE, I MIGHT AS WELL ASK HELP FROM AN EXPERT!
LEMMEE SHOW YOU...
ASWANGS... hmm..
I GUESS YOU ALREADY KNOW THIS ONE.
PALEOGLYPH INSCRIPTION
LEGEND OF ASWANGS
BAD GUYS.
LEGEND HAS IT THAT THEY ALL TURN INTO DOGS AT DAWN AND BACK INTO ASWANGS AT DUSK. THEY ALSO HAVE THE ABILITY TO FOLLOW THE SCENT OF AN OBJECT ALLOWING THEM TO TRACE IT'S POINT OF ORIGIN OR... WORSE... THE PERSON WHO HANDLED THE OBJECT.
THAT'S ALL I KNOW. MAYBE YOU COULD EXPLAIN IT TO ME MORE, KUBIN.
ARTIFACT # 8ZQ
MMM
WWW
WELL... THIS INSCRIPTION TELLS THE STORY OF A GREAT WARRIOR, LAM-ANG, THE FIRST ONE TO ENCOUNTER THE ASWANGS. BUT BECAUSE OF HIS RESPECT FOR ALL CREATURES GOOD OR EVIL, HE TRAPPED THEM INSIDE A VESSEL INSTEAD OF SLAYING THEM.
AND THIS ONE SHOWS LAM-ANG BURYING THE VESSEL BENEATH THE ASWANG'S SACRED TEMPLE. DEEP INTO THE EARTH HE BURIED THEM...
... ALONG WITH THE TERROR THAT HAS PLAGUED THE CHILDREN OF BATHALA.
I NEVER KNEW LAM-ANG THAT WELL. AND HE NEVER REVEALED THE LOCATION OF THE SACRED TEMPLE.
WHICH I THINK WAS A DAMN GOOD IDEA, TOO! BESIDES, DIDN'T THESE CREATURES EAT... Y'KNOW.... PEOPLE?

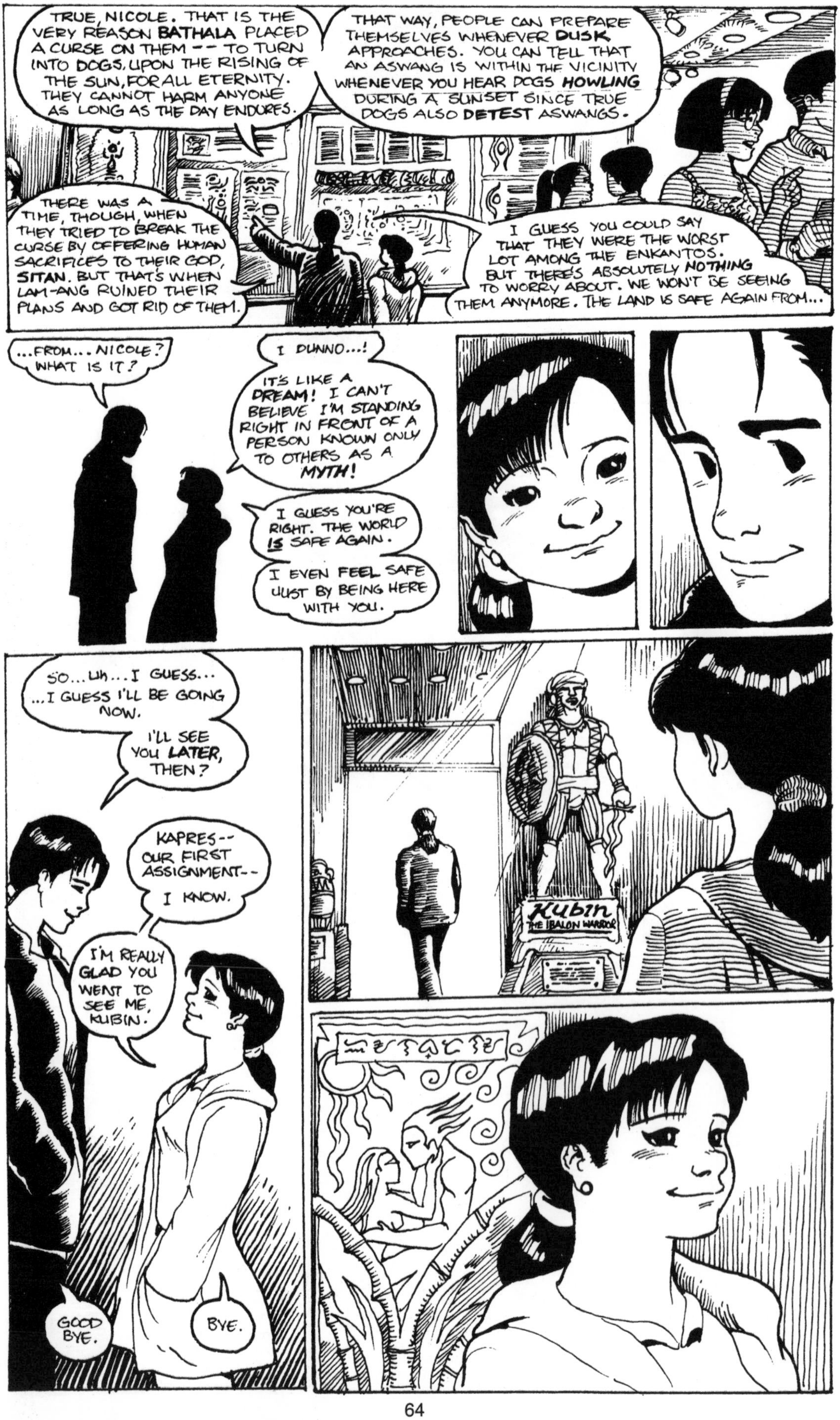
TRUE, NICOLE. THAT IS THE VERY REASON BATHALA PLACED A CURSE ON THEM -- TO TURN INTO DOGS, UPON THE RISING OF THE SUN, FOR ALL ETERNITY. THEY CANNOT HARM ANYONE AS LONG AS THE DAY ENDURES.
THAT WAY, PEOPLE CAN PREPARE THEMSELVES WHENEVER DUSK APPROACHES. YOU CAN TELL THAT AN ASWANG IS WITHIN THE VICINITY WHENEVER YOU HEAR DOGS HOWLING DURING A SUNSET SINCE TRUE DOGS ALSO DETEST ASWANGS.
THERE WAS A TIME, THOUGH, WHEN THEY TRIED TO BREAK THE CURSE BY OFFERING HUMAN SACRIFICES TO THEIR GOD, SITAN. BUT THAT'S WHEN LAM-ANG RUINED THEIR PLANS AND GOT RID OF THEM.
I GUESS YOU COULD SAY THAT THEY WERE THE WORST LOT AMONG THE ENKANTOS. BUT THERE'S ABSOLUTELY NOTHING TO WORRY ABOUT. WE WON'T BE SEEING THEM ANYMORE. THE LAND IS SAFE AGAIN FROM...
...FROM... NICOLE? WHAT IS IT?
I DUNNO...!
IT'S LIKE A DREAM! I CAN'T BELIEVE I'M STANDING RIGHT IN FRONT OF A PERSON KNOWN ONLY TO OTHERS AS A MYTH!
I GUESS YOU'RE RIGHT. THE WORLD IS SAFE AGAIN.
I EVEN FEEL SAFE JUST BY BEING HERE WITH YOU.
SO... UH... I GUESS... ...I GUESS I'LL BE GOING NOW.
I'LL SEE YOU LATER, THEN?
KAPRES-- OUR FIRST ASSIGNMENT--
I KNOW.
I'M REALLY GLAD YOU WENT TO SEE ME, KUBIN.
GOOD BYE.
BYE.
KUBIN
THE IBALON WARRIOR

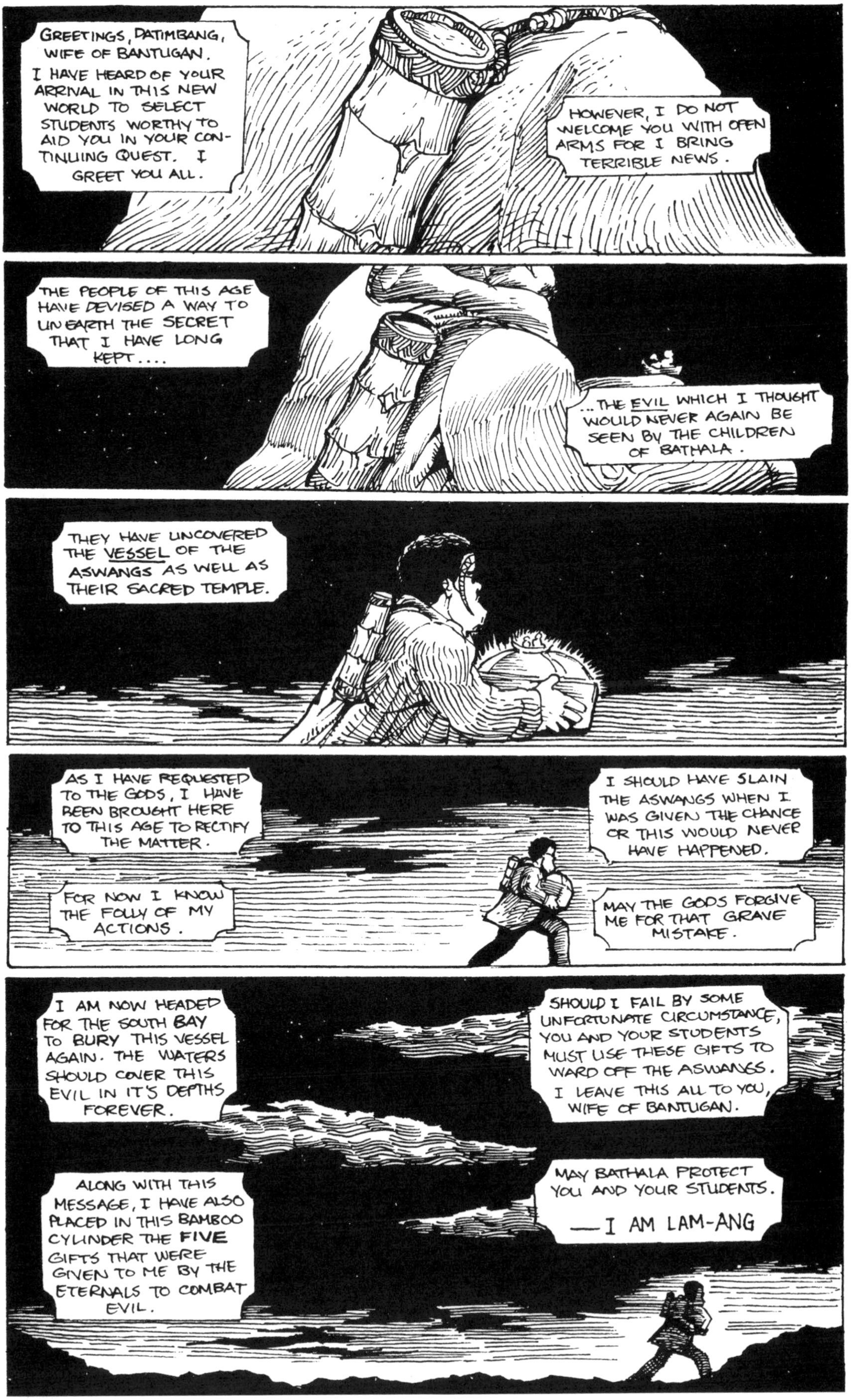
GREETINGS, DATIMBANG, WIFE OF BANTUGAN. I HAVE HEARD OF YOUR ARRIVAL IN THIS NEW WORLD TO SELECT STUDENTS WORTHY TO AID YOU IN YOUR CONTINUING QUEST. I GREET YOU ALL.
HOWEVER, I DO NOT WELCOME YOU WITH OPEN ARMS FOR I BRING TERRIBLE NEWS.
THE PEOPLE OF THIS AGE HAVE DEVISED A WAY TO UNEARTH THE SECRET THAT I HAVE LONG KEPT....
...THE EVIL WHICH I THOUGHT WOULD NEVER AGAIN BE SEEN BY THE CHILDREN OF BATHALA.
THEY HAVE UNCOVERED THE VESSEL OF THE ASWANGS AS WELL AS THEIR SACRED TEMPLE.
AS I HAVE REQUESTED TO THE GODS, I HAVE BEEN BROUGHT HERE TO THIS AGE TO RECTIFY THE MATTER.
FOR NOW I KNOW THE FOLLY OF MY ACTIONS.
I SHOULD HAVE SLAIN THE ASWANGS WHEN I WAS GIVEN THE CHANCE OR THIS WOULD NEVER HAVE HAPPENED.
MAY THE GODS FORGIVE ME FOR THAT GRAVE MISTAKE.
I AM NOW HEADED FOR THE SOUTH BAY TO BURY THIS VESSEL AGAIN. THE WATERS SHOULD COVER THIS EVIL IN IT'S DEPTHS FOREVER.
SHOULD I FAIL BY SOME UNFORTUNATE CIRCUMSTANCE, YOU AND YOUR STUDENTS MUST USE THESE GIFTS TO WARD OFF THE ASWANGS.
I LEAVE THIS ALL TO YOU, WIFE OF BANTUGAN.
ALONG WITH THIS MESSAGE, I HAVE ALSO PLACED IN THIS BAMBOO CYLINDER THE FIVE GIFTS THAT WERE GIVEN TO ME BY THE ETERNALS TO COMBAT EVIL.
MAY BATHALA PROTECT YOU AND YOUR STUDENTS.
—I AM LAM-ANG

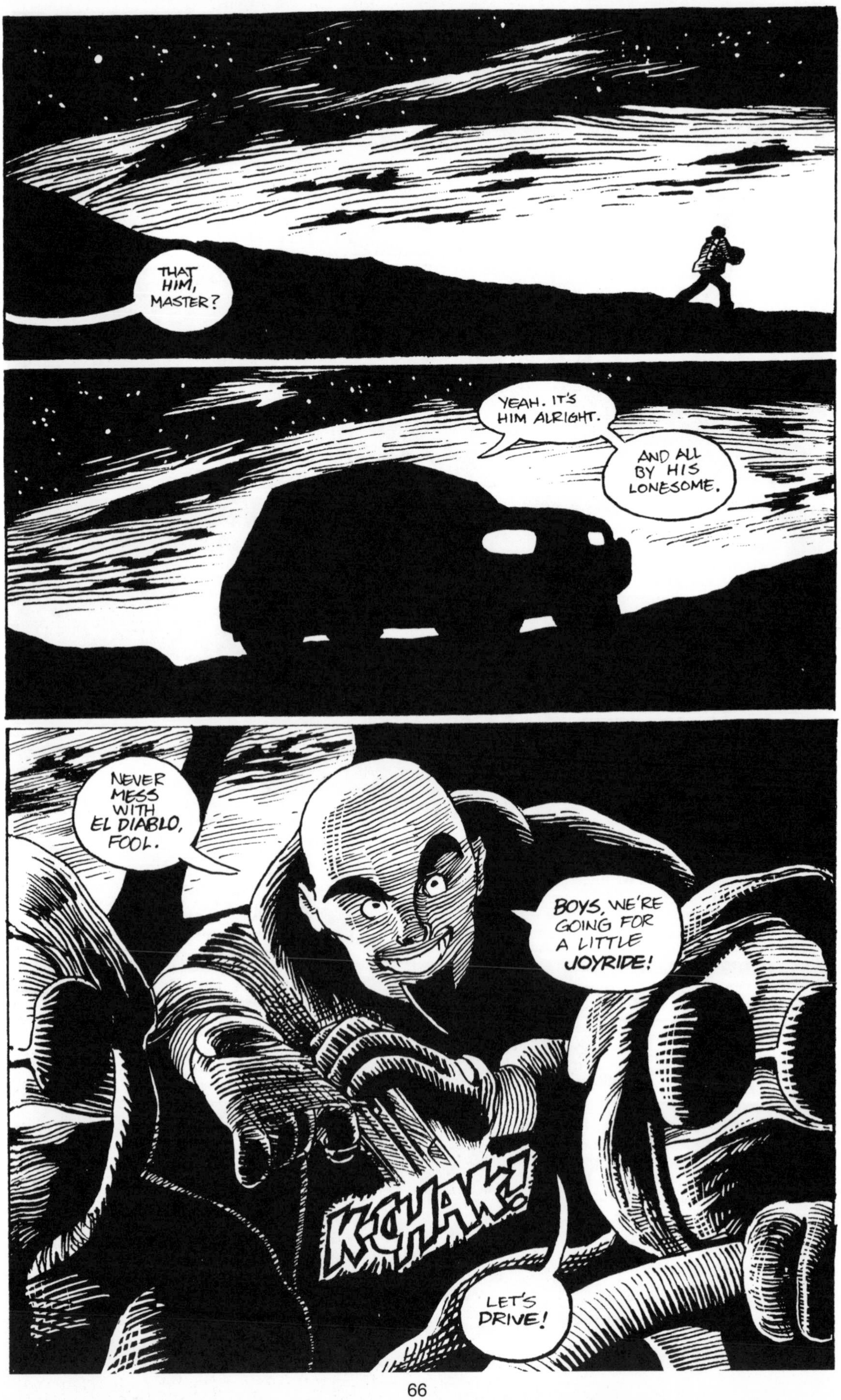
THAT HIM, MASTER?
YEAH. IT'S HIM ALRIGHT.
AND ALL BY HIS LONESOME.
NEVER MESS WITH EL DIABLO, FOOL.
BOYS, WE'RE GOING FOR A LITTLE JOYRIDE!
K-CHAK!
LET'S DRIVE!

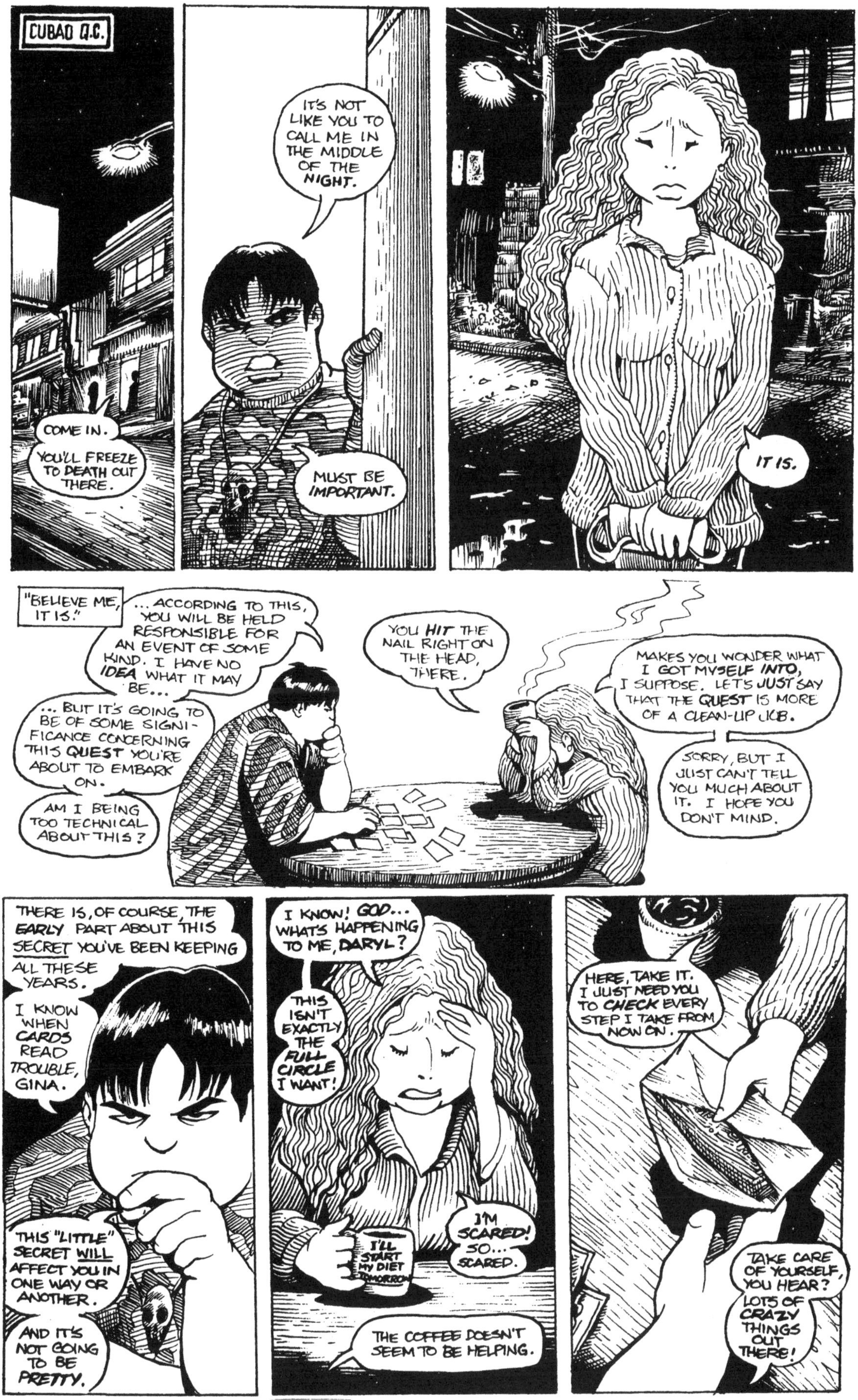
CUBAO Q.C.
IT'S NOT LIKE YOU TO CALL ME IN THE MIDDLE OF THE NIGHT.
COME IN.
YOU'LL FREEZE TO DEATH OUT THERE.
MUST BE IMPORTANT.
IT IS.
"BELIEVE ME, IT IS."
... ACCORDING TO THIS, YOU WILL BE HELD RESPONSIBLE FOR AN EVENT OF SOME KIND. I HAVE NO IDEA WHAT IT MAY BE...
... BUT IT'S GOING TO BE OF SOME SIGNIFICANCE CONCERNING THIS QUEST YOU'RE ABOUT TO EMBARK ON.
AM I BEING TOO TECHNICAL ABOUT THIS?
YOU HIT THE NAIL RIGHT ON THE HEAD, THERE.
MAKES YOU WONDER WHAT I GOT MYSELF INTO, I SUPPOSE. LET'S JUST SAY THAT THE QUEST IS MORE OF A CLEAN-UP JOB.
SORRY, BUT I JUST CAN'T TELL YOU MUCH ABOUT IT. I HOPE YOU DON'T MIND.
THERE IS, OF COURSE, THE EARLY PART ABOUT THIS SECRET YOU'VE BEEN KEEPING ALL THESE YEARS.
I KNOW WHEN CARDS READ TROUBLE, GINA.
THIS "LITTLE" SECRET WILL AFFECT YOU IN ONE WAY OR ANOTHER.
AND IT'S NOT GOING TO BE PRETTY.
I KNOW! GOD... WHAT'S HAPPENING TO ME, DARYL?
THIS ISN'T EXACTLY THE FULL CIRCLE I WANT!
I'LL START MY DIET TOMORROW
I'M SCARED! SO... SCARED.
THE COFFEE DOESN'T SEEM TO BE HELPING.
HERE, TAKE IT. I JUST NEED YOU TO CHECK EVERY STEP I TAKE FROM NOW ON.
TAKE CARE OF YOURSELF, YOU HEAR?
LOTS OF CRAZY THINGS OUT THERE!

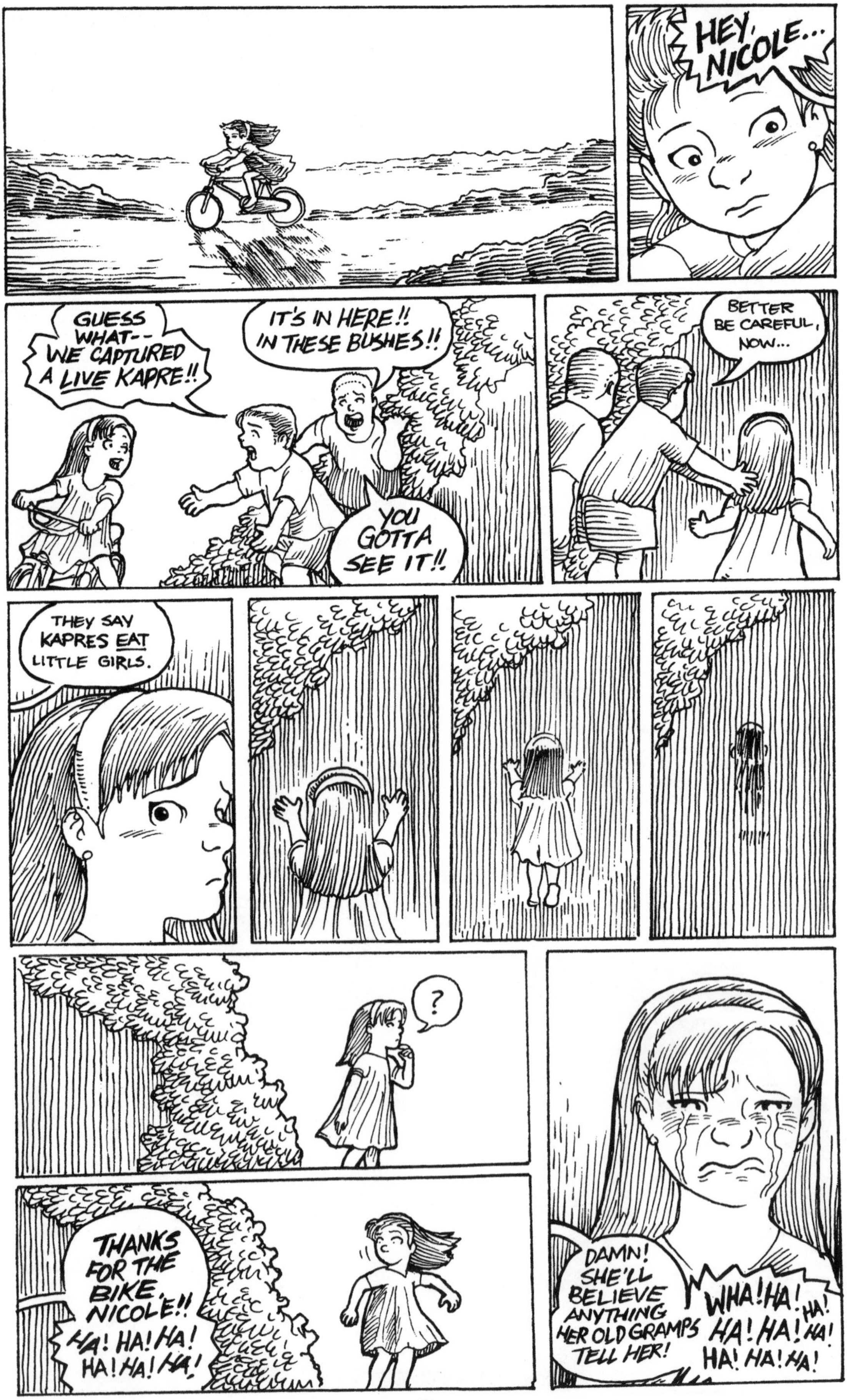

HEY, NICOLE...
GUESS WHAT-- WE CAPTURED A LIVE KAPRE!!
IT'S IN HERE!! IN THESE BUSHES!!
YOU GOTTA SEE IT!!
BETTER BE CAREFUL, NOW...
THEY SAY KAPRES EAT LITTLE GIRLS.
?
THANKS FOR THE BIKE, NICOLE!! HA! HA! HA! HA! HA! HA!
DAMN! SHE'LL BELIEVE ANYTHING HER OLD GRAMPS TELL HER!
WHA! HA! HA! HA! HA! HA! HA! HA! HA!

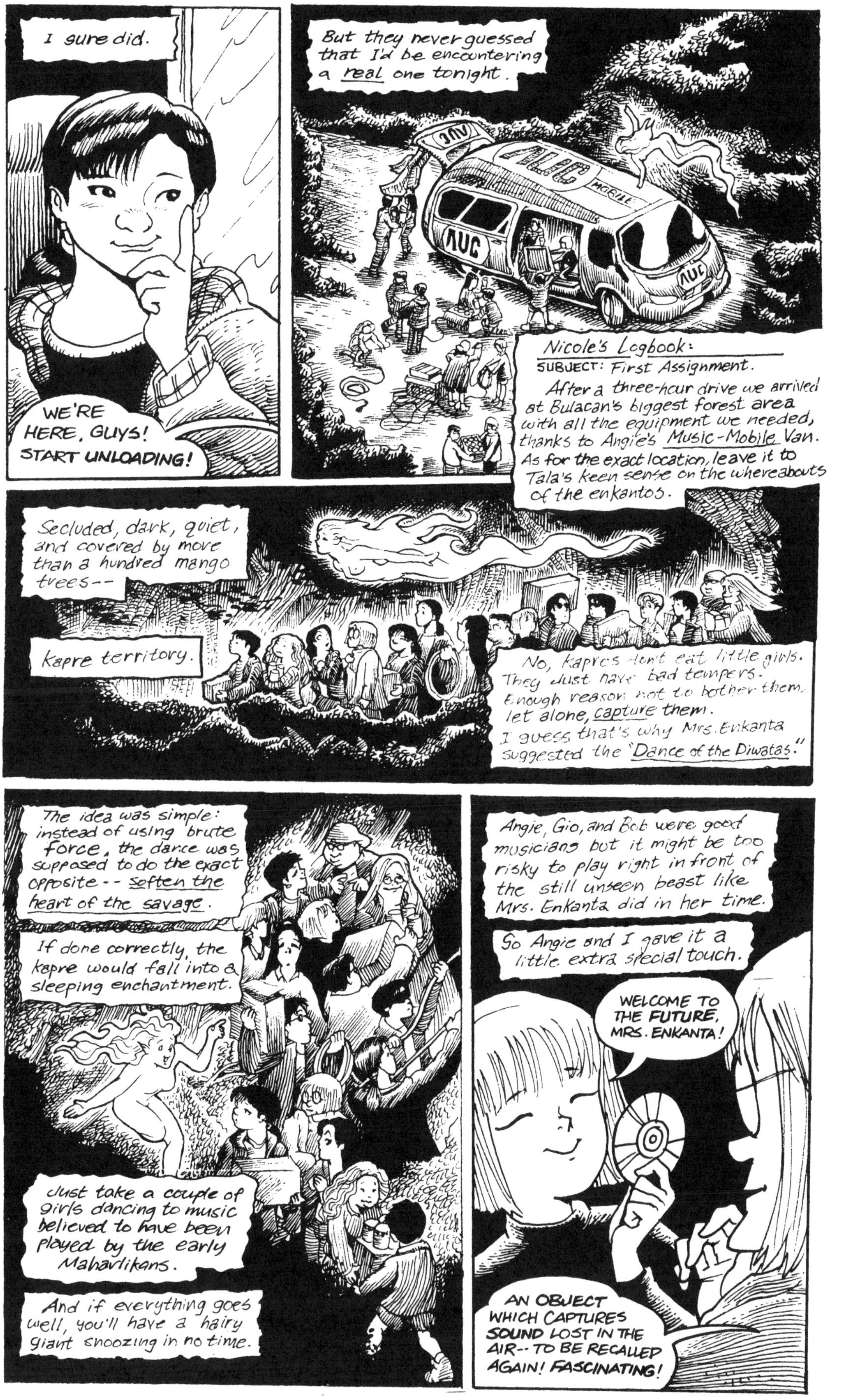
I sure did.
But they never guessed that I'd be encountering a real one tonight.
WE'RE HERE, GUYS! START UNLOADING!
Nicole's Logbook:
SUBJECT: First Assignment.
After a three-hour drive we arrived at Bulacan's biggest forest area with all the equipment we needed, thanks to Angie's Music-Mobile Van. As for the exact location, leave it to Tala's keen sense on the whereabouts of the enkantos.
Secluded, dark, quiet, and covered by more than a hundred mango trees--
Kapre territory.
No, kapres don't eat little girls. They just have bad tempers. Enough reason not to bother them, let alone, capture them.
I guess that's why Mrs. Enkanta suggested the "Dance of the Diwatas."
The idea was simple: instead of using brute force, the dance was supposed to do the exact opposite -- soften the heart of the savage.
If done correctly, the kapre would fall into a sleeping enchantment.
Just take a couple of girls dancing to music believed to have been played by the early Maharlikans.
And if everything goes well, you'll have a hairy giant snoozing in no time.
Angie, Gio, and Bob were good musicians but it might be too risky to play right in front of the still unseen beast like Mrs. Enkanta did in her time.
So Angie and I gave it a little extra special touch.
WELCOME TO THE FUTURE, MRS. ENKANTA!
AN OBJECT WHICH CAPTURES SOUND LOST IN THE AIR-- TO BE RECALLED AGAIN! FASCINATING!

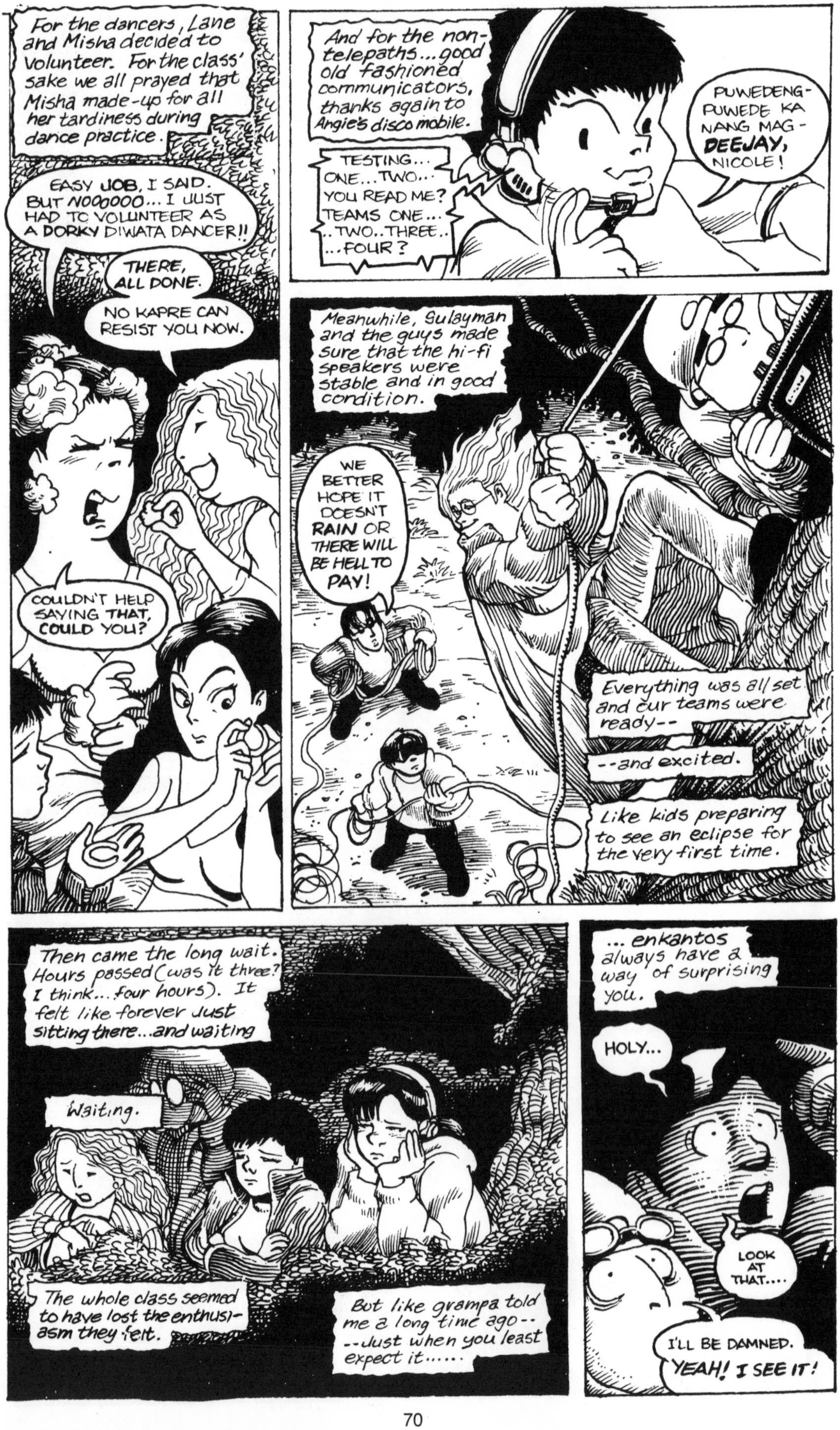
For the dancers, Lane and Misha decided to volunteer. For the class' sake we all prayed that Misha made-up for all her tardiness during dance practice.
EASY JOB, I SAID. BUT NOOOOOO... I JUST HAD TO VOLUNTEER AS A DORKY DIWATA DANCER!!
THERE, ALL DONE.
NO KAPRE CAN RESIST YOU NOW.
COULDN'T HELP SAYING THAT, COULD YOU?
And for the non-telepaths...good old fashioned communicators, thanks again to Angie's disco mobile.
TESTING... ONE...TWO... YOU READ ME? TEAMS ONE... ..TWO..THREE.. ...FOUR?
PUWEDENG-PUWEDE KA NANG MAG-DEEJAY, NICOLE!
Meanwhile, Sulayman and the guys made sure that the hi-fi speakers were stable and in good condition.
WE BETTER HOPE IT DOESN'T RAIN OR THERE WILL BE HELL TO PAY!
Everything was all set and our teams were ready--
--and excited.
Like kids preparing to see an eclipse for the very first time.
Then came the long wait. Hours passed (was it three? I think...four hours). It felt like forever just sitting there...and waiting
Waiting.
The whole class seemed to have lost the enthusiasm they felt.
But like grampa told me a long time ago-- --Just when you least expect it.....
...enkantos always have a way of surprising you.
HOLY...
LOOK AT THAT....
I'LL BE DAMNED. YEAH! I SEE IT!

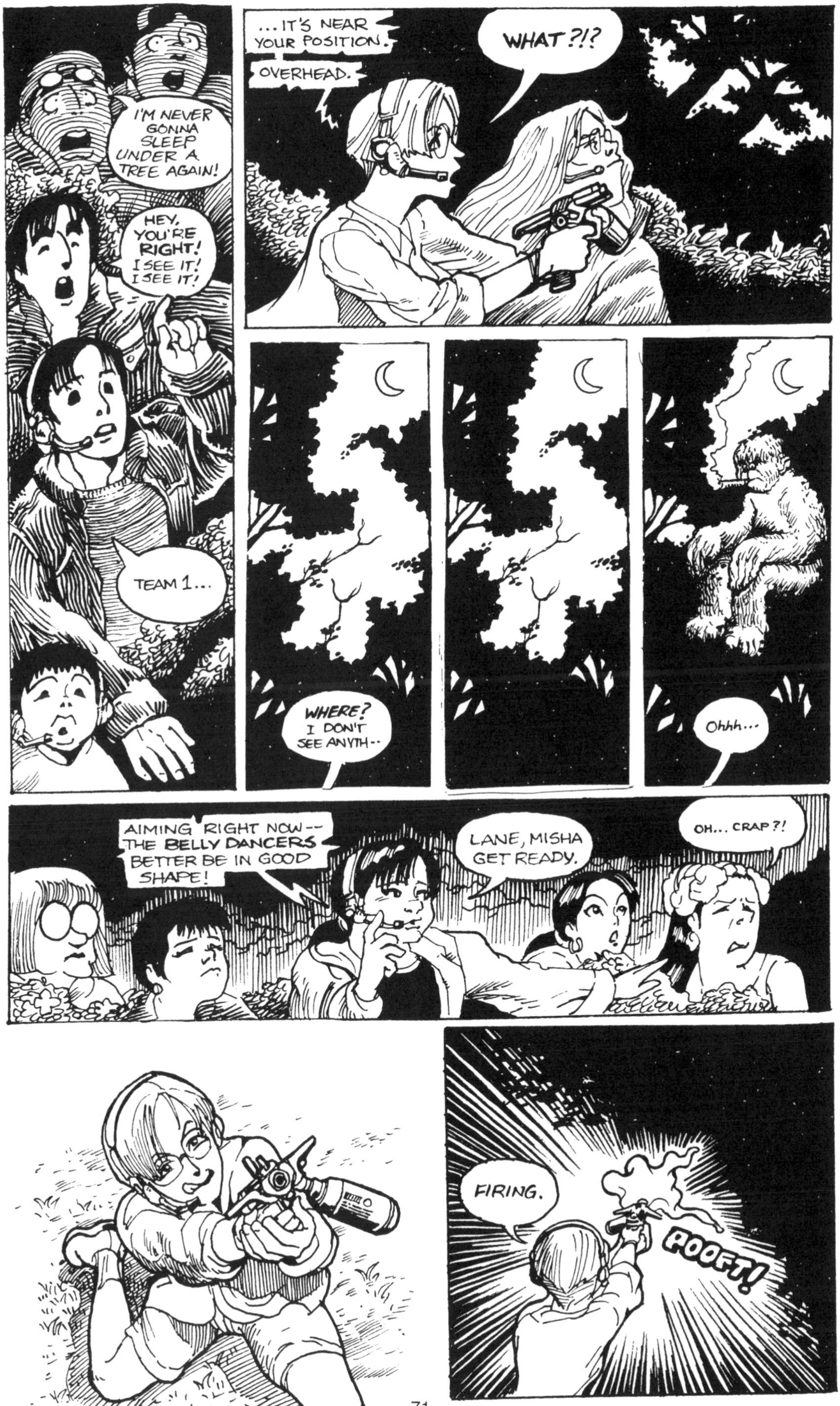

I'M NEVER GONNA SLEEP UNDER A TREE AGAIN!
HEY, YOU'RE RIGHT! I SEE IT! I SEE IT!
TEAM 1...
...IT'S NEAR YOUR POSITION.
OVERHEAD.
WHAT?!?
WHERE? I DON'T SEE ANYTH--
Ohhh...
AIMING RIGHT NOW-- THE BELLY DANCERS BETTER BE IN GOOD SHAPE!
LANE, MISHA GET READY.
OH... CRAP?!
FIRING.
POOFT!

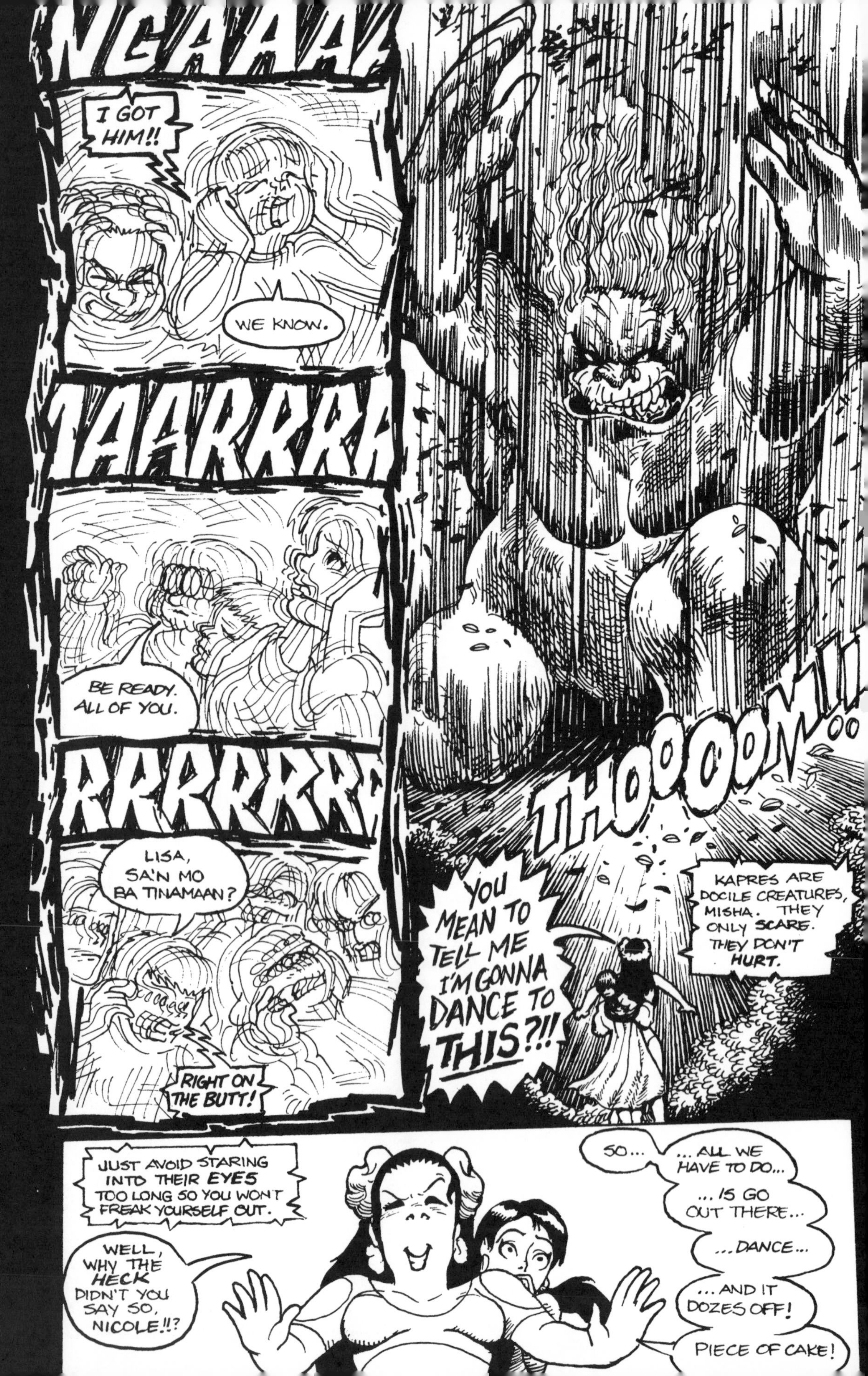
NGAAAA
I GOT HIM!!
WE KNOW.
AARRRR
BE READY. ALL OF YOU.
RRRRRR
LISA, SA'N MO BA TINAMAAN?
RIGHT ON THE BUTT!
THOOOOM!!
YOU MEAN TO TELL ME I'M GONNA DANCE TO THIS?!!
KAPRES ARE DOCILE CREATURES, MISHA. THEY ONLY SCARE. THEY DON'T HURT.
JUST AVOID STARING INTO THEIR EYES TOO LONG SO YOU WON'T FREAK YOURSELF OUT.
WELL, WHY THE HECK DIDN'T YOU SAY SO, NICOLE!!?
SO...
...ALL WE HAVE TO DO...
...IS GO OUT THERE...
...DANCE...
...AND IT DOZES OFF!
PIECE OF CAKE!

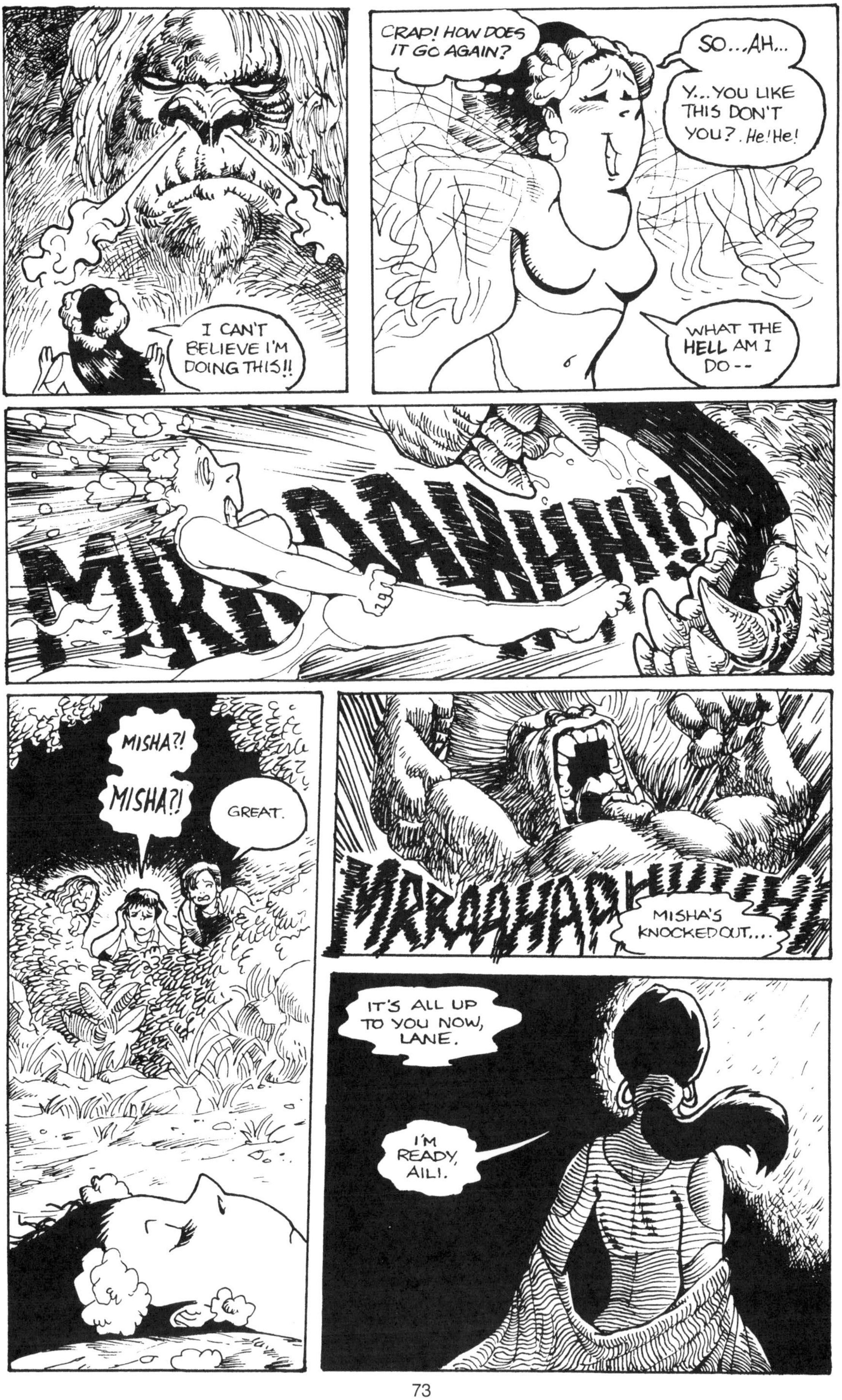
I CAN'T BELIEVE I'M DOING THIS!!
CRAP! HOW DOES IT GO AGAIN?
SO...AH...
Y...YOU LIKE THIS DON'T YOU? . He! He!
WHAT THE HELL AM I DO--
MRRDAHHHH!!
MISHA?!
MISHA?!
GREAT.
MRRAAHARHHHH!
MISHA'S KNOCKED OUT....
IT'S ALL UP TO YOU NOW, LANE.
I'M READY, AILI.

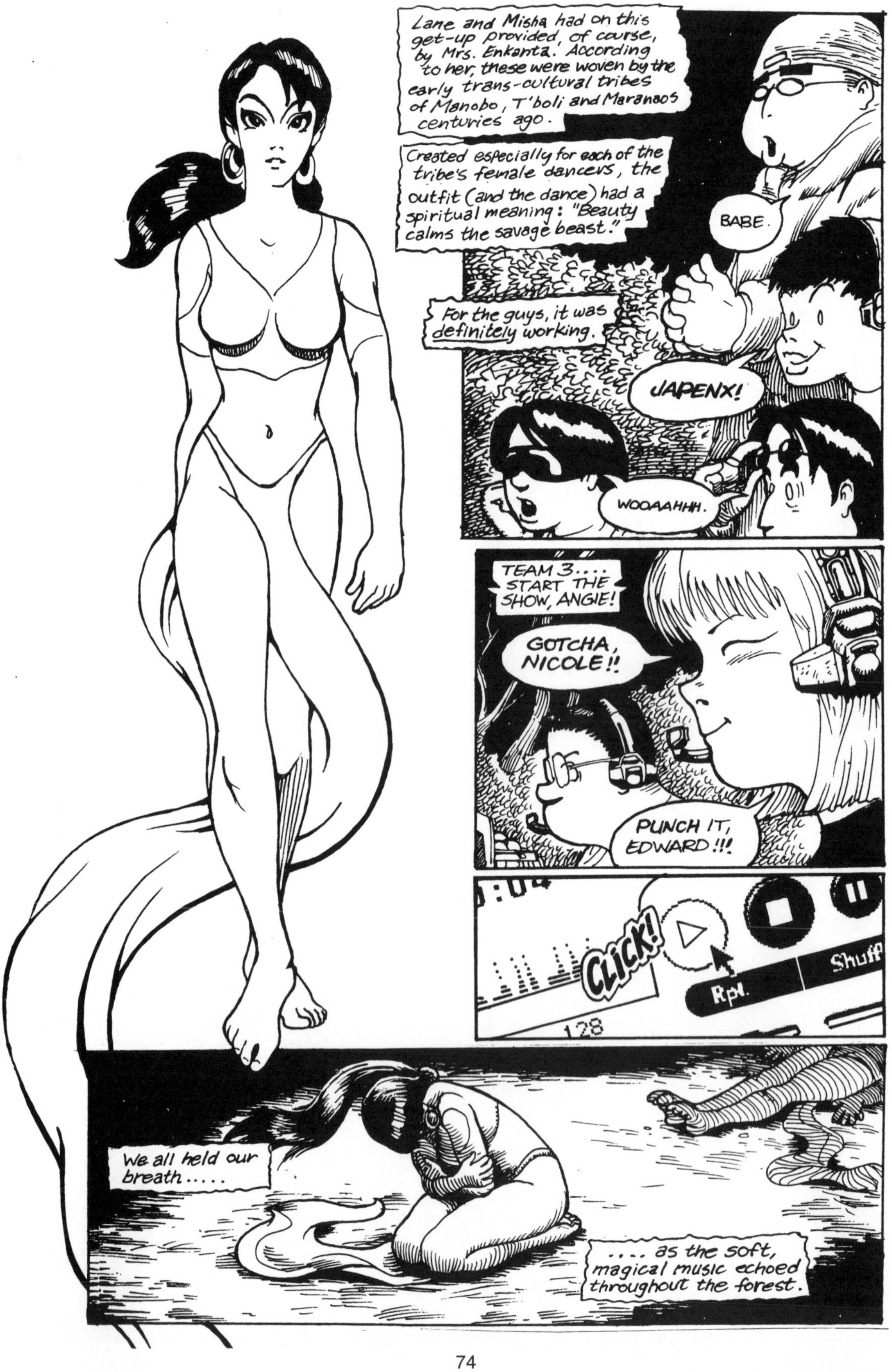
Lane and Misha had on this get-up provided, of course, by Mrs. Enkanta. According to her, these were woven by the early trans-cultural tribes of Manobo, T'boli and Maranaos centuries ago.
Created especially for each of the tribe's female dancers, the outfit (and the dance) had a spiritual meaning: "Beauty calms the savage beast."
BABE.
For the guys, it was definitely working.
JAPENX!
WOOAAHHH.
TEAM 3.... START THE SHOW, ANGIE!
GOTCHA, NICOLE!!
PUNCH IT, EDWARD!!!
CLICK!
Rpt.
128
We all held our breath.....
.... as the soft, magical music echoed throughout the forest.

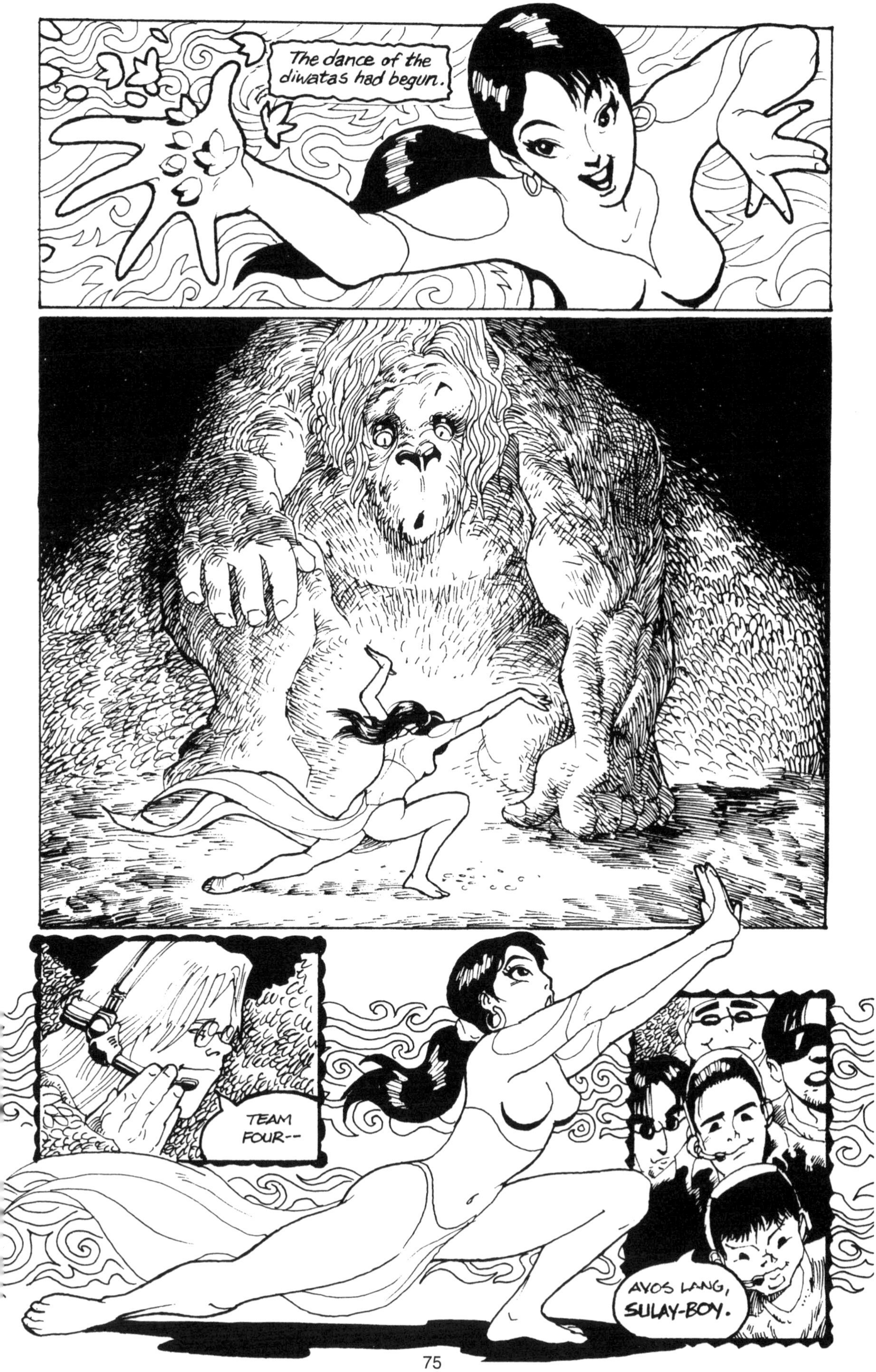
The dance of the diwatas had begun.
TEAM FOUR--
AVOS LANG, SULAY-BOY.

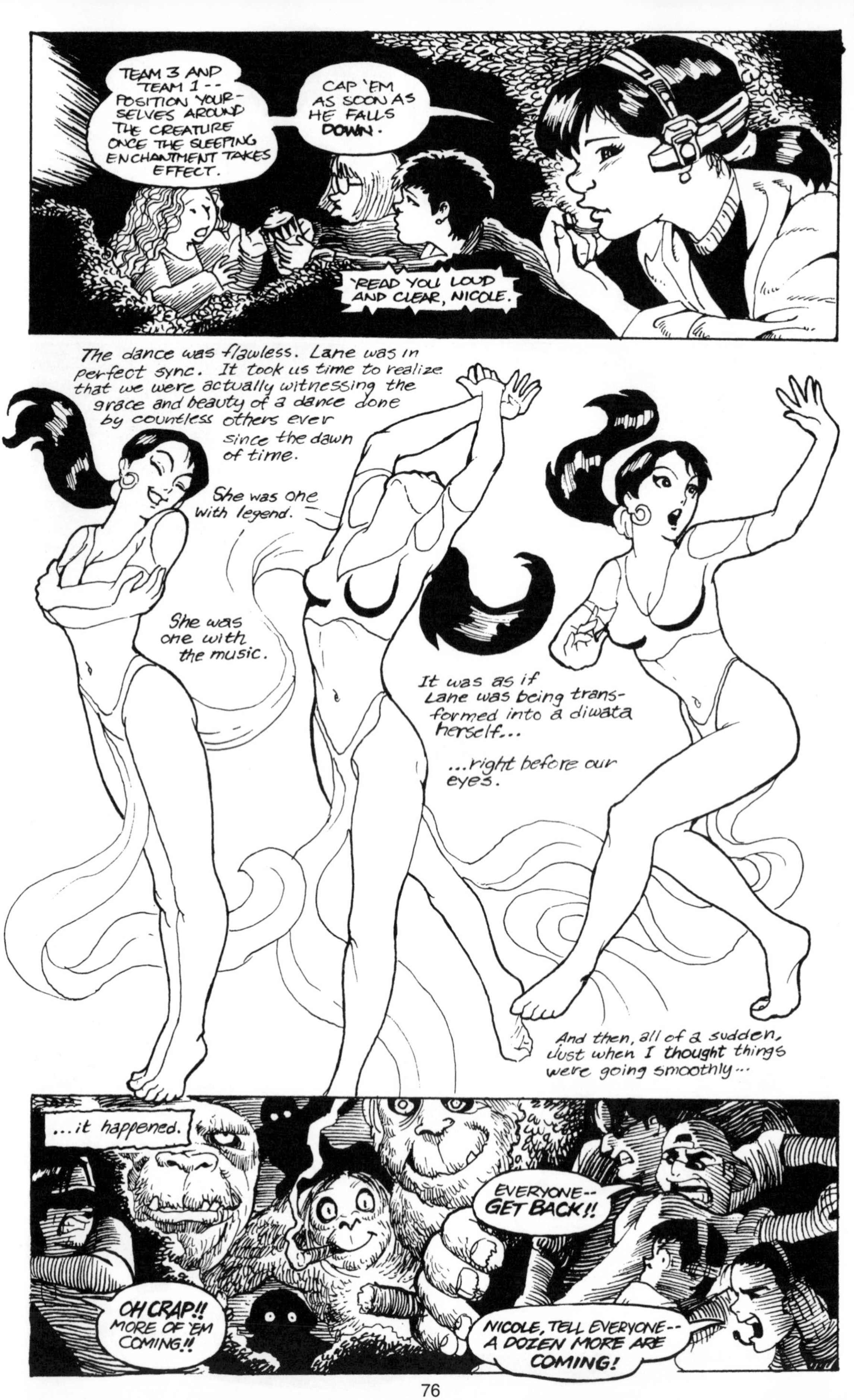
TEAM 3 AND TEAM 1 -- POSITION YOURSELVES AROUND THE CREATURE ONCE THE SLEEPING ENCHANTMENT TAKES EFFECT.
CAP 'EM AS SOON AS HE FALLS DOWN.
'READ YOU LOUD AND CLEAR, NICOLE.
The dance was flawless. Lane was in perfect sync. It took us time to realize that we were actually witnessing the grace and beauty of a dance done by countless others ever since the dawn of time.
She was one with legend.
She was one with the music.
It was as if Lane was being transformed into a diwata herself...
...right before our eyes.
And then, all of a sudden, just when I thought things were going smoothly...
...it happened.
EVERYONE-- GET BACK!!
OH CRAP!! MORE OF 'EM COMING!!
NICOLE, TELL EVERYONE-- A DOZEN MORE ARE COMING!

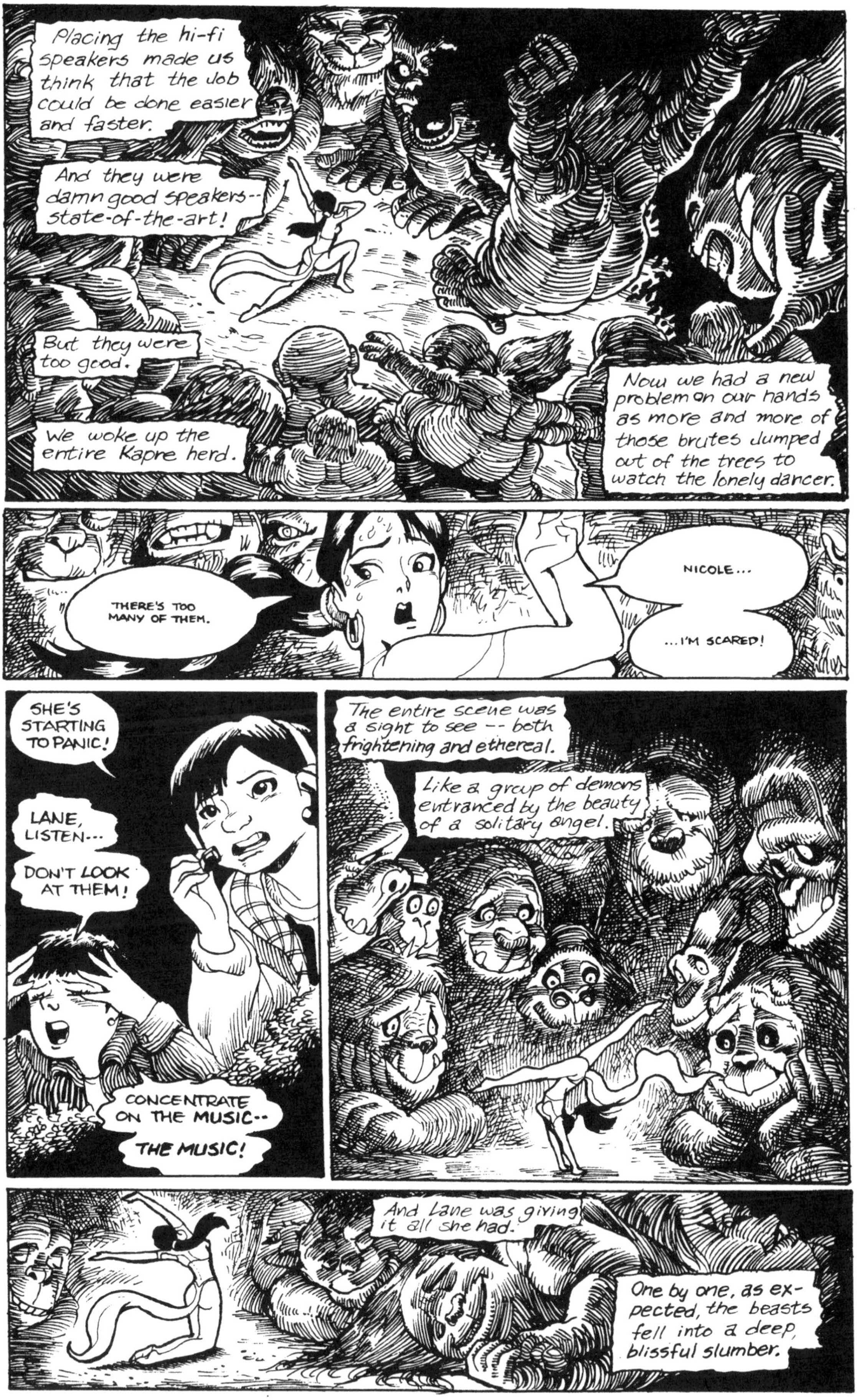
Placing the hi-fi speakers made us think that the job could be done easier and faster.
And they were damn good speakers-- state-of-the-art!
But they were too good.
We woke up the entire Kapre herd.
Now we had a new problem on our hands as more and more of those brutes jumped out of the trees to watch the lonely dancer.
THERE'S TOO MANY OF THEM.
NICOLE...
...I'M SCARED!
SHE'S STARTING TO PANIC!
LANE, LISTEN...
DON'T LOOK AT THEM!
CONCENTRATE ON THE MUSIC-- THE MUSIC!
The entire scene was a sight to see -- both frightening and ethereal.
Like a group of demons entranced by the beauty of a solitary angel.
And Lane was giving it all she had.
One by one, as expected, the beasts fell into a deep, blissful slumber.

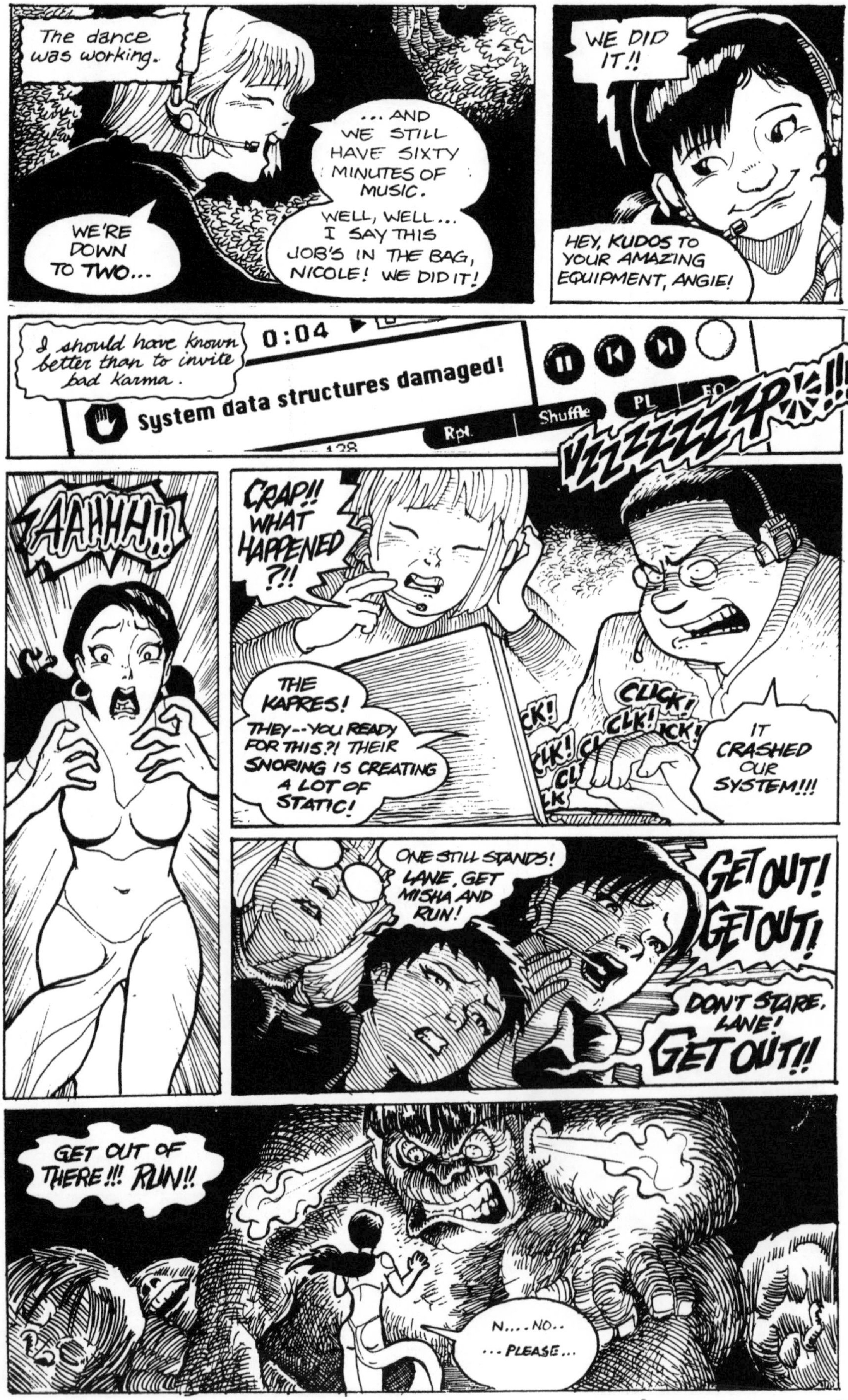
The dance was working.
WE'RE DOWN TO TWO...
...AND WE STILL HAVE SIXTY MINUTES OF MUSIC.
WELL, WELL... I SAY THIS JOB'S IN THE BAG, NICOLE! WE DID IT!
WE DID IT!!
HEY, KUDOS TO YOUR AMAZING EQUIPMENT, ANGIE!
I should have known better than to invite bad karma.
0:04
System data structures damaged!
Shuffle
PL
EQ
Rpt.
VZZZZZZZP!!!
AAHHH!!!
CRAP!! WHAT HAPPENED?!!
THE KAPRES!
THEY--YOU READY FOR THIS?! THEIR SNORING IS CREATING A LOT OF STATIC!
CLICK! CLK!
IT CRASHED OUR SYSTEM!!!
ONE STILL STANDS! LANE, GET MISHA AND RUN!
GET OUT! GET OUT!
DON'T STARE, LANE! GET OUT!!
GET OUT OF THERE!!! RUN!!
N....NO.. ...PLEASE...

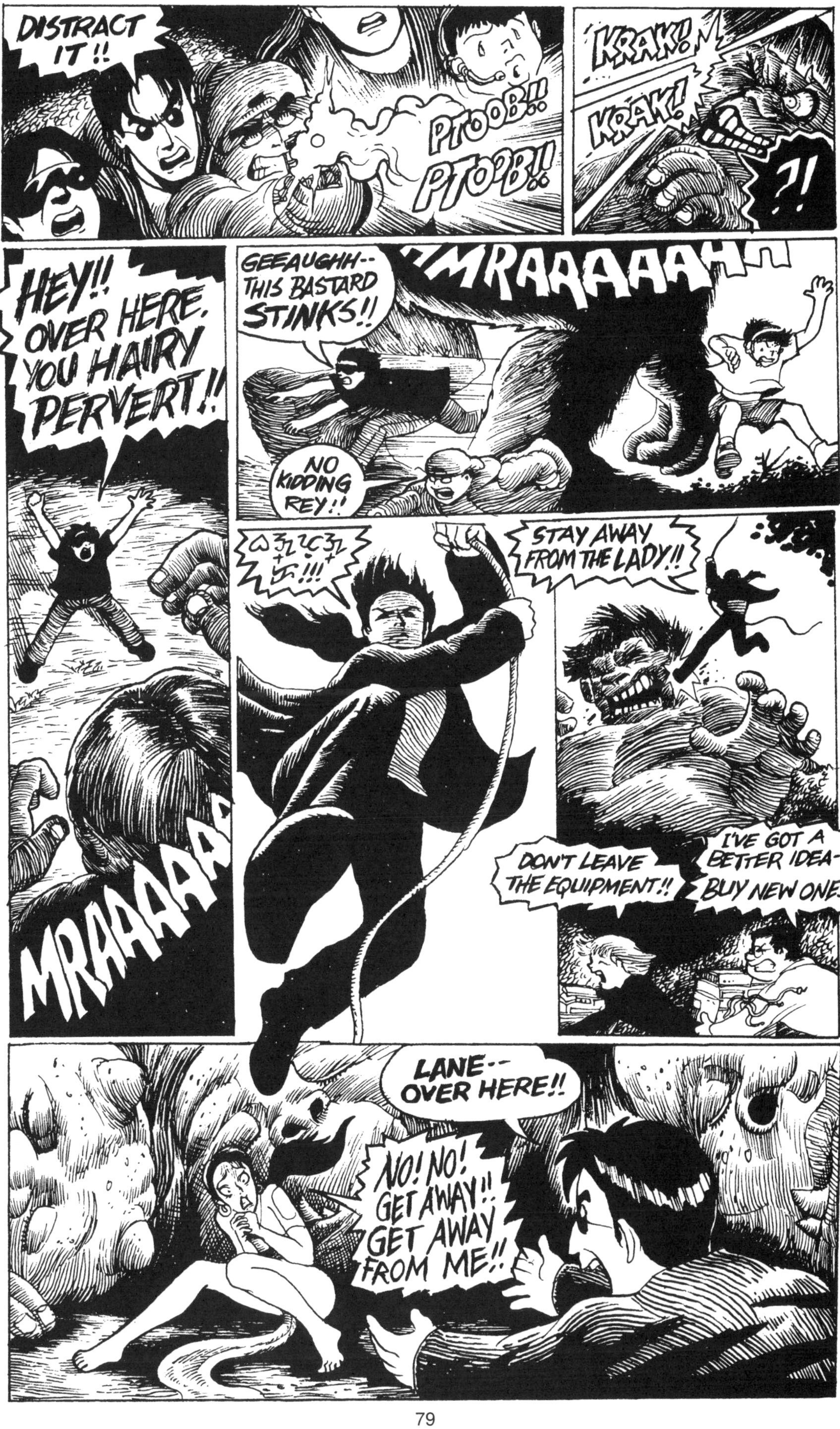
DISTRACT IT!!
PTOOB!!
PTOOB!!
KRAK!
KRAK!
?!
HEY!! OVER HERE, YOU HAIRY PERVERT!!
GEEAUGHH-- THIS BASTARD STINKS!!
MRAAAAAAHH
NO KIDDING REY!!
MRAAAAA
STAY AWAY FROM THE LADY!!
DON'T LEAVE THE EQUIPMENT!!
I'VE GOT A BETTER IDEA-- BUY NEW ONES!!
LANE-- OVER HERE!!
NO! NO! GET AWAY!! GET AWAY FROM ME!!

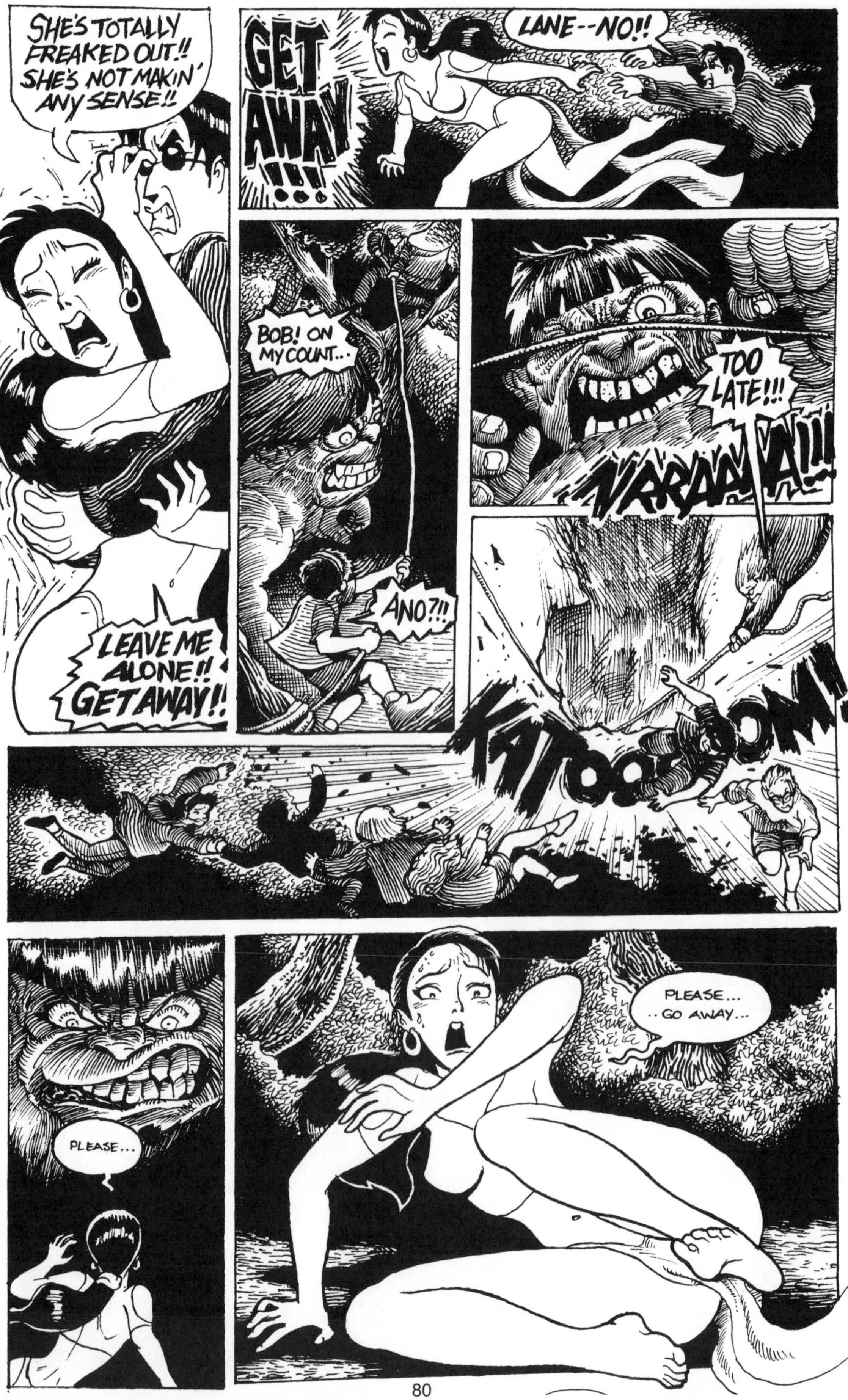
SHE'S TOTALLY FREAKED OUT!! SHE'S NOT MAKIN' ANY SENSE!!
LEAVE ME ALONE!! GET AWAY!!
GET AWAY!!!!
LANE--NO!!
BOB! ON MY COUNT...
ANO?!!
TOO LATE!!!
NRRAAAA!!!
KATOOOOOM!!
PLEASE...
PLEASE... ..GO AWAY...

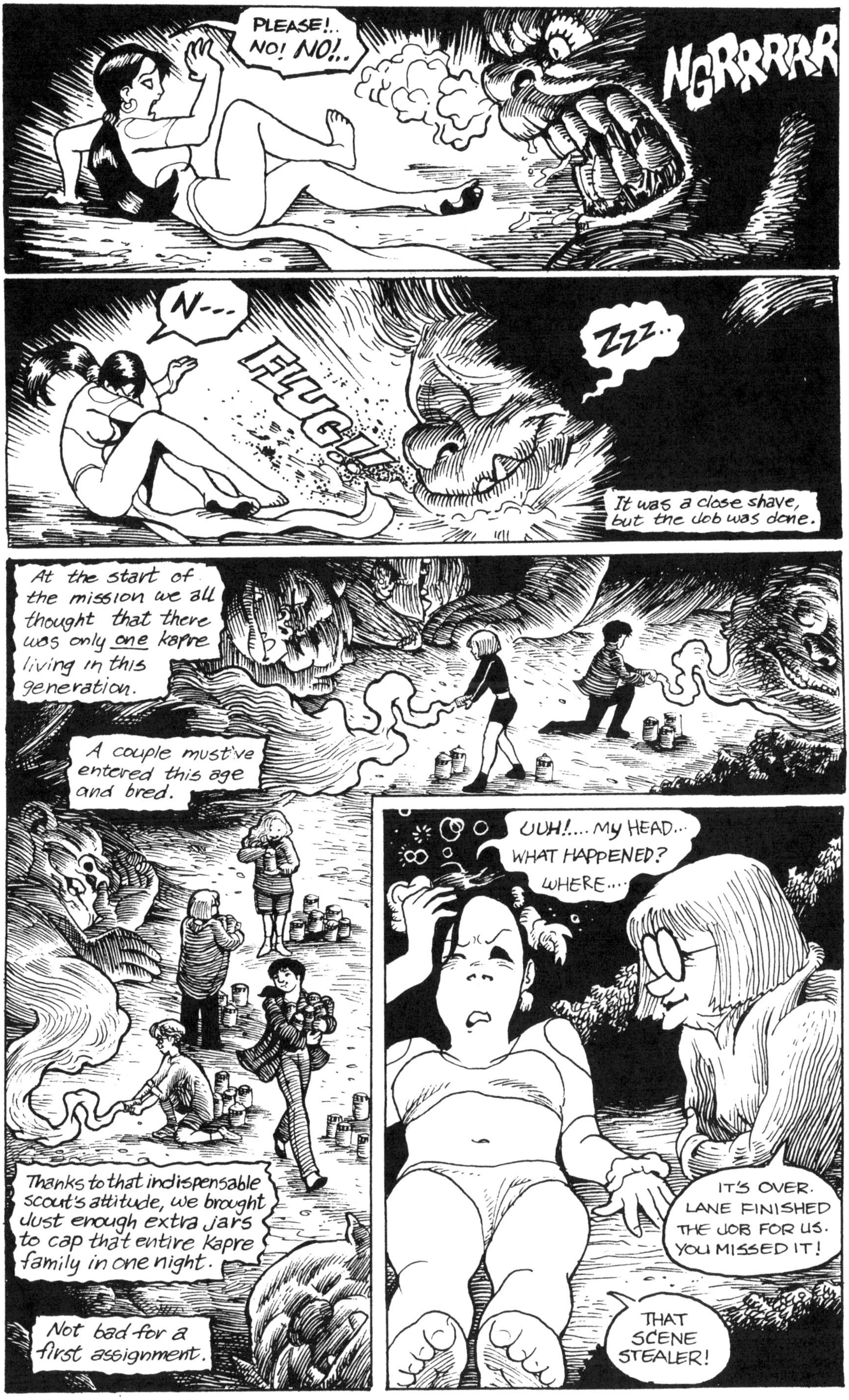
PLEASE!.. NO! NO!..
NGRRRRR
N---
FLUG!!
ZZZ..
It was a close shave, but the job was done.
At the start of the mission we all thought that there was only one kapre living in this generation.
A couple must've entered this age and bred.
Thanks to that indispensable scout's attitude, we brought just enough extra jars to cap that entire kapre family in one night.
Not bad for a first assignment.
UUH!.... MY HEAD... WHAT HAPPENED? WHERE....
IT'S OVER. LANE FINISHED THE JOB FOR US. YOU MISSED IT!
THAT SCENE STEALER!

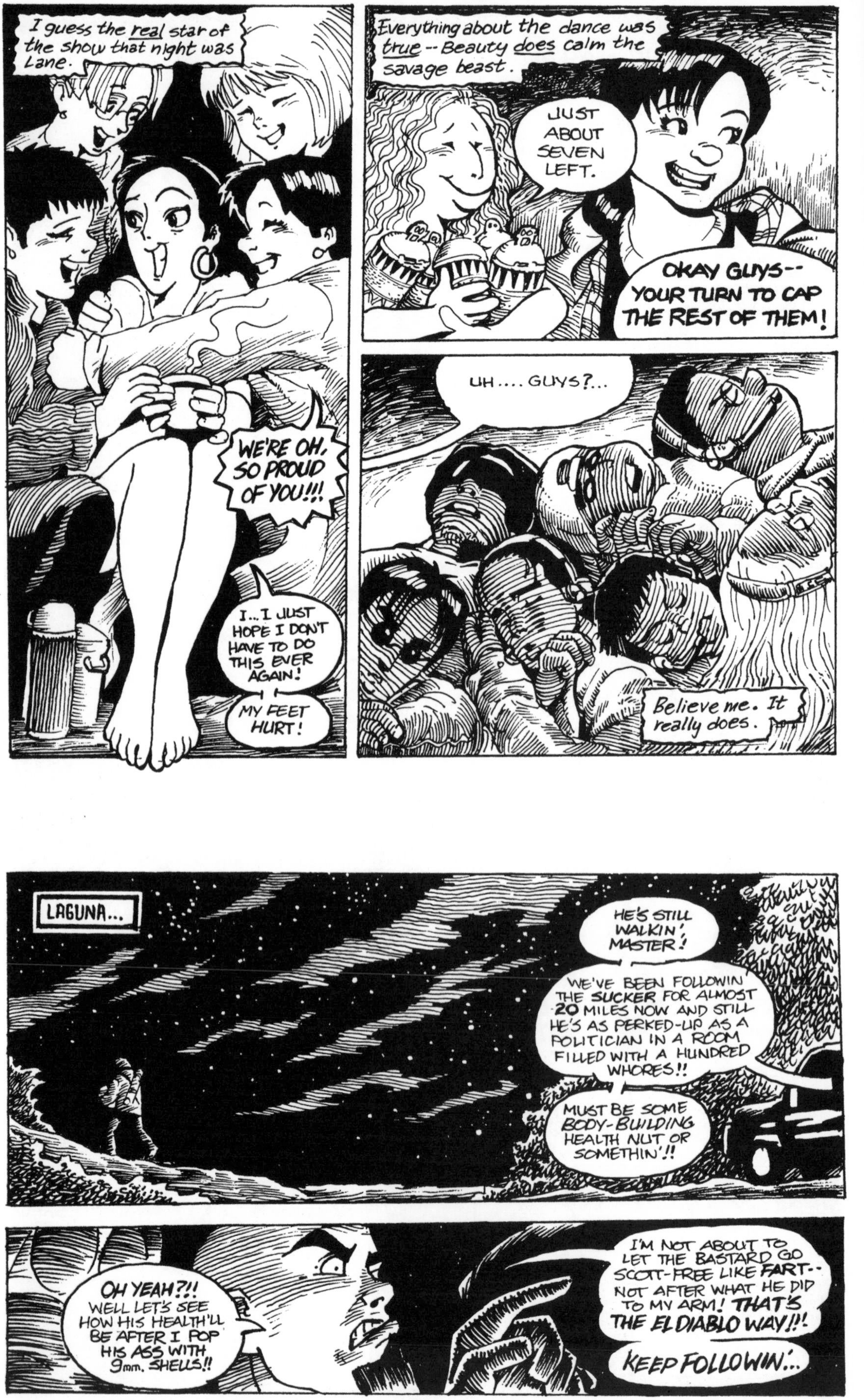

I guess the real star of the show that night was Lane.
WE'RE OH, SO PROUD OF YOU!!!
I...I JUST HOPE I DON'T HAVE TO DO THIS EVER AGAIN!
MY FEET HURT!
Everything about the dance was true -- Beauty does calm the savage beast.
JUST ABOUT SEVEN LEFT.
OKAY GUYS-- YOUR TURN TO CAP THE REST OF THEM!
UH .... GUYS?...
Believe me. It really does.
LAGUNA...
HE'S STILL WALKIN', MASTER!
WE'VE BEEN FOLLOWIN THE SUCKER FOR ALMOST 20 MILES NOW AND STILL HE'S AS PERKED-UP AS A POLITICIAN IN A ROOM FILLED WITH A HUNDRED WHORES!!
MUST BE SOME BODY-BUILDING HEALTH NUT OR SOMETHIN'!!
OH YEAH?!! WELL LET'S SEE HOW HIS HEALTH'LL BE AFTER I POP HIS ASS WITH 9mm. SHELLS!!
I'M NOT ABOUT TO LET THE BASTARD GO SCOTT-FREE LIKE FART-- NOT AFTER WHAT HE DID TO MY ARM! THAT'S THE EL DIABLO WAY!!!
KEEP FOLLOWIN'...

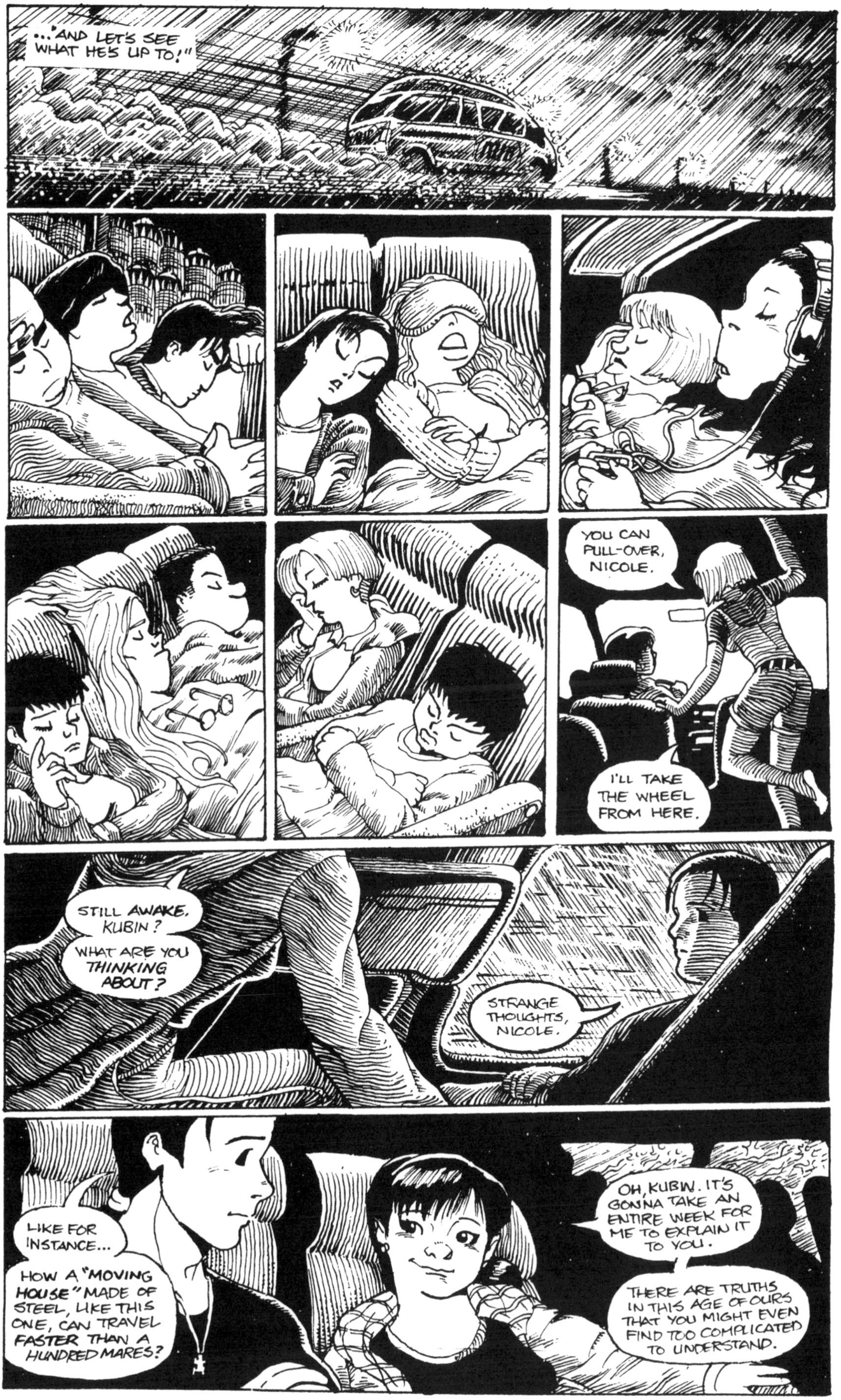
..."AND LET'S SEE WHAT HE'S UP TO!"
YOU CAN PULL-OVER, NICOLE.
I'LL TAKE THE WHEEL FROM HERE.
STILL AWAKE, KUBIN? WHAT ARE YOU THINKING ABOUT?
STRANGE THOUGHTS, NICOLE.
LIKE FOR INSTANCE...
HOW A "MOVING HOUSE" MADE OF STEEL, LIKE THIS ONE, CAN TRAVEL FASTER THAN A HUNDRED MARES?
OH, KUBIN. IT'S GONNA TAKE AN ENTIRE WEEK FOR ME TO EXPLAIN IT TO YOU.
THERE ARE TRUTHS IN THIS AGE OF OURS THAT YOU MIGHT EVEN FIND TOO COMPLICATED TO UNDERSTAND.

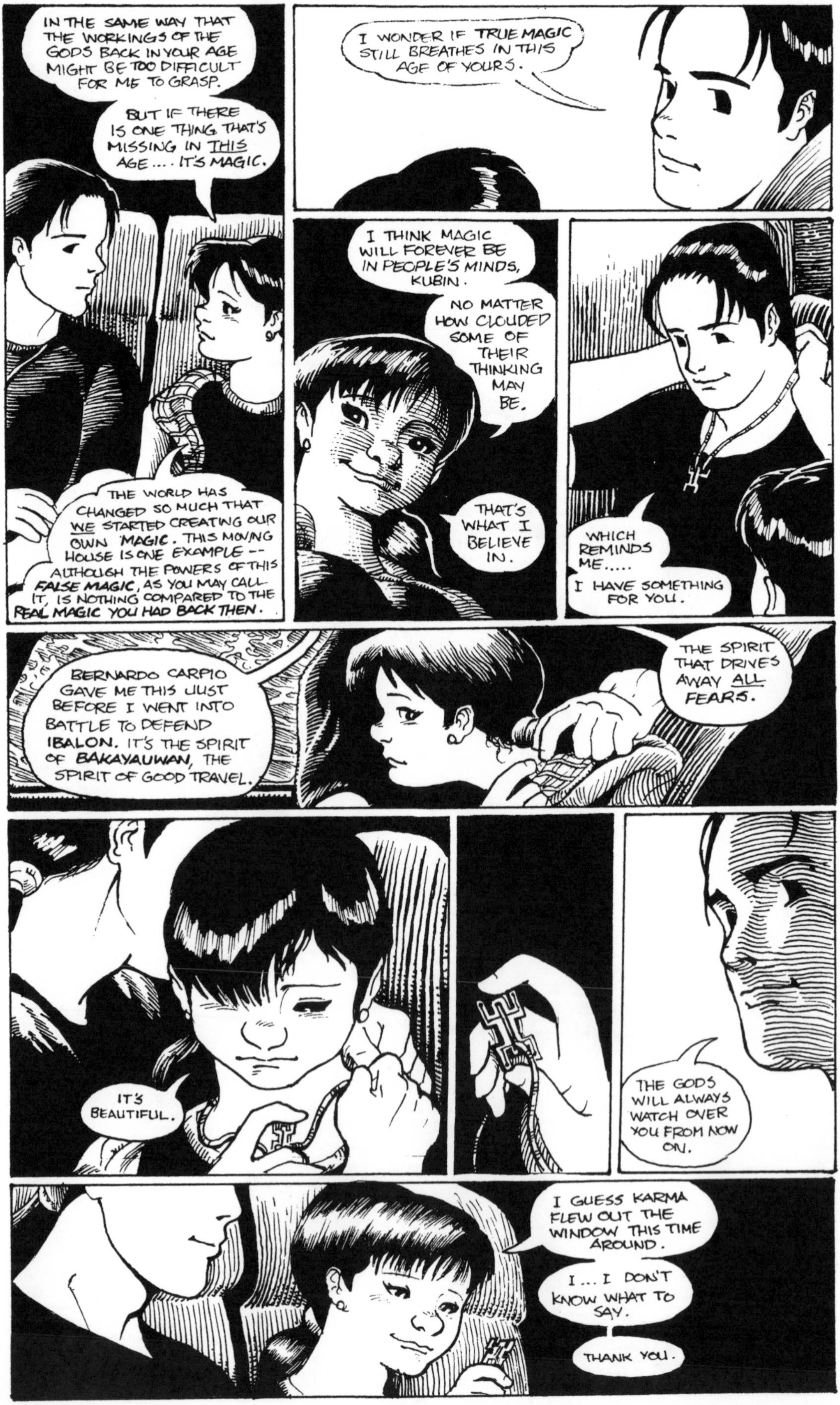
IN THE SAME WAY THAT THE WORKINGS OF THE GODS BACK IN YOUR AGE MIGHT BE TOO DIFFICULT FOR ME TO GRASP.
BUT IF THERE IS ONE THING THAT'S MISSING IN THIS AGE.... IT'S MAGIC.
THE WORLD HAS CHANGED SO MUCH THAT WE STARTED CREATING OUR OWN 'MAGIC'. THIS MOVING HOUSE IS ONE EXAMPLE -- ALTHOUGH THE POWERS OF THIS FALSE MAGIC, AS YOU MAY CALL IT, IS NOTHING COMPARED TO THE REAL MAGIC YOU HAD BACK THEN.
I WONDER IF TRUE MAGIC STILL BREATHES IN THIS AGE OF YOURS.
I THINK MAGIC WILL FOREVER BE IN PEOPLE'S MINDS, KUBIN.
NO MATTER HOW CLOUDED SOME OF THEIR THINKING MAY BE.
THAT'S WHAT I BELIEVE IN.
WHICH REMINDS ME.....
I HAVE SOMETHING FOR YOU.
BERNARDO CARPIO GAVE ME THIS JUST BEFORE I WENT INTO BATTLE TO DEFEND IBALON. IT'S THE SPIRIT OF BAKAYAUWAN, THE SPIRIT OF GOOD TRAVEL.
THE SPIRIT THAT DRIVES AWAY ALL FEARS.
IT'S BEAUTIFUL.
THE GODS WILL ALWAYS WATCH OVER YOU FROM NOW ON.
I GUESS KARMA FLEW OUT THE WINDOW THIS TIME AROUND.
I... I DON'T KNOW WHAT TO SAY.
THANK YOU.

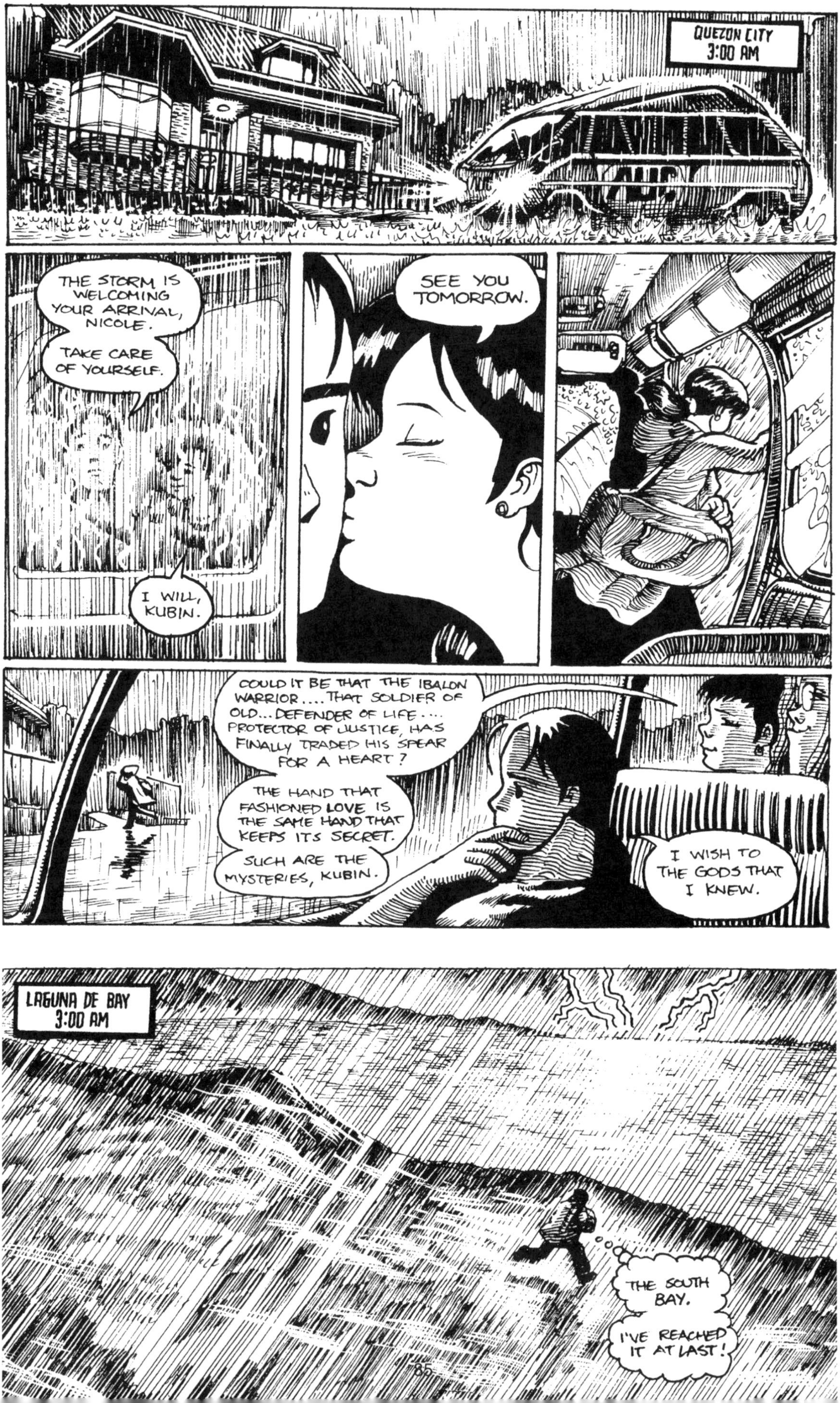
QUEZON CITY
3:00 AM
THE STORM IS WELCOMING YOUR ARRIVAL, NICOLE.
TAKE CARE OF YOURSELF.
I WILL, KUBIN.
SEE YOU TOMORROW.
COULD IT BE THAT THE IBALON WARRIOR.... THAT SOLDIER OF OLD... DEFENDER OF LIFE... PROTECTOR OF JUSTICE, HAS FINALLY TRADED HIS SPEAR FOR A HEART?
THE HAND THAT FASHIONED LOVE IS THE SAME HAND THAT KEEPS ITS SECRET.
SUCH ARE THE MYSTERIES, KUBIN.
I WISH TO THE GODS THAT I KNEW.
LAGUNA DE BAY
3:00 AM
THE SOUTH BAY.
I'VE REACHED IT AT LAST!

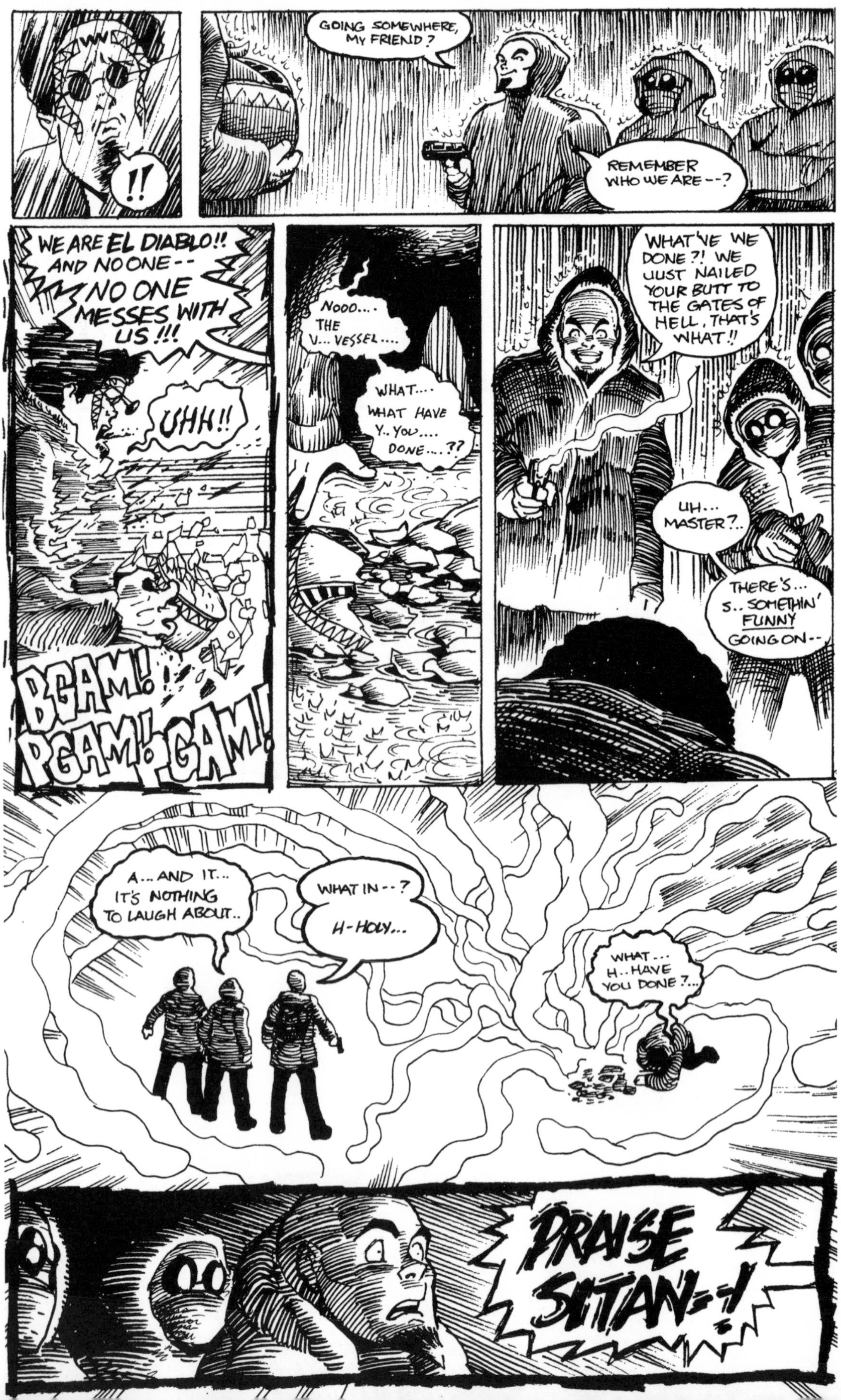
!!
GOING SOMEWHERE, MY FRIEND?
REMEMBER WHO WE ARE--?
WE ARE EL DIABLO!! AND NO ONE-- NO ONE MESSES WITH US!!!
UHH!!
BGAM! PGAM! PGAM!
NOOO... THE V... VESSEL....
WHAT.... WHAT HAVE Y.. YOU.... DONE....??
WHAT'VE WE DONE?! WE JUST NAILED YOUR BUTT TO THE GATES OF HELL, THAT'S WHAT!!
UH... MASTER?..
THERE'S... S.. SOMETHIN' FUNNY GOING ON--
A... AND IT... IT'S NOTHING TO LAUGH ABOUT..
WHAT IN--?
H-HOLY...
WHAT... H.. HAVE YOU DONE?...
PRAISE SATAN--!

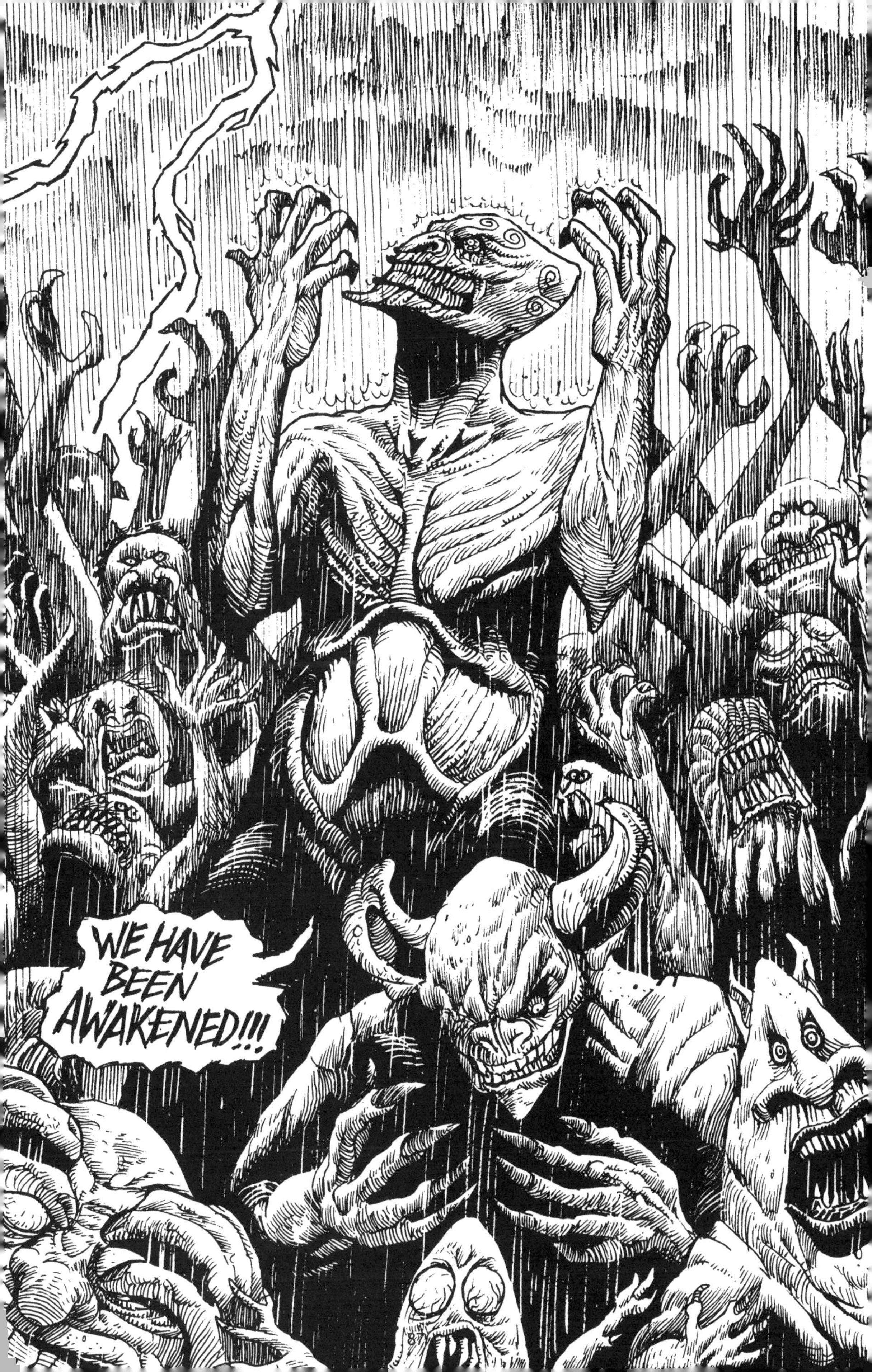
WE HAVE BEEN AWAKENED!!!

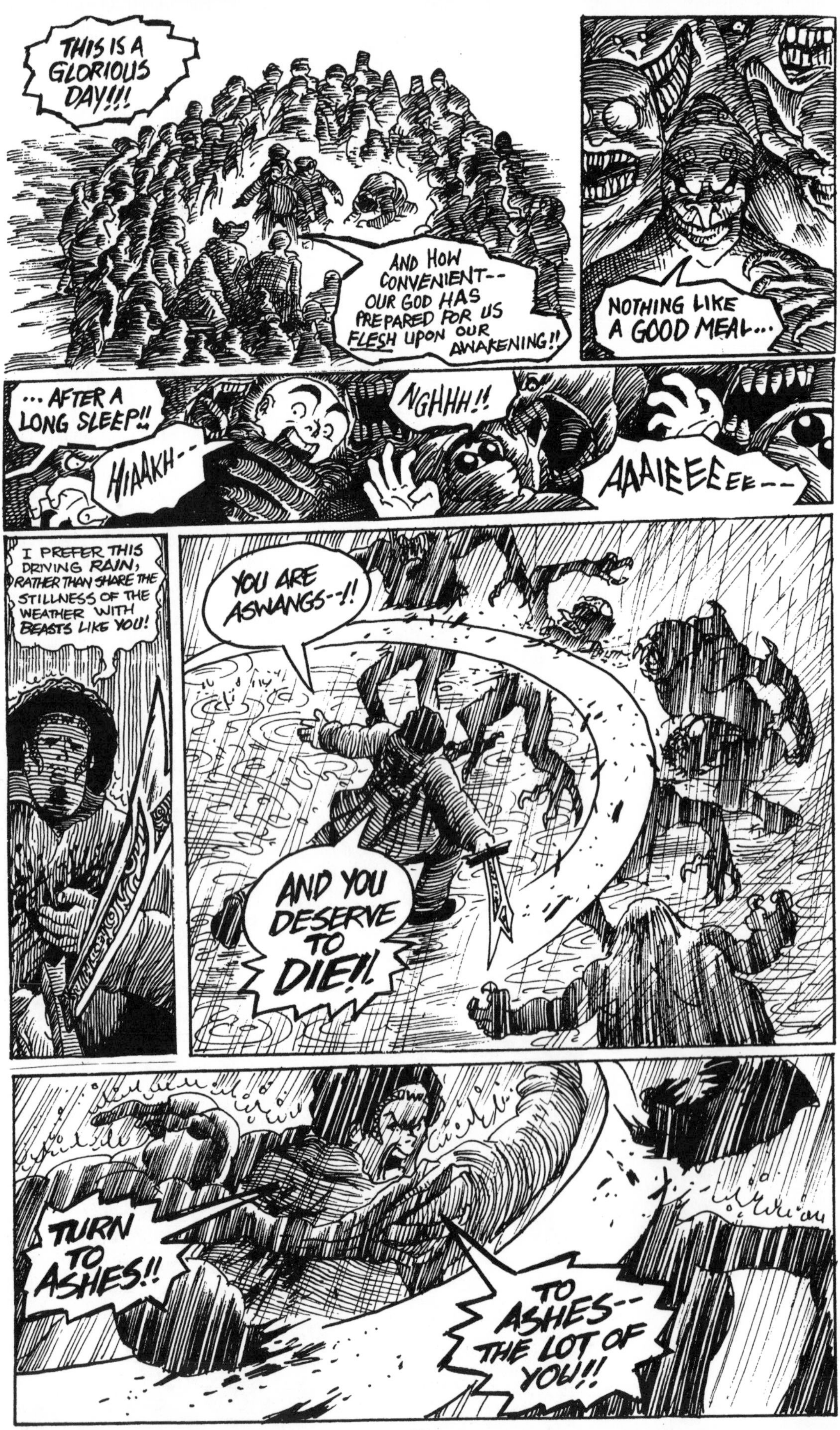

THIS IS A GLORIOUS DAY!!!
AND HOW CONVENIENT-- OUR GOD HAS PREPARED FOR US FLESH UPON OUR AWAKENING!!
NOTHING LIKE A GOOD MEAL...
... AFTER A LONG SLEEP!!
HIAAKH--
NGHHH!!
AAAIEEEEE---
I PREFER THIS DRIVING RAIN, RATHER THAN SHARE THE STILLNESS OF THE WEATHER WITH BEASTS LIKE YOU!
YOU ARE ASWANGS--!!
AND YOU DESERVE TO DIE!!
TURN TO ASHES!!
TO ASHES-- THE LOT OF YOU!!

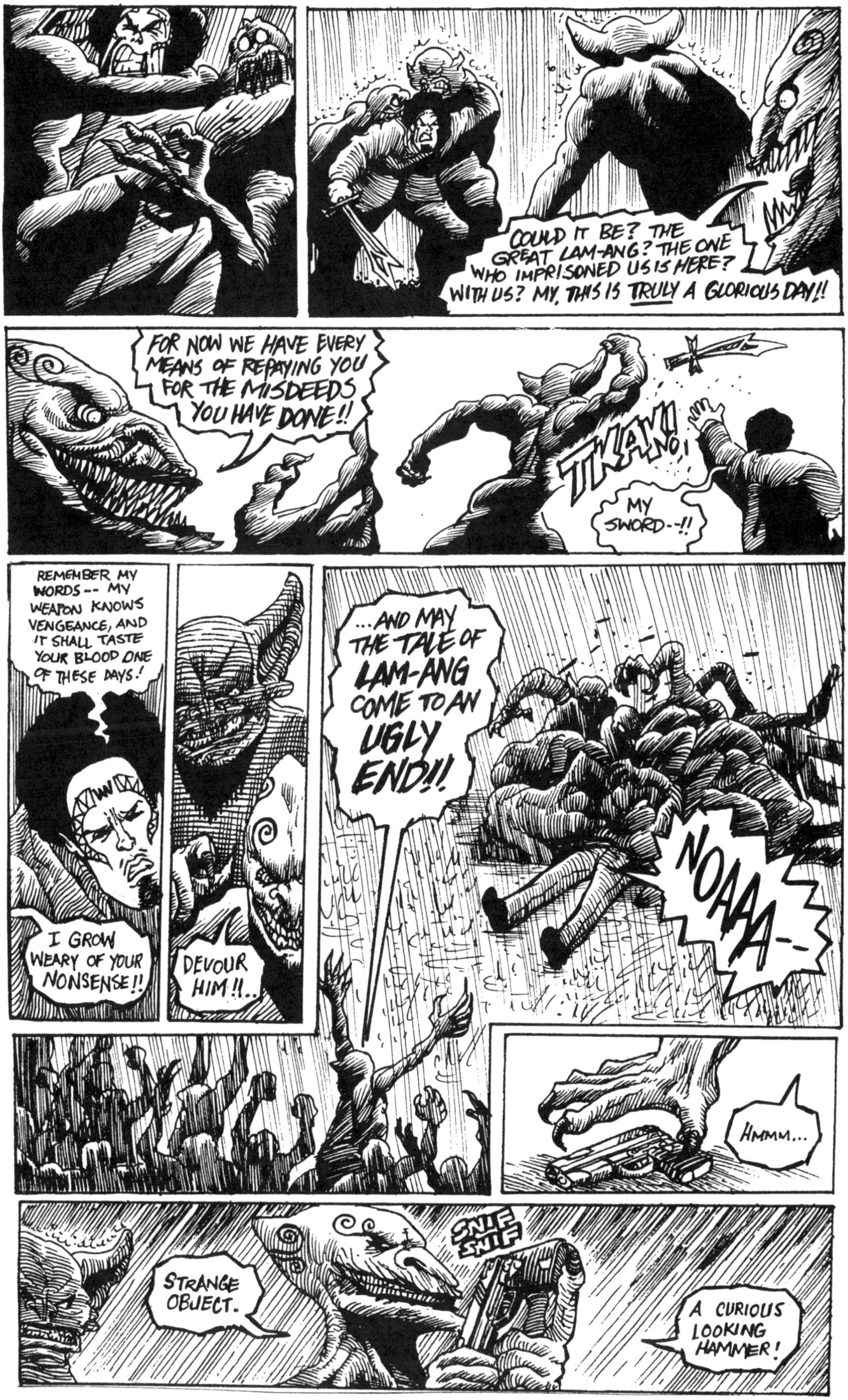
COULD IT BE? THE GREAT LAM-ANG? THE ONE WHO IMPRISONED US IS HERE? WITH US? MY, THIS IS TRULY A GLORIOUS DAY!!
FOR NOW WE HAVE EVERY MEANS OF REPAYING YOU FOR THE MISDEEDS YOU HAVE DONE!!
TKAN!
NO!
MY SWORD--!!
REMEMBER MY WORDS -- MY WEAPON KNOWS VENGEANCE, AND IT SHALL TASTE YOUR BLOOD ONE OF THESE DAYS!
I GROW WEARY OF YOUR NONSENSE!!
DEVOUR HIM!!..
...AND MAY THE TALE OF LAM-ANG COME TO AN UGLY END!!!
NOAAAA--
HMMM...
SNIF SNIF
STRANGE OBJECT.
A CURIOUS LOOKING HAMMER!

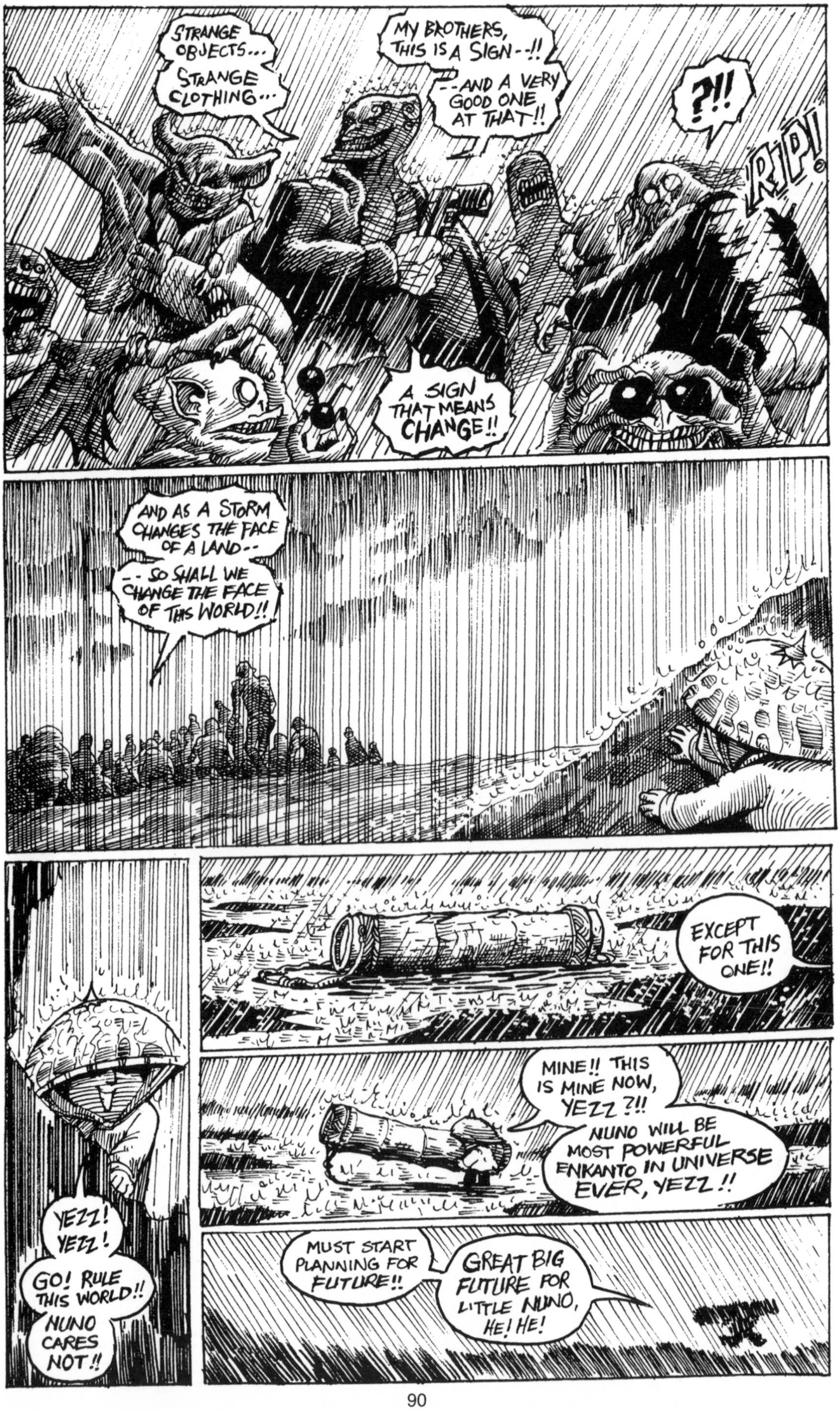
STRANGE OBJECTS... STRANGE CLOTHING...
MY BROTHERS, THIS IS A SIGN--!!
--AND A VERY GOOD ONE AT THAT!!
?!!
RIP!
A SIGN THAT MEANS CHANGE!!
AND AS A STORM CHANGES THE FACE OF A LAND--
--SO SHALL WE CHANGE THE FACE OF THIS WORLD!!
YEZZ! YEZZ!
GO! RULE THIS WORLD!!
NUNO CARES NOT!!
EXCEPT FOR THIS ONE!!
MINE!! THIS IS MINE NOW, YEZZ?!!
NUNO WILL BE MOST POWERFUL ENKANTO IN UNIVERSE EVER, YEZZ!!
MUST START PLANNING FOR FUTURE!!
GREAT BIG FUTURE FOR LITTLE NUNO, HE! HE!

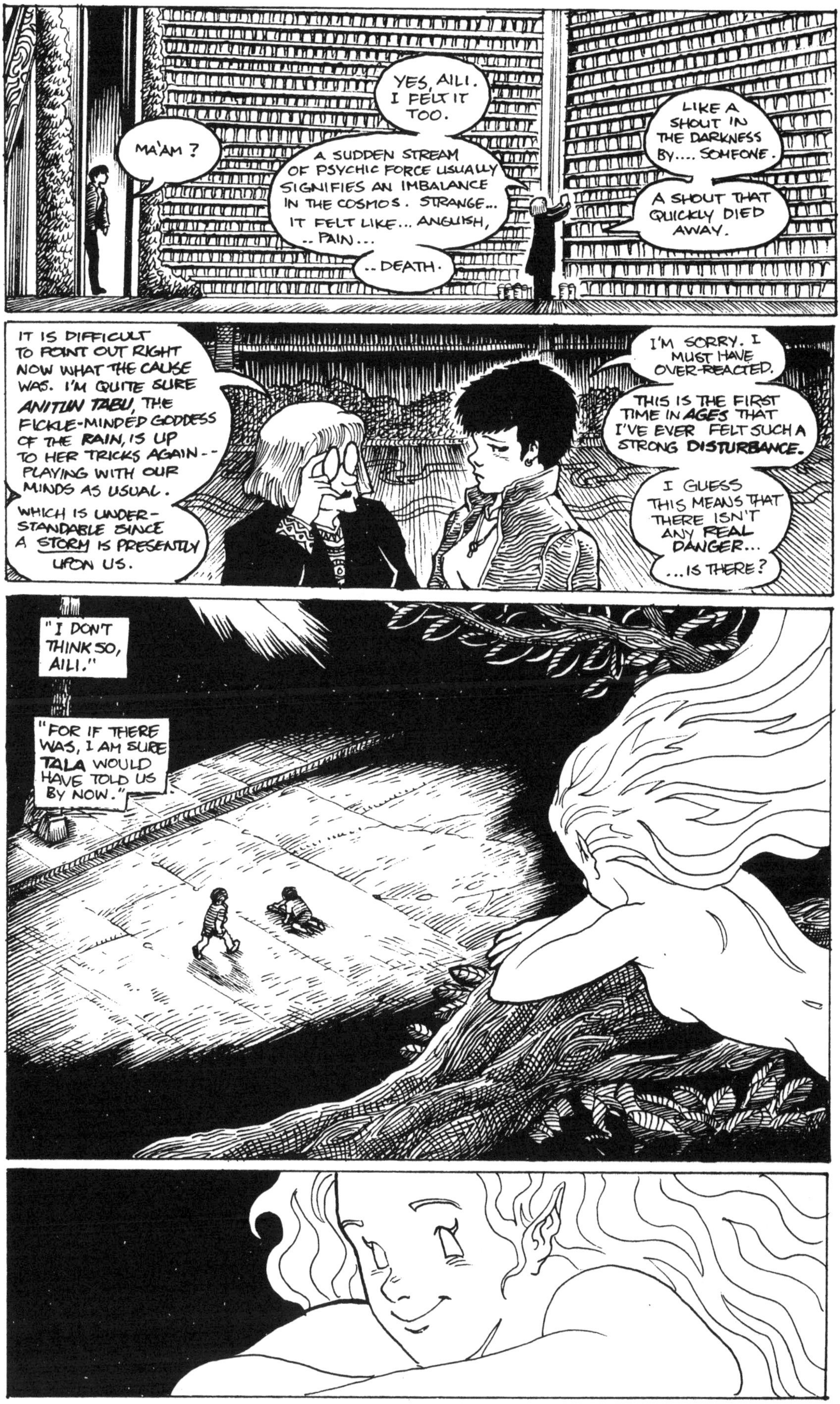

MA'AM ?
YES, AILI. I FELT IT TOO.
A SUDDEN STREAM OF PSYCHIC FORCE USUALLY SIGNIFIES AN IMBALANCE IN THE COSMOS. STRANGE... IT FELT LIKE... ANGUISH, ..PAIN...
..DEATH.
LIKE A SHOUT IN THE DARKNESS BY.... SOMEONE.
A SHOUT THAT QUICKLY DIED AWAY.
IT IS DIFFICULT TO POINT OUT RIGHT NOW WHAT THE CAUSE WAS. I'M QUITE SURE ANITUN TABU, THE FICKLE-MINDED GODDESS OF THE RAIN, IS UP TO HER TRICKS AGAIN-- PLAYING WITH OUR MINDS AS USUAL.
WHICH IS UNDERSTANDABLE SINCE A STORM IS PRESENTLY UPON US.
I'M SORRY. I MUST HAVE OVER-REACTED.
THIS IS THE FIRST TIME IN AGES THAT I'VE EVER FELT SUCH A STRONG DISTURBANCE.
I GUESS THIS MEANS THAT THERE ISN'T ANY REAL DANGER...
...IS THERE?
"I DON'T THINK SO, AILI."
"FOR IF THERE WAS, I AM SURE TALA WOULD HAVE TOLD US BY NOW."

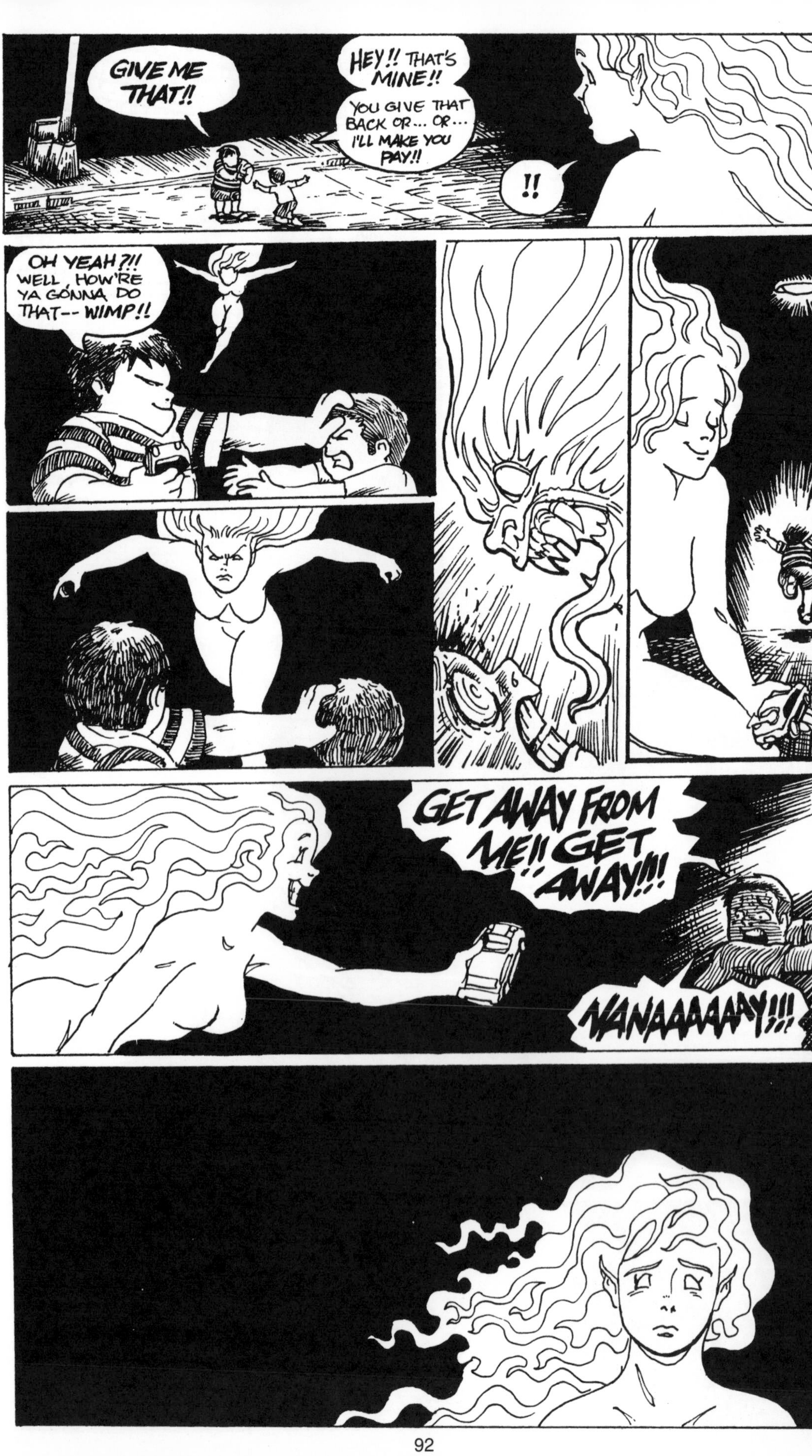
GIVE ME THAT!!
HEY!! THAT'S MINE!!
YOU GIVE THAT BACK OR... OR... I'LL MAKE YOU PAY!!
!!
OH YEAH?!! WELL, HOW'RE YA GONNA DO THAT-- WIMP!!
GET AWAY FROM ME!! GET AWAY!!!
WAAAAAAAY!!!

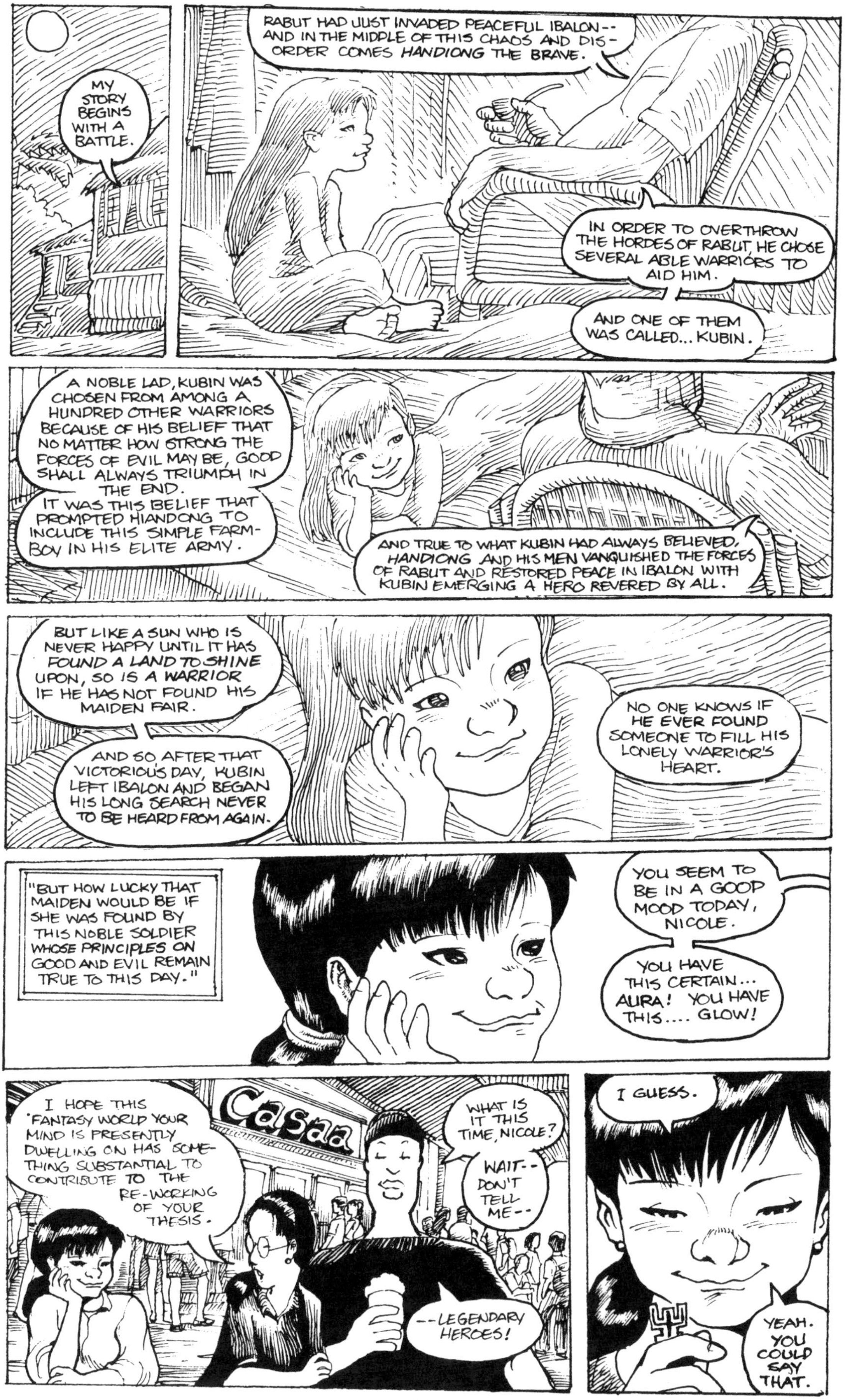
MY STORY BEGINS WITH A BATTLE.
RABUT HAD JUST INVADED PEACEFUL IBALON-- AND IN THE MIDDLE OF THIS CHAOS AND DIS-ORDER COMES HANDIONG THE BRAVE.
IN ORDER TO OVERTHROW THE HORDES OF RABUT, HE CHOSE SEVERAL ABLE WARRIORS TO AID HIM.
AND ONE OF THEM WAS CALLED... KUBIN.
A NOBLE LAD, KUBIN WAS CHOSEN FROM AMONG A HUNDRED OTHER WARRIORS BECAUSE OF HIS BELIEF THAT NO MATTER HOW STRONG THE FORCES OF EVIL MAY BE, GOOD SHALL ALWAYS TRIUMPH IN THE END.
IT WAS THIS BELIEF THAT PROMPTED HIANDONG TO INCLUDE THIS SIMPLE FARM-BOY IN HIS ELITE ARMY.
AND TRUE TO WHAT KUBIN HAD ALWAYS BELIEVED, HANDIONG AND HIS MEN VANQUISHED THE FORCES OF RABUT AND RESTORED PEACE IN IBALON WITH KUBIN EMERGING A HERO REVERED BY ALL.
BUT LIKE A SUN WHO IS NEVER HAPPY UNTIL IT HAS FOUND A LAND TO SHINE UPON, SO IS A WARRIOR IF HE HAS NOT FOUND HIS MAIDEN FAIR.
AND SO AFTER THAT VICTORIOUS DAY, KUBIN LEFT IBALON AND BEGAN HIS LONG SEARCH NEVER TO BE HEARD FROM AGAIN.
NO ONE KNOWS IF HE EVER FOUND SOMEONE TO FILL HIS LONELY WARRIOR'S HEART.
"BUT HOW LUCKY THAT MAIDEN WOULD BE IF SHE WAS FOUND BY THIS NOBLE SOLDIER WHOSE PRINCIPLES ON GOOD AND EVIL REMAIN TRUE TO THIS DAY."
YOU SEEM TO BE IN A GOOD MOOD TODAY, NICOLE.
YOU HAVE THIS CERTAIN... AURA! YOU HAVE THIS.... GLOW!
Casaa
I HOPE THIS "FANTASY WORLD YOUR MIND IS PRESENTLY DWELLING ON HAS SOME-THING SUBSTANTIAL TO CONTRIBUTE TO THE RE-WORKING OF YOUR THESIS.
WHAT IS IT THIS TIME, NICOLE?
WAIT-- DON'T TELL ME--
--LEGENDARY HEROES!
I GUESS.
YEAH. YOU COULD SAY THAT.

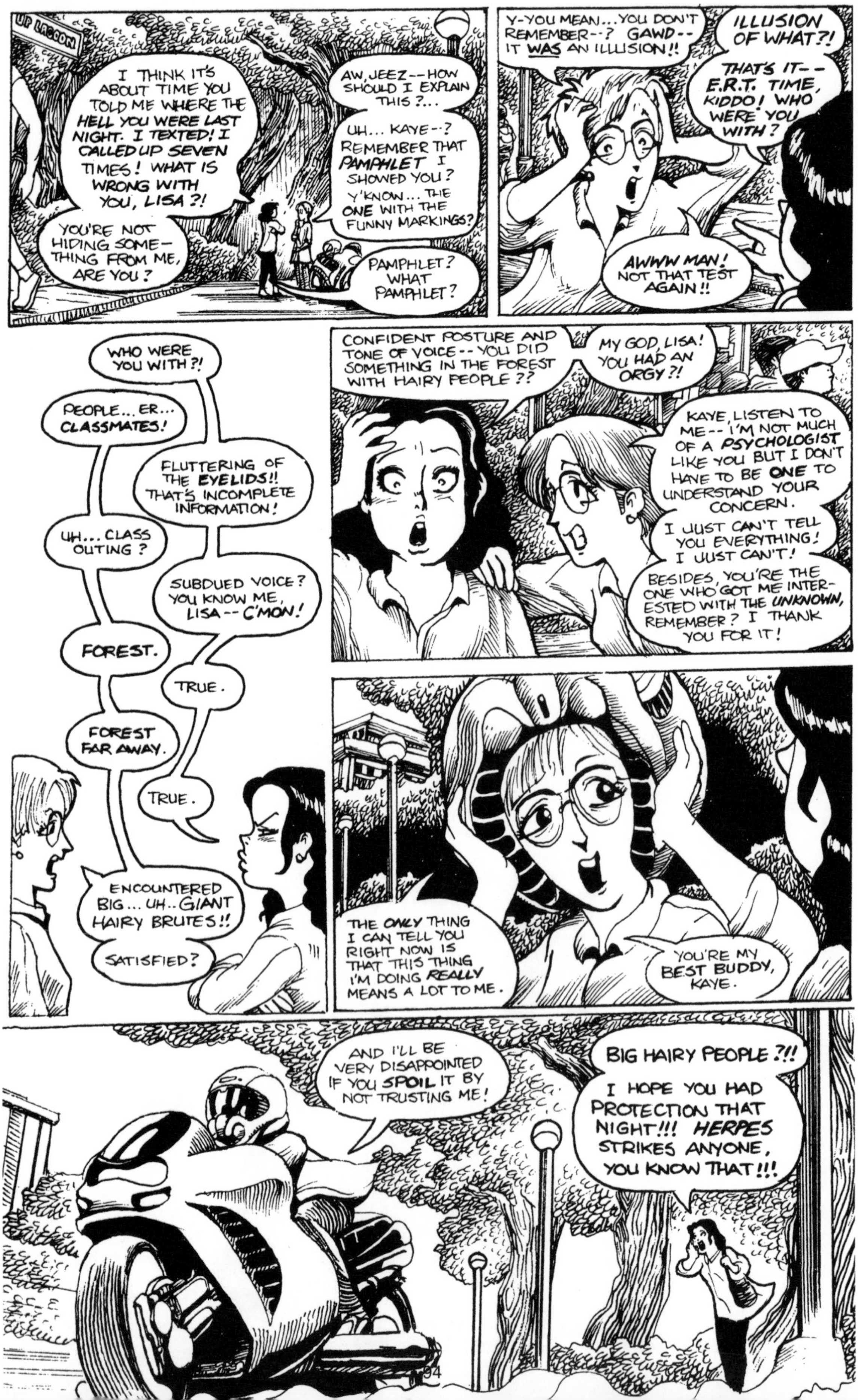
UP LAGOON
I THINK IT'S ABOUT TIME YOU TOLD ME WHERE THE HELL YOU WERE LAST NIGHT. I TEXTED! I CALLED UP SEVEN TIMES! WHAT IS WRONG WITH YOU, LISA?!
YOU'RE NOT HIDING SOME-THING FROM ME, ARE YOU?
AW, JEEZ--HOW SHOULD I EXPLAIN THIS?...
UH... KAYE--? REMEMBER THAT PAMPHLET I SHOWED YOU? Y'KNOW... THE ONE WITH THE FUNNY MARKINGS?
PAMPHLET? WHAT PAMPHLET?
Y-YOU MEAN... YOU DON'T REMEMBER--? GAWD-- IT WAS AN ILLUSION!!
ILLUSION OF WHAT?!
THAT'S IT-- E.R.T. TIME, KIDDO! WHO WERE YOU WITH?
AWWW MAN! NOT THAT TEST AGAIN!!
WHO WERE YOU WITH?!
PEOPLE... ER... CLASSMATES!
FLUTTERING OF THE EYELIDS!! THAT'S INCOMPLETE INFORMATION!
UH... CLASS OUTING?
SUBDUED VOICE? YOU KNOW ME, LISA--C'MON!
FOREST.
TRUE.
FOREST FAR AWAY.
TRUE.
ENCOUNTERED BIG... UH.. GIANT HAIRY BRUTES!!
SATISFIED?
CONFIDENT POSTURE AND TONE OF VOICE--YOU DID SOMETHING IN THE FOREST WITH HAIRY PEOPLE??
MY GOD, LISA! YOU HAD AN ORGY?!
KAYE, LISTEN TO ME--I'M NOT MUCH OF A PSYCHOLOGIST LIKE YOU BUT I DON'T HAVE TO BE ONE TO UNDERSTAND YOUR CONCERN.
I JUST CAN'T TELL YOU EVERYTHING! I JUST CAN'T!
BESIDES, YOU'RE THE ONE WHO GOT ME INTER-ESTED WITH THE UNKNOWN, REMEMBER? I THANK YOU FOR IT!
THE ONLY THING I CAN TELL YOU RIGHT NOW IS THAT THIS THING I'M DOING REALLY MEANS A LOT TO ME.
YOU'RE MY BEST BUDDY, KAYE.
AND I'LL BE VERY DISAPPOINTED IF YOU SPOIL IT BY NOT TRUSTING ME!
BIG HAIRY PEOPLE?!!
I HOPE YOU HAD PROTECTION THAT NIGHT!!! HERPES STRIKES ANYONE, YOU KNOW THAT!!!

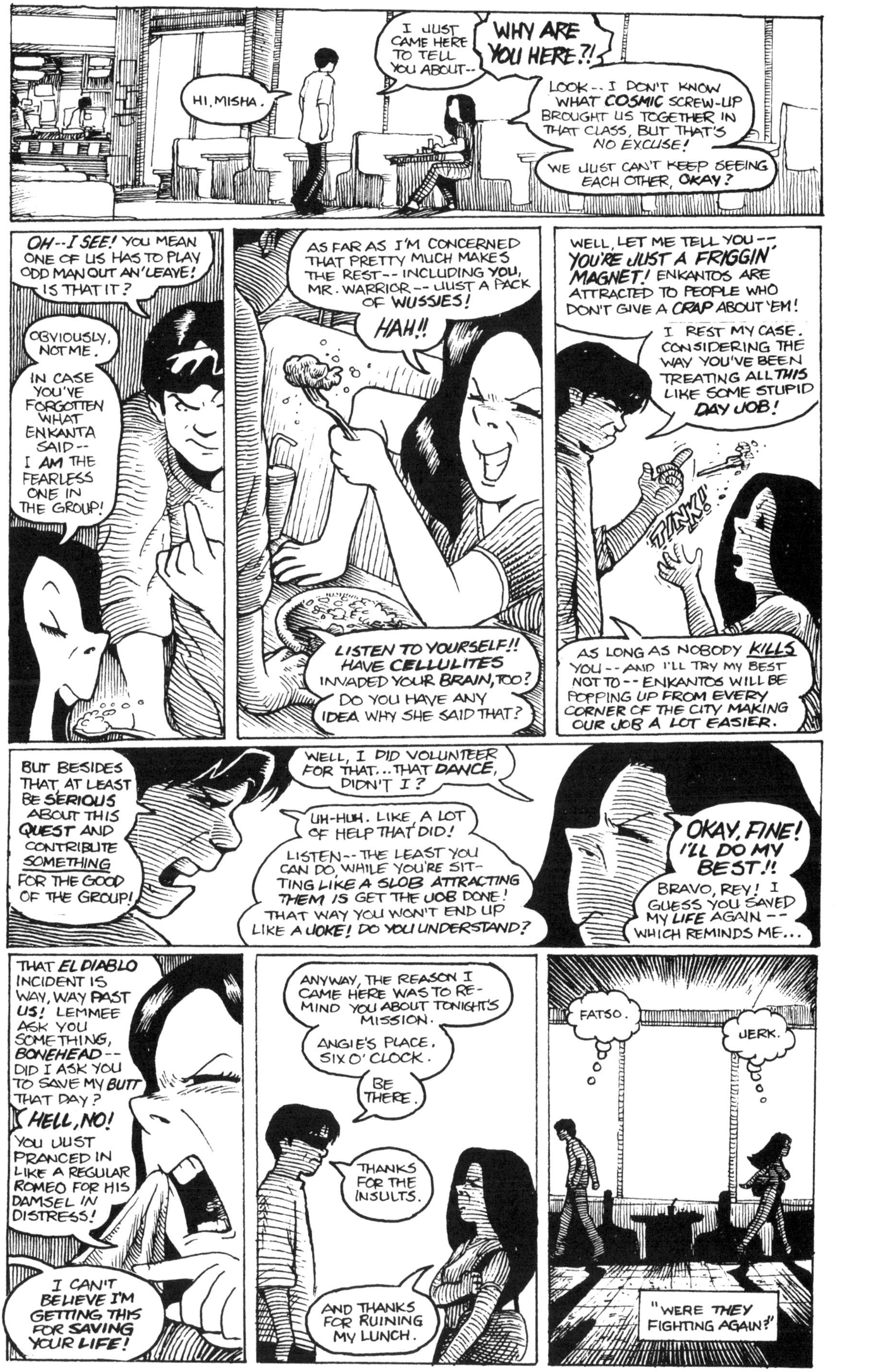
HI, MISHA.
I JUST CAME HERE TO TELL YOU ABOUT--
WHY ARE YOU HERE?!
LOOK--I DON'T KNOW WHAT COSMIC SCREW-UP BROUGHT US TOGETHER IN THAT CLASS, BUT THAT'S NO EXCUSE!
WE JUST CAN'T KEEP SEEING EACH OTHER, OKAY?
OH--I SEE! YOU MEAN ONE OF US HAS TO PLAY ODD MAN OUT AN' LEAVE! IS THAT IT?
OBVIOUSLY, NOT ME.
IN CASE YOU'VE FORGOTTEN WHAT ENKANTA SAID-- I AM THE FEARLESS ONE IN THE GROUP!
AS FAR AS I'M CONCERNED THAT PRETTY MUCH MAKES THE REST--INCLUDING YOU, MR. WARRIOR--JUST A PACK OF WUSSIES!
HAH!!
LISTEN TO YOURSELF!! HAVE CELLULITES INVADED YOUR BRAIN, TOO?
DO YOU HAVE ANY IDEA WHY SHE SAID THAT?
WELL, LET ME TELL YOU-- YOU'RE JUST A FRIGGIN' MAGNET! ENKANTOS ARE ATTRACTED TO PEOPLE WHO DON'T GIVE A CRAP ABOUT 'EM!
I REST MY CASE. CONSIDERING THE WAY YOU'VE BEEN TREATING ALL THIS LIKE SOME STUPID DAY JOB!
TINK!
AS LONG AS NOBODY KILLS YOU--AND I'LL TRY MY BEST NOT TO--ENKANTOS WILL BE POPPING UP FROM EVERY CORNER OF THE CITY MAKING OUR JOB A LOT EASIER.
BUT BESIDES THAT, AT LEAST BE SERIOUS ABOUT THIS QUEST AND CONTRIBUTE SOMETHING FOR THE GOOD OF THE GROUP!
WELL, I DID VOLUNTEER FOR THAT...THAT DANCE, DIDN'T I?
UH-HUH. LIKE A LOT OF HELP THAT DID!
LISTEN--THE LEAST YOU CAN DO WHILE YOU'RE SITTING LIKE A SLOB ATTRACTING THEM IS GET THE JOB DONE! THAT WAY YOU WON'T END UP LIKE A JOKE! DO YOU UNDERSTAND?
OKAY, FINE! I'LL DO MY BEST!!
BRAVO, REY! I GUESS YOU SAVED MY LIFE AGAIN-- WHICH REMINDS ME...
THAT EL DIABLO INCIDENT IS WAY, WAY PAST US! LEMMEE ASK YOU SOMETHING, BONEHEAD-- DID I ASK YOU TO SAVE MY BUTT THAT DAY?
HELL, NO!
YOU JUST PRANCED IN LIKE A REGULAR ROMEO FOR HIS DAMSEL IN DISTRESS!
I CAN'T BELIEVE I'M GETTING THIS FOR SAVING YOUR LIFE!
ANYWAY, THE REASON I CAME HERE WAS TO REMIND YOU ABOUT TONIGHT'S MISSION.
ANGIE'S PLACE. SIX O'CLOCK.
BE THERE.
THANKS FOR THE INSULTS.
AND THANKS FOR RUINING MY LUNCH.
FATSO.
JERK.
"WERE THEY FIGHTING AGAIN?"

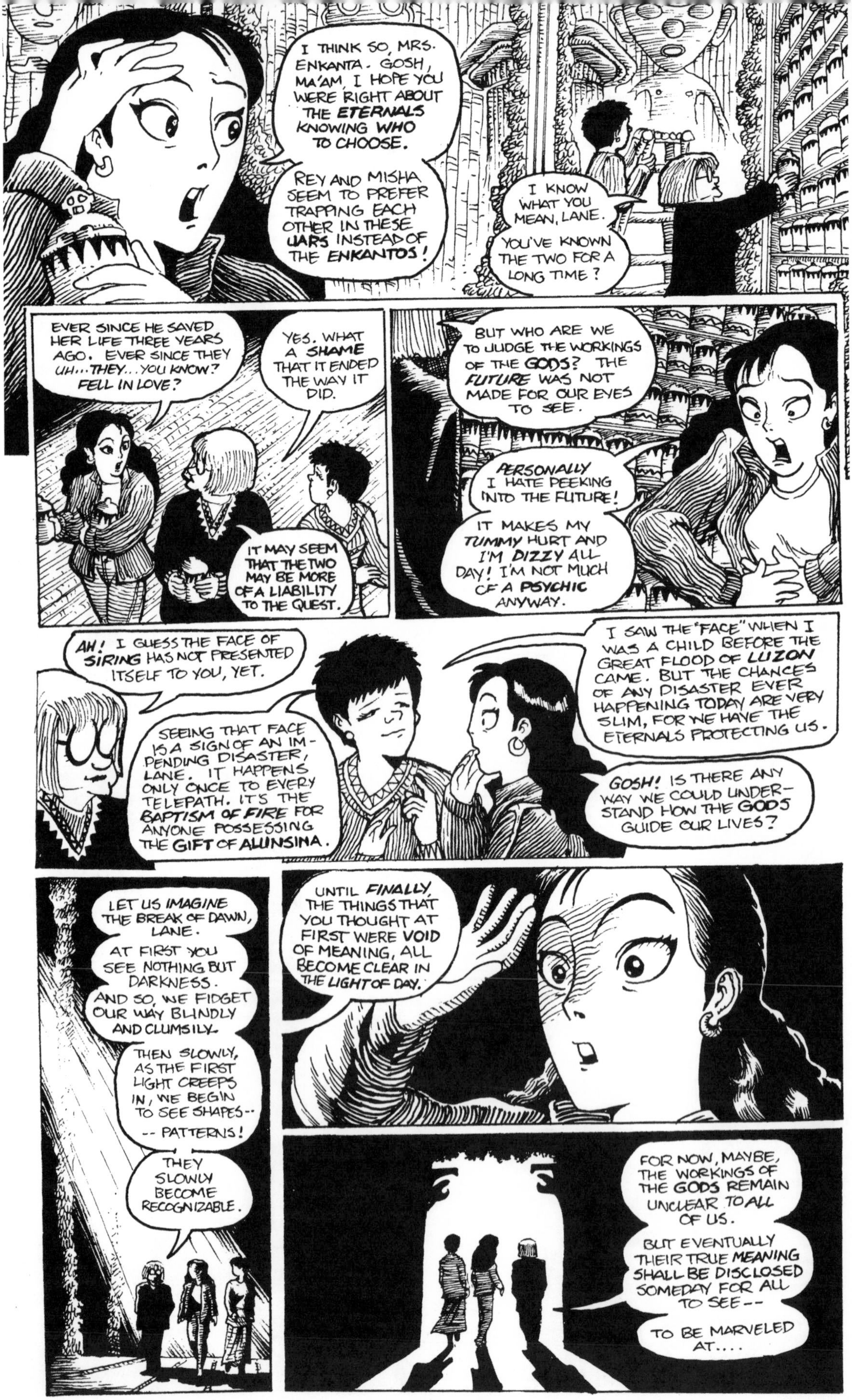
I THINK SO, MRS. ENKANTA. GOSH, MA'AM, I HOPE YOU WERE RIGHT ABOUT THE ETERNALS KNOWING WHO TO CHOOSE.
REY AND MISHA SEEM TO PREFER TRAPPING EACH OTHER IN THESE JARS INSTEAD OF THE ENKANTOS!
I KNOW WHAT YOU MEAN, LANE.
YOU'VE KNOWN THE TWO FOR A LONG TIME?
EVER SINCE HE SAVED HER LIFE THREE YEARS AGO. EVER SINCE THEY UH... THEY... YOU KNOW? FELL IN LOVE?
YES. WHAT A SHAME THAT IT ENDED THE WAY IT DID.
IT MAY SEEM THAT THE TWO MAY BE MORE OF A LIABILITY TO THE QUEST.
BUT WHO ARE WE TO JUDGE THE WORKINGS OF THE GODS? THE FUTURE WAS NOT MADE FOR OUR EYES TO SEE.
PERSONALLY I HATE PEEKING INTO THE FUTURE!
IT MAKES MY TUMMY HURT AND I'M DIZZY ALL DAY! I'M NOT MUCH OF A PSYCHIC ANYWAY.
AH! I GUESS THE FACE OF SIRING HAS NOT PRESENTED ITSELF TO YOU, YET.
SEEING THAT FACE IS A SIGN OF AN IMPENDING DISASTER, LANE. IT HAPPENS ONLY ONCE TO EVERY TELEPATH. IT'S THE BAPTISM OF FIRE FOR ANYONE POSSESSING THE GIFT OF ALUNSINA.
I SAW THE "FACE" WHEN I WAS A CHILD BEFORE THE GREAT FLOOD OF LUZON CAME. BUT THE CHANCES OF ANY DISASTER EVER HAPPENING TODAY ARE VERY SLIM, FOR WE HAVE THE ETERNALS PROTECTING US.
GOSH! IS THERE ANY WAY WE COULD UNDERSTAND HOW THE GODS GUIDE OUR LIVES?
LET US IMAGINE THE BREAK OF DAWN, LANE.
AT FIRST YOU SEE NOTHING BUT DARKNESS.
AND SO, WE FIDGET OUR WAY BLINDLY AND CLUMSILY.
THEN SLOWLY, AS THE FIRST LIGHT CREEPS IN, WE BEGIN TO SEE SHAPES--
-- PATTERNS!
THEY SLOWLY BECOME RECOGNIZABLE.
UNTIL FINALLY, THE THINGS THAT YOU THOUGHT AT FIRST WERE VOID OF MEANING, ALL BECOME CLEAR IN THE LIGHT OF DAY.
FOR NOW, MAYBE, THE WORKINGS OF THE GODS REMAIN UNCLEAR TO ALL OF US.
BUT EVENTUALLY THEIR TRUE MEANING SHALL BE DISCLOSED SOMEDAY FOR ALL TO SEE--
TO BE MARVELED AT....

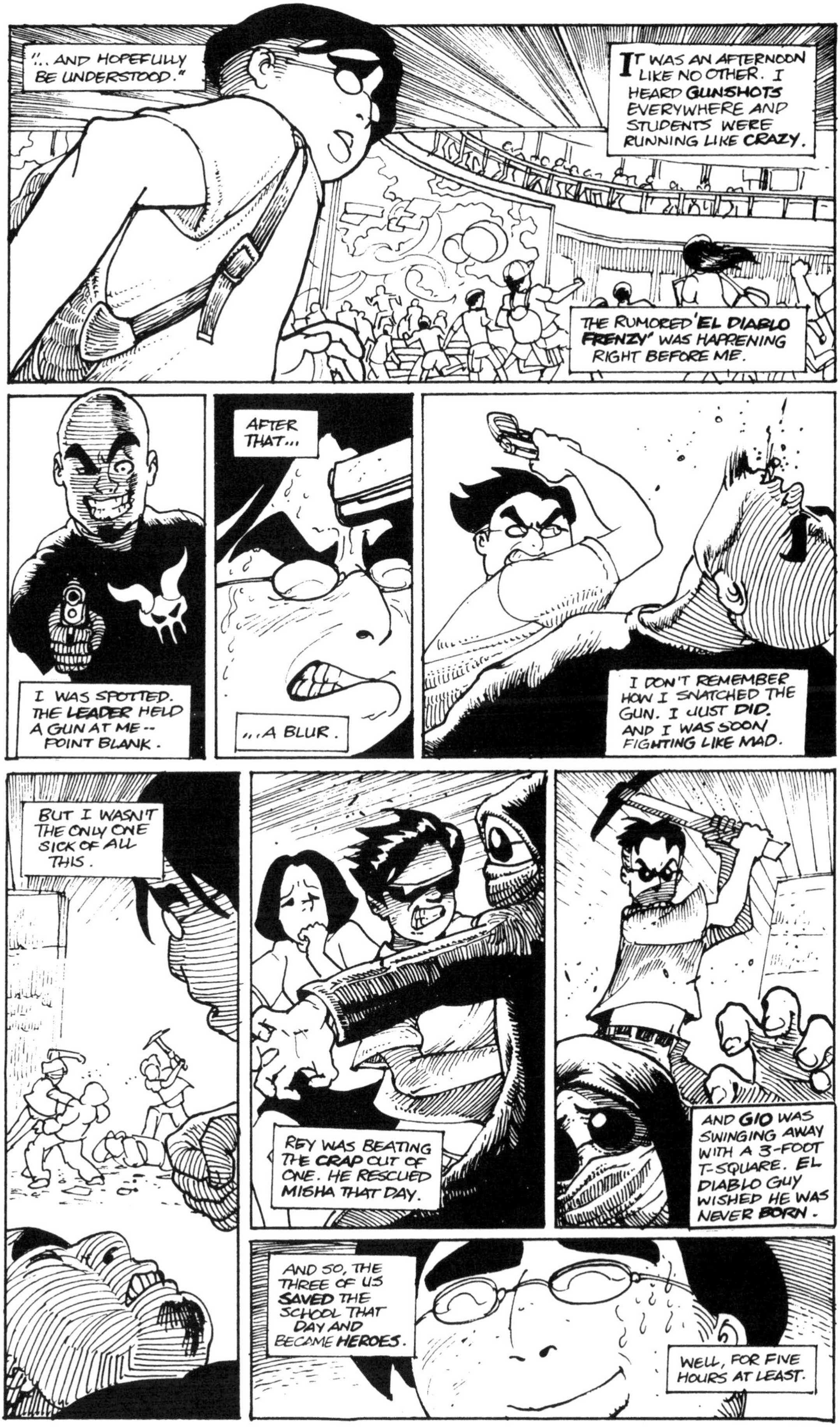
"... AND HOPEFULLY BE UNDERSTOOD."
IT WAS AN AFTERNOON LIKE NO OTHER. I HEARD GUNSHOTS EVERYWHERE AND STUDENTS WERE RUNNING LIKE CRAZY.
THE RUMORED 'EL DIABLO FRENZY' WAS HAPPENING RIGHT BEFORE ME.
I WAS SPOTTED. THE LEADER HELD A GUN AT ME -- POINT BLANK.
AFTER THAT...
...A BLUR.
I DON'T REMEMBER HOW I SNATCHED THE GUN. I JUST DID. AND I WAS SOON FIGHTING LIKE MAD.
BUT I WASN'T THE ONLY ONE SICK OF ALL THIS.
REY WAS BEATING THE CRAP OUT OF ONE. HE RESCUED MISHA THAT DAY.
AND GIO WAS SWINGING AWAY WITH A 3-FOOT T-SQUARE. EL DIABLO GUY WISHED HE WAS NEVER BORN.
AND SO, THE THREE OF US SAVED THE SCHOOL THAT DAY AND BECAME HEROES.
WELL, FOR FIVE HOURS AT LEAST.

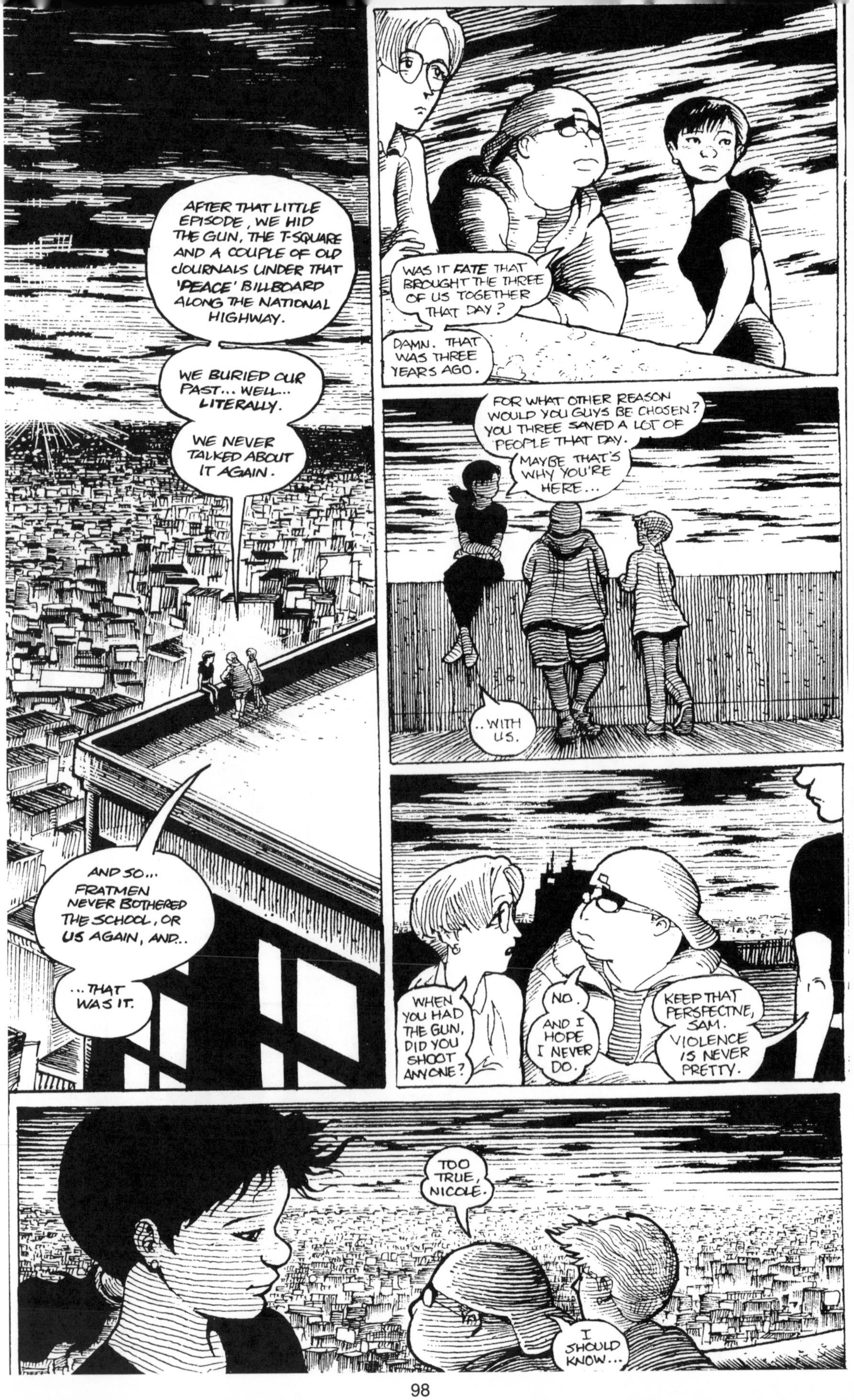
AFTER THAT LITTLE EPISODE, WE HID THE GUN, THE T-SQUARE AND A COUPLE OF OLD JOURNALS UNDER THAT 'PEACE' BILLBOARD ALONG THE NATIONAL HIGHWAY.
WE BURIED OUR PAST... WELL... LITERALLY.
WE NEVER TALKED ABOUT IT AGAIN.
AND SO... FRATMEN NEVER BOTHERED THE SCHOOL, OR US AGAIN, AND...
...THAT WAS IT.
WAS IT FATE THAT BROUGHT THE THREE OF US TOGETHER THAT DAY?
DAMN. THAT WAS THREE YEARS AGO.
FOR WHAT OTHER REASON WOULD YOU GUYS BE CHOSEN? YOU THREE SAVED A LOT OF PEOPLE THAT DAY.
MAYBE THAT'S WHY YOU'RE HERE...
..WITH US.
WHEN YOU HAD THE GUN, DID YOU SHOOT ANYONE?
NO.
AND I HOPE I NEVER DO.
KEEP THAT PERSPECTIVE, SAM. VIOLENCE IS NEVER PRETTY.
TOO TRUE, NICOLE.
I SHOULD KNOW...

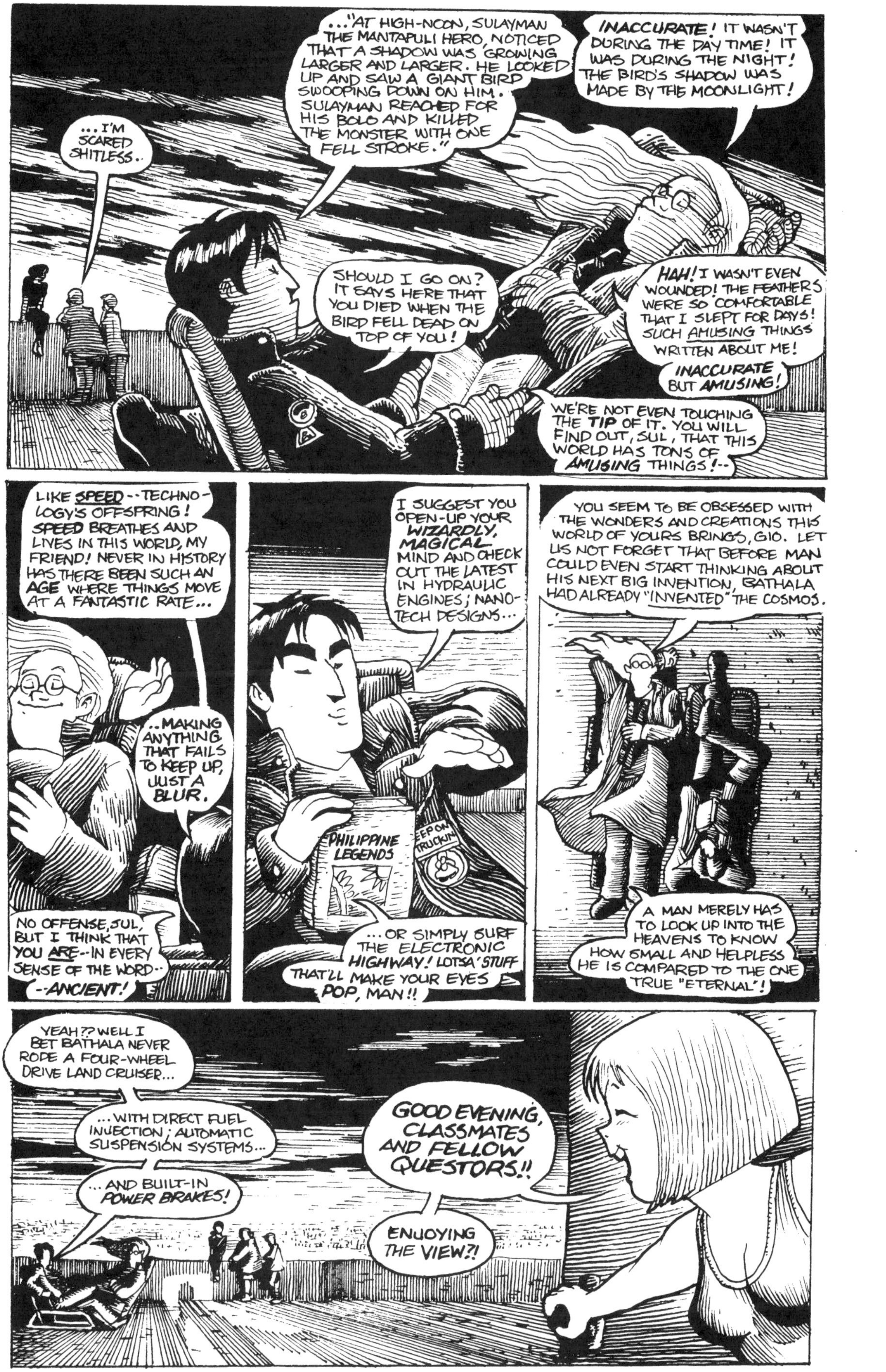

...I'M SCARED SHITLESS..
..."AT HIGH-NOON, SULAYMAN THE MANTAPULI HERO, NOTICED THAT A SHADOW WAS GROWING LARGER AND LARGER. HE LOOKED UP AND SAW A GIANT BIRD SWOOPING DOWN ON HIM. SULAYMAN REACHED FOR HIS BOLO AND KILLED THE MONSTER WITH ONE FELL STROKE."
INACCURATE! IT WASN'T DURING THE DAY TIME! IT WAS DURING THE NIGHT! THE BIRD'S SHADOW WAS MADE BY THE MOONLIGHT!
SHOULD I GO ON? IT SAYS HERE THAT YOU DIED WHEN THE BIRD FELL DEAD ON TOP OF YOU!
HAH! I WASN'T EVEN WOUNDED! THE FEATHERS WERE SO COMFORTABLE THAT I SLEPT FOR DAYS! SUCH AMUSING THINGS WRITTEN ABOUT ME!
INACCURATE BUT AMUSING!
WE'RE NOT EVEN TOUCHING THE TIP OF IT. YOU WILL FIND OUT, SUL, THAT THIS WORLD HAS TONS OF AMUSING THINGS!--
LIKE SPEED--TECHNOLOGY'S OFFSPRING! SPEED BREATHES AND LIVES IN THIS WORLD, MY FRIEND! NEVER IN HISTORY HAS THERE BEEN SUCH AN AGE WHERE THINGS MOVE AT A FANTASTIC RATE...
..MAKING ANYTHING THAT FAILS TO KEEP UP, JUST A BLUR.
NO OFFENSE, SUL, BUT I THINK THAT YOU ARE--IN EVERY SENSE OF THE WORD.. --ANCIENT!
I SUGGEST YOU OPEN-UP YOUR WIZARDLY, MAGICAL MIND AND CHECK OUT THE LATEST IN HYDRAULIC ENGINES; NANO-TECH DESIGNS...
PHILIPPINE LEGENDS
KEEP ON TRUCKIN
...OR SIMPLY SURF THE ELECTRONIC HIGHWAY! LOTSA' STUFF THAT'LL MAKE YOUR EYES POP, MAN!!
YOU SEEM TO BE OBSESSED WITH THE WONDERS AND CREATIONS THIS WORLD OF YOURS BRINGS, GIO. LET US NOT FORGET THAT BEFORE MAN COULD EVEN START THINKING ABOUT HIS NEXT BIG INVENTION, BATHALA HAD ALREADY "INVENTED" THE COSMOS.
A MAN MERELY HAS TO LOOK UP INTO THE HEAVENS TO KNOW HOW SMALL AND HELPLESS HE IS COMPARED TO THE ONE TRUE "ETERNAL"!
YEAH?? WELL I BET BATHALA NEVER RODE A FOUR-WHEEL DRIVE LAND CRUISER...
...WITH DIRECT FUEL INJECTION; AUTOMATIC SUSPENSION SYSTEMS...
...AND BUILT-IN POWER BRAKES!
GOOD EVENING, CLASSMATES AND FELLOW QUESTORS!!
ENJOYING THE VIEW?!

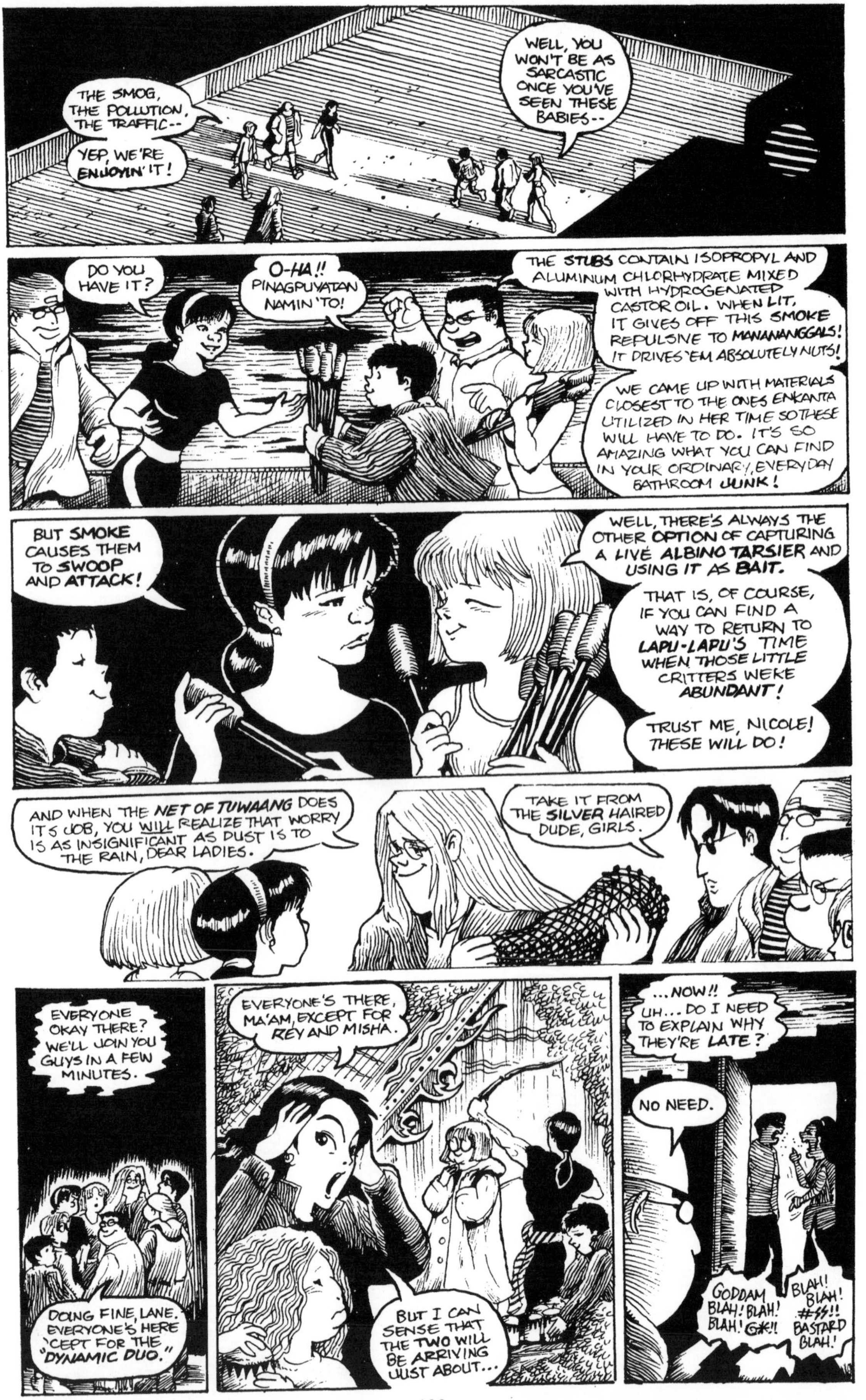
THE SMOG, THE POLLUTION, THE TRAFFIC--
YEP, WE'RE ENJOYIN' IT!
WELL, YOU WON'T BE AS SARCASTIC ONCE YOU'VE SEEN THESE BABIES--
DO YOU HAVE IT?
O-HA!! PINAGPUYATAN NAMIN'TO!
THE STUBS CONTAIN ISOPROPYL AND ALUMINUM CHLORHYDRATE MIXED WITH HYDROGENATED CASTOR OIL. WHEN LIT, IT GIVES OFF THIS SMOKE REPULSIVE TO MANANANGGALS! IT DRIVES 'EM ABSOLUTELY NUTS!
WE CAME UP WITH MATERIALS CLOSEST TO THE ONES ENKANTA UTILIZED IN HER TIME SO THESE WILL HAVE TO DO. IT'S SO AMAZING WHAT YOU CAN FIND IN YOUR ORDINARY, EVERYDAY BATHROOM JUNK!
BUT SMOKE CAUSES THEM TO SWOOP AND ATTACK!
WELL, THERE'S ALWAYS THE OTHER OPTION OF CAPTURING A LIVE ALBINO TARSIER AND USING IT AS BAIT.
THAT IS, OF COURSE, IF YOU CAN FIND A WAY TO RETURN TO LAPU-LAPU'S TIME WHEN THOSE LITTLE CRITTERS WERE ABUNDANT!
TRUST ME, NICOLE! THESE WILL DO!
AND WHEN THE NET OF TUWAANG DOES ITS JOB, YOU WILL REALIZE THAT WORRY IS AS INSIGNIFICANT AS DUST IS TO THE RAIN, DEAR LADIES.
TAKE IT FROM THE SILVER HAIRED DUDE, GIRLS.
EVERYONE OKAY THERE? WE'LL JOIN YOU GUYS IN A FEW MINUTES.
DOING FINE, LANE. EVERYONE'S HERE 'CEPT FOR THE "DYNAMIC DUO."
EVERYONE'S THERE, MA'AM, EXCEPT FOR REY AND MISHA.
BUT I CAN SENSE THAT THE TWO WILL BE ARRIVING JUST ABOUT...
...NOW!! UH... DO I NEED TO EXPLAIN WHY THEY'RE LATE?
NO NEED.
GODDAM BLAH! BLAH! BLAH! G#!!
BLAH! BLAH! #$$!! BASTARD BLAH!

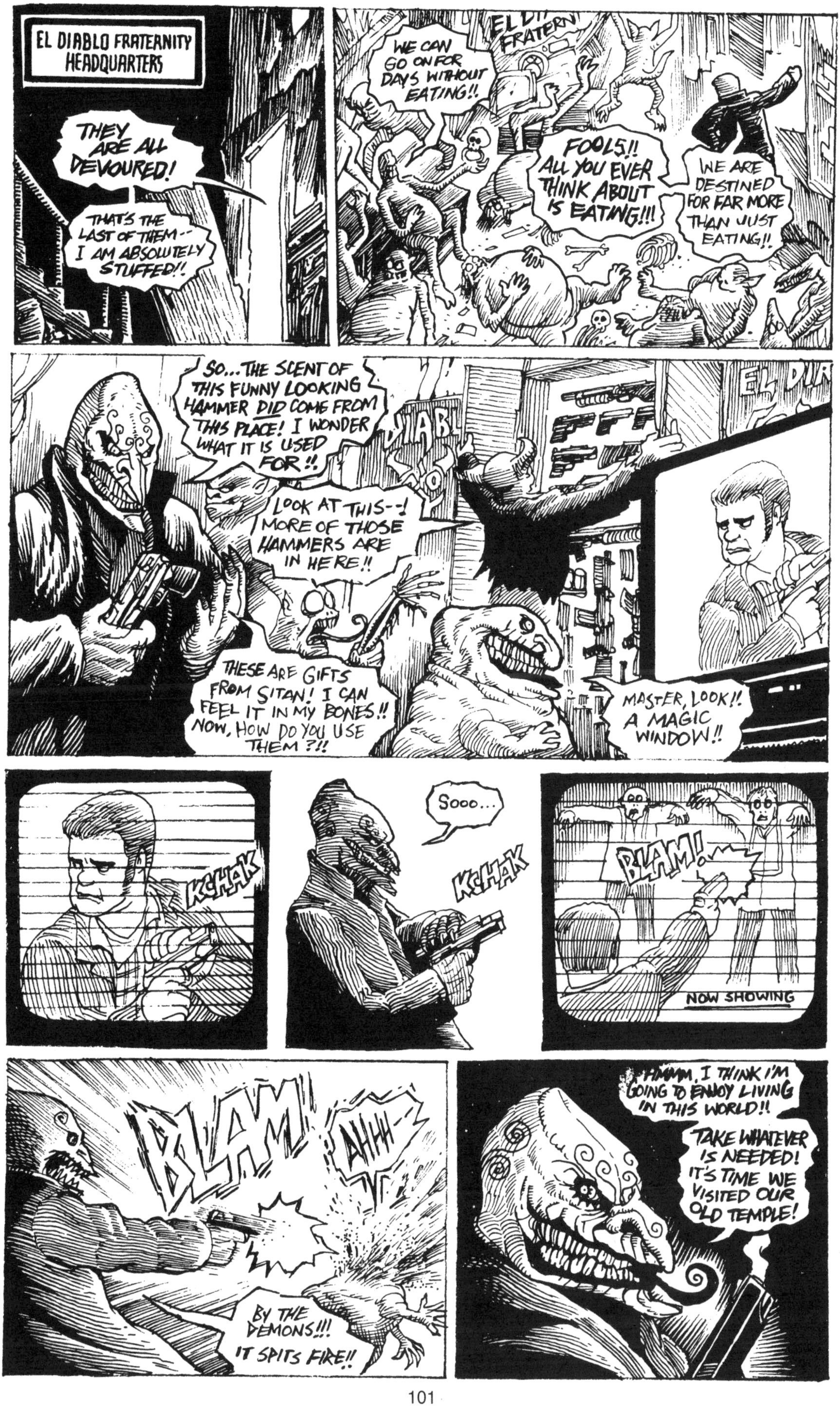
EL DIABLO FRATERNITY HEADQUARTERS
THEY ARE ALL DEVOURED!
THAT'S THE LAST OF THEM-- I AM ABSOLUTELY STUFFED!!
WE CAN GO ON FOR DAYS WITHOUT EATING!!
FOOLS!! ALL YOU EVER THINK ABOUT IS EATING!!!
WE ARE DESTINED FOR FAR MORE THAN JUST EATING!!
SO...THE SCENT OF THIS FUNNY LOOKING HAMMER DID COME FROM THIS PLACE! I WONDER WHAT IT IS USED FOR!!
LOOK AT THIS--! MORE OF THOSE HAMMERS ARE IN HERE!!
THESE ARE GIFTS FROM SITAN! I CAN FEEL IT IN MY BONES!! NOW, HOW DO YOU USE THEM?!!
MASTER, LOOK!! A MAGIC WINDOW!!
KCHAK
Sooo...
KCHAK
BLAM!
NOW SHOWING
BLAM
AHHH
BY THE DEMONS!!! IT SPITS FIRE!!
HMMM, I THINK I'M GOING TO ENJOY LIVING IN THIS WORLD!!
TAKE WHATEVER IS NEEDED! IT'S TIME WE VISITED OUR OLD TEMPLE!

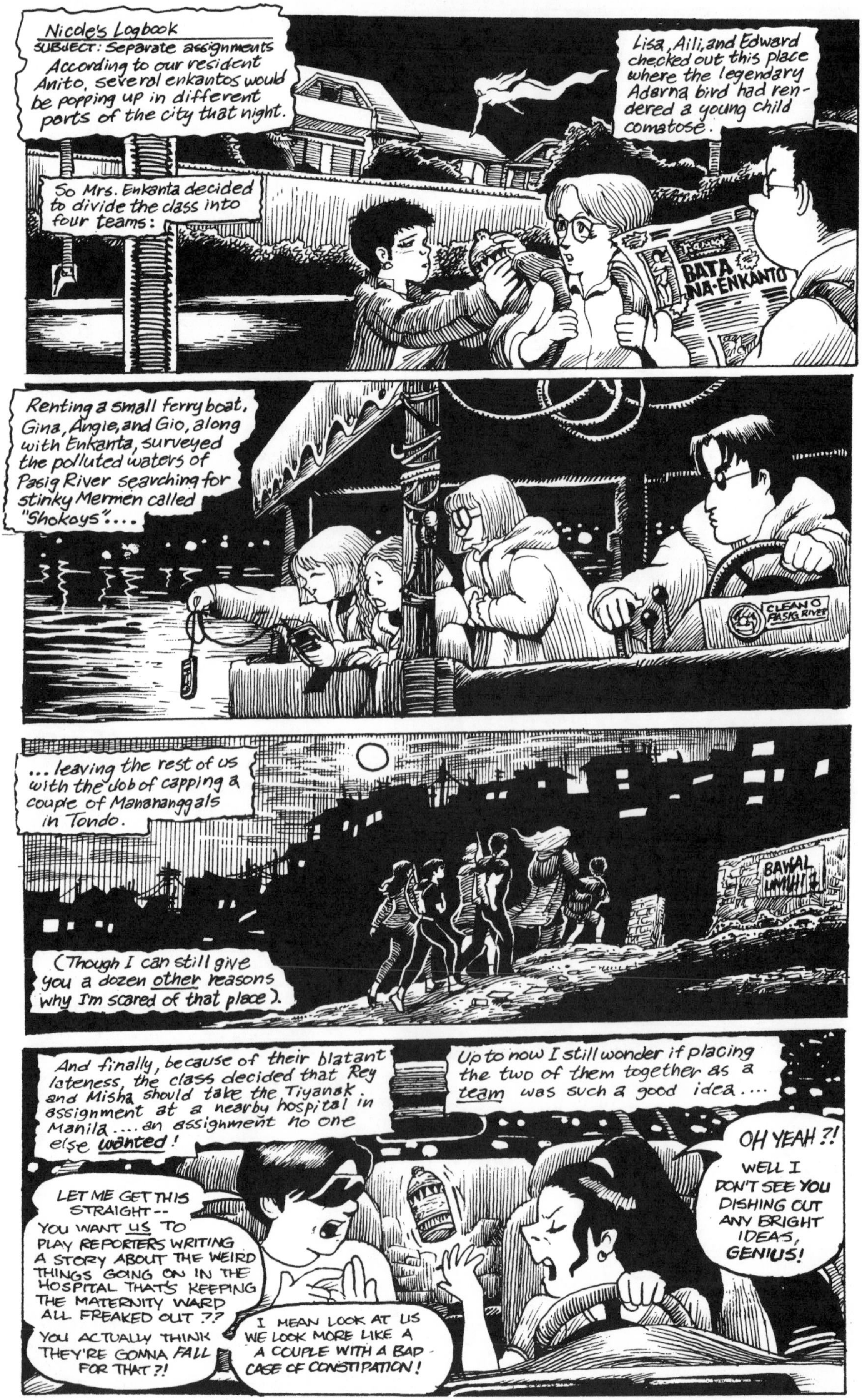
Nicole's Logbook
SUBJECT: Separate assignments
According to our resident Anito, several enkantos would be popping up in different parts of the city that night.
Lisa, Aili, and Edward checked out this place where the legendary Adarna bird had rendered a young child comatose.
So Mrs. Enkanta decided to divide the class into four teams:
BATA NA-ENKANTO
Renting a small ferry boat, Gina, Angie, and Gio, along with Enkanta, surveyed the polluted waters of Pasig River searching for stinky Mermen called "Shokoys"....
CLEAN O PASIG RIVER
... leaving the rest of us with the job of capping a couple of Manananggals in Tondo.
BAWAL
(Though I can still give you a dozen other reasons why I'm scared of that place).
And finally, because of their blatant lateness, the class decided that Rey and Misha should take the Tiyanak assignment at a nearby hospital in Manila.... an assignment no one else wanted!
Up to now I still wonder if placing the two of them together as a team was such a good idea....
LET ME GET THIS STRAIGHT -- YOU WANT US TO PLAY REPORTERS WRITING A STORY ABOUT THE WEIRD THINGS GOING ON IN THE HOSPITAL THAT'S KEEPING THE MATERNITY WARD ALL FREAKED OUT ?? YOU ACTUALLY THINK THEY'RE GONNA FALL FOR THAT ?!
I MEAN LOOK AT US WE LOOK MORE LIKE A A COUPLE WITH A BAD CASE OF CONSTIPATION!
OH YEAH ?! WELL I DON'T SEE YOU DISHING OUT ANY BRIGHT IDEAS, GENIUS!

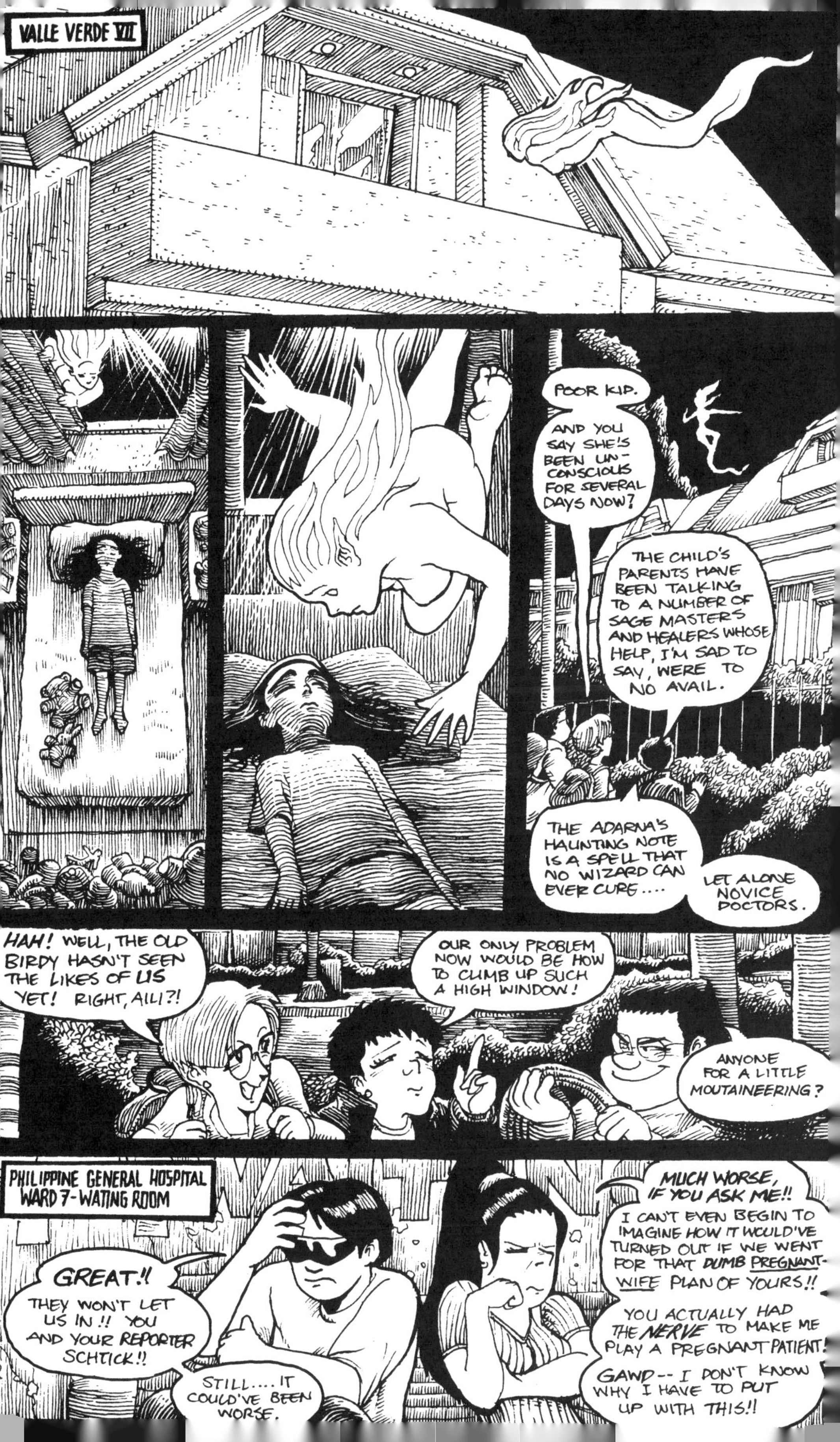

VALLE VERDE VII
POOR KIP.
AND YOU SAY SHE'S BEEN UN-CONSCIOUS FOR SEVERAL DAYS NOW?
THE CHILD'S PARENTS HAVE BEEN TALKING TO A NUMBER OF SAGE MASTERS AND HEALERS WHOSE HELP, I'M SAD TO SAY, WERE TO NO AVAIL.
THE ADARNA'S HAUNTING NOTE IS A SPELL THAT NO WIZARD CAN EVER CURE....
LET ALONE NOVICE DOCTORS.
HAH! WELL, THE OLD BIRDY HASN'T SEEN THE LIKES OF US YET! RIGHT, AILI?!
OUR ONLY PROBLEM NOW WOULD BE HOW TO CLIMB UP SUCH A HIGH WINDOW!
ANYONE FOR A LITTLE MOUTAINEERING?
PHILIPPINE GENERAL HOSPITAL WARD 7-WATING ROOM
GREAT!! THEY WON'T LET US IN!! YOU AND YOUR REPORTER SCHTICK!!
STILL.... IT COULD'VE BEEN WORSE.
MUCH WORSE, IF YOU ASK ME!! I CAN'T EVEN BEGIN TO IMAGINE HOW IT WOULD'VE TURNED OUT IF WE WENT FOR THAT DUMB PREGNANT-WIFE PLAN OF YOURS!!
YOU ACTUALLY HAD THE NERVE TO MAKE ME PLAY A PREGNANT PATIENT!
GAWD-- I DON'T KNOW WHY I HAVE TO PUT UP WITH THIS!!

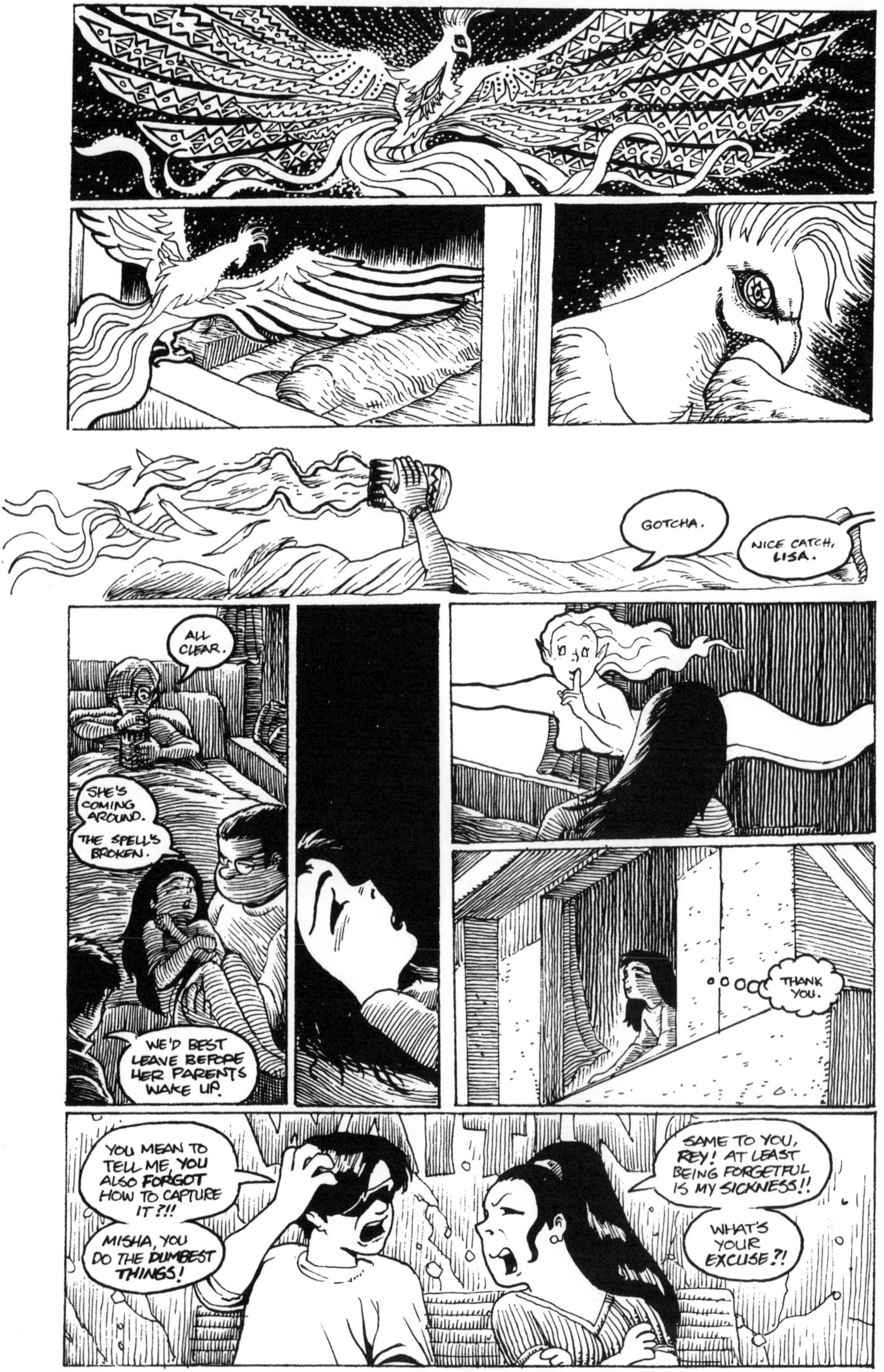
GOTCHA.
NICE CATCH, LISA.
ALL CLEAR.
SHE'S COMING AROUND.
THE SPELL'S BROKEN.
WE'D BEST LEAVE BEFORE HER PARENTS WAKE UP.
THANK YOU.
YOU MEAN TO TELL ME, YOU ALSO FORGOT HOW TO CAPTURE IT?!!
MISHA, YOU DO THE DUMBEST THINGS!
SAME TO YOU, REY! AT LEAST BEING FORGETFUL IS MY SICKNESS!!
WHAT'S YOUR EXCUSE?!

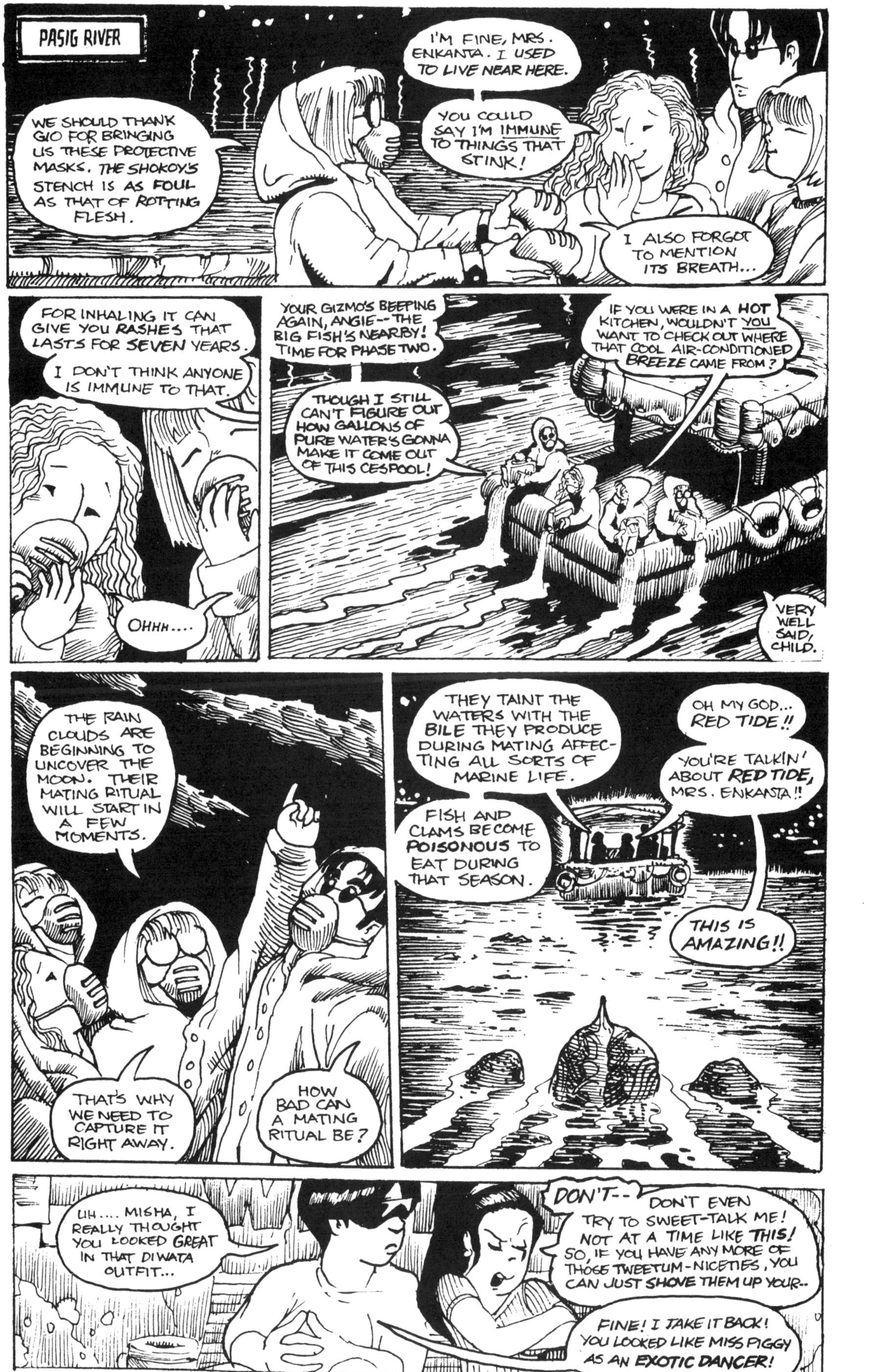
PASIG RIVER
WE SHOULD THANK GIO FOR BRINGING US THESE PROTECTIVE MASKS. THE SHOKOY'S STENCH IS AS FOUL AS THAT OF ROTTING FLESH.
I'M FINE, MRS. ENKANTA. I USED TO LIVE NEAR HERE.
YOU COULD SAY I'M IMMUNE TO THINGS THAT STINK!
I ALSO FORGOT TO MENTION ITS BREATH...
FOR INHALING IT CAN GIVE YOU RASHES THAT LASTS FOR SEVEN YEARS.
I DON'T THINK ANYONE IS IMMUNE TO THAT.
OHHH....
YOUR GIZMO'S BEEPING AGAIN, ANGIE-- THE BIG FISH'S NEARBY! TIME FOR PHASE TWO.
THOUGH I STILL CAN'T FIGURE OUT HOW GALLONS OF PURE WATER'S GONNA MAKE IT COME OUT OF THIS CESPOOL!
IF YOU WERE IN A HOT KITCHEN, WOULDN'T YOU WANT TO CHECK OUT WHERE THAT COOL AIR-CONDITIONED BREEZE CAME FROM?
VERY WELL SAID, CHILD.
THE RAIN CLOUDS ARE BEGINNING TO UNCOVER THE MOON. THEIR MATING RITUAL WILL START IN A FEW MOMENTS.
THAT'S WHY WE NEED TO CAPTURE IT RIGHT AWAY.
HOW BAD CAN A MATING RITUAL BE?
THEY TAINT THE WATERS WITH THE BILE THEY PRODUCE DURING MATING AFFECTING ALL SORTS OF MARINE LIFE.
FISH AND CLAMS BECOME POISONOUS TO EAT DURING THAT SEASON.
OH MY GOD... RED TIDE!!
YOU'RE TALKIN' ABOUT RED TIDE, MRS. ENKANTA!!
THIS IS AMAZING!!
UH.... MISHA, I REALLY THOUGHT YOU LOOKED GREAT IN THAT DIWATA OUTFIT...
DON'T-- DON'T EVEN TRY TO SWEET-TALK ME! NOT AT A TIME LIKE THIS! SO, IF YOU HAVE ANY MORE OF THOSE TWEETUM-NICETIES, YOU CAN JUST SHOVE THEM UP YOUR..
FINE! I TAKE IT BACK! YOU LOOKED LIKE MISS PIGGY AS AN EXOTIC DANCER!

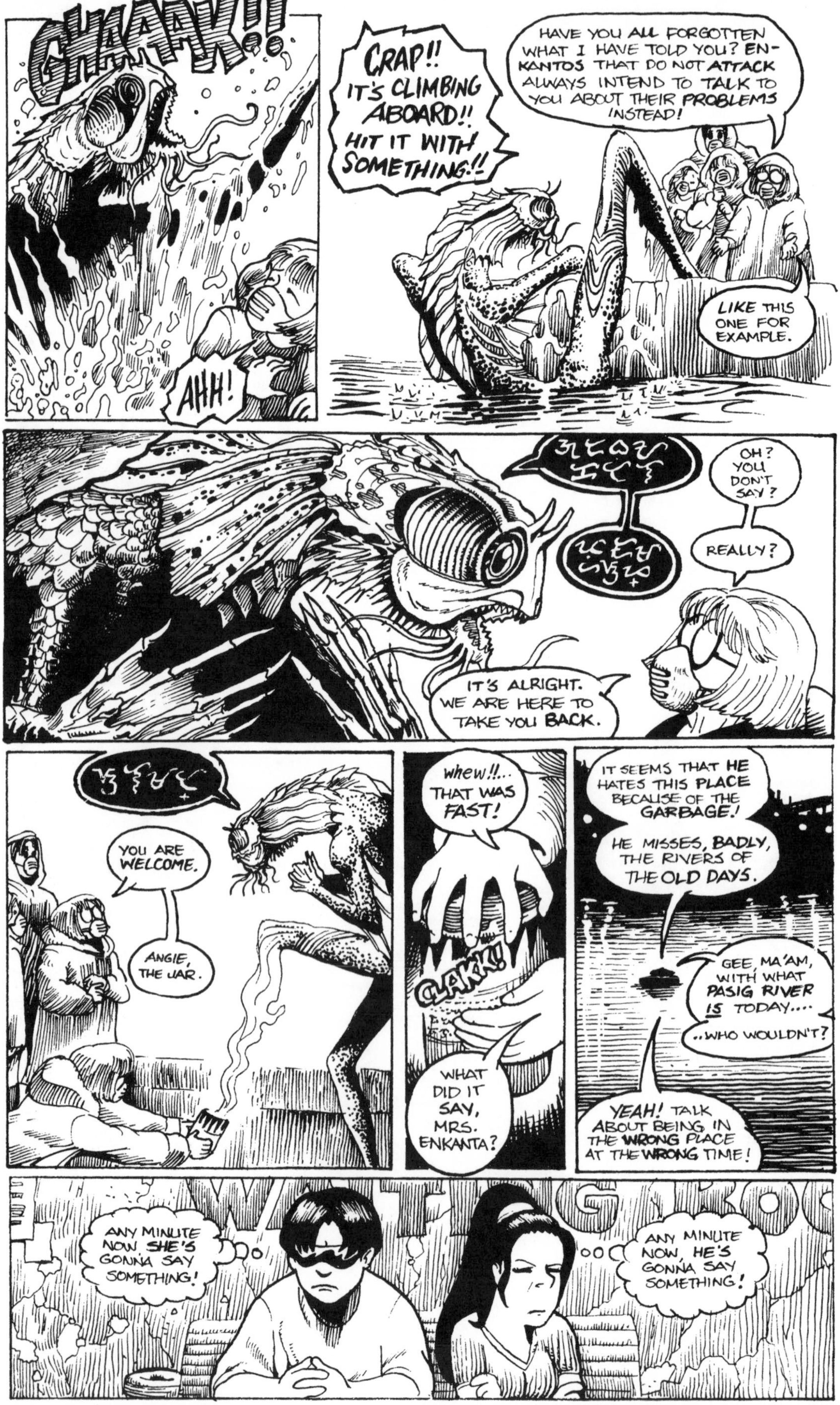

GHAAAK!!
AHH!
CRAP!! IT'S CLIMBING ABOARD!! HIT IT WITH SOMETHING!!
HAVE YOU ALL FORGOTTEN WHAT I HAVE TOLD YOU? EN-KANTOS THAT DO NOT ATTACK ALWAYS INTEND TO TALK TO YOU ABOUT THEIR PROBLEMS INSTEAD!
LIKE THIS ONE FOR EXAMPLE.
OH? YOU DON'T SAY?
REALLY?
IT'S ALRIGHT. WE ARE HERE TO TAKE YOU BACK.
YOU ARE WELCOME.
ANGIE, THE JAR.
whew!!... THAT WAS FAST!
CLAKK!
WHAT DID IT SAY, MRS. ENKANTA?
IT SEEMS THAT HE HATES THIS PLACE BECAUSE OF THE GARBAGE!
HE MISSES, BADLY, THE RIVERS OF THE OLD DAYS.
GEE, MA'AM, WITH WHAT PASIG RIVER IS TODAY....
..WHO WOULDN'T?
YEAH! TALK ABOUT BEING IN THE WRONG PLACE AT THE WRONG TIME!
ANY MINUTE NOW SHE'S GONNA SAY SOMETHING!
ANY MINUTE NOW, HE'S GONNA SAY SOMETHING!

TONDO MLA.

THEY'RE FLYING IN CIRCLES-- WORSHIPPING MAYARI, GODDESS OF THE MOON.

THEIR DEITY.

I SEE THAT YOU'VE BROUGHT YOUR OWN. YOUR VARIETY OF SKILLS IMPRESS ME.

NAH. JUST ARCHERY CLASS.

WELL?

SHALL WE?

SMOKE ALWAYS ANNOYS THEM.

THEY LOOK....

...THEY LOOK HIDEOUS!

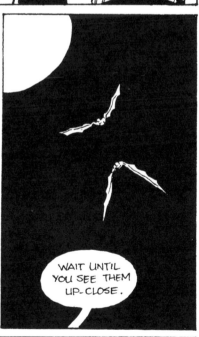

WAIT UNTIL YOU SEE THEM UP-CLOSE.

SHE'S GONNA BRING-UP THAT OLD TOPIC! I JUST KNOW IT!

HE'S GONNA BRING THAT TOPIC BACK AGAIN! I CAN FEEL IT!!

107

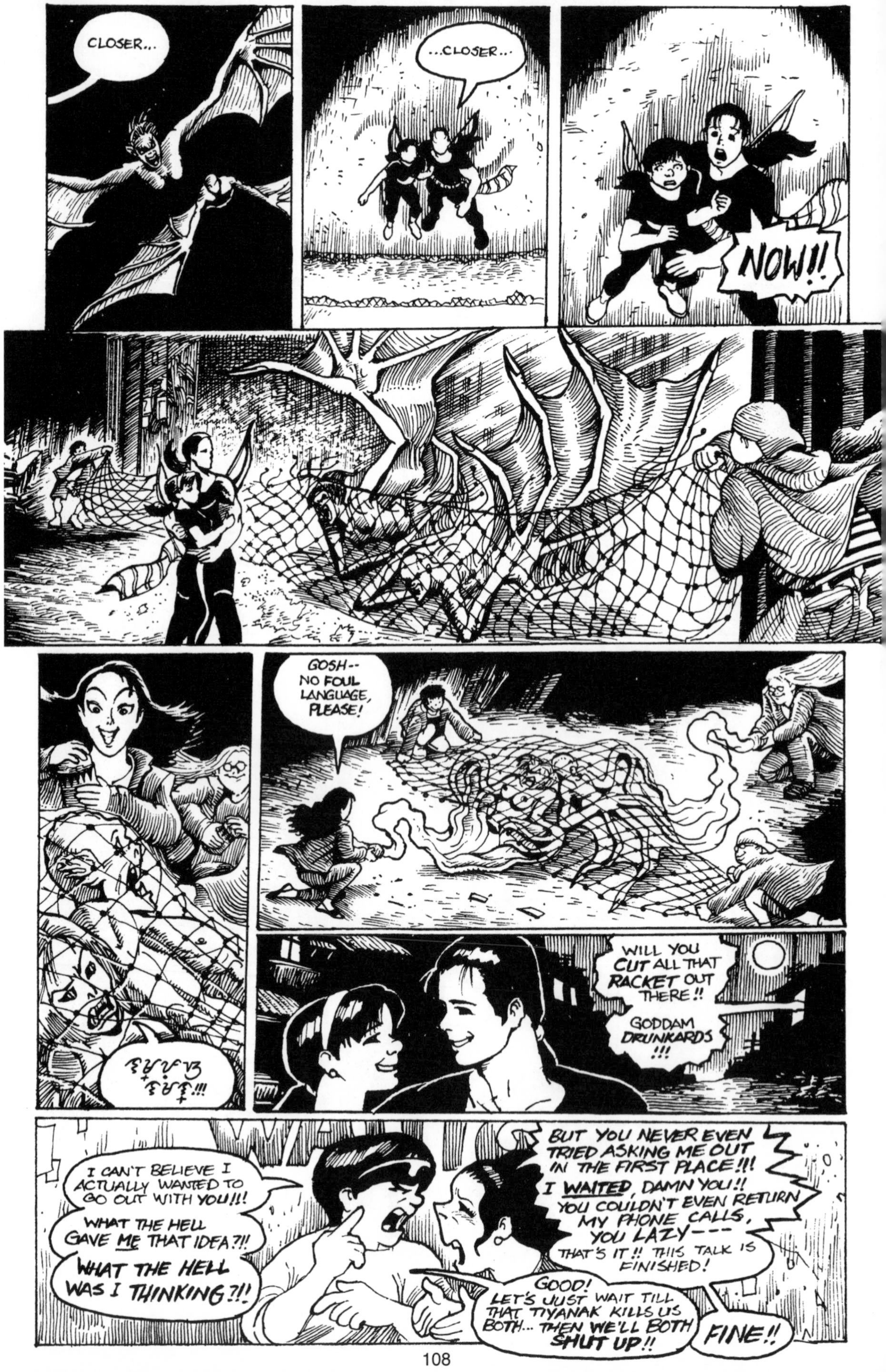
CLOSER...
...CLOSER...
NOW!!
GOSH-- NO FOUL LANGUAGE, PLEASE!
WILL YOU CUT ALL THAT RACKET OUT THERE!!
GODDAM DRUNKARDS!!!
I CAN'T BELIEVE I ACTUALLY WANTED TO GO OUT WITH YOU!!!
WHAT THE HELL GAVE ME THAT IDEA?!!
WHAT THE HELL WAS I THINKING?!!
BUT YOU NEVER EVEN TRIED ASKING ME OUT IN THE FIRST PLACE!!!
I WAITED, DAMN YOU!! YOU COULDN'T EVEN RETURN MY PHONE CALLS, YOU LAZY---
THAT'S IT!! THIS TALK IS FINISHED!
GOOD! LET'S JUST WAIT TILL THAT TIYANAK KILLS US BOTH... THEN WE'LL BOTH SHUT UP!!
FINE!!

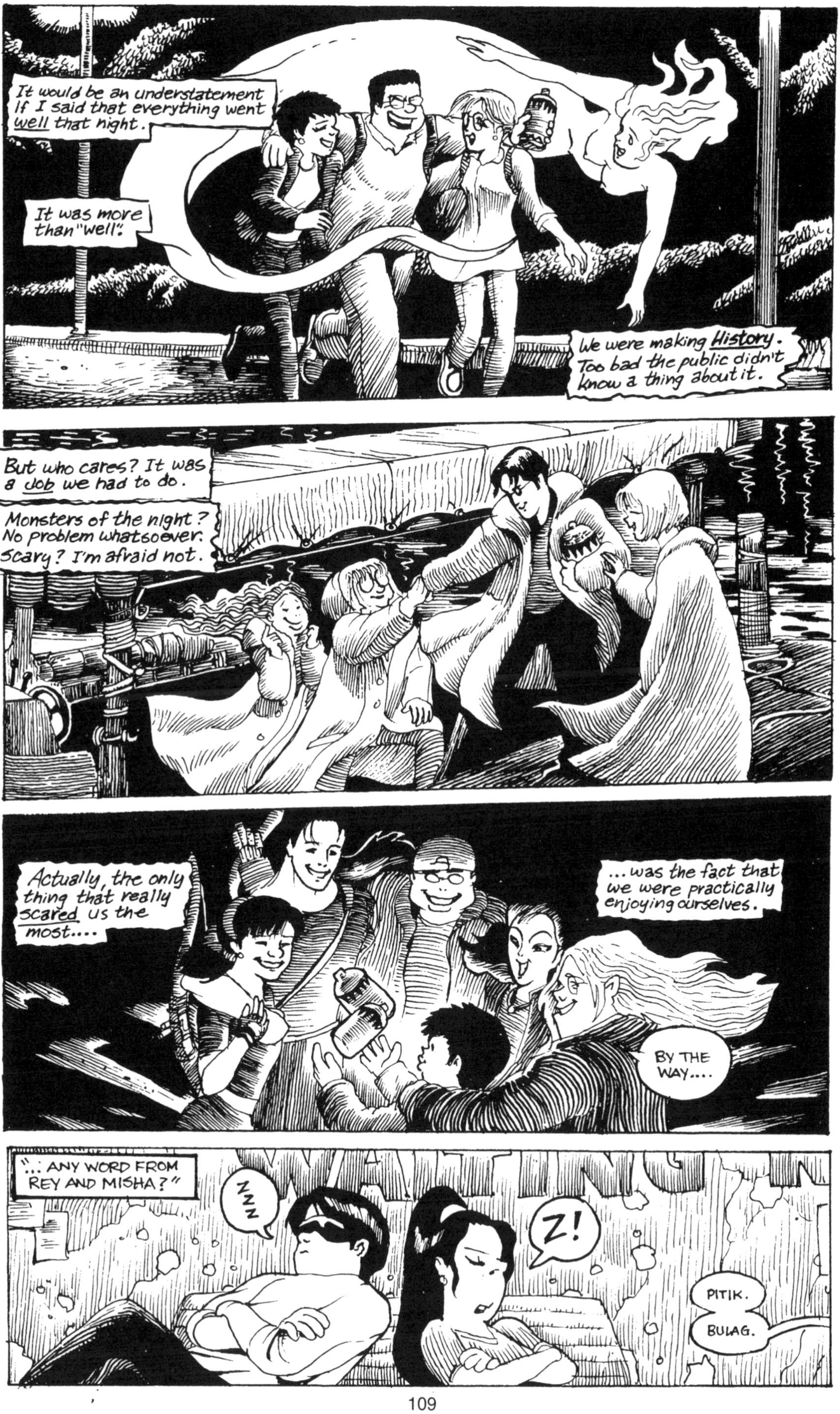
It would be an understatement if I said that everything went well that night.
It was more than "well".
We were making History. Too bad the public didn't know a thing about it.
But who cares? It was a job we had to do.
Monsters of the night? No problem whatsoever. Scary? I'm afraid not.
Actually, the only thing that really scared us the most....
...was the fact that we were practically enjoying ourselves.
BY THE WAY....
"...ANY WORD FROM REY AND MISHA?"
ZZZ
Z!
PITIK.
BULAG.

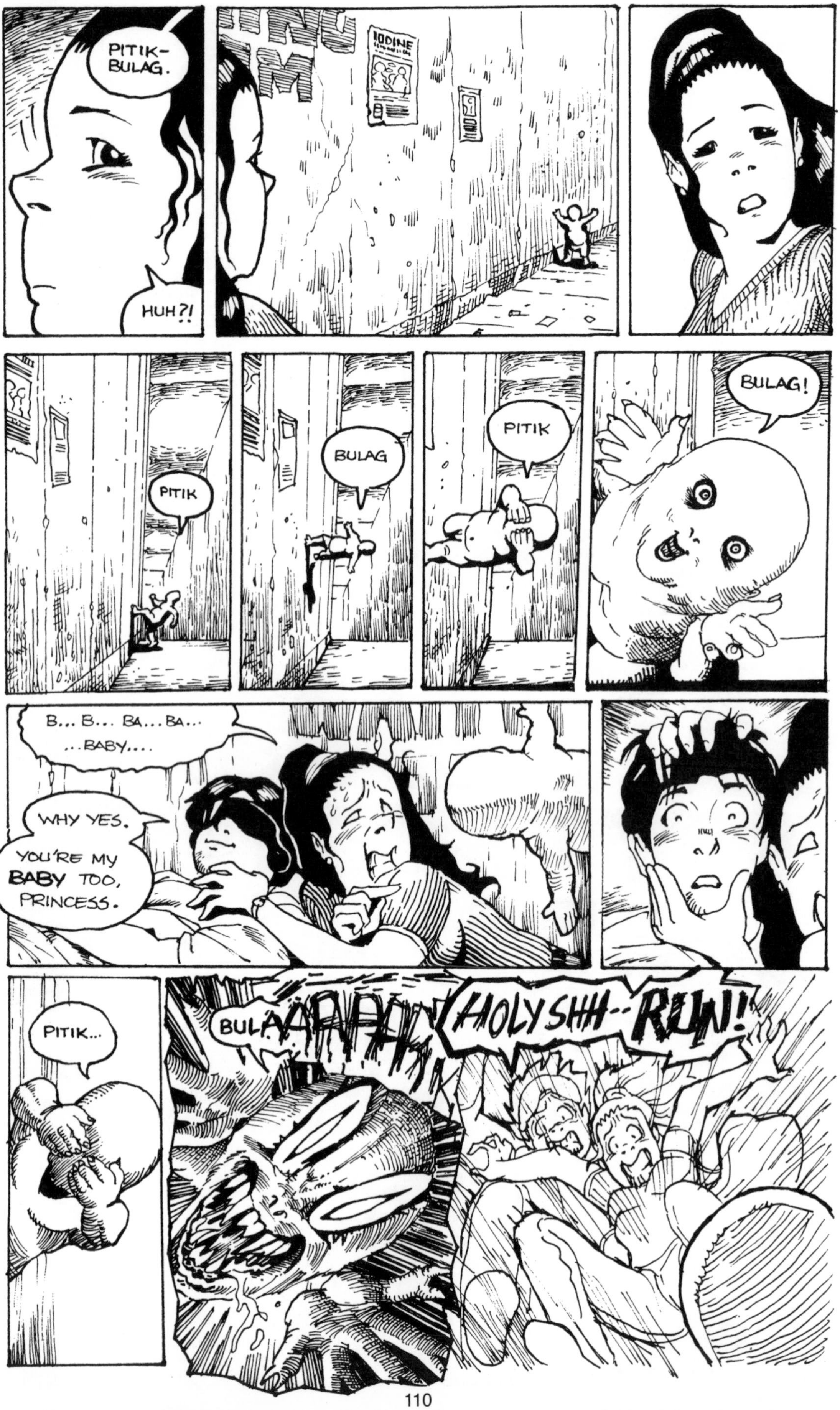

PITIK-BULAG.
HUH?!
IODINE
PITIK
BULAG
PITIK
BULAG!
B... B... BA... BA... ...BABY....
WHY YES.
YOU'RE MY BABY TOO, PRINCESS.
PITIK...
BULAAARHH
HOLY SHH--RUN!

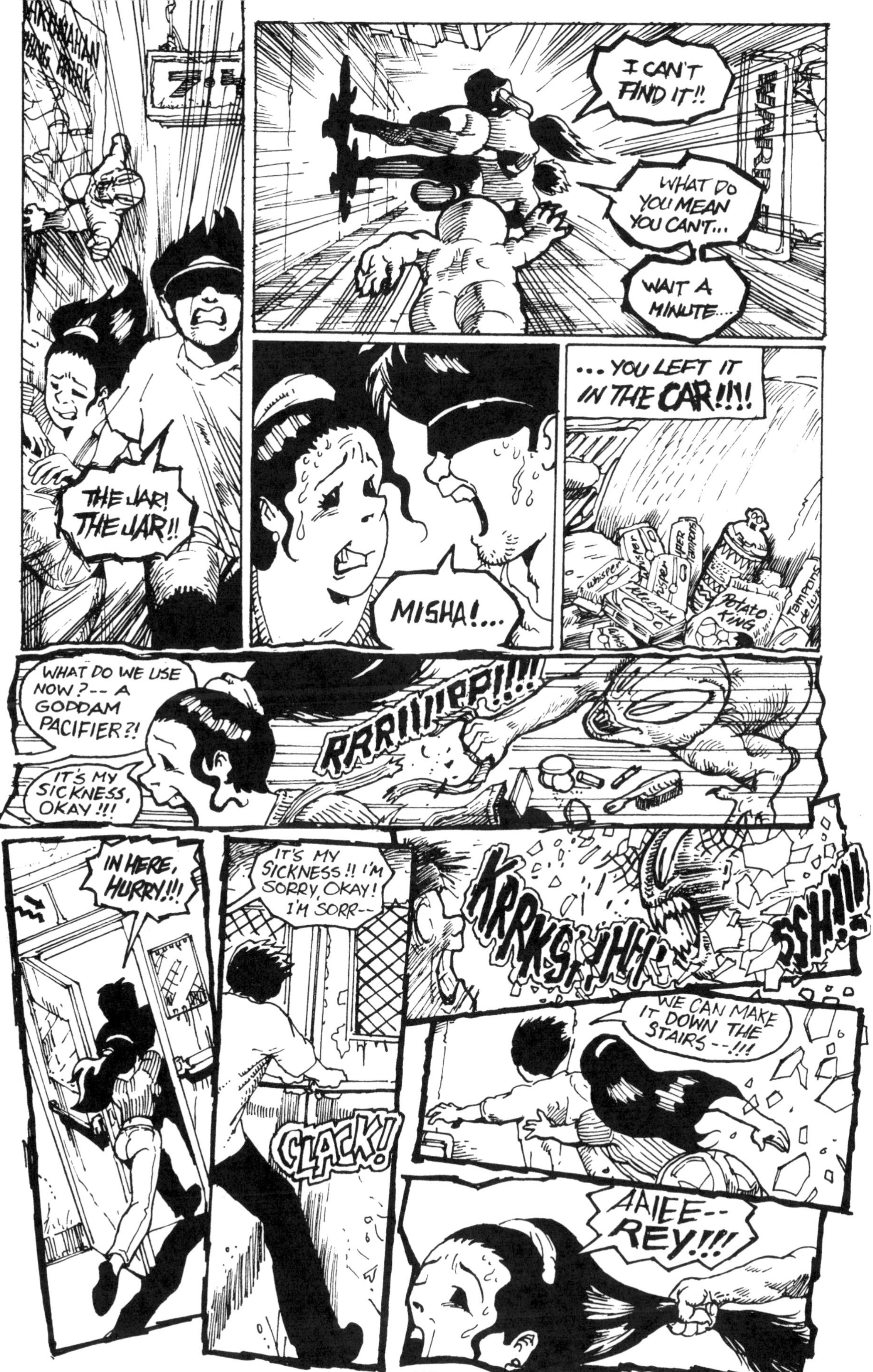
I CAN'T FIND IT!!
WHAT DO YOU MEAN YOU CAN'T...
WAIT A MINUTE....
THE JAR! THE JAR!!
MISHA!...
...YOU LEFT IT IN THE CAR!!!!
whisper
Kleenex
Potato King
tampons de luxe
WHAT DO WE USE NOW?-- A GODDAM PACIFIER?!
IT'S MY SICKNESS, OKAY!!!
RRRIIIIPP!!!!
IN HERE, HURRY!!!
IT'S MY SICKNESS!! I'M SORRY, OKAY! I'M SORR--
CLACK!
KRRKSHHH SSH!!!
WE CAN MAKE IT DOWN THE STAIRS--!!!
AAIEE-- REY!!!

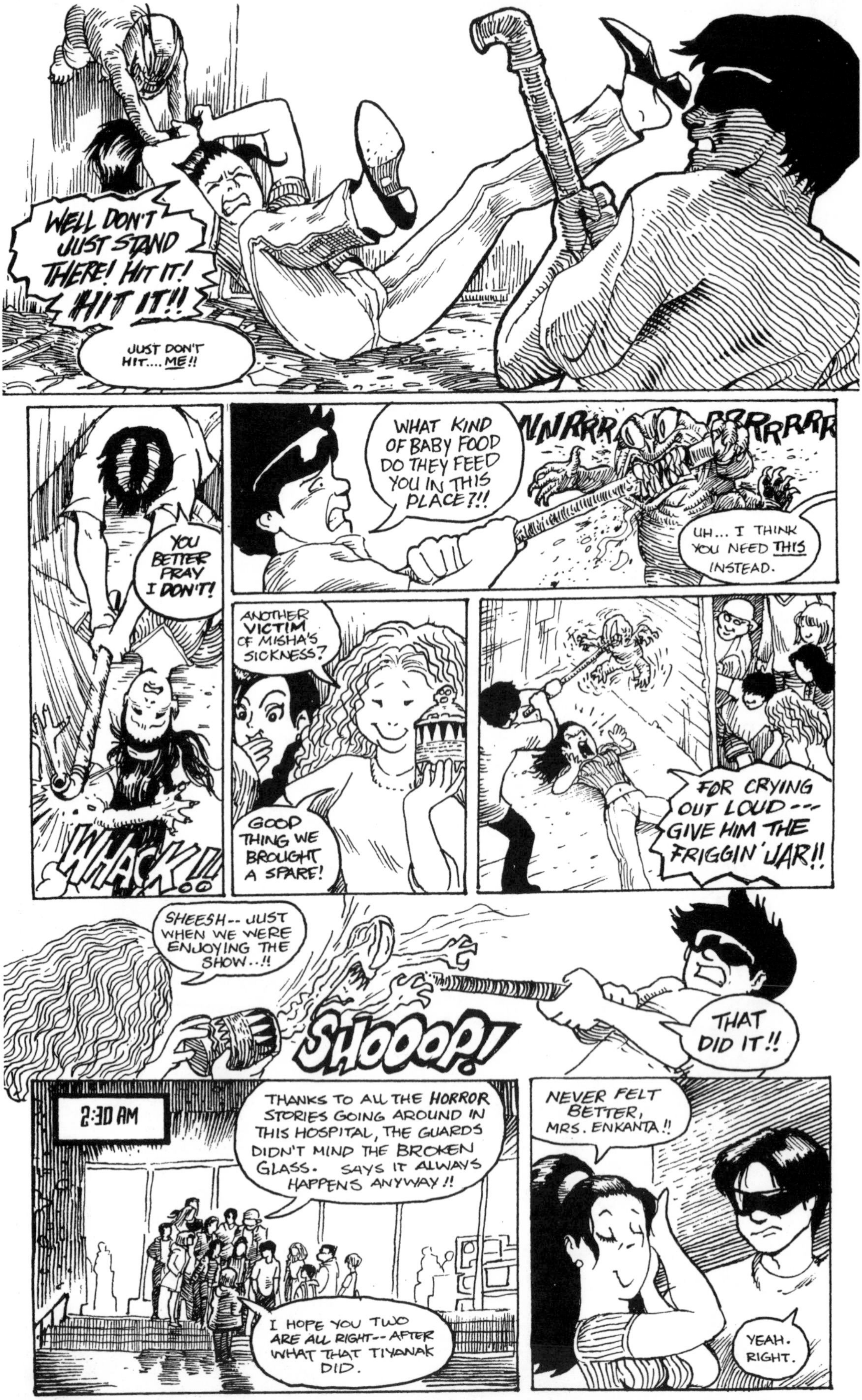

WELL DON'T JUST STAND THERE! HIT IT! HIT IT!!
JUST DON'T HIT.... ME!!
YOU BETTER PRAY I DON'T!
WHACK!!
WHAT KIND OF BABY FOOD DO THEY FEED YOU IN THIS PLACE?!!
NNRRR RRRRRRR
UH... I THINK YOU NEED THIS INSTEAD.
ANOTHER VICTIM OF MISHA'S SICKNESS?
GOOD THING WE BROUGHT A SPARE!
FOR CRYING OUT LOUD--- GIVE HIM THE FRIGGIN' JAR!!
SHEESH-- JUST WHEN WE WERE ENJOYING THE SHOW..!!
SHOOOP!
THAT DID IT!!
2:30 AM
THANKS TO ALL THE HORROR STORIES GOING AROUND IN THIS HOSPITAL, THE GUARDS DIDN'T MIND THE BROKEN GLASS. SAYS IT ALWAYS HAPPENS ANYWAY!!
I HOPE YOU TWO ARE ALL RIGHT-- AFTER WHAT THAT TIYANAK DID.
NEVER FELT BETTER, MRS. ENKANTA!!
YEAH. RIGHT.

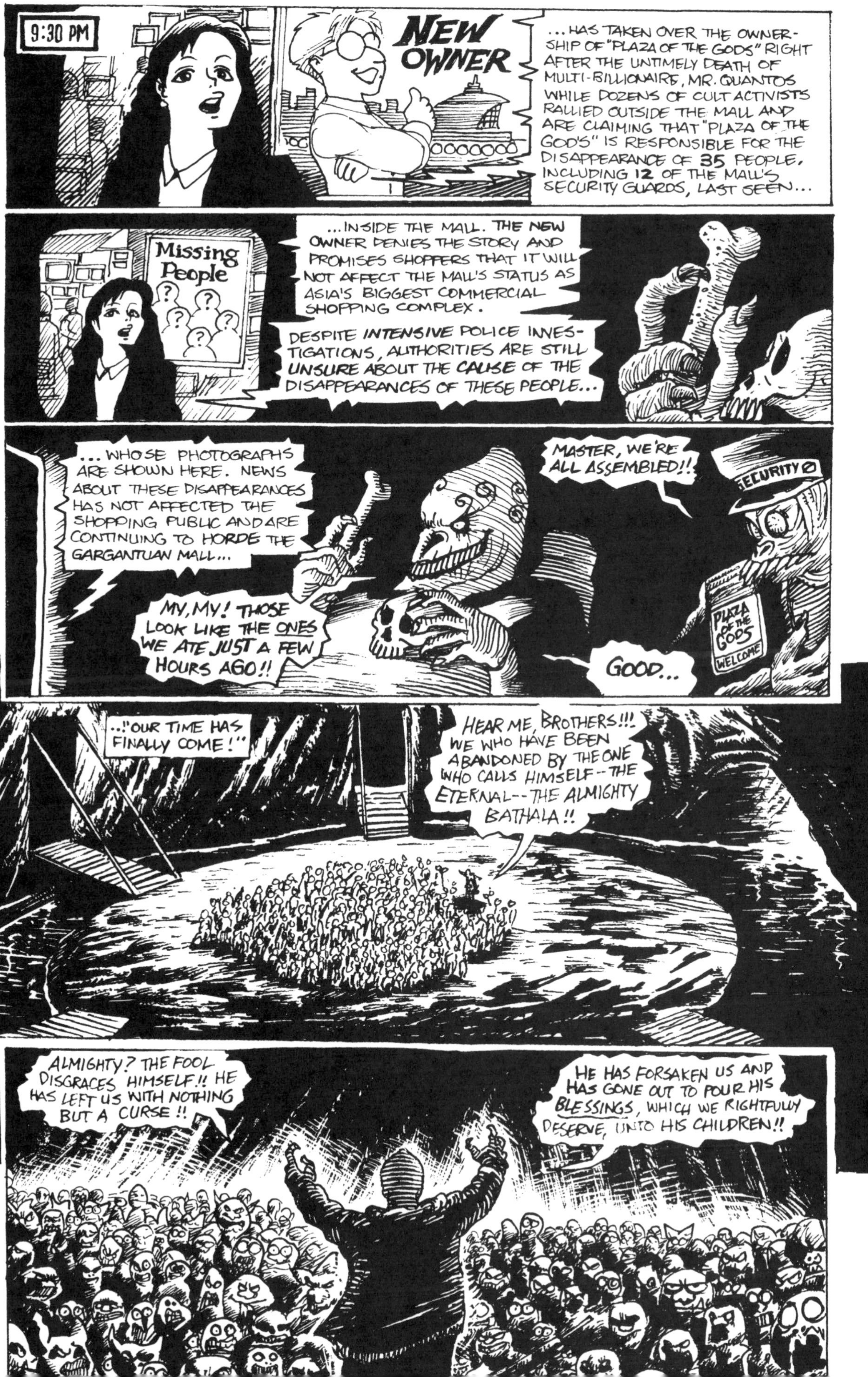

9:30 PM
NEW OWNER
...HAS TAKEN OVER THE OWNERSHIP OF "PLAZA OF THE GODS" RIGHT AFTER THE UNTIMELY DEATH OF MULTI-BILLIONAIRE, MR. QUANTOS WHILE DOZENS OF CULT ACTIVISTS RALLIED OUTSIDE THE MALL AND ARE CLAIMING THAT "PLAZA OF THE GOD'S" IS RESPONSIBLE FOR THE DISAPPEARANCE OF 35 PEOPLE, INCLUDING 12 OF THE MALL'S SECURITY GUARDS, LAST SEEN...
Missing People
...INSIDE THE MALL. THE NEW OWNER DENIES THE STORY AND PROMISES SHOPPERS THAT IT WILL NOT AFFECT THE MALL'S STATUS AS ASIA'S BIGGEST COMMERCIAL SHOPPING COMPLEX.
DESPITE INTENSIVE POLICE INVESTIGATIONS, AUTHORITIES ARE STILL UNSURE ABOUT THE CAUSE OF THE DISAPPEARANCES OF THESE PEOPLE...
...WHOSE PHOTOGRAPHS ARE SHOWN HERE. NEWS ABOUT THESE DISAPPEARANCES HAS NOT AFFECTED THE SHOPPING PUBLIC AND ARE CONTINUING TO HORDE THE GARGANTUAN MALL...
MY, MY! THOSE LOOK LIKE THE ONES WE ATE JUST A FEW HOURS AGO!!
MASTER, WE'RE ALL ASSEMBLED!!
SECURITY
PLAZA OF THE GODS WELCOME
GOOD...
..."OUR TIME HAS FINALLY COME!"
HEAR ME, BROTHERS!!! WE WHO HAVE BEEN ABANDONED BY THE ONE WHO CALLS HIMSELF--THE ETERNAL--THE ALMIGHTY BATHALA!!
ALMIGHTY? THE FOOL DISGRACES HIMSELF!! HE HAS LEFT US WITH NOTHING BUT A CURSE!!
HE HAS FORSAKEN US AND HAS GONE OUT TO POUR HIS BLESSINGS, WHICH WE RIGHTFULLY DESERVE, UNTO HIS CHILDREN!!

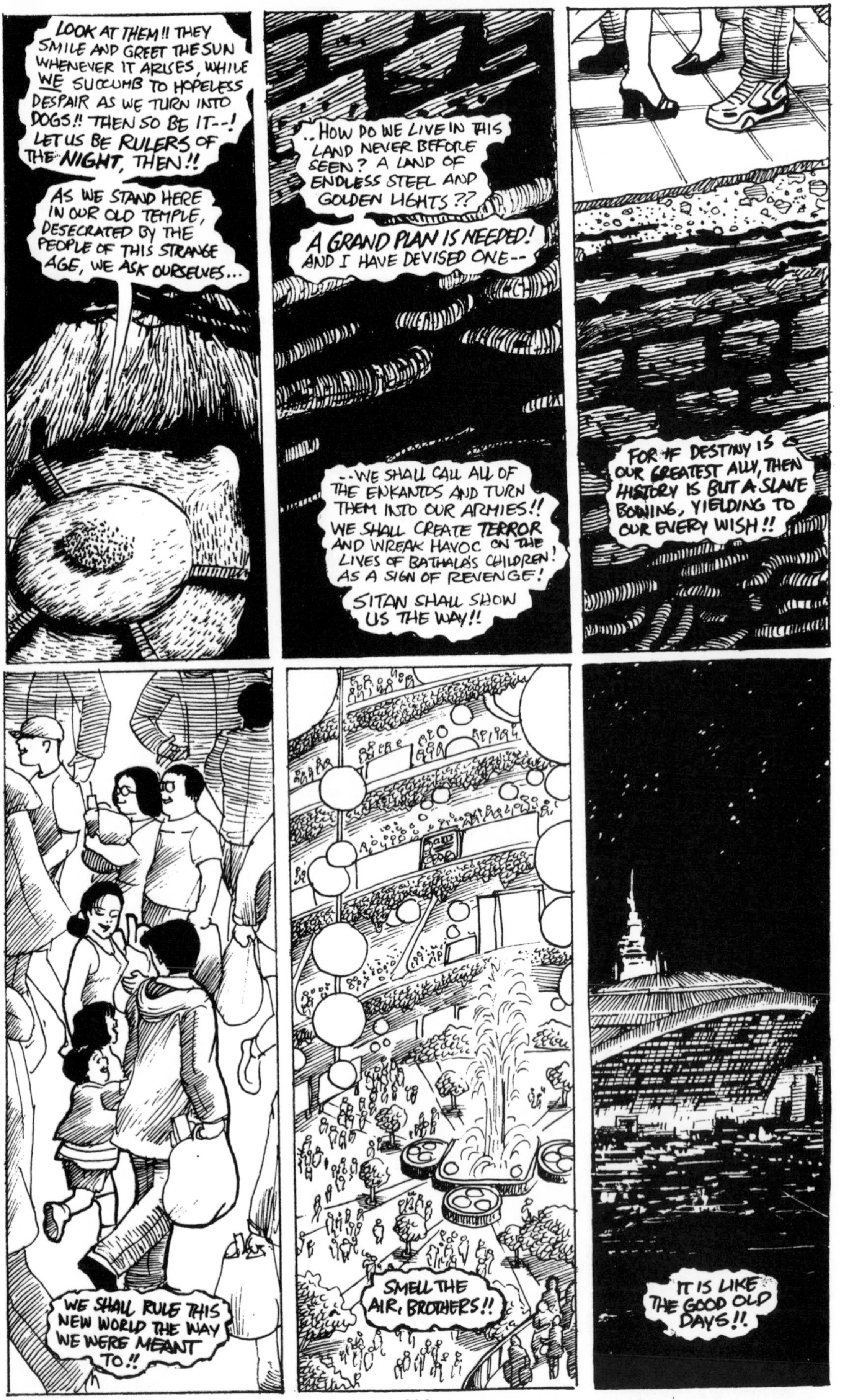
LOOK AT THEM!! THEY SMILE AND GREET THE SUN WHENEVER IT ARISES, WHILE WE SUCCUMB TO HOPELESS DESPAIR AS WE TURN INTO DOGS!! THEN SO BE IT--! LET US BE RULERS OF THE NIGHT, THEN!!
AS WE STAND HERE IN OUR OLD TEMPLE, DESECRATED BY THE PEOPLE OF THIS STRANGE AGE, WE ASK OURSELVES...
..HOW DO WE LIVE IN THIS LAND NEVER BEFORE SEEN? A LAND OF ENDLESS STEEL AND GOLDEN LIGHTS??
A GRAND PLAN IS NEEDED! AND I HAVE DEVISED ONE--
--WE SHALL CALL ALL OF THE ENKANTOS AND TURN THEM INTO OUR ARMIES!! WE SHALL CREATE TERROR AND WREAK HAVOC ON THE LIVES OF BATHALA'S CHILDREN! AS A SIGN OF REVENGE!
SITAN SHALL SHOW US THE WAY!!
FOR IF DESTINY IS OUR GREATEST ALLY, THEN HISTORY IS BUT A SLAVE BOWING, YIELDING TO OUR EVERY WISH!!
WE SHALL RULE THIS NEW WORLD THE WAY WE WERE MEANT TO!!
SMELL THE AIR, BROTHERS!!
IT IS LIKE THE GOOD OLD DAYS!!

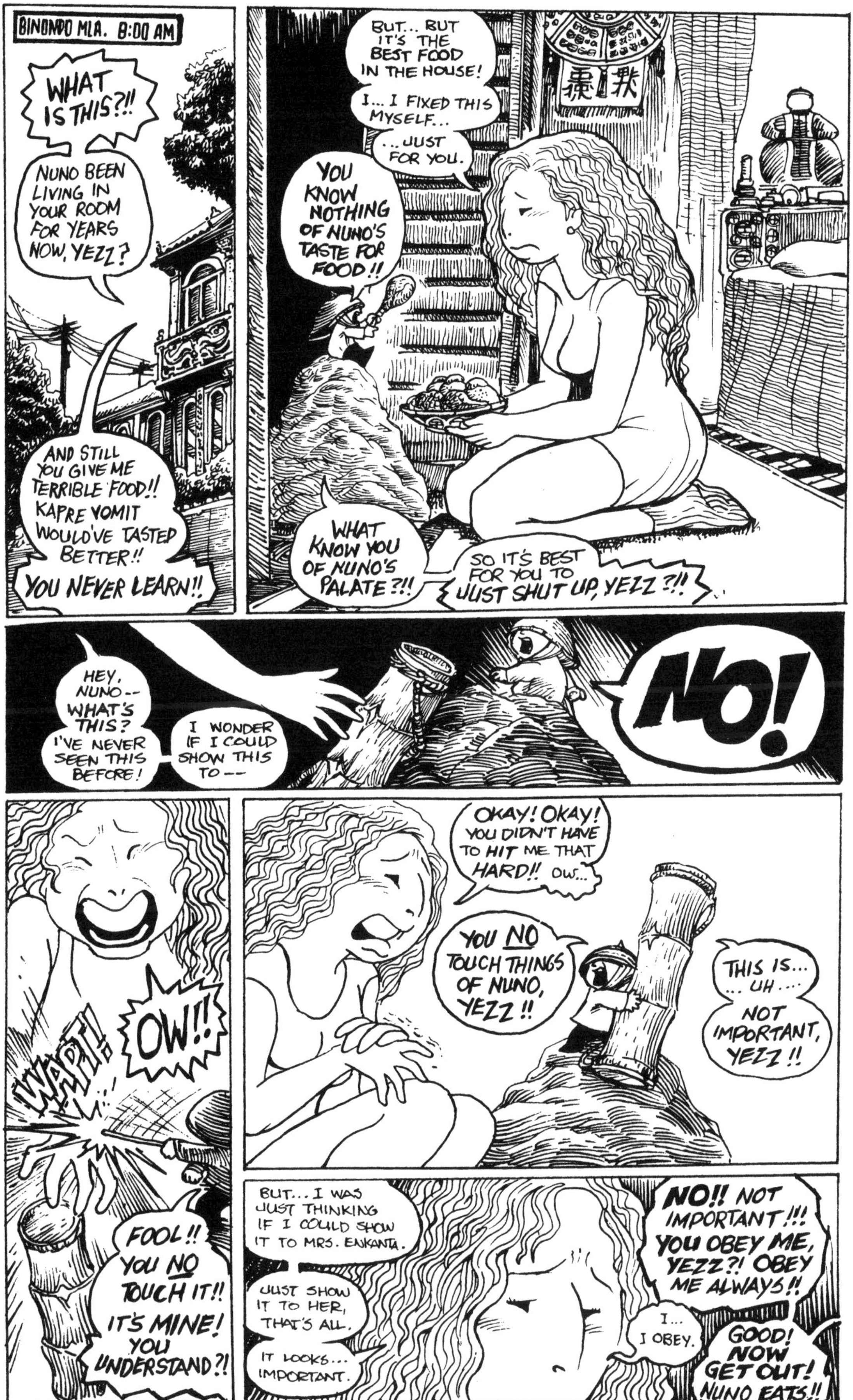
BINONDO MLA. 8:00 AM
WHAT IS THIS?!!
NUNO BEEN LIVING IN YOUR ROOM FOR YEARS NOW, YEZZ?
AND STILL YOU GIVE ME TERRIBLE FOOD!! KAPRE VOMIT WOULD'VE TASTED BETTER!!
YOU NEVER LEARN!!
BUT... BUT IT'S THE BEST FOOD IN THE HOUSE!
I... I FIXED THIS MYSELF...
...JUST FOR YOU.
YOU KNOW NOTHING OF NUNO'S TASTE FOR FOOD!!
WHAT KNOW YOU OF NUNO'S PALATE?!!
SO IT'S BEST FOR YOU TO JUST SHUT UP, YEZZ?!!
HEY, NUNO-- WHAT'S THIS? I'VE NEVER SEEN THIS BEFORE!
I WONDER IF I COULD SHOW THIS TO--
NO!
WAPP!!
OW!!
FOOL!! YOU NO TOUCH IT!! IT'S MINE! YOU UNDERSTAND?!!
OKAY! OKAY! YOU DIDN'T HAVE TO HIT ME THAT HARD!! OW...
YOU NO TOUCH THINGS OF NUNO, YEZZ!!
THIS IS... ...UH... NOT IMPORTANT, YEZZ!!
BUT... I WAS JUST THINKING IF I COULD SHOW IT TO MRS. ENKANTA.
JUST SHOW IT TO HER, THAT'S ALL.
IT LOOKS... IMPORTANT.
NO!! NOT IMPORTANT!!! YOU OBEY ME, YEZZ?! OBEY ME ALWAYS!!
I... I OBEY.
GOOD! NOW GET OUT! NUNO EATS!!

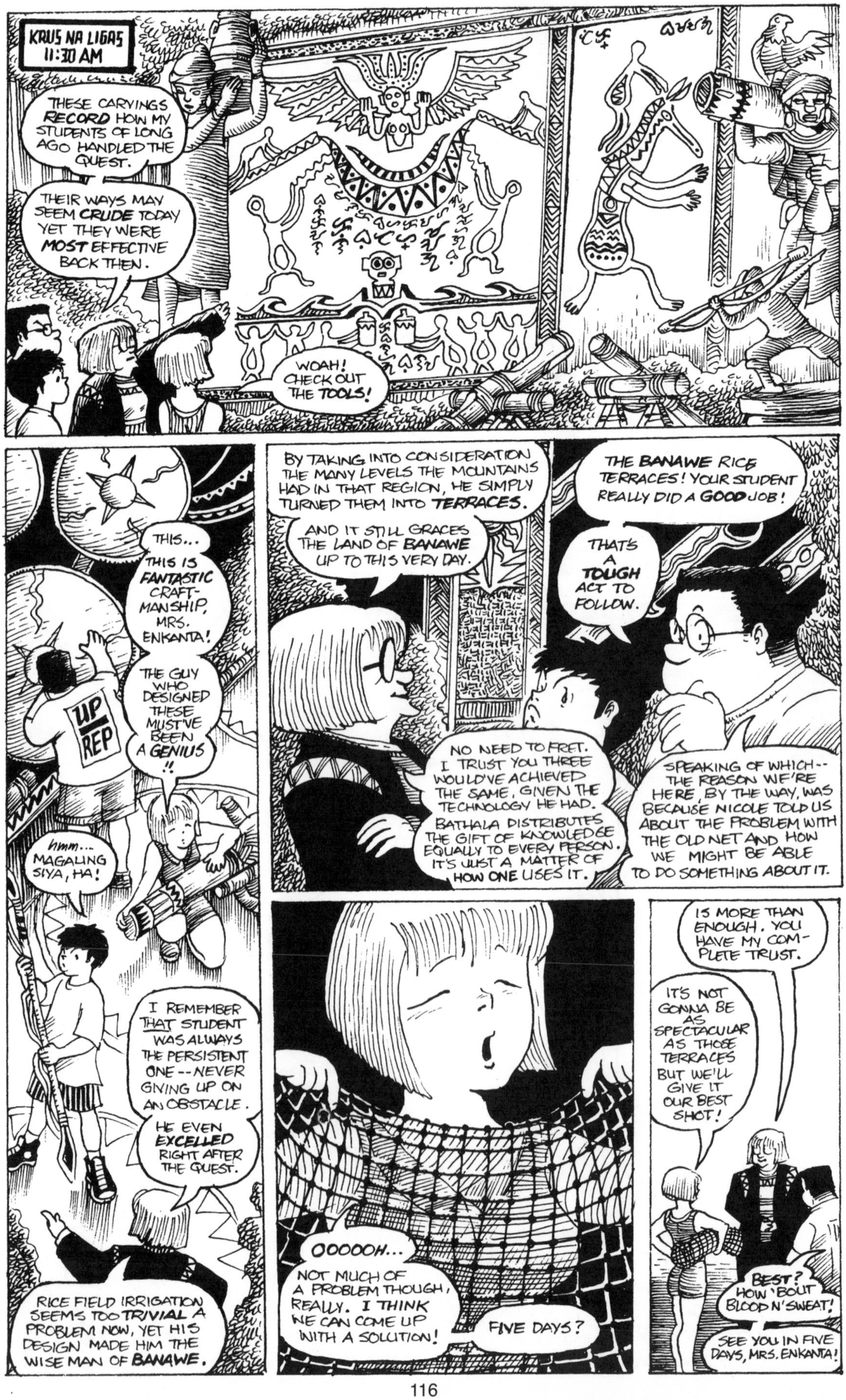
KRUS NA LIGAS 11:30 AM
THESE CARVINGS RECORD HOW MY STUDENTS OF LONG AGO HANDLED THE QUEST.
THEIR WAYS MAY SEEM CRUDE TODAY YET THEY WERE MOST EFFECTIVE BACK THEN.
WOAH! CHECK OUT THE TOOLS!
THIS... THIS IS FANTASTIC CRAFT-MANSHIP, MRS. ENKANTA!
THE GUY WHO DESIGNED THESE MUST'VE BEEN A GENIUS!!
UP REP
hmm... MAGALING SIYA, HA!
I REMEMBER THAT STUDENT WAS ALWAYS THE PERSISTENT ONE--NEVER GIVING UP ON AN OBSTACLE.
HE EVEN EXCELLED RIGHT AFTER THE QUEST.
RICE FIELD IRRIGATION SEEMS TOO TRIVIAL A PROBLEM NOW, YET HIS DESIGN MADE HIM THE WISE MAN OF BANAWE.
BY TAKING INTO CONSIDERATION THE MANY LEVELS THE MOUNTAINS HAD IN THAT REGION, HE SIMPLY TURNED THEM INTO TERRACES.
AND IT STILL GRACES THE LAND OF BANAWE UP TO THIS VERY DAY.
THE BANAWE RICE TERRACES! YOUR STUDENT REALLY DID A GOOD JOB!
THAT'S A TOUGH ACT TO FOLLOW.
NO NEED TO FRET. I TRUST YOU THREE WOULD'VE ACHIEVED THE SAME, GIVEN THE TECHNOLOGY HE HAD.
BATHALA DISTRIBUTES THE GIFT OF KNOWLEDGE EQUALLY TO EVERY PERSON. IT'S JUST A MATTER OF HOW ONE USES IT.
SPEAKING OF WHICH--THE REASON WE'RE HERE, BY THE WAY, WAS BECAUSE NICOLE TOLD US ABOUT THE PROBLEM WITH THE OLD NET AND HOW WE MIGHT BE ABLE TO DO SOMETHING ABOUT IT.
OOOOOH...
NOT MUCH OF A PROBLEM THOUGH, REALLY. I THINK WE CAN COME UP WITH A SOLUTION!
FIVE DAYS?
IS MORE THAN ENOUGH. YOU HAVE MY COM-PLETE TRUST.
IT'S NOT GONNA BE AS SPECTACULAR AS THOSE TERRACES BUT WE'LL GIVE IT OUR BEST SHOT!
BEST? HOW 'BOUT BLOOD N' SWEAT!
SEE YOU IN FIVE DAYS, MRS. ENKANTA!

YOUR HELP WITH THE EQUIPMENT AND ALL IS WELL APPRECIATED.

BUT YOU HAVE BEEN WORKING TOO LONG.

JUST FINISHING OFF THESE JARS, MA'AM.

YOU NEED REST.

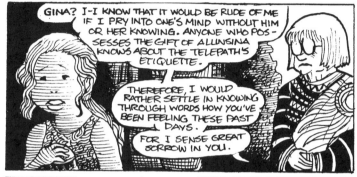

GINA? I-I KNOW THAT IT WOULD BE RUDE OF ME IF I PRY INTO ONE'S MIND WITHOUT HIM OR HER KNOWING. ANYONE WHO POSSESSES THE GIFT OF ALUNSINA KNOWS ABOUT THE TELEPATH'S ETIQUETTE.

THEREFORE, I WOULD RATHER SETTLE IN KNOWING THROUGH WORDS HOW YOU'VE BEEN FEELING THESE PAST DAYS.

FOR I SENSE GREAT SORROW IN YOU.

YOU DON'T SEEM TO GET ALONG WELL WITH THE OTHERS. BOB EVEN SAYS THAT YOU'RE TOO SILENT. WHY IS THAT??

WE ARE A FAMILY, GINA. SHARING ONE'S THOUGHTS WITH OTHERS HEALS THE INNER SOUL-- THE SAME IS TRUE IF ONE IS BURDENED BY SORROW. BATHALA MEANT "SHARING" TO BE JUST LIKE THAT.

I WOULD BE MORE THAN HAPPY TO HELP.... IF YOU CAN JUST TELL ME.

IS SOMETHING WRONG, CHILD?

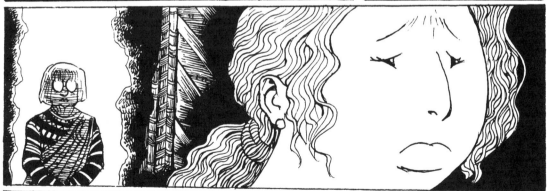

I'M FINE, MRS. ENKANTA.

REALLY, I AM.

117

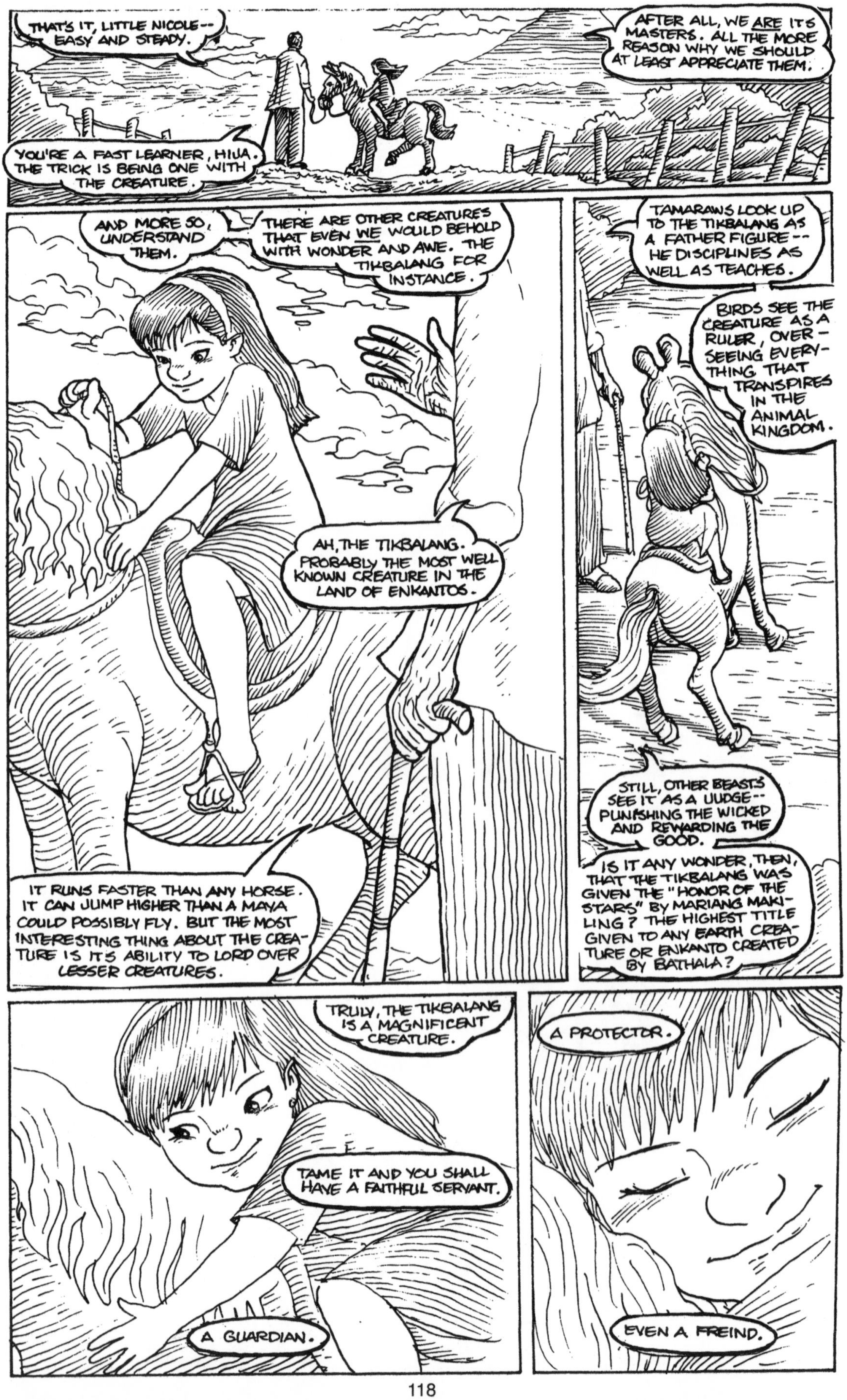
THAT'S IT, LITTLE NICOLE-- EASY AND STEADY.
AFTER ALL, WE ARE ITS MASTERS. ALL THE MORE REASON WHY WE SHOULD AT LEAST APPRECIATE THEM.
YOU'RE A FAST LEARNER, HIJA. THE TRICK IS BEING ONE WITH THE CREATURE.
AND MORE SO, UNDERSTAND THEM.
THERE ARE OTHER CREATURES THAT EVEN WE WOULD BEHOLD WITH WONDER AND AWE. THE TIKBALANG FOR INSTANCE.
AH, THE TIKBALANG. PROBABLY THE MOST WELL KNOWN CREATURE IN THE LAND OF ENKANTOS.
IT RUNS FASTER THAN ANY HORSE. IT CAN JUMP HIGHER THAN A MAYA COULD POSSIBLY FLY. BUT THE MOST INTERESTING THING ABOUT THE CREATURE IS ITS ABILITY TO LORD OVER LESSER CREATURES.
TAMARAWS LOOK UP TO THE TIKBALANG AS A FATHER FIGURE-- HE DISCIPLINES AS WELL AS TEACHES.
BIRDS SEE THE CREATURE AS A RULER, OVERSEEING EVERYTHING THAT TRANSPIRES IN THE ANIMAL KINGDOM.
STILL, OTHER BEASTS SEE IT AS A JUDGE-- PUNISHING THE WICKED AND REWARDING THE GOOD.
IS IT ANY WONDER, THEN, THAT THE TIKBALANG WAS GIVEN THE "HONOR OF THE STARS" BY MARIANG MAKILING? THE HIGHEST TITLE GIVEN TO ANY EARTH CREATURE OR ENKANTO CREATED BY BATHALA?
TRULY, THE TIKBALANG IS A MAGNIFICENT CREATURE.
TAME IT AND YOU SHALL HAVE A FAITHFUL SERVANT.
A GUARDIAN.
A PROTECTOR.
EVEN A FREIND.

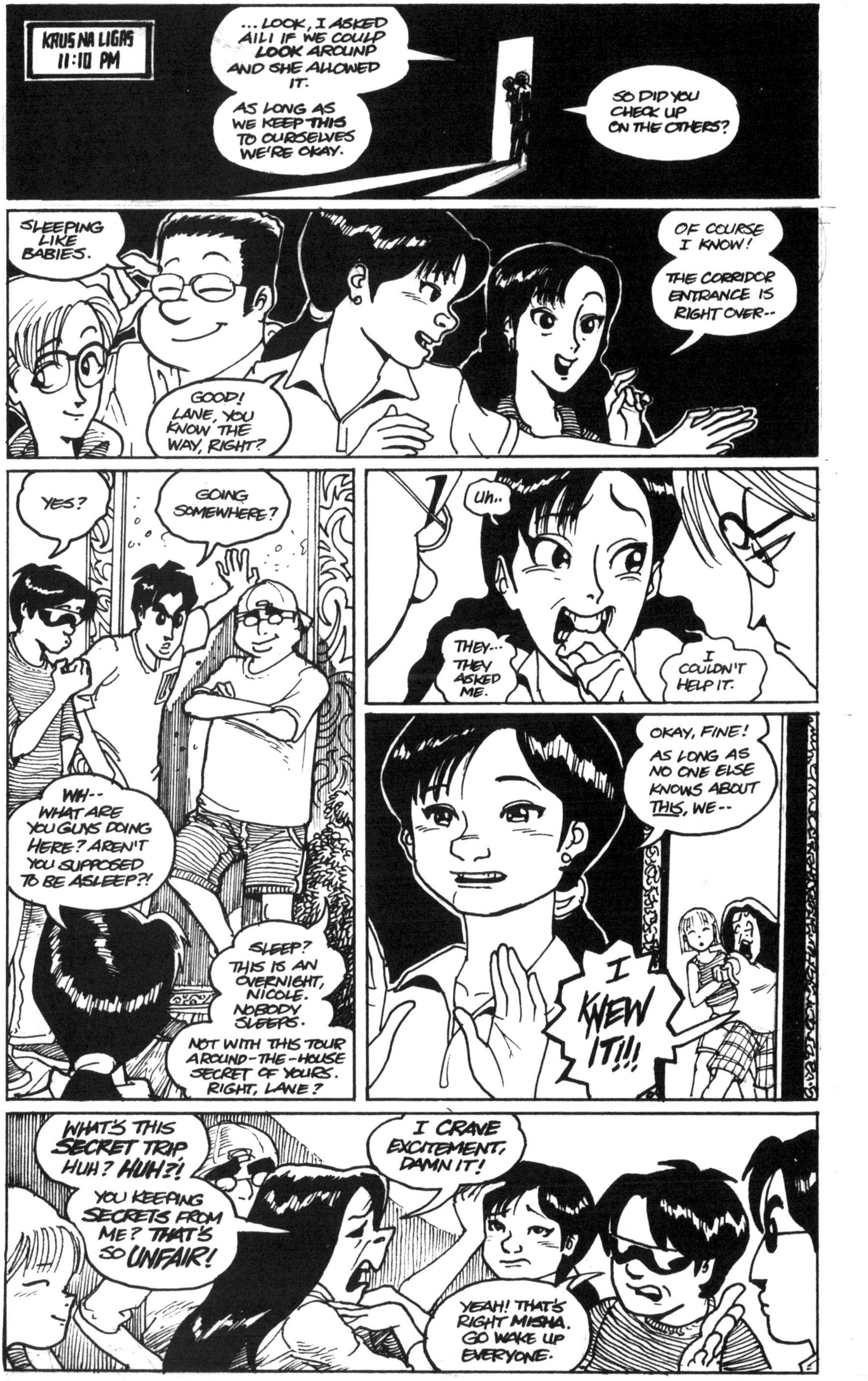
KRUS NA LIGAS
11:10 PM
... LOOK, I ASKED AILI IF WE COULD LOOK AROUND AND SHE ALLOWED IT.
AS LONG AS WE KEEP THIS TO OURSELVES WE'RE OKAY.
SO DID YOU CHECK UP ON THE OTHERS?
SLEEPING LIKE BABIES.
GOOD! LANE, YOU KNOW THE WAY, RIGHT?
OF COURSE I KNOW!
THE CORRIDOR ENTRANCE IS RIGHT OVER--
YES?
GOING SOMEWHERE?
WH-- WHAT ARE YOU GUYS DOING HERE? AREN'T YOU SUPPOSED TO BE ASLEEP?!
SLEEP? THIS IS AN OVERNIGHT, NICOLE. NOBODY SLEEPS.
NOT WITH THIS TOUR AROUND-THE-HOUSE SECRET OF YOURS. RIGHT, LANE?
Uh..
THEY... THEY ASKED ME.
I COULDN'T HELP IT.
OKAY, FINE! AS LONG AS NO ONE ELSE KNOWS ABOUT THIS, WE--
I KNEW IT!!!
WHAT'S THIS SECRET TRIP HUH? HUH?!
YOU KEEPING SECRETS FROM ME? THAT'S SO UNFAIR!
I CRAVE EXCITEMENT, DAMN IT!
YEAH! THAT'S RIGHT MISHA. GO WAKE UP EVERYONE.

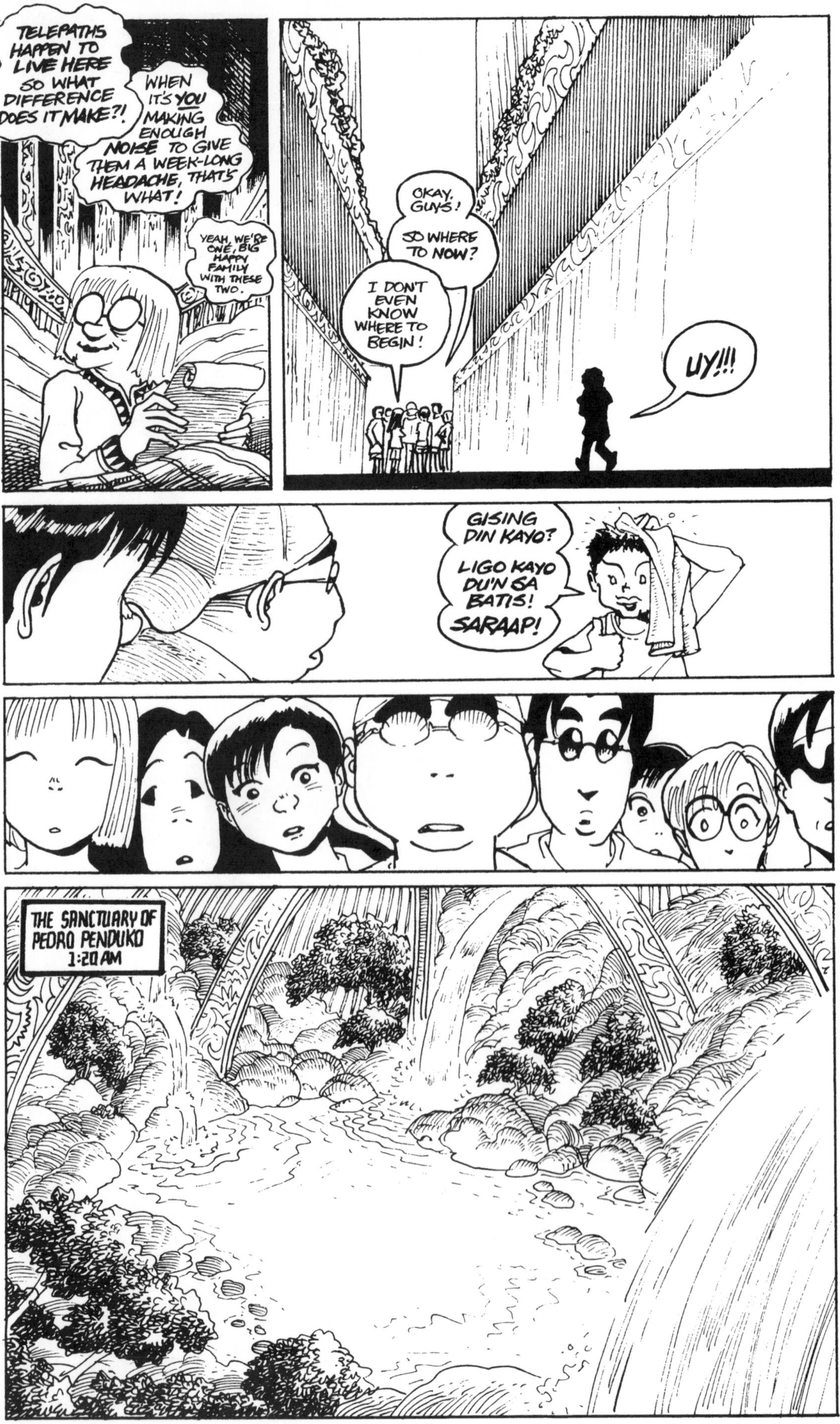
TELEPATHS HAPPEN TO LIVE HERE SO WHAT DIFFERENCE DOES IT MAKE?!
WHEN IT'S YOU MAKING ENOUGH NOISE TO GIVE THEM A WEEK-LONG HEADACHE, THAT'S WHAT!
YEAH, WE'RE ONE, BIG HAPPY FAMILY WITH THESE TWO.
OKAY, GUYS!
SO WHERE TO NOW?
I DON'T EVEN KNOW WHERE TO BEGIN!
UY!!!
GISING DIN KAYO?
LIGO KAYO DU'N SA BATIS!
SARAAP!
THE SANCTUARY OF PEDRO PENDUKO 1:20 AM

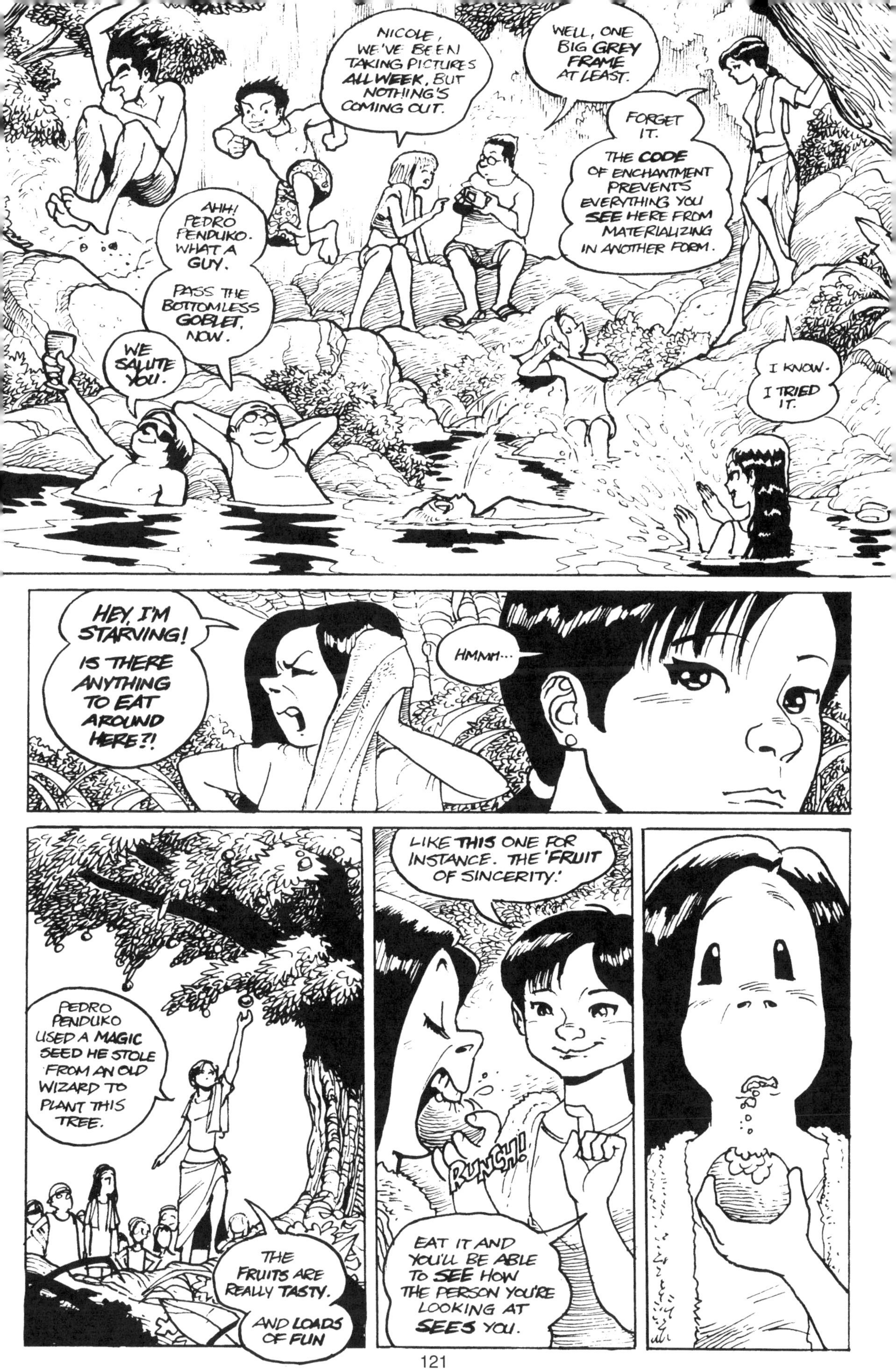
NICOLE, WE'VE BEEN TAKING PICTURES ALL WEEK, BUT NOTHING'S COMING OUT.
WELL, ONE BIG GREY FRAME AT LEAST.
FORGET IT.
THE CODE OF ENCHANTMENT PREVENTS EVERYTHING YOU SEE HERE FROM MATERIALIZING IN ANOTHER FORM.
AHH! PEDRO PENDUKO. WHAT A GUY.
PASS THE BOTTOMLESS GOBLET, NOW.
WE SALUTE YOU.
I KNOW. I TRIED IT.
HEY, I'M STARVING!
IS THERE ANYTHING TO EAT AROUND HERE?!
HMMM...
PEDRO PENDUKO USED A MAGIC SEED HE STOLE FROM AN OLD WIZARD TO PLANT THIS TREE.
THE FRUITS ARE REALLY TASTY.
AND LOADS OF FUN
LIKE THIS ONE FOR INSTANCE. THE 'FRUIT OF SINCERITY.'
RUNCH!
EAT IT AND YOU'LL BE ABLE TO SEE HOW THE PERSON YOU'RE LOOKING AT SEES YOU.

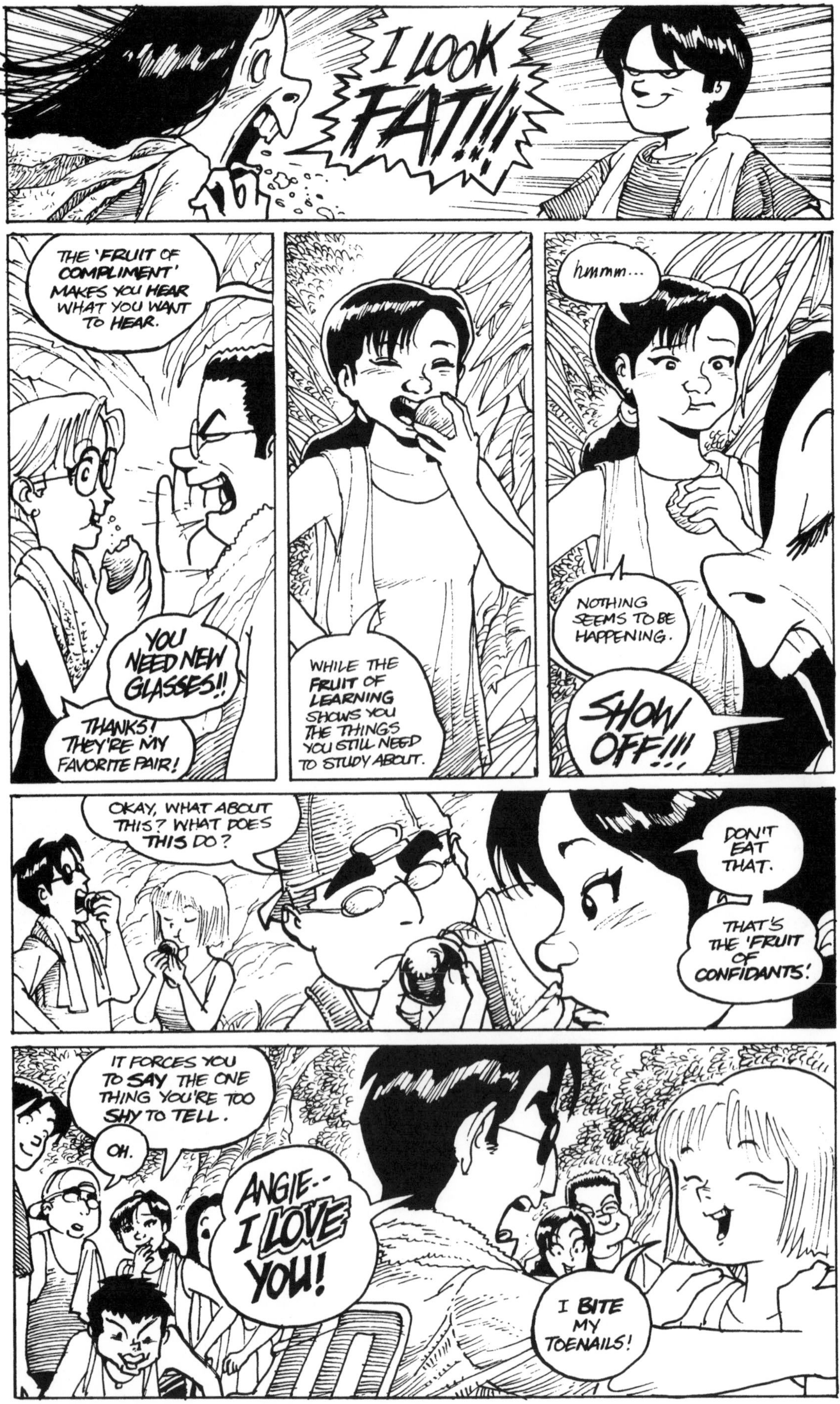
I LOOK FAT!!
THE 'FRUIT OF COMPLIMENT' MAKES YOU HEAR WHAT YOU WANT TO HEAR.
YOU NEED NEW GLASSES!!
THANKS! THEY'RE MY FAVORITE PAIR!
WHILE THE FRUIT OF LEARNING SHOWS YOU THE THINGS YOU STILL NEED TO STUDY ABOUT.
hmmm...
NOTHING SEEMS TO BE HAPPENING.
SHOW OFF!!!
OKAY, WHAT ABOUT THIS? WHAT DOES THIS DO?
DON'T EAT THAT.
THAT'S THE 'FRUIT OF CONFIDANTS'.
IT FORCES YOU TO SAY THE ONE THING YOU'RE TOO SHY TO TELL.
OH.
ANGIE-- I LOVE YOU!
I BITE MY TOENAILS!

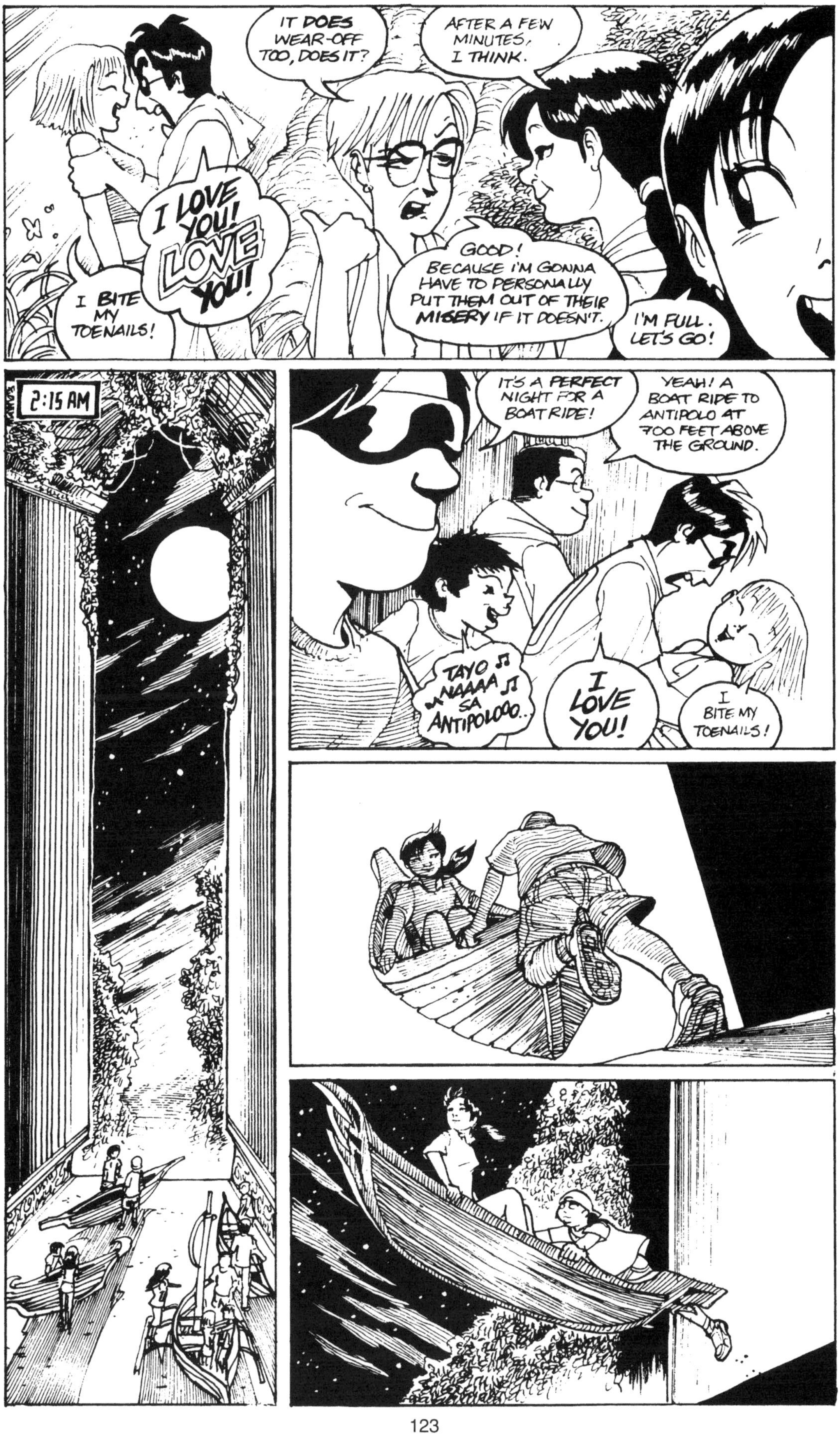

IT DOES WEAR-OFF TOO, DOES IT?
AFTER A FEW MINUTES, I THINK.
I LOVE YOU! LOVE YOU!
I BITE MY TOENAILS!
GOOD! BECAUSE I'M GONNA HAVE TO PERSONALLY PUT THEM OUT OF THEIR MISERY IF IT DOESN'T.
I'M FULL. LET'S GO!
2:15 AM
IT'S A PERFECT NIGHT FOR A BOAT RIDE!
YEAH! A BOAT RIDE TO ANTIPOLO AT 700 FEET ABOVE THE GROUND.
TAYO NAAAA SA ANTIPOLOOO..
I LOVE YOU!
I BITE MY TOENAILS!

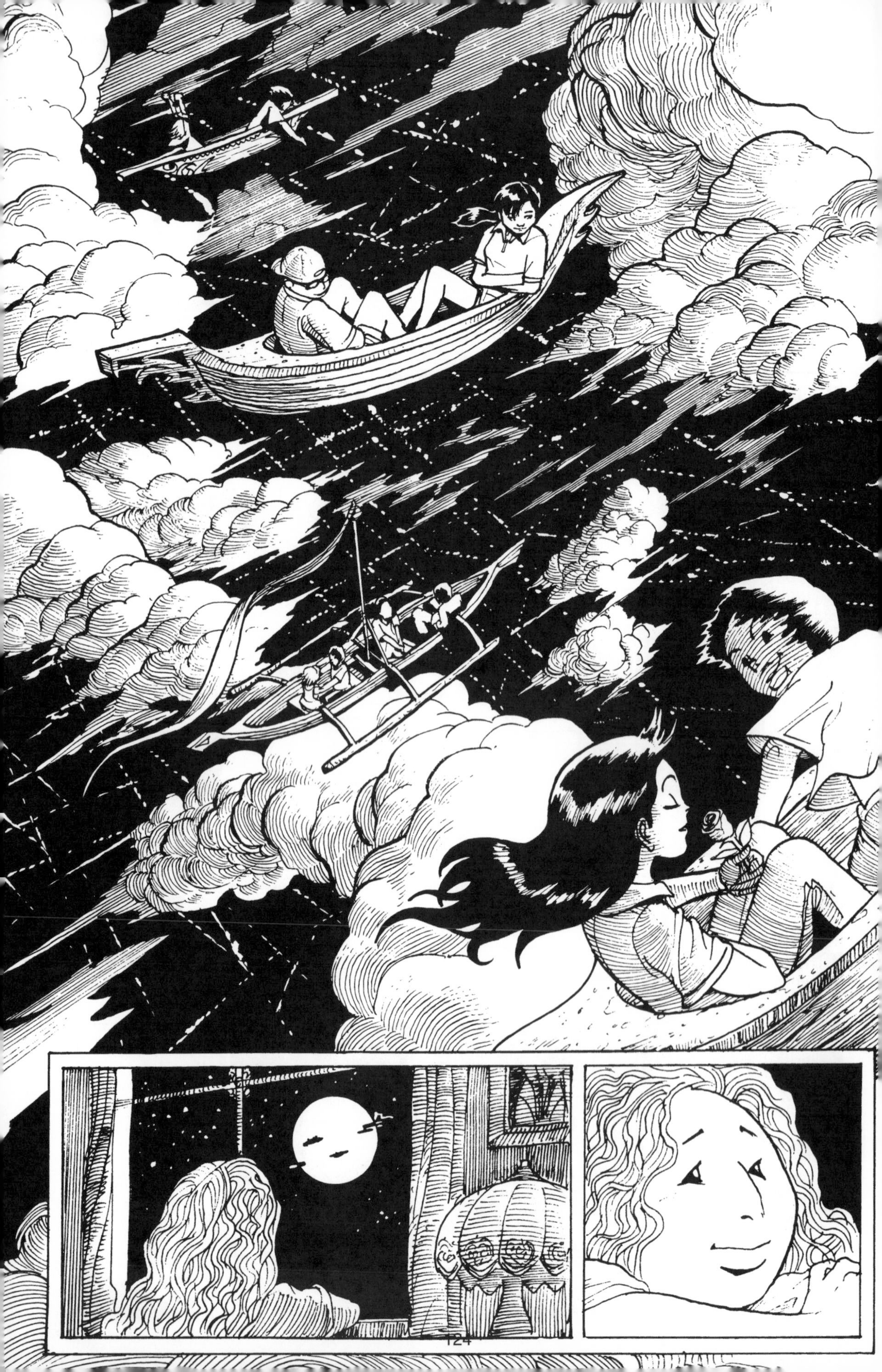

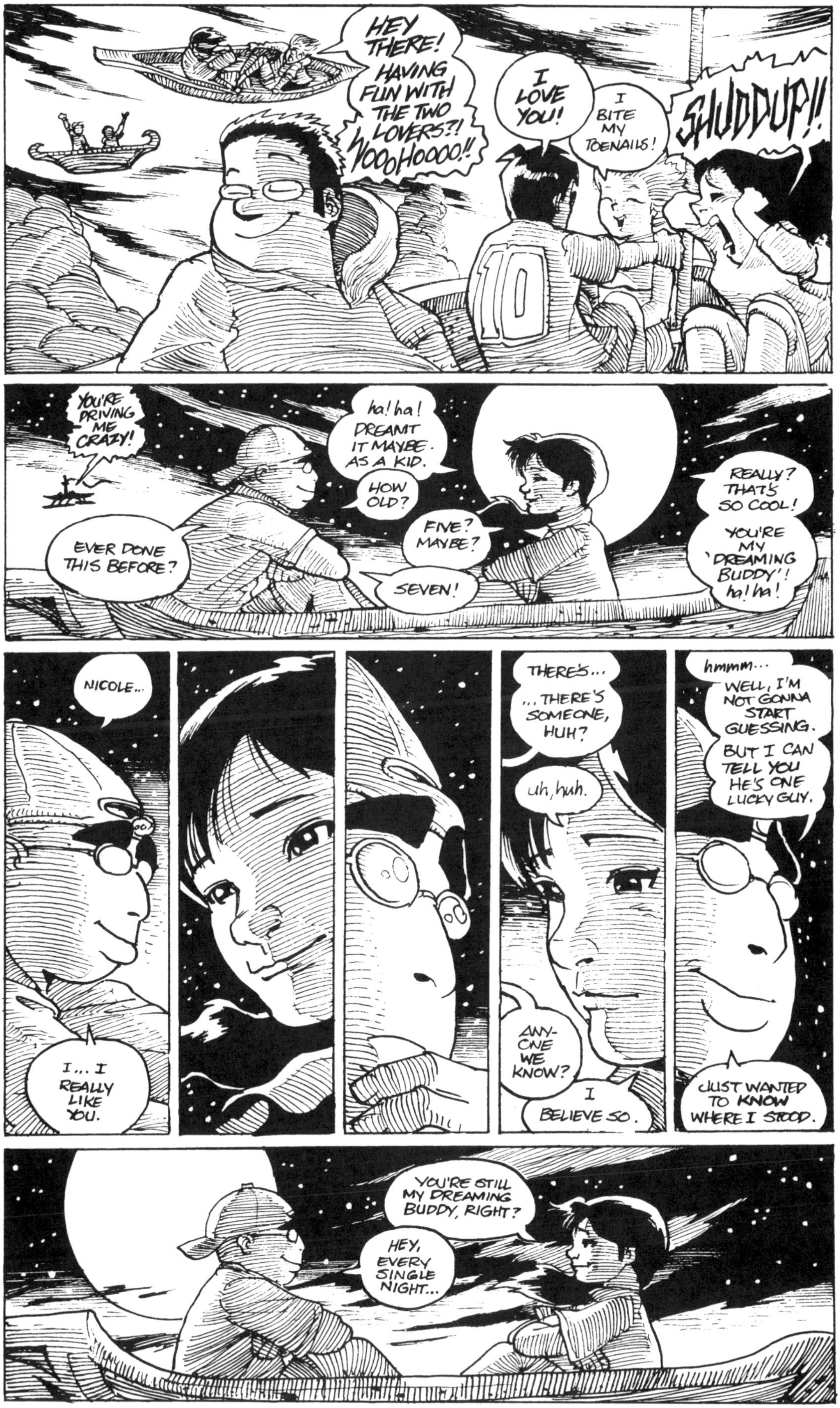
HEY THERE! HAVING FUN WITH THE TWO LOVERS?! WOOOHOOOO!!
I LOVE YOU!
I BITE MY TOENAILS!
SHUDDUP!!
YOU'RE DRIVING ME CRAZY!
EVER DONE THIS BEFORE?
ha! ha! DREAMT IT MAYBE. AS A KID.
HOW OLD?
FIVE? MAYBE?
SEVEN!
REALLY? THAT'S SO COOL!
YOU'RE MY 'DREAMING BUDDY'! ha! ha!
NICOLE...
I... I REALLY LIKE YOU.
THERE'S...
...THERE'S SOMEONE, HUH?
uh, huh.
ANY-ONE WE KNOW?
I BELIEVE SO.
hmmm...
WELL, I'M NOT GONNA START GUESSING.
BUT I CAN TELL YOU HE'S ONE LUCKY GUY.
JUST WANTED TO KNOW WHERE I STOOD.
YOU'RE STILL MY DREAMING BUDDY, RIGHT?
HEY, EVERY SINGLE NIGHT...

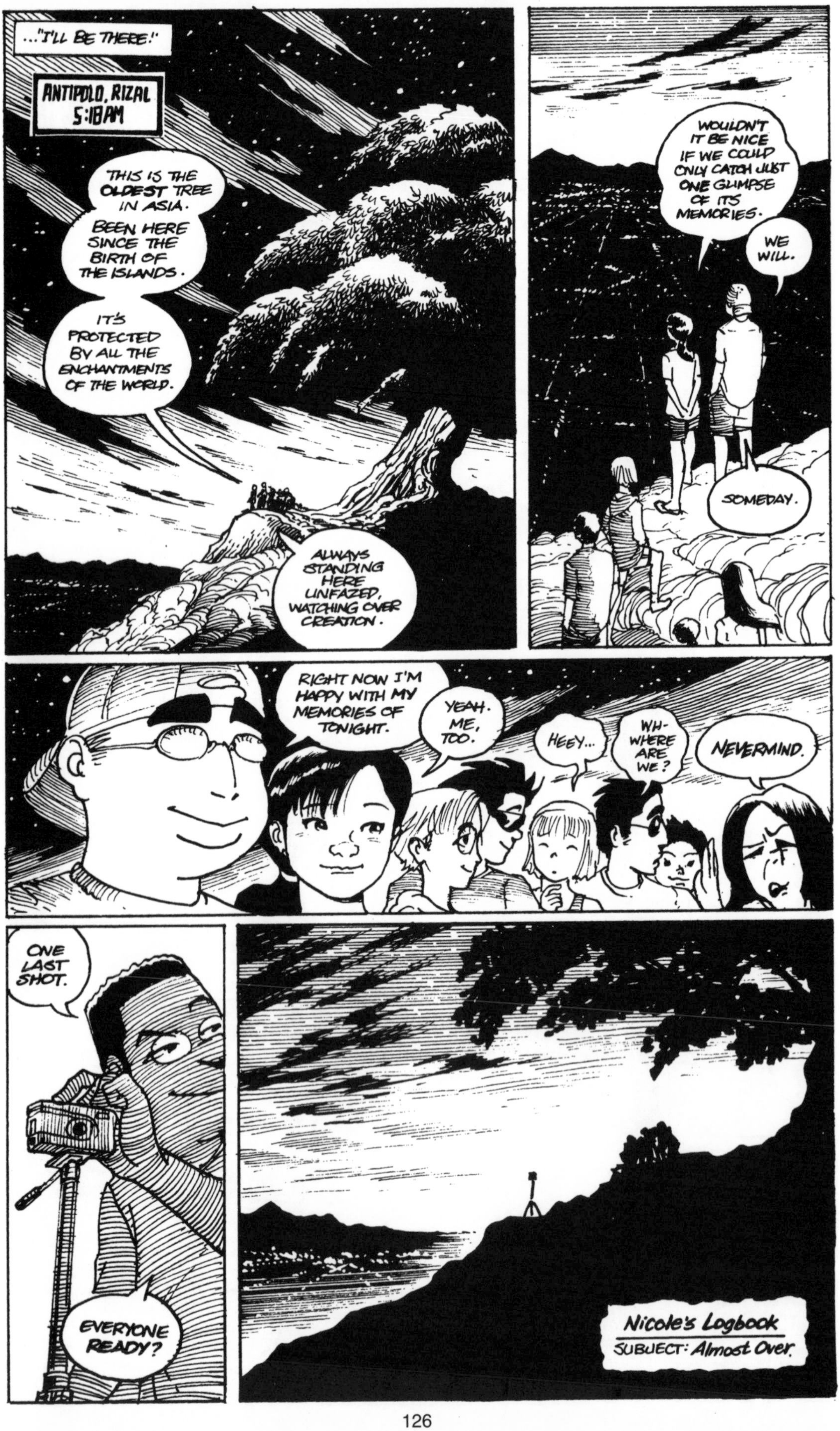
..."I'LL BE THERE!"
ANTIPOLO, RIZAL 5:18AM
THIS IS THE OLDEST TREE IN ASIA.
BEEN HERE SINCE THE BIRTH OF THE ISLANDS.
IT'S PROTECTED BY ALL THE ENCHANTMENTS OF THE WORLD.
ALWAYS STANDING HERE UNFAZED, WATCHING OVER CREATION.
WOULDN'T IT BE NICE IF WE COULD ONLY CATCH JUST ONE GLIMPSE OF ITS MEMORIES.
WE WILL.
SOMEDAY.
RIGHT NOW I'M HAPPY WITH MY MEMORIES OF TONIGHT.
YEAH. ME, TOO.
HEEY...
WH- WHERE ARE WE?
NEVERMIND.
ONE LAST SHOT.
EVERYONE READY?
Nicole's Logbook
SUBJECT: Almost Over.

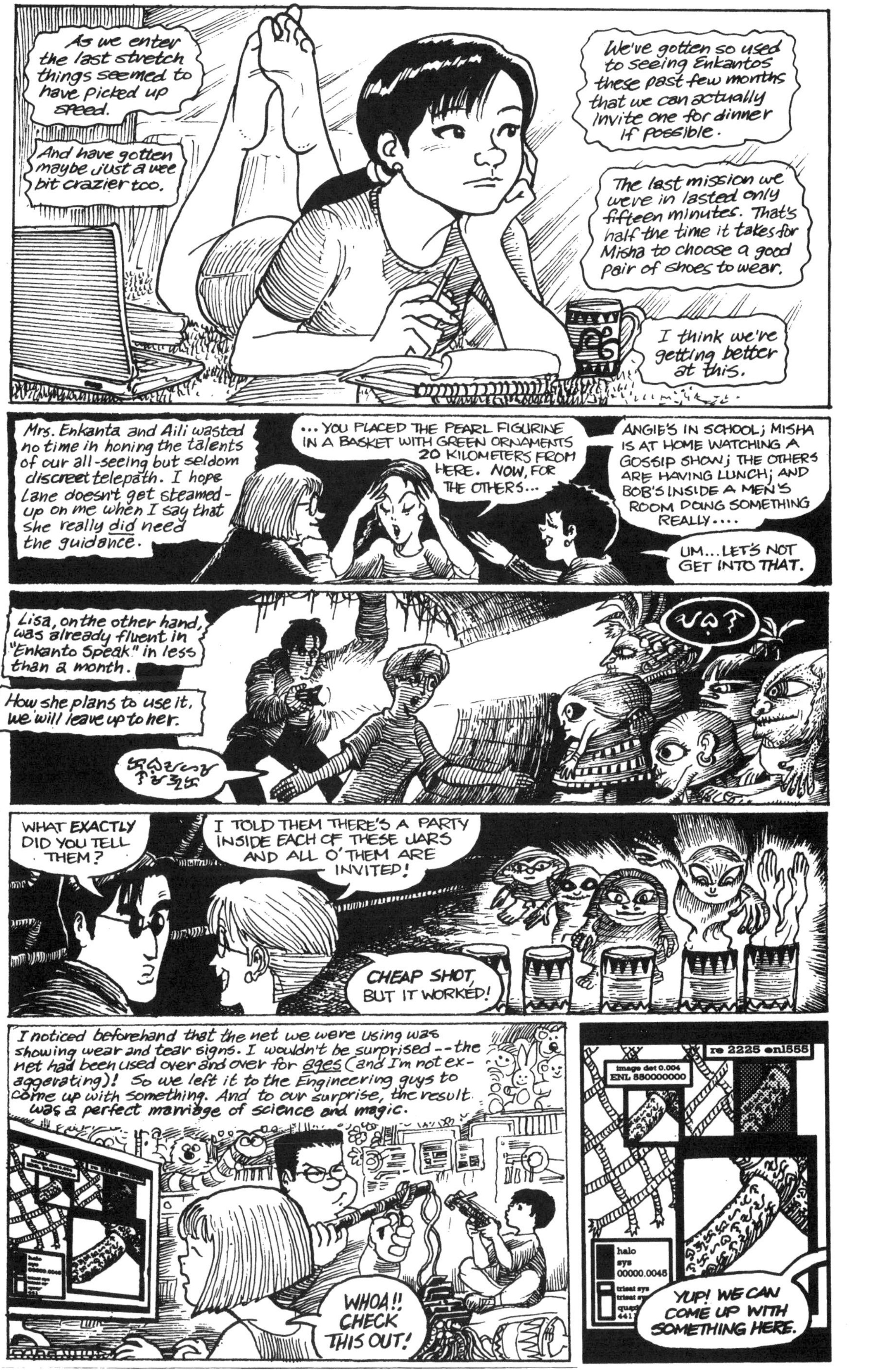
As we enter the last stretch things seemed to have picked up speed.
And have gotten maybe just a wee bit crazier too.
We've gotten so used to seeing Enkantos these past few months that we can actually invite one for dinner if possible.
The last mission we were in lasted only fifteen minutes. That's half the time it takes for Misha to choose a good pair of shoes to wear.
I think we're getting better at this.
Mrs. Enkanta and Aili wasted no time in honing the talents of our all-seeing but seldom discreet telepath. I hope Lane doesn't get steamed-up on me when I say that she really did need the guidance.
...YOU PLACED THE PEARL FIGURINE IN A BASKET WITH GREEN ORNAMENTS 20 KILOMETERS FROM HERE. NOW, FOR THE OTHERS...
ANGIE'S IN SCHOOL; MISHA IS AT HOME WATCHING A GOSSIP SHOW; THE OTHERS ARE HAVING LUNCH; AND BOB'S INSIDE A MEN'S ROOM DOING SOMETHING REALLY....
UM...LET'S NOT GET INTO THAT.
Lisa, on the other hand, was already fluent in "Enkanto Speak" in less than a month.
How she plans to use it, we will leave up to her.
WHAT EXACTLY DID YOU TELL THEM?
I TOLD THEM THERE'S A PARTY INSIDE EACH OF THESE JARS AND ALL O' THEM ARE INVITED!
CHEAP SHOT, BUT IT WORKED!
I noticed beforehand that the net we were using was showing wear and tear signs. I wouldn't be surprised -- the net had been used over and over for ages (and I'm not exaggerating)! So we left it to the Engineering guys to come up with something. And to our surprise, the result was a perfect marriage of science and magic.
WHOA!! CHECK THIS OUT!
re 2225 enl555
image det 0.004
ENL 550000000
halo
sys
00000.0045
YUP! WE CAN COME UP WITH SOMETHING HERE.

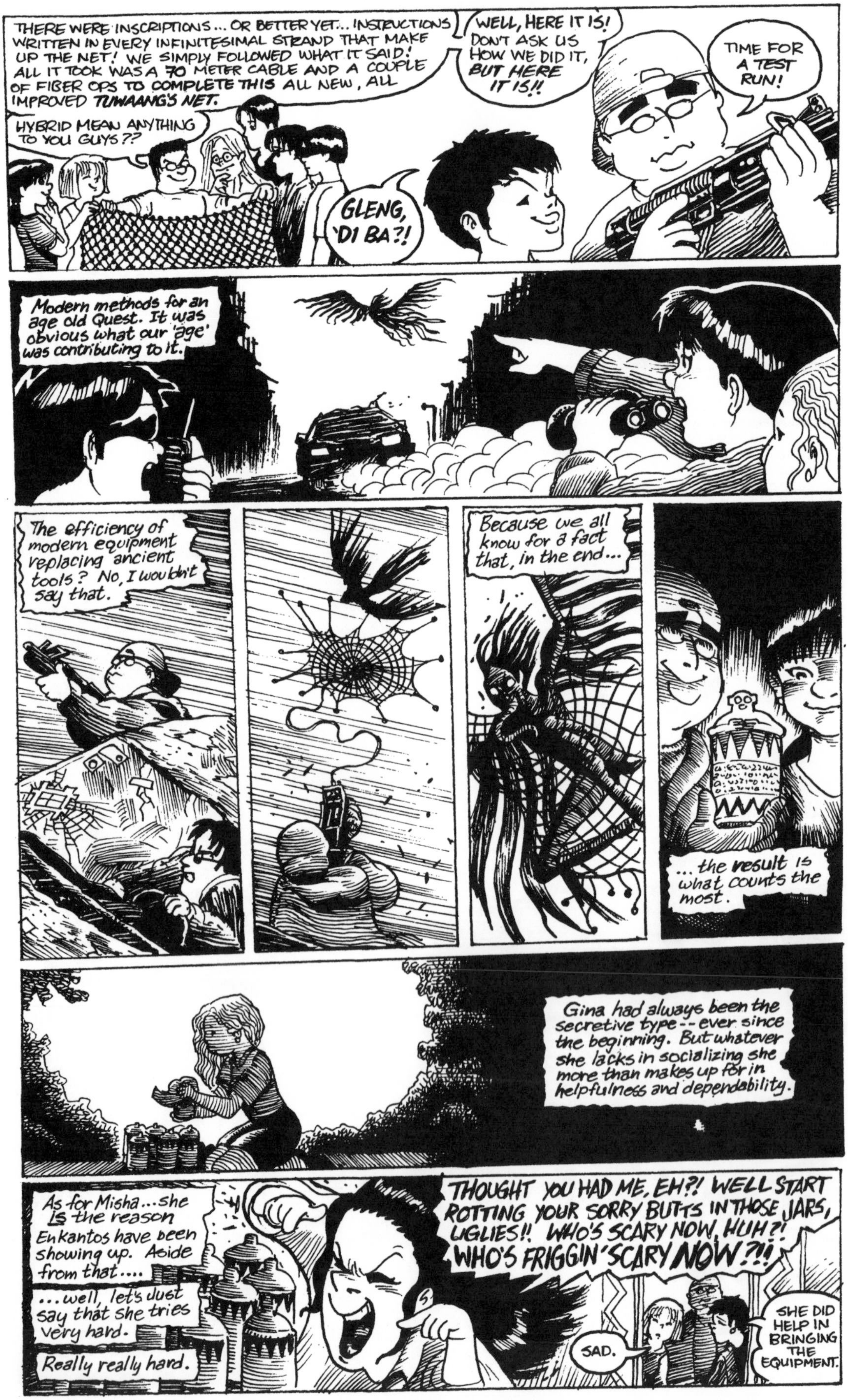

THERE WERE INSCRIPTIONS... OR BETTER YET... INSTRUCTIONS WRITTEN IN EVERY INFINITESIMAL STRAND THAT MAKE UP THE NET! WE SIMPLY FOLLOWED WHAT IT SAID! ALL IT TOOK WAS A 70 METER CABLE AND A COUPLE OF FIBER OPS TO COMPLETE THIS ALL NEW, ALL IMPROVED TUWAANG'S NET.
HYBRID MEAN ANYTHING TO YOU GUYS??
WELL, HERE IT IS! DON'T ASK US HOW WE DID IT, BUT HERE IT IS!!
TIME FOR A TEST RUN!
GLENG, 'DI BA?!
Modern methods for an age old Quest. It was obvious what our 'age' was contributing to it.
The efficiency of modern equipment replacing ancient tools? No, I wouldn't say that.
Because we all know for a fact that, in the end...
... the result is what counts the most.
Gina had always been the secretive type -- ever since the beginning. But whatever she lacks in socializing she more than makes up for in helpfulness and dependability.
As for Misha... she IS the reason Enkantos have been showing up. Aside from that....
... well, let's just say that she tries very hard.
Really really hard.
THOUGHT YOU HAD ME, EH?! WELL START ROTTING YOUR SORRY BUTTS IN THOSE JARS, UGLIES!! WHO'S SCARY NOW, HUH?! WHO'S FRIGGIN' SCARY NOW?!!
SAD.
SHE DID HELP IN BRINGING THE EQUIPMENT.

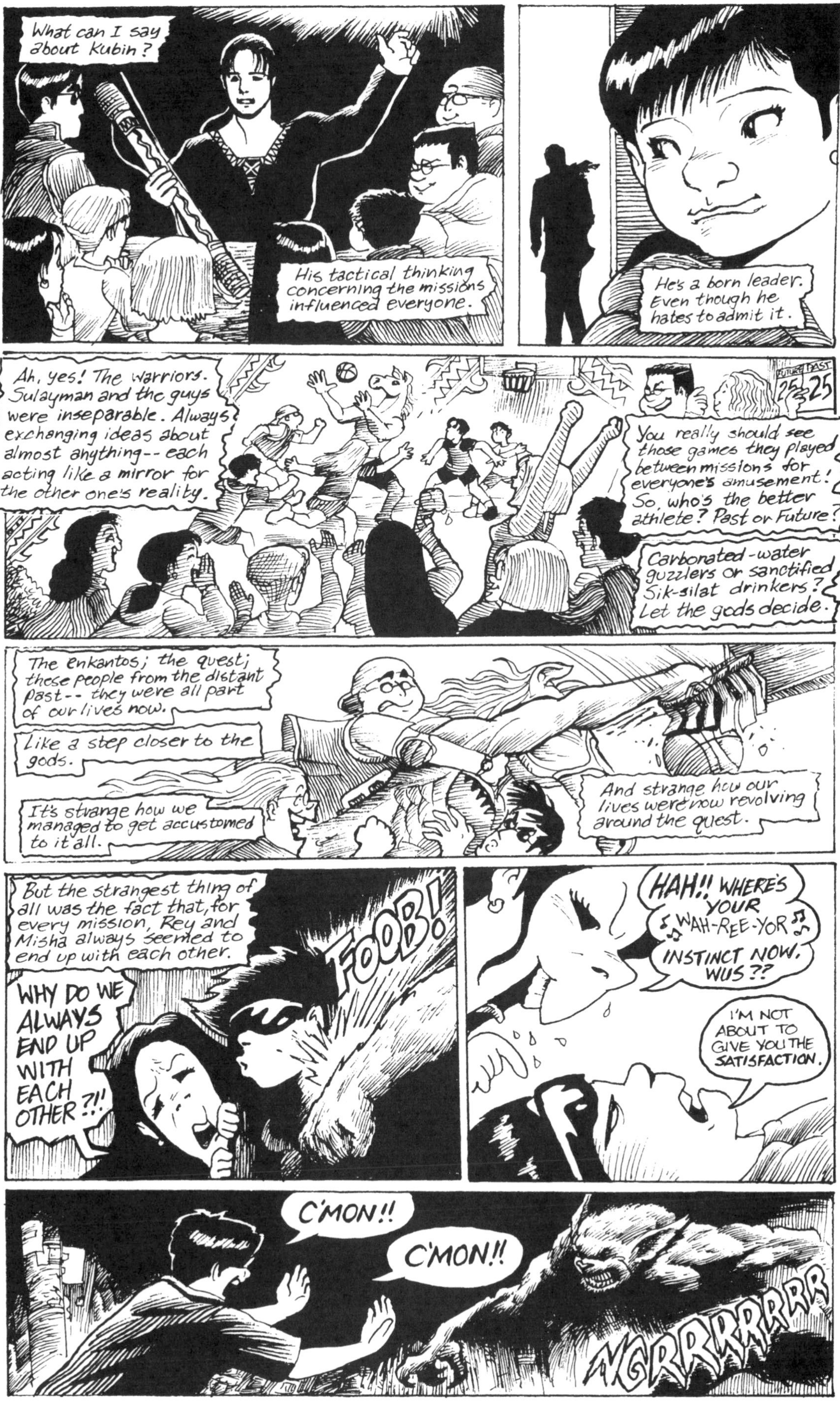
What can I say about Kubin?
His tactical thinking concerning the missions influenced everyone.
He's a born leader. Even though he hates to admit it.
Ah, yes! The warriors. Sulayman and the guys were inseparable. Always exchanging ideas about almost anything-- each acting like a mirror for the other one's reality.
FUTURE 25
PAST 25
You really should see those games they played between missions for everyone's amusement! So, who's the better athlete? Past or Future?
Carbonated-water guzzlers or sanctified Sik-silat drinkers? Let the gods decide.
The enkantos; the quest; these people from the distant past-- they were all part of our lives now.
Like a step closer to the gods.
It's strange how we managed to get accustomed to it all.
And strange how our lives were now revolving around the quest.
But the strangest thing of all was the fact that, for every mission, Rey and Misha always seemed to end up with each other.
FOOB!
WHY DO WE ALWAYS END UP WITH EACH OTHER?!!
HAH!! WHERE'S YOUR ♫WAH-REE-YOR♫ INSTINCT NOW, WUS??
I'M NOT ABOUT TO GIVE YOU THE SATISFACTION.
C'MON!!
C'MON!!
NGRRRRRRR

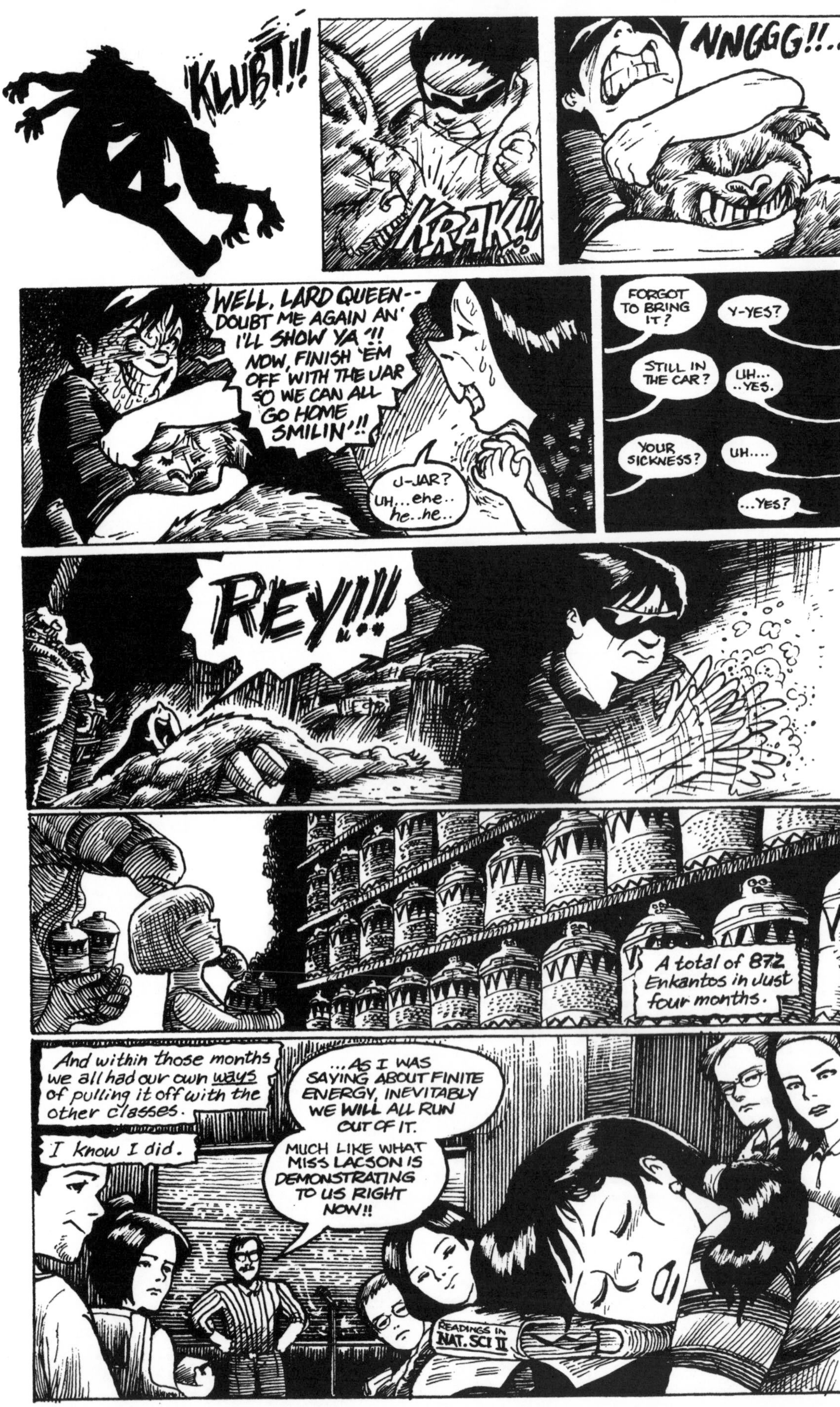
KLUBT!!
KRAK!!
NNGGG!!..
WELL, LARD QUEEN-- DOUBT ME AGAIN AN' I'LL SHOW YA'!! NOW, FINISH 'EM OFF WITH THE JAR SO WE CAN ALL GO HOME SMILIN'!!
J-JAR? UH...ehe.. he..he..
FORGOT TO BRING IT?
Y-YES?
STILL IN THE CAR?
UH... ..YES.
YOUR SICKNESS?
UH....
...YES?
REY!!!
A total of 872 Enkantos in just four months.
And within those months we all had our own ways of pulling it off with the other classes.
I know I did.
...AS I WAS SAYING ABOUT FINITE ENERGY, INEVITABLY WE WILL ALL RUN OUT OF IT.
MUCH LIKE WHAT MISS LACSON IS DEMONSTRATING TO US RIGHT NOW!!
READINGS IN NAT. SCI II

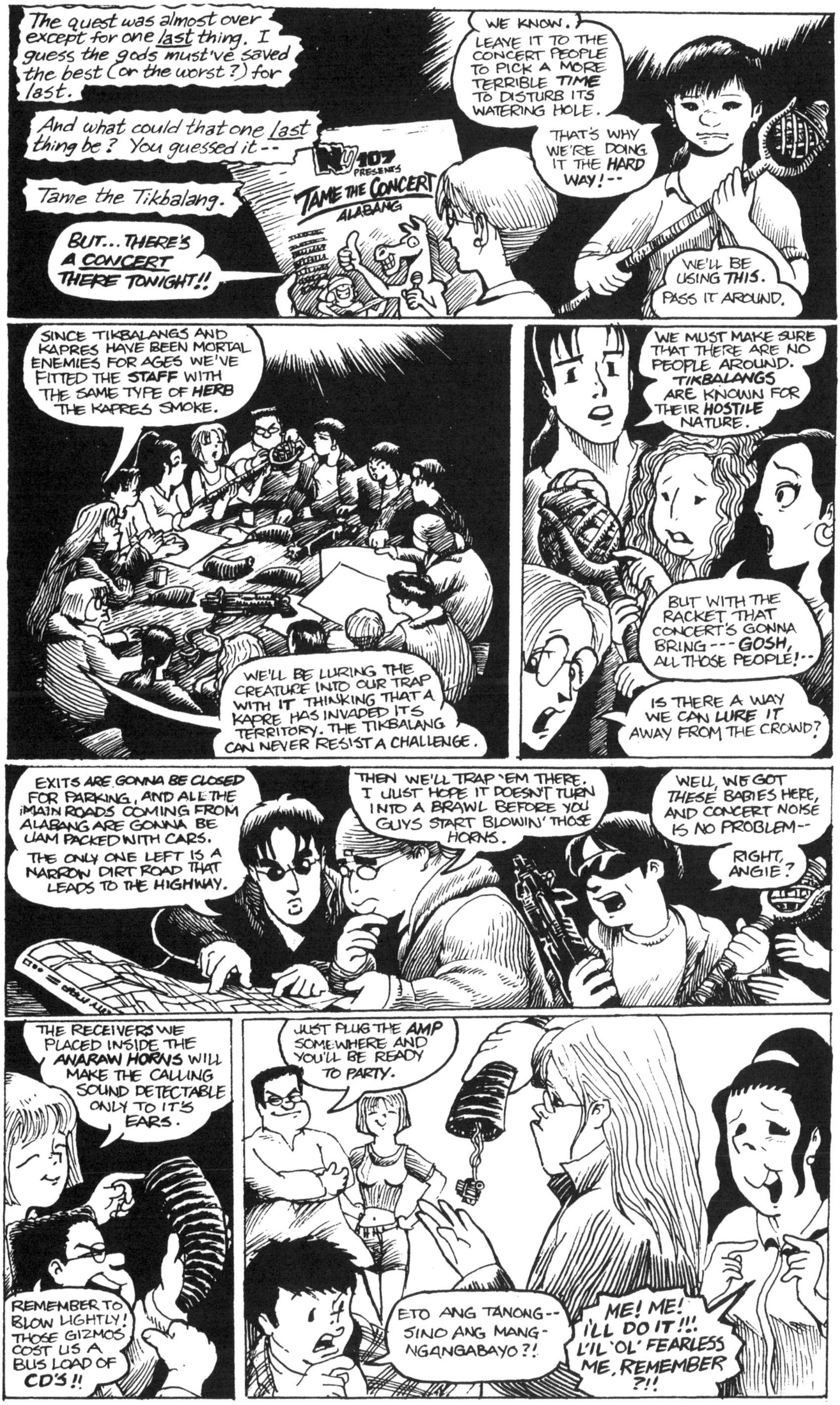

The quest was almost over except for one last thing. I guess the gods must've saved the best (or the worst?) for last.
And what could that one last thing be? You guessed it --
Tame the Tikbalang.
BUT... THERE'S A CONCERT THERE TONIGHT!!
NU 107 PRESENTS TAME THE CONCERT ALABANG
WE KNOW.
LEAVE IT TO THE CONCERT PEOPLE TO PICK A MORE TERRIBLE TIME TO DISTURB ITS WATERING HOLE.
THAT'S WHY WE'RE DOING IT THE HARD WAY! --
WE'LL BE USING THIS.
PASS IT AROUND.
SINCE TIKBALANGS AND KAPRES HAVE BEEN MORTAL ENEMIES FOR AGES WE'VE FITTED THE STAFF WITH THE SAME TYPE OF HERB THE KAPRES SMOKE.
WE'LL BE LURING THE CREATURE INTO OUR TRAP WITH IT THINKING THAT A KAPRE HAS INVADED ITS TERRITORY. THE TIKBALANG CAN NEVER RESIST A CHALLENGE.
WE MUST MAKE SURE THAT THERE ARE NO PEOPLE AROUND. TIKBALANGS ARE KNOWN FOR THEIR HOSTILE NATURE.
BUT WITH THE RACKET THAT CONCERT'S GONNA BRING --- GOSH, ALL THOSE PEOPLE! --
IS THERE A WAY WE CAN LURE IT AWAY FROM THE CROWD?
EXITS ARE GONNA BE CLOSED FOR PARKING, AND ALL THE MAIN ROADS COMING FROM ALABANG ARE GONNA BE JAM PACKED WITH CARS.
THE ONLY ONE LEFT IS A NARROW DIRT ROAD THAT LEADS TO THE HIGHWAY.
THEN WE'LL TRAP 'EM THERE. I JUST HOPE IT DOESN'T TURN INTO A BRAWL BEFORE YOU GUYS START BLOWIN' THOSE HORNS.
WELL, WE GOT THESE BABIES HERE, AND CONCERT NOISE IS NO PROBLEM --
RIGHT, ANGIE?
THE RECEIVERS WE PLACED INSIDE THE ANARAW HORNS WILL MAKE THE CALLING SOUND DETECTABLE ONLY TO IT'S EARS.
REMEMBER TO BLOW LIGHTLY! THOSE GIZMOS COST US A BUS LOAD OF CD'S!!
JUST PLUG THE AMP SOMEWHERE AND YOU'LL BE READY TO PARTY.
ETO ANG TANONG -- SINO ANG MANG-NGANGABAYO?!
ME! ME! I'LL DO IT!!! L'IL 'OL' FEARLESS ME, REMEMBER?!!

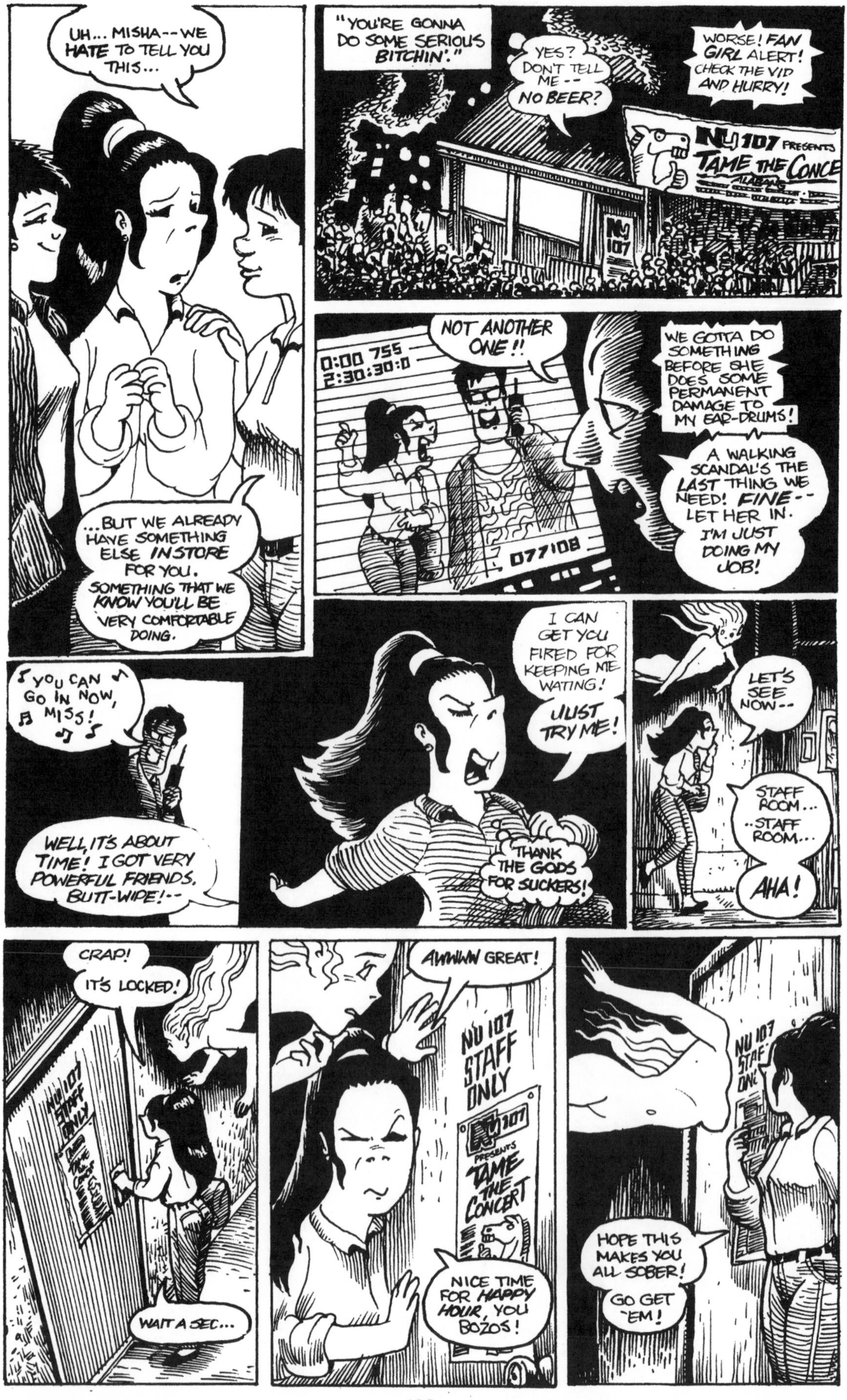
UH... MISHA--WE HATE TO TELL YOU THIS...
...BUT WE ALREADY HAVE SOMETHING ELSE INSTORE FOR YOU. SOMETHING THAT WE KNOW YOU'LL BE VERY COMFORTABLE DOING.
"YOU'RE GONNA DO SOME SERIOUS BITCHIN'."
YES? DON'T TELL ME -- NO BEER?
WORSE! FAN GIRL ALERT! CHECK THE VID AND HURRY!
NU 107 PRESENTS
TAME THE CONCE
0:00 755
2:30:30:0
NOT ANOTHER ONE!!
077108
WE GOTTA DO SOMETHING BEFORE SHE DOES SOME PERMANENT DAMAGE TO MY EAR-DRUMS!
A WALKING SCANDAL'S THE LAST THING WE NEED! FINE-- LET HER IN. I'M JUST DOING MY JOB!
YOU CAN GO IN NOW, MISS!
WELL, IT'S ABOUT TIME! I GOT VERY POWERFUL FRIENDS. BUTT-WIPE!--
I CAN GET YOU FIRED FOR KEEPING ME WAITING!
JUST TRY ME!
THANK THE GODS FOR SUCKERS!
LET'S SEE NOW--
STAFF ROOM... ..STAFF ROOM...
AHA!
CRAP!
IT'S LOCKED!
NU 107 STAFF ONLY
WAIT A SEC...
AWWWW GREAT!
NU 107 STAFF ONLY
NU 107 PRESENTS TAME THE CONCERT
NICE TIME FOR HAPPY HOUR, YOU BOZOS!
HOPE THIS MAKES YOU ALL SOBER!
GO GET 'EM!

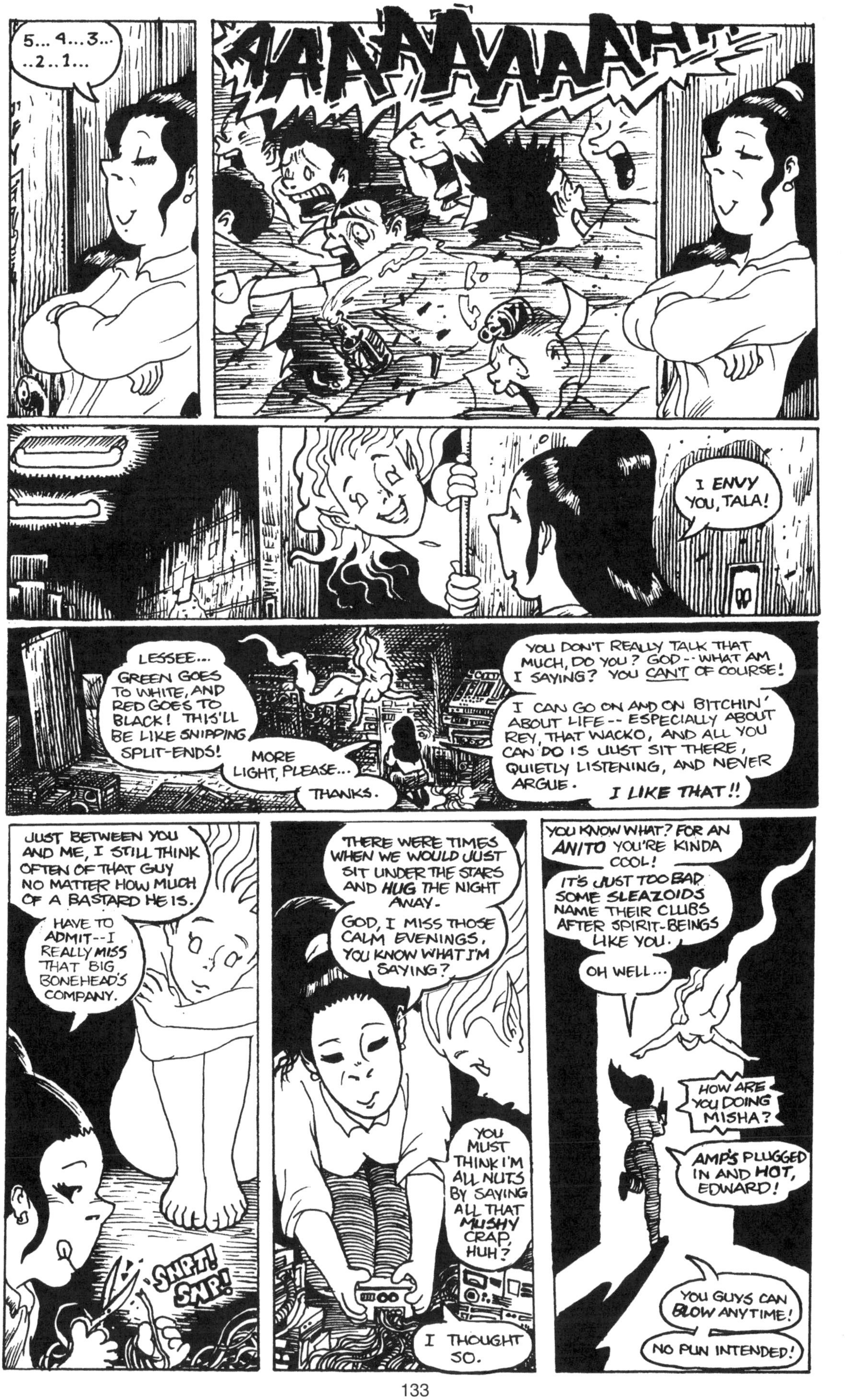
5... 4... 3... ..2..1...
AAAAAAAAAAH!
I ENVY YOU, TALA!
LESSEE... GREEN GOES TO WHITE, AND RED GOES TO BLACK! THIS'LL BE LIKE SNIPPING SPLIT-ENDS!
MORE LIGHT, PLEASE...
THANKS.
YOU DON'T REALLY TALK THAT MUCH, DO YOU? GOD--WHAT AM I SAYING? YOU CAN'T OF COURSE!
I CAN GO ON AND ON BITCHIN' ABOUT LIFE-- ESPECIALLY ABOUT REY, THAT WACKO, AND ALL YOU CAN DO IS JUST SIT THERE, QUIETLY LISTENING, AND NEVER ARGUE. I LIKE THAT!!
JUST BETWEEN YOU AND ME, I STILL THINK OFTEN OF THAT GUY NO MATTER HOW MUCH OF A BASTARD HE IS.
HAVE TO ADMIT--I REALLY MISS THAT BIG BONEHEAD'S COMPANY.
SNPT! SNP!
THERE WERE TIMES WHEN WE WOULD JUST SIT UNDER THE STARS AND HUG THE NIGHT AWAY.
GOD, I MISS THOSE CALM EVENINGS, YOU KNOW WHAT I'M SAYING?
YOU MUST THINK I'M ALL NUTS BY SAYING ALL THAT MUSHY CRAP, HUH?
I THOUGHT SO.
YOU KNOW WHAT? FOR AN ANITO YOU'RE KINDA COOL!
IT'S JUST TOO BAD SOME SLEAZOIDS NAME THEIR CLUBS AFTER SPIRIT-BEINGS LIKE YOU.
OH WELL...
HOW ARE YOU DOING MISHA?
AMP'S PLUGGED IN AND HOT, EDWARD!
YOU GUYS CAN BLOW ANYTIME!
NO PUN INTENDED!

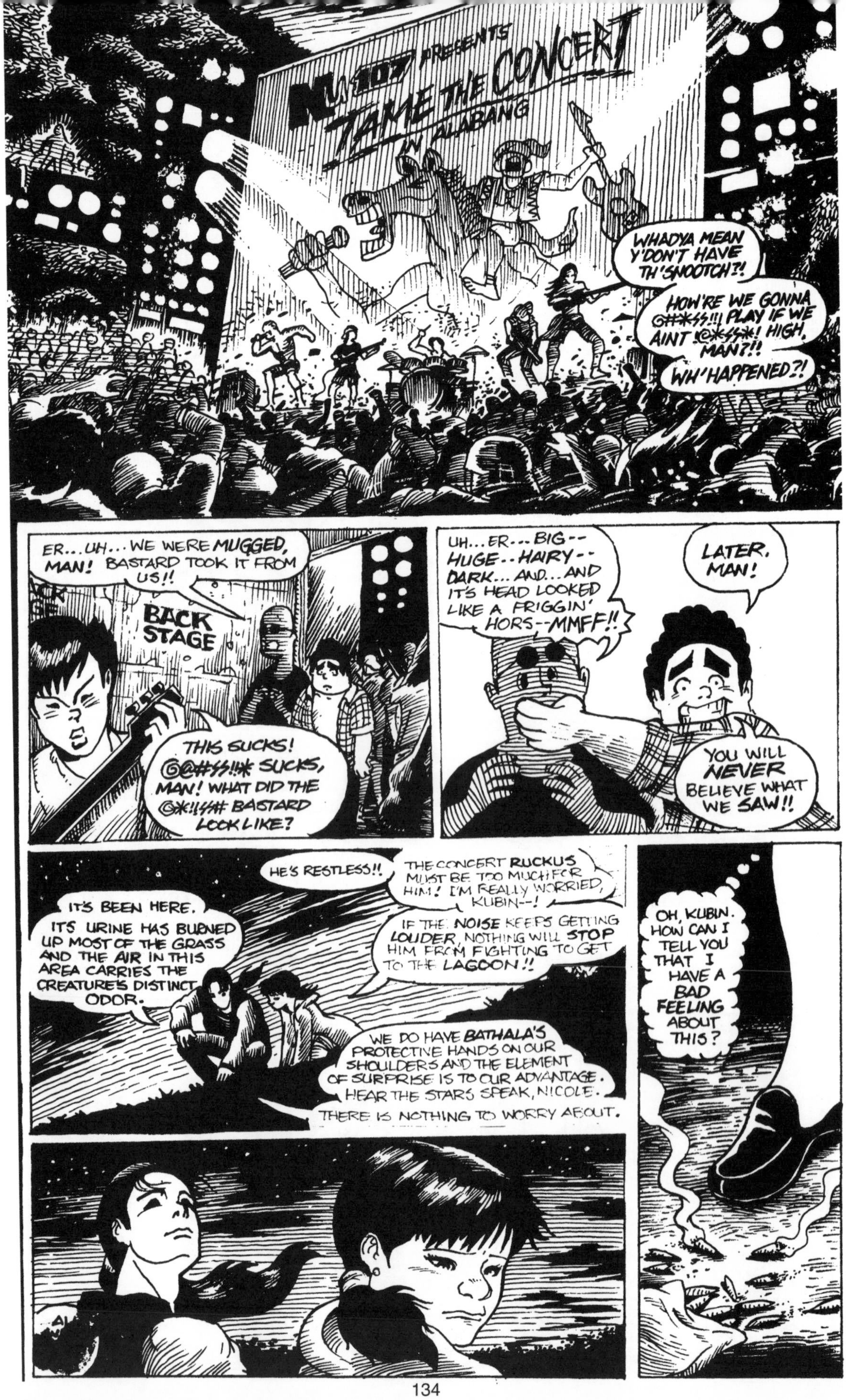

TAME THE CONCERT
IN ALABANG
WHADYA MEAN Y'DON'T HAVE TH'SNOOTCH?!
HOW'RE WE GONNA @#*$$!!! PLAY IF WE AINT !@*$$*! HIGH, MAN?!!
WH'HAPPENED?!
ER...UH...WE WERE MUGGED, MAN! BASTARD TOOK IT FROM US!!
BACK STAGE
THIS SUCKS! @@#$$!!* SUCKS, MAN! WHAT DID THE @*!!$$# BASTARD LOOK LIKE?
UH...ER...BIG--HUGE--HAIRY--DARK...AND...AND IT'S HEAD LOOKED LIKE A FRIGGIN' HORS--MMFF!!
LATER, MAN!
YOU WILL NEVER BELIEVE WHAT WE SAW!!
HE'S RESTLESS!!
THE CONCERT RUCKUS MUST BE TOO MUCH FOR HIM! I'M REALLY WORRIED, KUBIN--!
IT'S BEEN HERE. ITS URINE HAS BURNED UP MOST OF THE GRASS AND THE AIR IN THIS AREA CARRIES THE CREATURE'S DISTINCT ODOR.
IF THE NOISE KEEPS GETTING LOUDER, NOTHING WILL STOP HIM FROM FIGHTING TO GET TO THE LAGOON!!
WE DO HAVE BATHALA'S PROTECTIVE HANDS ON OUR SHOULDERS AND THE ELEMENT OF SURPRISE IS TO OUR ADVANTAGE. HEAR THE STARS SPEAK, NICOLE.
THERE IS NOTHING TO WORRY ABOUT.
OH, KUBIN. HOW CAN I TELL YOU THAT I HAVE A BAD FEELING ABOUT THIS?

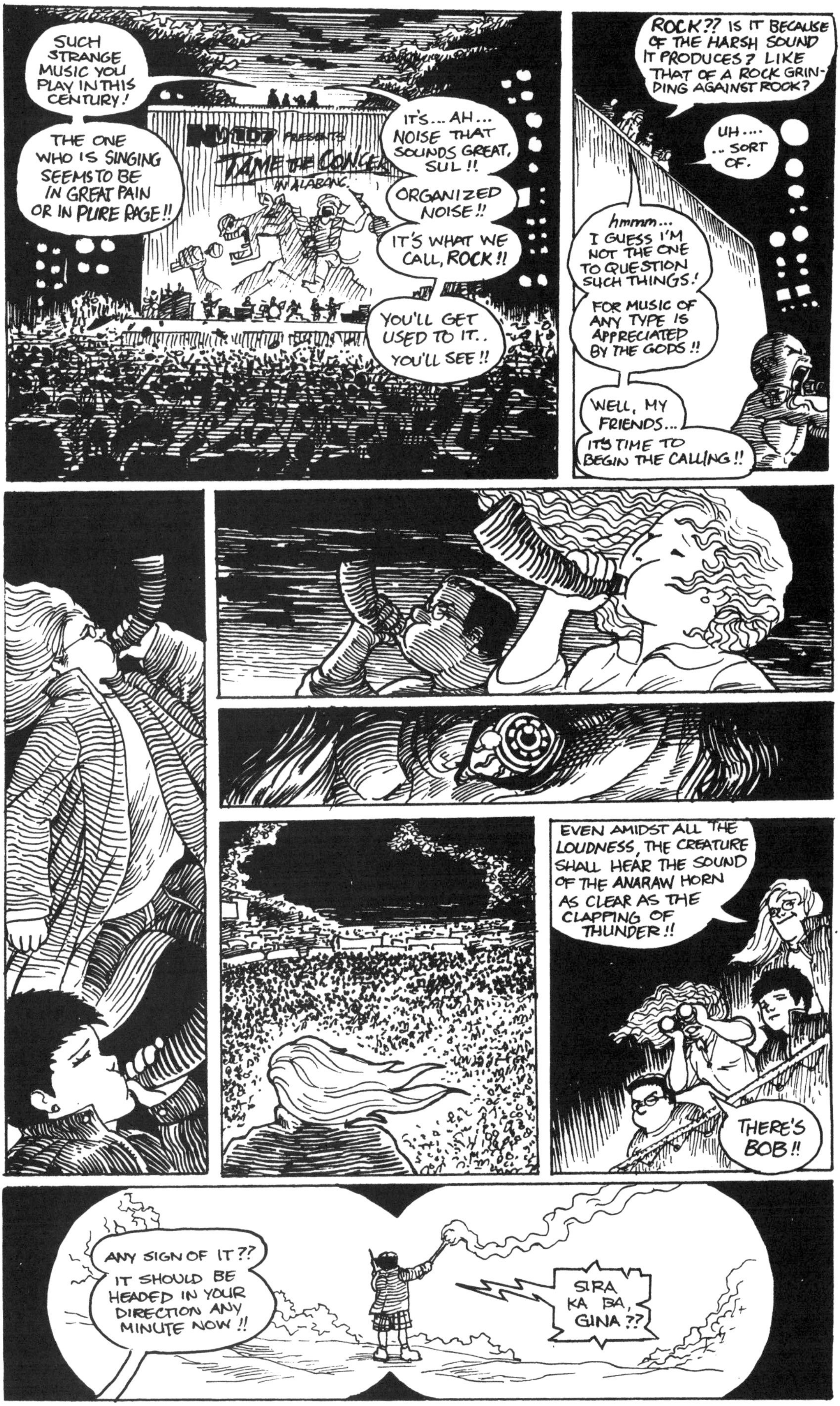
SUCH STRANGE MUSIC YOU PLAY IN THIS CENTURY!
THE ONE WHO IS SINGING SEEMS TO BE IN GREAT PAIN OR IN PURE RAGE!!
IT'S... AH... NOISE THAT SOUNDS GREAT, SUL!!
ORGANIZED NOISE!!
IT'S WHAT WE CALL, ROCK!!
YOU'LL GET USED TO IT.. YOU'LL SEE!!
ROCK?? IS IT BECAUSE OF THE HARSH SOUND IT PRODUCES? LIKE THAT OF A ROCK GRINDING AGAINST ROCK?
UH.... .. SORT OF.
hmmm... I GUESS I'M NOT THE ONE TO QUESTION SUCH THINGS!
FOR MUSIC OF ANY TYPE IS APPRECIATED BY THE GODS!!
WELL, MY FRIENDS...
IT'S TIME TO BEGIN THE CALLING!!
EVEN AMIDST ALL THE LOUDNESS, THE CREATURE SHALL HEAR THE SOUND OF THE ANARAW HORN AS CLEAR AS THE CLAPPING OF THUNDER!!
THERE'S BOB!!
ANY SIGN OF IT?? IT SHOULD BE HEADED IN YOUR DIRECTION ANY MINUTE NOW!!
SIRA KA BA, GINA??

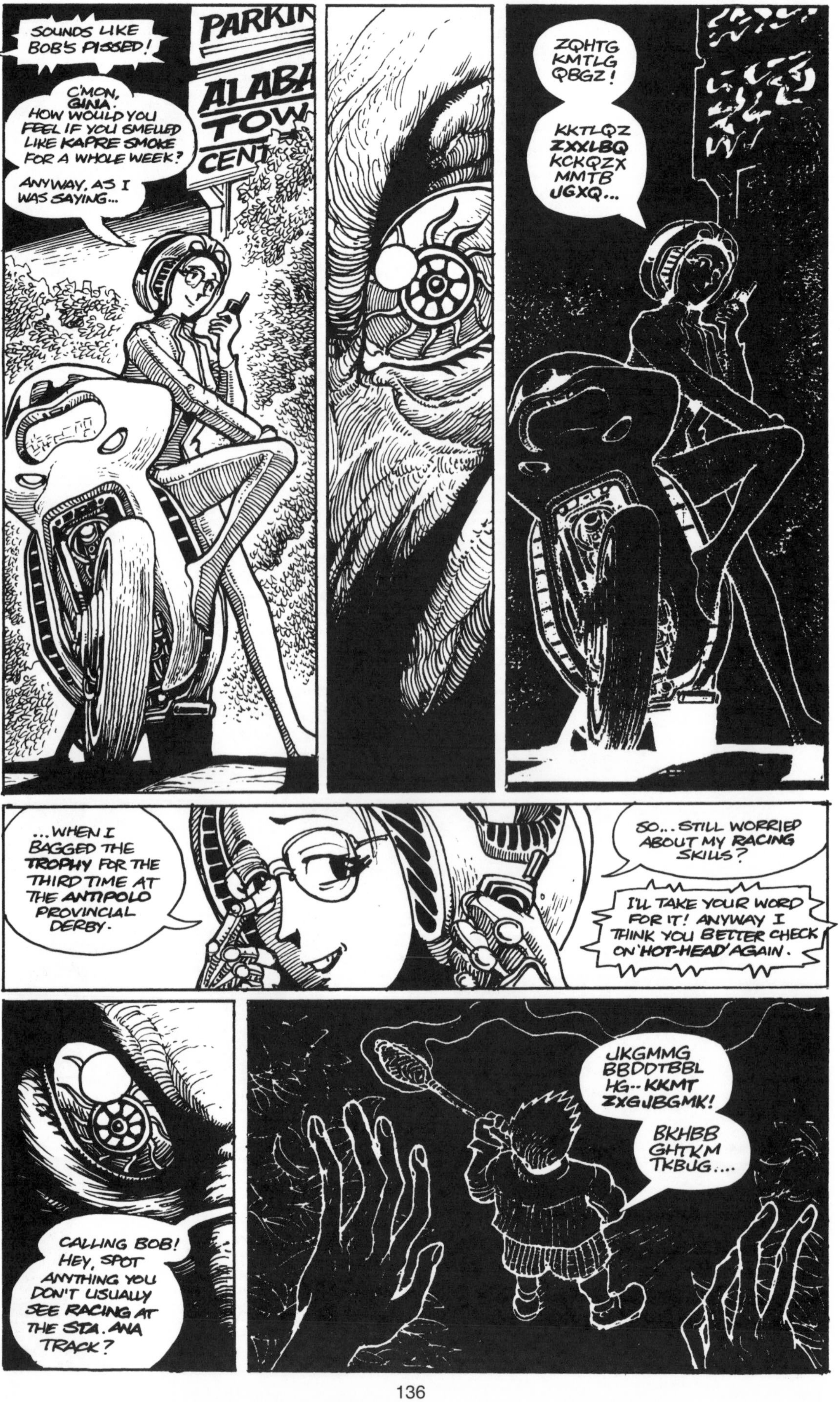
SOUNDS LIKE BOB'S PISSED!
PARKIN
ALABA TOW CENT
C'MON, GINA. HOW WOULD YOU FEEL IF YOU SMELLED LIKE KAPRE SMOKE FOR A WHOLE WEEK?
ANYWAY, AS I WAS SAYING...
ZQHTG KMTLG QBGZ!
KKTLQZ ZXXLBQ KCKQZX MMTB UGXQ...
...WHEN I BAGGED THE TROPHY FOR THE THIRD TIME AT THE ANTIPOLO PROVINCIAL DERBY.
SO... STILL WORRIED ABOUT MY RACING SKILLS?
I'LL TAKE YOUR WORD FOR IT! ANYWAY I THINK YOU BETTER CHECK ON 'HOT-HEAD' AGAIN.
CALLING BOB! HEY, SPOT ANYTHING YOU DON'T USUALLY SEE RACING AT THE STA. ANA TRACK?
JKGMMG BBDDTBBL HG-- KKMT ZXGJBGMK!
BKHBB GHTKM TKBUG....

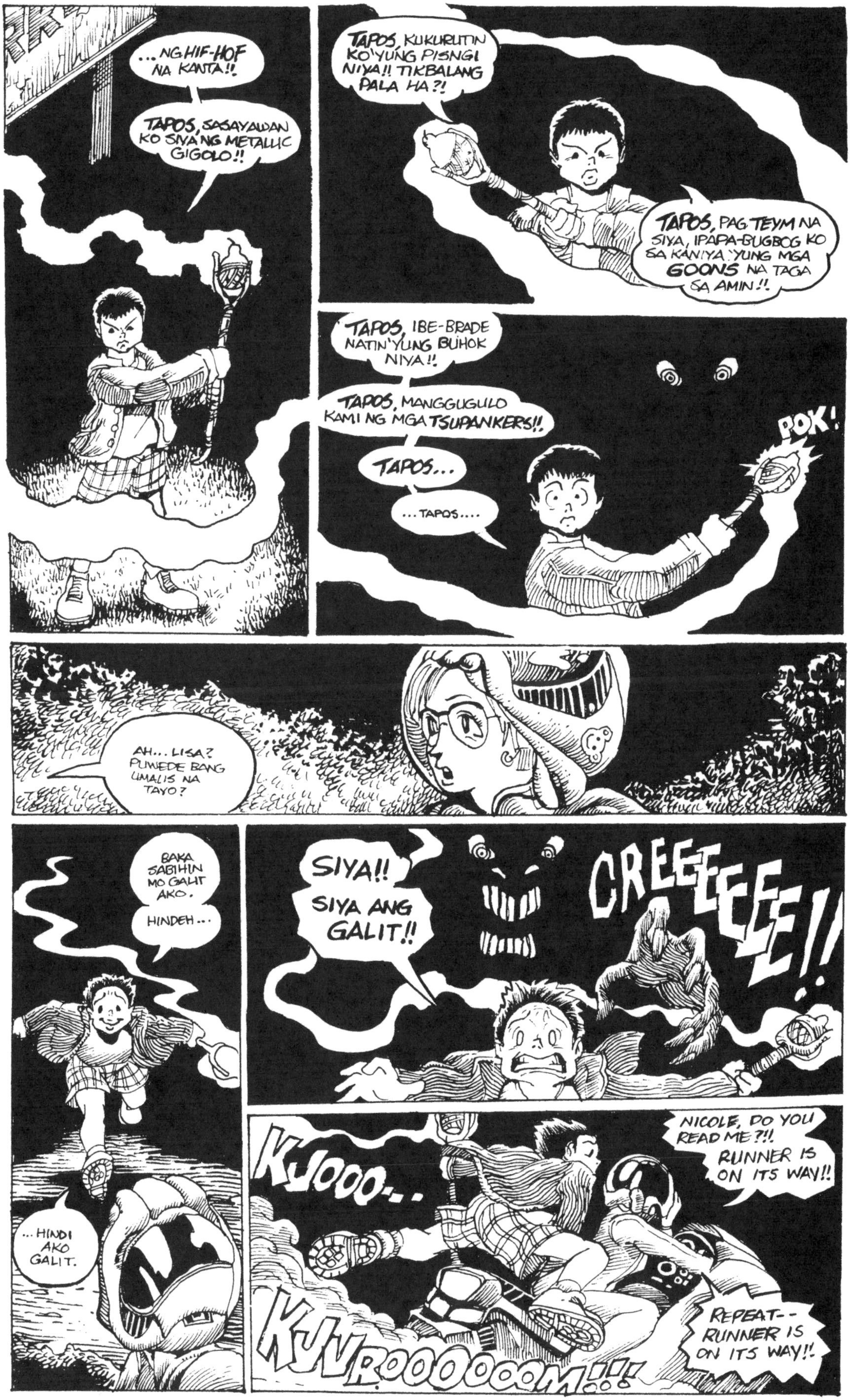
...NG HIF-HOF NA KANTA!!
TAPOS, SASAYAWAN KO SIYA'NG METALLIC GIGOLO!!
TAPOS, KUKURUTIN KO'YUNG PISNGI NIYA!! TIKBALANG PALA HA?!
TAPOS, PAG TEYM NA SIYA, IPAPA-BUGBOG KO SA KANIYA 'YUNG MGA GOONS NA TAGA SA AMIN!!
TAPOS, IBE-BRADE NATIN'YUNG BUHOK NIYA!!
TAPOS, MANGGUGULO KAMI NG MGA TSUPANKERS!!
TAPOS...
...TAPOS....
POK!
AH... LISA? PUWEDE BANG UMALIS NA TAYO?
BAKA SABIHIN MO GALIT AKO.
HINDEH...
...HINDI AKO GALIT.
SIYA!! SIYA ANG GALIT!!
CREEEEEEEE!!
KJOOO-..
NICOLE, DO YOU READ ME?!!
RUNNER IS ON ITS WAY!!
KJVROOOOOOM!!!
REPEAT-- RUNNER IS ON ITS WAY!!

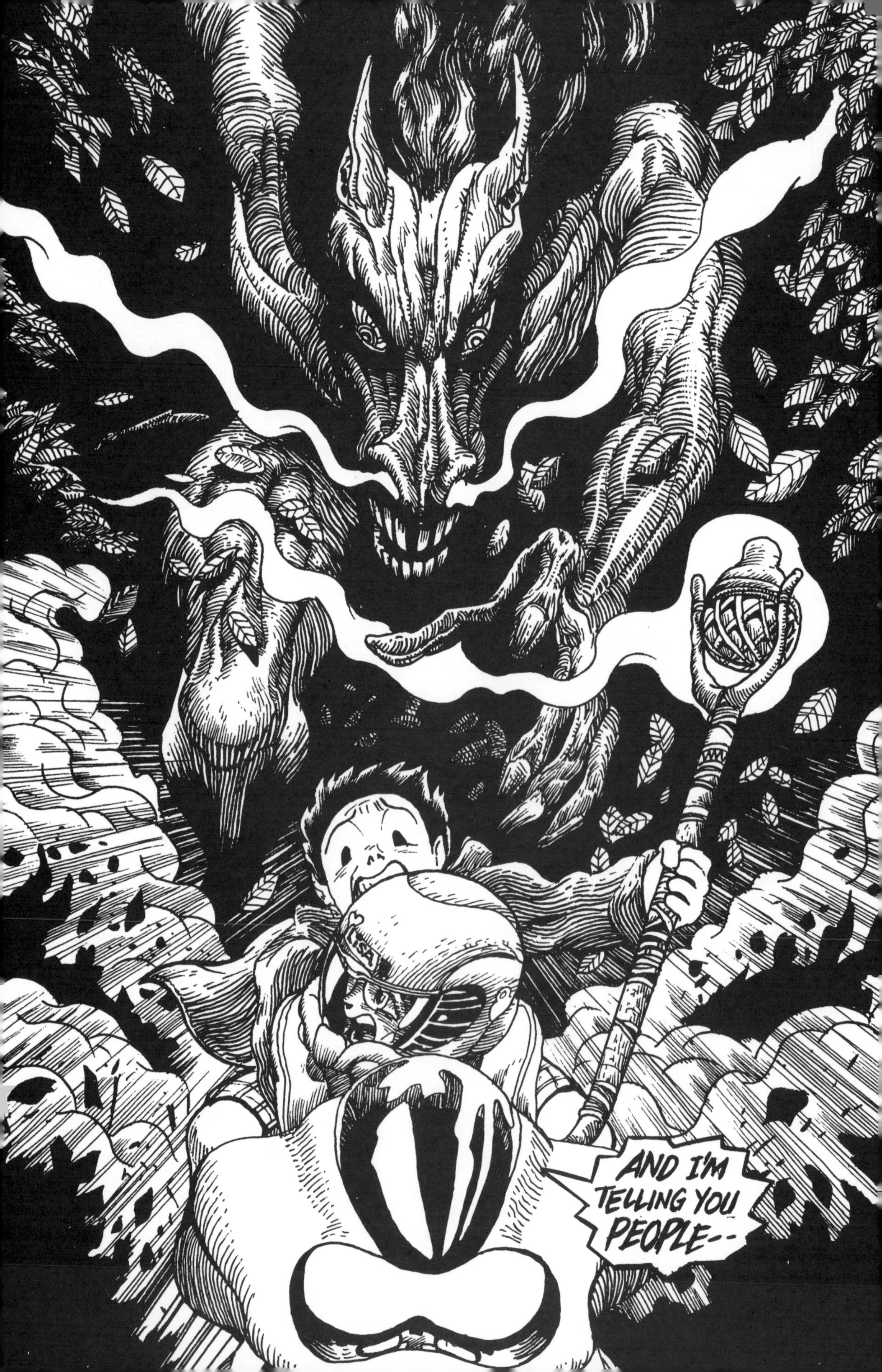
AND I'M TELLING YOU PEOPLE--

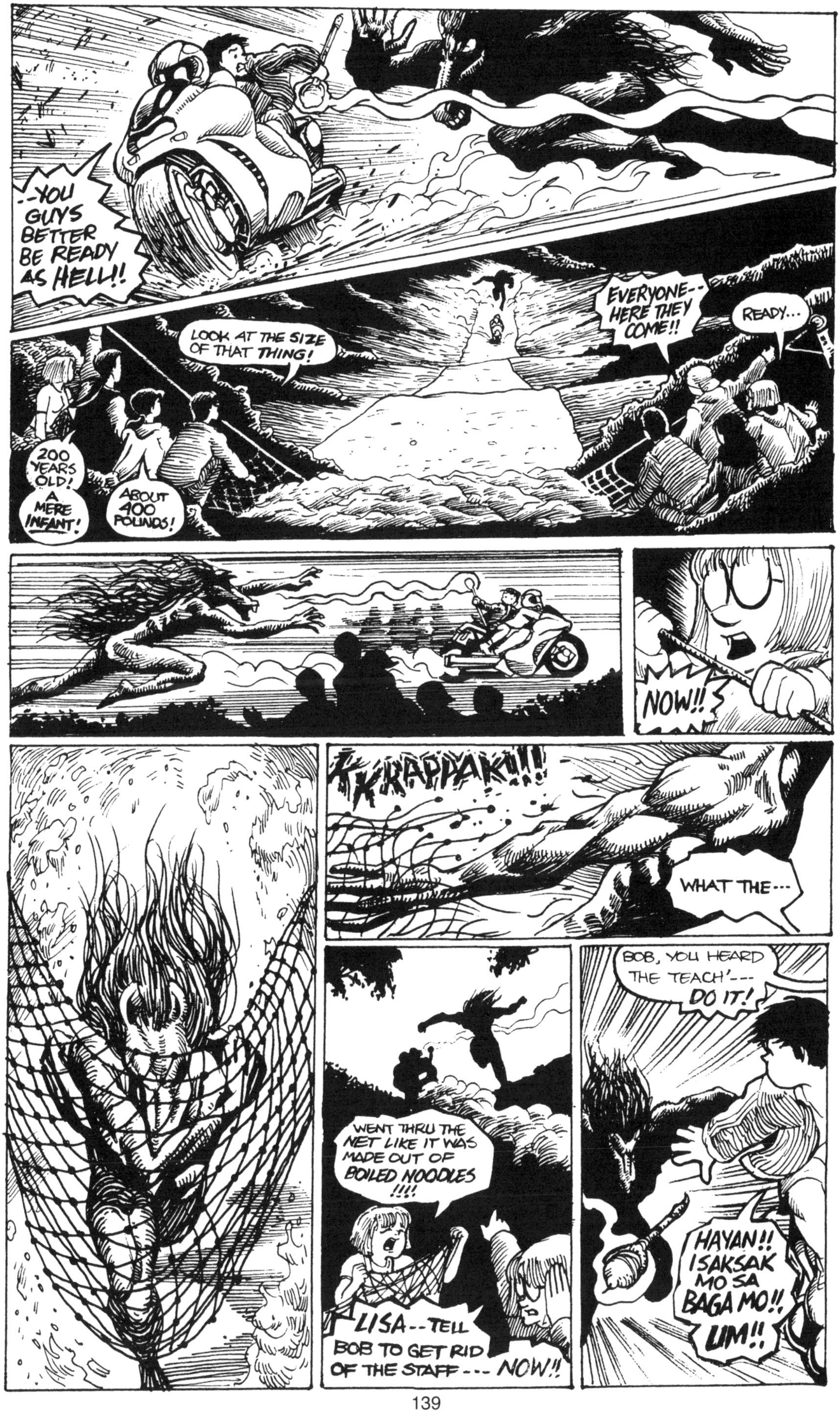
--YOU GUYS BETTER BE READY AS HELL!!
LOOK AT THE SIZE OF THAT THING!
EVERYONE-- HERE THEY COME!!
READY...
200 YEARS OLD! A MERE INFANT!
ABOUT 400 POUNDS!
NOW!!
KKRAPPAK!!!
WHAT THE---
WENT THRU THE NET LIKE IT WAS MADE OUT OF BOILED NOODLES !!!!
LISA--TELL BOB TO GET RID OF THE STAFF--- NOW!!
BOB, YOU HEARD THE TEACH'--- DO IT!
HAYAN!! ISAKSAK MO SA BAGA MO!! UM!!

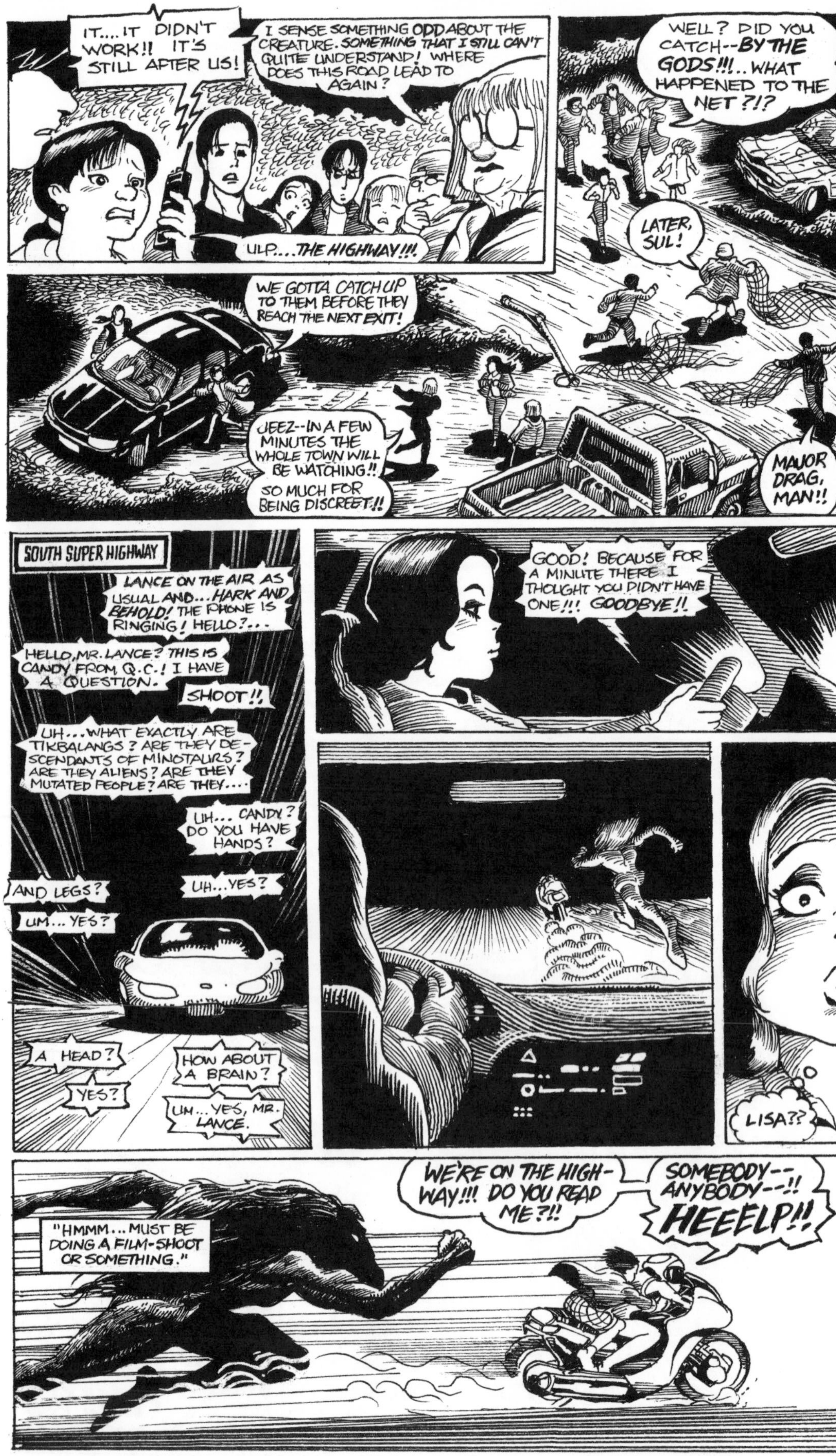
IT.... IT DIDN'T WORK!! IT'S STILL AFTER US!
I SENSE SOMETHING ODD ABOUT THE CREATURE. SOMETHING THAT I STILL CAN'T QUITE UNDERSTAND! WHERE DOES THIS ROAD LEAD TO AGAIN?
ULP.... THE HIGHWAY!!!
WELL? DID YOU CATCH--BY THE GODS!!!... WHAT HAPPENED TO THE NET?!?
LATER, SUL!
WE GOTTA CATCH UP TO THEM BEFORE THEY REACH THE NEXT EXIT!
JEEZ--IN A FEW MINUTES THE WHOLE TOWN WILL BE WATCHING!!
SO MUCH FOR BEING DISCREET!!
MAJOR DRAG, MAN!!
SOUTH SUPER HIGHWAY
LANCE ON THE AIR AS USUAL AND... HARK AND BEHOLD! THE PHONE IS RINGING! HELLO?...
HELLO, MR. LANCE? THIS IS CANDY FROM Q.C.! I HAVE A QUESTION.
SHOOT!!
UH... WHAT EXACTLY ARE TIKBALANGS? ARE THEY DESCENDANTS OF MINOTAURS? ARE THEY ALIENS? ARE THEY MUTATED PEOPLE? ARE THEY....
UH... CANDY? DO YOU HAVE HANDS?
UH... YES?
AND LEGS?
UM... YES?
A HEAD?
YES?
HOW ABOUT A BRAIN?
UM... YES, MR. LANCE.
GOOD! BECAUSE FOR A MINUTE THERE I THOUGHT YOU DIDN'T HAVE ONE!!! GOODBYE!!
LISA??
"HMMM... MUST BE DOING A FILM-SHOOT OR SOMETHING."
WE'RE ON THE HIGHWAY!!! DO YOU READ ME?!!
SOMEBODY--ANYBODY--!! HEEELP!!

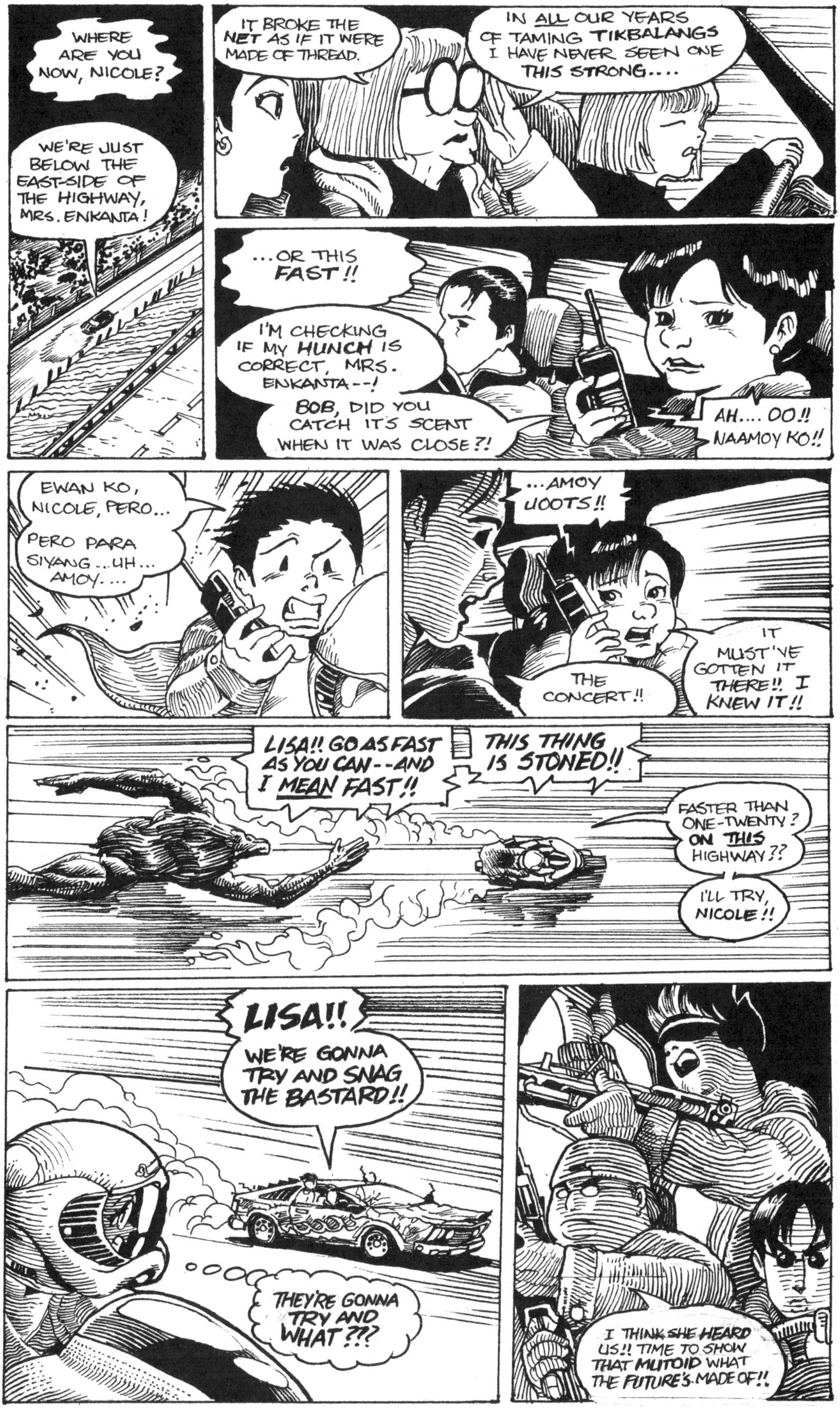
WHERE ARE YOU NOW, NICOLE?
WE'RE JUST BELOW THE EAST-SIDE OF THE HIGHWAY, MRS. ENKANTA!
IT BROKE THE NET AS IF IT WERE MADE OF THREAD.
IN ALL OUR YEARS OF TAMING TIKBALANGS I HAVE NEVER SEEN ONE THIS STRONG....
...OR THIS FAST!!
I'M CHECKING IF MY HUNCH IS CORRECT, MRS. ENKANTA--!
BOB, DID YOU CATCH IT'S SCENT WHEN IT WAS CLOSE?!
AH.... OO!! NAAMOY KO!!
EWAN KO, NICOLE, PERO...
PERO PARA SIYANG ...UH... AMOY....
...AMOY UOOTS!!
THE CONCERT!!
IT MUST'VE GOTTEN IT THERE!! I KNEW IT!!
LISA!! GO AS FAST AS YOU CAN--AND I MEAN FAST!!
THIS THING IS STONED!!
FASTER THAN ONE-TWENTY? ON THIS HIGHWAY??
I'LL TRY, NICOLE!!
LISA!!
WE'RE GONNA TRY AND SNAG THE BASTARD!!
THEY'RE GONNA TRY AND WHAT???
I THINK SHE HEARD US!! TIME TO SHOW THAT MUTOID WHAT THE FUTURE'S MADE OF!!

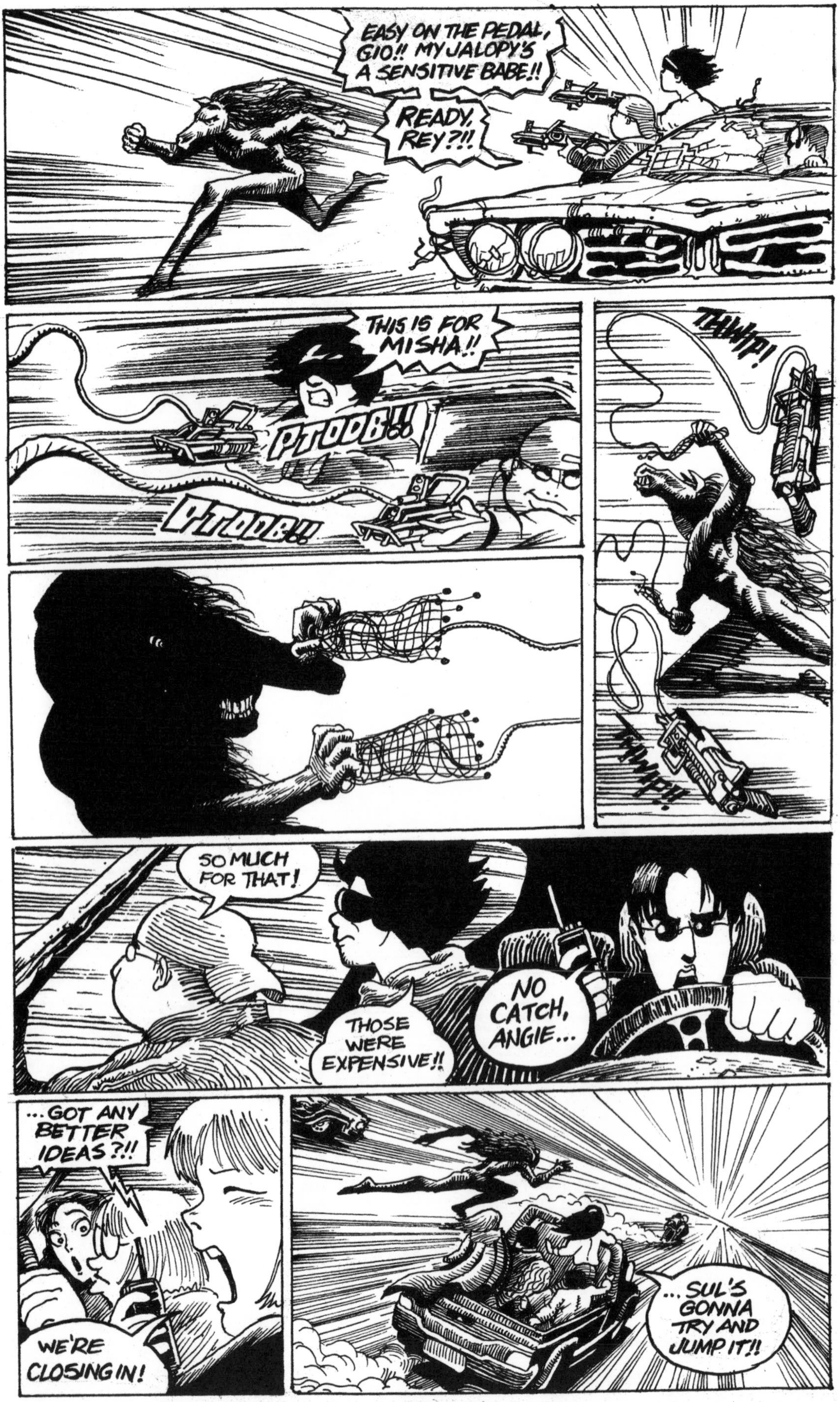
EASY ON THE PEDAL, GIO!! MY JALOPY'S A SENSITIVE BABE!!
READY, REY?!!
THIS IS FOR MISHA!!
PTOOB!!
PTOOB!!
THWIP!
THWIP!!
SO MUCH FOR THAT!
THOSE WERE EXPENSIVE!!
NO CATCH, ANGIE...
...GOT ANY BETTER IDEAS?!!
WE'RE CLOSING IN!
...SUL'S GONNA TRY AND JUMP IT!!

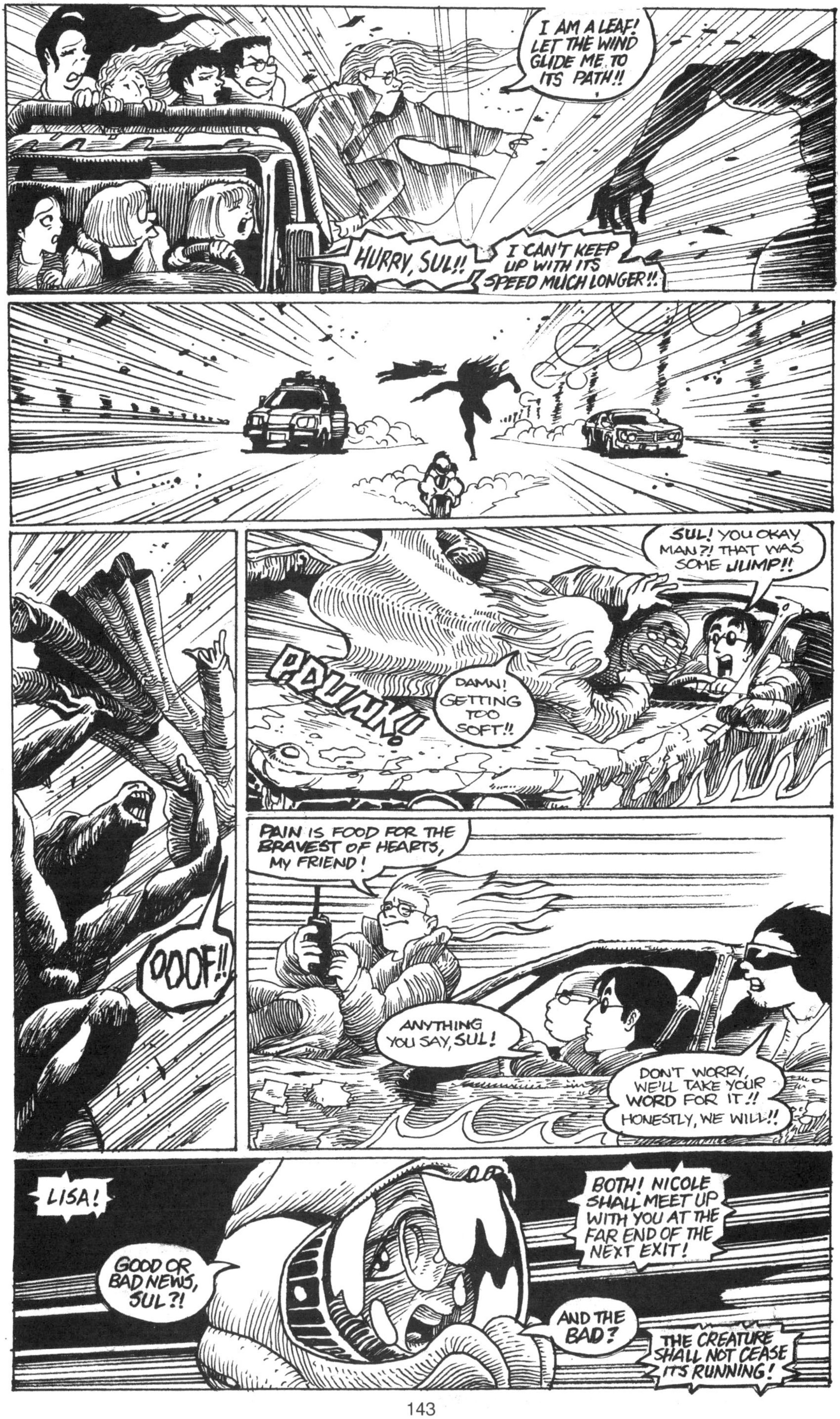
I AM A LEAF! LET THE WIND GLIDE ME TO ITS PATH!!
HURRY, SUL!!
I CAN'T KEEP UP WITH ITS SPEED MUCH LONGER!!
SUL! YOU OKAY MAN?! THAT WAS SOME JUMP!!
POUNK!
DAMN! GETTING TOO SOFT!!
OOOF!!
PAIN IS FOOD FOR THE BRAVEST OF HEARTS, MY FRIEND!
ANYTHING YOU SAY, SUL!
DON'T WORRY, WE'LL TAKE YOUR WORD FOR IT!! HONESTLY, WE WILL!!
LISA!
GOOD OR BAD NEWS, SUL?!
BOTH! NICOLE SHALL MEET UP WITH YOU AT THE FAR END OF THE NEXT EXIT!
AND THE BAD?
THE CREATURE SHALL NOT CEASE ITS RUNNING!

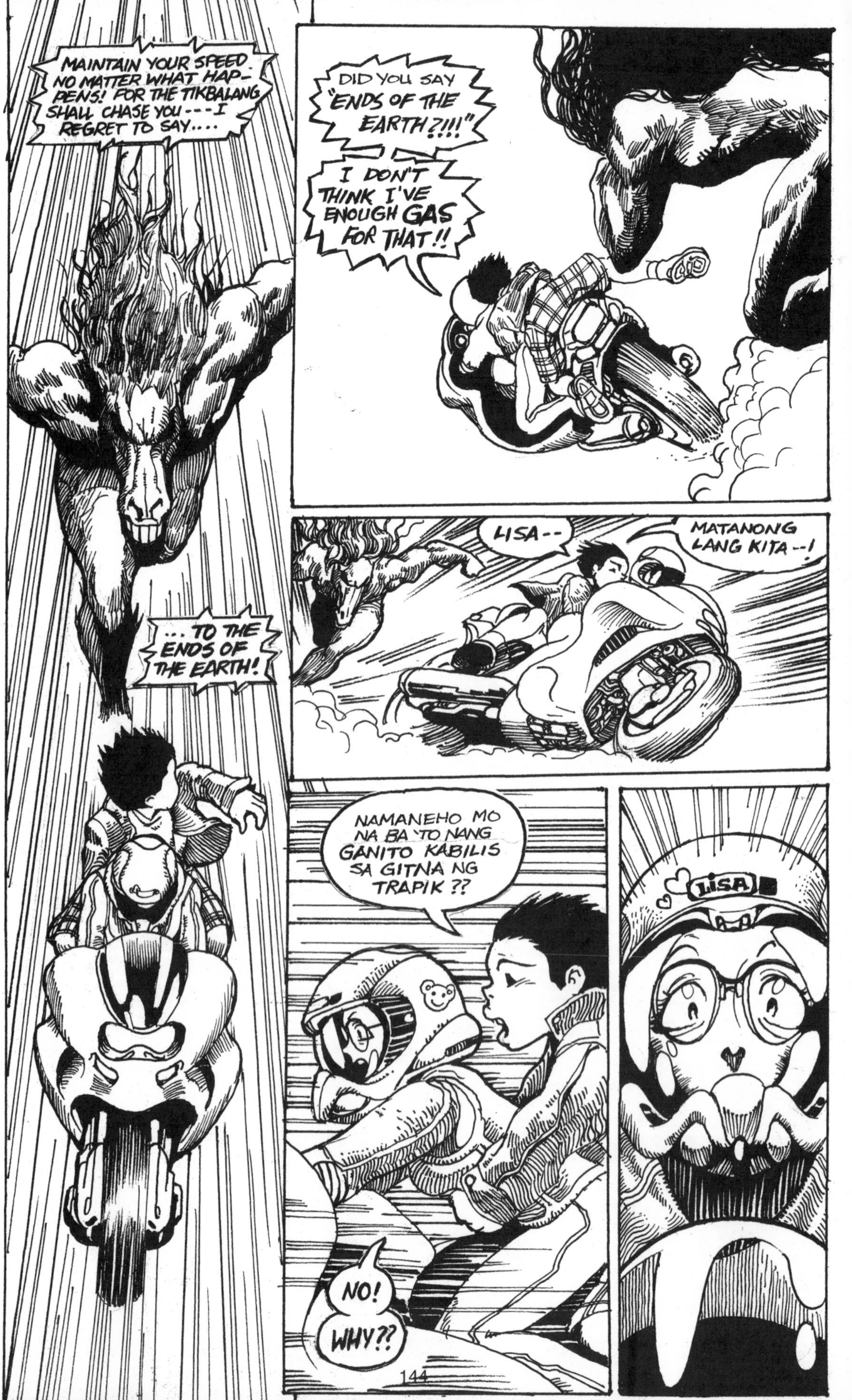
MAINTAIN YOUR SPEED NO MATTER WHAT HAP-PENS! FOR THE TIKBALANG SHALL CHASE YOU---I REGRET TO SAY....
...TO THE ENDS OF THE EARTH!
DID YOU SAY "ENDS OF THE EARTH?!!!"
I DON'T THINK I'VE ENOUGH GAS FOR THAT!!
LISA--
MATANONG LANG KITA--!
NAMANEHO MO NA BA 'TO NANG GANITO KABILIS SA GITNA NG TRAPIK??
NO!
WHY??
LISA

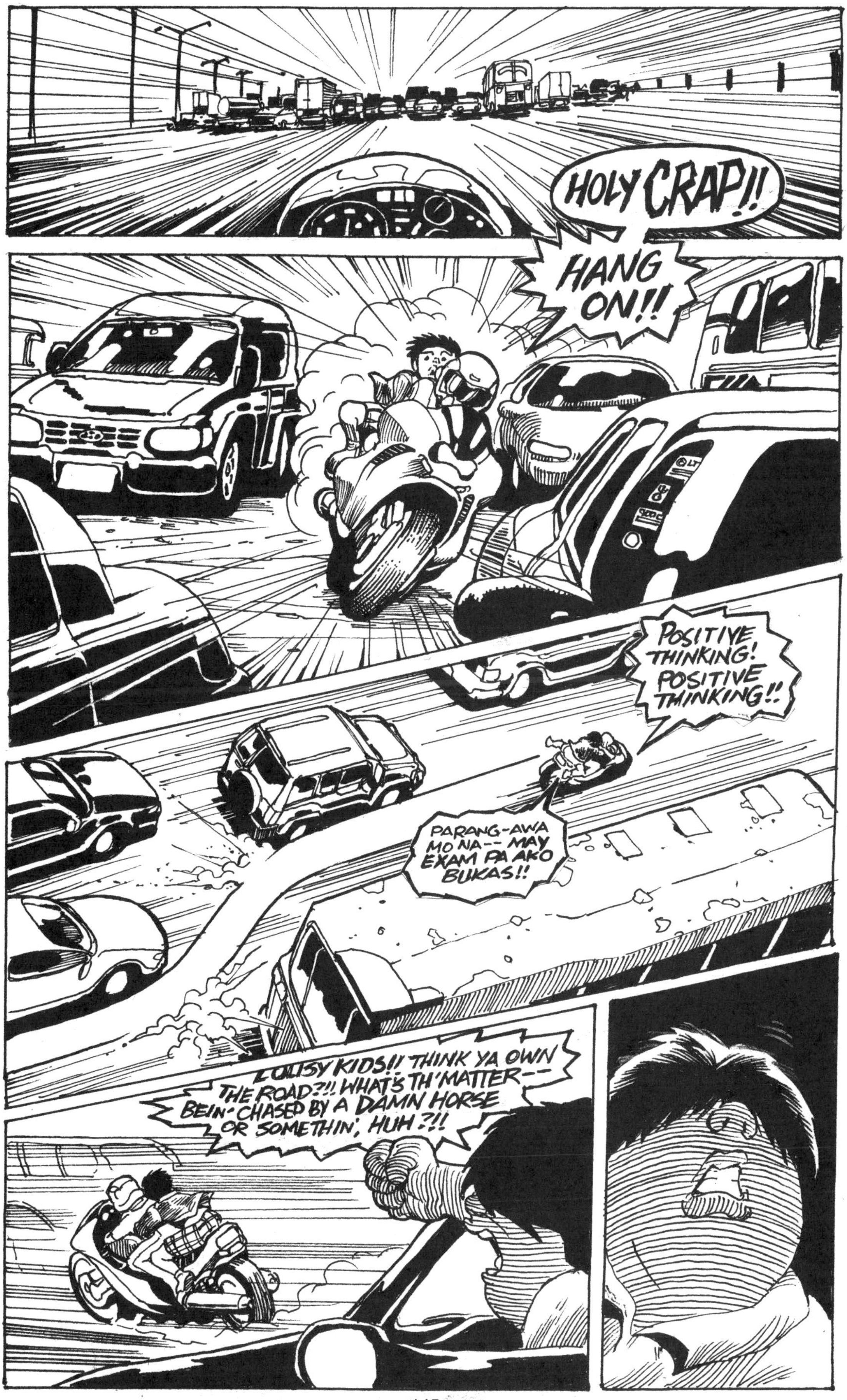
HOLY CRAP!!
HANG ON!!
POSITIVE THINKING! POSITIVE THINKING!!
PARANG-AWA MO NA-- MAY EXAM PA AKO BUKAS!!
LOUSY KIDS!! THINK YA OWN THE ROAD?!! WHAT'S TH' MATTER-- BEIN' CHASED BY A DAMN HORSE OR SOMETHIN', HUH?!!

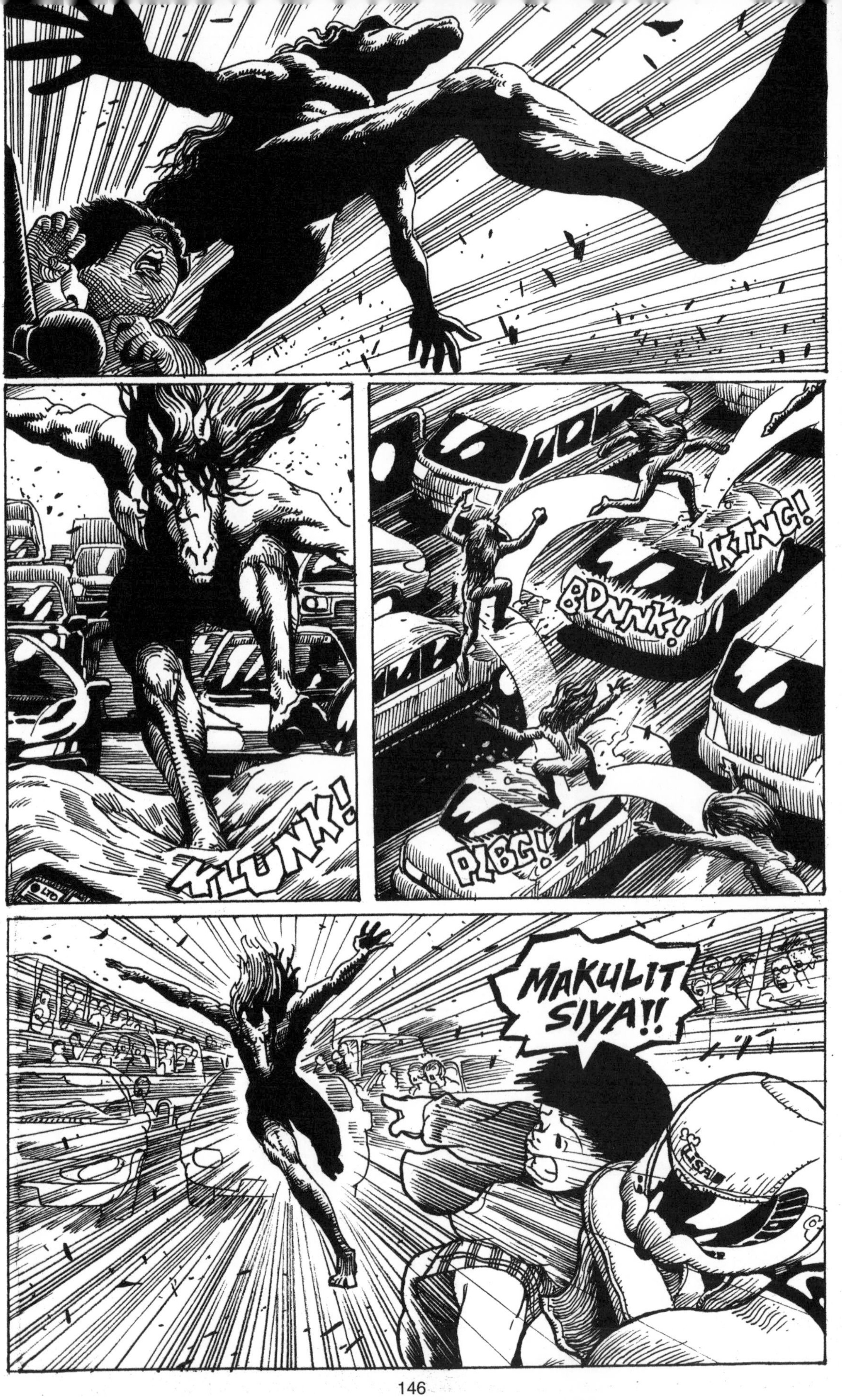
KLUNK!
KTNG!
BDNNK!
PLBG!
MAKULIT SIYA!!

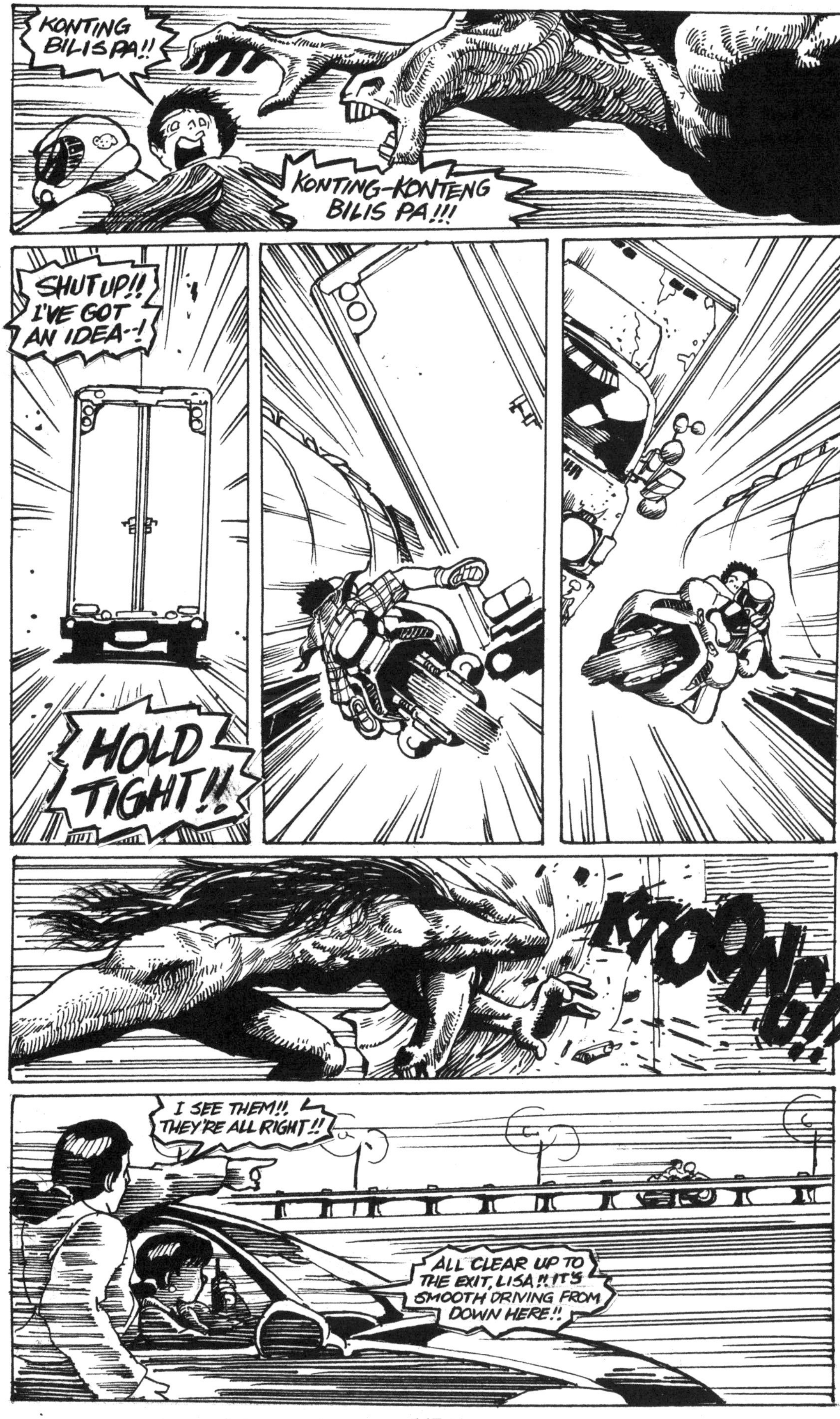
KONTING BILIS PA!!
KONTING-KONTENG BILIS PA!!!
SHUT UP!! I'VE GOT AN IDEA--!
HOLD TIGHT!!
KTOONG!!
I SEE THEM!! THEY'RE ALL RIGHT!!
ALL CLEAR UP TO THE EXIT, LISA!! IT'S SMOOTH DRIVING FROM DOWN HERE!!

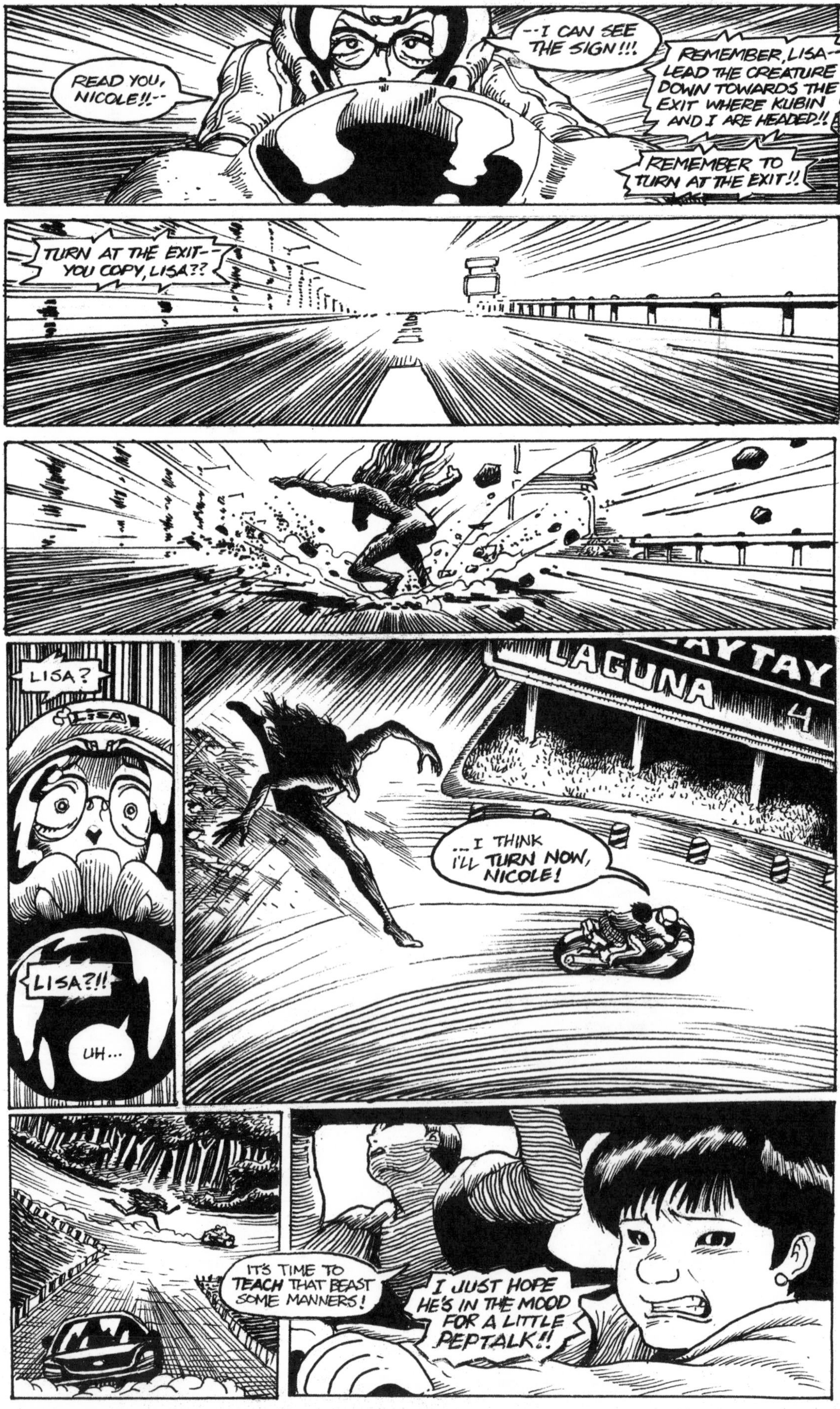
READ YOU, NICOLE!!--
--I CAN SEE THE SIGN!!!
REMEMBER, LISA-- LEAD THE CREATURE DOWN TOWARDS THE EXIT WHERE KUBIN AND I ARE HEADED!!
REMEMBER TO TURN AT THE EXIT!!
TURN AT THE EXIT-- YOU COPY, LISA??
LISA?
LISA
LISA?!!
UH...
LAGUNA
AYTAY
4
...I THINK I'LL TURN NOW, NICOLE!
IT'S TIME TO TEACH THAT BEAST SOME MANNERS!
I JUST HOPE HE'S IN THE MOOD FOR A LITTLE PEPTALK!!

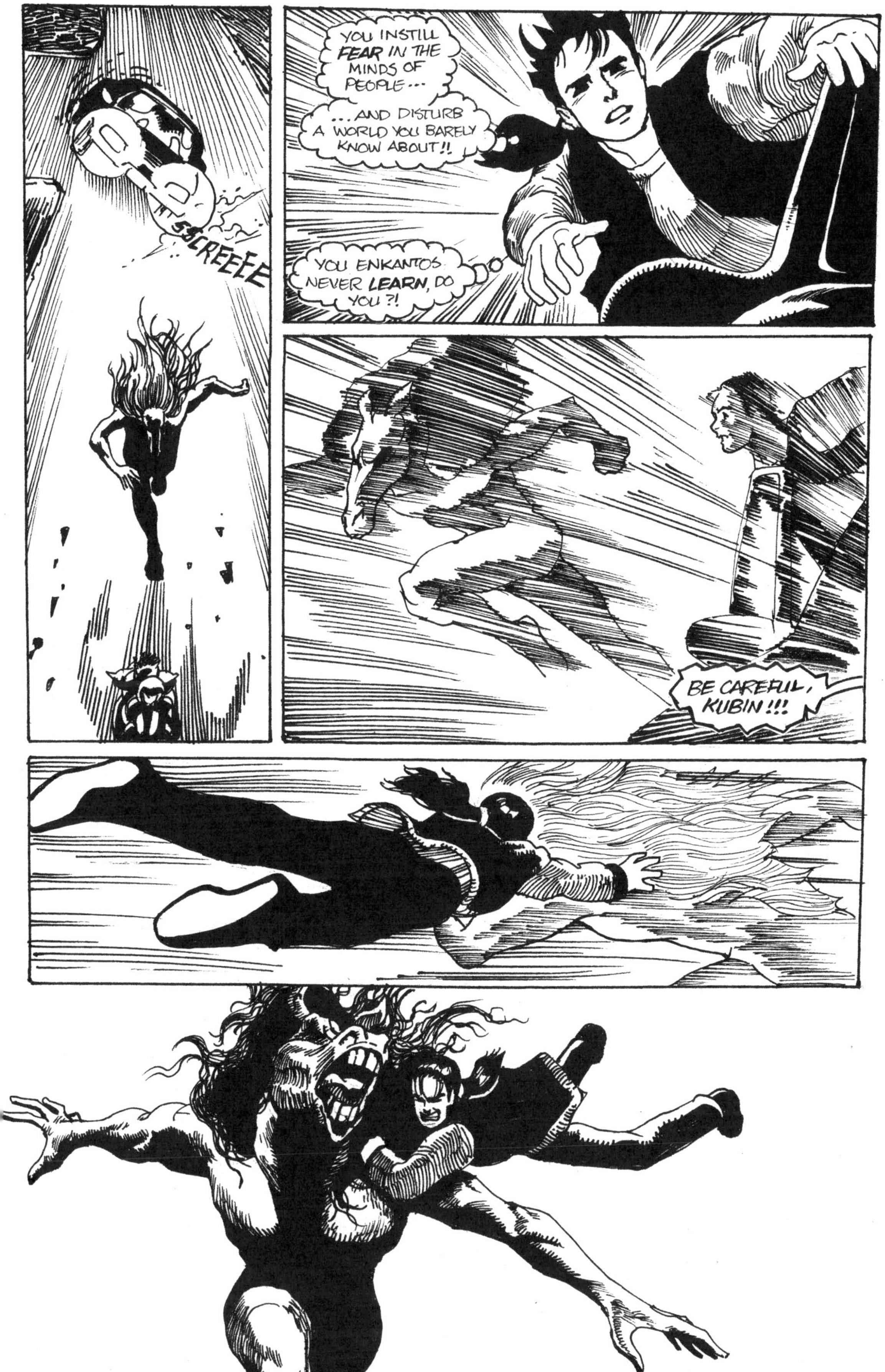
SSCREEEEE
YOU INSTILL FEAR IN THE MINDS OF PEOPLE...
...AND DISTURB A WORLD YOU BARELY KNOW ABOUT!!
YOU ENKANTOS NEVER LEARN, DO YOU ?!
BE CAREFUL, KUBIN!!!

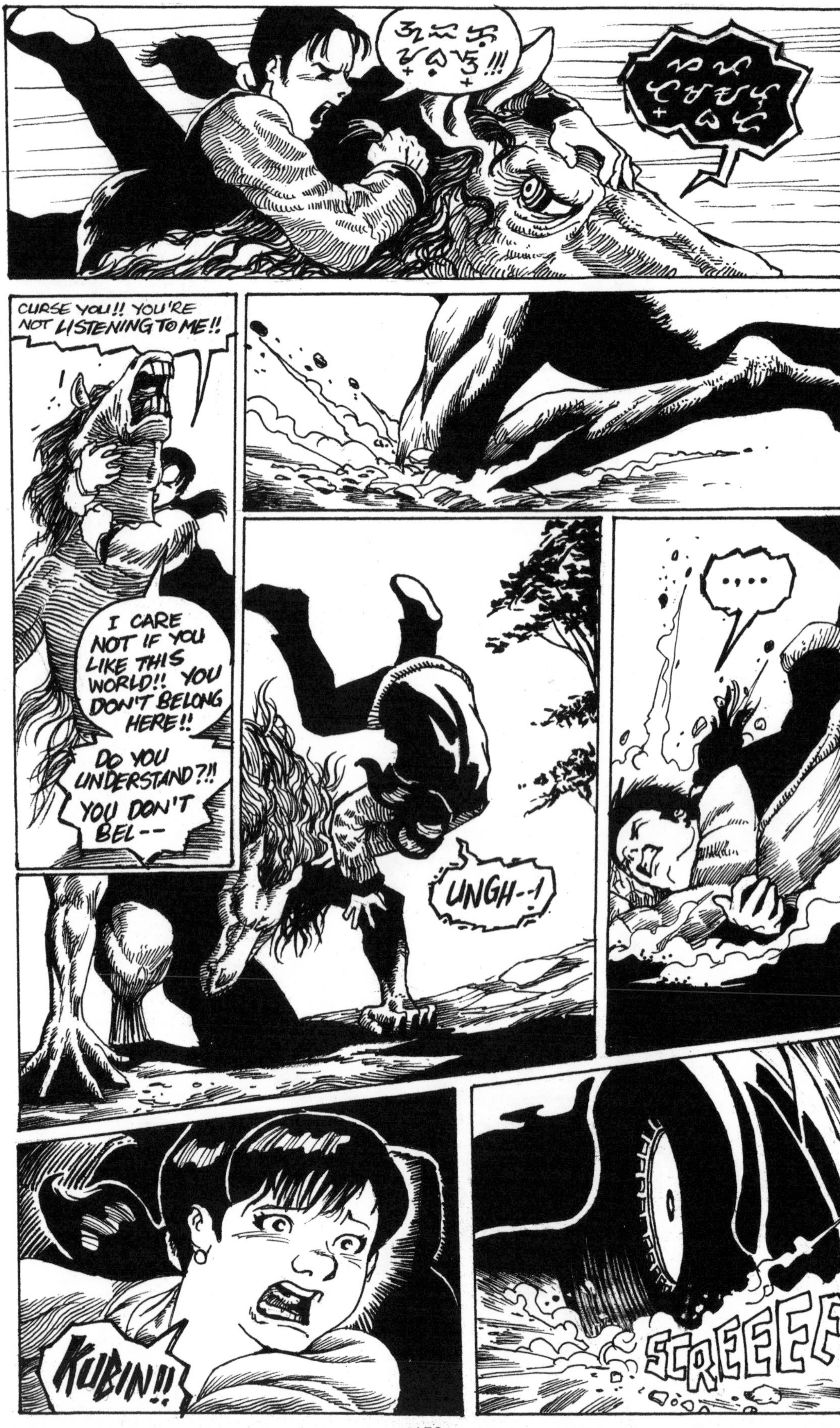
CURSE YOU!! YOU'RE NOT LISTENING TO ME!!
I CARE NOT IF YOU LIKE THIS WORLD!! YOU DON'T BELONG HERE!!
DO YOU UNDERSTAND?!! YOU DON'T BEL--
UNGH--!
...
KUBIN!!
SCREEEE

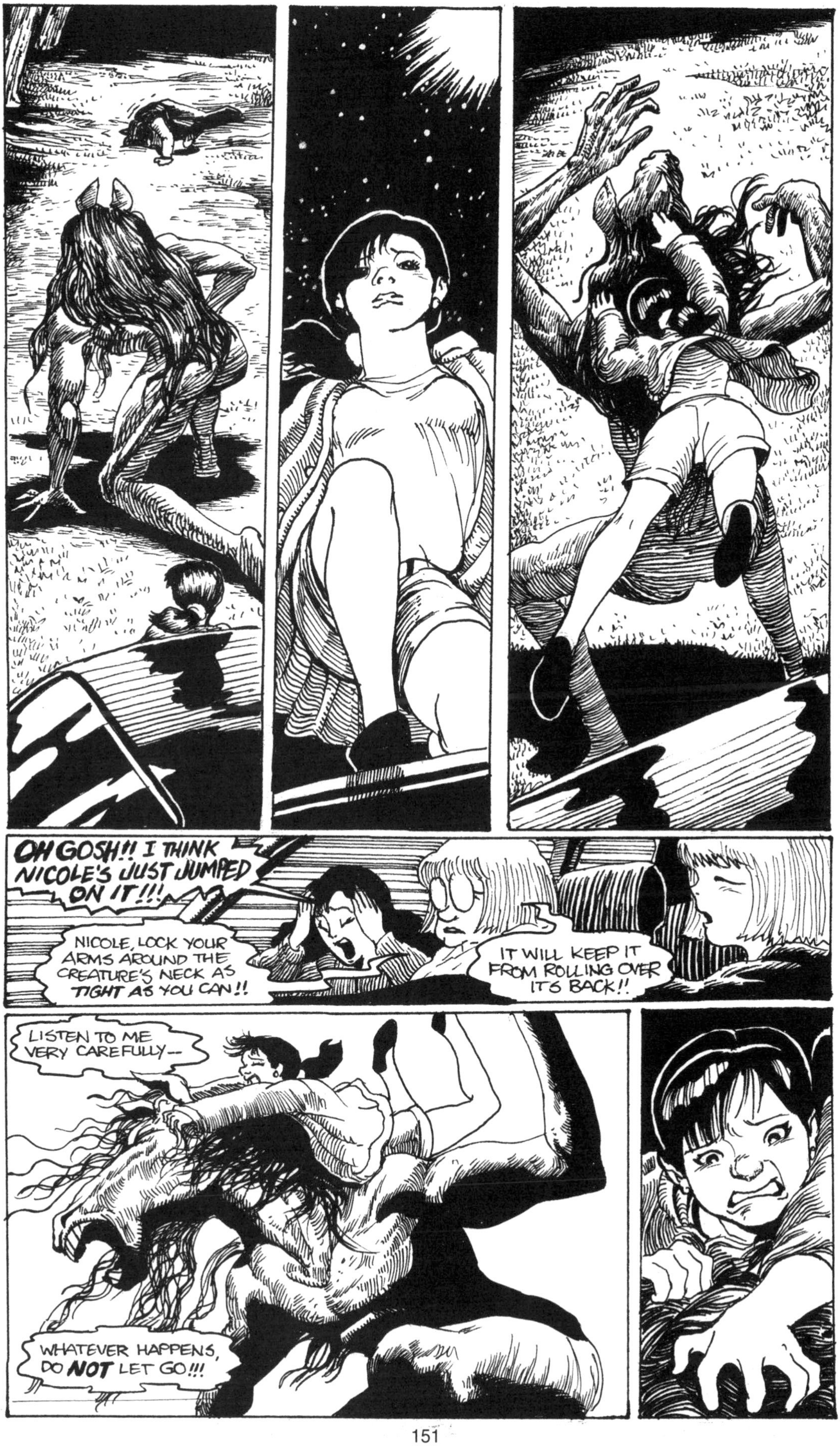
OH GOSH!! I THINK NICOLE'S JUST JUMPED ON IT!!!
NICOLE, LOCK YOUR ARMS AROUND THE CREATURE'S NECK AS TIGHT AS YOU CAN!!
IT WILL KEEP IT FROM ROLLING OVER IT'S BACK!!
LISTEN TO ME VERY CAREFULLY--
WHATEVER HAPPENS, DO NOT LET GO!!!

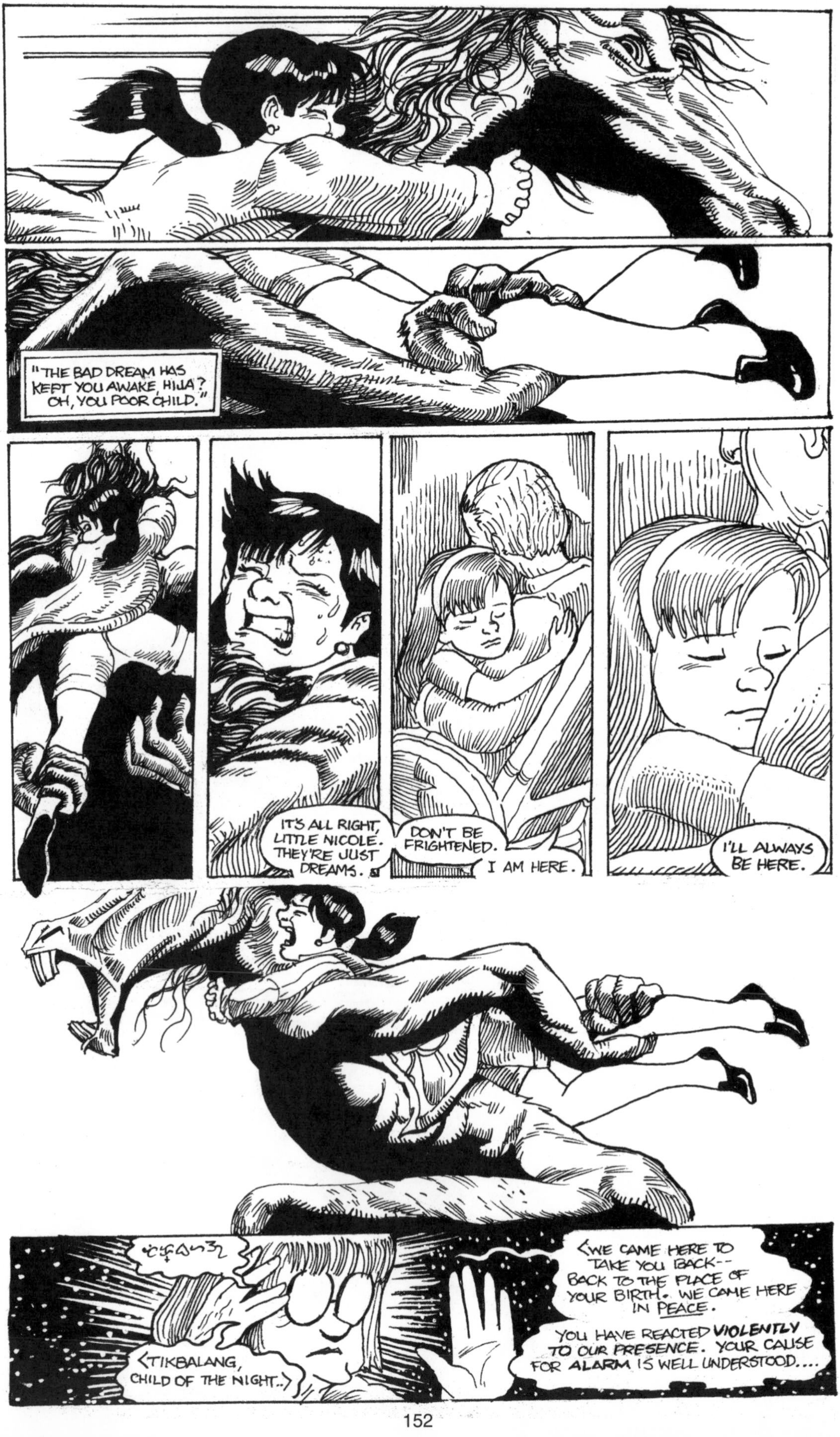
"THE BAD DREAM HAS KEPT YOU AWAKE, HIJA? OH, YOU POOR CHILD."
IT'S ALL RIGHT, LITTLE NICOLE. THEY'RE JUST DREAMS.
DON'T BE FRIGHTENED.
I AM HERE.
I'LL ALWAYS BE HERE.
<TIKBALANG, CHILD OF THE NIGHT..>
<WE CAME HERE TO TAKE YOU BACK-- BACK TO THE PLACE OF YOUR BIRTH. WE CAME HERE IN PEACE.
YOU HAVE REACTED VIOLENTLY TO OUR PRESENCE. YOUR CAUSE FOR ALARM IS WELL UNDERSTOOD....

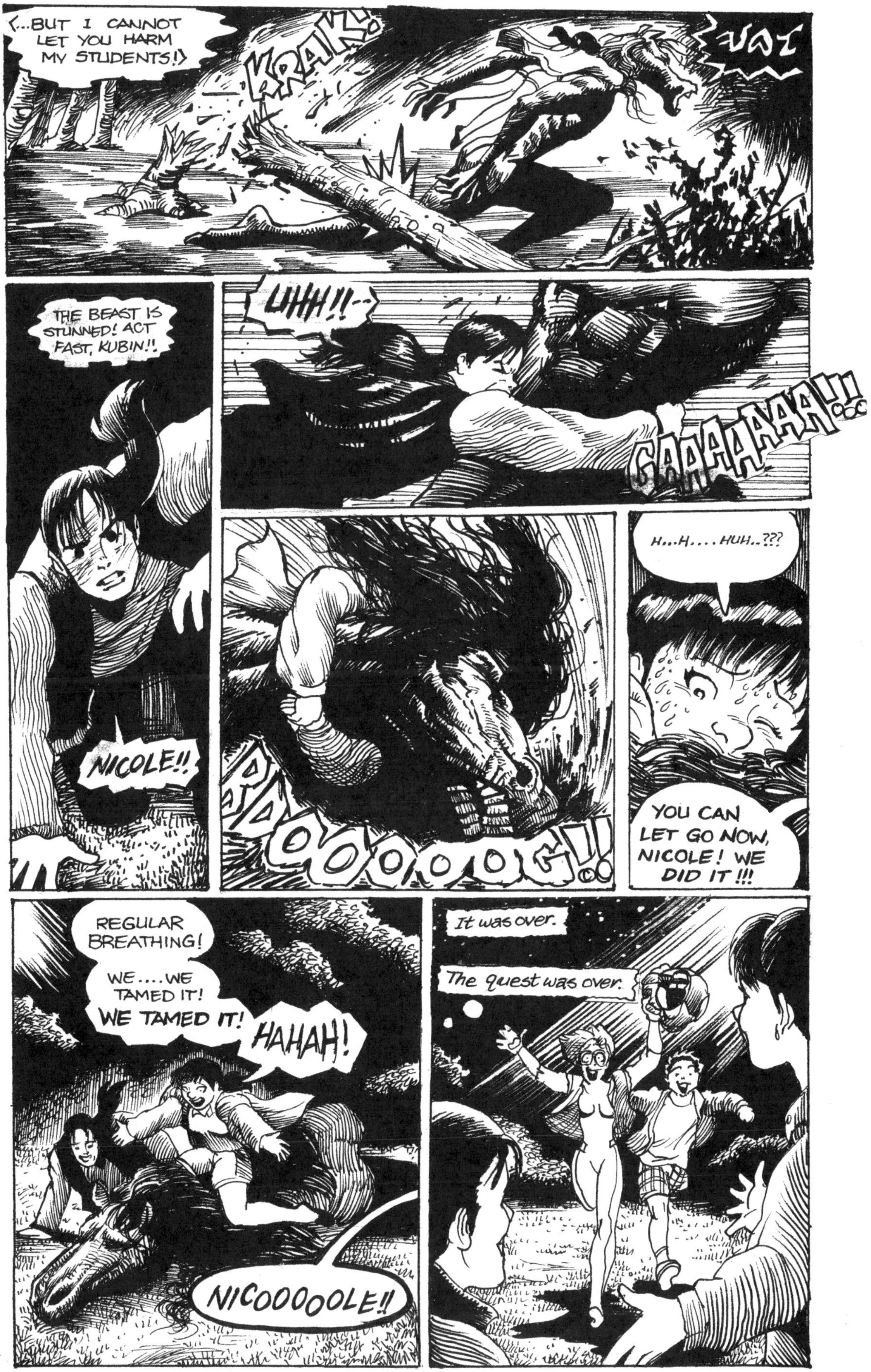

<...BUT I CANNOT LET YOU HARM MY STUDENTS!>
KRAK!
THE BEAST IS STUNNED! ACT FAST, KUBIN!!
UHH!!
GAAAAAAR!!
NICOLE!!
BROOOOOOG!!
H...H....HUH..???
YOU CAN LET GO NOW, NICOLE! WE DID IT!!!
REGULAR BREATHING!
WE....WE TAMED IT!
WE TAMED IT!
HAHAH!
NICOOOOOLE!!
It was over.
The quest was over.

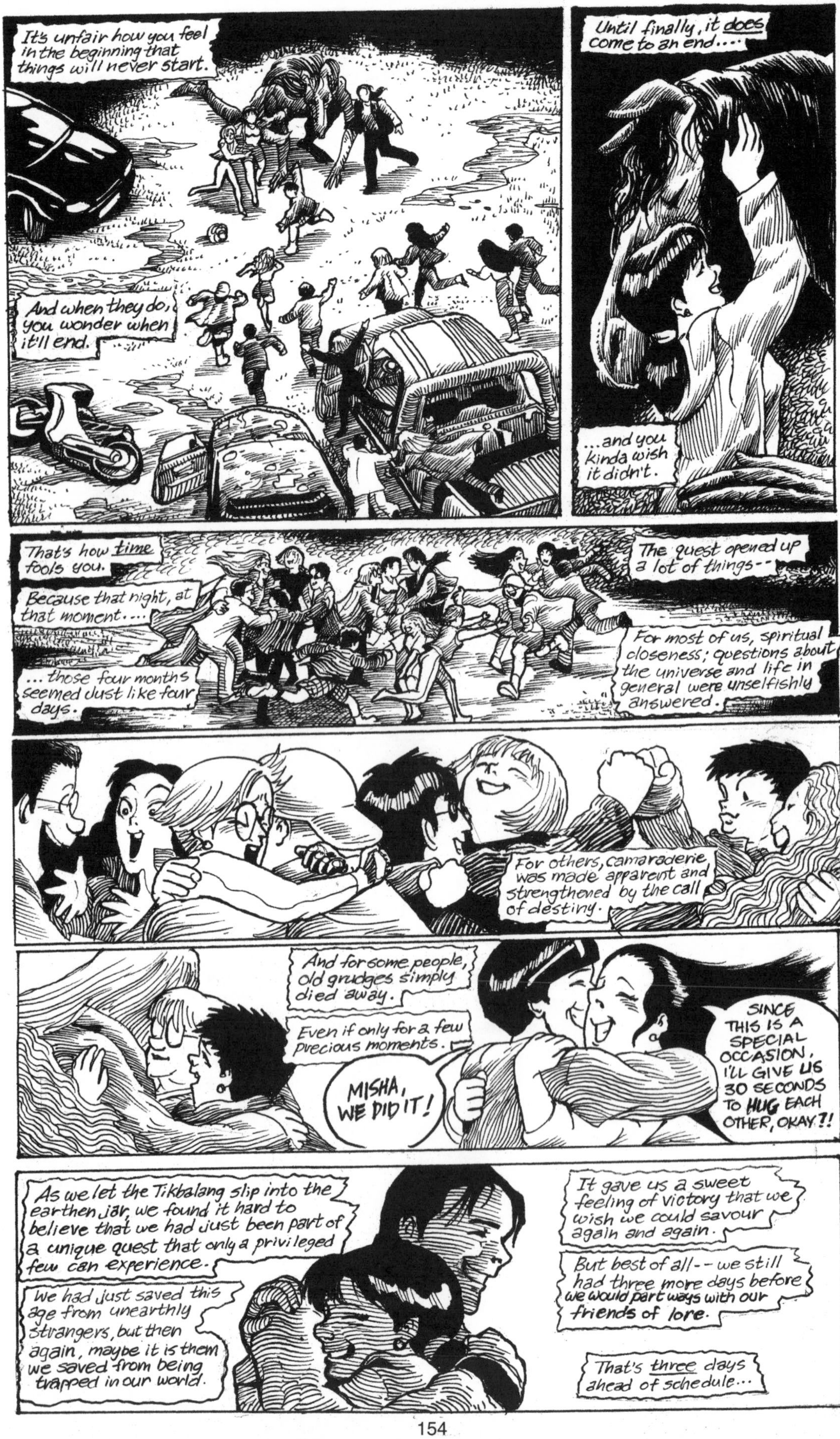
It's unfair how you feel in the beginning that things will never start.
And when they do, you wonder when it'll end.
Until finally, it does come to an end....
...and you kinda wish it didn't.
That's how time fools you.
Because that night, at that moment....
...those four months seemed just like four days.
The quest opened up a lot of things--
For most of us, spiritual closeness; questions about the universe and life in general were unselfishly answered.
For others, camaraderie was made apparent and strengthened by the call of destiny.
And for some people, old grudges simply died away.
Even if only for a few precious moments.
MISHA, WE DID IT!
SINCE THIS IS A SPECIAL OCCASION, I'LL GIVE US 30 SECONDS TO HUG EACH OTHER, OKAY?!
As we let the Tikbalang slip into the earthen jar, we found it hard to believe that we had just been part of a unique quest that only a privileged few can experience.
We had just saved this age from unearthly strangers, but then again, maybe it is them we saved from being trapped in our world.
It gave us a sweet feeling of victory that we wish we could savour again and again.
But best of all--we still had three more days before we would part ways with our friends of lore.
That's three days ahead of schedule...

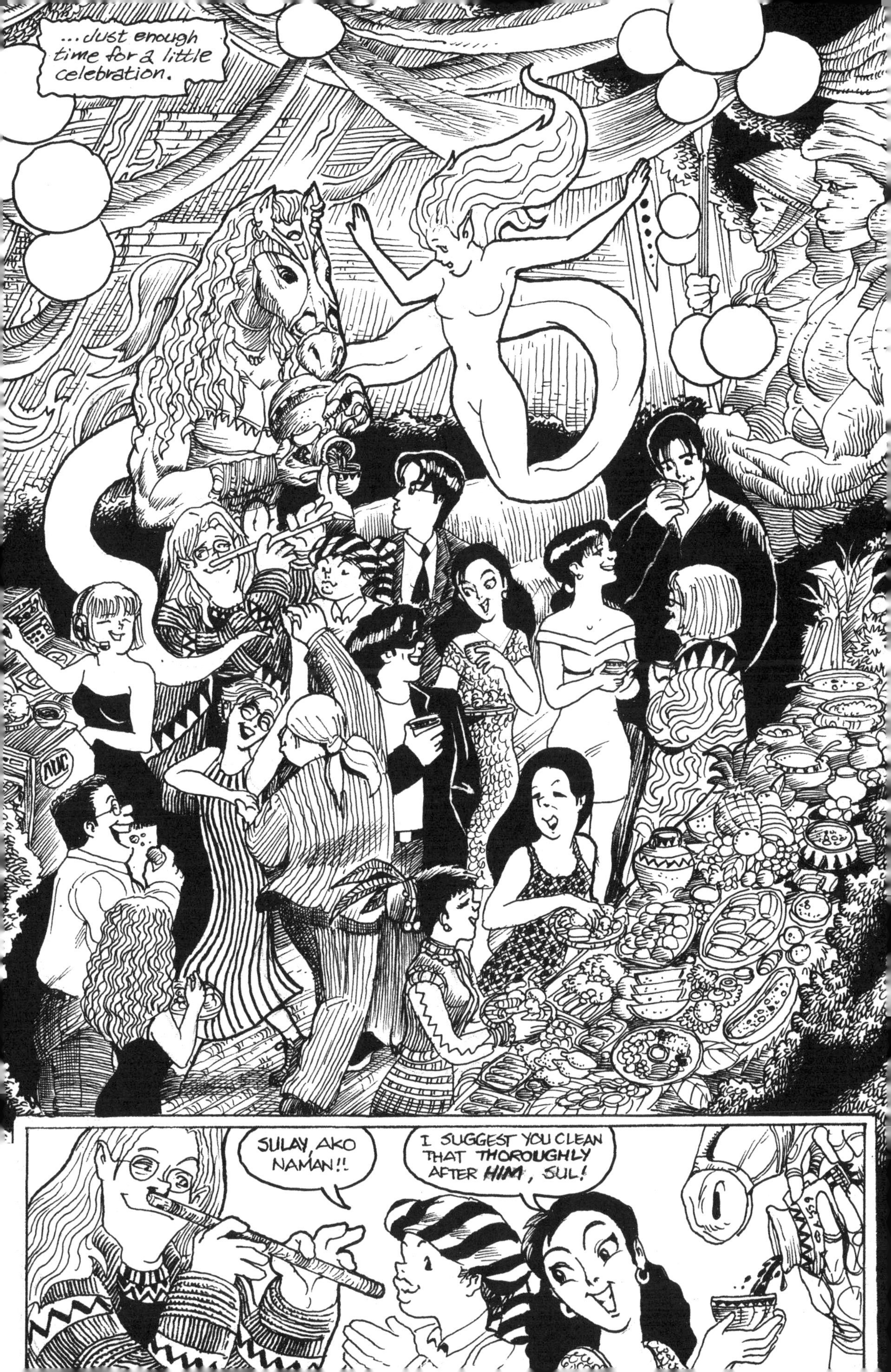
...Just enough time for a little celebration.
SULAY, AKO NAMAN!!
I SUGGEST YOU CLEAN THAT THOROUGHLY AFTER HIM, SUL!

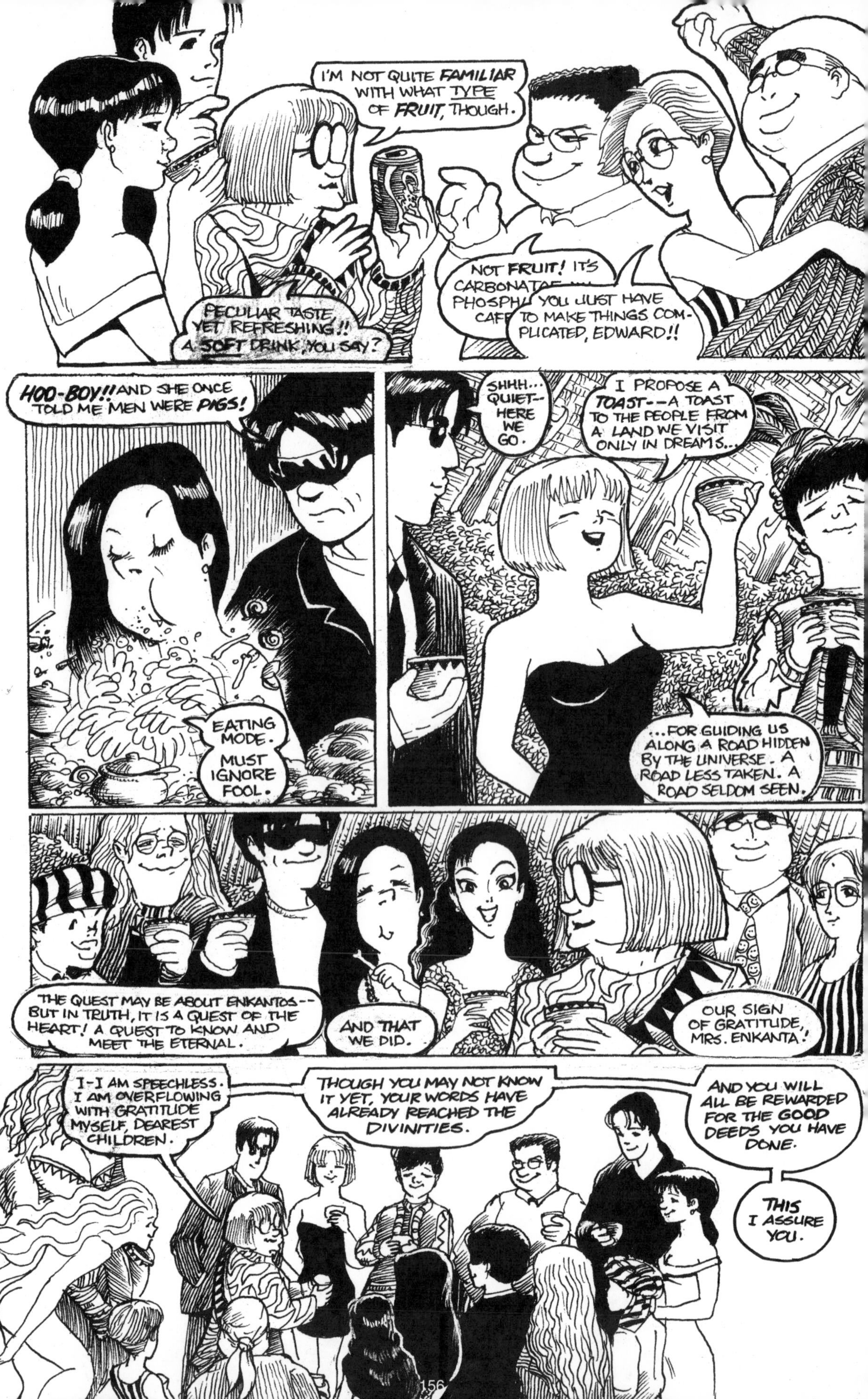
I'M NOT QUITE FAMILIAR WITH WHAT TYPE OF FRUIT, THOUGH.
PECULIAR TASTE, YET REFRESHING!! A SOFT DRINK, YOU SAY?
NOT FRUIT! IT'S
YOU JUST HAVE TO MAKE THINGS COM-PLICATED, EDWARD!!
HOO-BOY!! AND SHE ONCE TOLD ME MEN WERE PIGS!
EATING MODE. MUST IGNORE FOOL.
SHHH... QUIET-- HERE WE GO.
I PROPOSE A TOAST--A TOAST TO THE PEOPLE FROM A LAND WE VISIT ONLY IN DREAMS...
...FOR GUIDING US ALONG A ROAD HIDDEN BY THE UNIVERSE. A ROAD LESS TAKEN. A ROAD SELDOM SEEN.
THE QUEST MAY BE ABOUT ENKANTOS-- BUT IN TRUTH, IT IS A QUEST OF THE HEART! A QUEST TO KNOW AND MEET THE ETERNAL.
AND THAT WE DID.
OUR SIGN OF GRATITUDE, MRS. ENKANTA!
I-I AM SPEECHLESS. I AM OVERFLOWING WITH GRATITUDE MYSELF, DEAREST CHILDREN.
THOUGH YOU MAY NOT KNOW IT YET, YOUR WORDS HAVE ALREADY REACHED THE DIVINITIES.
AND YOU WILL ALL BE REWARDED FOR THE GOOD DEEDS YOU HAVE DONE.
THIS I ASSURE YOU.

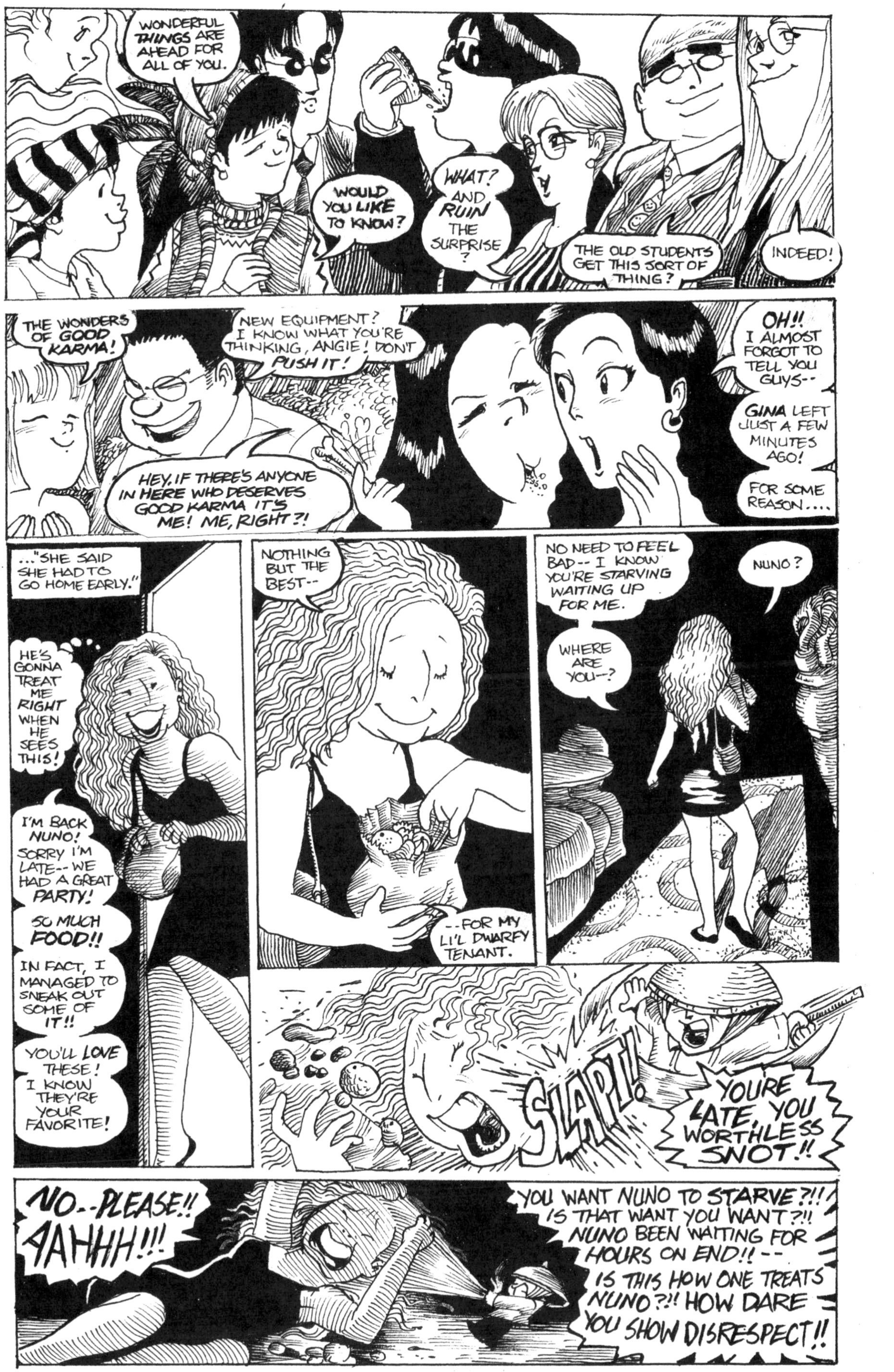
WONDERFUL THINGS ARE AHEAD FOR ALL OF YOU.
WOULD YOU LIKE TO KNOW?
WHAT? AND RUIN THE SURPRISE?
THE OLD STUDENTS GET THIS SORT OF THING?
INDEED!
THE WONDERS OF GOOD KARMA!
NEW EQUIPMENT? I KNOW WHAT YOU'RE THINKING, ANGIE! DON'T PUSH IT!
HEY, IF THERE'S ANYONE IN HERE WHO DESERVES GOOD KARMA IT'S ME! ME, RIGHT?!
OH!! I ALMOST FORGOT TO TELL YOU GUYS--
GINA LEFT JUST A FEW MINUTES AGO!
FOR SOME REASON....
..."SHE SAID SHE HAD TO GO HOME EARLY."
HE'S GONNA TREAT ME RIGHT WHEN HE SEES THIS!
I'M BACK NUNO! SORRY I'M LATE-- WE HAD A GREAT PARTY!
SO MUCH FOOD!!
IN FACT, I MANAGED TO SNEAK OUT SOME OF IT!!
YOU'LL LOVE THESE! I KNOW THEY'RE YOUR FAVORITE!
NOTHING BUT THE BEST--
--FOR MY LI'L DWARFY TENANT.
NO NEED TO FEEL BAD-- I KNOW YOU'RE STARVING WAITING UP FOR ME.
WHERE ARE YOU--?
NUNO?
SLAP!!
YOU'RE LATE, YOU WORTHLESS SNOT!!
NO--PLEASE!! AAHHH!!!
YOU WANT NUNO TO STARVE?!! IS THAT WANT YOU WANT?!! NUNO BEEN WAITING FOR HOURS ON END!! --
IS THIS HOW ONE TREATS NUNO?!! HOW DARE YOU SHOW DISRESPECT!!

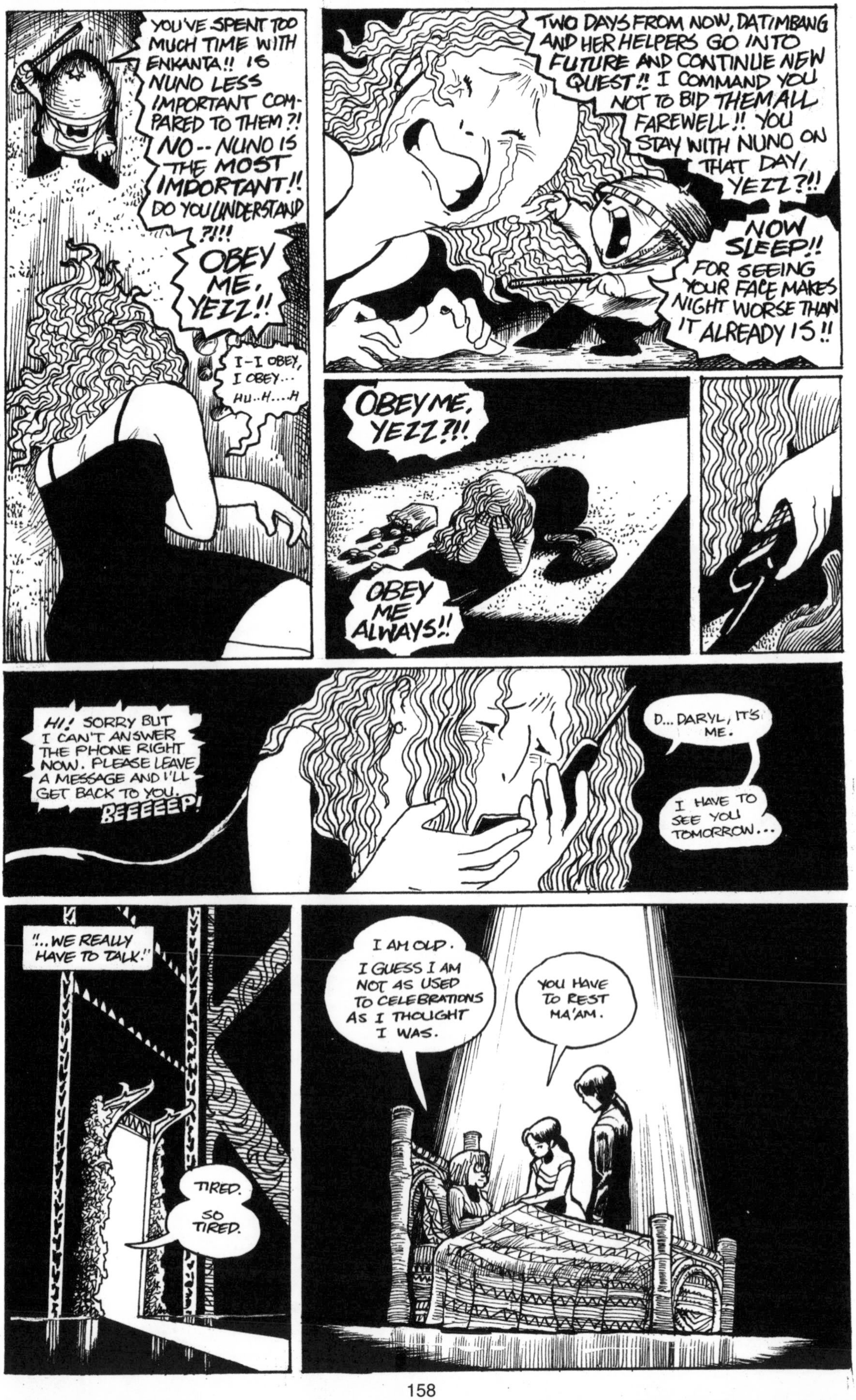

YOU'VE SPENT TOO MUCH TIME WITH ENKANTA!! IS NUNO LESS IMPORTANT COMPARED TO THEM?! NO--NUNO IS THE MOST IMPORTANT!! DO YOU UNDERSTAND?!!!
OBEY ME, YEZZ!!
I-I OBEY, I OBEY... HU..H....H
TWO DAYS FROM NOW, DATIMBANG AND HER HELPERS GO INTO FUTURE AND CONTINUE NEW QUEST!! I COMMAND YOU NOT TO BID THEM ALL FAREWELL!! YOU STAY WITH NUNO ON THAT DAY, YEZZ?!!
NOW SLEEP!! FOR SEEING YOUR FACE MAKES NIGHT WORSE THAN IT ALREADY IS!!
OBEY ME, YEZZ?!!
OBEY ME ALWAYS!!
HI! SORRY BUT I CAN'T ANSWER THE PHONE RIGHT NOW. PLEASE LEAVE A MESSAGE AND I'LL GET BACK TO YOU. BEEEEEP!
D... DARYL, IT'S ME.
I HAVE TO SEE YOU TOMORROW...
"...WE REALLY HAVE TO TALK."
TIRED.
SO TIRED.
I AM OLD.
I GUESS I AM NOT AS USED TO CELEBRATIONS AS I THOUGHT I WAS.
YOU HAVE TO REST MA'AM.

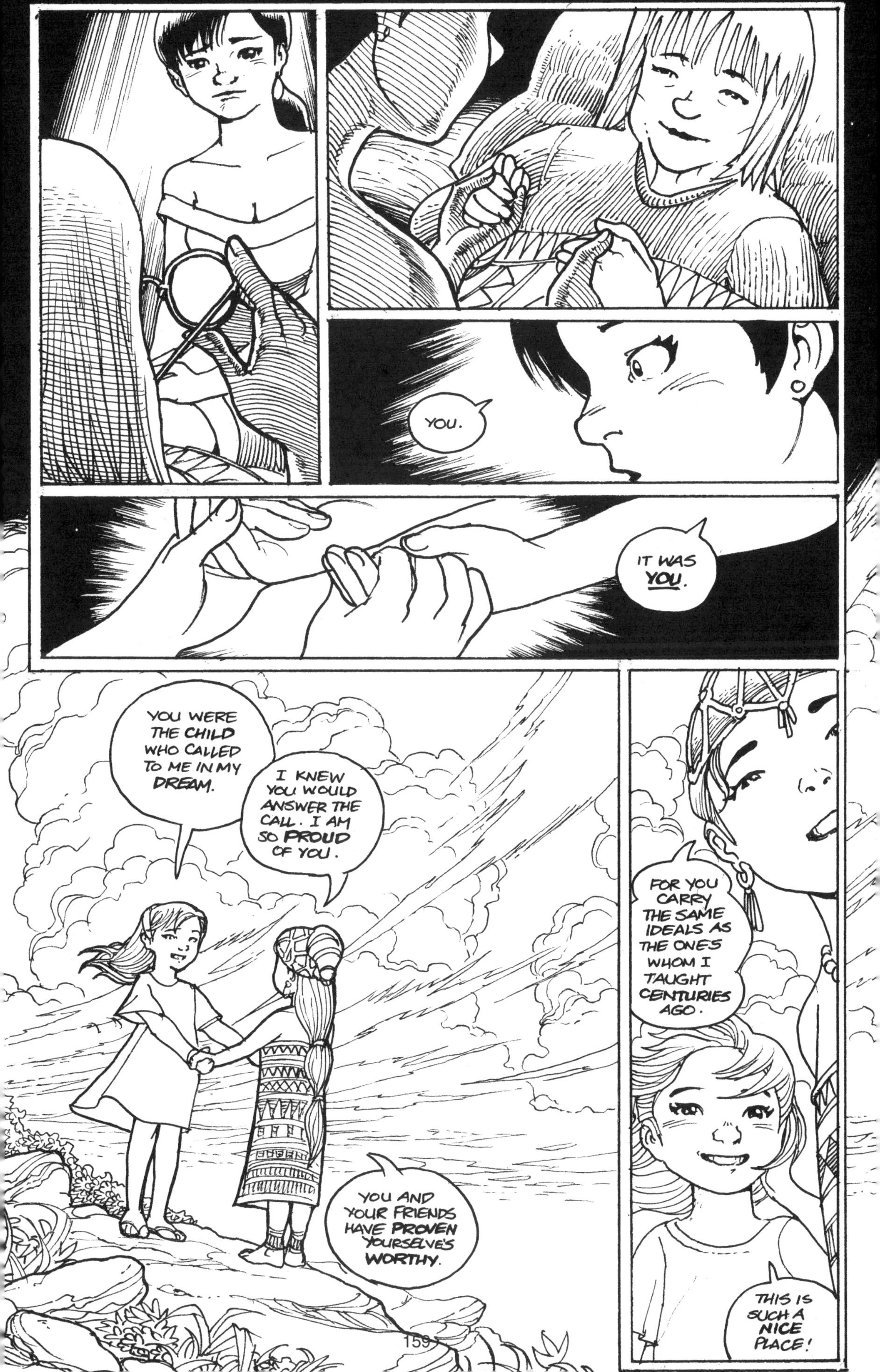
YOU.
IT WAS YOU.
YOU WERE THE CHILD WHO CALLED TO ME IN MY DREAM.
I KNEW YOU WOULD ANSWER THE CALL. I AM SO PROUD OF YOU.
YOU AND YOUR FRIENDS HAVE PROVEN YOURSELVE'S WORTHY.
FOR YOU CARRY THE SAME IDEALS AS THE ONES WHOM I TAUGHT CENTURIES AGO.
THIS IS SUCH A NICE PLACE!

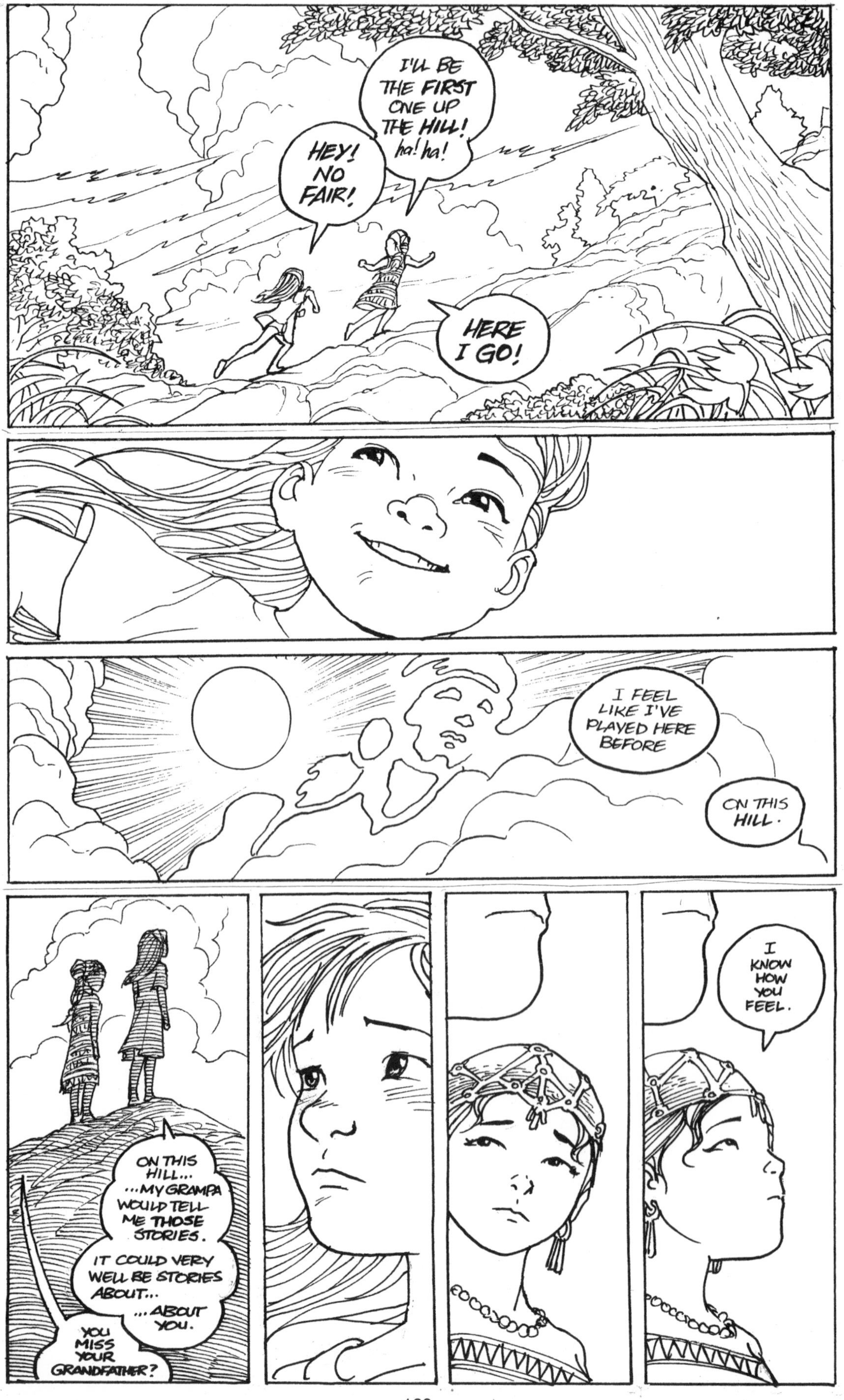
I'LL BE THE FIRST ONE UP THE HILL! ha! ha!
HEY! NO FAIR!
HERE I GO!
I FEEL LIKE I'VE PLAYED HERE BEFORE
ON THIS HILL.
ON THIS HILL... ...MY GRAMPA WOULD TELL ME THOSE STORIES.
IT COULD VERY WELL BE STORIES ABOUT... ...ABOUT YOU.
YOU MISS YOUR GRANDFATHER?
I KNOW HOW YOU FEEL.

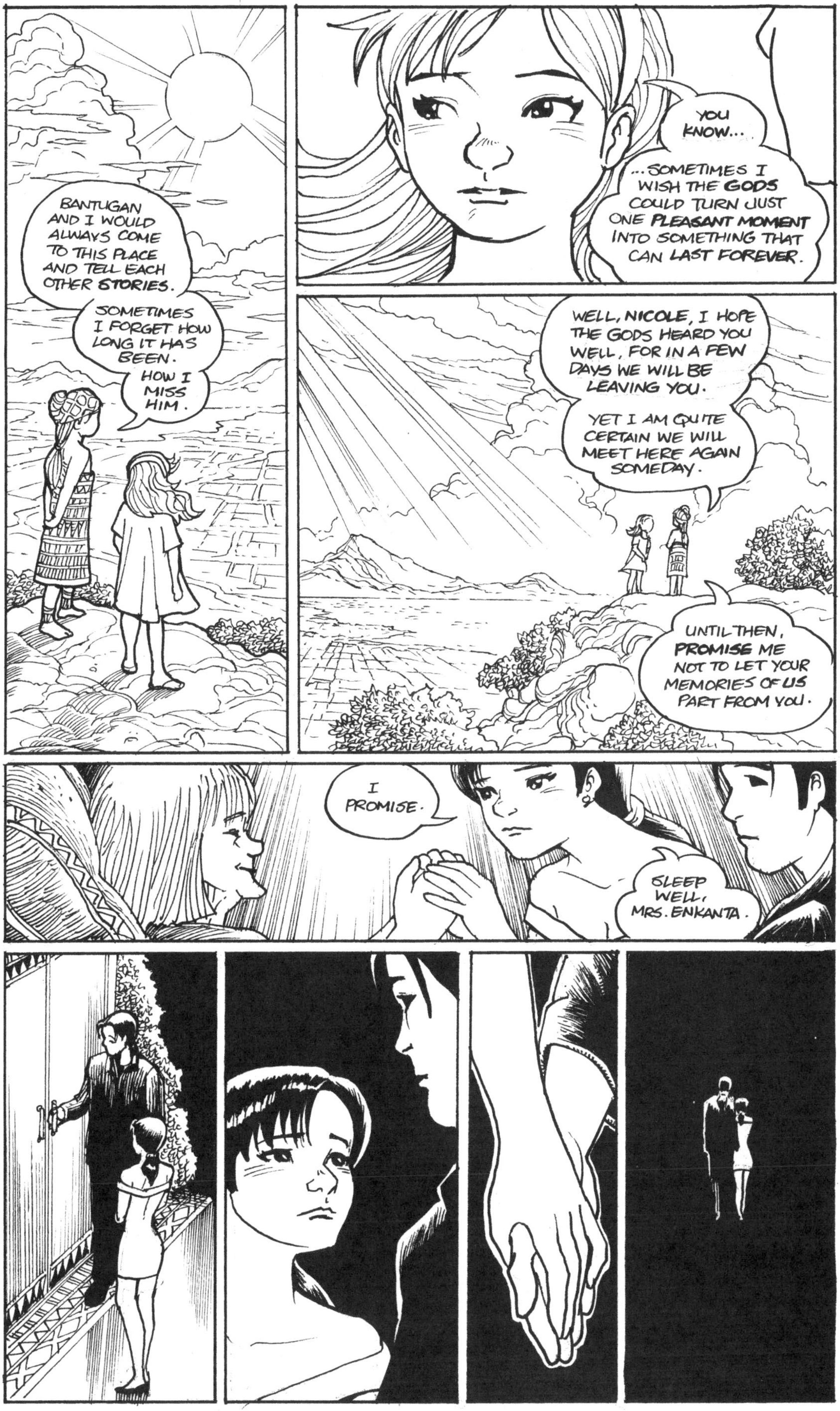
BANTUGAN AND I WOULD ALWAYS COME TO THIS PLACE AND TELL EACH OTHER STORIES.
SOMETIMES I FORGET HOW LONG IT HAS BEEN.
HOW I MISS HIM.
YOU KNOW...
...SOMETIMES I WISH THE GODS COULD TURN JUST ONE PLEASANT MOMENT INTO SOMETHING THAT CAN LAST FOREVER.
WELL, NICOLE, I HOPE THE GODS HEARD YOU WELL, FOR IN A FEW DAYS WE WILL BE LEAVING YOU.
YET I AM QUITE CERTAIN WE WILL MEET HERE AGAIN SOMEDAY.
UNTIL THEN, PROMISE ME NOT TO LET YOUR MEMORIES OF US PART FROM YOU.
I PROMISE.
SLEEP WELL, MRS. ENKANTA.

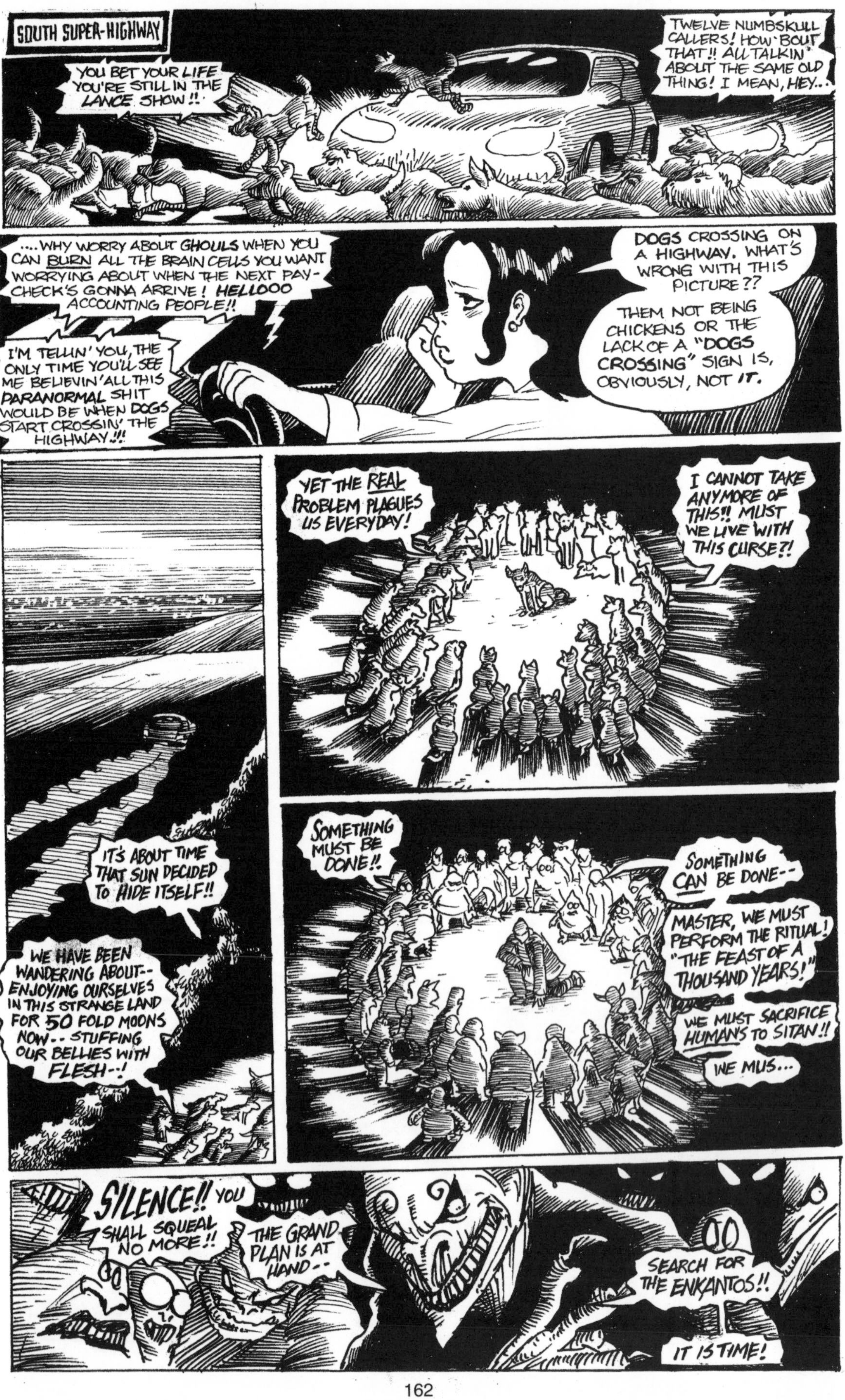
SOUTH SUPER-HIGHWAY
YOU BET YOUR LIFE YOU'RE STILL IN THE LANCE SHOW!!
TWELVE NUMBSKULL CALLERS! HOW 'BOUT THAT!! ALL TALKIN' ABOUT THE SAME OLD THING! I MEAN, HEY...
...WHY WORRY ABOUT GHOULS WHEN YOU CAN BURN ALL THE BRAIN CELLS YOU WANT WORRYING ABOUT WHEN THE NEXT PAY-CHECK'S GONNA ARRIVE! HELLOOO ACCOUNTING PEOPLE!!
I'M TELLIN' YOU, THE ONLY TIME YOU'LL SEE ME BELIEVIN' ALL THIS PARANORMAL SHIT WOULD BE WHEN DOGS START CROSSIN' THE HIGHWAY!!!
DOGS CROSSING ON A HIGHWAY. WHAT'S WRONG WITH THIS PICTURE??
THEM NOT BEING CHICKENS OR THE LACK OF A "DOGS CROSSING" SIGN IS, OBVIOUSLY, NOT IT.
YET THE REAL PROBLEM PLAGUES US EVERYDAY!
I CANNOT TAKE ANYMORE OF THIS!! MUST WE LIVE WITH THIS CURSE?!
IT'S ABOUT TIME THAT SUN DECIDED TO HIDE ITSELF!!
WE HAVE BEEN WANDERING ABOUT-- ENJOYING OURSELVES IN THIS STRANGE LAND FOR 50 FOLD MOONS NOW-- STUFFING OUR BELLIES WITH FLESH--!
SOMETHING MUST BE DONE!!
SOMETHING CAN BE DONE--
MASTER, WE MUST PERFORM THE RITUAL! "THE FEAST OF A THOUSAND YEARS!"
WE MUST SACRIFICE HUMANS TO SITAN!!
WE MUS...
SILENCE!! YOU SHALL SQUEAL NO MORE!!
THE GRAND PLAN IS AT HAND--
SEARCH FOR THE ENKANTOS!!
IT IS TIME!

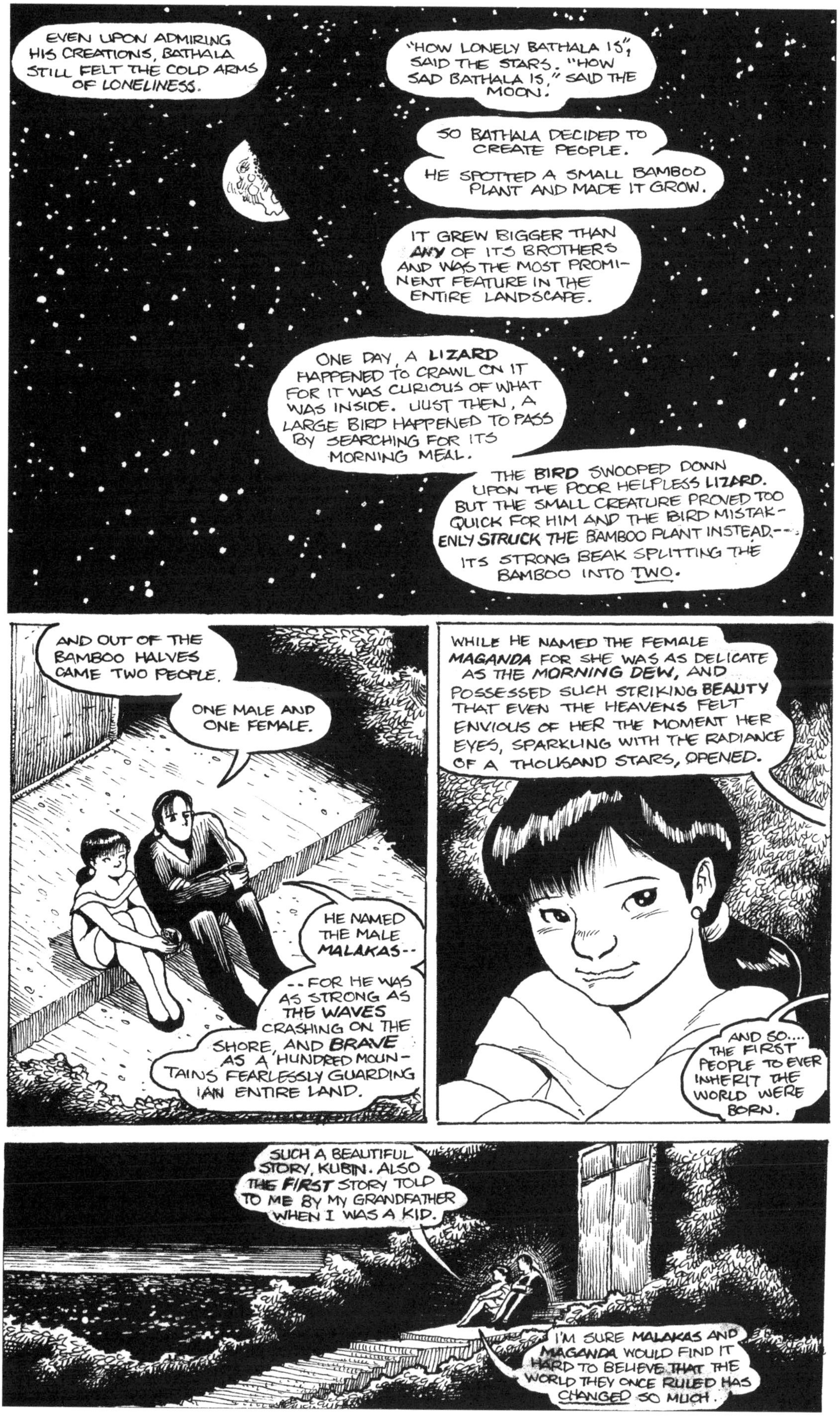
EVEN UPON ADMIRING HIS CREATIONS, BATHALA STILL FELT THE COLD ARMS OF LONELINESS.
"HOW LONELY BATHALA IS," SAID THE STARS. "HOW SAD BATHALA IS," SAID THE MOON.
SO BATHALA DECIDED TO CREATE PEOPLE.
HE SPOTTED A SMALL BAMBOO PLANT AND MADE IT GROW.
IT GREW BIGGER THAN ANY OF ITS BROTHERS AND WAS THE MOST PROMINENT FEATURE IN THE ENTIRE LANDSCAPE.
ONE DAY, A LIZARD HAPPENED TO CRAWL ON IT FOR IT WAS CURIOUS OF WHAT WAS INSIDE. JUST THEN, A LARGE BIRD HAPPENED TO PASS BY SEARCHING FOR ITS MORNING MEAL.
THE BIRD SWOOPED DOWN UPON THE POOR HELPLESS LIZARD. BUT THE SMALL CREATURE PROVED TOO QUICK FOR HIM AND THE BIRD MISTAKENLY STRUCK THE BAMBOO PLANT INSTEAD--- ITS STRONG BEAK SPLITTING THE BAMBOO INTO TWO.
AND OUT OF THE BAMBOO HALVES CAME TWO PEOPLE.
ONE MALE AND ONE FEMALE.
HE NAMED THE MALE MALAKAS--
--FOR HE WAS AS STRONG AS THE WAVES CRASHING ON THE SHORE, AND BRAVE AS A HUNDRED MOUNTAINS FEARLESSLY GUARDING AN ENTIRE LAND.
WHILE HE NAMED THE FEMALE MAGANDA FOR SHE WAS AS DELICATE AS THE MORNING DEW, AND POSSESSED SUCH STRIKING BEAUTY THAT EVEN THE HEAVENS FELT ENVIOUS OF HER THE MOMENT HER EYES, SPARKLING WITH THE RADIANCE OF A THOUSAND STARS, OPENED.
AND SO.... THE FIRST PEOPLE TO EVER INHERIT THE WORLD WERE BORN.
SUCH A BEAUTIFUL STORY, KUBIN. ALSO THE FIRST STORY TOLD TO ME BY MY GRANDFATHER WHEN I WAS A KID.
I'M SURE MALAKAS AND MAGANDA WOULD FIND IT HARD TO BELIEVE THAT THE WORLD THEY ONCE RULED HAS CHANGED SO MUCH.

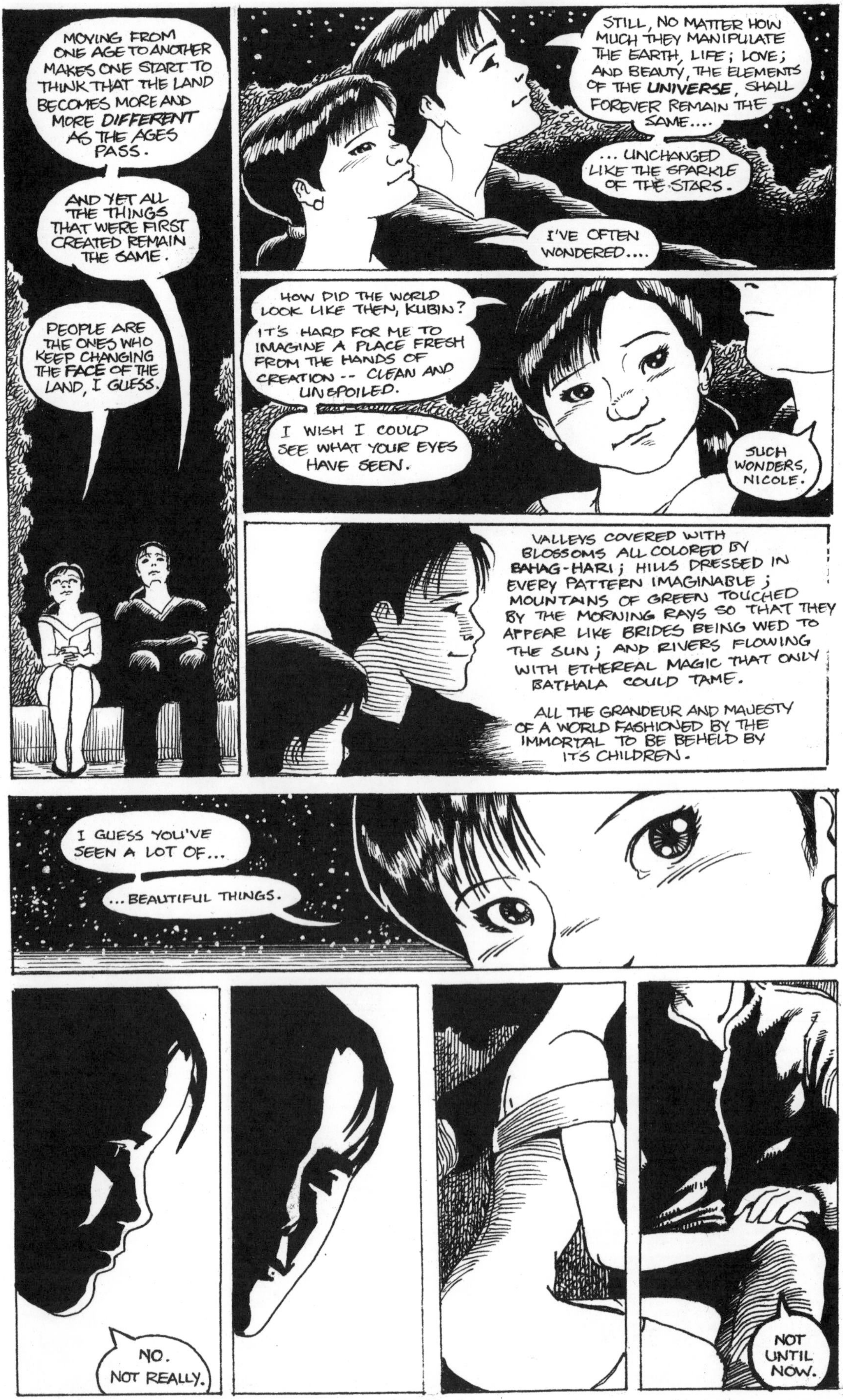
MOVING FROM ONE AGE TO ANOTHER MAKES ONE START TO THINK THAT THE LAND BECOMES MORE AND MORE DIFFERENT AS THE AGES PASS.
AND YET ALL THE THINGS THAT WERE FIRST CREATED REMAIN THE SAME.
PEOPLE ARE THE ONES WHO KEEP CHANGING THE FACE OF THE LAND, I GUESS.
STILL, NO MATTER HOW MUCH THEY MANIPULATE THE EARTH, LIFE; LOVE; AND BEAUTY, THE ELEMENTS OF THE UNIVERSE, SHALL FOREVER REMAIN THE SAME....
... UNCHANGED LIKE THE SPARKLE OF THE STARS.
I'VE OFTEN WONDERED....
HOW DID THE WORLD LOOK LIKE THEN, KUBIN?
IT'S HARD FOR ME TO IMAGINE A PLACE FRESH FROM THE HANDS OF CREATION -- CLEAN AND UNSPOILED.
I WISH I COULD SEE WHAT YOUR EYES HAVE SEEN.
SUCH WONDERS, NICOLE.
VALLEYS COVERED WITH BLOSSOMS ALL COLORED BY BAHAG-HARI; HILLS DRESSED IN EVERY PATTERN IMAGINABLE; MOUNTAINS OF GREEN TOUCHED BY THE MORNING RAYS SO THAT THEY APPEAR LIKE BRIDES BEING WED TO THE SUN; AND RIVERS FLOWING WITH ETHEREAL MAGIC THAT ONLY BATHALA COULD TAME.
ALL THE GRANDEUR AND MAJESTY OF A WORLD FASHIONED BY THE IMMORTAL TO BE BEHELD BY ITS CHILDREN.
I GUESS YOU'VE SEEN A LOT OF...
...BEAUTIFUL THINGS.
NO. NOT REALLY.
NOT UNTIL NOW.

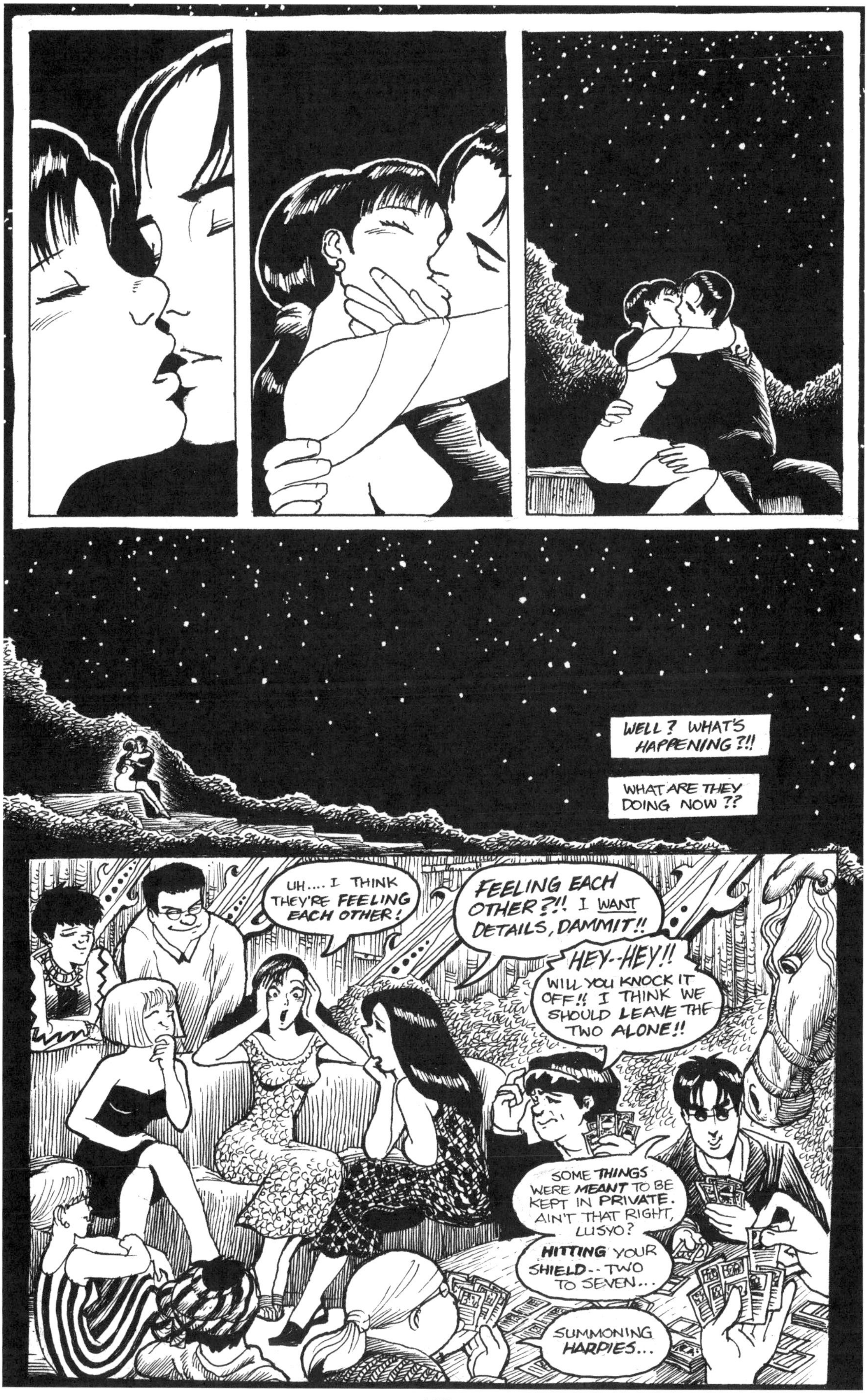

WELL? WHAT'S HAPPENING?!!
WHAT ARE THEY DOING NOW??
UH.... I THINK THEY'RE FEELING EACH OTHER!
FEELING EACH OTHER?!! I WANT DETAILS, DAMMIT!!
HEY--HEY!! WILL YOU KNOCK IT OFF!! I THINK WE SHOULD LEAVE THE TWO ALONE!!
SOME THINGS WERE MEANT TO BE KEPT IN PRIVATE. AIN'T THAT RIGHT, LUSYO?
HITTING YOUR SHIELD-- TWO TO SEVEN...
SUMMONING HARPIES...

HEY SUL, EVER GOT TIRED OF BATTLING MONSTERS? HOW DID YOU LIVE BACK THEN?

YEAH.

JUST THINK-- GEEKS LIKE US WOULD DO ANYTHING JUST TO LIVE THE LIFE OF A HERO LIKE YOURSELF.

I'M ATTACKING YOUR MINOTAUR, BY THE WAY.

MY FRIENDS, IT IS A DIFFICULT LIFE NOT KNOWING WHAT DANGER LURKS.

WE CAN IMAGINE.

HEY, BUT... ...WE SURE WILL MISS YOU ALL.

YEAH! IMPS, GHOULS, HAIRY STINKY GIANTS? GIVE ME FOUR-HOUR TRAFFIC ANYTIME!

THAT WAS ONE HECK OF AN ADVENTURE WE HAD WITH YOU.

WOULDN'T TRADE IT FOR ANYTHING.

AKO RIN.

YOU THINK WE'LL SEE EACH OTHER AGAIN IN DREAMS?

OR FACE TO FACE? IN AN ENTIRELY NEW QUEST EVEN?

WHO KNOWS?

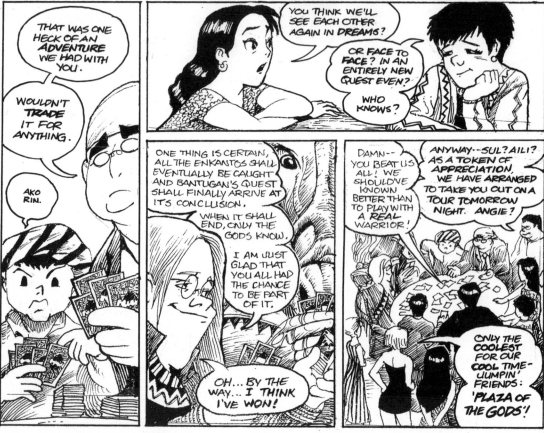

ONE THING IS CERTAIN, ALL THE ENKANTOS SHALL EVENTUALLY BE CAUGHT AND BANTUGAN'S QUEST SHALL FINALLY ARRIVE AT ITS CONCLUSION.

WHEN IT SHALL END, ONLY THE GODS KNOW.

I AM JUST GLAD THAT YOU ALL HAD THE CHANCE TO BE PART OF IT.

OH.... BY THE WAY... I THINK I'VE WON!

DAMN-- YOU BEAT US ALL! WE SHOULD'VE KNOWN BETTER THAN TO PLAY WITH A REAL WARRIOR!

ANYWAY--SUL? AILI? AS A TOKEN OF APPRECIATION, WE HAVE ARRANGED TO TAKE YOU OUT ON A TOUR TOMORROW NIGHT. ANGIE?

ONLY THE COOLEST FOR OUR COOL TIME-JUMPIN' FRIENDS: 'PLAZA OF THE GODS'!

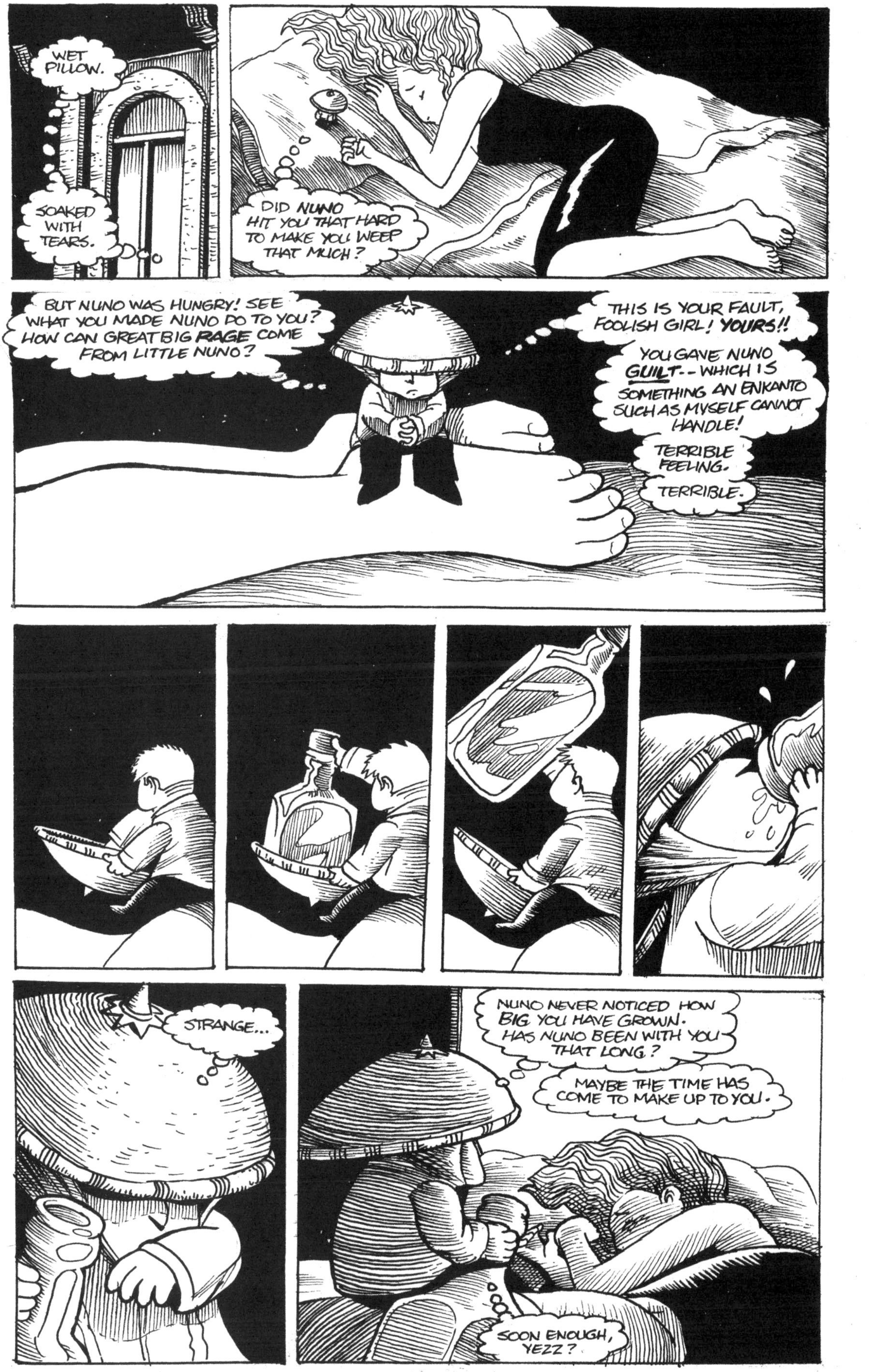
WET PILLOW.
SOAKED WITH TEARS.
DID NUNO HIT YOU THAT HARD TO MAKE YOU WEEP THAT MUCH?
BUT NUNO WAS HUNGRY! SEE WHAT YOU MADE NUNO DO TO YOU? HOW CAN GREAT BIG RAGE COME FROM LITTLE NUNO?
THIS IS YOUR FAULT, FOOLISH GIRL! YOURS!!
YOU GAVE NUNO GUILT-- WHICH IS SOMETHING AN ENKANTO SUCH AS MYSELF CANNOT HANDLE!
TERRIBLE FEELING.
TERRIBLE.
STRANGE...
NUNO NEVER NOTICED HOW BIG YOU HAVE GROWN. HAS NUNO BEEN WITH YOU THAT LONG?
MAYBE THE TIME HAS COME TO MAKE UP TO YOU.
SOON ENOUGH, YEZZ?

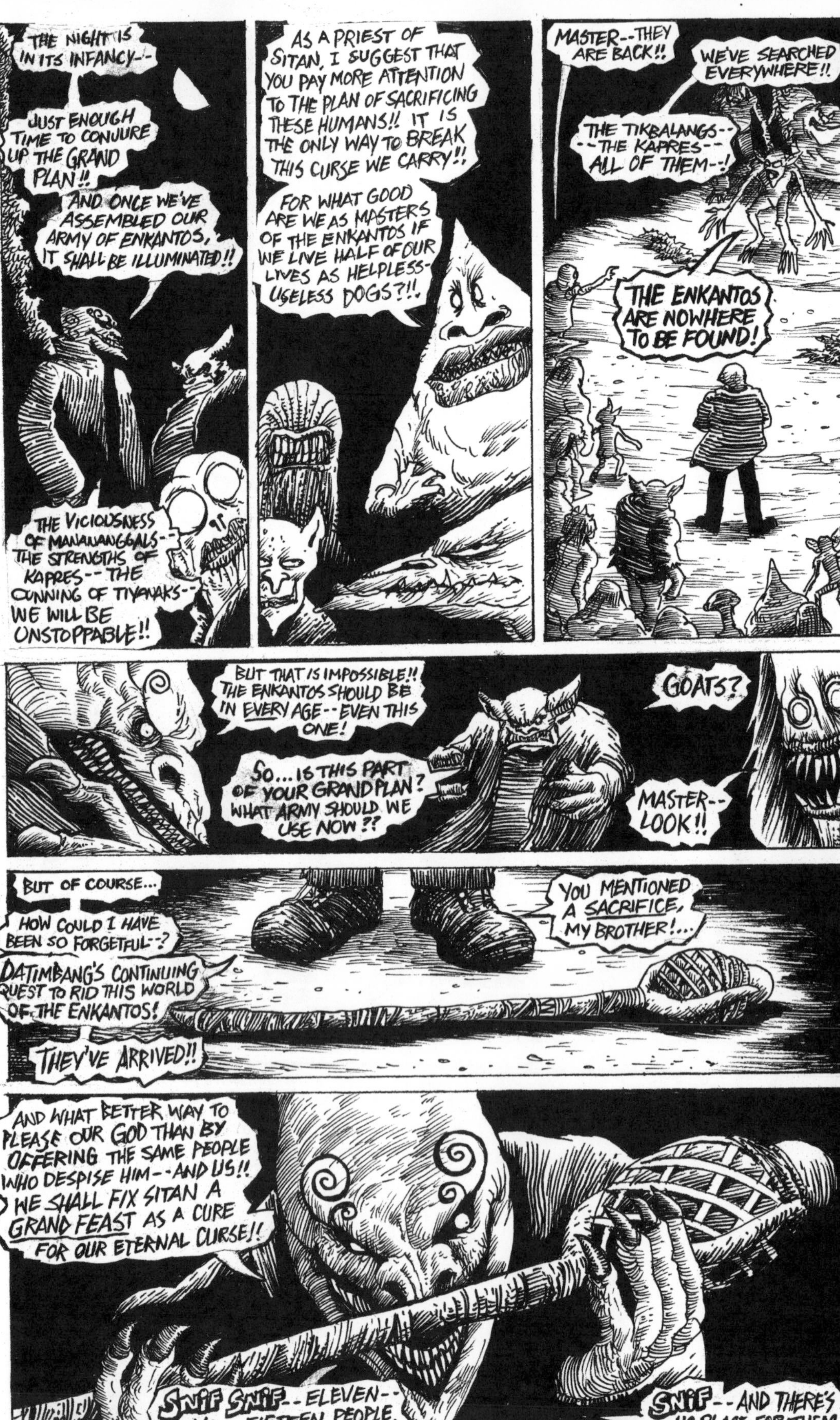
THE NIGHT IS IN ITS INFANCY--
JUST ENOUGH TIME TO CONJURE UP THE GRAND PLAN!!
AND ONCE WE'VE ASSEMBLED OUR ARMY OF ENKANTOS, IT SHALL BE ILLUMINATED!!
THE VICIOUSNESS OF MANANANGGALS-- THE STRENGTHS OF KAPRES-- THE CUNNING OF TIYANAKS-- WE WILL BE UNSTOPPABLE!!
AS A PRIEST OF SITAN, I SUGGEST THAT YOU PAY MORE ATTENTION TO THE PLAN OF SACRIFICING THESE HUMANS!! IT IS THE ONLY WAY TO BREAK THIS CURSE WE CARRY!!
FOR WHAT GOOD ARE WE AS MASTERS OF THE ENKANTOS IF WE LIVE HALF OF OUR LIVES AS HELPLESS-USELESS DOGS?!!
MASTER--THEY ARE BACK!!
WE'VE SEARCHED EVERYWHERE!!
THE TIKBALANGS-- --THE KAPRES-- ALL OF THEM--!
THE ENKANTOS ARE NOWHERE TO BE FOUND!
BUT THAT IS IMPOSSIBLE!! THE ENKANTOS SHOULD BE IN EVERY AGE--EVEN THIS ONE!
SO... IS THIS PART OF YOUR GRAND PLAN? WHAT ARMY SHOULD WE USE NOW??
GOATS?
MASTER-- LOOK!!
BUT OF COURSE...
HOW COULD I HAVE BEEN SO FORGETFUL--?
DATIMBANG'S CONTINUING QUEST TO RID THIS WORLD OF THE ENKANTOS!
THEY'VE ARRIVED!!
YOU MENTIONED A SACRIFICE, MY BROTHER!...
AND WHAT BETTER WAY TO PLEASE OUR GOD THAN BY OFFERING THE SAME PEOPLE WHO DESPISE HIM--AND US!! WE SHALL FIX SITAN A GRAND FEAST AS A CURE FOR OUR ETERNAL CURSE!!
SNIF SNIF--ELEVEN-- NO--FIFTEEN PEOPLE, INCLUDING THE ACCURSED MISTRESS!!
SNIF--AND THERE'S NO PLACE FOR THEM TO HIDE!!

III

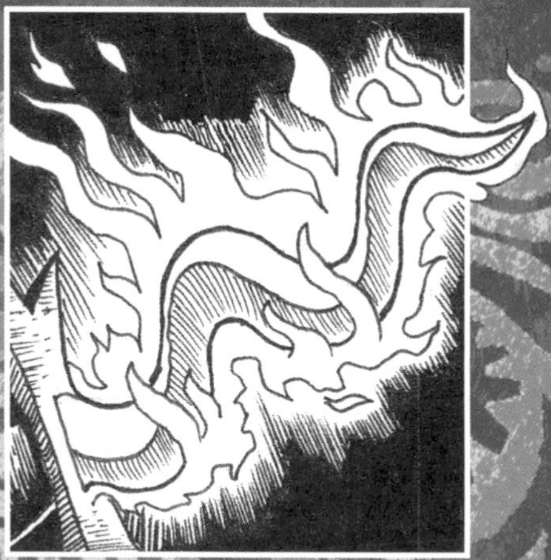

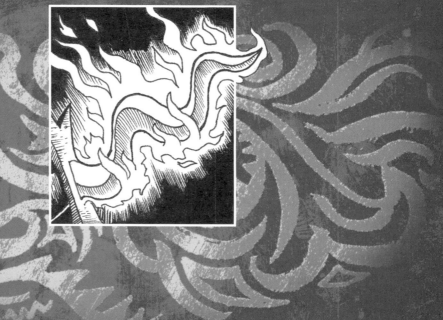

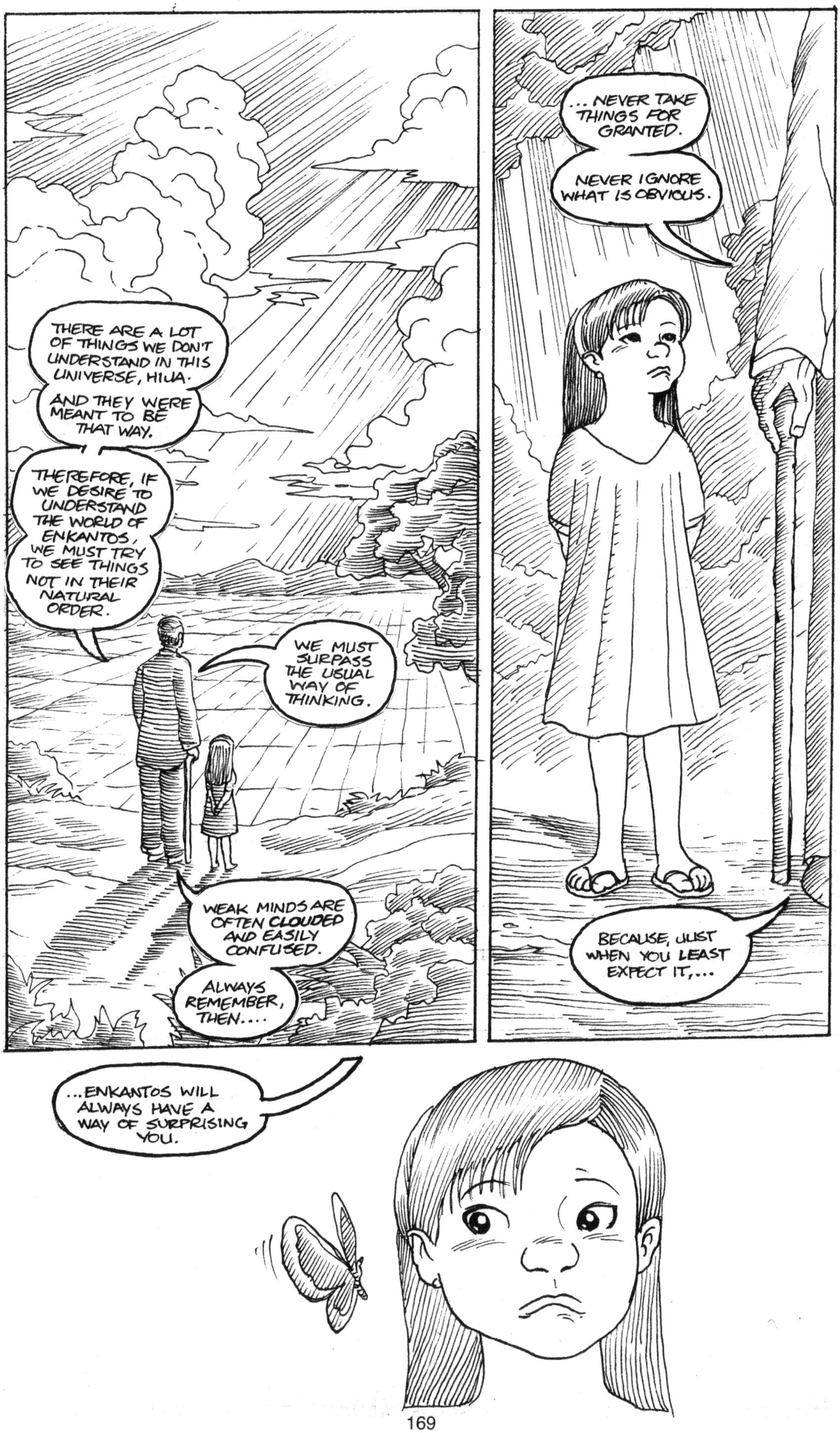
THERE ARE A LOT OF THINGS WE DON'T UNDERSTAND IN THIS UNIVERSE, HIJA.
AND THEY WERE MEANT TO BE THAT WAY.
THEREFORE, IF WE DESIRE TO UNDERSTAND THE WORLD OF ENKANTOS, WE MUST TRY TO SEE THINGS NOT IN THEIR NATURAL ORDER.
WE MUST SURPASS THE USUAL WAY OF THINKING.
WEAK MINDS ARE OFTEN CLOUDED AND EASILY CONFUSED.
ALWAYS REMEMBER, THEN....
...NEVER TAKE THINGS FOR GRANTED.
NEVER IGNORE WHAT IS OBVIOUS.
BECAUSE, JUST WHEN YOU LEAST EXPECT IT,...
...ENKANTOS WILL ALWAYS HAVE A WAY OF SURPRISING YOU.

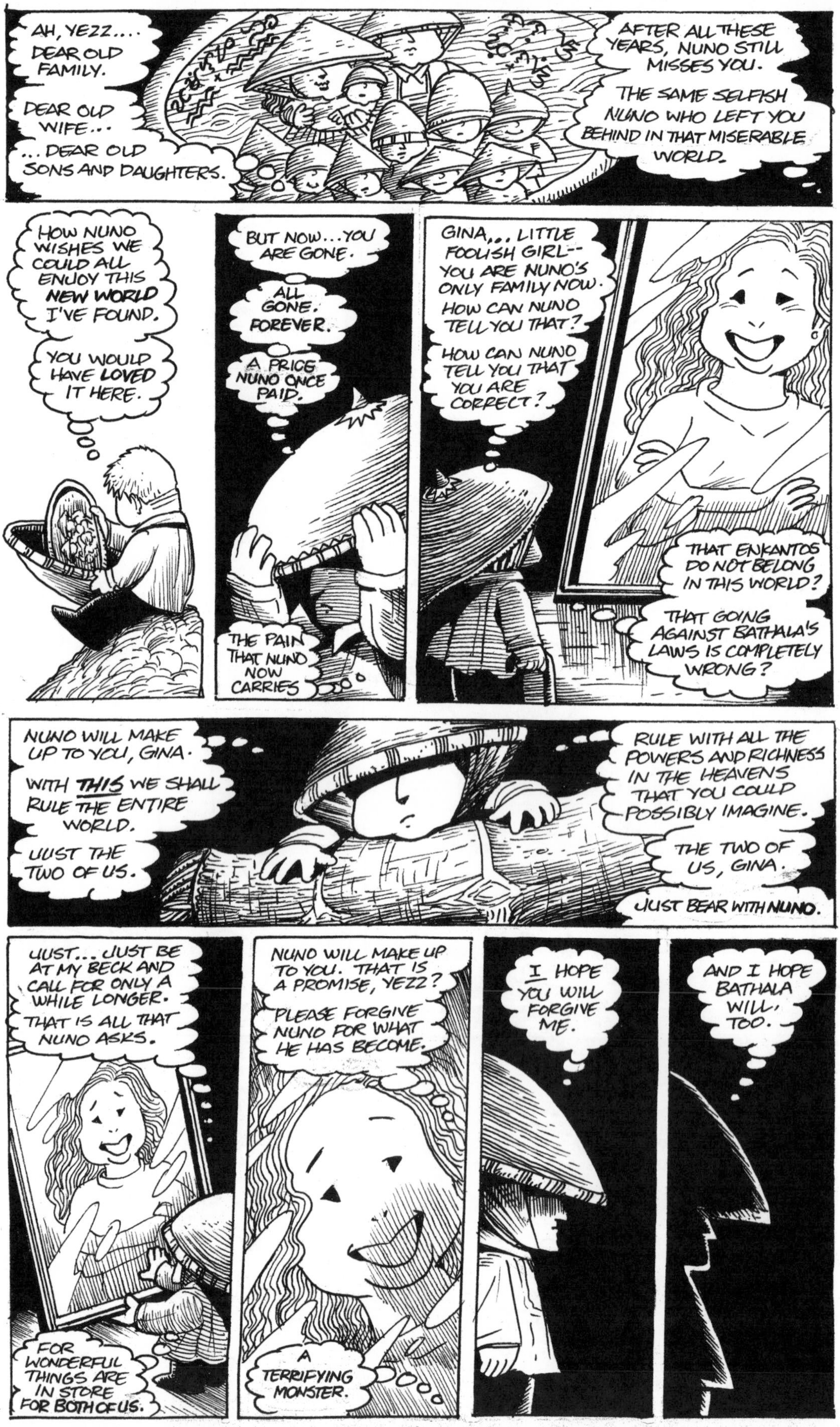
AH, YEZZ.... DEAR OLD FAMILY.
DEAR OLD WIFE...
...DEAR OLD SONS AND DAUGHTERS.
AFTER ALL THESE YEARS, NUNO STILL MISSES YOU.
THE SAME SELFISH NUNO WHO LEFT YOU BEHIND IN THAT MISERABLE WORLD.
HOW NUNO WISHES WE COULD ALL ENJOY THIS NEW WORLD I'VE FOUND.
YOU WOULD HAVE LOVED IT HERE.
BUT NOW...YOU ARE GONE.
ALL GONE. FOREVER.
A PRICE NUNO ONCE PAID.
THE PAIN THAT NUNO NOW CARRIES
GINA... LITTLE FOOLISH GIRL-- YOU ARE NUNO'S ONLY FAMILY NOW.
HOW CAN NUNO TELL YOU THAT?
HOW CAN NUNO TELL YOU THAT YOU ARE CORRECT?
THAT ENKANTOS DO NOT BELONG IN THIS WORLD?
THAT GOING AGAINST BATHALA'S LAWS IS COMPLETELY WRONG?
NUNO WILL MAKE UP TO YOU, GINA.
WITH THIS WE SHALL RULE THE ENTIRE WORLD.
JUST THE TWO OF US.
RULE WITH ALL THE POWERS AND RICHNESS IN THE HEAVENS THAT YOU COULD POSSIBLY IMAGINE.
THE TWO OF US, GINA.
JUST BEAR WITH NUNO.
JUST... JUST BE AT MY BECK AND CALL FOR ONLY A WHILE LONGER.
THAT IS ALL THAT NUNO ASKS.
FOR WONDERFUL THINGS ARE IN STORE FOR BOTH OF US.
NUNO WILL MAKE UP TO YOU. THAT IS A PROMISE, YEZZ?
PLEASE FORGIVE NUNO FOR WHAT HE HAS BECOME.
A TERRIFYING MONSTER.
I HOPE YOU WILL FORGIVE ME.
AND I HOPE BATHALA WILL, TOO.

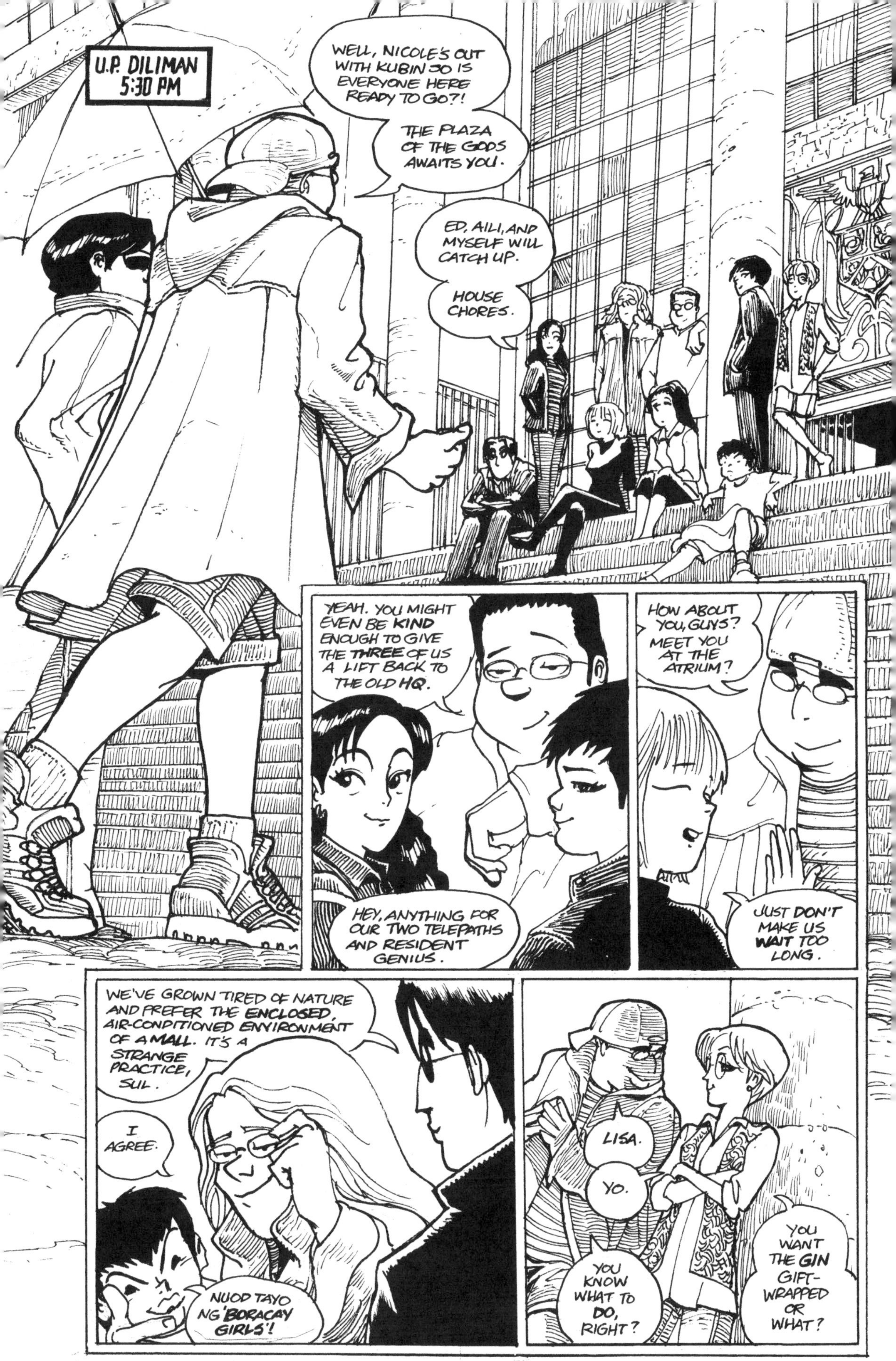
U.P. DILIMAN 5:30 PM
WELL, NICOLE'S OUT WITH KUBIN SO IS EVERYONE HERE READY TO GO?!
THE PLAZA OF THE GODS AWAITS YOU.
ED, AILI, AND MYSELF WILL CATCH UP.
HOUSE CHORES.
YEAH. YOU MIGHT EVEN BE KIND ENOUGH TO GIVE THE THREE OF US A LIFT BACK TO THE OLD HQ.
HEY, ANYTHING FOR OUR TWO TELEPATHS AND RESIDENT GENIUS.
HOW ABOUT YOU, GUYS? MEET YOU AT THE ATRIUM?
JUST DON'T MAKE US WAIT TOO LONG.
WE'VE GROWN TIRED OF NATURE AND PREFER THE ENCLOSED, AIR-CONDITIONED ENVIRONMENT OF A MALL. IT'S A STRANGE PRACTICE, SUL.
I AGREE.
NUOD TAYO NG 'BORACAY GIRLS'!
LISA.
YO.
YOU KNOW WHAT TO DO, RIGHT?
YOU WANT THE GIN GIFT-WRAPPED OR WHAT?

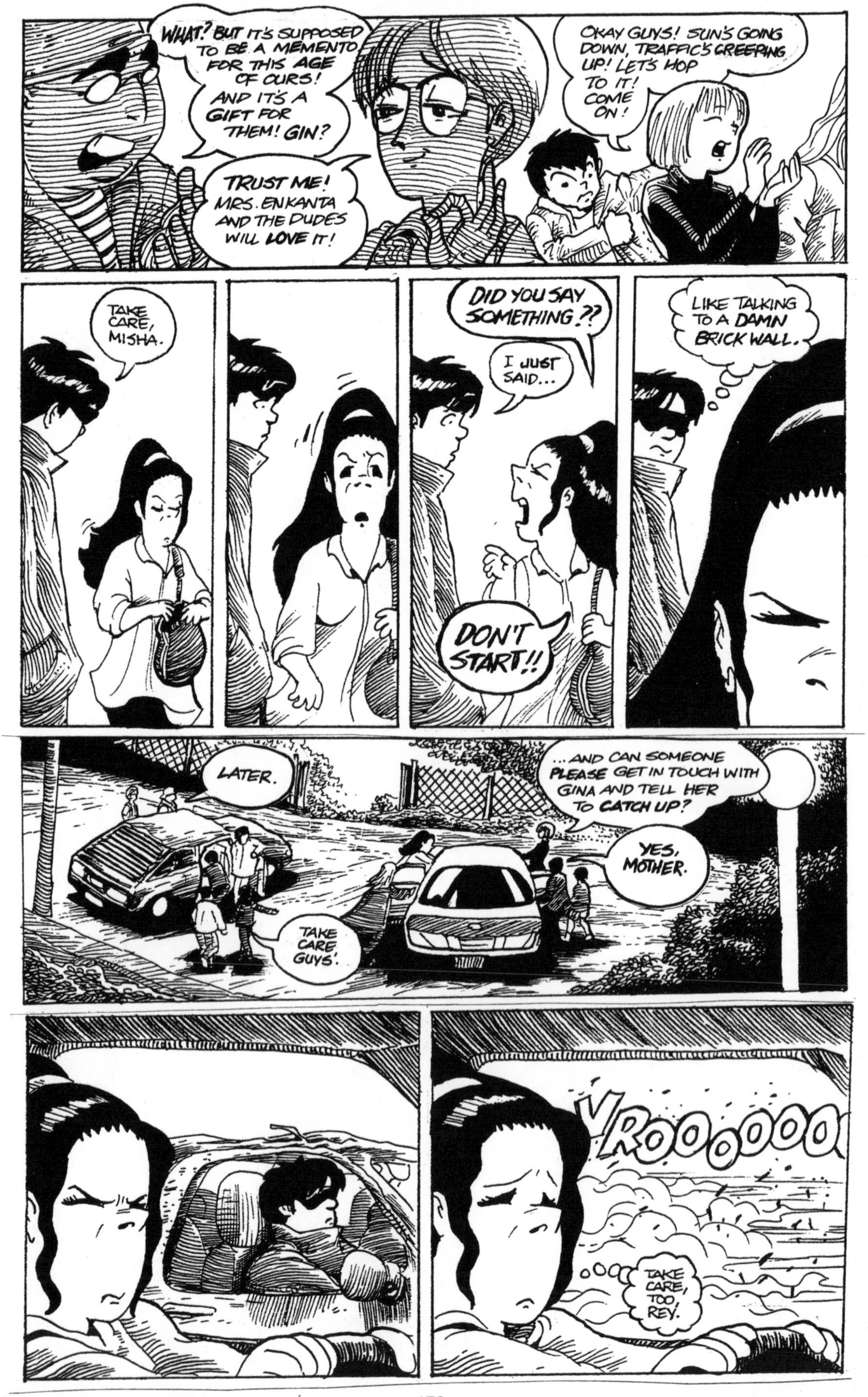

WHAT? BUT IT'S SUPPOSED TO BE A MEMENTO FOR THIS AGE OF OURS! AND IT'S A GIFT FOR THEM! GIN?
TRUST ME! MRS. ENKANTA AND THE DUDES WILL LOVE IT!
OKAY GUYS! SUN'S GOING DOWN, TRAFFIC'S CREEPING UP! LET'S HOP TO IT! COME ON!
TAKE CARE, MISHA.
DID YOU SAY SOMETHING??
I JUST SAID...
DON'T START!!
LIKE TALKING TO A DAMN BRICK WALL.
LATER.
...AND CAN SOMEONE PLEASE GET IN TOUCH WITH GINA AND TELL HER TO CATCH UP?
YES, MOTHER.
TAKE CARE GUYS!
VROOOOOO
TAKE CARE, TOO, REY.

CUBAO 5:30 PM

...A ROOM. IT'S DARK.

WHAT ELSE?

I CAN'T SEE ANYTHING ELSE. BUT I FEEL...

WHAT DO YOU FEEL?

SOMETHING IN MY HAND...

...I'VE CRUSHED SOMETHING.

...I'M SCARED.

IT'S ALL RIGHT. OPEN YOUR EYES.

THERE'S NO ESCAPING IT, IS THERE? I WILL BE HELD RESPONSIBLE FOR SOMETHING.

IN THAT THREAD OF DESTINY...

...YES.

I CAN STILL CHANGE IT.

YOU CAN'T.

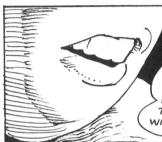

WHY CAN'T I?

BECAUSE THE ROAD IS MADE. YOU ARE WALKING ON IT, NOW, AT THIS VERY MOMENT. YOU CAN'T CHANGE THE PATH. JUST BEAR WITNESS TO ANYTHING THAT COMES ALONG.

"ONLY THEN WILL YOU KNOW WHERE IT LEADS."

AFTER ALL THESE YEARS I FINALLY UNDERSTAND.

THIS IS IT THEN.

I KNOW WHAT I MUST DO.

IT ALL ENDS TONIGHT, NUNO.

ONE WAY OR ANOTHER.

U.P. DILIMAN

173

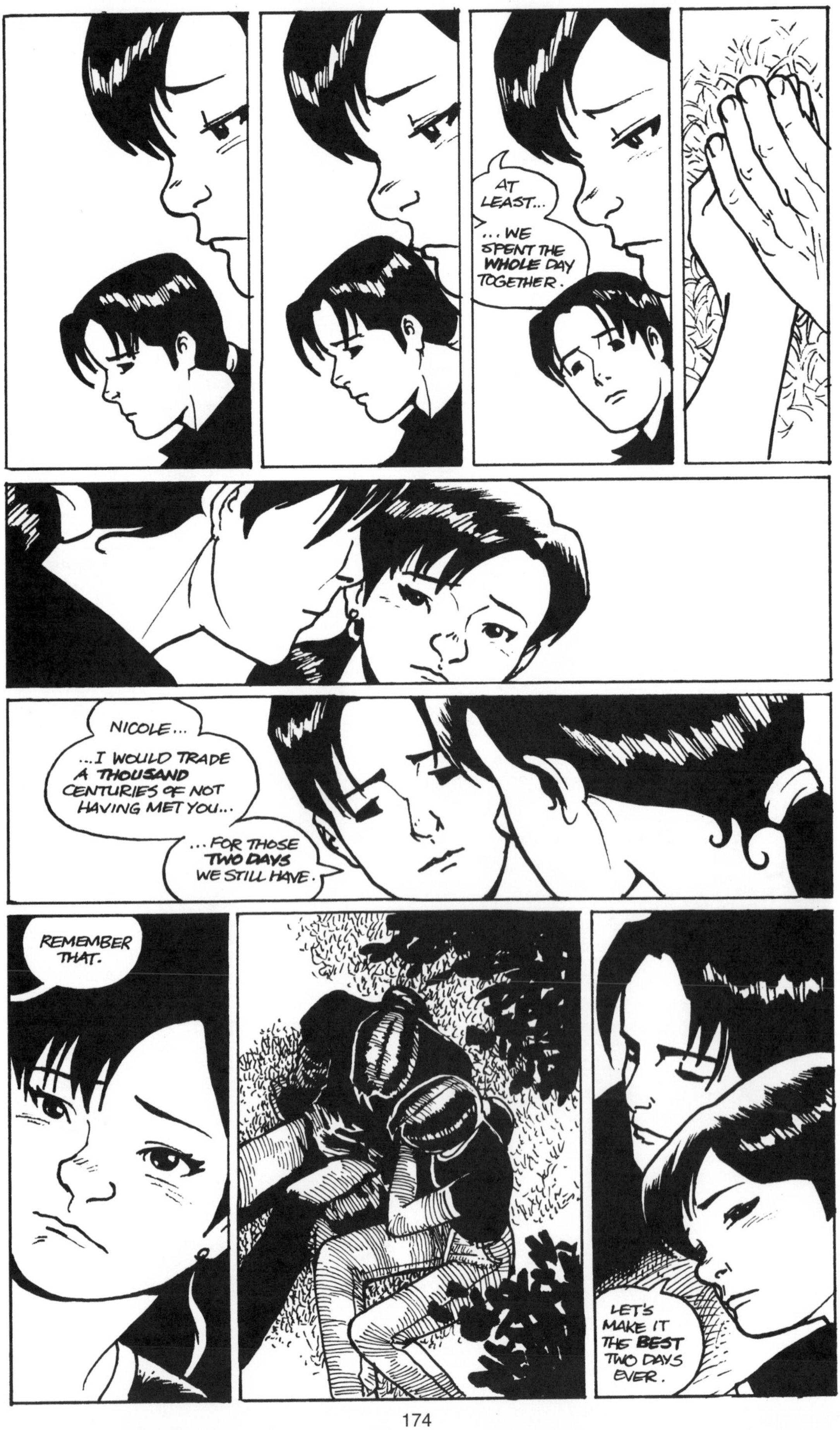
AT LEAST...
...WE SPENT THE WHOLE DAY TOGETHER.
NICOLE...
...I WOULD TRADE A THOUSAND CENTURIES OF NOT HAVING MET YOU...
...FOR THOSE TWO DAYS WE STILL HAVE.
REMEMBER THAT.
LET'S MAKE IT THE BEST TWO DAYS EVER.

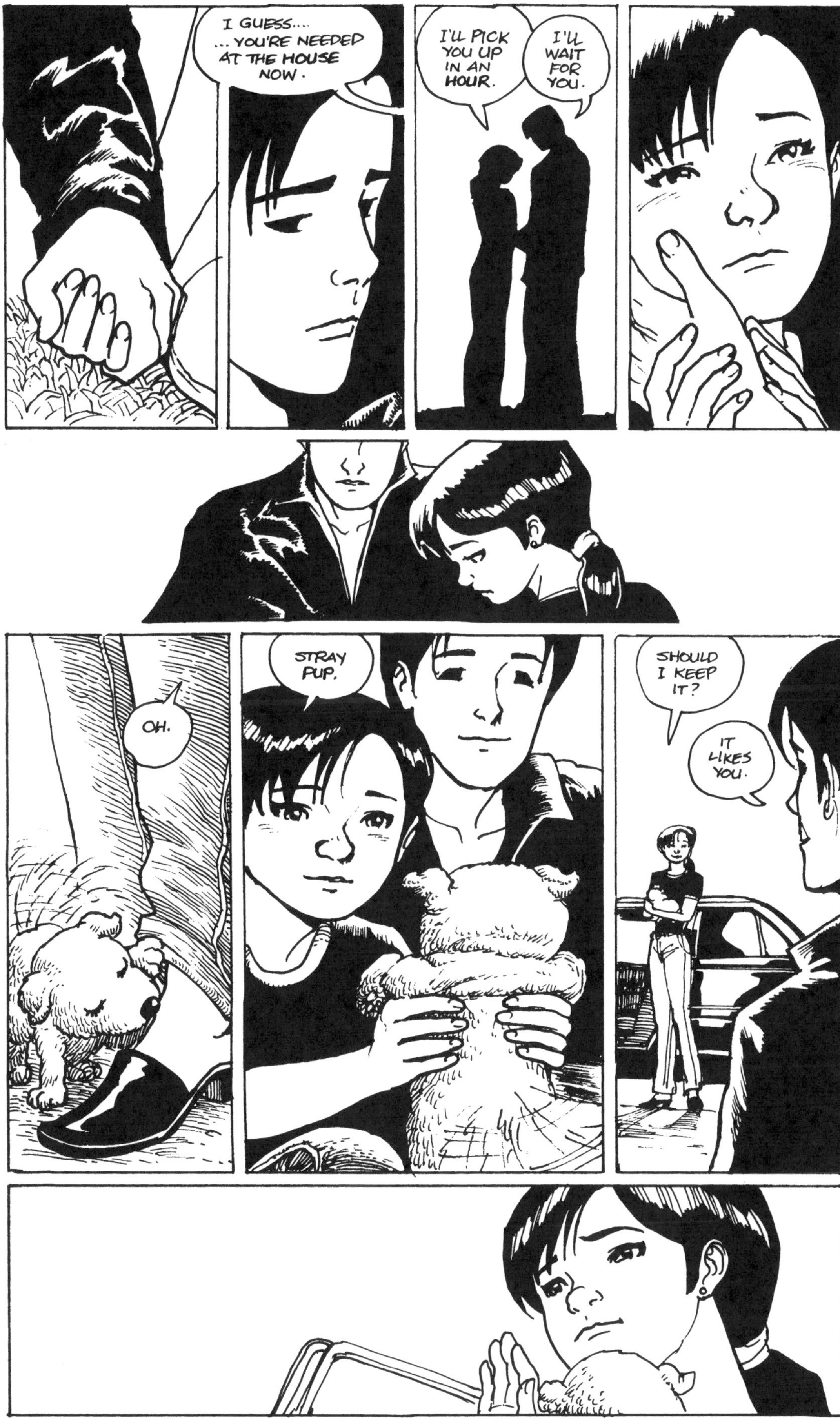
I GUESS....
... YOU'RE NEEDED AT THE HOUSE NOW.
I'LL PICK YOU UP IN AN HOUR.
I'LL WAIT FOR YOU.
OH.
STRAY PUP.
SHOULD I KEEP IT?
IT LIKES YOU.

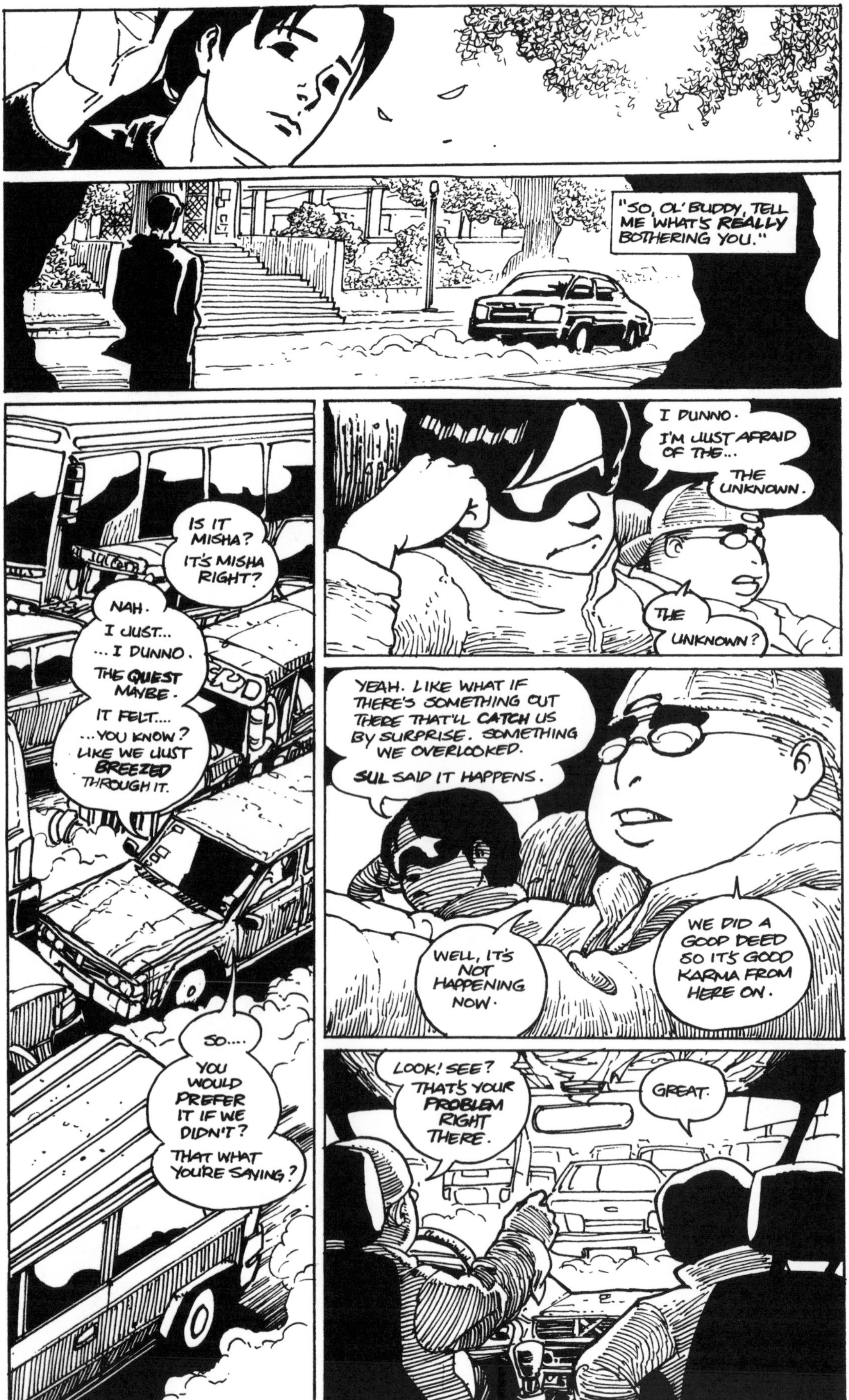
"SO, OL' BUDDY, TELL ME WHAT'S REALLY BOTHERING YOU."
IS IT MISHA? IT'S MISHA RIGHT?
NAH. I JUST... ...I DUNNO. THE QUEST MAYBE. IT FELT.... ...YOU KNOW? LIKE WE JUST BREEZED THROUGH IT.
SO.... YOU WOULD PREFER IT IF WE DIDN'T? THAT WHAT YOU'RE SAYING?
I DUNNO. I'M JUST AFRAID OF THE... THE UNKNOWN.
THE UNKNOWN?
YEAH. LIKE WHAT IF THERE'S SOMETHING OUT THERE THAT'LL CATCH US BY SURPRISE. SOMETHING WE OVERLOOKED. SUL SAID IT HAPPENS.
WELL, IT'S NOT HAPPENING NOW.
WE DID A GOOD DEED SO IT'S GOOD KARMA FROM HERE ON.
LOOK! SEE? THAT'S YOUR PROBLEM RIGHT THERE.
GREAT.

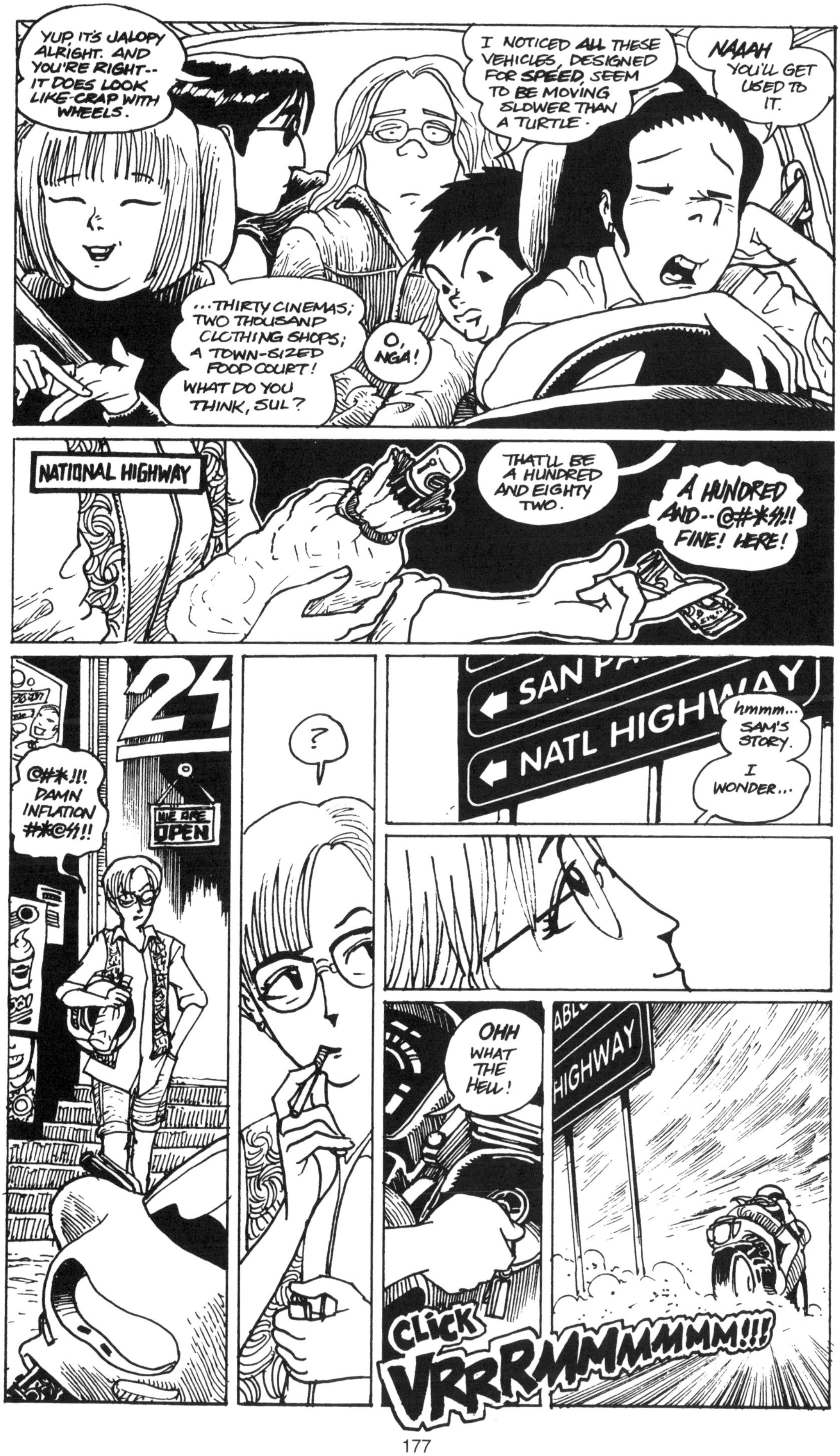
YUP, IT'S JALOPY ALRIGHT. AND YOU'RE RIGHT-- IT DOES LOOK LIKE CRAP WITH WHEELS.
I NOTICED ALL THESE VEHICLES, DESIGNED FOR SPEED, SEEM TO BE MOVING SLOWER THAN A TURTLE.
NAAAH YOU'LL GET USED TO IT.
...THIRTY CINEMAS; TWO THOUSAND CLOTHING SHOPS; A TOWN-SIZED FOOD COURT!
WHAT DO YOU THINK, SUL?
O, NGA!
NATIONAL HIGHWAY
THAT'LL BE A HUNDRED AND EIGHTY TWO.
A HUNDRED AND--@#*$!! FINE! HERE!
24
@#*!!. DAMN INFLATION #*@$!!
WE ARE OPEN
?
SAN PA
NATL HIGHWAY
hmmm... SAM'S STORY.
I WONDER...
OHH WHAT THE HELL!
HIGHWAY
CLICK
VRRRMMMMMMM!!!

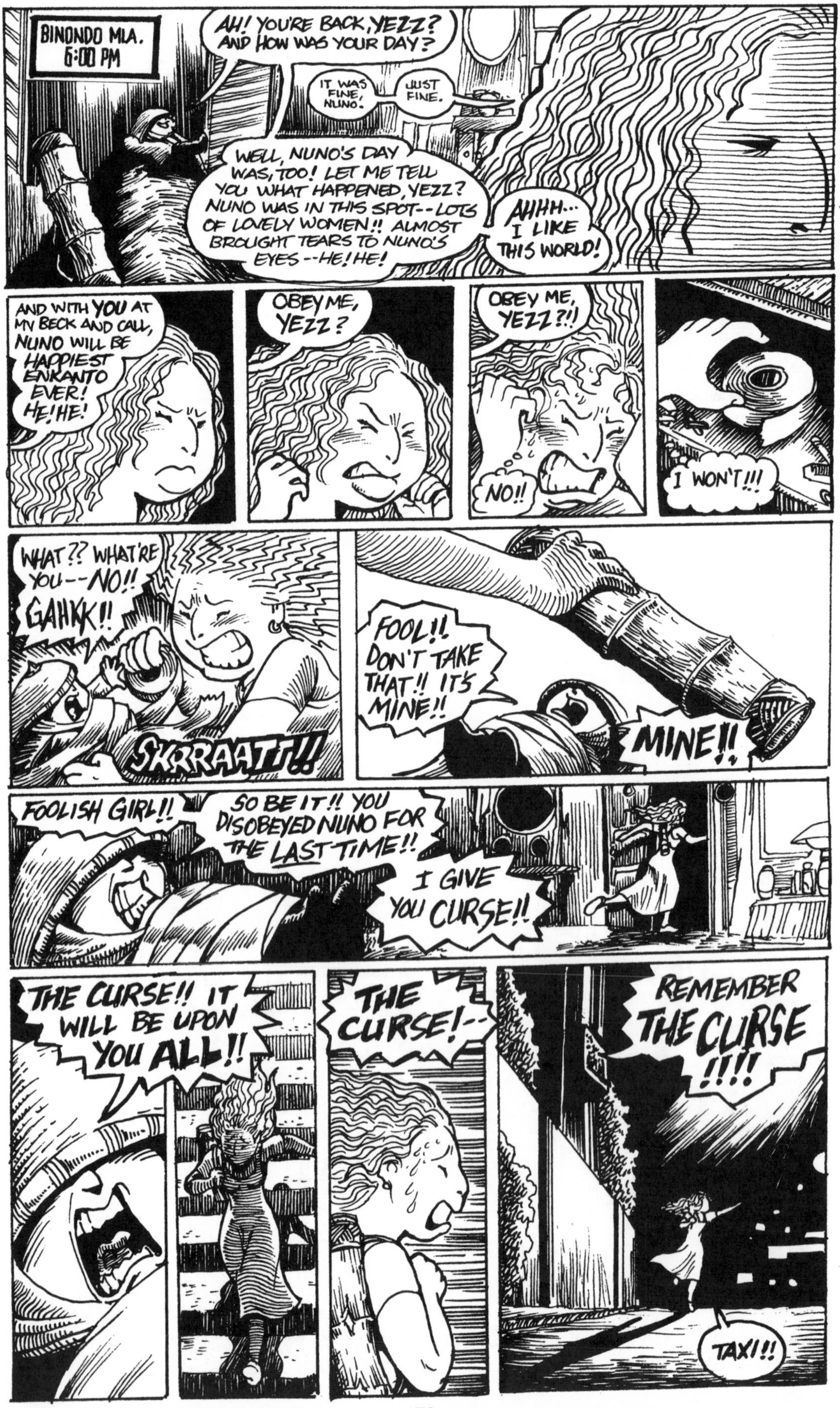
BINONDO MLA. 6:00 PM
AH! YOU'RE BACK, YEZZ? AND HOW WAS YOUR DAY?
IT WAS FINE, NUNO.
JUST FINE.
WELL, NUNO'S DAY WAS, TOO! LET ME TELL YOU WHAT HAPPENED, YEZZ? NUNO WAS IN THIS SPOT--LOTS OF LOVELY WOMEN!! ALMOST BROUGHT TEARS TO NUNO'S EYES--HE! HE!
AHHH... I LIKE THIS WORLD!
AND WITH YOU AT MY BECK AND CALL, NUNO WILL BE HAPPIEST ENKANTO EVER! HE! HE!
OBEY ME, YEZZ?
OBEY ME, YEZZ?!!
NO!!
I WON'T!!!
WHAT?? WHAT'RE YOU--NO!! GAHKK!!
SKRRAATT!!
FOOL!! DON'T TAKE THAT!! IT'S MINE!!
MINE!!
FOOLISH GIRL!!
SO BE IT!! YOU DISOBEYED NUNO FOR THE LAST TIME!!
I GIVE YOU CURSE!!
THE CURSE!! IT WILL BE UPON YOU ALL!!
THE CURSE!--
REMEMBER THE CURSE!!!!
TAXI!!

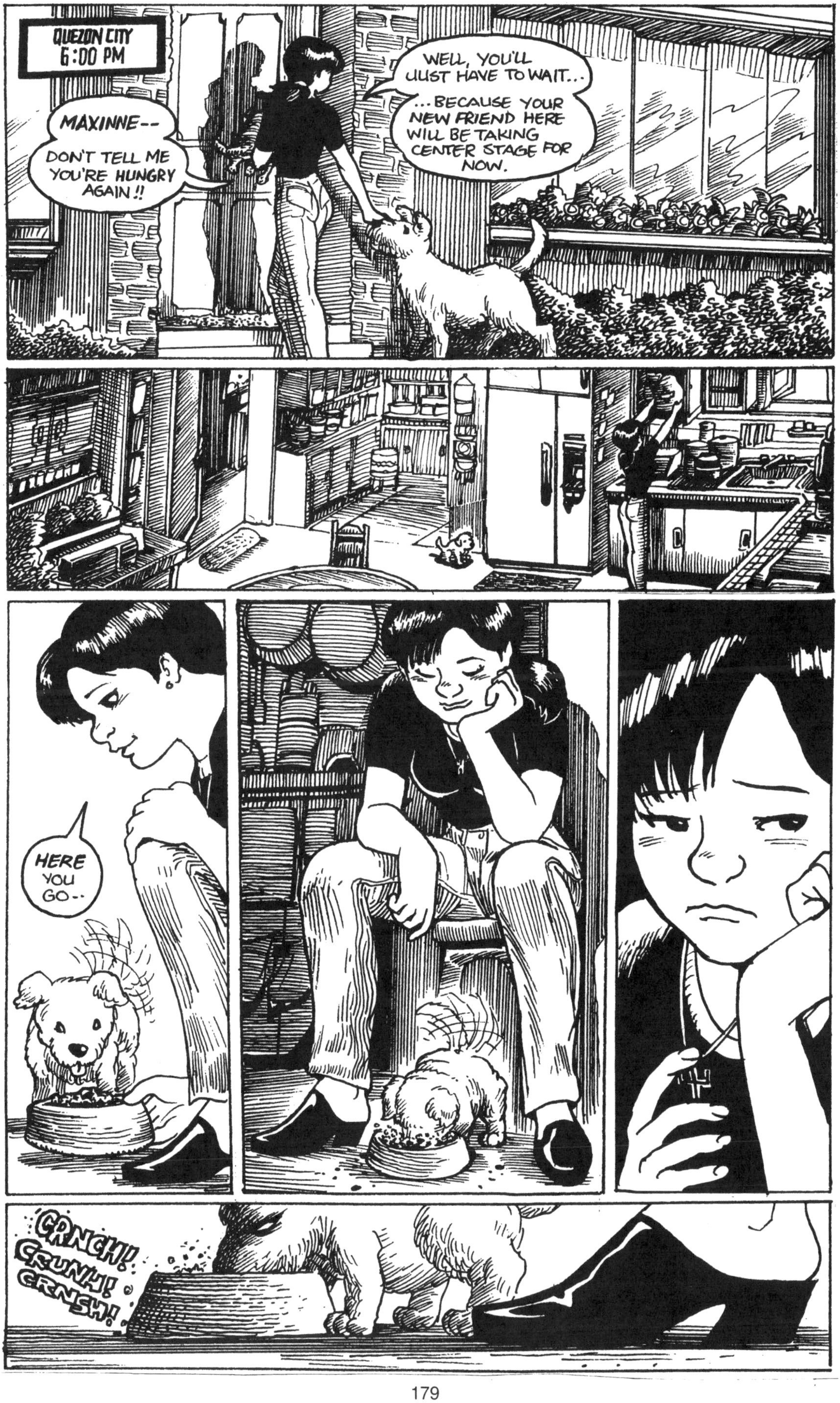
QUEZON CITY 6:00 PM
MAXINNE--
DON'T TELL ME YOU'RE HUNGRY AGAIN!!
WELL, YOU'LL JUST HAVE TO WAIT...
...BECAUSE YOUR NEW FRIEND HERE WILL BE TAKING CENTER STAGE FOR NOW.
HERE YOU GO--
GRNCH! CRUNH! GRNSH!

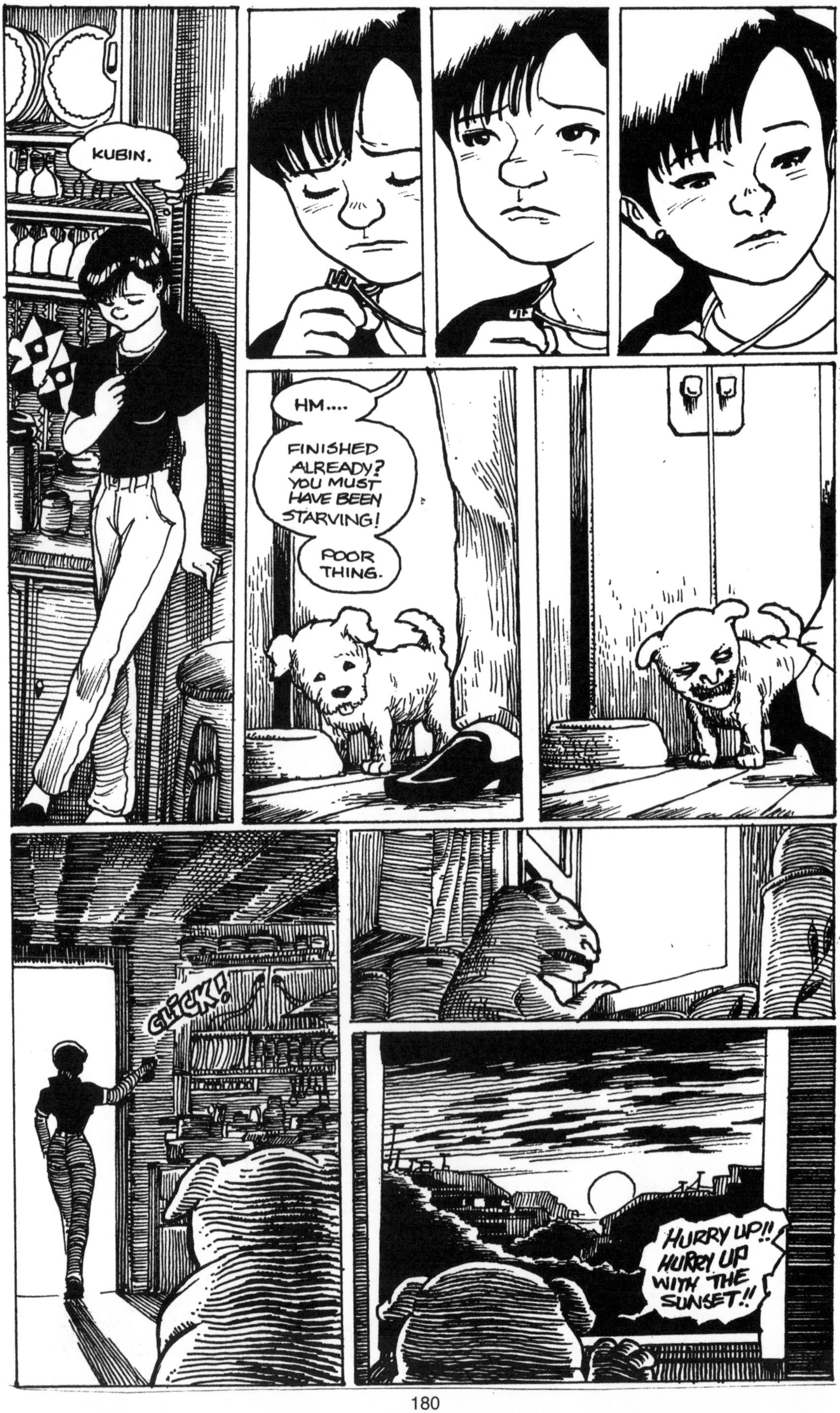
KUBIN.
HM....
FINISHED ALREADY? YOU MUST HAVE BEEN STARVING!
POOR THING.
CLICK!
HURRY UP!! HURRY UP WITH THE SUNSET!!

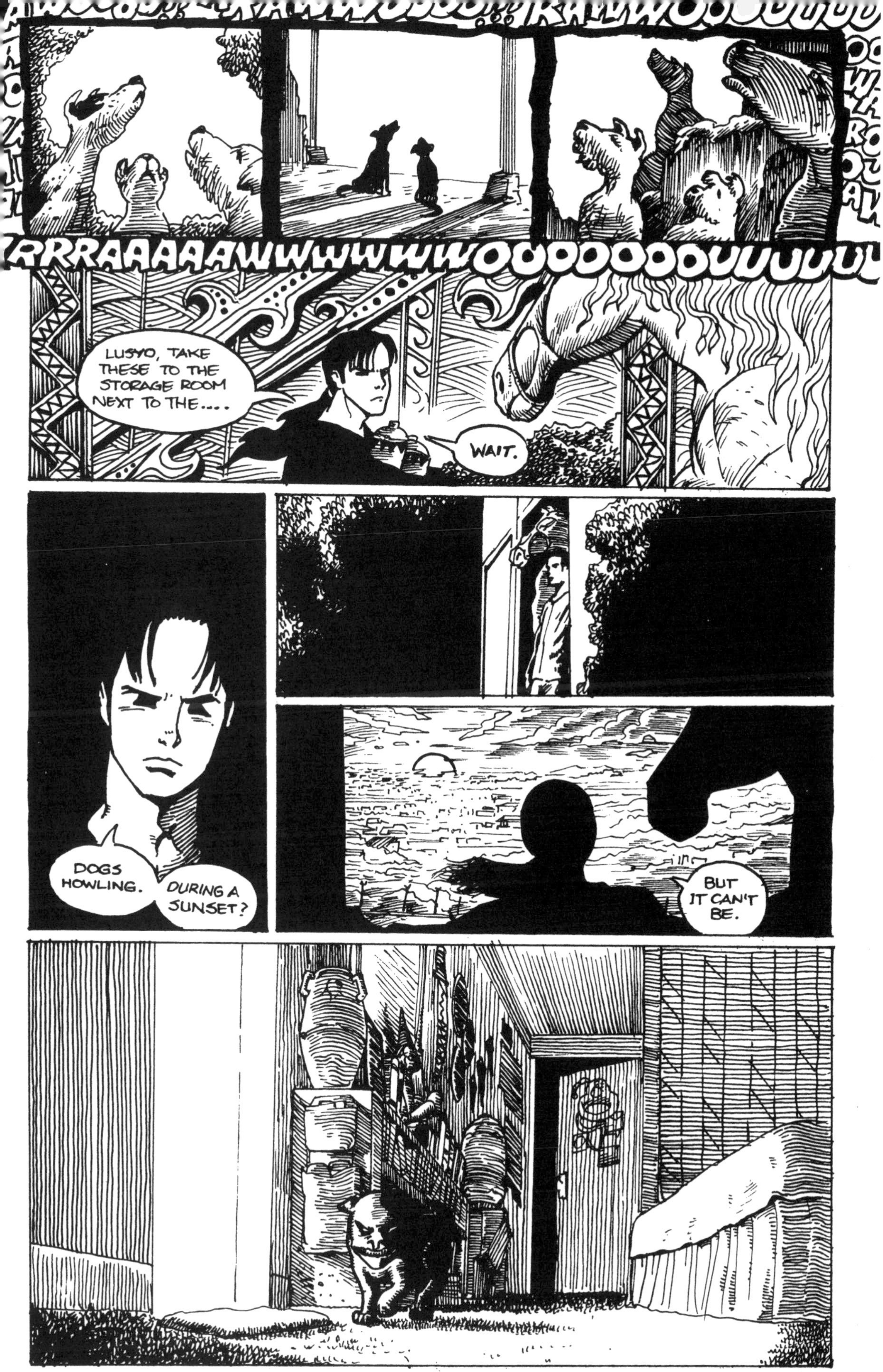
RRRAAAAAAWWWWWWWOOOOOOOOUUUUU
LUSYO, TAKE THESE TO THE STORAGE ROOM NEXT TO THE....
WAIT.
DOGS HOWLING.
DURING A SUNSET?
BUT IT CAN'T BE.

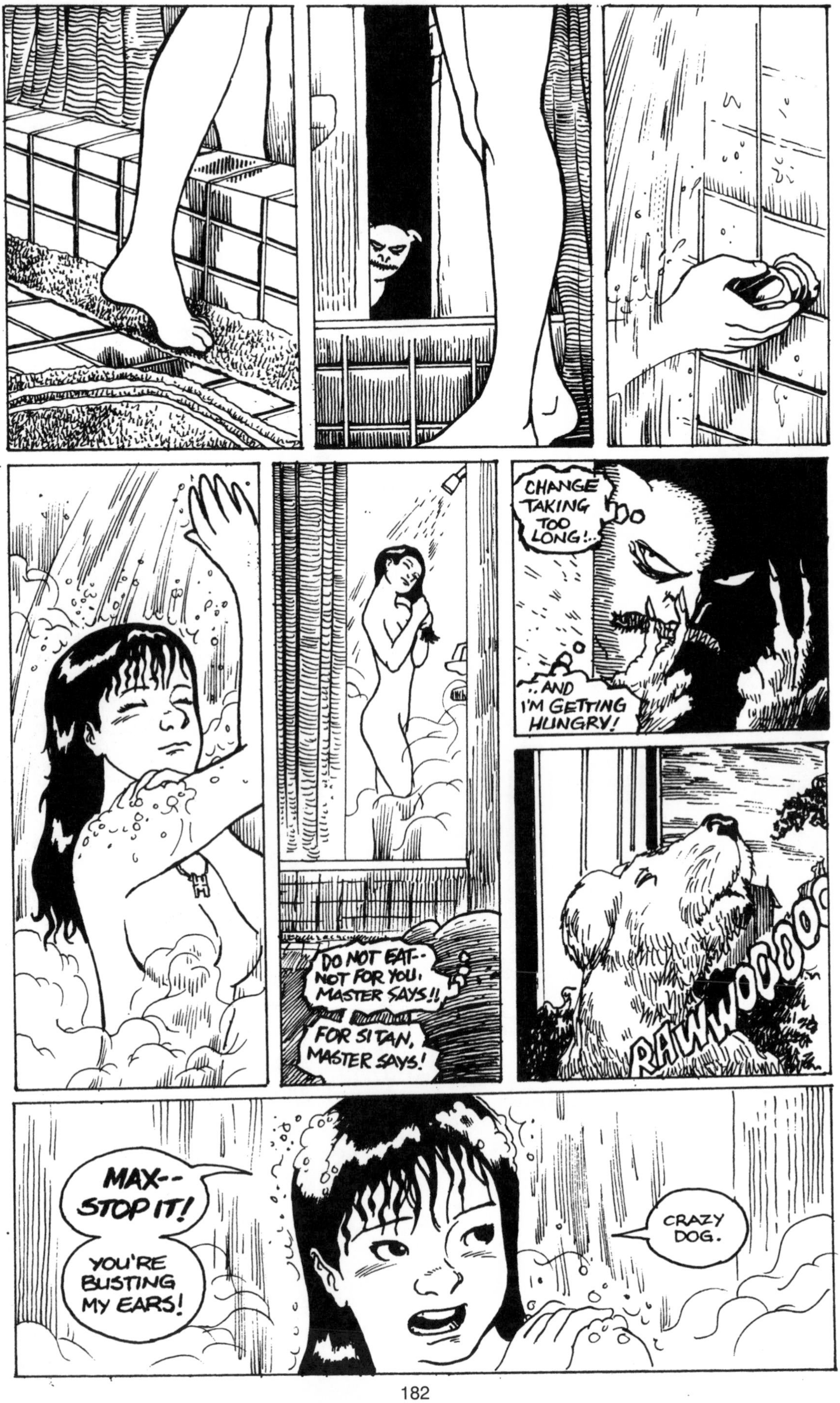
CHANGE TAKING TOO LONG!..
..AND I'M GETTING HUNGRY!
DO NOT EAT-NOT FOR YOU, MASTER SAYS!!
FOR SI TAN, MASTER SAYS!
RAWWOOOOOO
MAX--STOP IT!
YOU'RE BUSTING MY EARS!
CRAZY DOG.

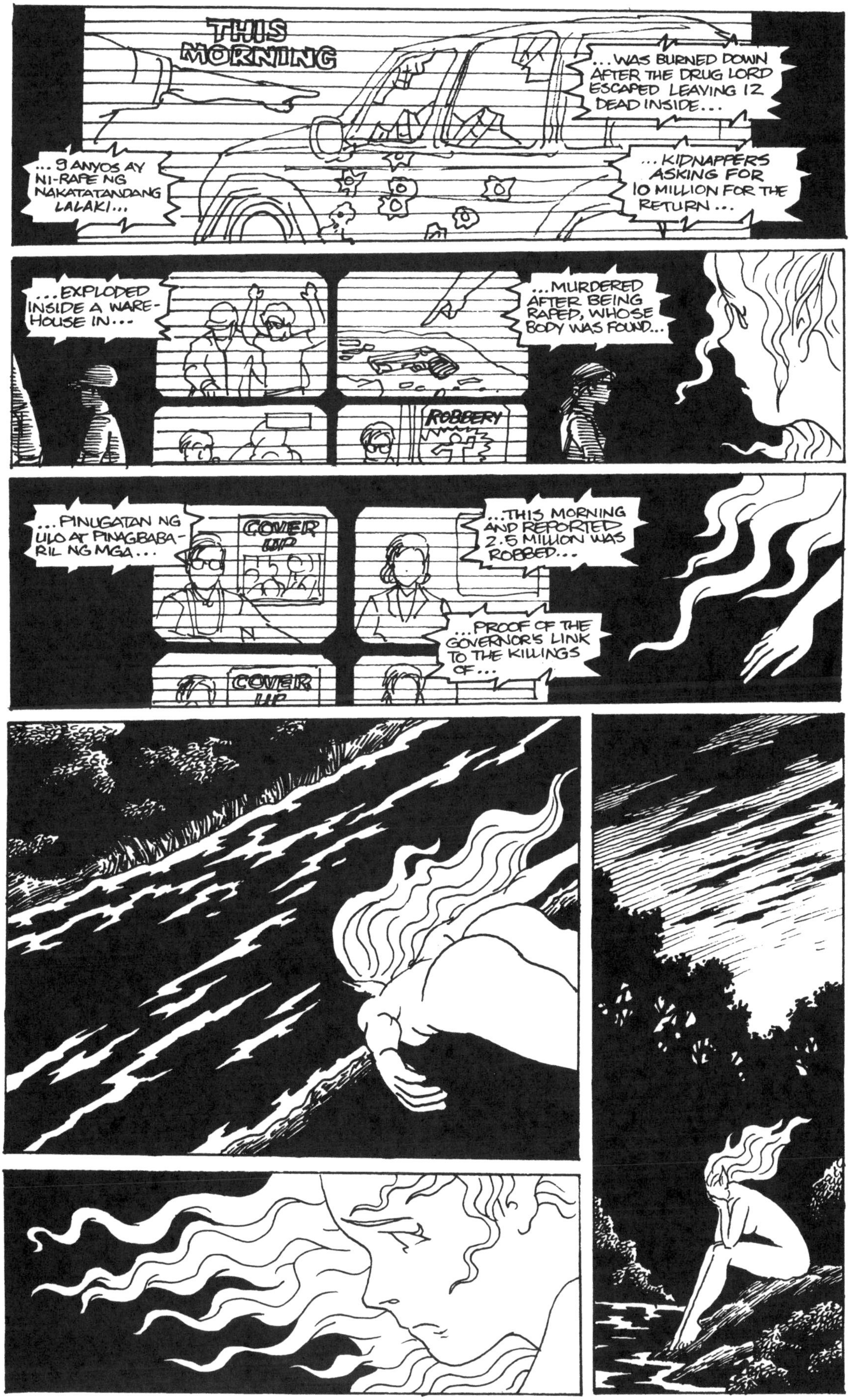
THIS MORNING
...WAS BURNED DOWN AFTER THE DRUG LORD ESCAPED LEAVING 12 DEAD INSIDE...
...9 ANYOS AY NI-RAPE NG NAKATATANDANG LALAKI...
...KIDNAPPERS ASKING FOR 10 MILLION FOR THE RETURN...
...EXPLODED INSIDE A WARE-HOUSE IN...
...MURDERED AFTER BEING RAPED, WHOSE BODY WAS FOUND...
ROBBERY
...PINUGATAN NG ULO AT PINAGBABA-RIL NG MGA...
COVER UP
...THIS MORNING AND REPORTED 2.5 MILLION WAS ROBBED...
...PROOF OF THE GOVERNOR'S LINK TO THE KILLINGS OF...
COVER UP

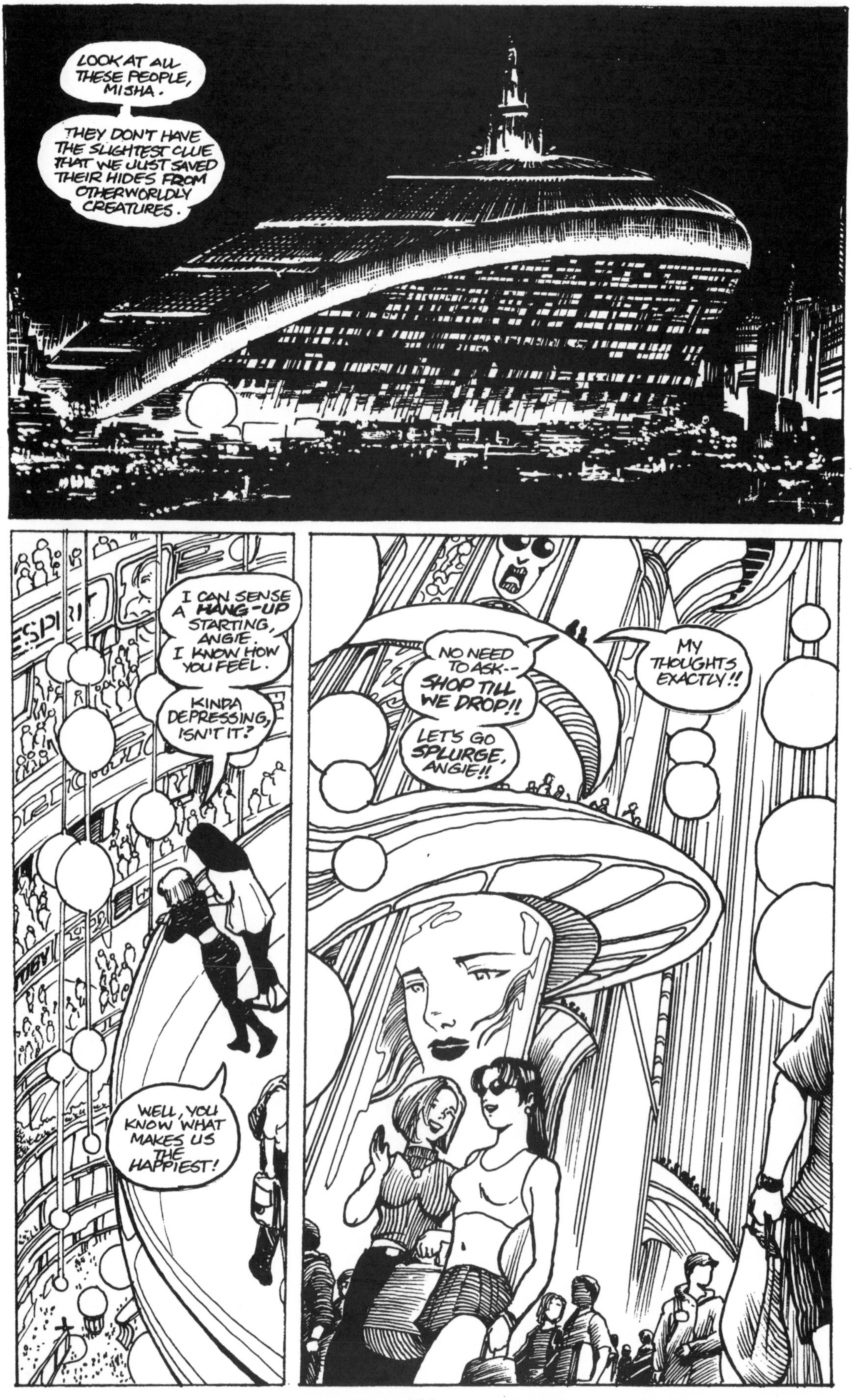
LOOK AT ALL THESE PEOPLE, MISHA.
THEY DON'T HAVE THE SLIGHTEST CLUE THAT WE JUST SAVED THEIR HIDES FROM OTHERWORLDLY CREATURES.
I CAN SENSE A HANG-UP STARTING, ANGIE. I KNOW HOW YOU FEEL.
KINDA DEPRESSING, ISN'T IT?
WELL, YOU KNOW WHAT MAKES US THE HAPPIEST!
NO NEED TO ASK-- SHOP TILL WE DROP!!
LET'S GO SPLURGE, ANGIE!!
MY THOUGHTS EXACTLY!!

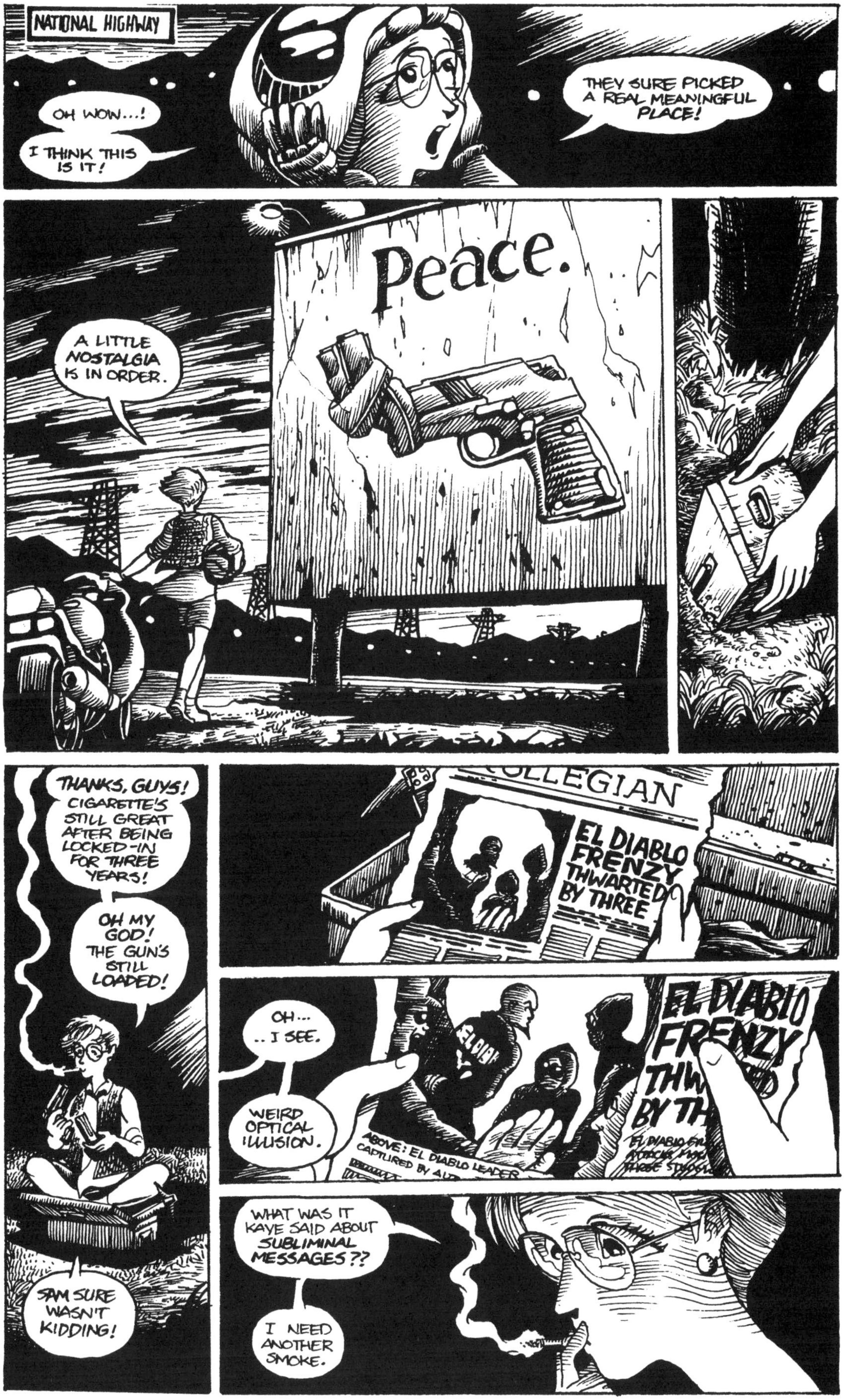
NATIONAL HIGHWAY
OH WOW...!
I THINK THIS IS IT!
THEY SURE PICKED A REAL MEANINGFUL PLACE!
Peace.
A LITTLE NOSTALGIA IS IN ORDER.
THANKS, GUYS! CIGARETTE'S STILL GREAT AFTER BEING LOCKED-IN FOR THREE YEARS!
OH MY GOD! THE GUN'S STILL LOADED!
SAM SURE WASN'T KIDDING!
COLLEGIAN
EL DIABLO FRENZY THWARTED BY THREE
OH... .. I SEE.
WEIRD OPTICAL ILLUSION.
EL DIABLO FRENZY
ABOVE: EL DIABLO LEADER CAPTURED BY AU
WHAT WAS IT KAYE SAID ABOUT SUBLIMINAL MESSAGES??
I NEED ANOTHER SMOKE.

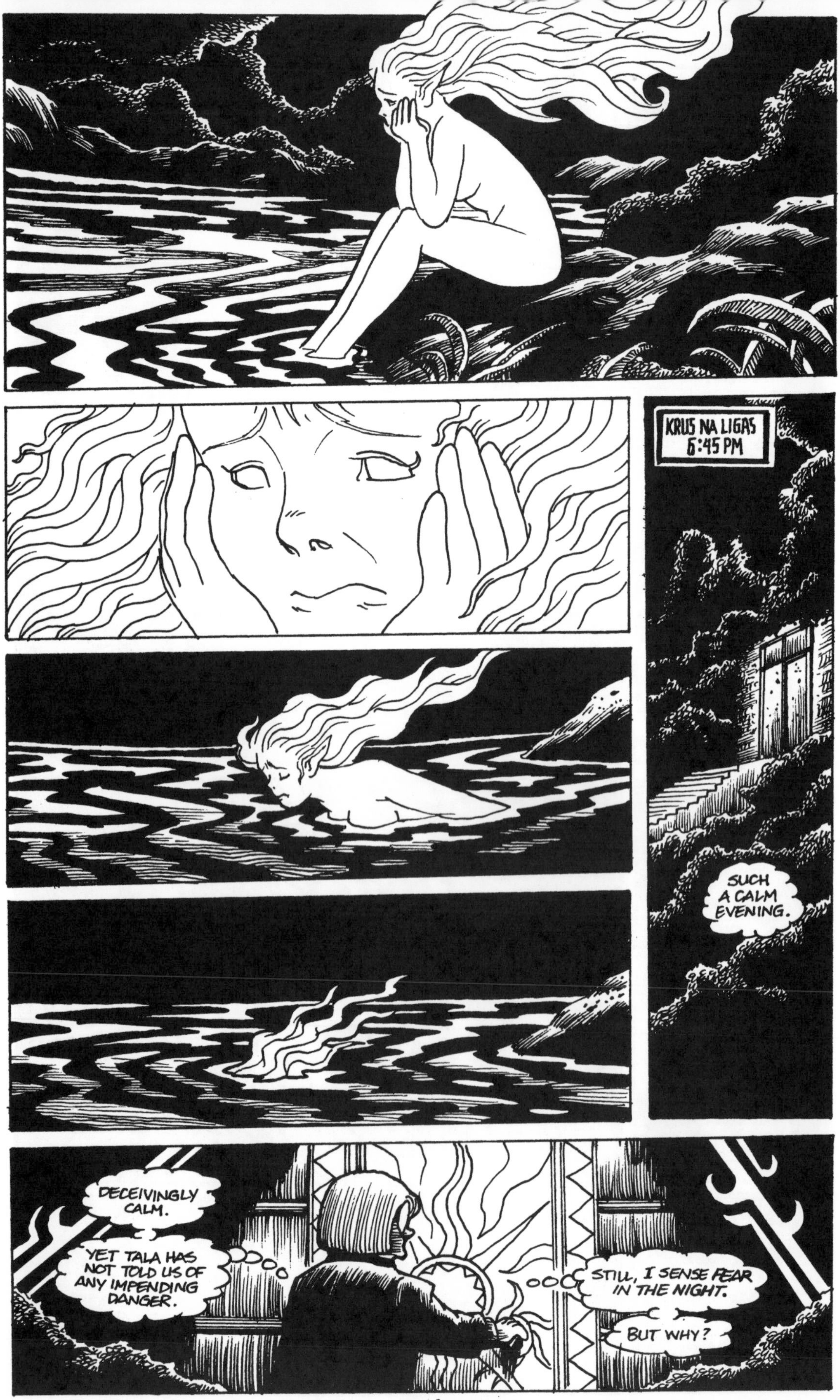
KRUS NA LIGAS 6:45 PM
SUCH A CALM EVENING.
DECEIVINGLY CALM.
YET TALA HAS NOT TOLD US OF ANY IMPENDING DANGER.
STILL, I SENSE FEAR IN THE NIGHT.
BUT WHY?

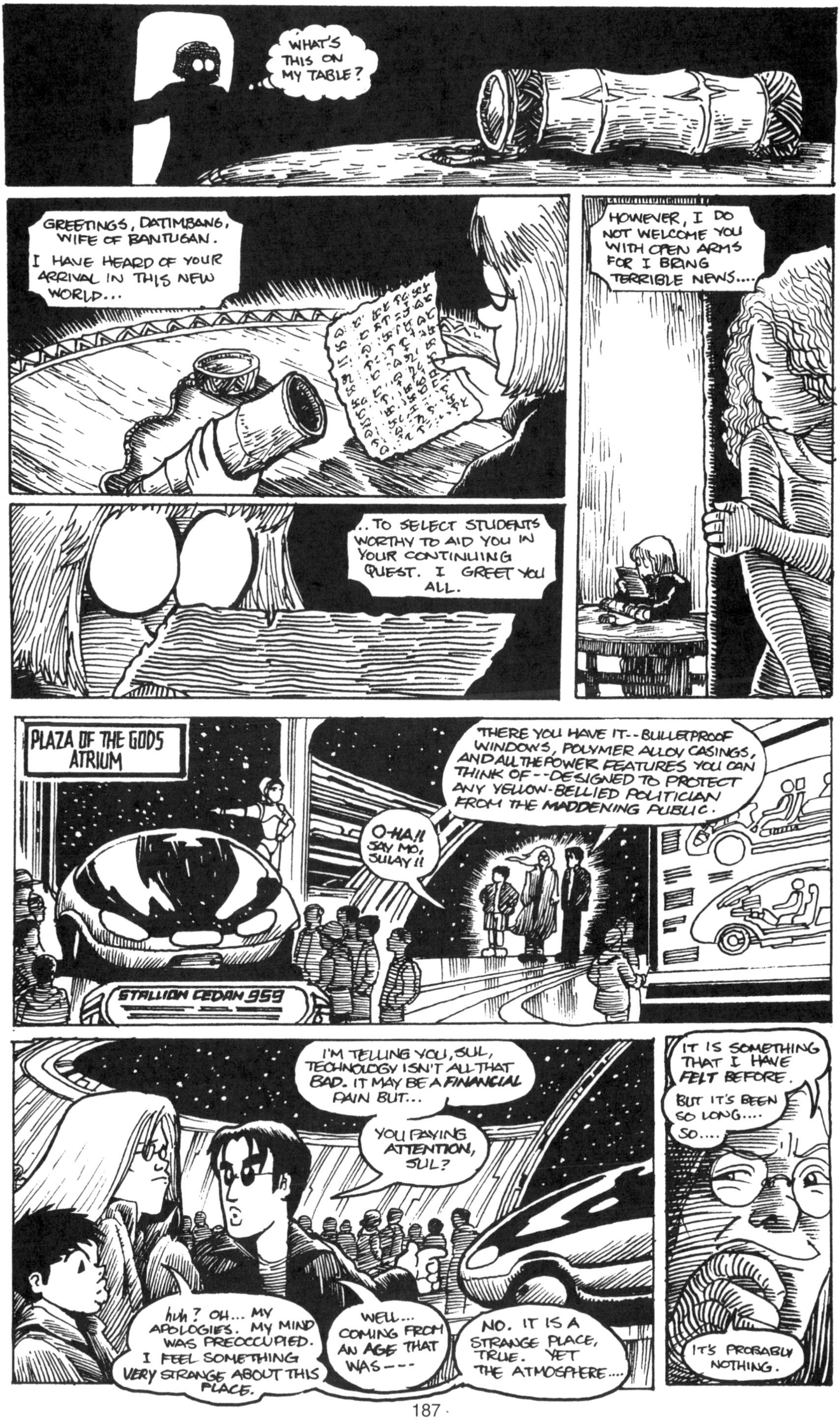

WHAT'S THIS ON MY TABLE?
GREETINGS, DATIMBANG, WIFE OF BANTUGAN.
I HAVE HEARD OF YOUR ARRIVAL IN THIS NEW WORLD...
HOWEVER, I DO NOT WELCOME YOU WITH OPEN ARMS FOR I BRING TERRIBLE NEWS....
..TO SELECT STUDENTS WORTHY TO AID YOU IN YOUR CONTINUING QUEST. I GREET YOU ALL.
PLAZA OF THE GODS ATRIUM
THERE YOU HAVE IT--BULLETPROOF WINDOWS, POLYMER ALLOY CASINGS, AND ALL THE POWER FEATURES YOU CAN THINK OF--DESIGNED TO PROTECT ANY YELLOW-BELLIED POLITICIAN FROM THE MADDENING PUBLIC.
O-HA!! SAY MO, SULAY!!
STALLION CEDAN 959
I'M TELLING YOU, SUL, TECHNOLOGY ISN'T ALL THAT BAD. IT MAY BE A FINANCIAL PAIN BUT...
YOU PAYING ATTENTION, SUL?
huh? OH... MY APOLOGIES. MY MIND WAS PREOCCUPIED. I FEEL SOMETHING VERY STRANGE ABOUT THIS PLACE.
WELL... COMING FROM AN AGE THAT WAS---
NO. IT IS A STRANGE PLACE, TRUE. YET THE ATMOSPHERE....
IT IS SOMETHING THAT I HAVE FELT BEFORE.
BUT IT'S BEEN SO LONG.... SO....
IT'S PROBABLY NOTHING.

HERE YOU ARE, MISS.

THIS BABY'S BEEN WAITING FOR MAMA ALL DAY!

SEVENTH CONE!

SEVENTH SHIRT!

INDULGE!!! HA! HA! HA! HA!

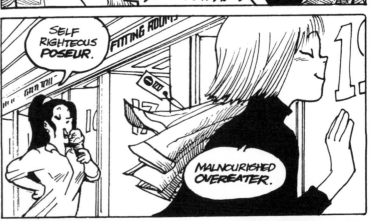

SELF RIGHTEOUS POSEUR.

MALNOURISHED OVEREATER.

IRONY.

AH, YES.

IRONY IS A CAR BREAKING DOWN JUST A FEW METERS FROM THE GAS STATION.

IRONY.

IRONY IS SAVING THE LAND FROM OTHER-WORLDLY GHOULS AND STILL ENDING UP CLEANING SPARK PLUGS.

OR SEALING RADIATOR HOLES-- WHICHEVER COMES FIRST.

HEY, LOOK AT THAT.

WHAT?

PLAZA OF THE GODS.

WHAT ABOUT?

IF YOU SQUINT A BIT IT LOOKS LIKE IT'S SMILING AT US.

OR GRINNING.

SO WHERE'S THE IRONY IN THAT?

I DON'T KNOW. I HOPE THERE ISN'T.

KRUS NA LIGAS.

...LOOK, LET'S CALM DOWN AND THINK.

SO LANE, YOU HAVEN'T SEEN LUSYO OR KUBIN ANYWHERE? RIGHT?

I CAN'T REALLY SEE THEM AS IN 'SEE' THEM.

MY TELEPATHY'S ALL FUZZY AND THIS...THIS SPLITTING HEADACHE...

I KNOW, LANE. MY MIND'S UNCLEAR TOO.

YOU GUYS SURE IT WASN'T THE SPICY SHRIMPS?

I SURE HOPE NOT.

ANYWAY, I BELIEVE IT'S BEST THAT WE ORGANIZE THE JARS OURSELVES.

WAIT FOR US HERE. GOT THAT?

OOOKAAY... BUT YOU GUYS BETTER HURRY.

UH... ...AILI?

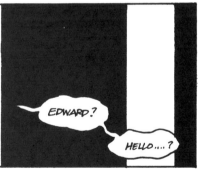

EDWARD?

HELLO....?

189

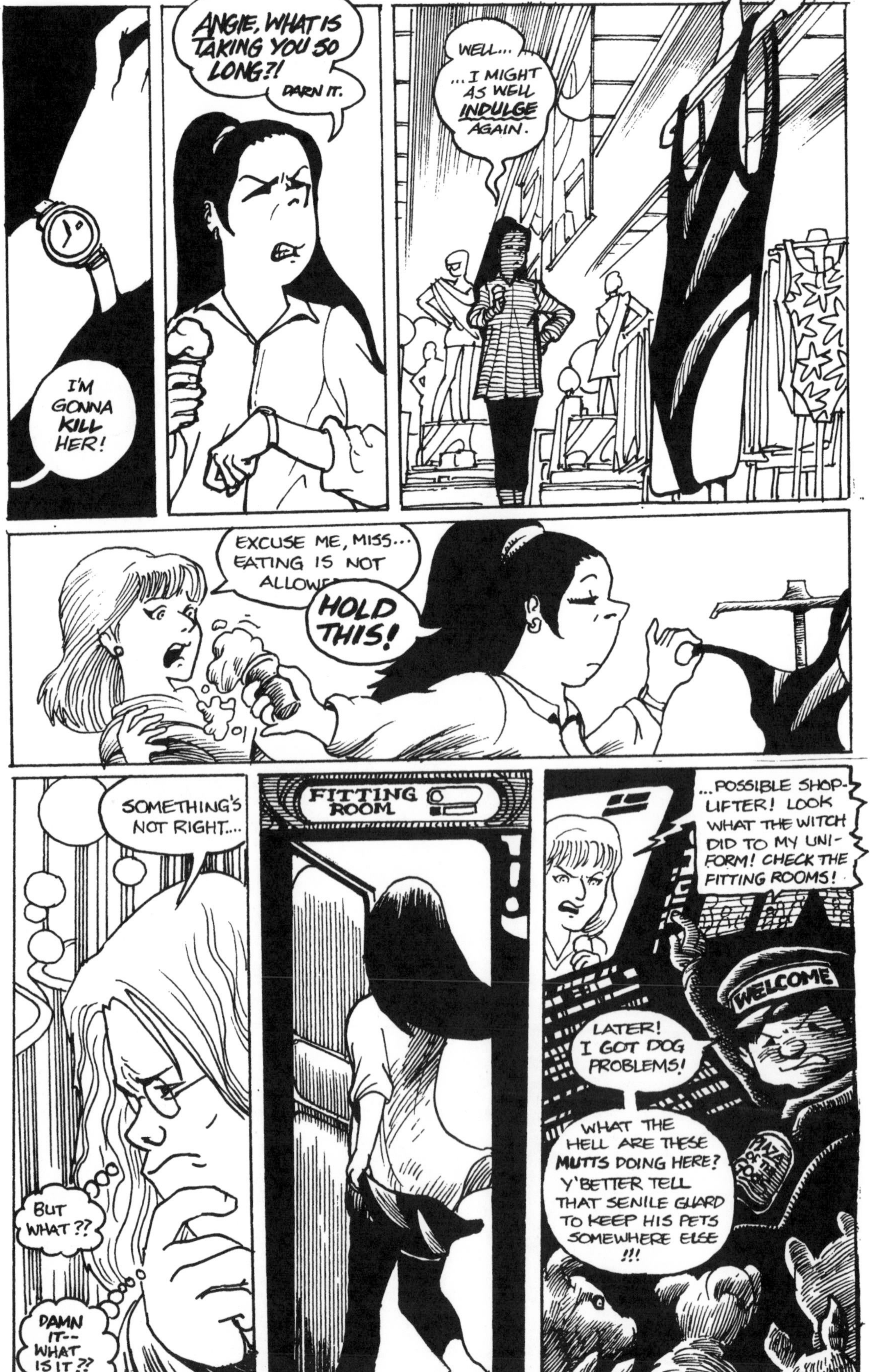

I'M GONNA KILL HER!
ANGIE, WHAT IS TAKING YOU SO LONG?!
DARN IT.
WELL...
...I MIGHT AS WELL INDULGE AGAIN.
EXCUSE ME, MISS... EATING IS NOT ALLOWE
HOLD THIS!
SOMETHING'S NOT RIGHT....
BUT WHAT??
DAMN IT-- WHAT IS IT??
FITTING ROOM
...POSSIBLE SHOP-LIFTER! LOOK WHAT THE WITCH DID TO MY UNI-FORM! CHECK THE FITTING ROOMS!
WELCOME
LATER! I GOT DOG PROBLEMS!
WHAT THE HELL ARE THESE MUTTS DOING HERE? Y'BETTER TELL THAT SENILE GUARD TO KEEP HIS PETS SOMEWHERE ELSE !!!

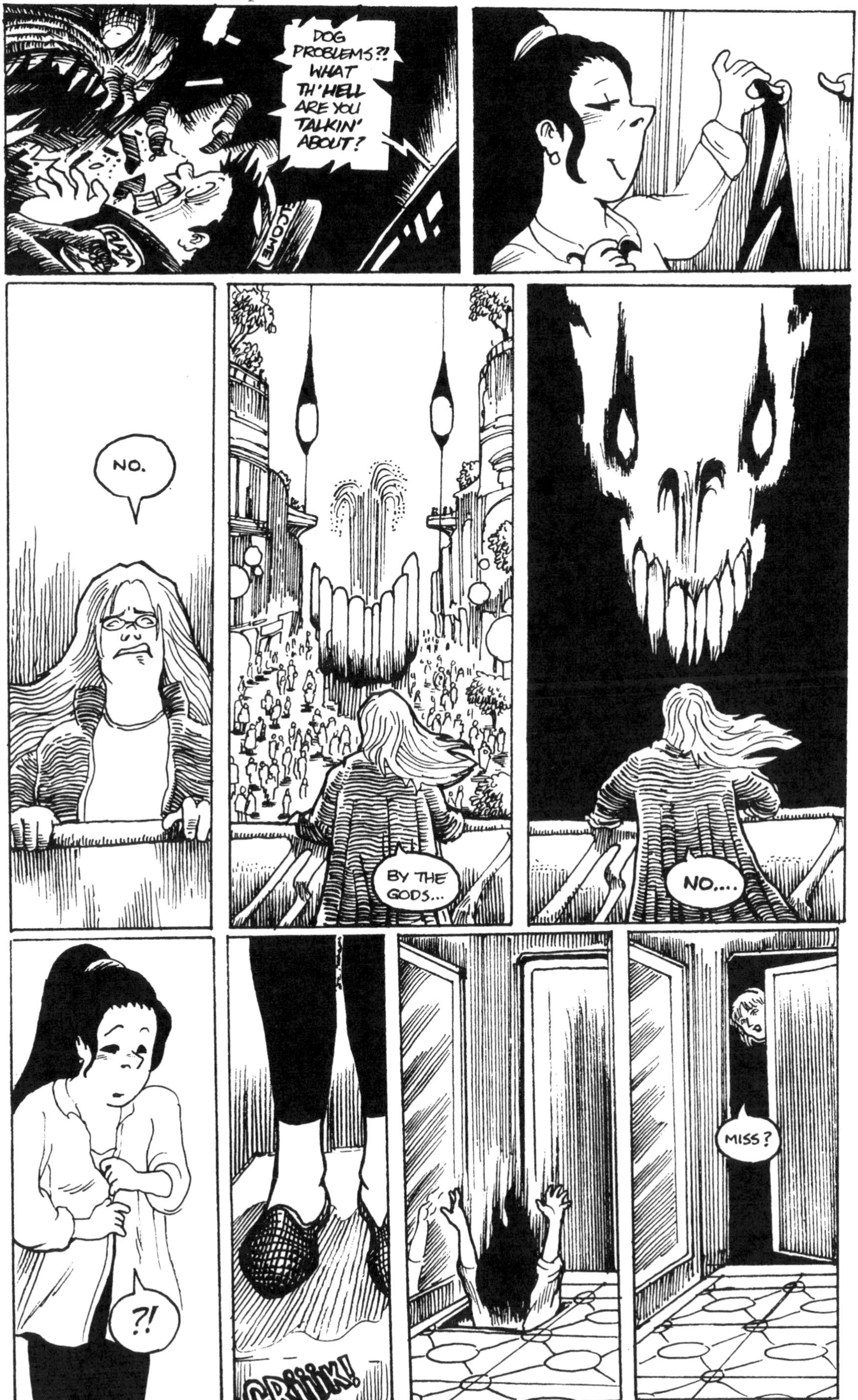
DOG PROBLEMS?! WHAT TH'HELL ARE YOU TALKIN' ABOUT?
NO.
BY THE GODS...
NO....
?!
CRIIIK!
MISS?

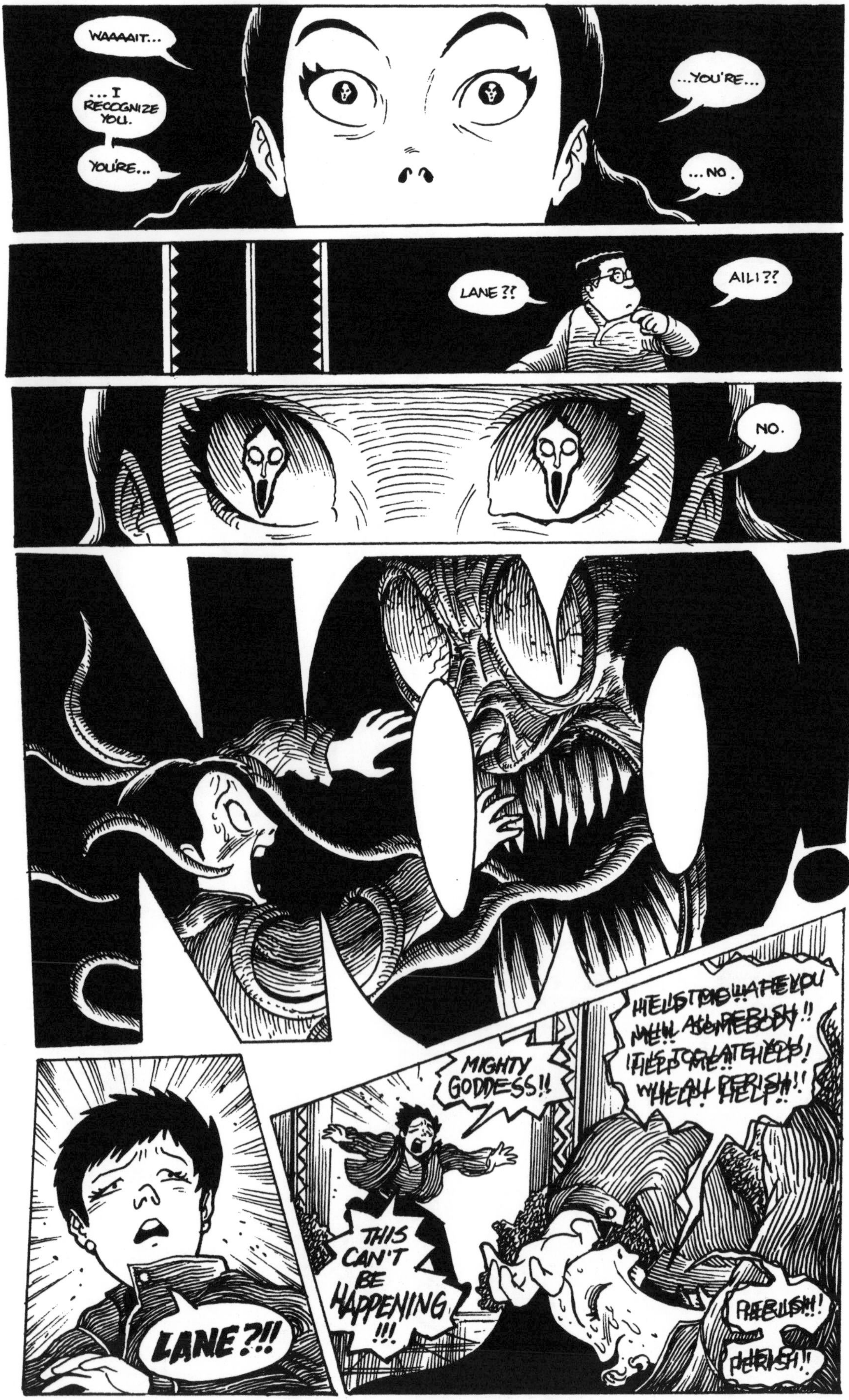
WAAAAIT...
...I RECOGNIZE YOU.
YOU'RE...
...YOU'RE...
...NO.
LANE ?!
AILI ?!
NO.
NO!
LANE ?!!
MIGHTY GODDESS!!
THIS CAN'T BE HAPPENING!!!

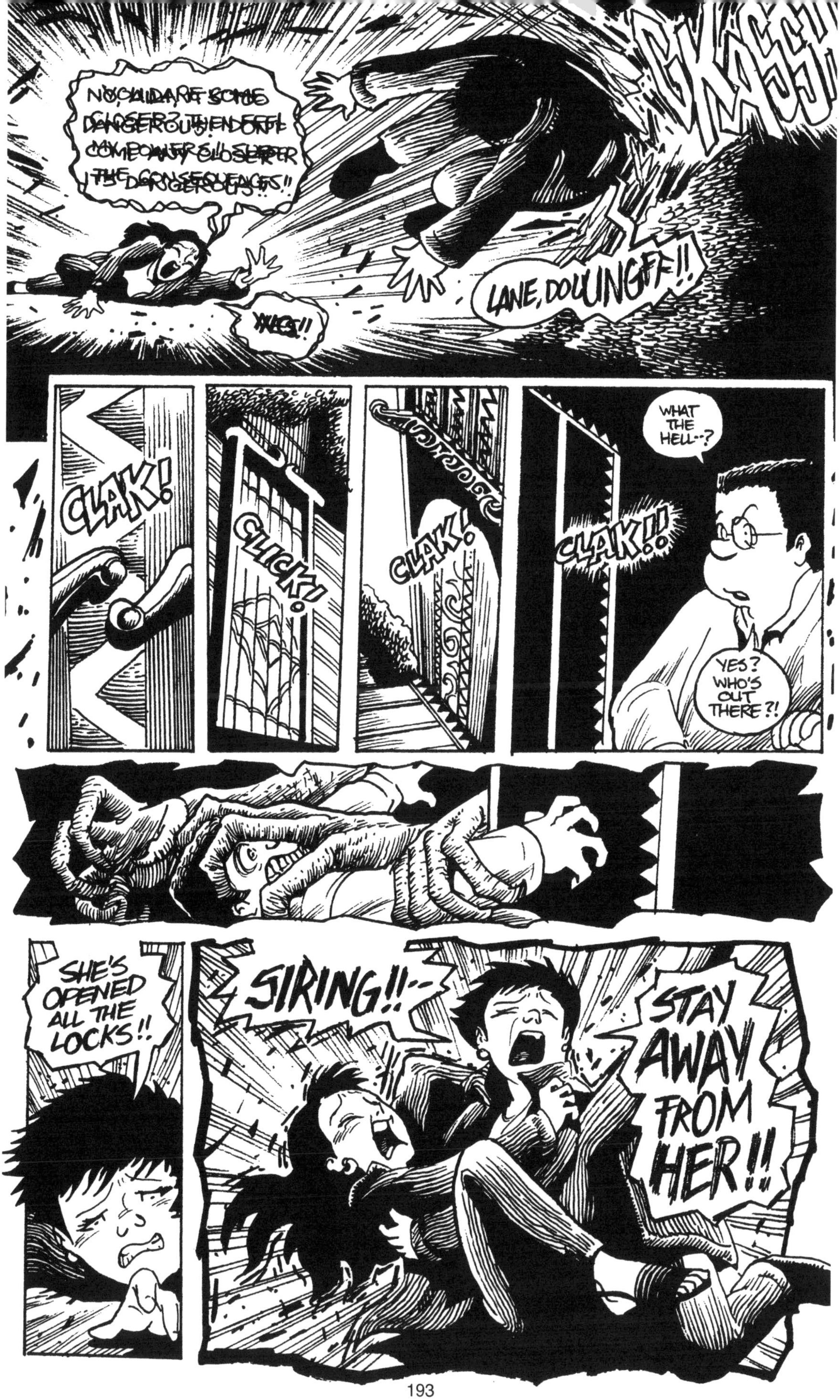
CLAK!
CLICK!
CLAK!
CLAK!!
WHAT THE HELL--?
YES? WHO'S OUT THERE?!
SHE'S OPENED ALL THE LOCKS!!
SIRING!!
STAY AWAY FROM HER!!

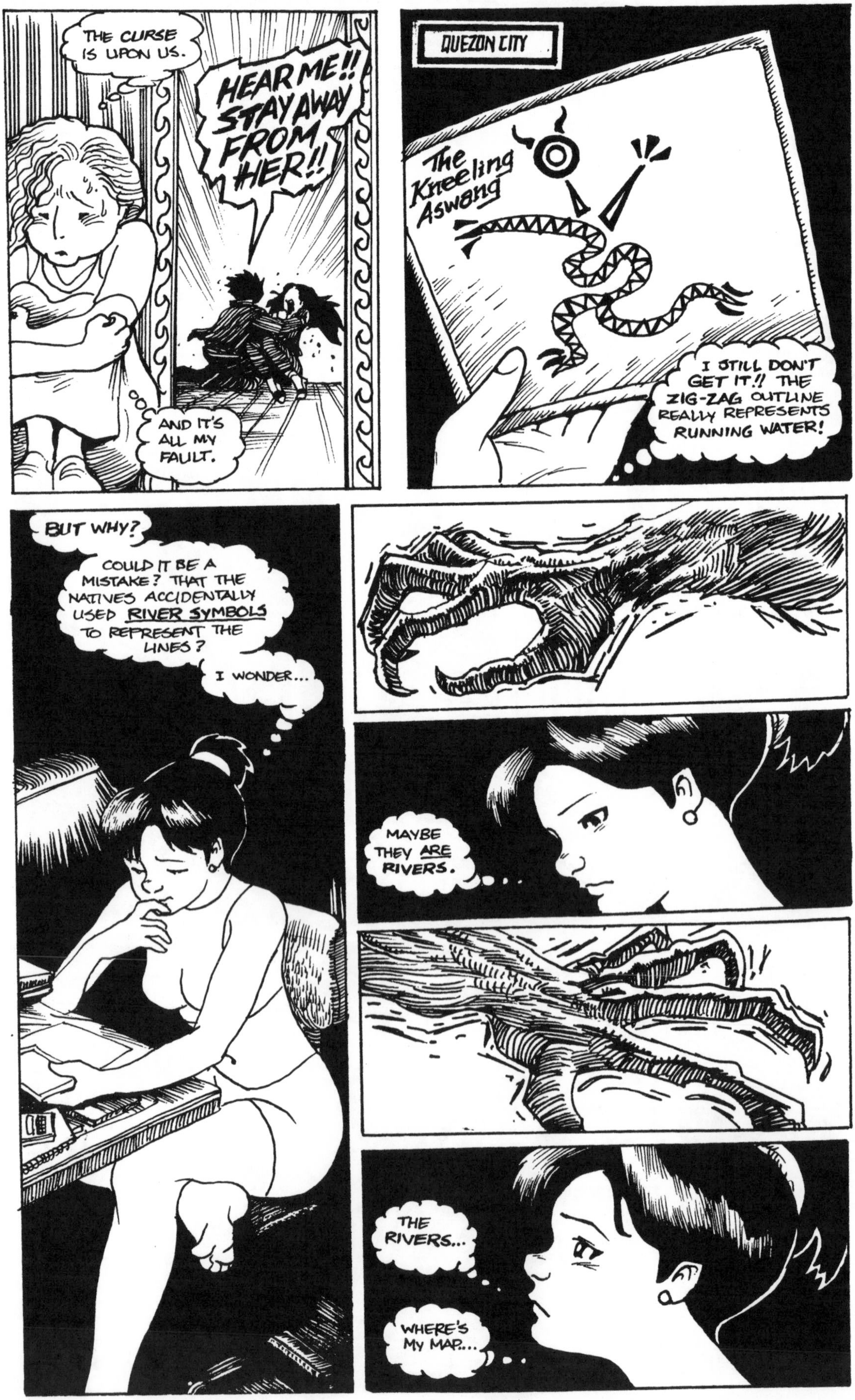
THE CURSE IS UPON US.
HEAR ME!! STAY AWAY FROM HER!!
AND IT'S ALL MY FAULT.
QUEZON CITY
The Kreeling Aswang
I STILL DON'T GET IT!! THE ZIG-ZAG OUTLINE REALLY REPRESENTS RUNNING WATER!
BUT WHY?
COULD IT BE A MISTAKE? THAT THE NATIVES ACCIDENTALLY USED RIVER SYMBOLS TO REPRESENT THE LINES?
I WONDER...
MAYBE THEY ARE RIVERS.
THE RIVERS...
WHERE'S MY MAP...

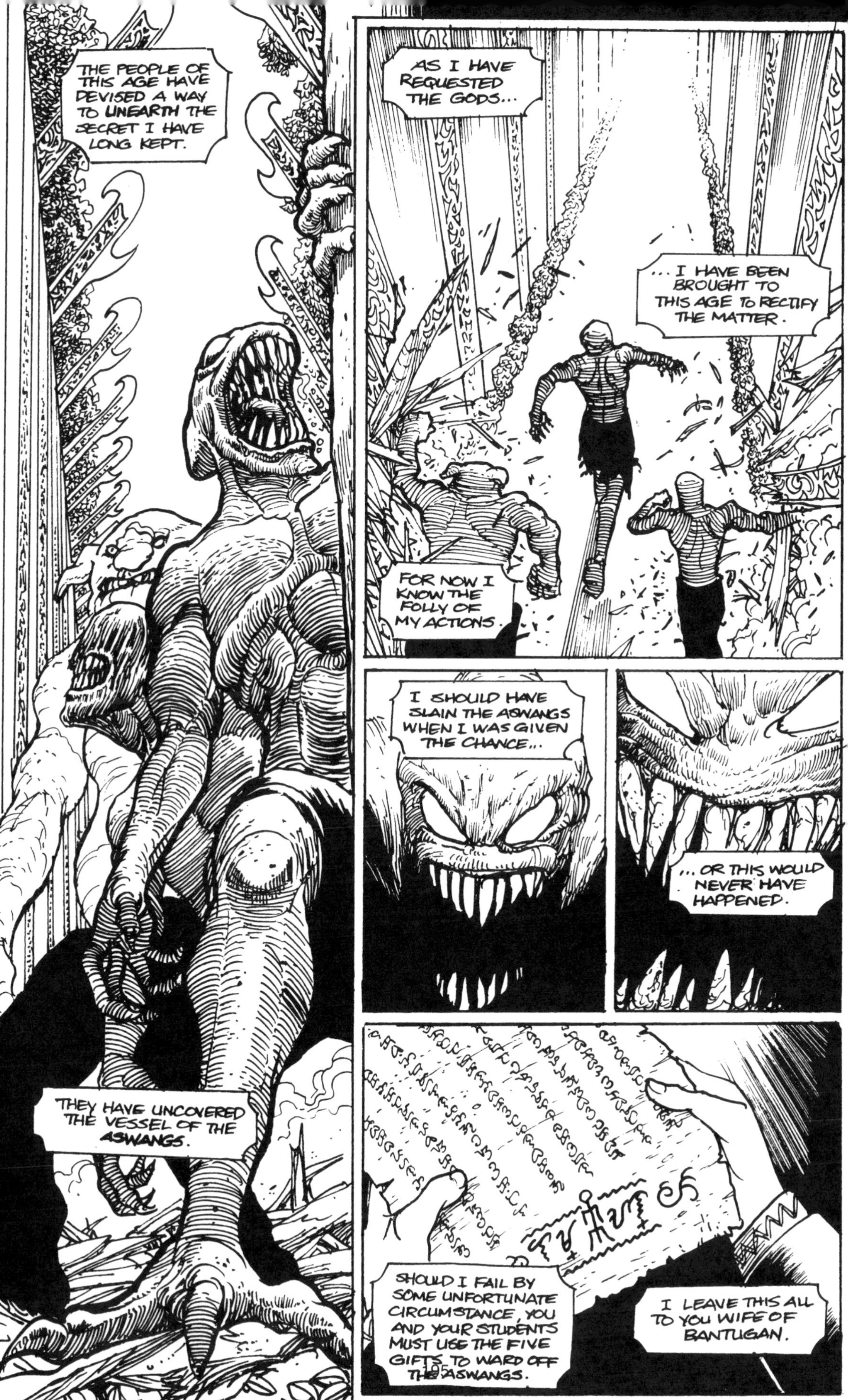
THE PEOPLE OF THIS AGE HAVE DEVISED A WAY TO UNEARTH THE SECRET I HAVE LONG KEPT.
THEY HAVE UNCOVERED THE VESSEL OF THE ASWANGS.
AS I HAVE REQUESTED THE GODS...
...I HAVE BEEN BROUGHT TO THIS AGE TO RECTIFY THE MATTER.
FOR NOW I KNOW THE FOLLY OF MY ACTIONS.
I SHOULD HAVE SLAIN THE ASWANGS WHEN I WAS GIVEN THE CHANCE...
...OR THIS WOULD NEVER HAVE HAPPENED.
SHOULD I FAIL BY SOME UNFORTUNATE CIRCUMSTANCE, YOU AND YOUR STUDENTS MUST USE THE FIVE GIFTS TO WARD OFF THE ASWANGS.
I LEAVE THIS ALL TO YOU WIFE OF BANTUGAN.

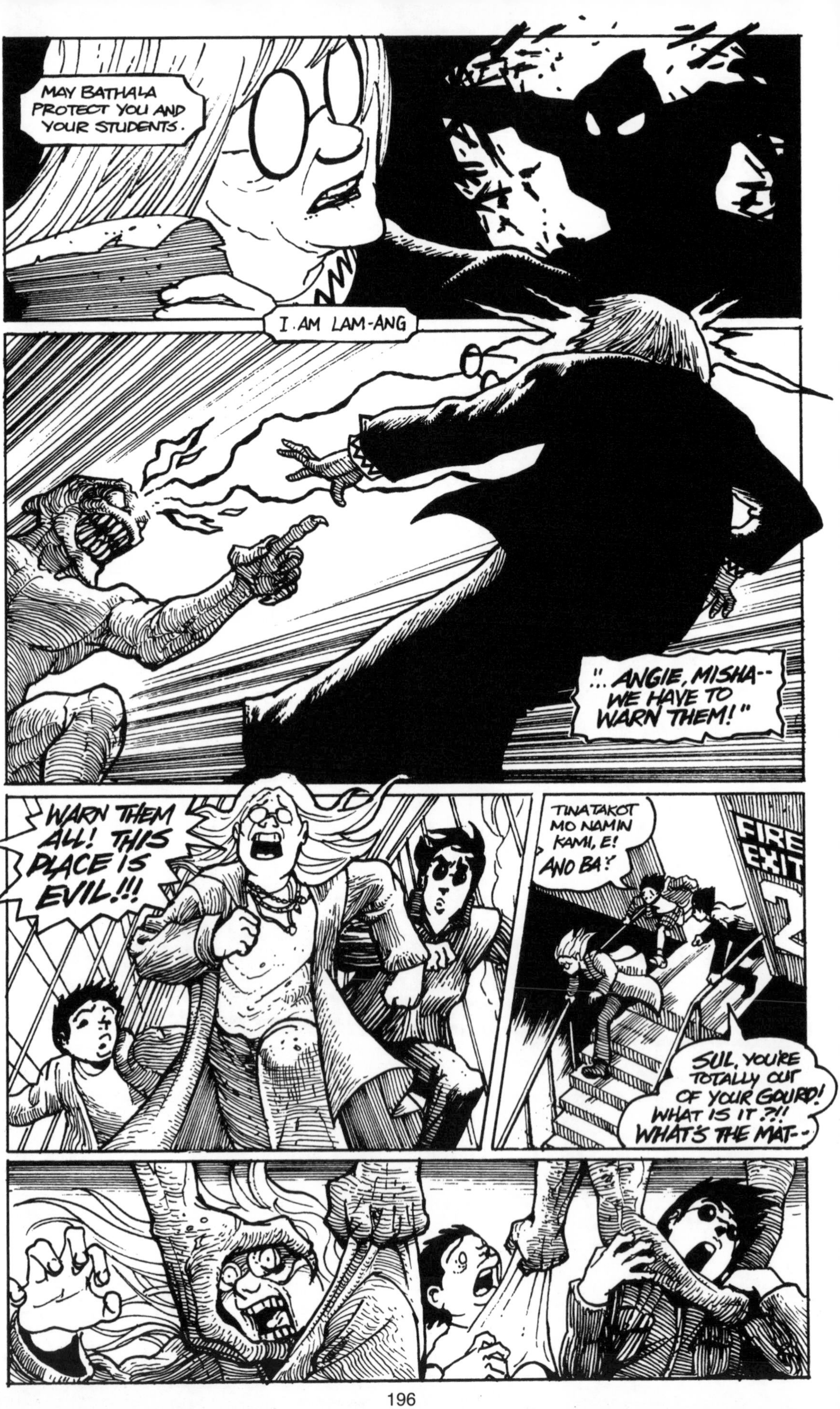
MAY BATHALA PROTECT YOU AND YOUR STUDENTS.
I AM LAM-ANG
"... ANGIE, MISHA-- WE HAVE TO WARN THEM!"
WARN THEM ALL! THIS PLACE IS EVIL!!!
TINATAKOT MO NAMIN KAMI, E! ANO BA?
FIRE EXIT
SUL, YOU'RE TOTALLY OUT OF YOUR GOURD! WHAT IS IT?!! WHAT'S THE MAT--

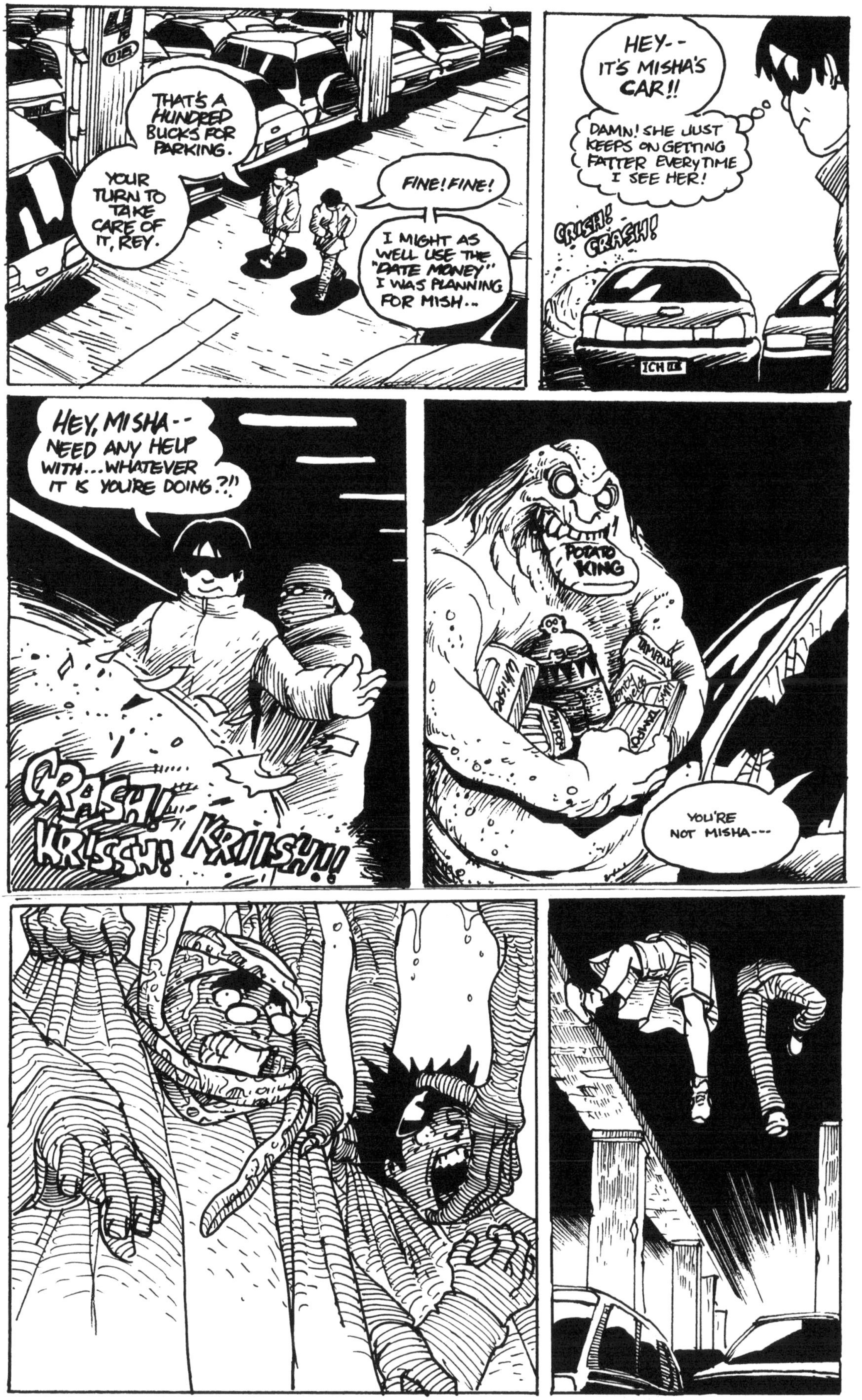
THAT'S A HUNDRED BUCKS FOR PARKING.
YOUR TURN TO TAKE CARE OF IT, REY.
FINE! FINE!
I MIGHT AS WELL USE THE "DATE MONEY" I WAS PLANNING FOR MISH..
HEY-- IT'S MISHA'S CAR!!
DAMN! SHE JUST KEEPS ON GETTING FATTER EVERYTIME I SEE HER!
CRASH! CRASH!
ICH
HEY, MISHA-- NEED ANY HELP WITH... WHATEVER IT IS YOU'RE DOING?!
CRASH! KRISSH! KRIISH!!
POTATO KING
YOU'RE NOT MISHA---

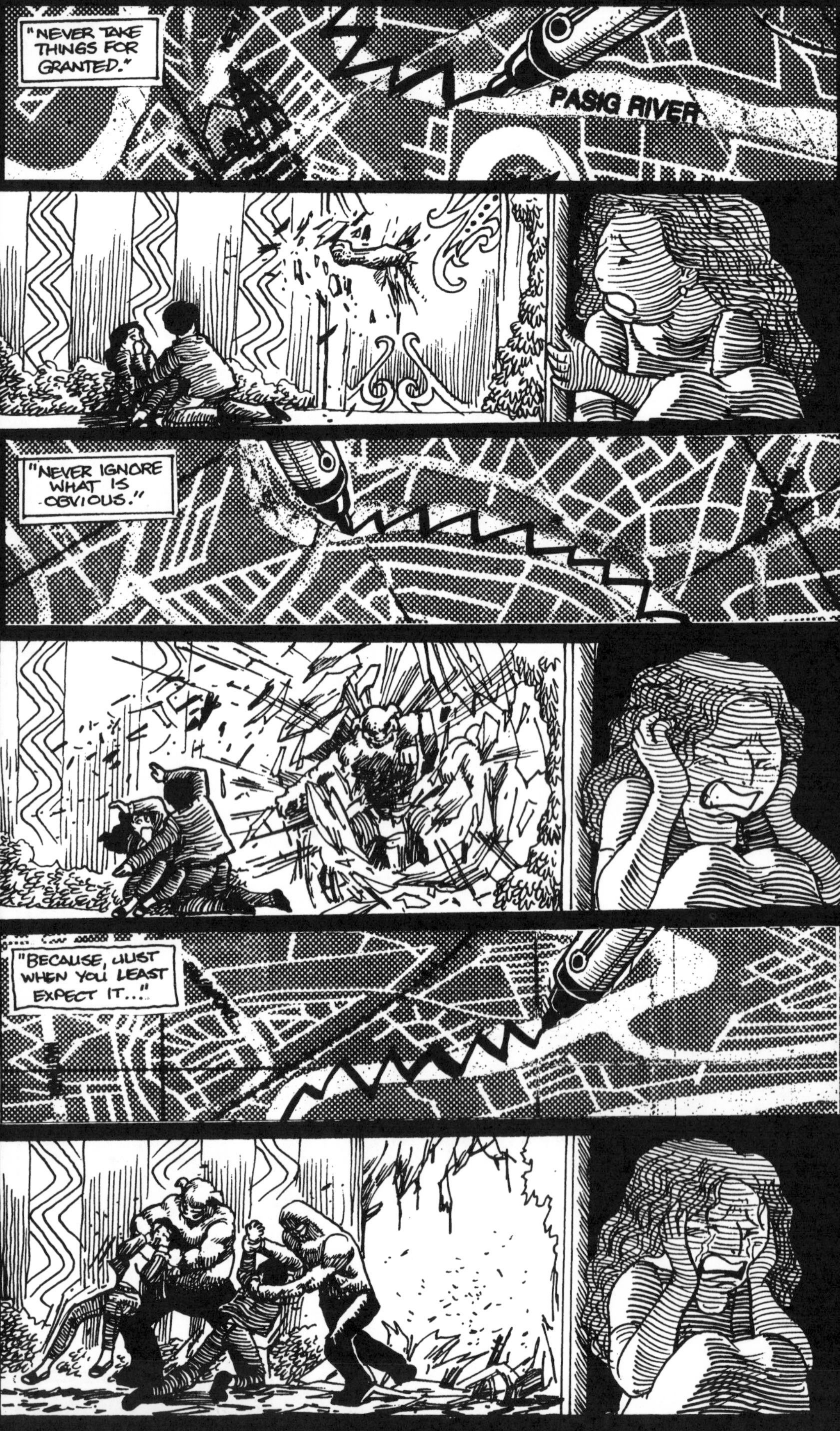
"NEVER TAKE THINGS FOR GRANTED."
PASIG RIVER
"NEVER IGNORE WHAT IS OBVIOUS."
"BECAUSE, JUST WHEN YOU LEAST EXPECT IT..."

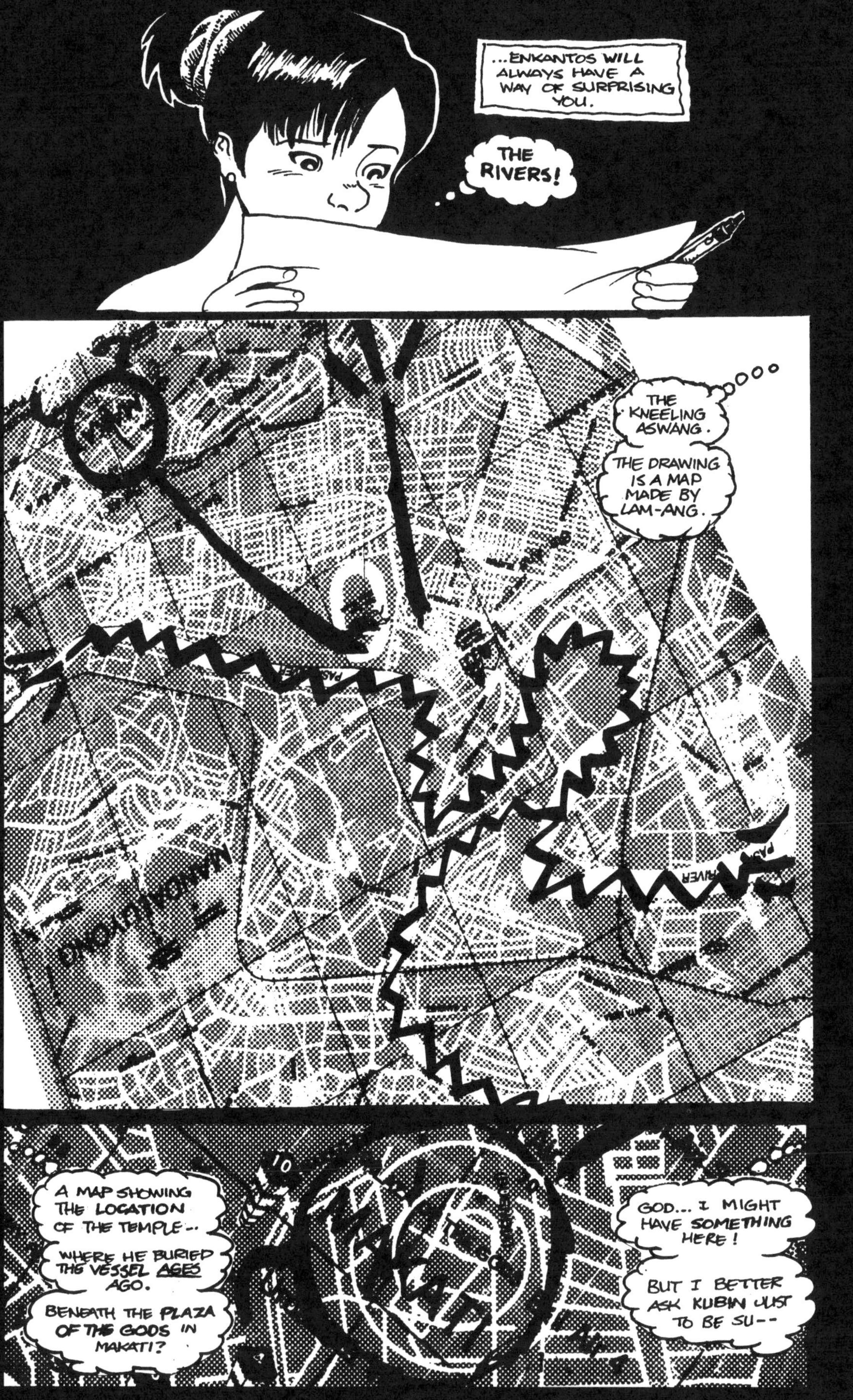
...ENKANTOS WILL ALWAYS HAVE A WAY OF SURPRISING YOU.
THE RIVERS!
THE KNEELING ASWANG.
THE DRAWING IS A MAP MADE BY LAM-ANG.
A MAP SHOWING THE LOCATION OF THE TEMPLE--
WHERE HE BURIED THE VESSEL AGES AGO.
BENEATH THE PLAZA OF THE GODS IN MAKATI?
GOD... I MIGHT HAVE SOMETHING HERE!
BUT I BETTER ASK KUBIN JUST TO BE SU--

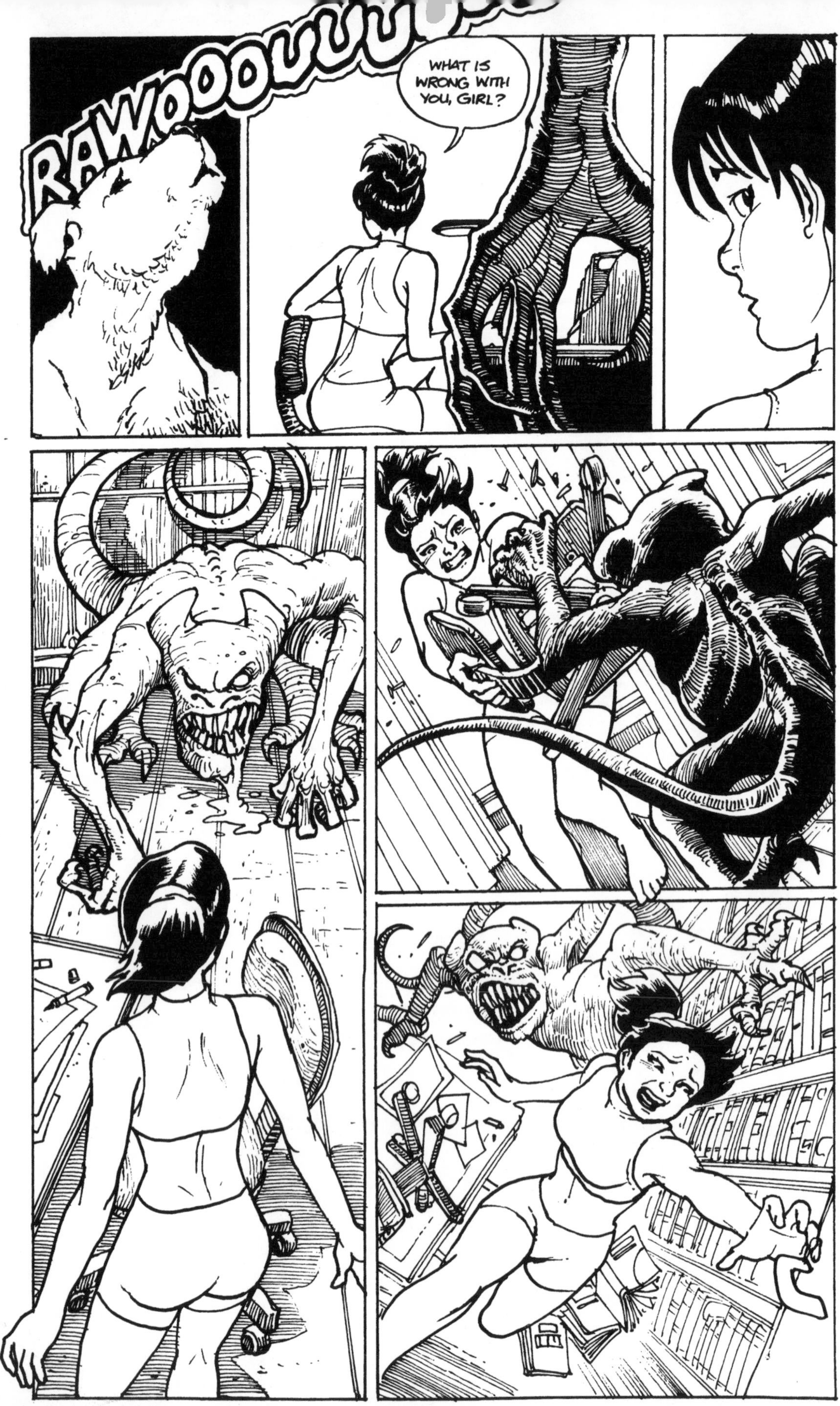
RAWOOOLUUU
WHAT IS WRONG WITH YOU, GIRL?

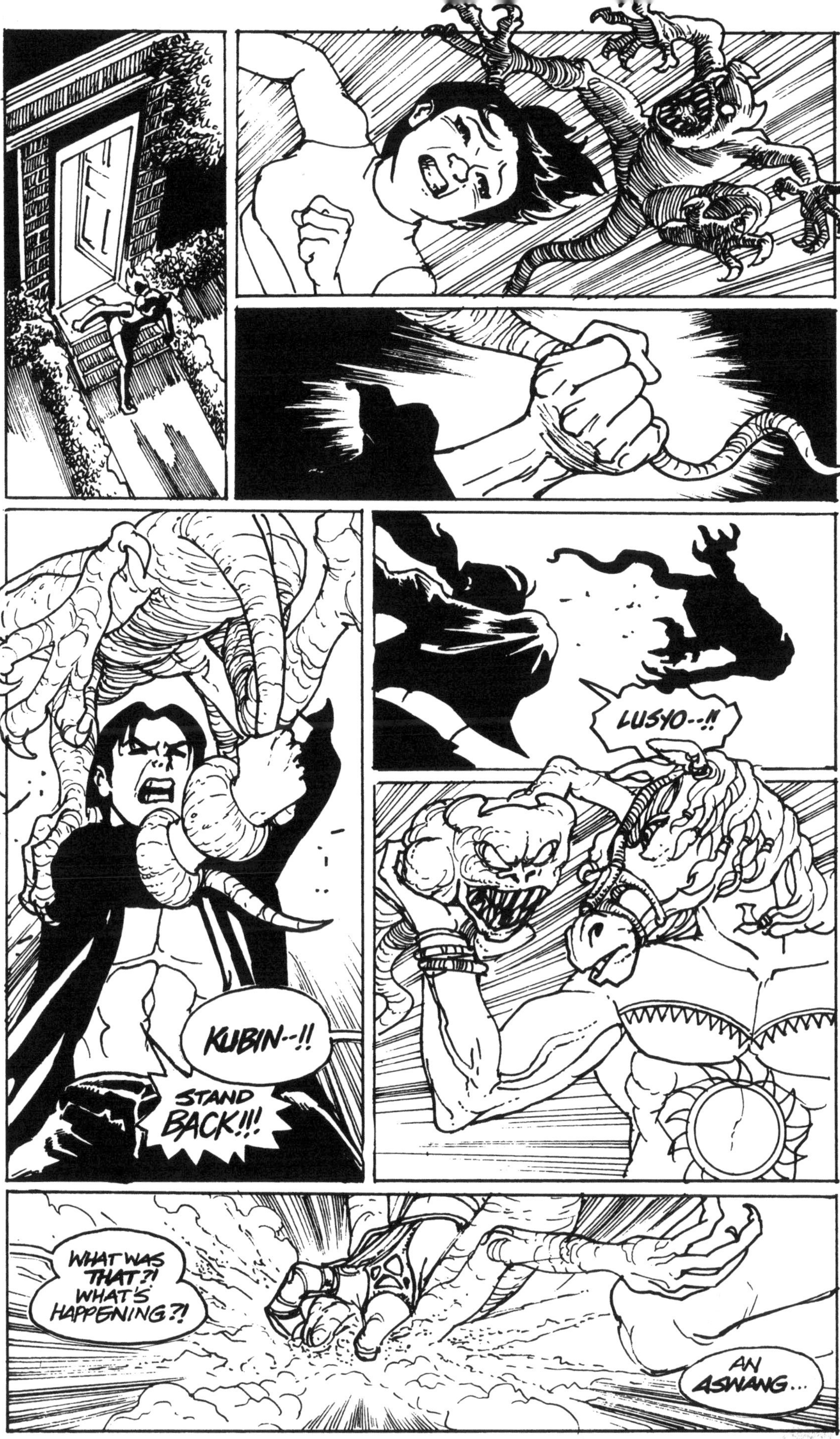
KUBIN--!!
STAND BACK!!!
LUSYO--!!
WHAT WAS THAT?! WHAT'S HAPPENING?!
AN ASWANG...

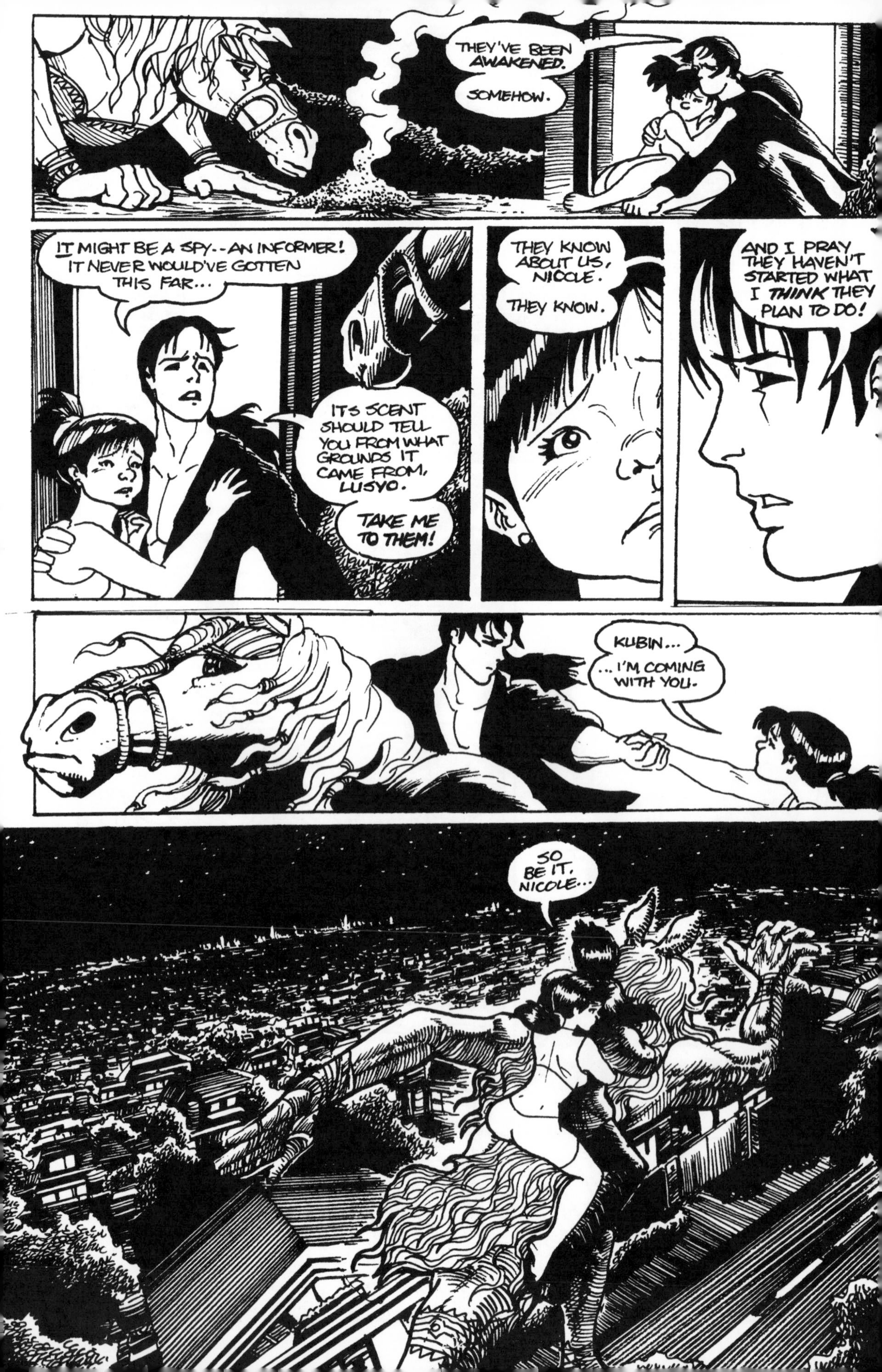
THEY'VE BEEN AWAKENED.
SOMEHOW.
IT MIGHT BE A SPY--AN INFORMER! IT NEVER WOULD'VE GOTTEN THIS FAR...
IT'S SCENT SHOULD TELL YOU FROM WHAT GROUNDS IT CAME FROM, LUSYO.
TAKE ME TO THEM!
THEY KNOW ABOUT US, NICOLE.
THEY KNOW.
AND I PRAY THEY HAVEN'T STARTED WHAT I THINK THEY PLAN TO DO!
KUBIN...
...I'M COMING WITH YOU.
SO BE IT, NICOLE...

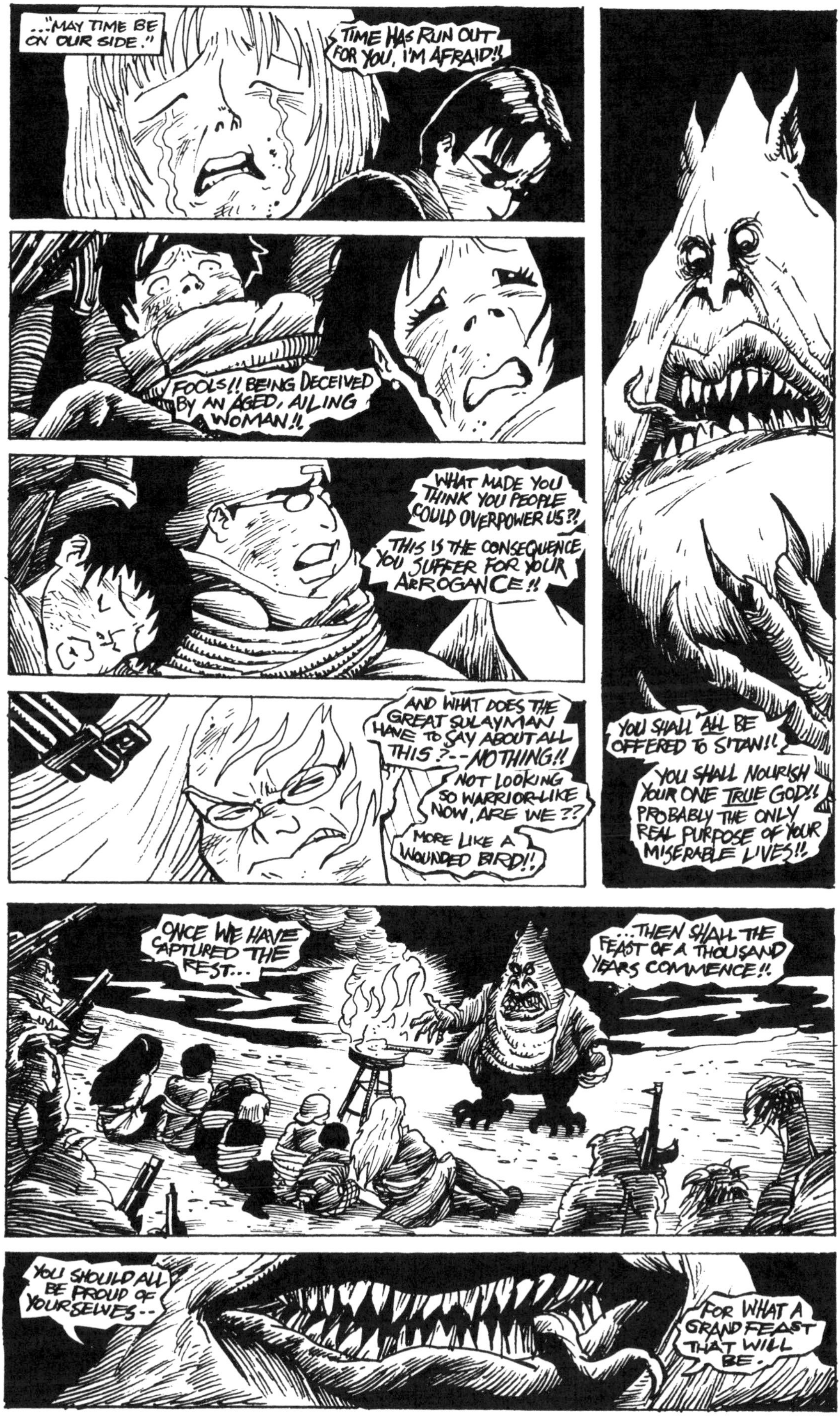
..."MAY TIME BE ON OUR SIDE."
TIME HAS RUN OUT FOR YOU, I'M AFRAID!!
FOOLS!! BEING DECEIVED BY AN AGED, AILING WOMAN!!
WHAT MADE YOU THINK YOU PEOPLE COULD OVERPOWER US?!
THIS IS THE CONSEQUENCE YOU SUFFER FOR YOUR ARROGANCE!!
AND WHAT DOES THE GREAT SULAYMAN HAVE TO SAY ABOUT ALL THIS?--NOTHING!!
NOT LOOKING SO WARRIOR-LIKE NOW, ARE WE??
MORE LIKE A WOUNDED BIRD!!
YOU SHALL ALL BE OFFERED TO SITAN!!
YOU SHALL NOURISH YOUR ONE TRUE GOD!! PROBABLY THE ONLY REAL PURPOSE OF YOUR MISERABLE LIVES!!
ONCE WE HAVE CAPTURED THE REST...
...THEN SHALL THE FEAST OF A THOUSAND YEARS COMMENCE!!
YOU SHOULD ALL BE PROUD OF YOURSELVES--
FOR WHAT A GRAND FEAST THAT WILL BE.

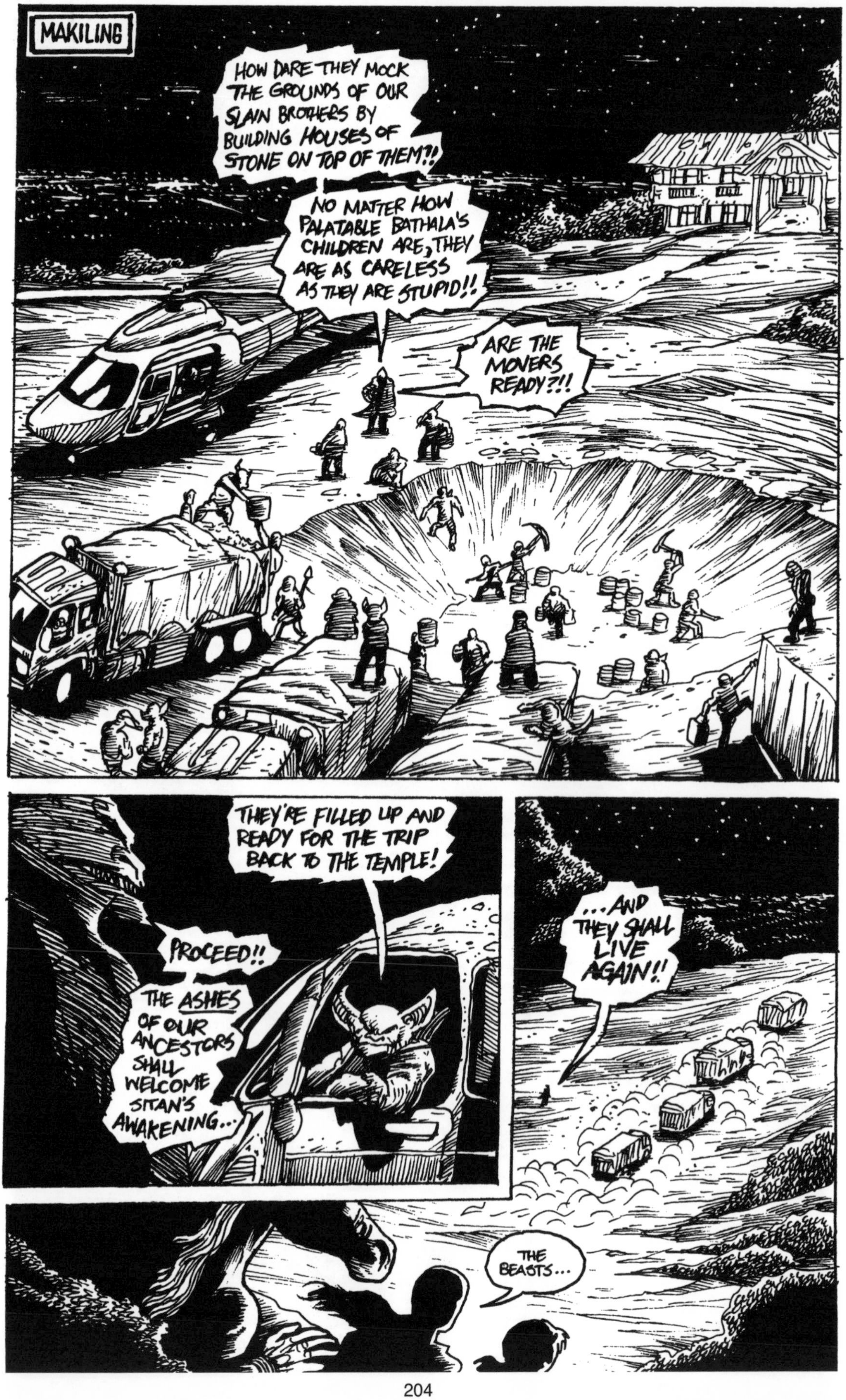
MAKILING
HOW DARE THEY MOCK THE GROUNDS OF OUR SLAIN BROTHERS BY BUILDING HOUSES OF STONE ON TOP OF THEM?!
NO MATTER HOW PALATABLE BATHALA'S CHILDREN ARE, THEY ARE AS CARELESS AS THEY ARE STUPID!!
ARE THE MOVERS READY?!!
THEY'RE FILLED UP AND READY FOR THE TRIP BACK TO THE TEMPLE!
PROCEED!!
THE ASHES OF OUR ANCESTORS SHALL WELCOME SITAN'S AWAKENING...
...AND THEY SHALL LIVE AGAIN!!
THE BEASTS...

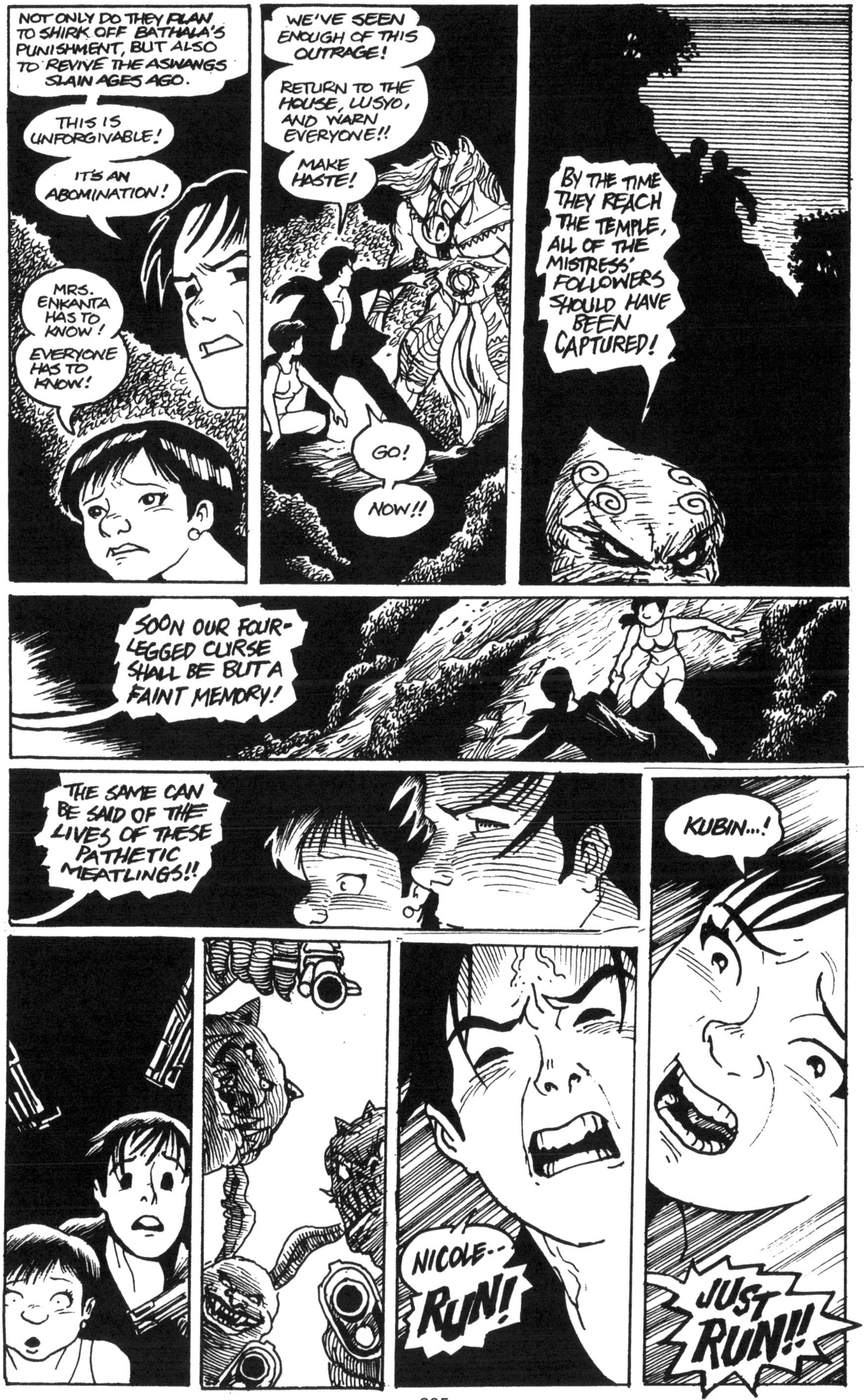
NOT ONLY DO THEY PLAN TO SHIRK OFF BATHALA'S PUNISHMENT, BUT ALSO TO REVIVE THE ASWANGS SLAIN AGES AGO.
THIS IS UNFORGIVABLE!
IT'S AN ABOMINATION!
MRS. ENKANTA HAS TO KNOW!
EVERYONE HAS TO KNOW!
WE'VE SEEN ENOUGH OF THIS OUTRAGE!
RETURN TO THE HOUSE, LUSYO, AND WARN EVERYONE!!
MAKE HASTE!
GO!
NOW!!
BY THE TIME THEY REACH THE TEMPLE, ALL OF THE MISTRESS' FOLLOWERS SHOULD HAVE BEEN CAPTURED!
SOON OUR FOUR-LEGGED CURSE SHALL BE BUT A FAINT MEMORY!
THE SAME CAN BE SAID OF THE LIVES OF THESE PATHETIC MEATLINGS!!
KUBIN...!
NICOLE... RUN!
JUST RUN!!

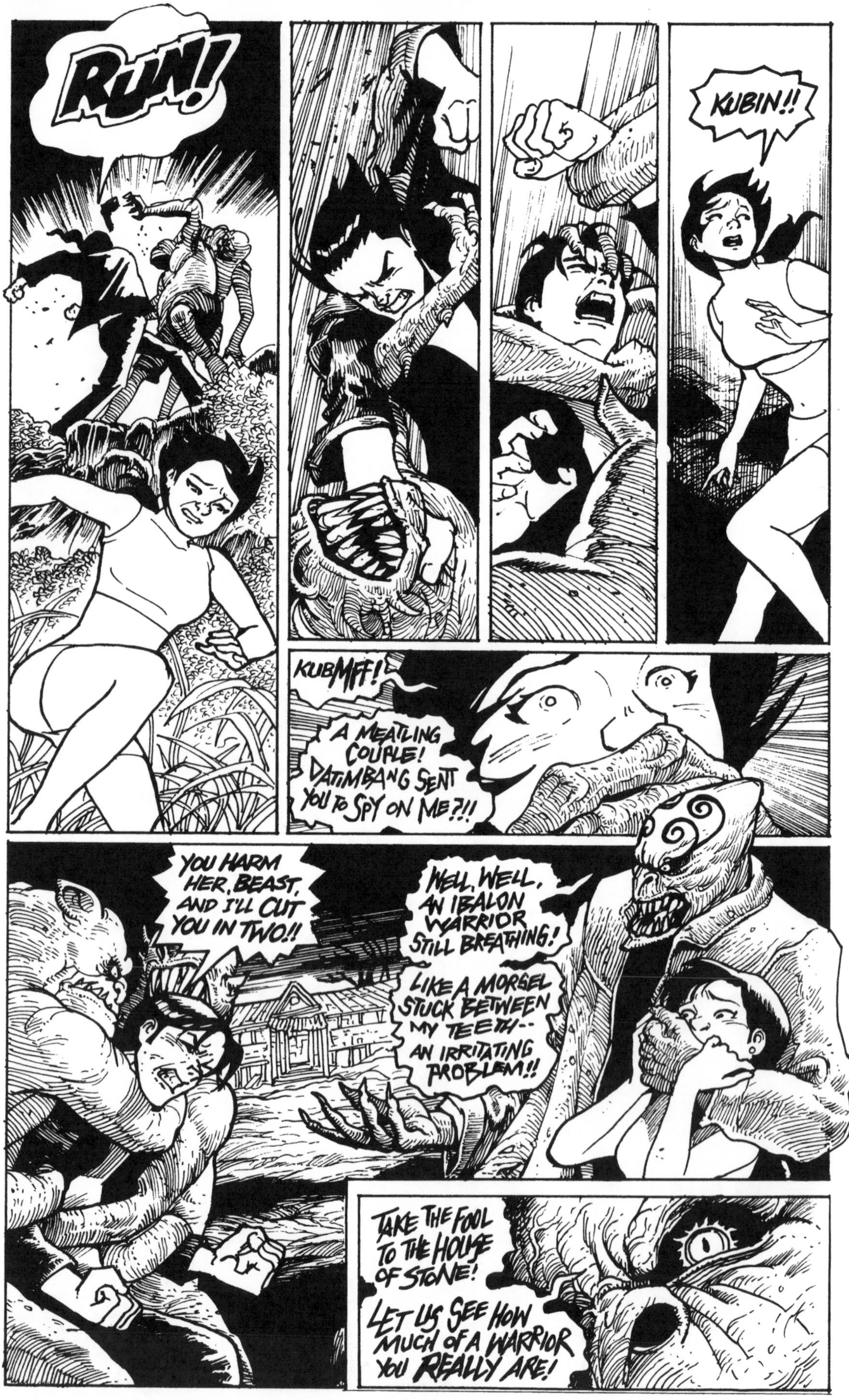
RUN!
KUBIN!!
KUBMFF!
A MEATLING COUPLE! DATIMBANG SENT YOU TO SPY ON ME?!!
YOU HARM HER, BEAST, AND I'LL CUT YOU IN TWO!!
WELL, WELL, AN IBALON WARRIOR STILL BREATHING!
LIKE A MORSEL STUCK BETWEEN MY TEETH-- AN IRRITATING PROBLEM!!
TAKE THE FOOL TO THE HOUSE OF STONE!
LET US SEE HOW MUCH OF A WARRIOR YOU REALLY ARE!

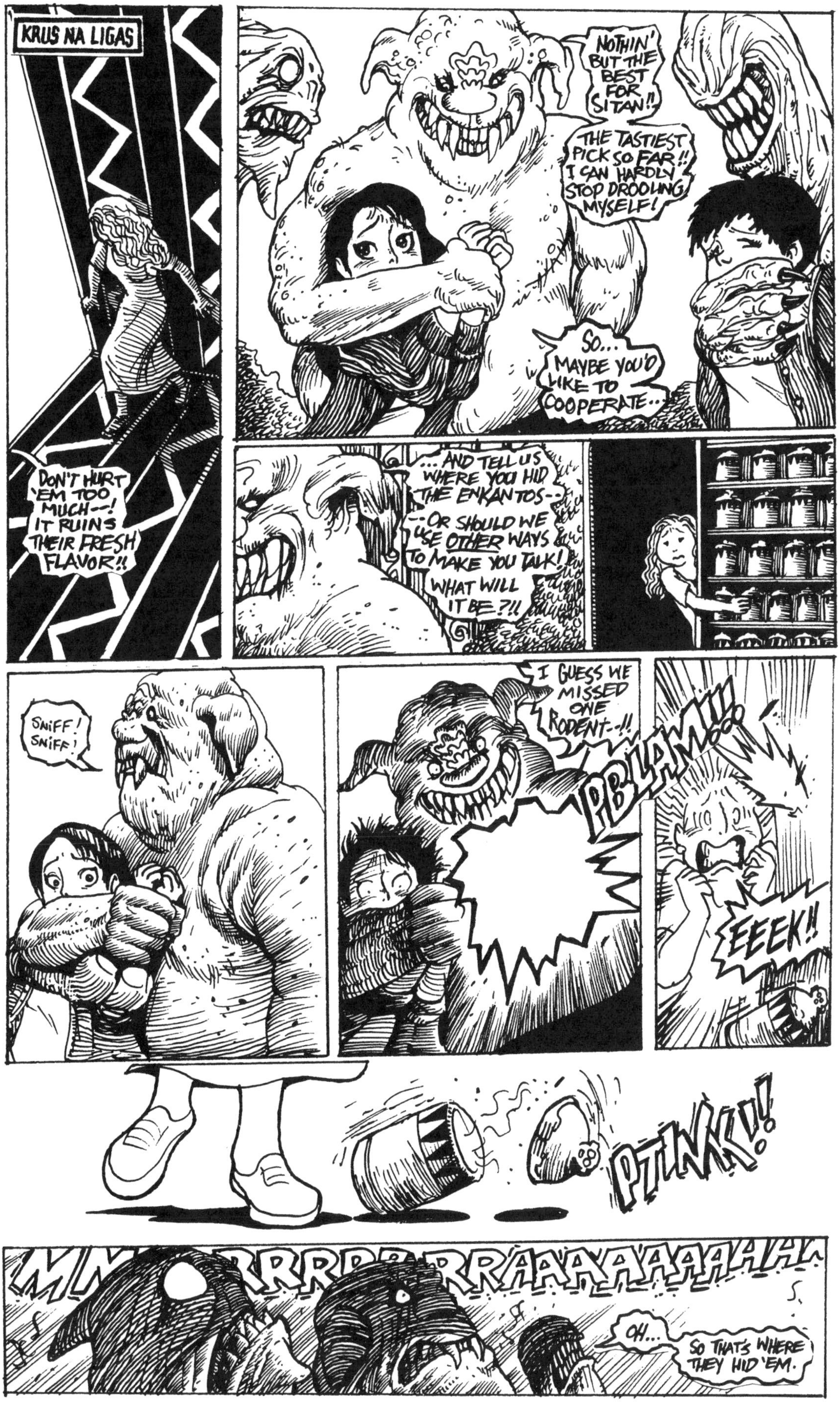
KRUS NA LIGAS
NOTHIN' BUT THE BEST FOR SITAN!!
THE TASTIEST PICK SO FAR!! I CAN HARDLY STOP DROOLING MYSELF!
SO... MAYBE YOU'D LIKE TO COOPERATE...
DON'T HURT 'EM TOO MUCH--! IT RUINS THEIR FRESH FLAVOR!!
...AND TELL US WHERE YOU HID THE ENKANTOS--
--OR SHOULD WE USE OTHER WAYS TO MAKE YOU TALK!
WHAT WILL IT BE?!!
SNIFF! SNIFF!
I GUESS WE MISSED ONE RODENT--!!
PBLAM!!!
EEEK!!
PTINK!!
MNRRRRRRAAAAAAAAH!
OH...
SO THAT'S WHERE THEY HID 'EM.

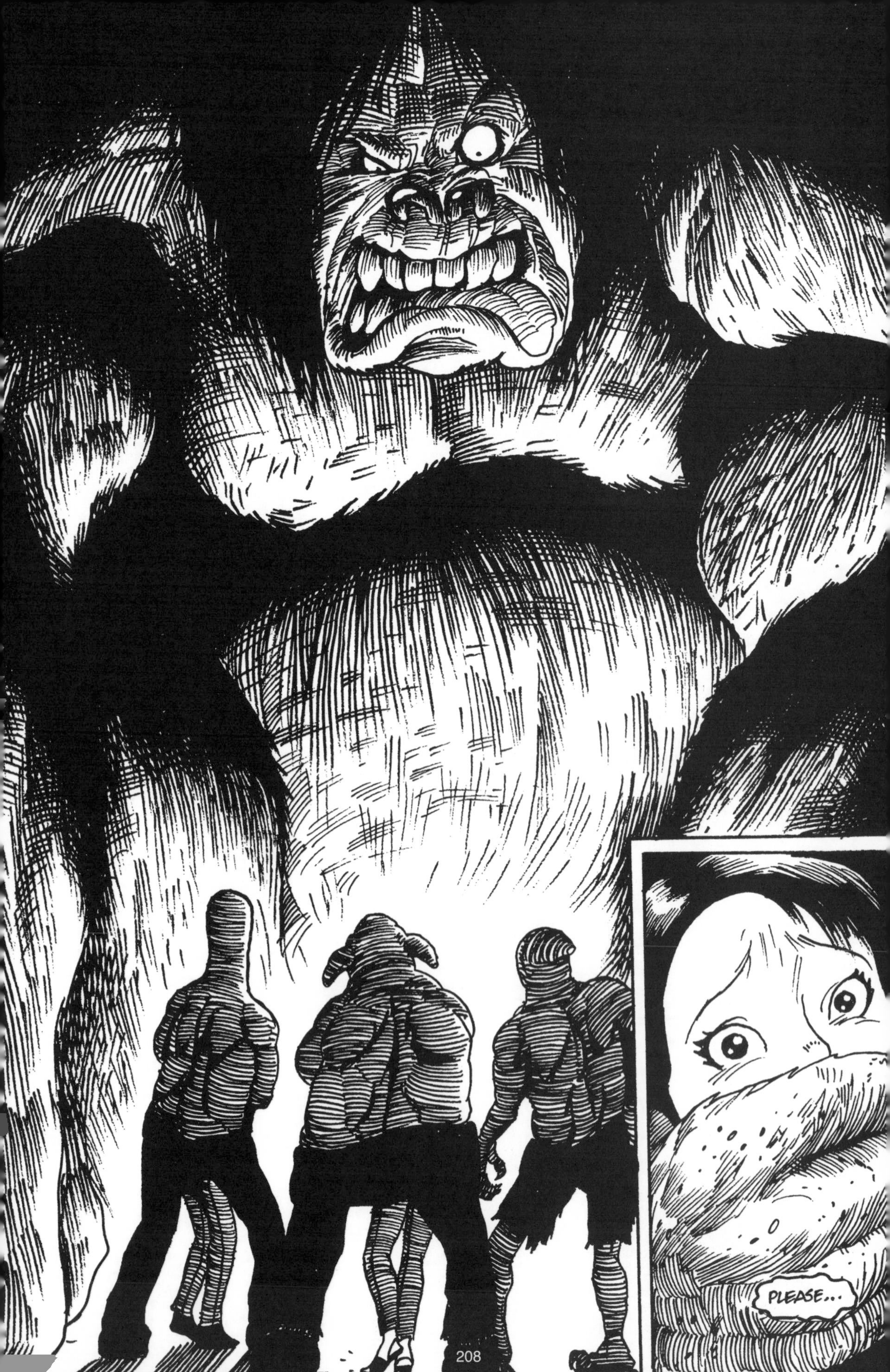
PLEASE...

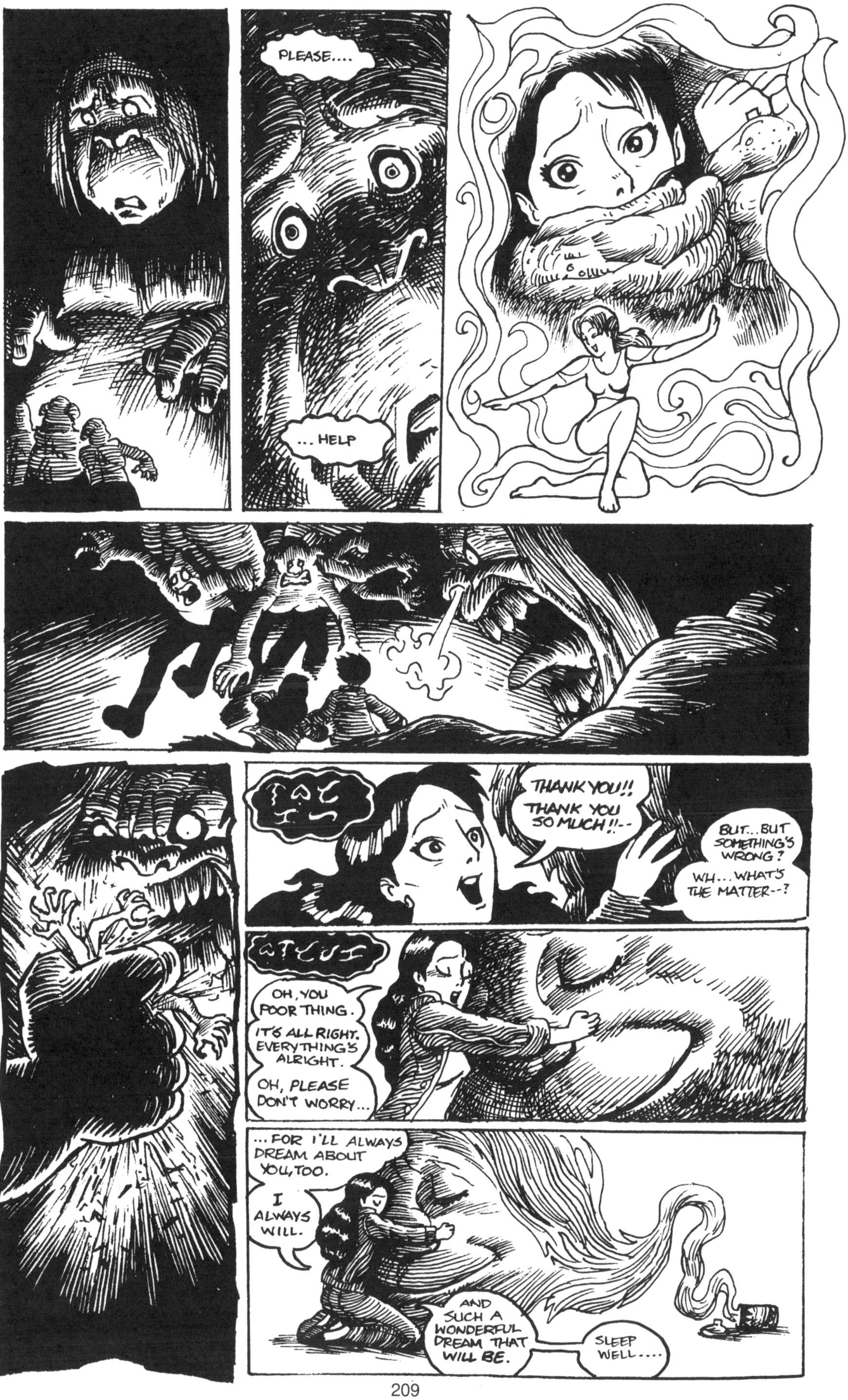
PLEASE....
... HELP
THANK YOU!!
THANK YOU SO MUCH!!--
BUT...BUT SOMETHING'S WRONG?
WH...WHAT'S THE MATTER--?
OH, YOU POOR THING.
IT'S ALL RIGHT. EVERYTHING'S ALRIGHT.
OH, PLEASE DON'T WORRY...
...FOR I'LL ALWAYS DREAM ABOUT YOU, TOO.
I ALWAYS WILL.
AND SUCH A WONDERFUL DREAM THAT WILL BE.
SLEEP WELL....

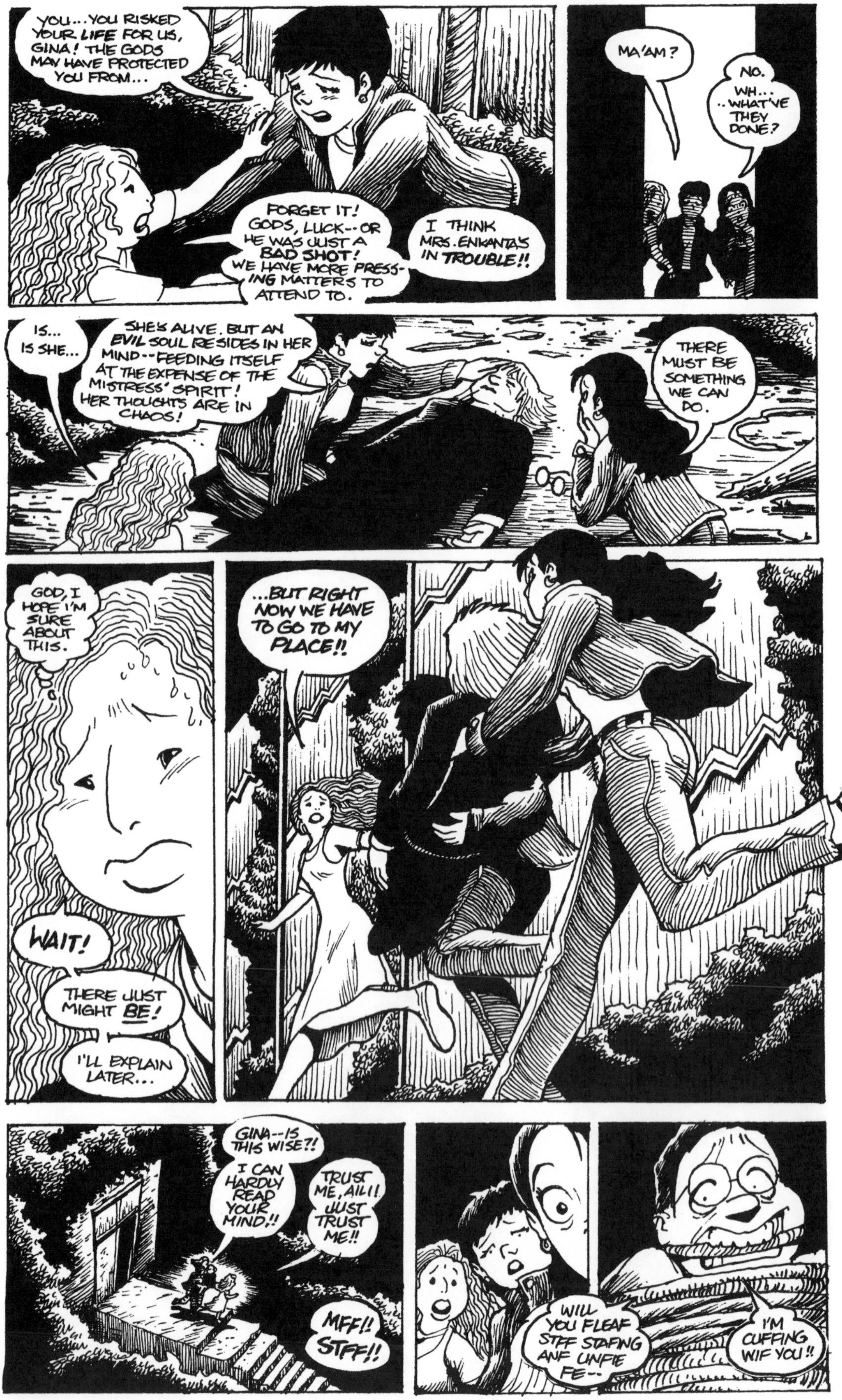
YOU...YOU RISKED YOUR LIFE FOR US, GINA! THE GODS MAY HAVE PROTECTED YOU FROM...
FORGET IT! GODS, LUCK--OR HE WAS JUST A BAD SHOT! WE HAVE MORE PRESSING MATTERS TO ATTEND TO.
I THINK MRS. ENKANTA'S IN TROUBLE!!
MA'AM?
NO. WH... ..WHAT'VE THEY DONE?
IS... IS SHE...
SHE'S ALIVE. BUT AN EVIL SOUL RESIDES IN HER MIND--FEEDING ITSELF AT THE EXPENSE OF THE MISTRESS' SPIRIT! HER THOUGHTS ARE IN CHAOS!
THERE MUST BE SOMETHING WE CAN DO.
GOD, I HOPE I'M SURE ABOUT THIS.
WAIT!
THERE JUST MIGHT BE!
I'LL EXPLAIN LATER...
...BUT RIGHT NOW WE HAVE TO GO TO MY PLACE!!
GINA--IS THIS WISE?!
I CAN HARDLY READ YOUR MIND!!
TRUST ME, AILI! JUST TRUST ME!!
MFF!! STFF!!
WILL YOU FLEAF STFF STAFING ANF UNFIE FE--
I'M CUFFING WIF YOU!!

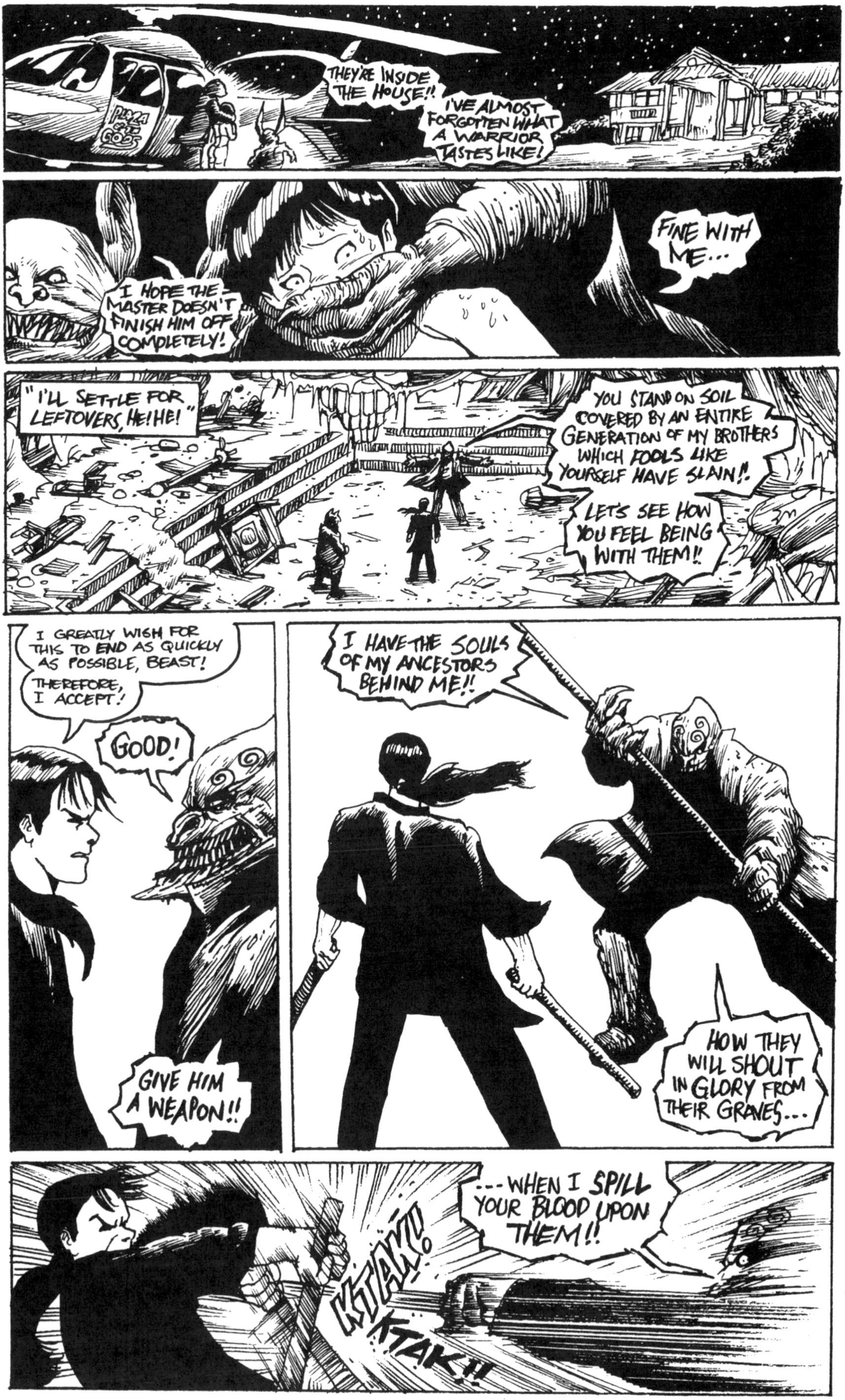
THEY'RE INSIDE THE HOUSE!!
I'VE ALMOST FORGOTTEN WHAT A WARRIOR TASTES LIKE!
PIZZA OF THE GODS
I HOPE THE MASTER DOESN'T FINISH HIM OFF COMPLETELY!
FINE WITH ME...
"I'LL SETTLE FOR LEFTOVERS, HE! HE!"
YOU STAND ON SOIL COVERED BY AN ENTIRE GENERATION OF MY BROTHERS WHICH FOOLS LIKE YOURSELF HAVE SLAIN!!
LET'S SEE HOW YOU FEEL BEING WITH THEM!!
I GREATLY WISH FOR THIS TO END AS QUICKLY AS POSSIBLE, BEAST!
THEREFORE, I ACCEPT!
GOOD!
GIVE HIM A WEAPON!!
I HAVE THE SOULS OF MY ANCESTORS BEHIND ME!!
HOW THEY WILL SHOUT IN GLORY FROM THEIR GRAVES...
...WHEN I SPILL YOUR BLOOD UPON THEM!!
KTAK!!
KTAK!!

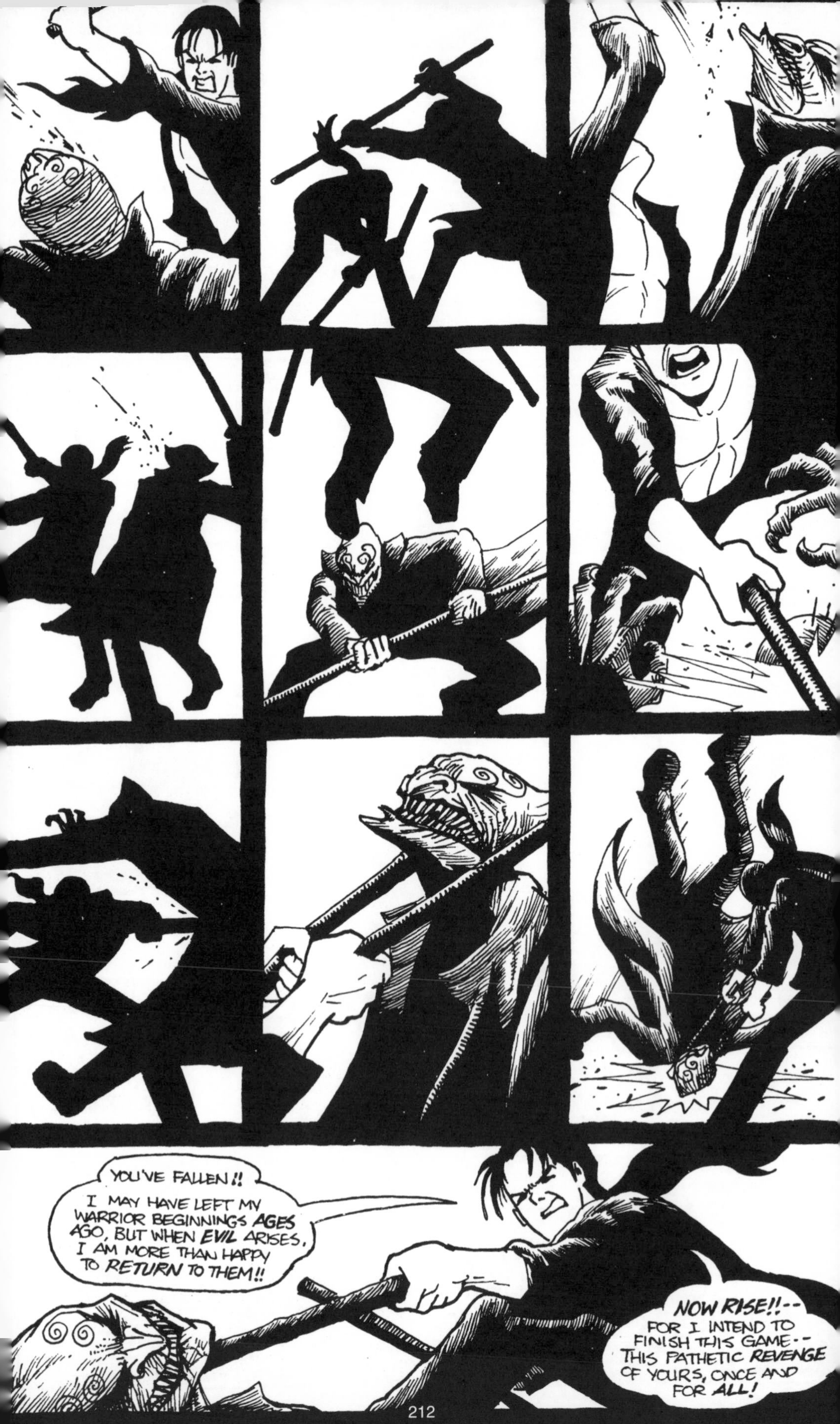
YOU'VE FALLEN!!
I MAY HAVE LEFT MY WARRIOR BEGINNINGS AGES AGO, BUT WHEN EVIL ARISES, I AM MORE THAN HAPPY TO RETURN TO THEM!!
NOW RISE!!-- FOR I INTEND TO FINISH THIS GAME-- THIS PATHETIC REVENGE OF YOURS, ONCE AND FOR ALL!

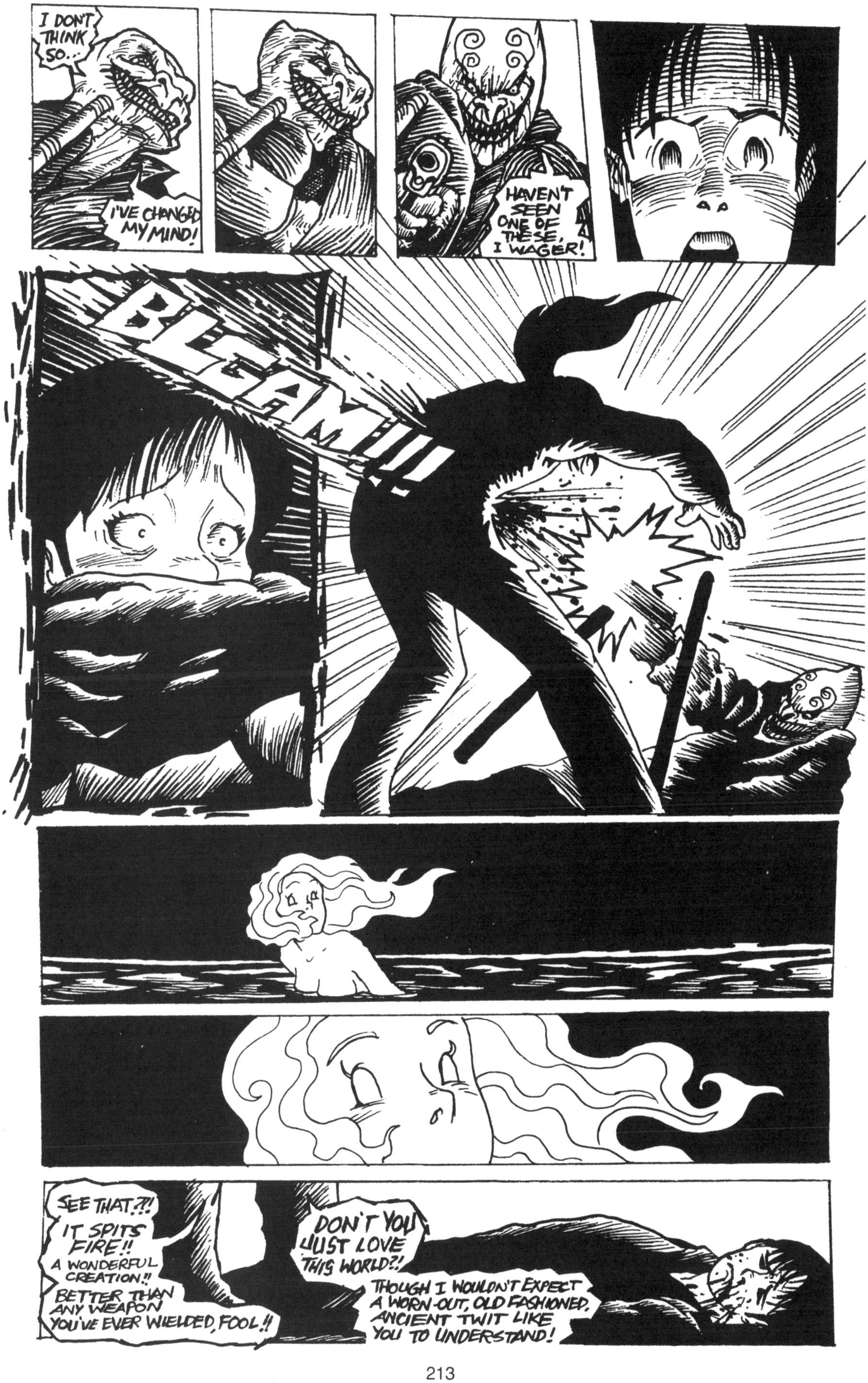
I DON'T THINK SO...
I'VE CHANGED MY MIND!
HAVEN'T SEEN ONE OF THESE, I WAGER!
BLAM!!!
SEE THAT?!! IT SPITS FIRE!! A WONDERFUL CREATION!! BETTER THAN ANY WEAPON YOU'VE EVER WIELDED, FOOL!!
DON'T YOU JUST LOVE THIS WORLD?!
THOUGH I WOULDN'T EXPECT A WORN-OUT, OLD FASHIONED, ANCIENT TWIT LIKE YOU TO UNDERSTAND!

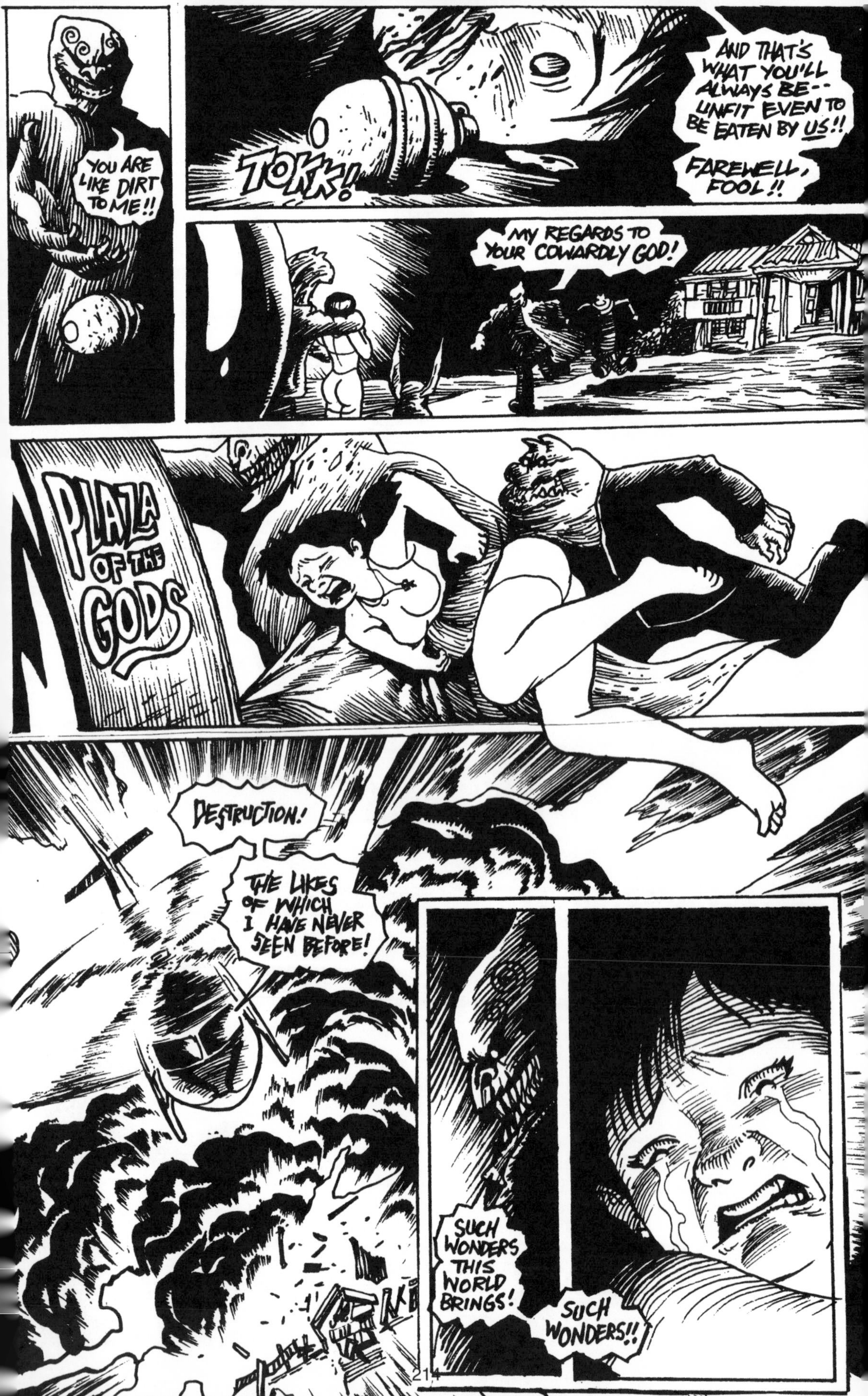
YOU ARE LIKE DIRT TO ME!!
TOKK!
AND THAT'S WHAT YOU'LL ALWAYS BE-- UNFIT EVEN TO BE EATEN BY US!!
FAREWELL, FOOL!!
MY REGARDS TO YOUR COWARDLY GOD!
PLAZA OF THE GODS
DESTRUCTION!
THE LIKES OF WHICH I HAVE NEVER SEEN BEFORE!
SUCH WONDERS THIS WORLD BRINGS!
SUCH WONDERS!!

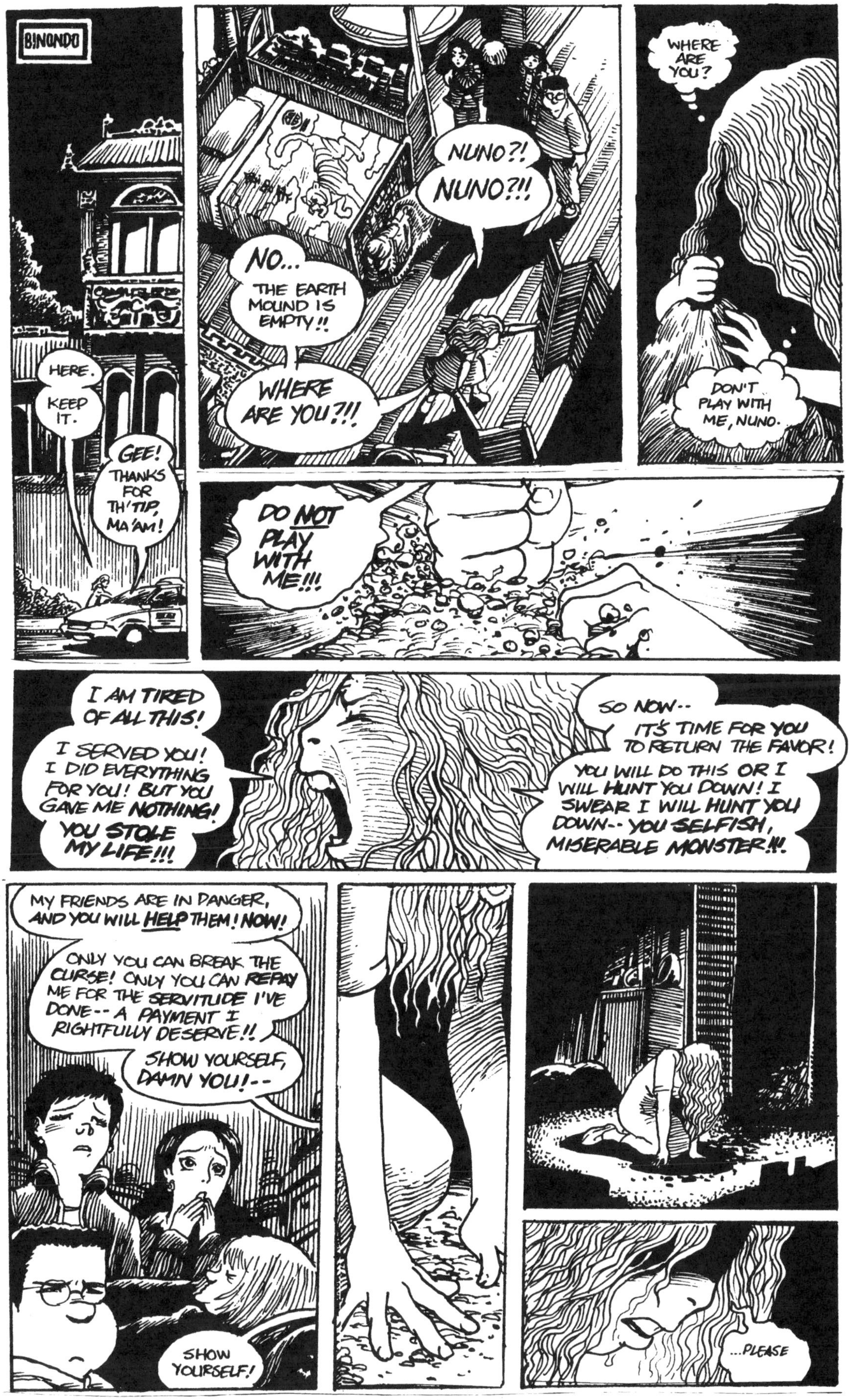
BINONDO
HERE. KEEP IT.
GEE! THANKS FOR TH'TIP, MA'AM!
NUNO?! NUNO?!!
NO... THE EARTH MOUND IS EMPTY!!
WHERE ARE YOU?!!
WHERE ARE YOU?
DON'T PLAY WITH ME, NUNO.
DO NOT PLAY WITH ME!!!
I AM TIRED OF ALL THIS!
I SERVED YOU! I DID EVERYTHING FOR YOU! BUT YOU GAVE ME NOTHING! YOU STOLE MY LIFE!!!
SO NOW-- IT'S TIME FOR YOU TO RETURN THE FAVOR!
YOU WILL DO THIS OR I WILL HUNT YOU DOWN! I SWEAR I WILL HUNT YOU DOWN-- YOU SELFISH, MISERABLE MONSTER!!!
MY FRIENDS ARE IN DANGER, AND YOU WILL HELP THEM! NOW!
ONLY YOU CAN BREAK THE CURSE! ONLY YOU CAN REPAY ME FOR THE SERVITUDE I'VE DONE-- A PAYMENT I RIGHTFULLY DESERVE!!
SHOW YOURSELF, DAMN YOU!--
SHOW YOURSELF!
...PLEASE

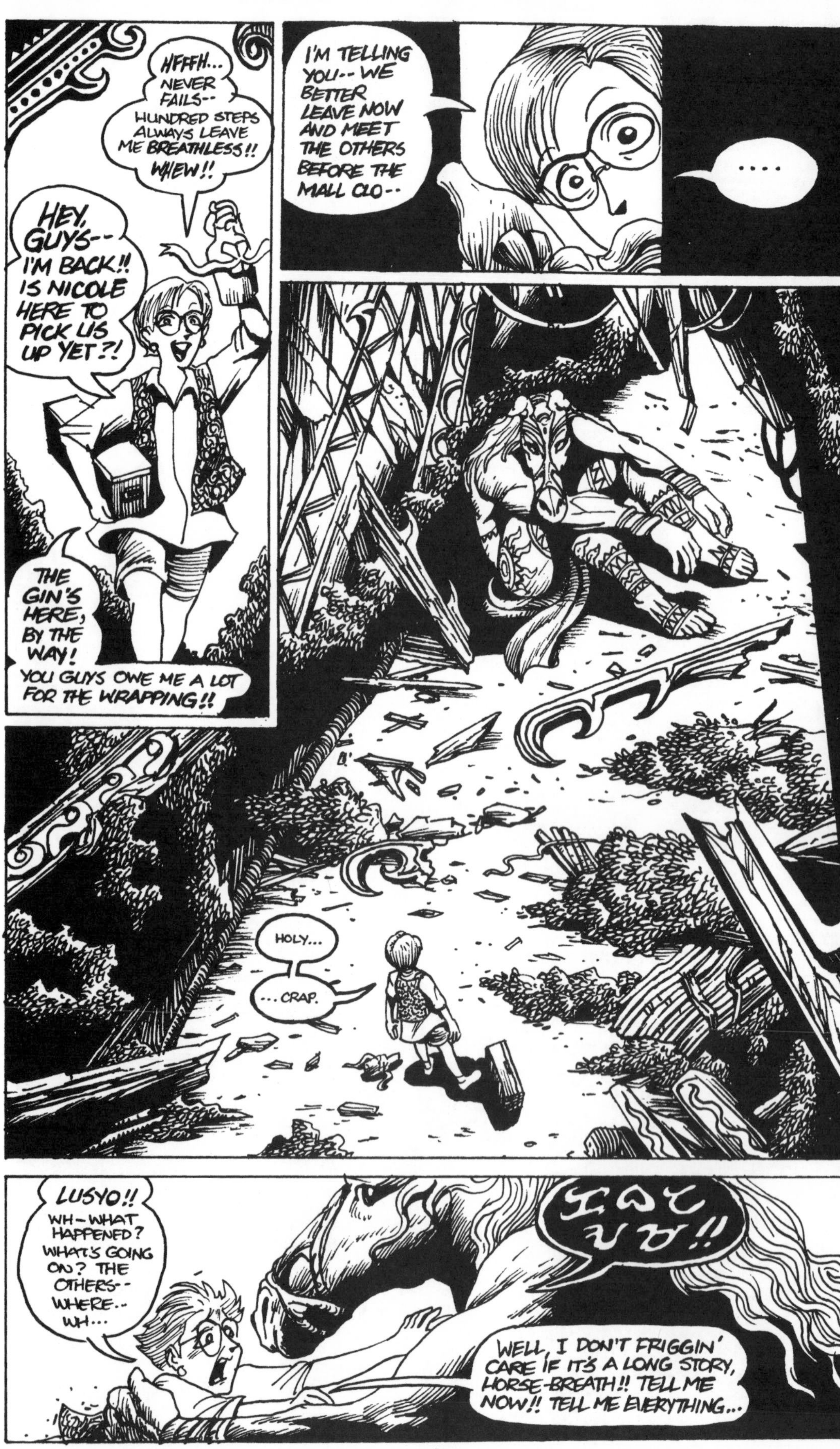
HFFFH... NEVER FAILS-- HUNDRED STEPS ALWAYS LEAVE ME BREATHLESS!! WHEW!!
HEY, GUYS-- I'M BACK!! IS NICOLE HERE TO PICK US UP YET?!
THE GIN'S HERE, BY THE WAY! YOU GUYS OWE ME A LOT FOR THE WRAPPING!!
I'M TELLING YOU-- WE BETTER LEAVE NOW AND MEET THE OTHERS BEFORE THE MALL CLO--
....
HOLY...
...CRAP.
LUSYO!! WH-WHAT HAPPENED? WHAT'S GOING ON? THE OTHERS-- WHERE.. WH...
WELL, I DON'T FRIGGIN' CARE IF IT'S A LONG STORY, HORSE-BREATH!! TELL ME NOW!! TELL ME EVERYTHING...

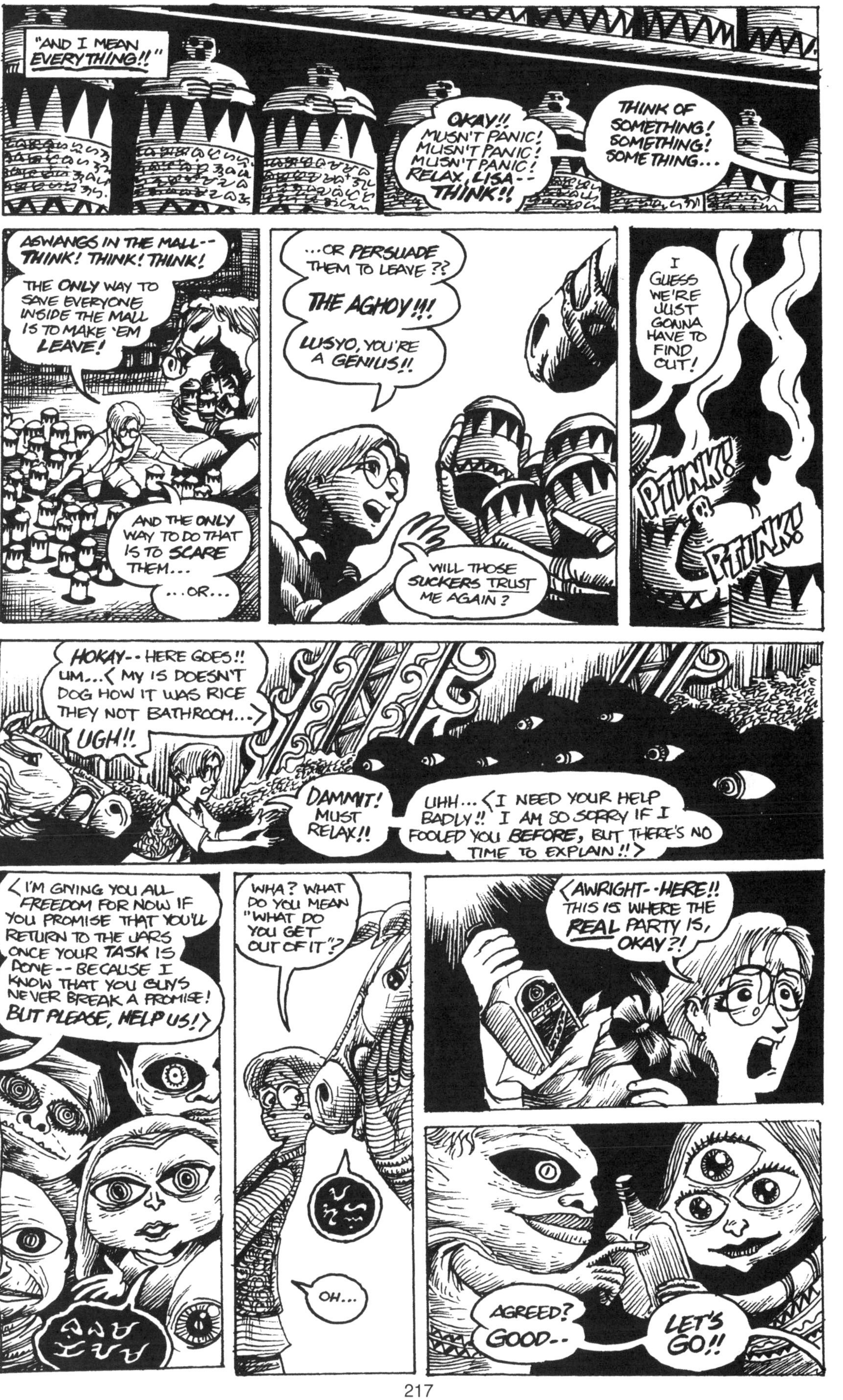
"AND I MEAN EVERYTHING!!"
OKAY!! MUSN'T PANIC! MUSN'T PANIC! MUSN'T PANIC! RELAX, LISA-- THINK!!
THINK OF SOMETHING! SOMETHING! SOMETHING...
ASWANGS IN THE MALL-- THINK! THINK! THINK!
THE ONLY WAY TO SAVE EVERYONE INSIDE THE MALL IS TO MAKE 'EM LEAVE!
AND THE ONLY WAY TO DO THAT IS TO SCARE THEM...
...OR...
...OR PERSUADE THEM TO LEAVE??
THE AGHOY!!!
LUSYO, YOU'RE A GENIUS!!
WILL THOSE SUCKERS TRUST ME AGAIN?
I GUESS WE'RE JUST GONNA HAVE TO FIND OUT!
PTINK!
PTINK!
HOKAY-- HERE GOES!! UM...< MY IS DOESN'T DOG HOW IT WAS RICE THEY NOT BATHROOM...>
UGH!!
DAMMIT! MUST RELAX!!
UHH...< I NEED YOUR HELP BADLY!! I AM SO SORRY IF I FOOLED YOU BEFORE, BUT THERE'S NO TIME TO EXPLAIN!!>
< I'M GIVING YOU ALL FREEDOM FOR NOW IF YOU PROMISE THAT YOU'LL RETURN TO THE JARS ONCE YOUR TASK IS DONE-- BECAUSE I KNOW THAT YOU GUYS NEVER BREAK A PROMISE! BUT PLEASE, HELP US!>
WHA? WHAT DO YOU MEAN "WHAT DO YOU GET OUT OF IT"?
OH...
< AWRIGHT--HERE!! THIS IS WHERE THE REAL PARTY IS, OKAY?!
AGREED? GOOD--
LET'S GO!!

"AND LUSYO, BE A NICE HORSE AND GUARD THE HOUSE!"

JUST A FEW MORE MINUTES, MASTER!!

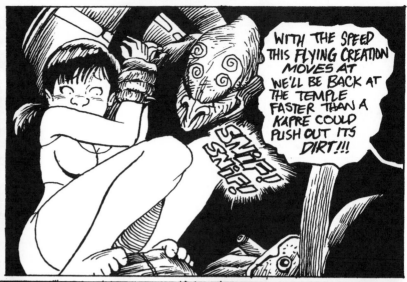

WITH THE SPEED THIS FLYING CREATION MOVES AT WE'LL BE BACK AT THE TEMPLE FASTER THAN A KAPRE COULD PUSH OUT ITS DIRT!!!

SNIF! SNIF! SNIF!

GOOD!! THAT MEANS ENOUGH TIME FOR A LITTLE.... FUN!

THOUGH WE CURSE BATHALA IN HIS NAME, I HAVE TO ADMIT HE DOES CREATE HIS BEINGS WELL!.. he he he

I CAN BE A REAL HOUND, MY PRETTY!! HE! HE! HE!

I SAW HER FIRST!! I WANNA HAVE FUN, TOO!!

YOU TAMARAW DUNG --- THE CONTROLS!!

THE CONTROLS!!

NWBRRRRR

STUPID DOG!! YOU'RE GOING TO GET US KILLED FOR THINKING WITH YOUR GROIN RATHER THAN YOUR BRAIN!!

KRIKK!!

AARRGH!!

218

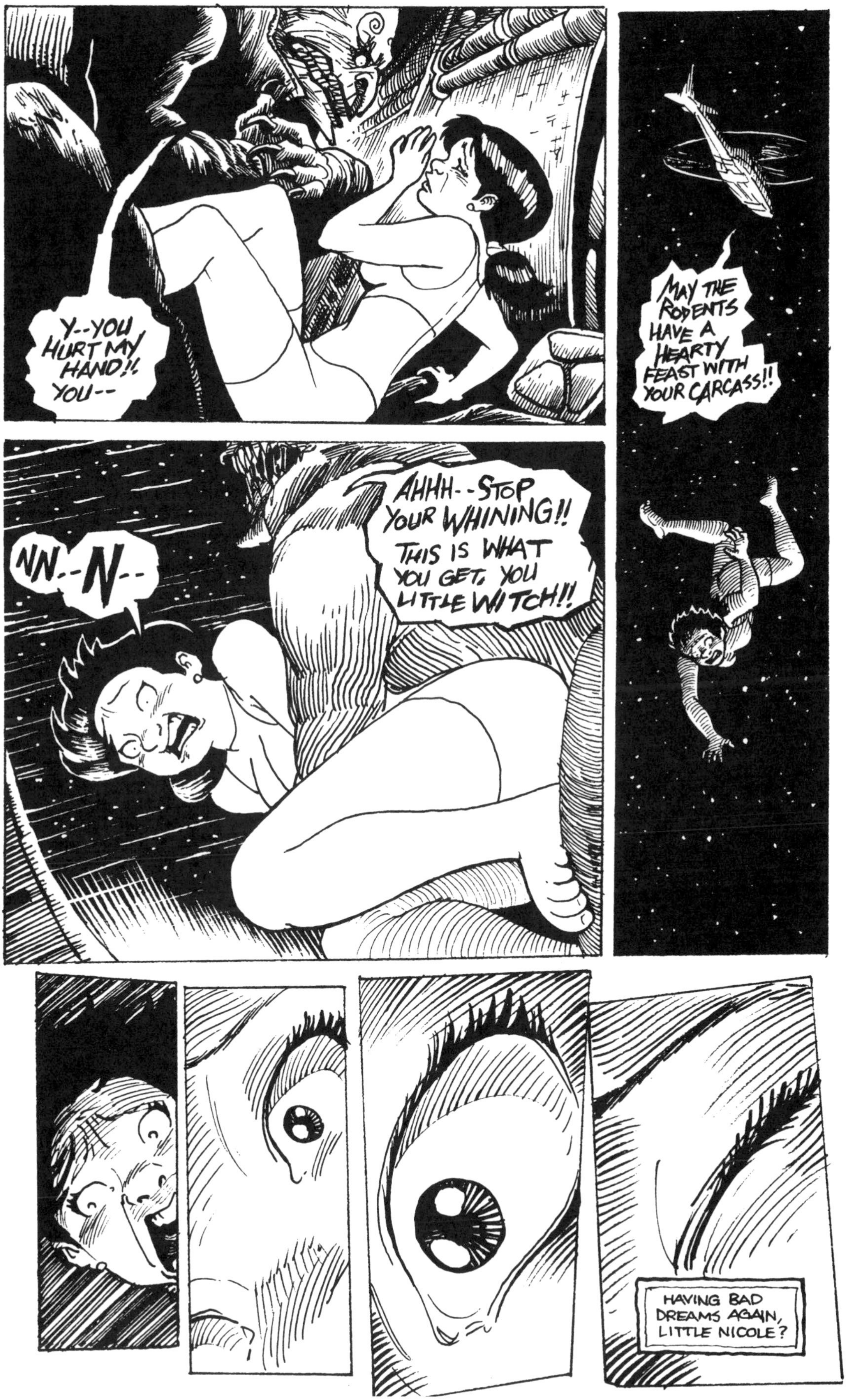
Y--YOU HURT MY HAND!! YOU--
MAY THE RODENTS HAVE A HEARTY FEAST WITH YOUR CARCASS!!
AHHH--STOP YOUR WHINING!! THIS IS WHAT YOU GET, YOU LITTLE WITCH!!
NN--N--
HAVING BAD DREAMS AGAIN, LITTLE NICOLE?

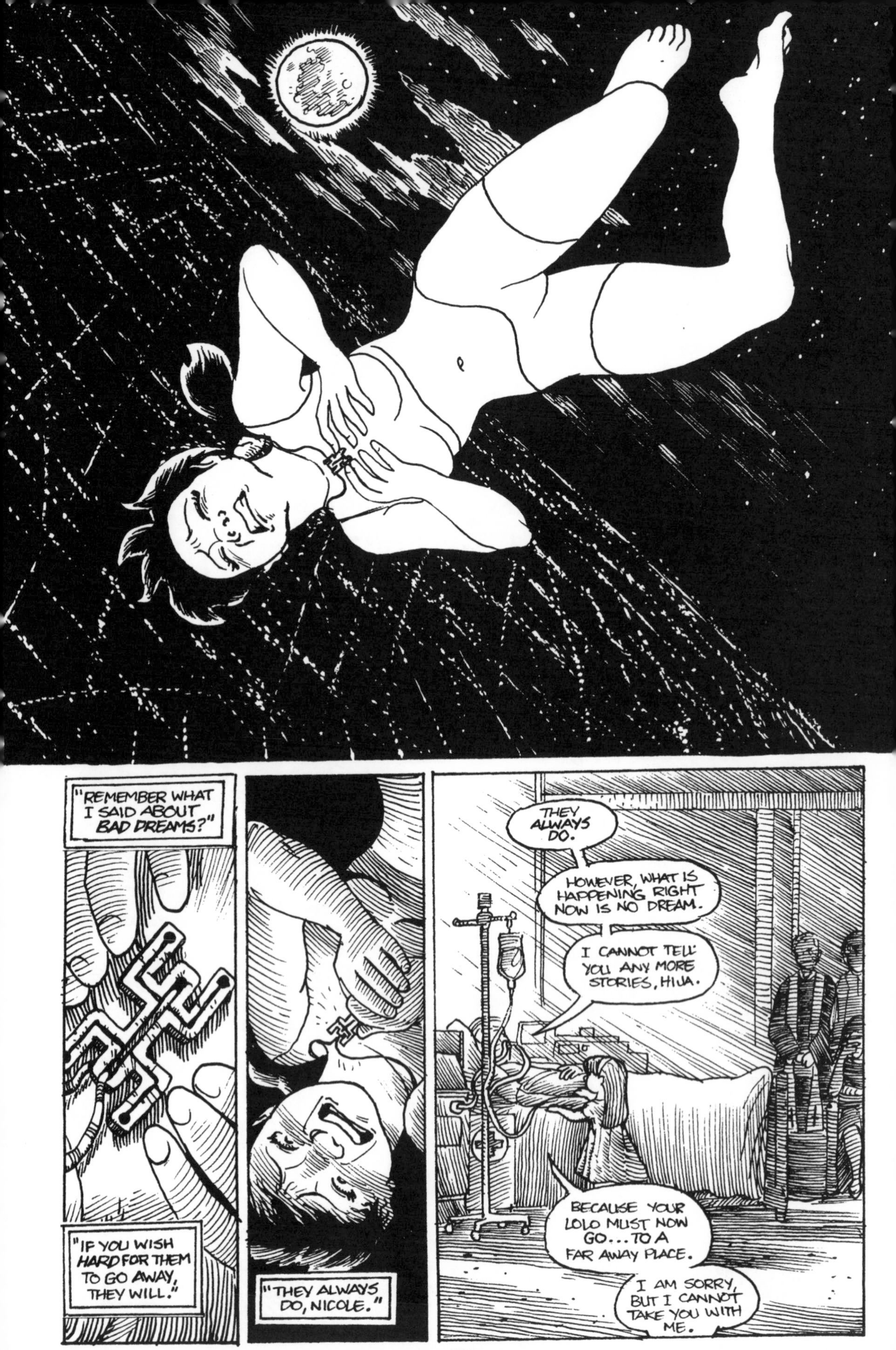

"REMEMBER WHAT I SAID ABOUT BAD DREAMS?"
"IF YOU WISH HARD FOR THEM TO GO AWAY, THEY WILL."
"THEY ALWAYS DO, NICOLE."
THEY ALWAYS DO.
HOWEVER, WHAT IS HAPPENING RIGHT NOW IS NO DREAM.
I CANNOT TELL YOU ANY MORE STORIES, HIJA.
BECAUSE YOUR LOLO MUST NOW GO... TO A FAR AWAY PLACE.
I AM SORRY, BUT I CANNOT TAKE YOU WITH ME.

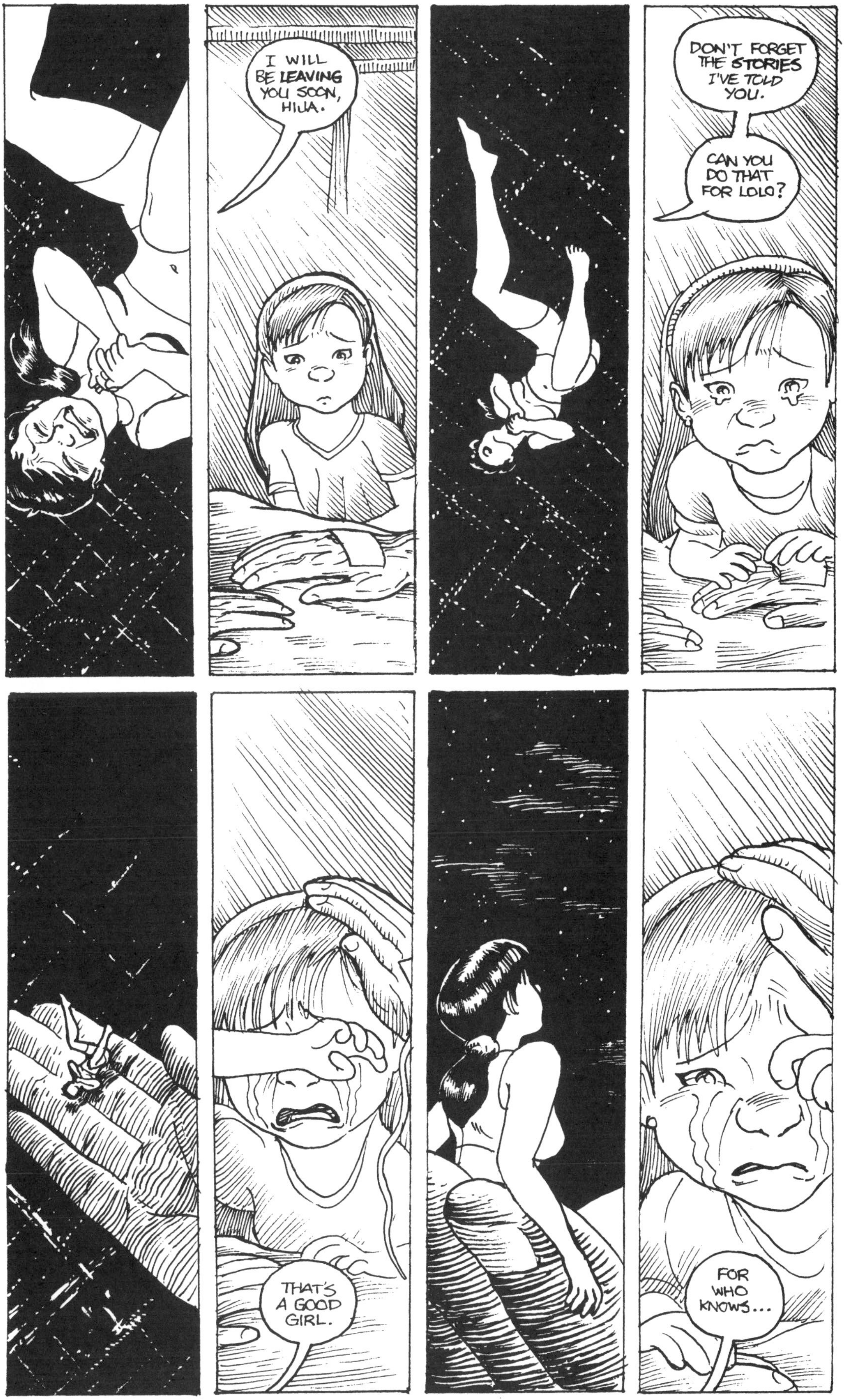
I WILL BE LEAVING YOU SOON, HIJA.
DON'T FORGET THE STORIES I'VE TOLD YOU.
CAN YOU DO THAT FOR LOLO?
THAT'S A GOOD GIRL.
FOR WHO KNOWS...

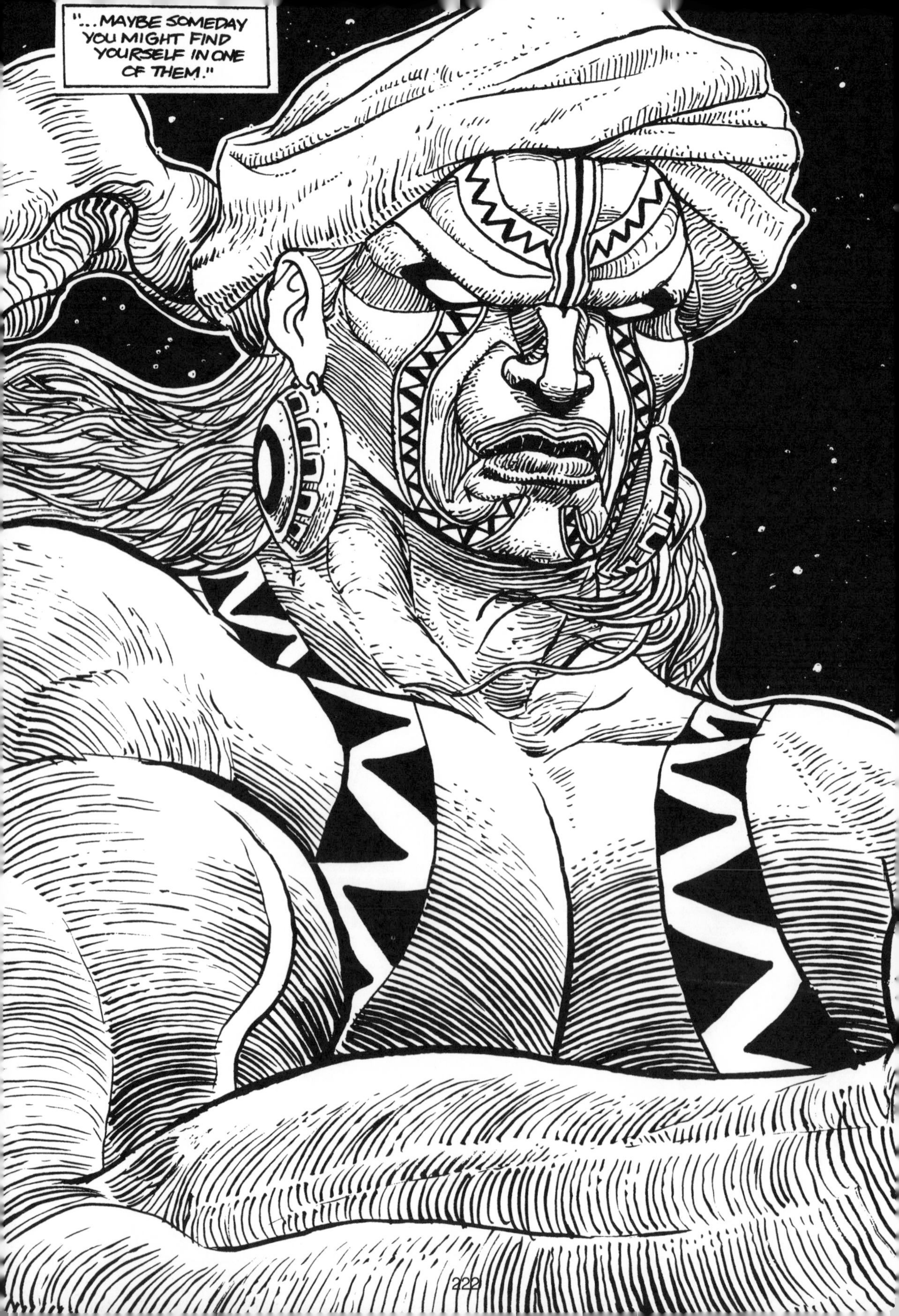
"...MAYBE SOMEDAY YOU MIGHT FIND YOURSELF IN ONE OF THEM."

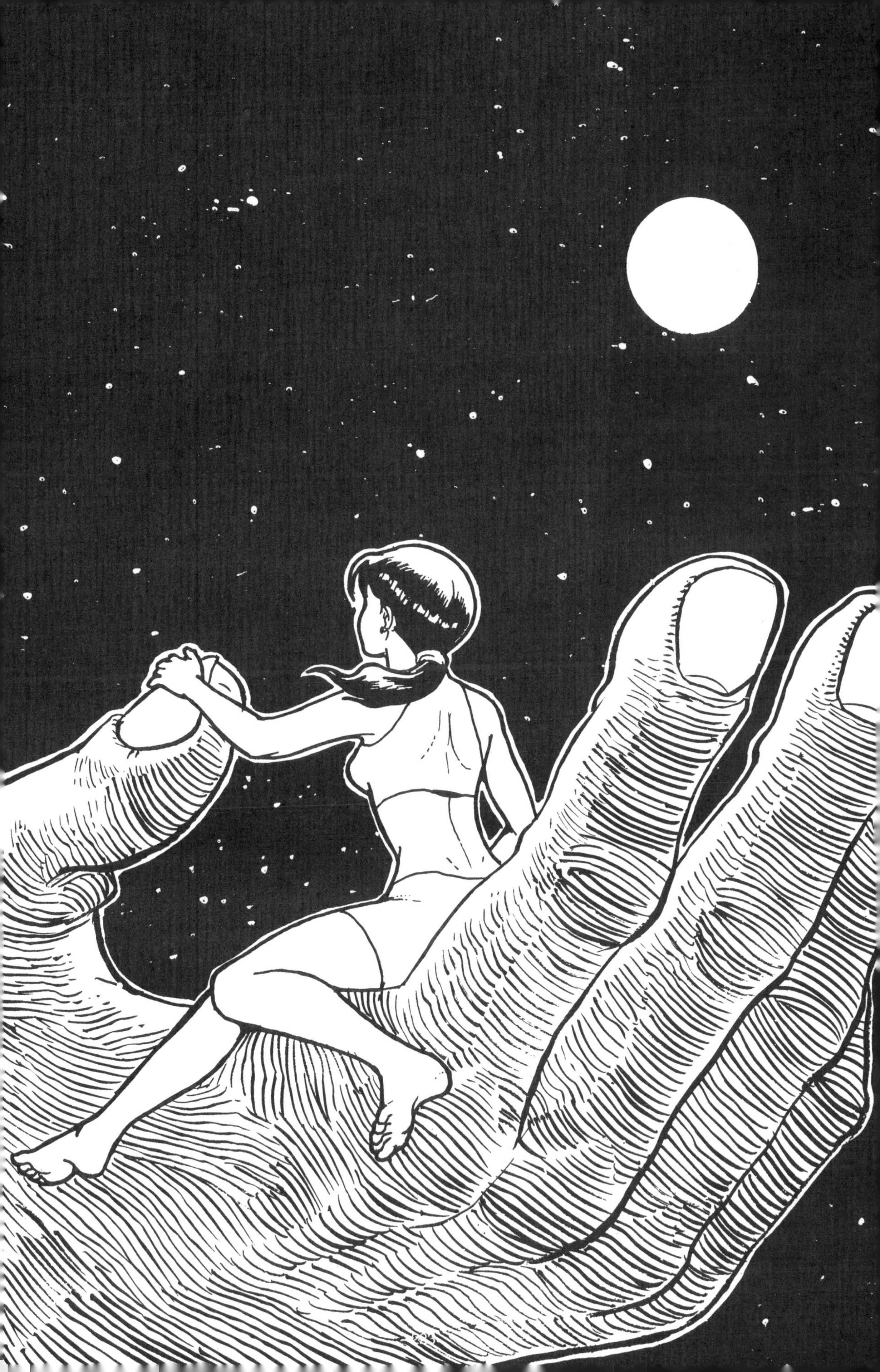

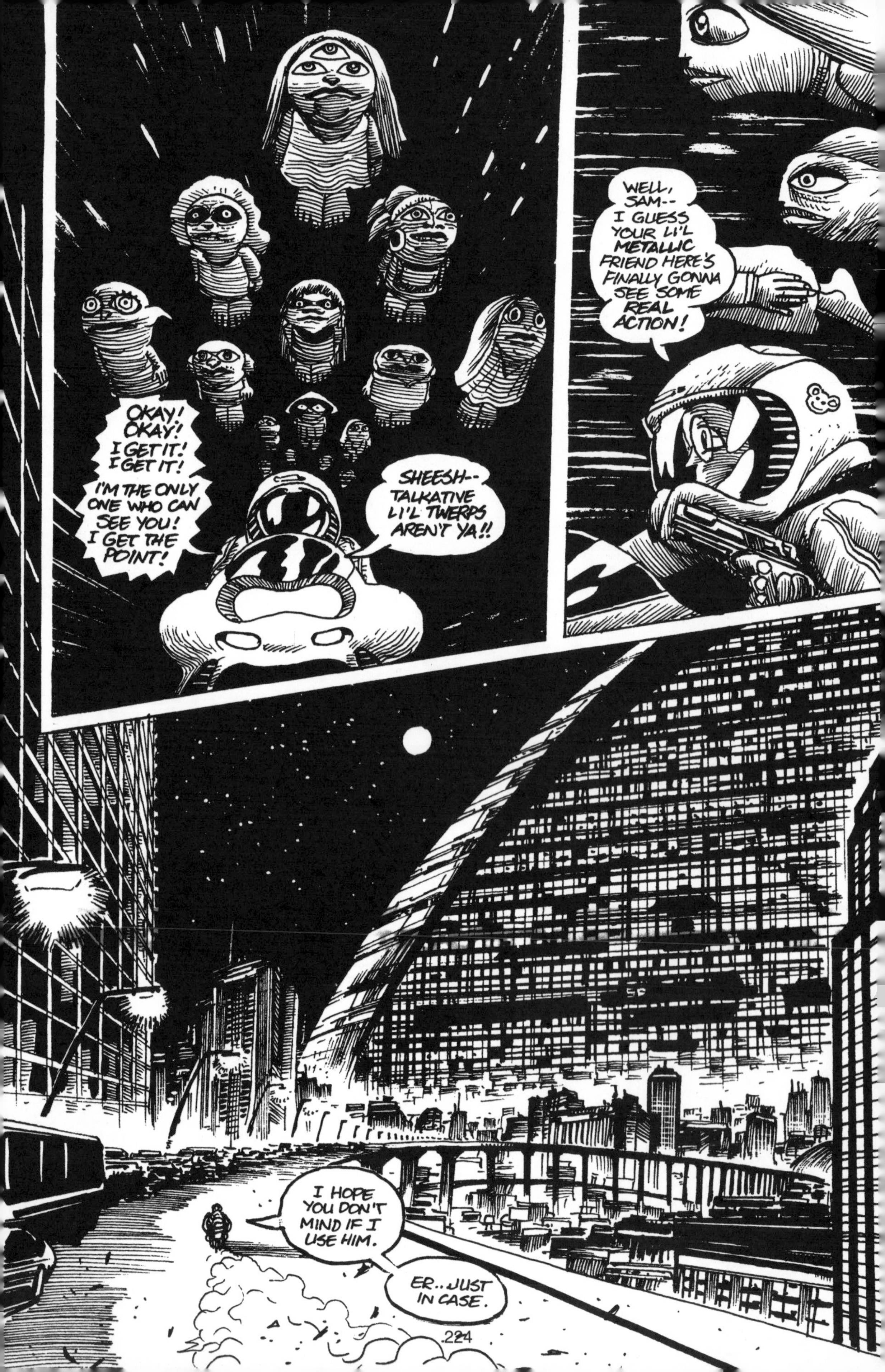
OKAY! OKAY! I GET IT! I GET IT! I'M THE ONLY ONE WHO CAN SEE YOU! I GET THE POINT!
SHEESH-- TALKATIVE LI'L TWERPS AREN'T YA!!
WELL, SAM-- I GUESS YOUR LI'L METALLIC FRIEND HERE'S FINALLY GONNA SEE SOME REAL ACTION!
I HOPE YOU DON'T MIND IF I USE HIM.
ER.. JUST IN CASE.

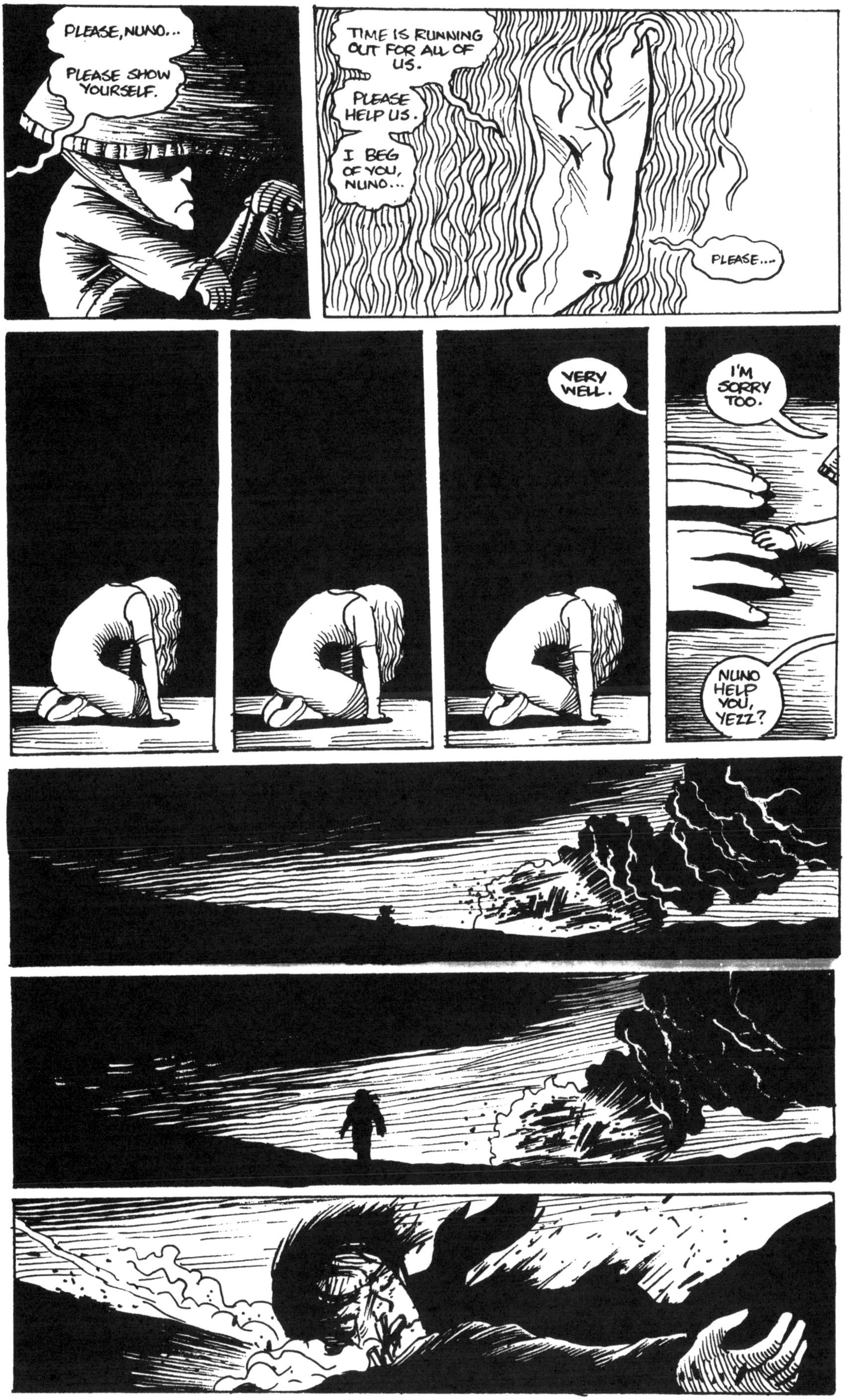
PLEASE, NUNO...
PLEASE SHOW YOURSELF.
TIME IS RUNNING OUT FOR ALL OF US.
PLEASE HELP US.
I BEG OF YOU, NUNO...
PLEASE...
VERY WELL.
I'M SORRY TOO.
NUNO HELP YOU, YEZZ?

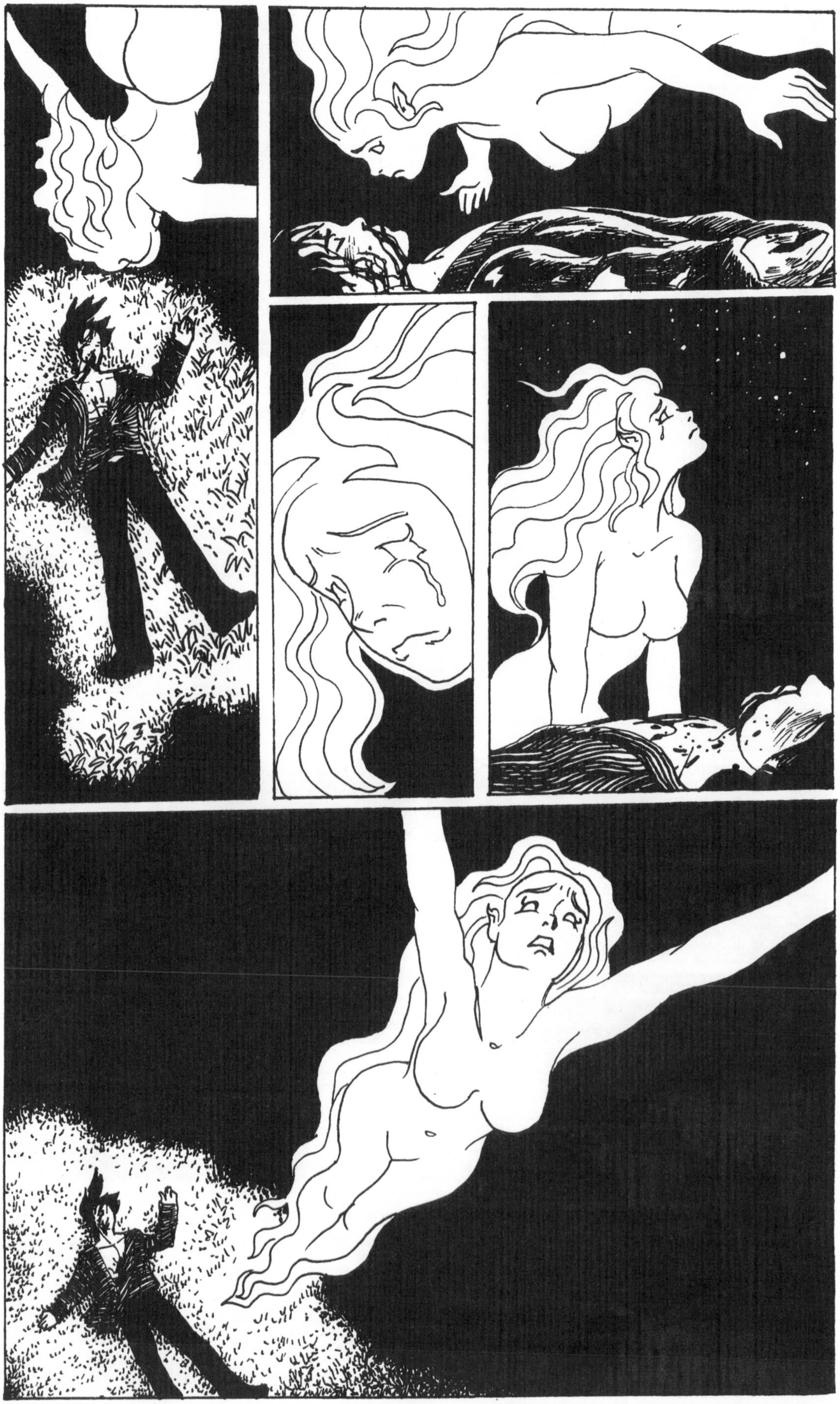

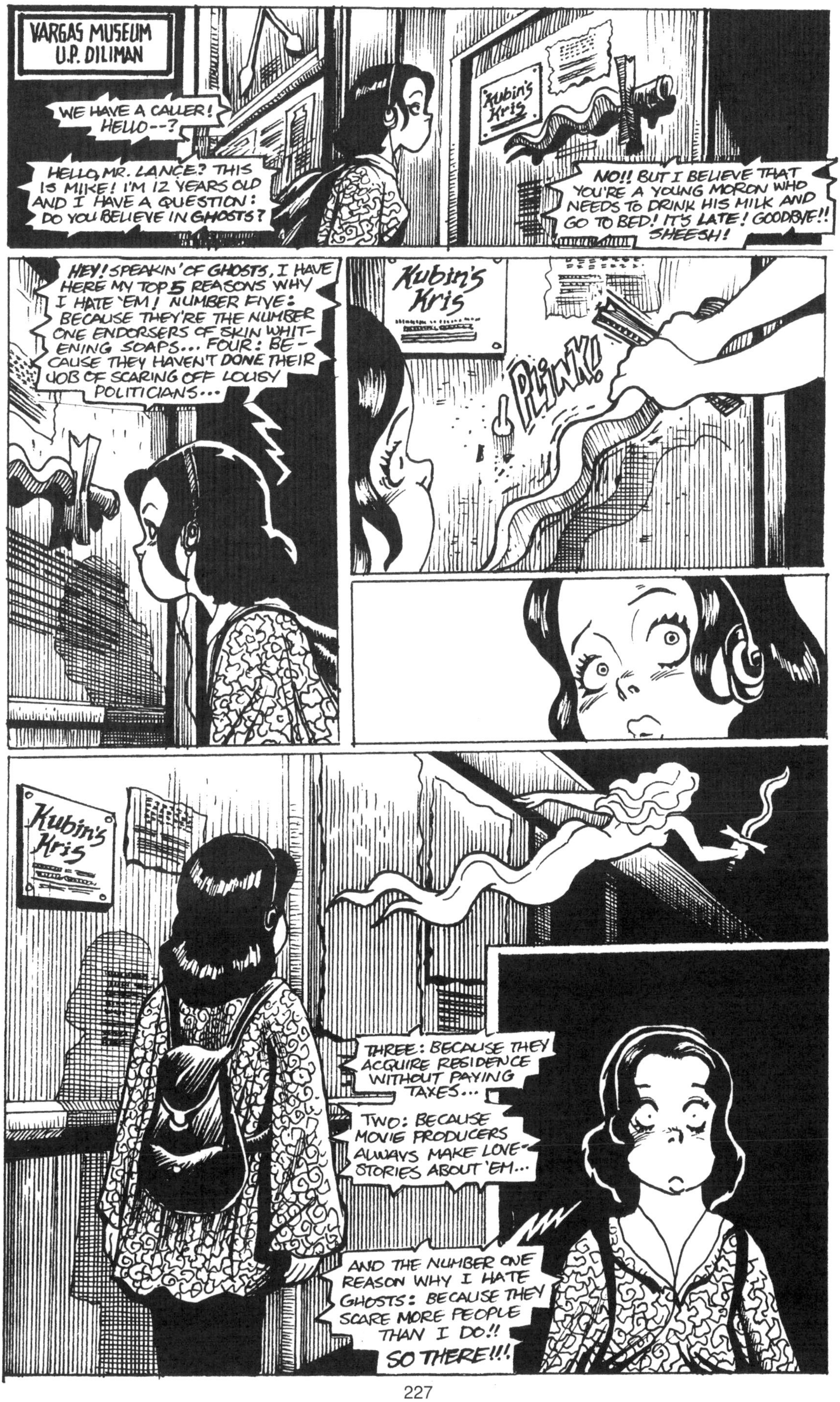
VARGAS MUSEUM
U.P. DILIMAN
WE HAVE A CALLER! HELLO--?
HELLO, MR. LANCE? THIS IS MIKE! I'M 12 YEARS OLD AND I HAVE A QUESTION: DO YOU BELIEVE IN GHOSTS?
Kubin's Kris
NO!! BUT I BELIEVE THAT YOU'RE A YOUNG MORON WHO NEEDS TO DRINK HIS MILK AND GO TO BED! IT'S LATE! GOODBYE!! SHEESH!
HEY! SPEAKIN' OF GHOSTS, I HAVE HERE MY TOP 5 REASONS WHY I HATE 'EM! NUMBER FIVE: BECAUSE THEY'RE THE NUMBER ONE ENDORSERS OF SKIN WHITENING SOAPS... FOUR: BECAUSE THEY HAVEN'T DONE THEIR JOB OF SCARING OFF LOUSY POLITICIANS...
Kubin's Kris
PLINK!
Kubin's Kris
THREE: BECAUSE THEY ACQUIRE RESIDENCE WITHOUT PAYING TAXES...
TWO: BECAUSE MOVIE PRODUCERS ALWAYS MAKE LOVE-STORIES ABOUT 'EM...
AND THE NUMBER ONE REASON WHY I HATE GHOSTS: BECAUSE THEY SCARE MORE PEOPLE THAN I DO!! SO THERE!!!

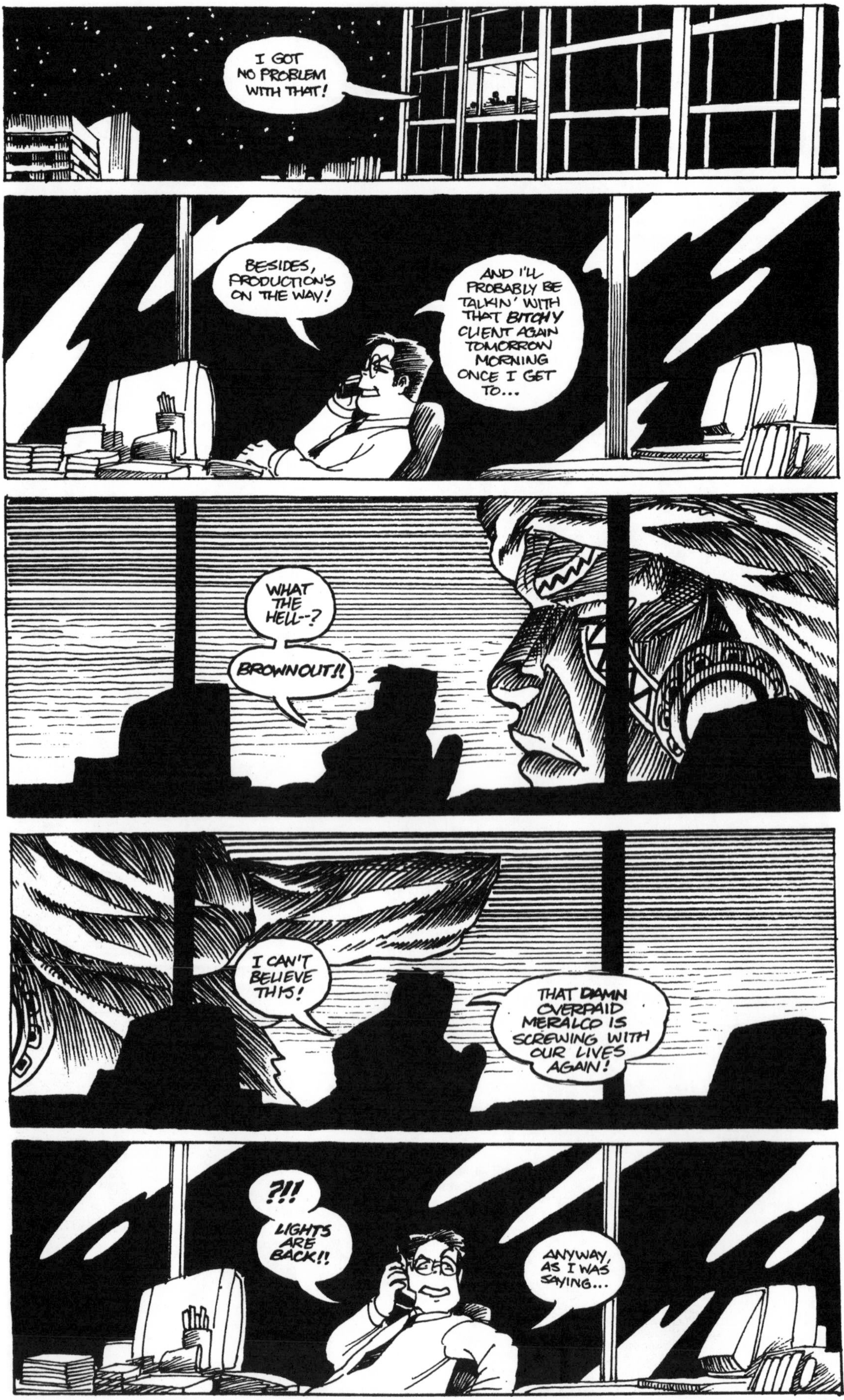
I GOT NO PROBLEM WITH THAT!
BESIDES, PRODUCTION'S ON THE WAY!
AND I'LL PROBABLY BE TALKIN' WITH THAT BITCHY CLIENT AGAIN TOMORROW MORNING ONCE I GET TO...
WHAT THE HELL--?
BROWNOUT!!
I CAN'T BELIEVE THIS!
THAT DAMN OVERPAID MERALCO IS SCREWING WITH OUR LIVES AGAIN!
?!!
LIGHTS ARE BACK!!
ANYWAY, AS I WAS SAYING...

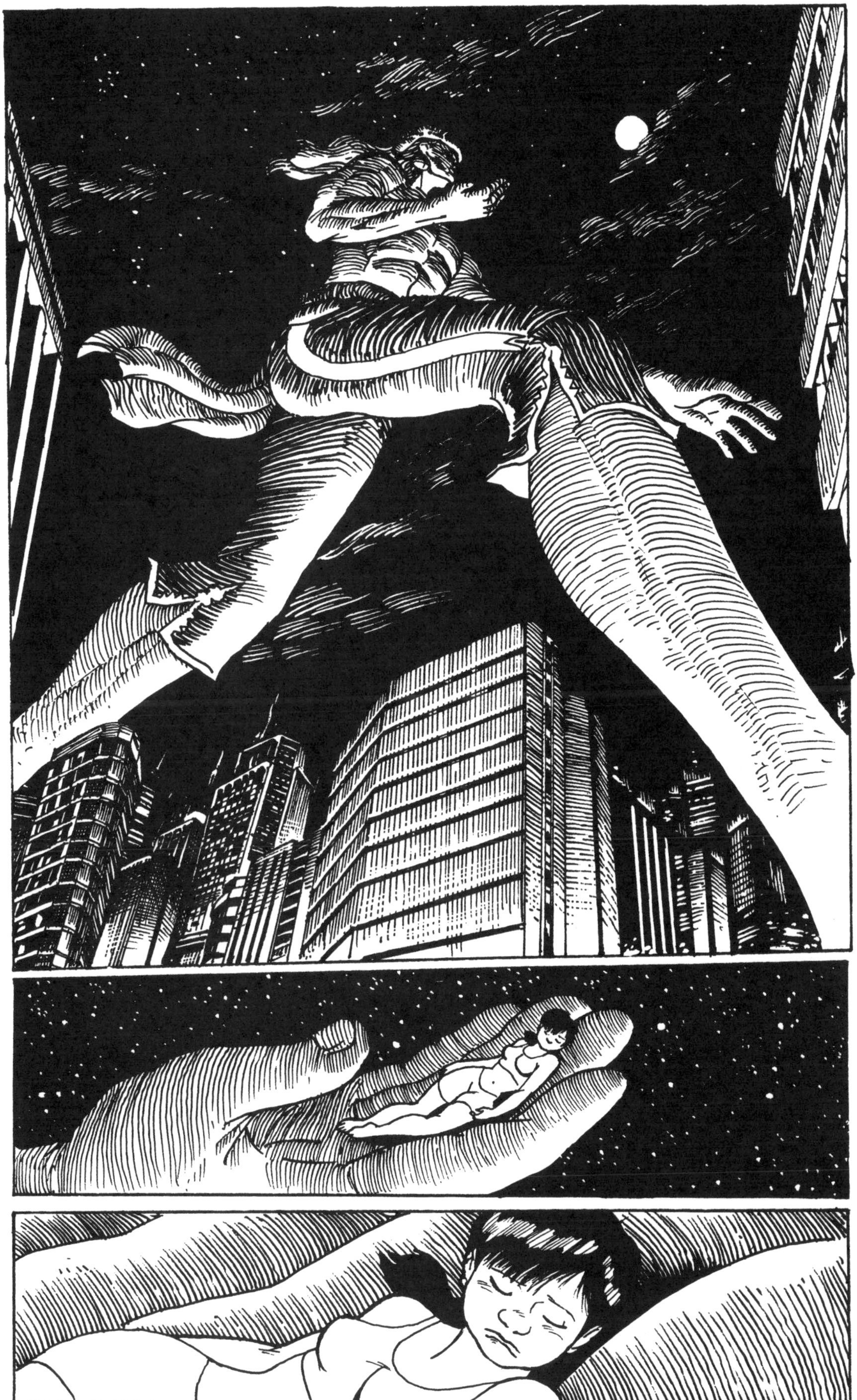

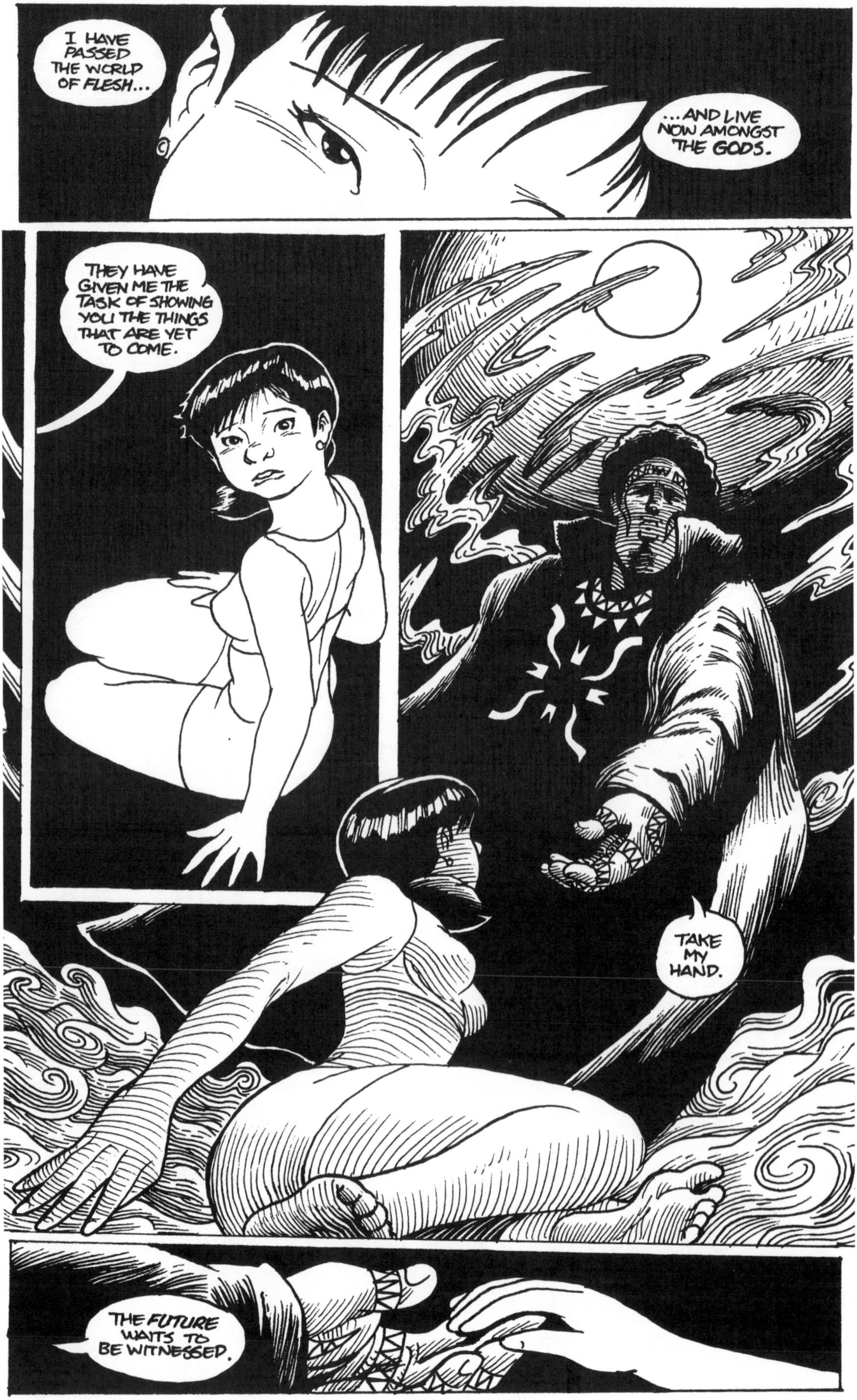
I HAVE PASSED THE WORLD OF FLESH...
...AND LIVE NOW AMONGST THE GODS.
THEY HAVE GIVEN ME THE TASK OF SHOWING YOU THE THINGS THAT ARE YET TO COME.
TAKE MY HAND.
THE FUTURE WAITS TO BE WITNESSED.

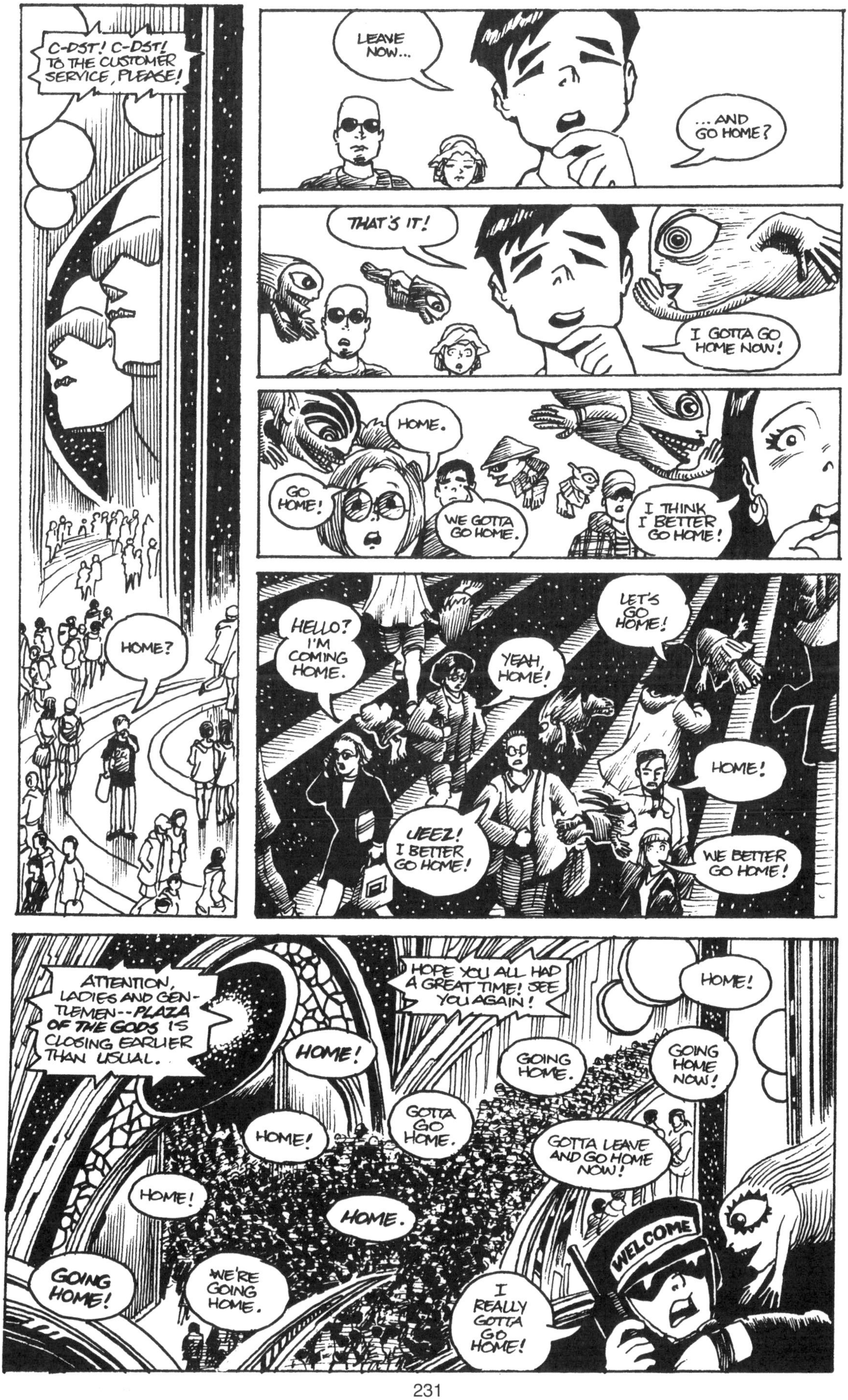

C-DST! C-DST! TO THE CUSTOMER SERVICE, PLEASE!
HOME?
LEAVE NOW...
...AND GO HOME?
THAT'S IT!
I GOTTA GO HOME NOW!
HOME.
GO HOME!
WE GOTTA GO HOME.
I THINK I BETTER GO HOME!
HELLO? I'M COMING HOME.
YEAH, HOME!
LET'S GO HOME!
HOME!
JEEZ! I BETTER GO HOME!
WE BETTER GO HOME!
ATTENTION, LADIES AND GENTLEMEN--PLAZA OF THE GODS IS CLOSING EARLIER THAN USUAL.
HOPE YOU ALL HAD A GREAT TIME! SEE YOU AGAIN!
HOME!
HOME!
GOING HOME.
GOING HOME NOW!
GOTTA GO HOME.
HOME!
GOTTA LEAVE AND GO HOME NOW!
HOME!
HOME.
GOING HOME!
WE'RE GOING HOME.
I REALLY GOTTA GO HOME!
WELCOME

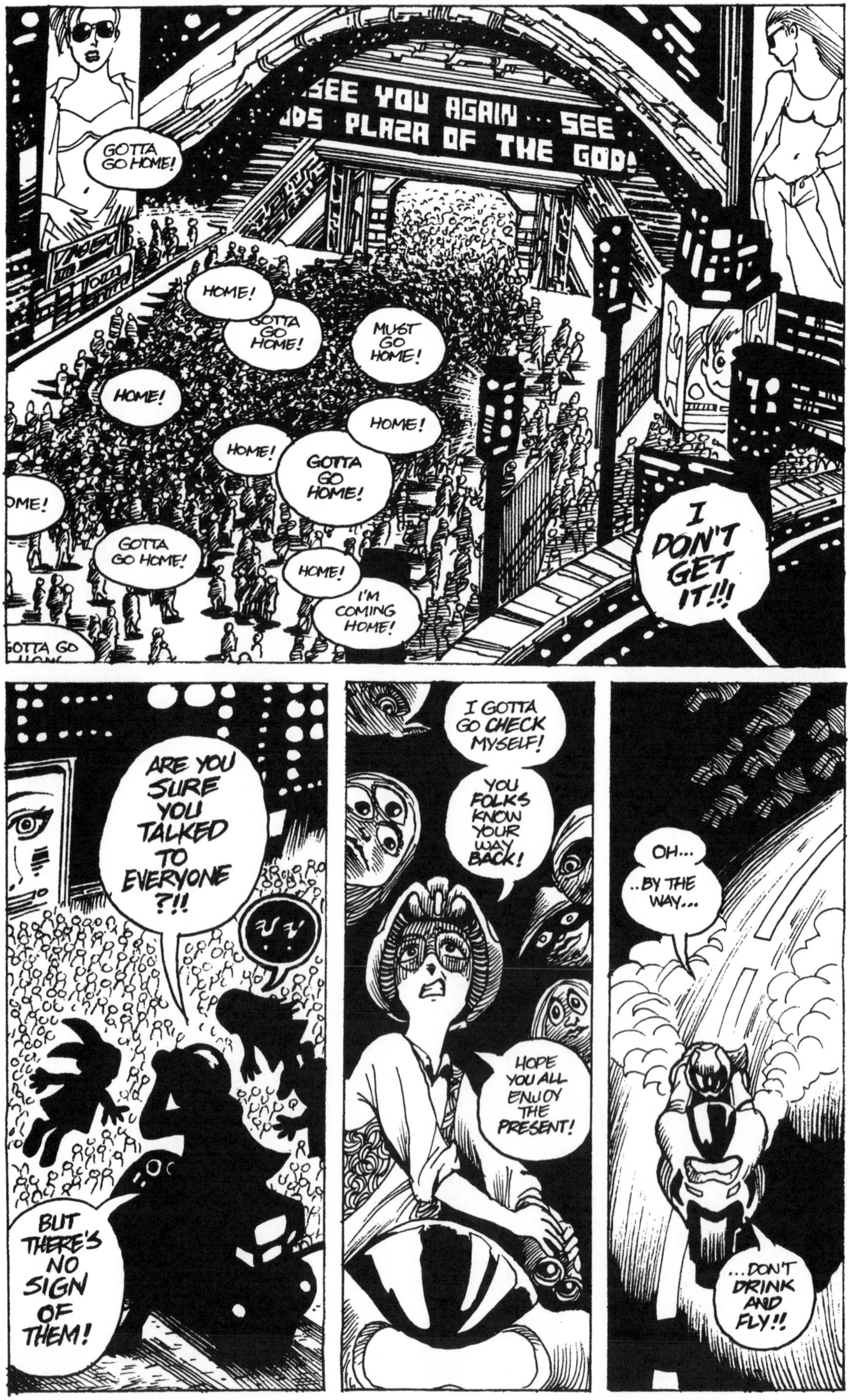
SEE YOU AGAIN ... SEE
PLAZA OF THE GOD
GOTTA GO HOME!
HOME!
GOTTA GO HOME!
MUST GO HOME!
HOME!
HOME!
HOME!
GOTTA GO HOME!
GOTTA GO HOME!
HOME!
I'M COMING HOME!
GOTTA GO
I DON'T GET IT!!!
ARE YOU SURE YOU TALKED TO EVERYONE ?!!
BUT THERE'S NO SIGN OF THEM!
I GOTTA GO CHECK MYSELF!
YOU FOLKS KNOW YOUR WAY BACK!
HOPE YOU ALL ENJOY THE PRESENT!
OH...
..BY THE WAY...
...DON'T DRINK AND FLY!!

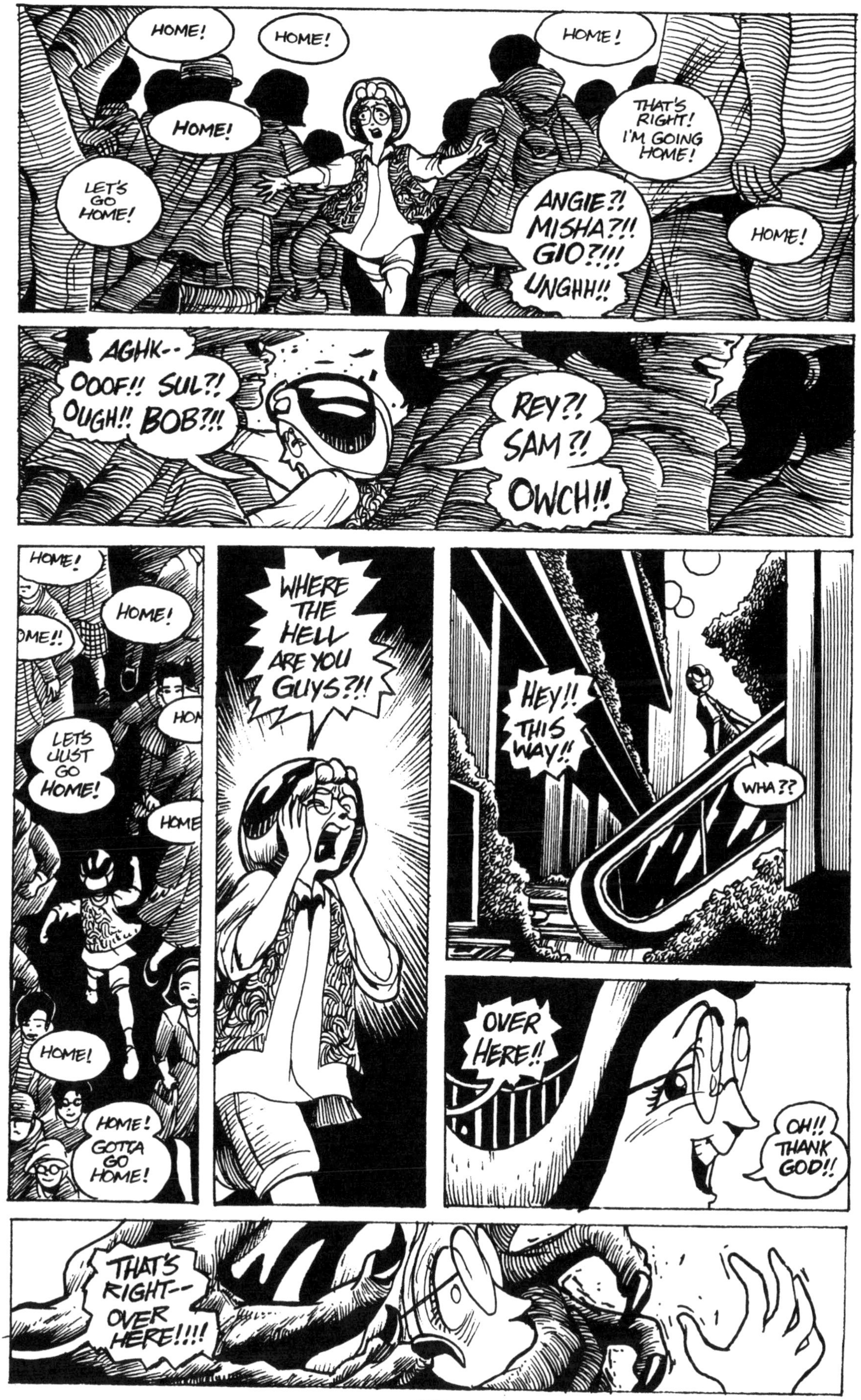
HOME!
HOME!
HOME!
HOME!
THAT'S RIGHT! I'M GOING HOME!
LET'S GO HOME!
ANGIE?! MISHA?!! GIO?!!! UNGHH!!
HOME!
AGHK--
OOOF!! SUL?!
OUGH!! BOB?!!
REY?! SAM?! OWCH!!
HOME!
HOME!
LET'S JUST GO HOME!
HOME!
HOME! GOTTA GO HOME!
WHERE THE HELL ARE YOU GUYS?!!
HEY!! THIS WAY!!
WHA??
OVER HERE!!
OH!! THANK GOD!!
THAT'S RIGHT-- OVER HERE!!!!

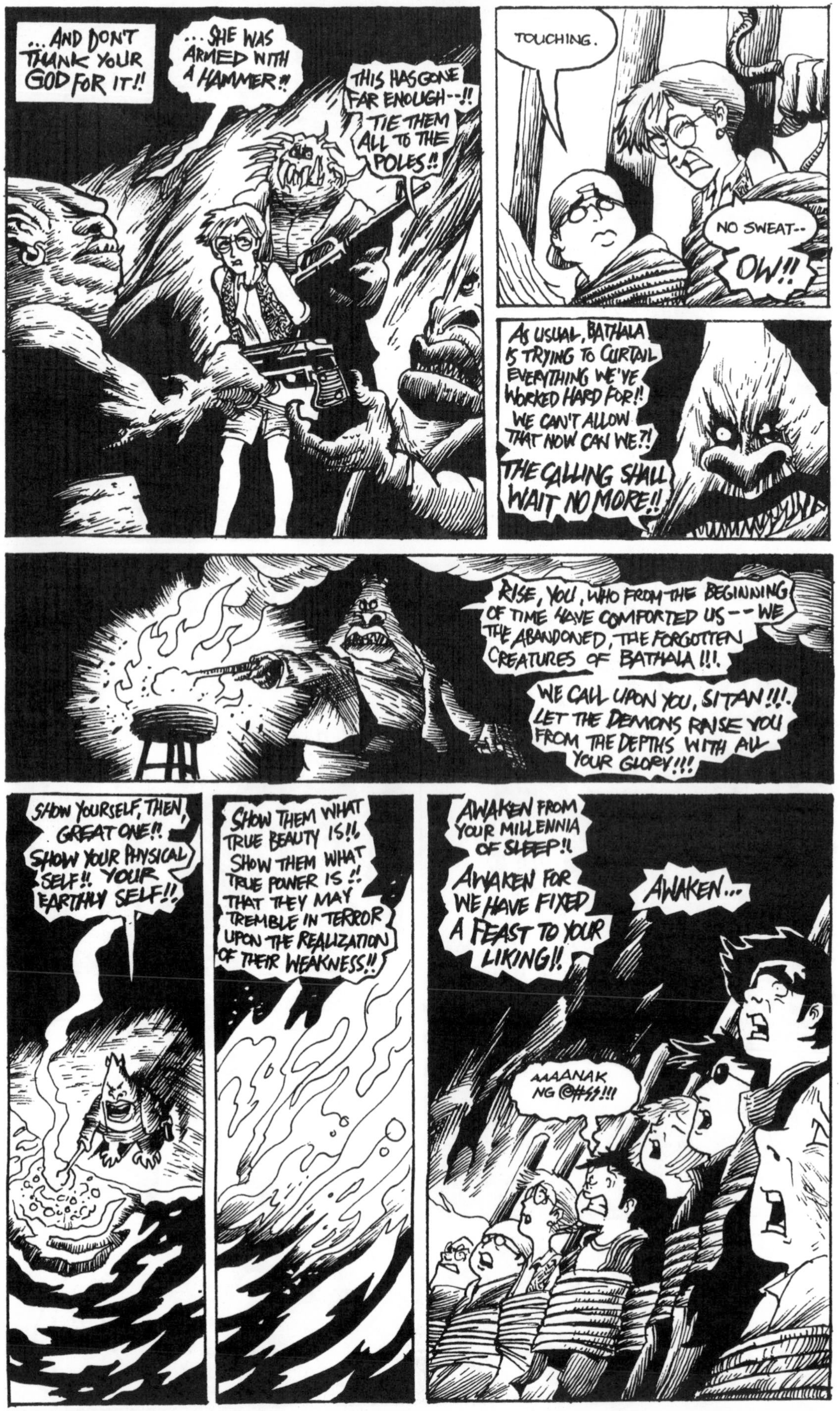
...AND DON'T THANK YOUR GOD FOR IT!!
...SHE WAS ARMED WITH A HAMMER!!
THIS HAS GONE FAR ENOUGH--!! TIE THEM ALL TO THE POLES!!
TOUCHING.
NO SWEAT--
OW!!
AS USUAL, BATHALA IS TRYING TO CURTAIL EVERYTHING WE'VE WORKED HARD FOR!! WE CAN'T ALLOW THAT NOW CAN WE?!
THE CALLING SHALL WAIT NO MORE!!
RISE, YOU, WHO FROM THE BEGINNING OF TIME HAVE COMFORTED US -- WE THE ABANDONED, THE FORGOTTEN CREATURES OF BATHALA!!!
WE CALL UPON YOU, SITAN!!! LET THE DEMONS RAISE YOU FROM THE DEPTHS WITH ALL YOUR GLORY!!!
SHOW YOURSELF, THEN, GREAT ONE!! SHOW YOUR PHYSICAL SELF!! YOUR EARTHLY SELF!!
SHOW THEM WHAT TRUE BEAUTY IS!! SHOW THEM WHAT TRUE POWER IS!! THAT THEY MAY TREMBLE IN TERROR UPON THE REALIZATION OF THEIR WEAKNESS!!
AWAKEN FROM YOUR MILLENNIA OF SLEEP!!
AWAKEN FOR WE HAVE FIXED A FEAST TO YOUR LIKING!!
AWAKEN...
AAAANAK NG @#$$!!!

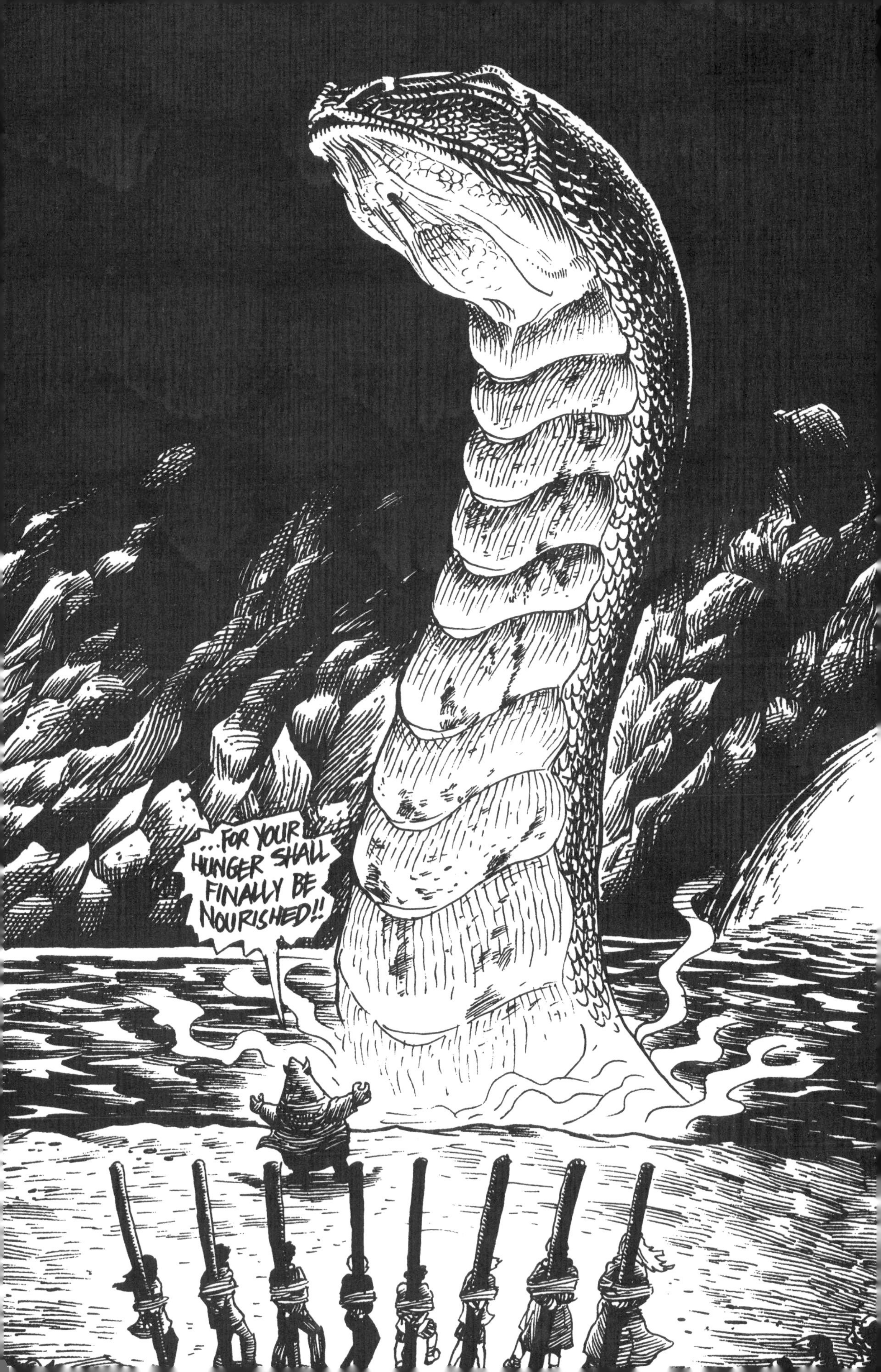
...FOR YOUR HUNGER SHALL FINALLY BE NOURISHED!!

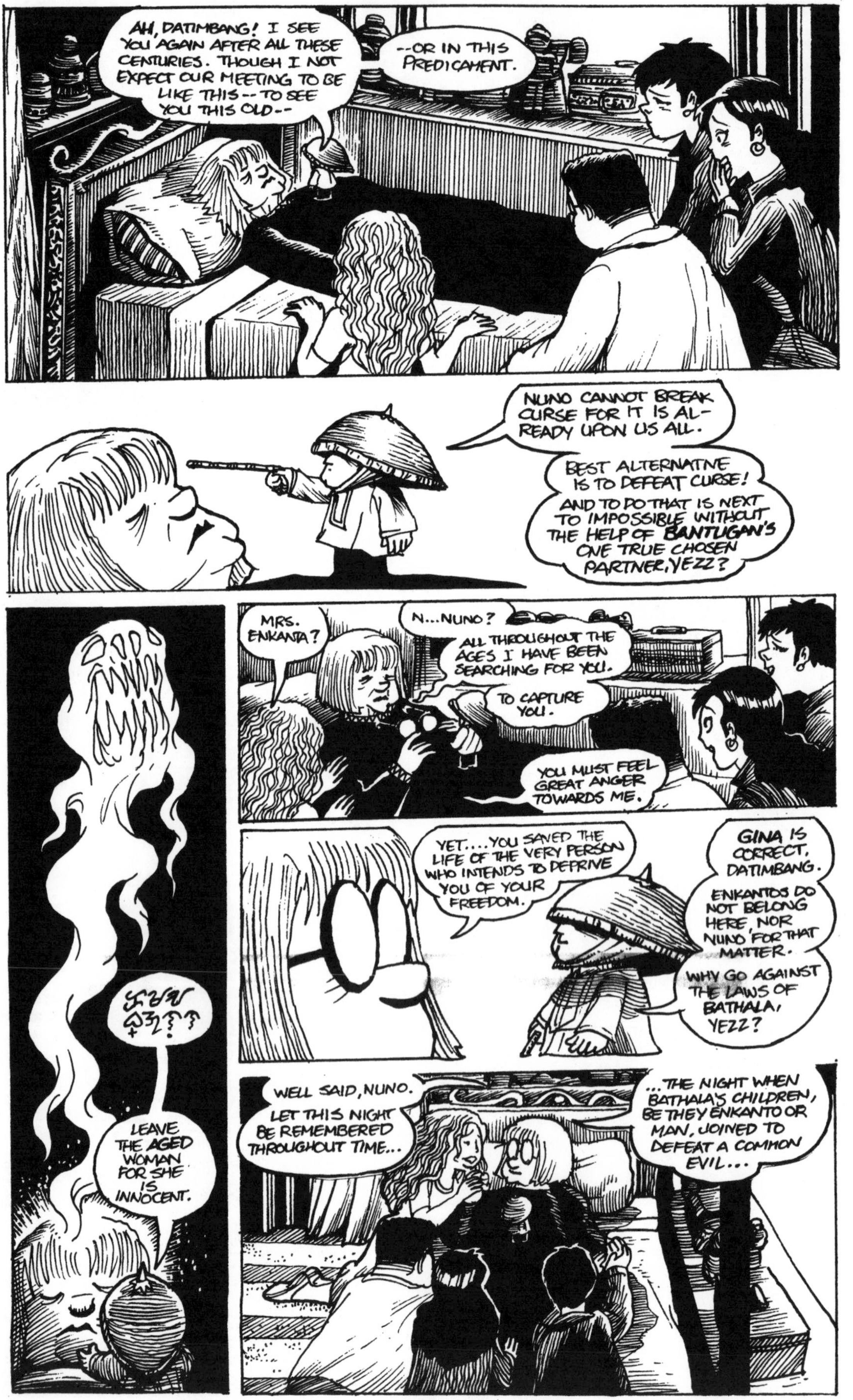
AH, DATIMBANG! I SEE YOU AGAIN AFTER ALL THESE CENTURIES. THOUGH I NOT EXPECT OUR MEETING TO BE LIKE THIS--TO SEE YOU THIS OLD--
--OR IN THIS PREDICAMENT.
NUNO CANNOT BREAK CURSE FOR IT IS ALREADY UPON US ALL.
BEST ALTERNATIVE IS TO DEFEAT CURSE! AND TO DO THAT IS NEXT TO IMPOSSIBLE WITHOUT THE HELP OF BANTUGAN'S ONE TRUE CHOSEN PARTNER, YEZZ?
LEAVE THE AGED WOMAN FOR SHE IS INNOCENT.
MRS. ENKANTA?
N...NUNO?
ALL THROUGHOUT THE AGES I HAVE BEEN SEARCHING FOR YOU.
TO CAPTURE YOU.
YOU MUST FEEL GREAT ANGER TOWARDS ME.
YET.... YOU SAVED THE LIFE OF THE VERY PERSON WHO INTENDS TO DEPRIVE YOU OF YOUR FREEDOM.
GINA IS CORRECT, DATIMBANG.
ENKANTOS DO NOT BELONG HERE, NOR NUNO FOR THAT MATTER.
WHY GO AGAINST THE LAWS OF BATHALA, YEZZ?
WELL SAID, NUNO.
LET THIS NIGHT BE REMEMBERED THROUGHOUT TIME...
...THE NIGHT WHEN BATHALA'S CHILDREN, BE THEY ENKANTO OR MAN, JOINED TO DEFEAT A COMMON EVIL...

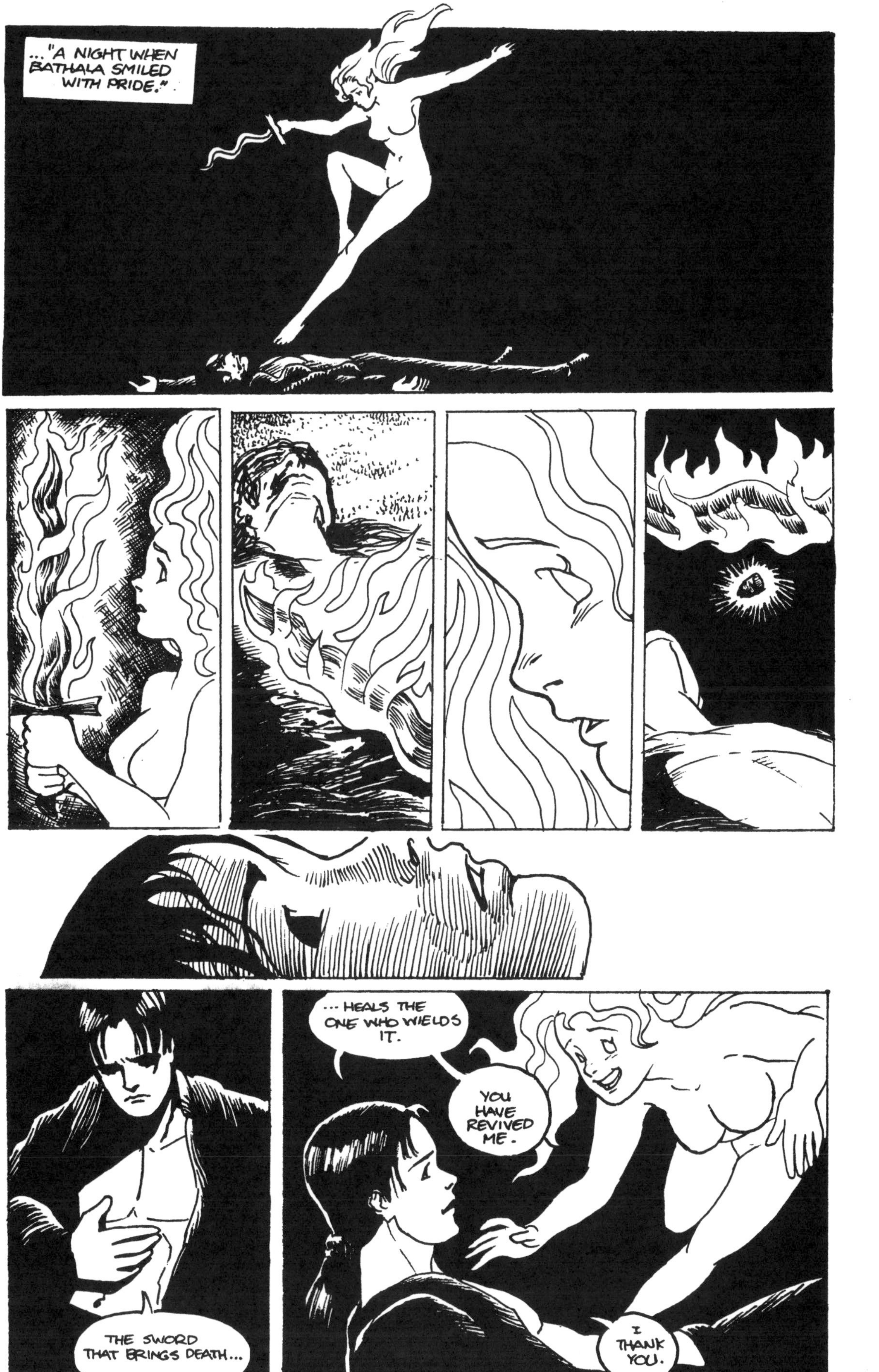
..."A NIGHT WHEN BATHALA SMILED WITH PRIDE."
THE SWORD THAT BRINGS DEATH...
...HEALS THE ONE WHO WIELDS IT.
YOU HAVE REVIVED ME.
I THANK YOU.

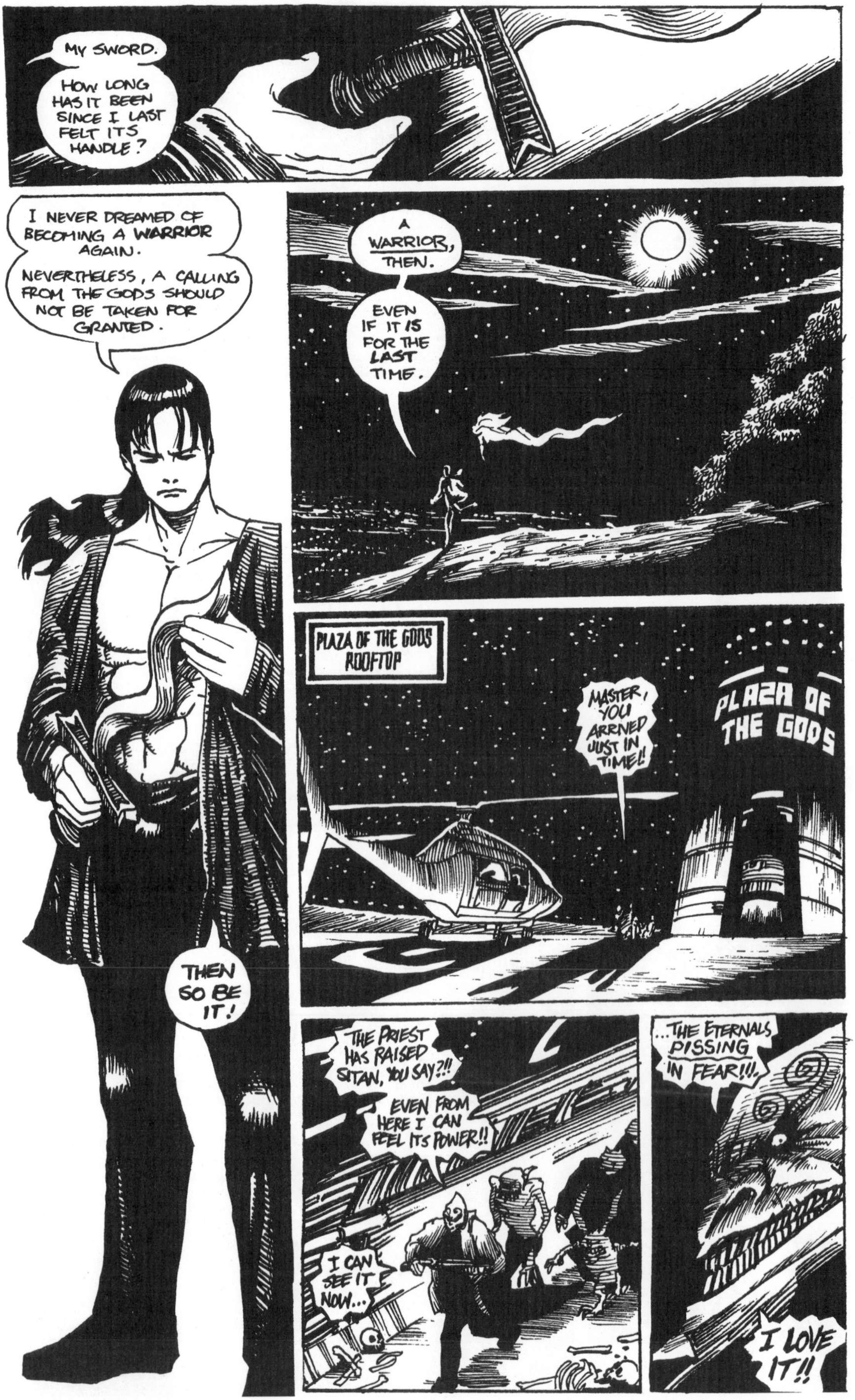
MY SWORD.
HOW LONG HAS IT BEEN SINCE I LAST FELT ITS HANDLE?
I NEVER DREAMED OF BECOMING A WARRIOR AGAIN.
NEVERTHELESS, A CALLING FROM THE GODS SHOULD NOT BE TAKEN FOR GRANTED.
A WARRIOR, THEN.
EVEN IF IT IS FOR THE LAST TIME.
THEN SO BE IT!
PLAZA OF THE GODS ROOFTOP
MASTER, YOU ARRIVED JUST IN TIME!!
PLAZA OF THE GODS
THE PRIEST HAS RAISED SITAN, YOU SAY?!!
EVEN FROM HERE I CAN FEEL ITS POWER!!
I CAN SEE IT NOW...
...THE ETERNALS PISSING IN FEAR!!!
I LOVE IT!!

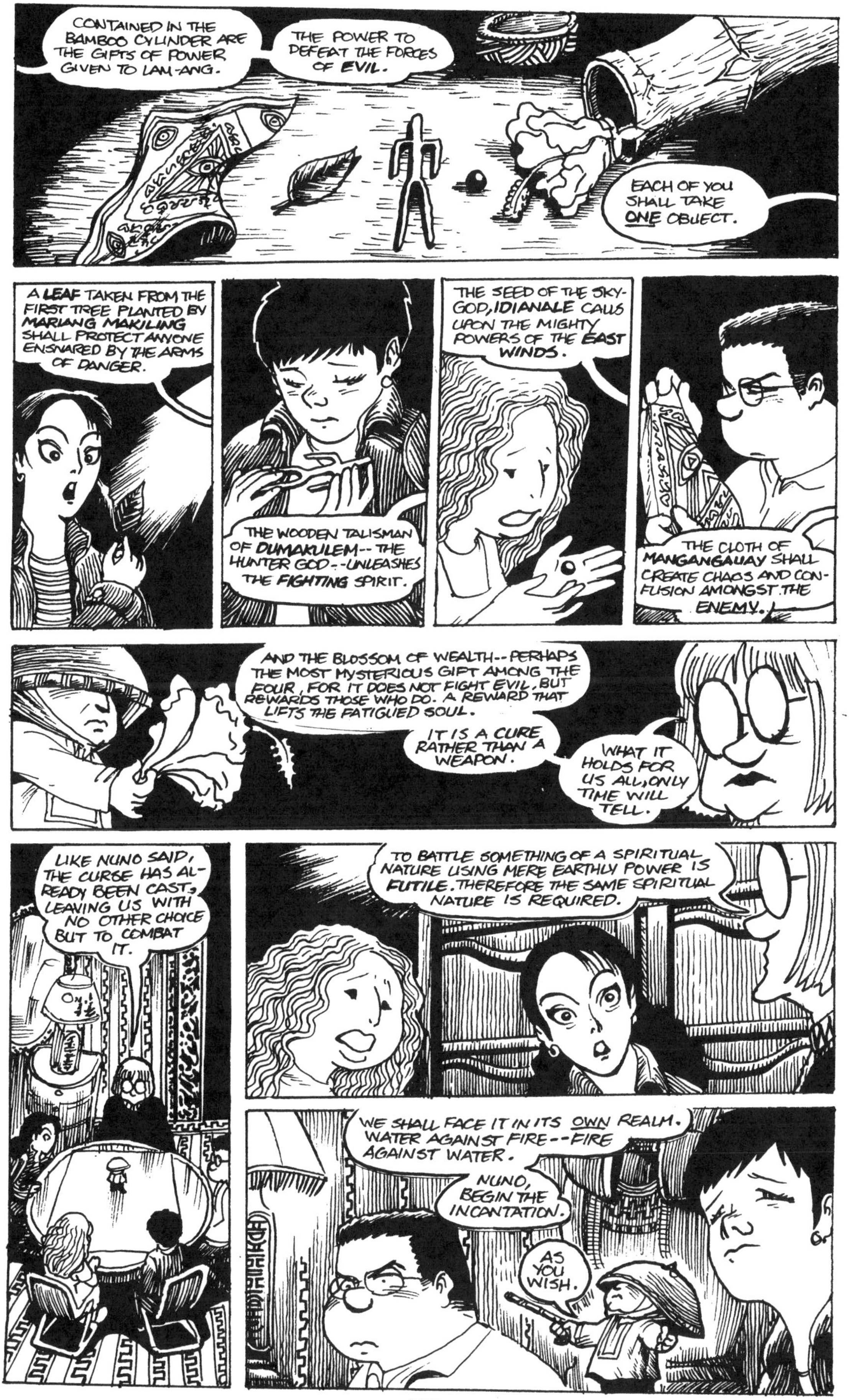

CONTAINED IN THE BAMBOO CYLINDER ARE THE GIFTS OF POWER GIVEN TO LAM-ANG.
THE POWER TO DEFEAT THE FORCES OF EVIL.
EACH OF YOU SHALL TAKE ONE OBJECT.
A LEAF TAKEN FROM THE FIRST TREE PLANTED BY MARIANG MAKILING SHALL PROTECT ANYONE ENSNARED BY THE ARMS OF DANGER.
THE WOODEN TALISMAN OF DUMAKULEM-- THE HUNTER GOD--UNLEASHES THE FIGHTING SPIRIT.
THE SEED OF THE SKY-GOD, IDIANALE CALLS UPON THE MIGHTY POWERS OF THE EAST WINDS.
THE CLOTH OF MANGANGAUAY SHALL CREATE CHAOS AND CONFUSION AMONGST THE ENEMY.
AND THE BLOSSOM OF WEALTH--PERHAPS THE MOST MYSTERIOUS GIFT AMONG THE FOUR, FOR IT DOES NOT FIGHT EVIL, BUT REWARDS THOSE WHO DO. A REWARD THAT LIFTS THE FATIGUED SOUL.
IT IS A CURE RATHER THAN A WEAPON.
WHAT IT HOLDS FOR US ALL, ONLY TIME WILL TELL.
LIKE NUNO SAID, THE CURSE HAS ALREADY BEEN CAST, LEAVING US WITH NO OTHER CHOICE BUT TO COMBAT IT.
TO BATTLE SOMETHING OF A SPIRITUAL NATURE USING MERE EARTHLY POWER IS FUTILE. THEREFORE THE SAME SPIRITUAL NATURE IS REQUIRED.
WE SHALL FACE IT IN ITS OWN REALM. WATER AGAINST FIRE--FIRE AGAINST WATER.
NUNO, BEGIN THE INCANTATION.
AS YOU WISH.

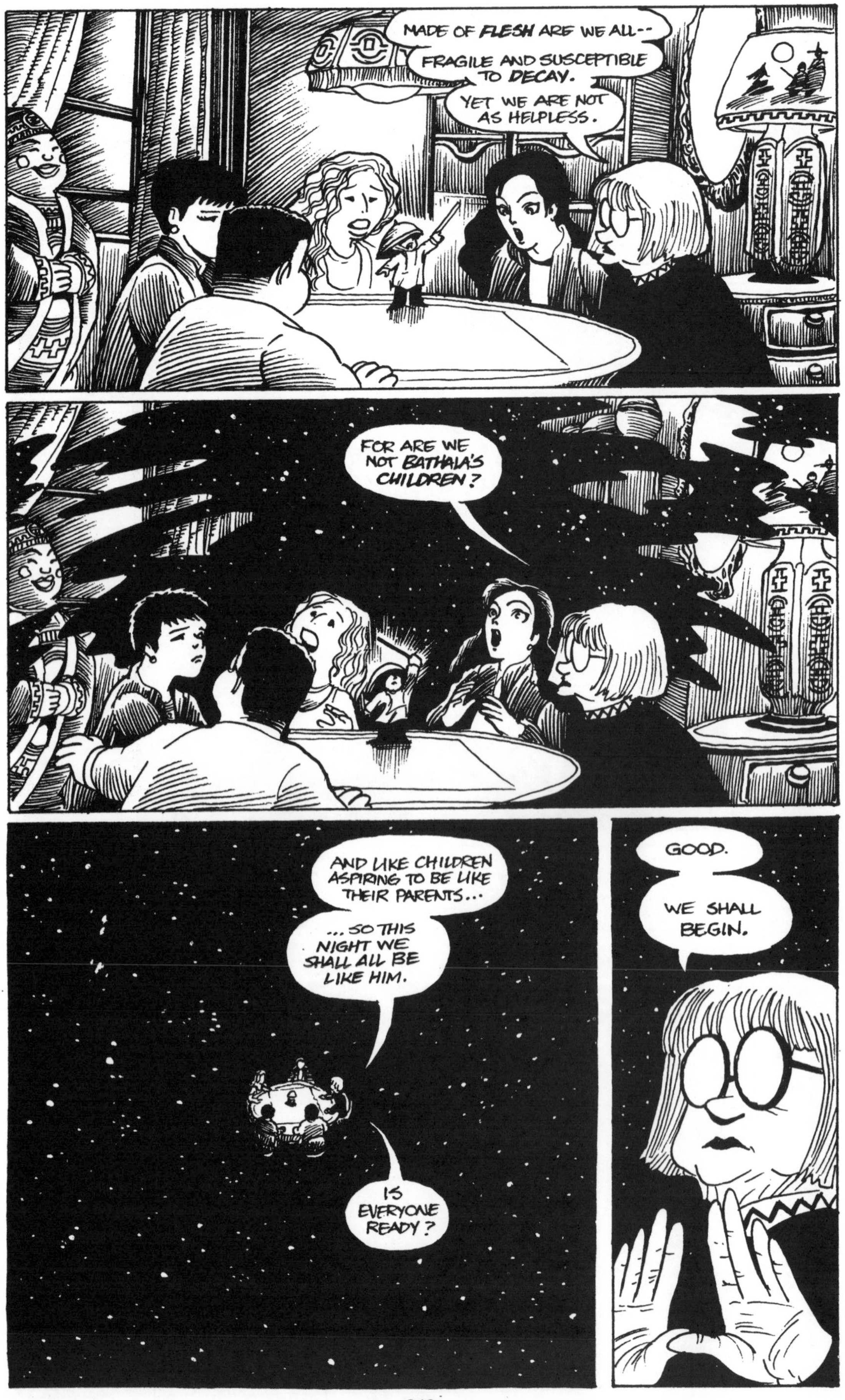
MADE OF FLESH ARE WE ALL--
FRAGILE AND SUSCEPTIBLE TO DECAY.
YET WE ARE NOT AS HELPLESS.
FOR ARE WE NOT BATHALA'S CHILDREN?
AND LIKE CHILDREN ASPIRING TO BE LIKE THEIR PARENTS...
...SO THIS NIGHT WE SHALL ALL BE LIKE HIM.
IS EVERYONE READY?
GOOD.
WE SHALL BEGIN.

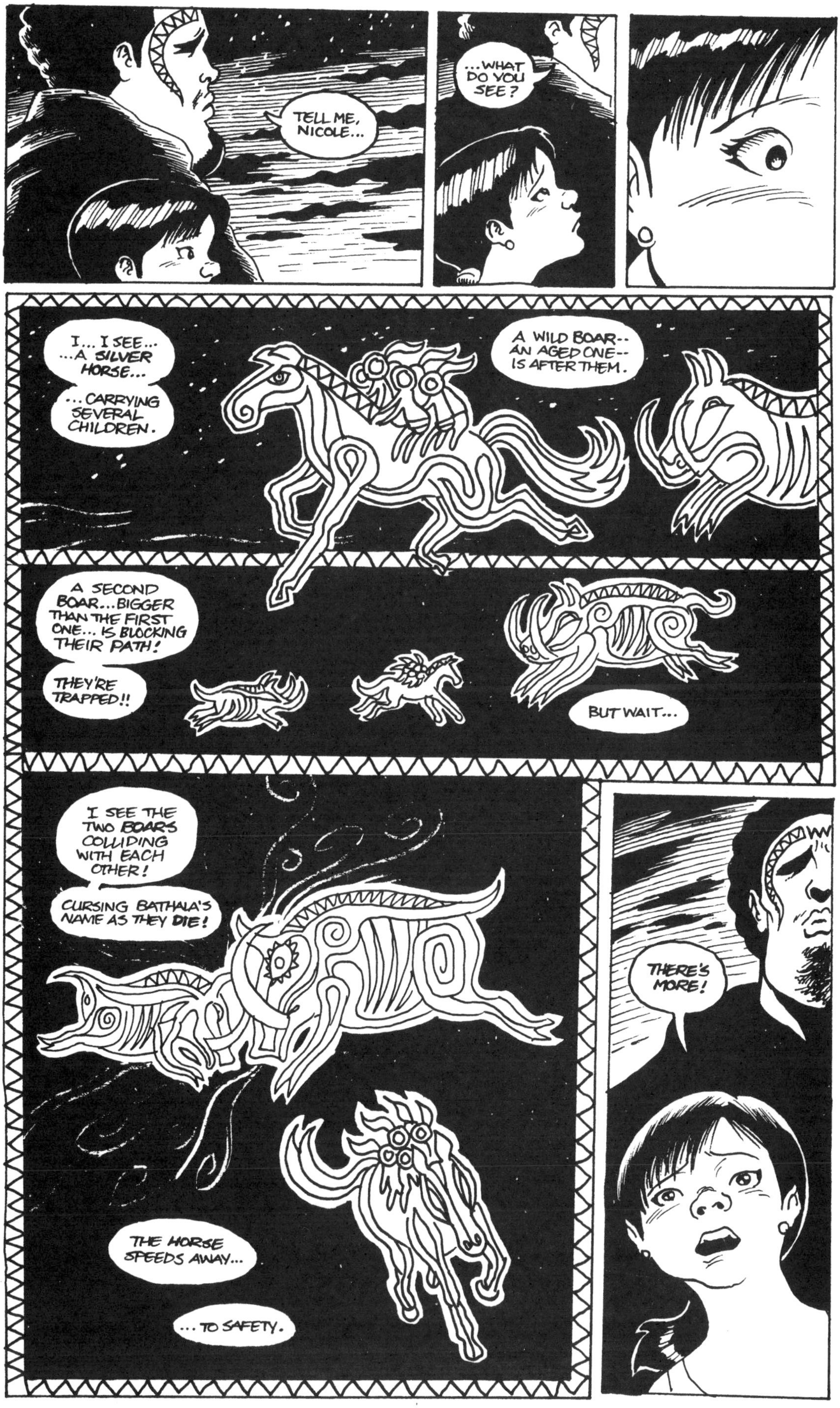
TELL ME, NICOLE...
...WHAT DO YOU SEE?
I... I SEE... ...A SILVER HORSE...
...CARRYING SEVERAL CHILDREN.
A WILD BOAR-- AN AGED ONE-- IS AFTER THEM.
A SECOND BOAR... BIGGER THAN THE FIRST ONE... IS BLOCKING THEIR PATH!
THEY'RE TRAPPED!!
BUT WAIT...
I SEE THE TWO BOARS COLLIDING WITH EACH OTHER!
CURSING BATHALA'S NAME AS THEY DIE!
THE HORSE SPEEDS AWAY...
...TO SAFETY.
THERE'S MORE!

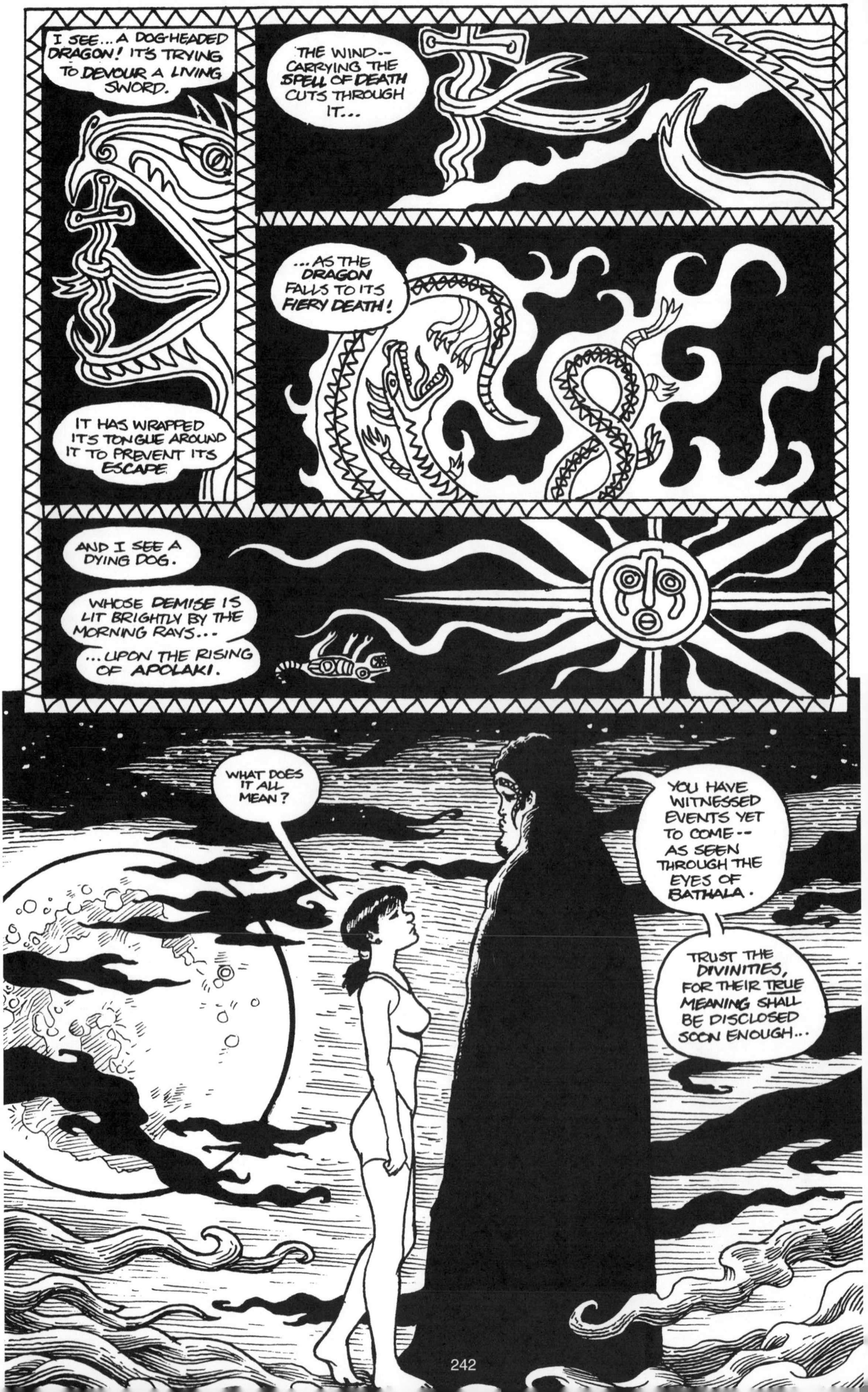

I SEE... A DOG-HEADED DRAGON! IT'S TRYING TO DEVOUR A LIVING SWORD.
IT HAS WRAPPED IT'S TONGUE AROUND IT TO PREVENT ITS ESCAPE
THE WIND-- CARRYING THE SPELL OF DEATH CUTS THROUGH IT...
...AS THE DRAGON FALLS TO ITS FIERY DEATH!
AND I SEE A DYING DOG.
WHOSE DEMISE IS LIT BRIGHTLY BY THE MORNING RAYS...
...UPON THE RISING OF APOLAKI.
WHAT DOES IT ALL MEAN?
YOU HAVE WITNESSED EVENTS YET TO COME-- AS SEEN THROUGH THE EYES OF BATHALA.
TRUST THE DIVINITIES, FOR THEIR TRUE MEANING SHALL BE DISCLOSED SOON ENOUGH...

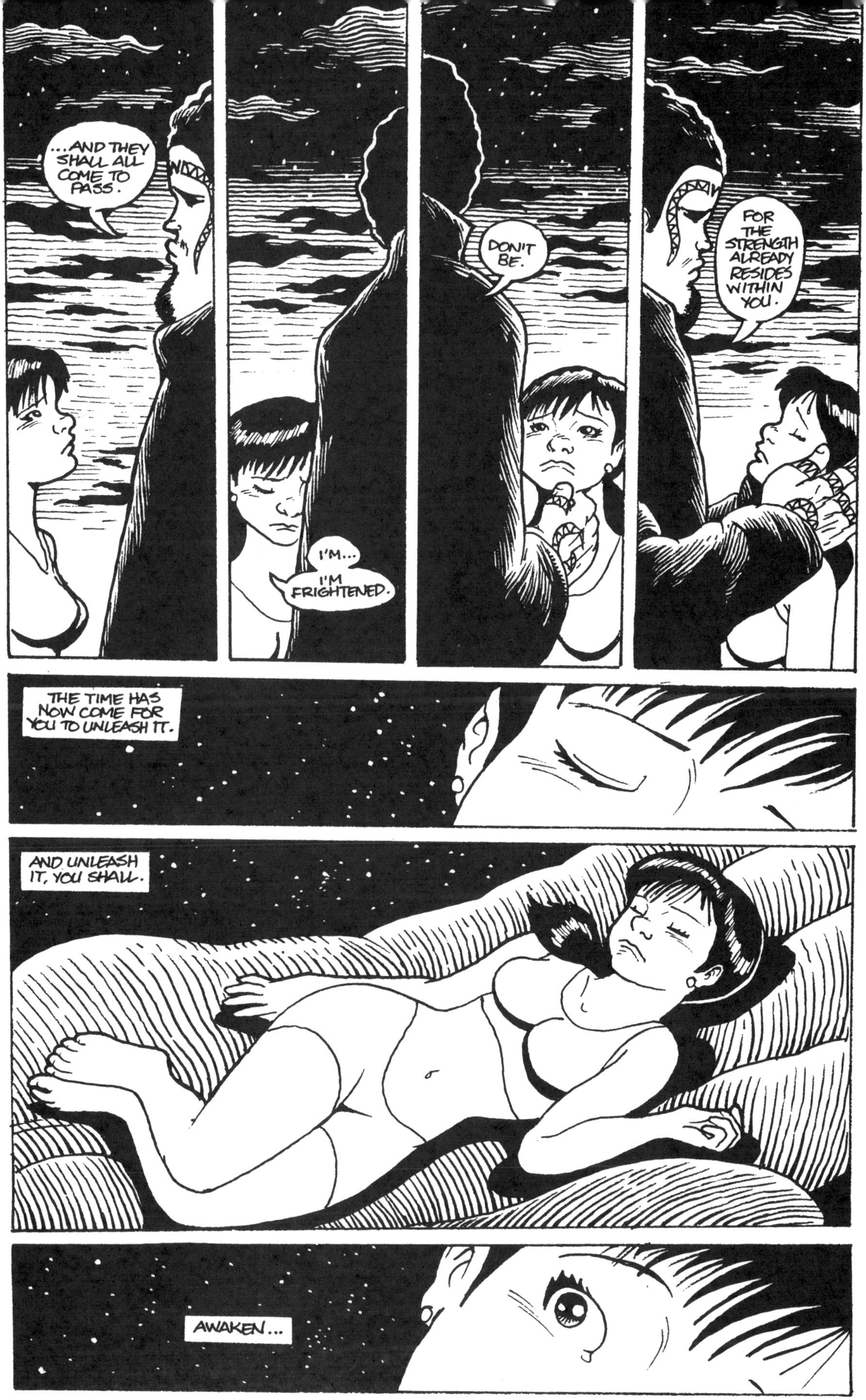
...AND THEY SHALL ALL COME TO PASS.
I'M... I'M FRIGHTENED.
DON'T BE.
FOR THE STRENGTH ALREADY RESIDES WITHIN YOU.
THE TIME HAS NOW COME FOR YOU TO UNLEASH IT.
AND UNLEASH IT, YOU SHALL.
AWAKEN...

"...AND MAY BATHALA GUIDE YOUR EVERY STEP."

PLAZA OF THE GODS

SERVICE ELEVATOR

NO UNAUTHORIZED PERSON

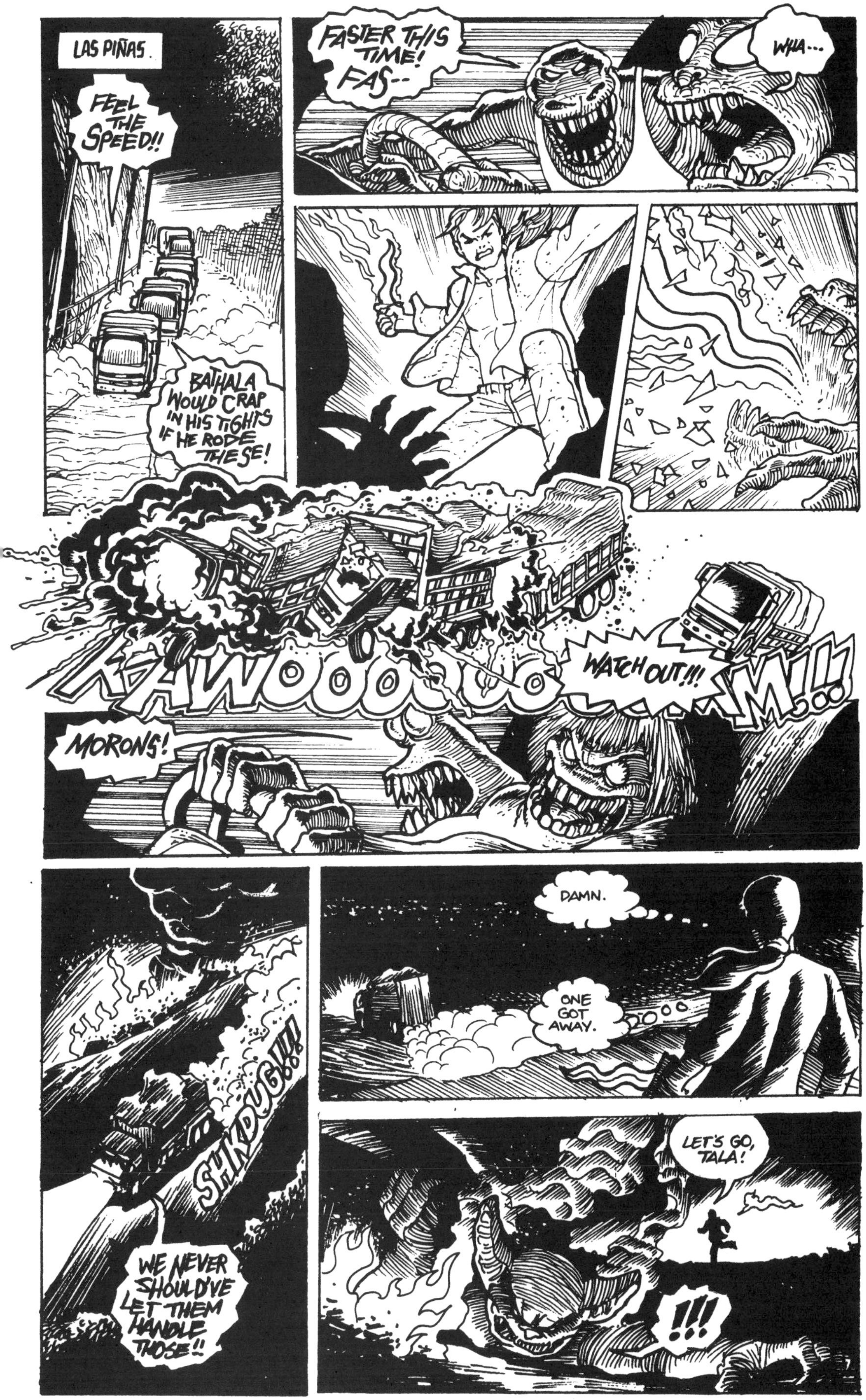
LAS PIÑAS.
FEEL THE SPEED!!
BATHALA WOULD CRAP IN HIS TIGHTS IF HE RODE THESE!
FASTER THIS TIME! FAS--
WHA...
KAWOOOOOO...M!!
WATCH OUT!!!
MORONS!
SHKDUGH!!!
WE NEVER SHOULD'VE LET THEM HANDLE THOSE!!
DAMN.
ONE GOT AWAY.
LET'S GO, TALA!
!!!

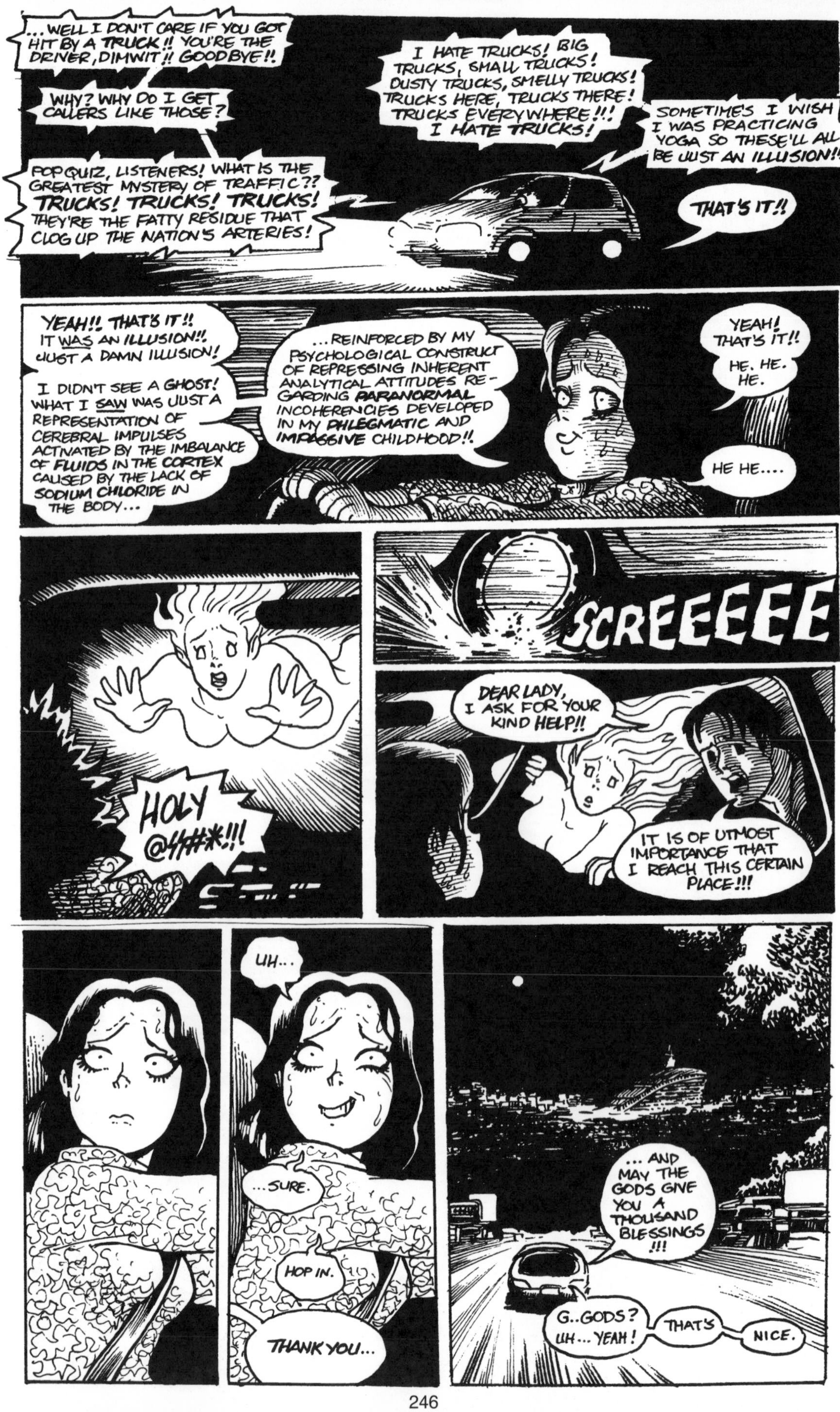
...WELL I DON'T CARE IF YOU GOT HIT BY A TRUCK!! YOU'RE THE DRIVER, DIMWIT!! GOODBYE!!
WHY? WHY DO I GET CALLERS LIKE THOSE?
POP QUIZ, LISTENERS! WHAT IS THE GREATEST MYSTERY OF TRAFFIC?? TRUCKS! TRUCKS! TRUCKS! THEY'RE THE FATTY RESIDUE THAT CLOG UP THE NATION'S ARTERIES!
I HATE TRUCKS! BIG TRUCKS, SMALL TRUCKS! DUSTY TRUCKS, SMELLY TRUCKS! TRUCKS HERE, TRUCKS THERE! TRUCKS EVERYWHERE!!! I HATE TRUCKS!
SOMETIMES I WISH I WAS PRACTICING YOGA SO THESE'LL ALL BE JUST AN ILLUSION!!
THAT'S IT!!
YEAH!! THAT'S IT!! IT WAS AN ILLUSION!! JUST A DAMN ILLUSION!
I DIDN'T SEE A GHOST! WHAT I SAW WAS JUST A REPRESENTATION OF CEREBRAL IMPULSES ACTIVATED BY THE IMBALANCE OF FLUIDS IN THE CORTEX CAUSED BY THE LACK OF SODIUM CHLORIDE IN THE BODY...
...REINFORCED BY MY PSYCHOLOGICAL CONSTRUCT OF REPRESSING INHERENT ANALYTICAL ATTITUDES REGARDING PARANORMAL INCOHERENCIES DEVELOPED IN MY PHLEGMATIC AND IMPASSIVE CHILDHOOD!!
YEAH! THAT'S IT!!
HE. HE. HE.
HE HE....
HOLY @$#*!!!
SCREEEEEE
DEAR LADY, I ASK FOR YOUR KIND HELP!!
IT IS OF UTMOST IMPORTANCE THAT I REACH THIS CERTAIN PLACE!!!
UH...
...SURE.
HOP IN.
THANK YOU...
...AND MAY THE GODS GIVE YOU A THOUSAND BLESSINGS!!!
G..GODS? UH...YEAH!
THAT'S
NICE.

IV

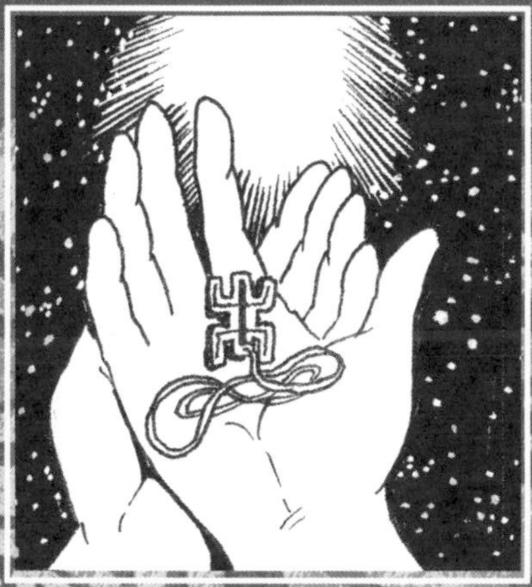

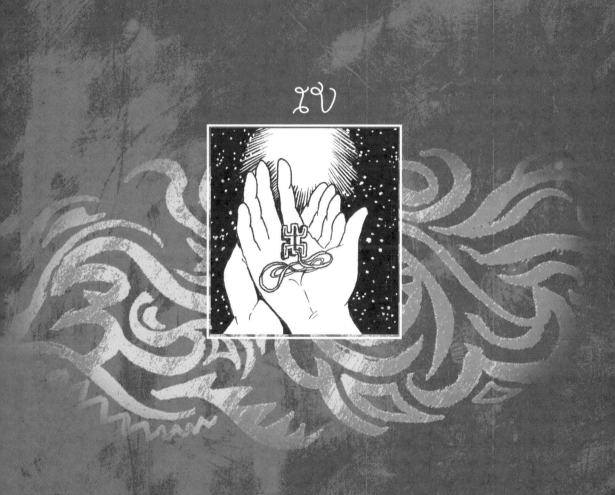

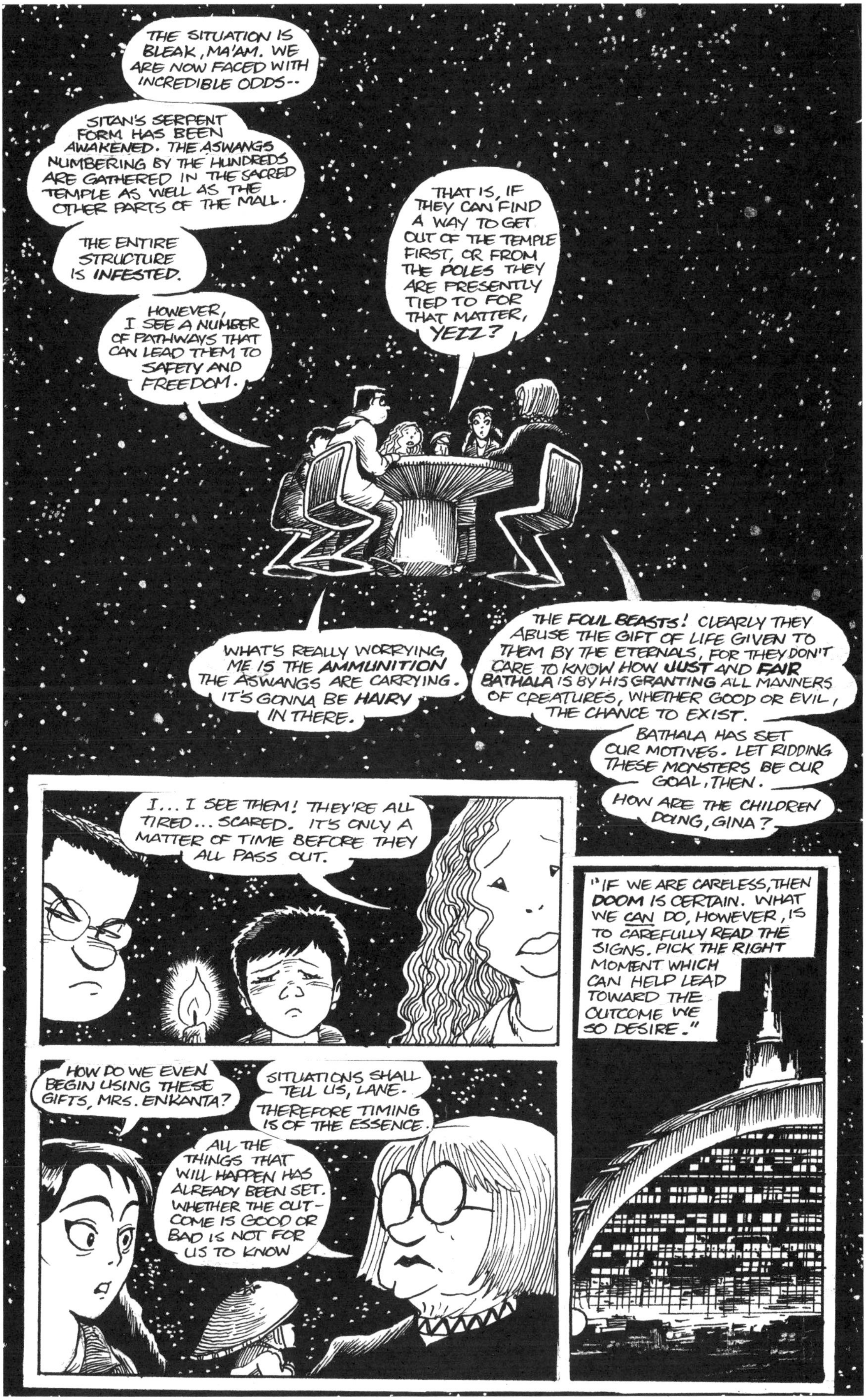
THE SITUATION IS BLEAK, MA'AM. WE ARE NOW FACED WITH INCREDIBLE ODDS--
SITAN'S SERPENT FORM HAS BEEN AWAKENED. THE ASWANGS NUMBERING BY THE HUNDREDS ARE GATHERED IN THE SACRED TEMPLE AS WELL AS THE OTHER PARTS OF THE MALL.
THE ENTIRE STRUCTURE IS INFESTED.
HOWEVER, I SEE A NUMBER OF PATHWAYS THAT CAN LEAD THEM TO SAFETY AND FREEDOM.
THAT IS, IF THEY CAN FIND A WAY TO GET OUT OF THE TEMPLE FIRST, OR FROM THE POLES THEY ARE PRESENTLY TIED TO FOR THAT MATTER, YEZZ?
WHAT'S REALLY WORRYING ME IS THE AMMUNITION THE ASWANGS ARE CARRYING. IT'S GONNA BE HAIRY IN THERE.
THE FOUL BEASTS! CLEARLY THEY ABUSE THE GIFT OF LIFE GIVEN TO THEM BY THE ETERNALS, FOR THEY DON'T CARE TO KNOW HOW JUST AND FAIR BATHALA IS BY HIS GRANTING ALL MANNERS OF CREATURES, WHETHER GOOD OR EVIL, THE CHANCE TO EXIST.
BATHALA HAS SET OUR MOTIVES. LET RIDDING THESE MONSTERS BE OUR GOAL, THEN.
HOW ARE THE CHILDREN DOING, GINA?
I... I SEE THEM! THEY'RE ALL TIRED... SCARED. IT'S ONLY A MATTER OF TIME BEFORE THEY ALL PASS OUT.
HOW DO WE EVEN BEGIN USING THESE GIFTS, MRS. ENKANTA?
SITUATIONS SHALL TELL US, LANE.
THEREFORE TIMING IS OF THE ESSENCE.
ALL THE THINGS THAT WILL HAPPEN HAS ALREADY BEEN SET. WHETHER THE OUT-COME IS GOOD OR BAD IS NOT FOR US TO KNOW
"IF WE ARE CARELESS, THEN DOOM IS CERTAIN. WHAT WE CAN DO, HOWEVER, IS TO CAREFULLY READ THE SIGNS. PICK THE RIGHT MOMENT WHICH CAN HELP LEAD TOWARD THE OUTCOME WE SO DESIRE."

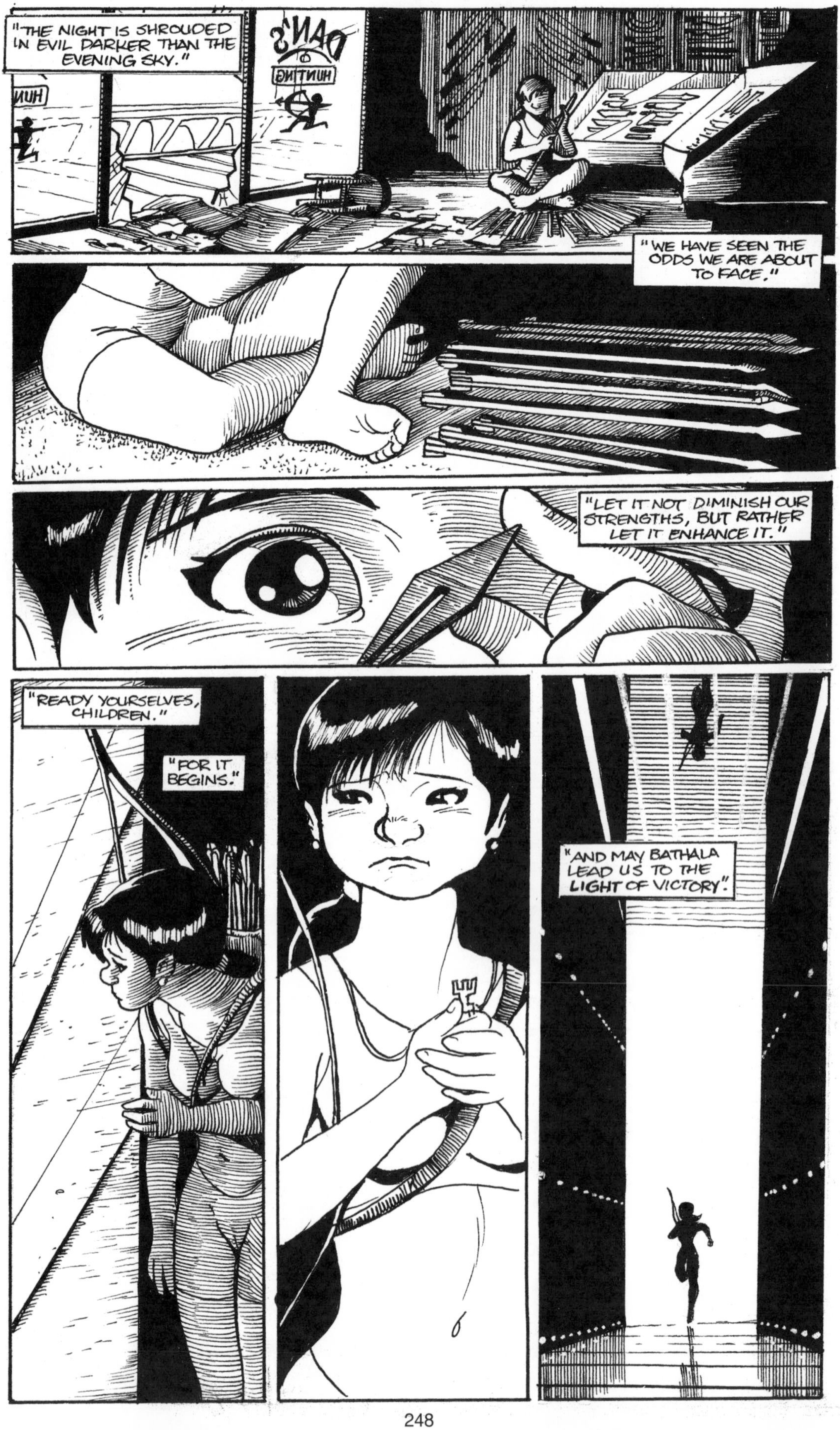

"THE NIGHT IS SHROUDED IN EVIL DARKER THAN THE EVENING SKY."
DAN'S
HUNTING
"WE HAVE SEEN THE ODDS WE ARE ABOUT TO FACE."
"LET IT NOT DIMINISH OUR STRENGTHS, BUT RATHER LET IT ENHANCE IT."
"READY YOURSELVES, CHILDREN."
"FOR IT BEGINS."
"AND MAY BATHALA LEAD US TO THE LIGHT OF VICTORY".

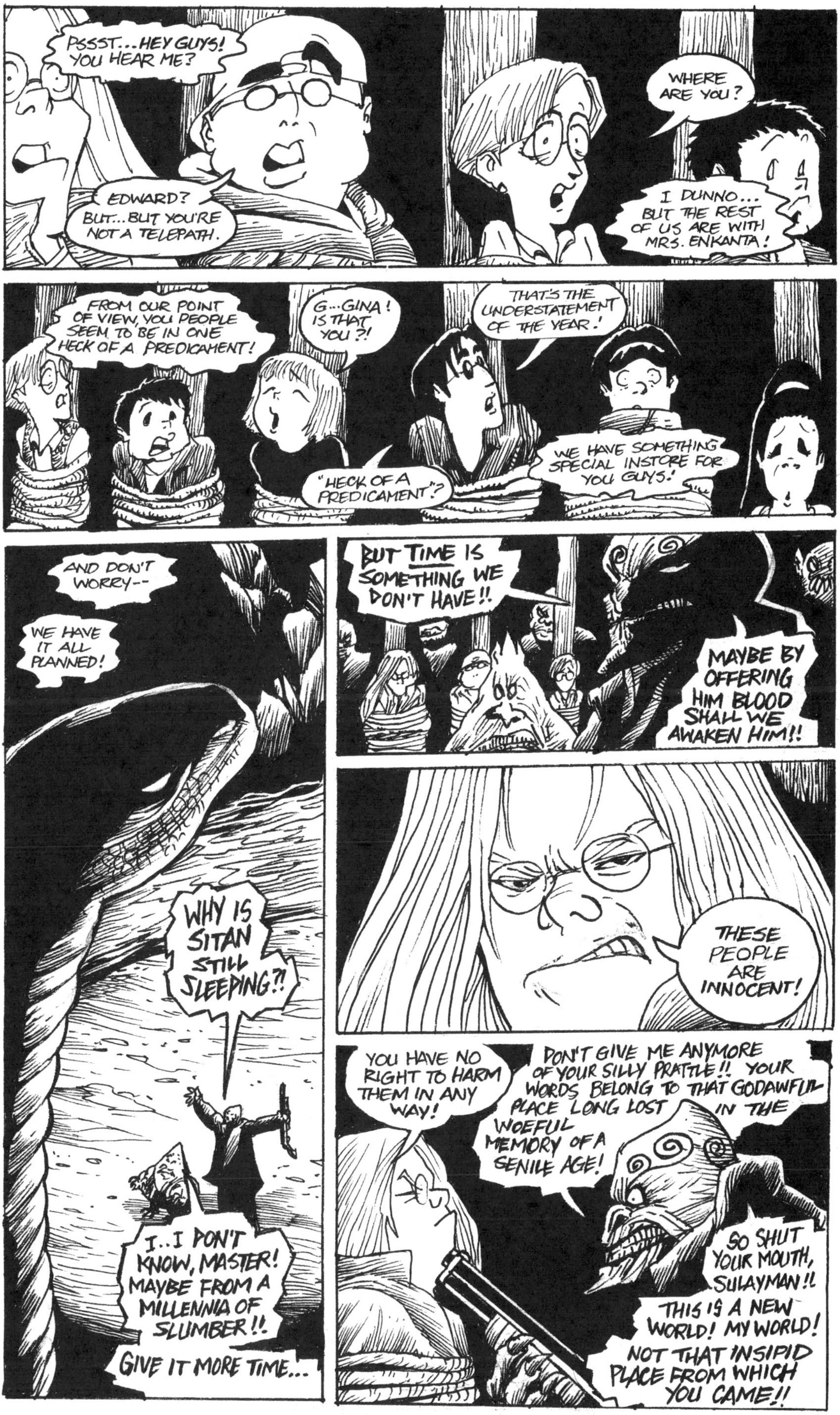

PSSST... HEY GUYS! YOU HEAR ME?
EDWARD? BUT... BUT YOU'RE NOT A TELEPATH.
WHERE ARE YOU?
I DUNNO... BUT THE REST OF US ARE WITH MRS. ENKANTA!
FROM OUR POINT OF VIEW, YOU PEOPLE SEEM TO BE IN ONE HECK OF A PREDICAMENT!
G...GINA! IS THAT YOU?!
"HECK OF A PREDICAMENT"?
THAT'S THE UNDERSTATEMENT OF THE YEAR!
WE HAVE SOMETHING SPECIAL INSTORE FOR YOU GUYS!
AND DON'T WORRY--
WE HAVE IT ALL PLANNED!
WHY IS SITAN STILL SLEEPING?!
I..I DON'T KNOW, MASTER! MAYBE FROM A MILLENNIA OF SLUMBER!!
GIVE IT MORE TIME...
BUT TIME IS SOMETHING WE DON'T HAVE!!
MAYBE BY OFFERING HIM BLOOD SHALL WE AWAKEN HIM!!
THESE PEOPLE ARE INNOCENT!
YOU HAVE NO RIGHT TO HARM THEM IN ANY WAY!
DON'T GIVE ME ANYMORE OF YOUR SILLY PRATTLE!! YOUR WORDS BELONG TO THAT GODAWFUL PLACE LONG LOST IN THE WOEFUL MEMORY OF A SENILE AGE!
SO SHUT YOUR MOUTH, SULAYMAN!!
THIS IS A NEW WORLD! MY WORLD!
NOT THAT INSIPID PLACE FROM WHICH YOU CAME!!

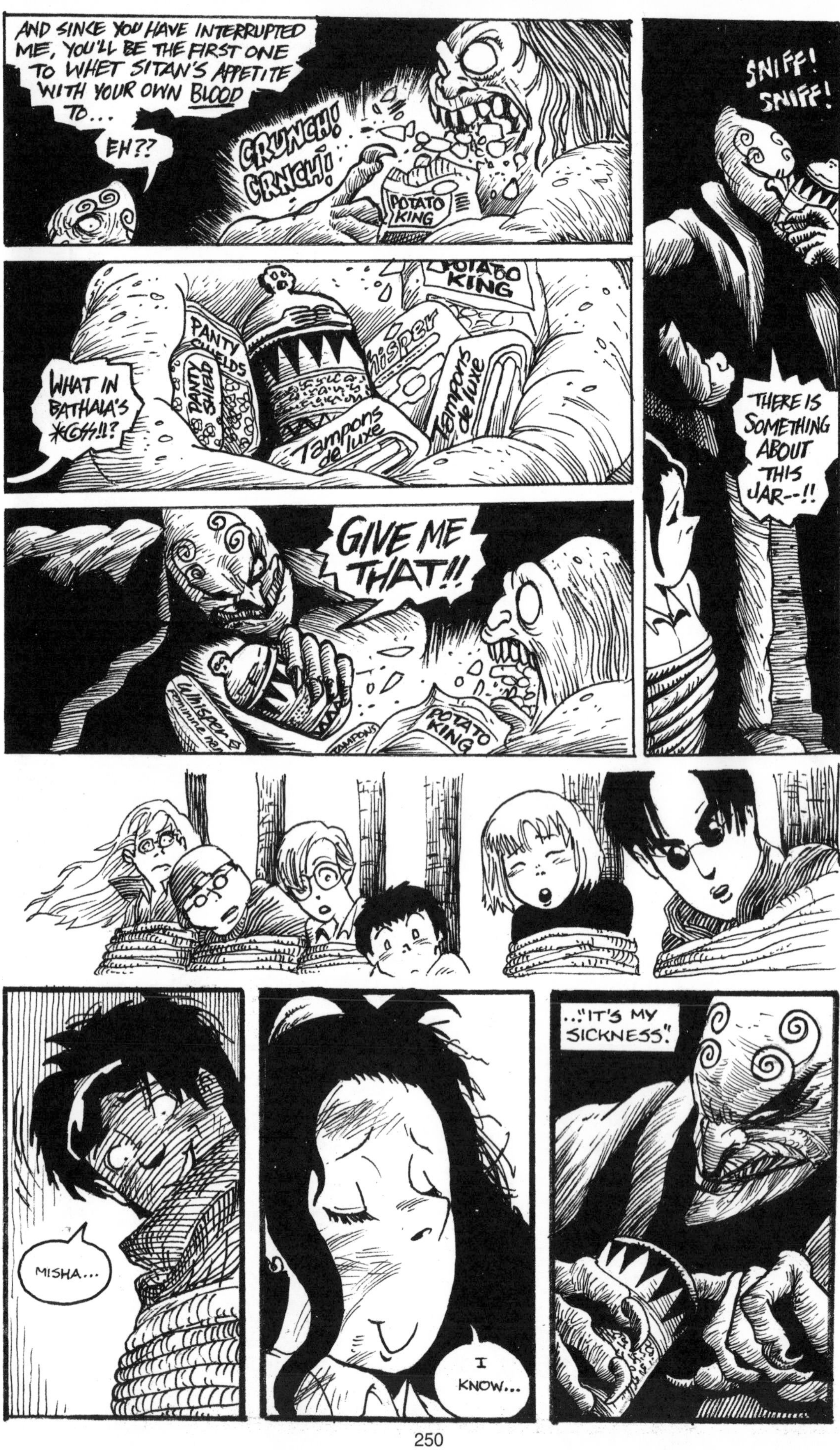
AND SINCE YOU HAVE INTERRUPTED ME, YOU'LL BE THE FIRST ONE TO WHET SITAN'S APPETITE WITH YOUR OWN BLOOD TO...
EH??
CRUNCH! CRNCH!
POTATO KING
SNIFF! SNIFF!
WHAT IN BATHALA'S *@$!!?
PANTY SHIELDS
PANTY SHIELD
POTATO KING
Whisper
Tampons de luxe
Tampons de luxe
Tampons de luxe
THERE IS SOMETHING ABOUT THIS JAR--!!
GIVE ME THAT!!
POTATO KING
TAMPONS
MISHA...
I KNOW...
..."IT'S MY SICKNESS."

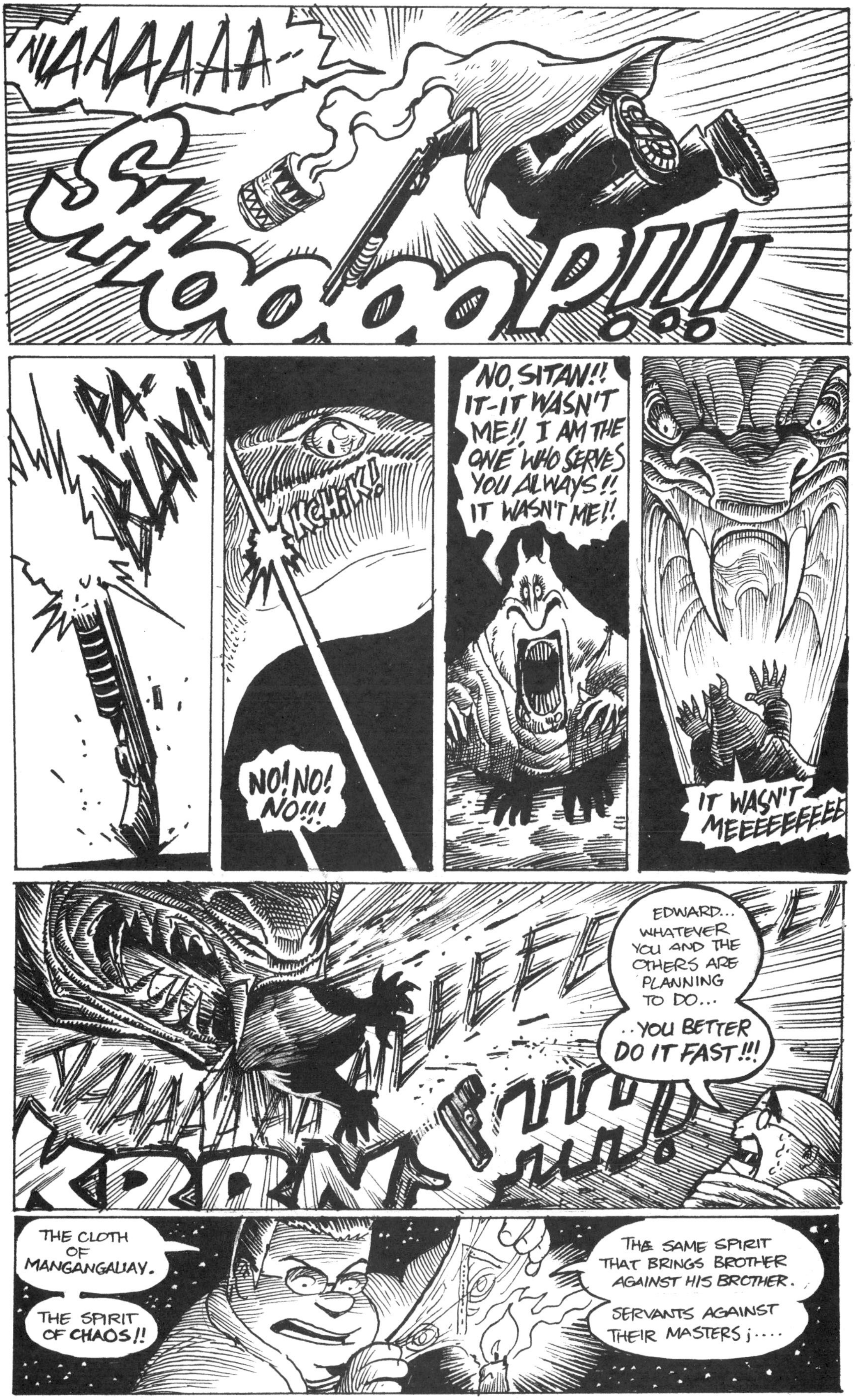
NIAAAAAA--
SHLOOOOOP!!!
PA-BLAM!
CHIK!
NO! NO! NO!!!
NO, SITAN!! IT-IT WASN'T ME!! I AM THE ONE WHO SERVES YOU ALWAYS!! IT WASN'T ME!!
IT WASN'T MEEEEEEEEE
EDWARD... WHATEVER YOU AND THE OTHERS ARE PLANNING TO DO...
..YOU BETTER DO IT FAST!!!
THE CLOTH OF MANGANGALIAY.
THE SPIRIT OF CHAOS!!
THE SAME SPIRIT THAT BRINGS BROTHER AGAINST HIS BROTHER.
SERVANTS AGAINST THEIR MASTERS ;....

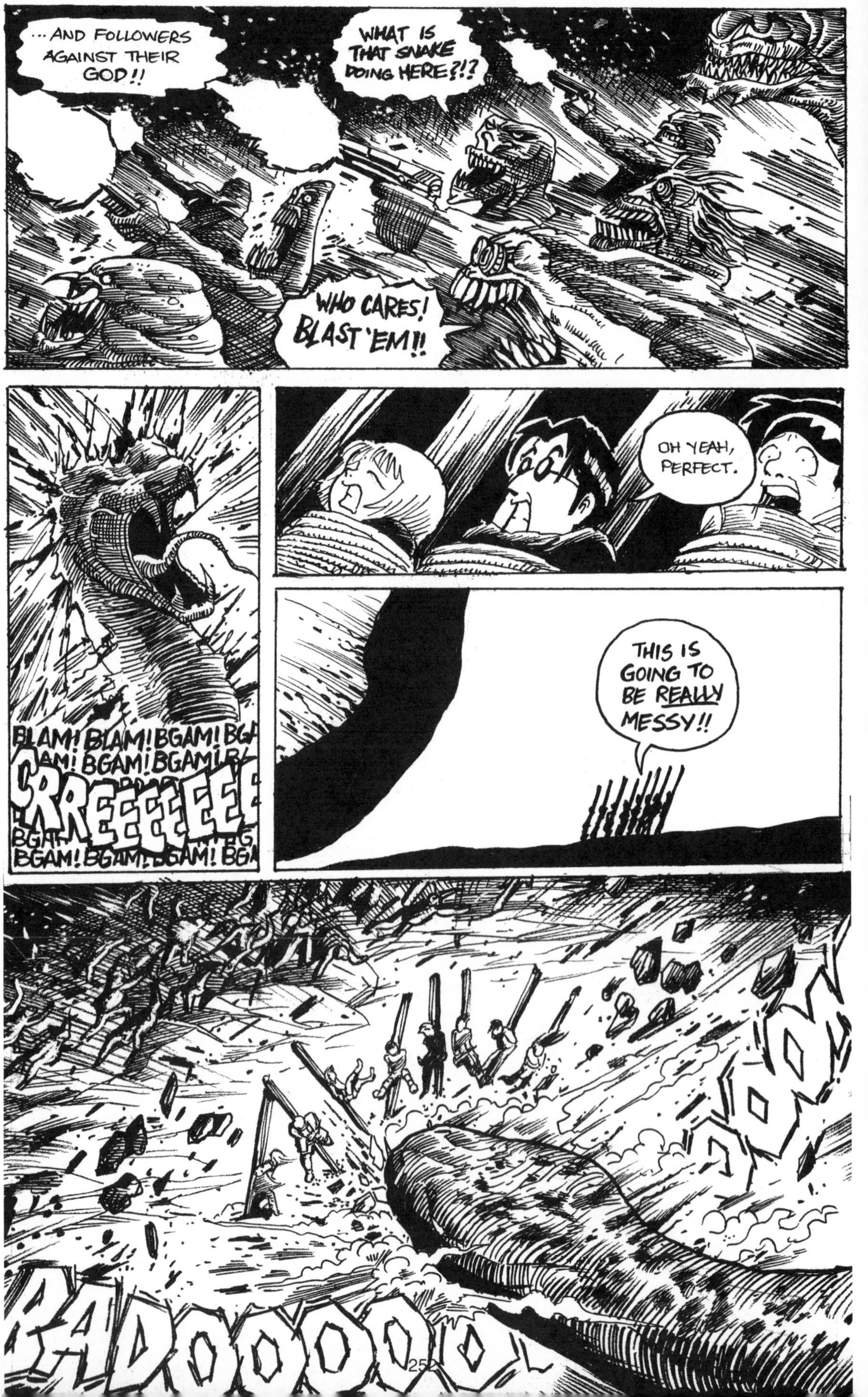
...AND FOLLOWERS AGAINST THEIR GOD!!
WHAT IS THAT SNAKE DOING HERE?!?
WHO CARES! BLAST 'EM!!
BLAM! BLAM! BGAM! BGAM! BGAM!
CRREEEEEEE
BGAM! BGAM! BGAM!
OH YEAH, PERFECT.
THIS IS GOING TO BE REALLY MESSY!!
BADOOOOOOM

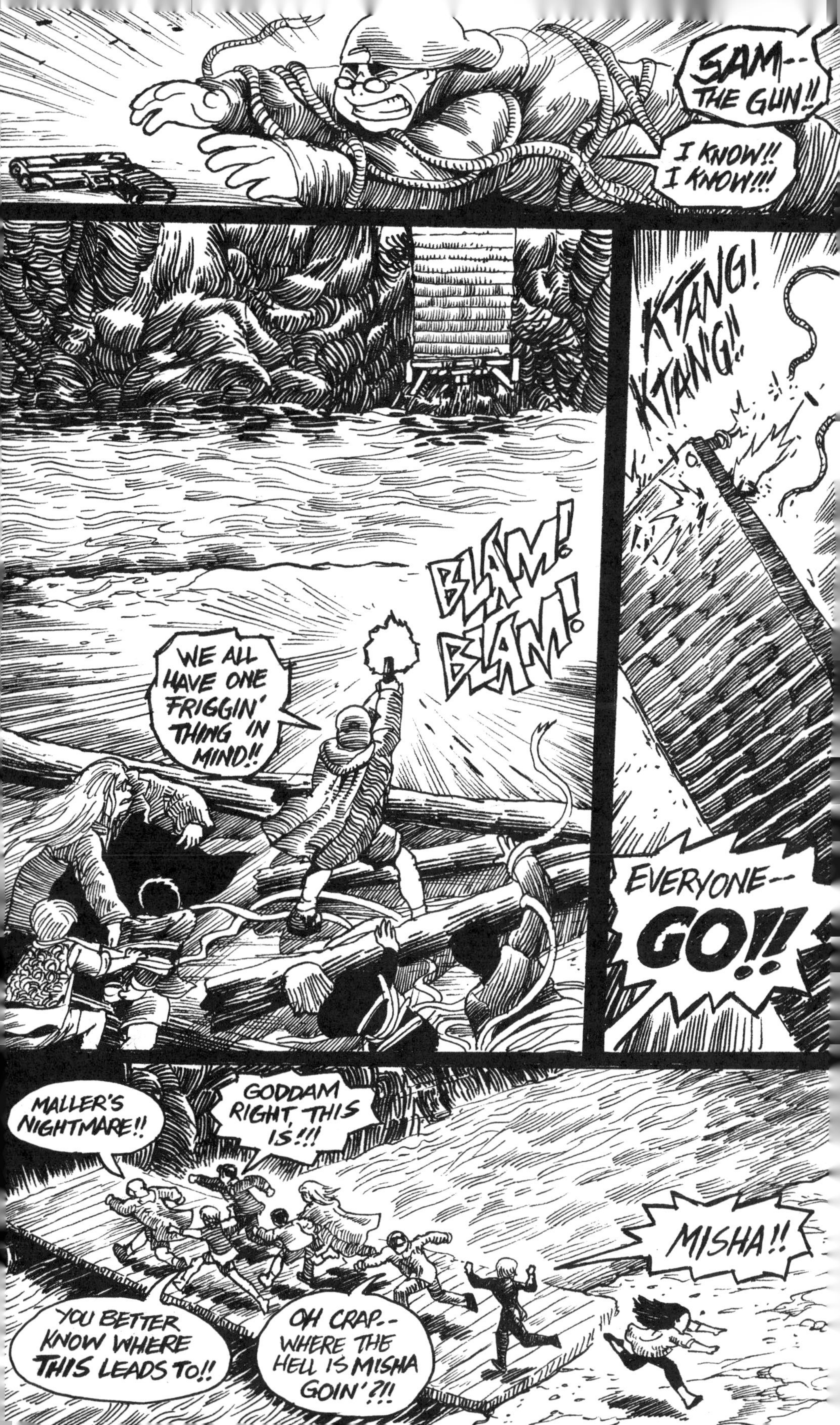
SAM-- THE GUN!!
I KNOW!! I KNOW!!!
KTANG! KTANG!!
BLAM! BLAM!
WE ALL HAVE ONE FRIGGIN' THING IN MIND!!
EVERYONE-- GO!!
MALLER'S NIGHTMARE!!
GODDAM RIGHT, THIS IS!!!
MISHA!!
YOU BETTER KNOW WHERE THIS LEADS TO!!
OH CRAP-- WHERE THE HELL IS MISHA GOIN'?!!

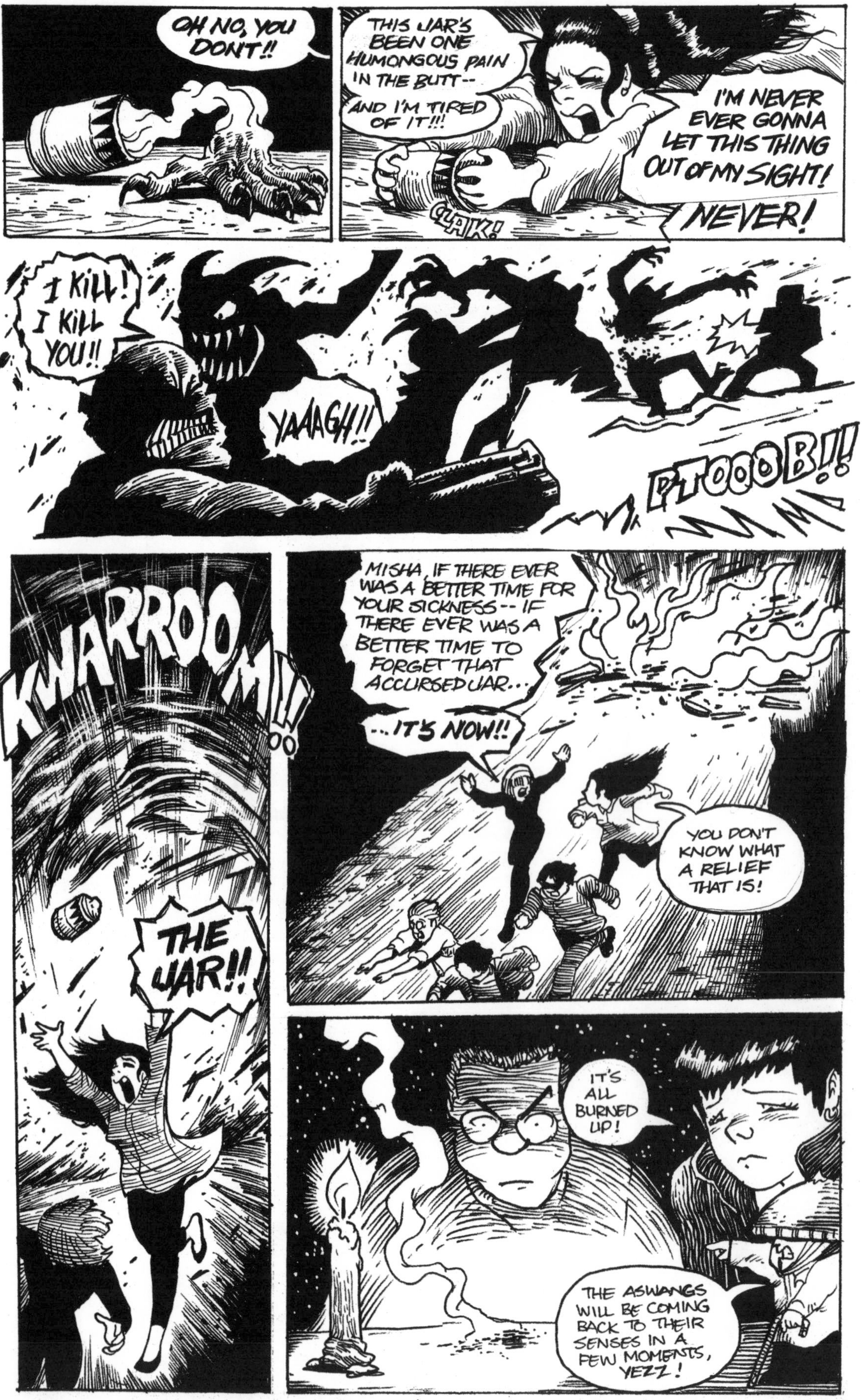
OH NO, YOU DON'T!!
THIS JAR'S BEEN ONE HUMONGOUS PAIN IN THE BUTT--
AND I'M TIRED OF IT!!!
I'M NEVER EVER GONNA LET THIS THING OUT OF MY SIGHT!
NEVER!
CLAK!
I KILL! I KILL YOU!!
YAAAGH!!
PTOOOB!!
KWARROOM!!
THE JAR!!
MISHA, IF THERE EVER WAS A BETTER TIME FOR YOUR SICKNESS-- IF THERE EVER WAS A BETTER TIME TO FORGET THAT ACCURSED JAR...
...IT'S NOW!!
YOU DON'T KNOW WHAT A RELIEF THAT IS!
IT'S ALL BURNED UP!
THE ASWANGS WILL BE COMING BACK TO THEIR SENSES IN A FEW MOMENTS, YEZZ!

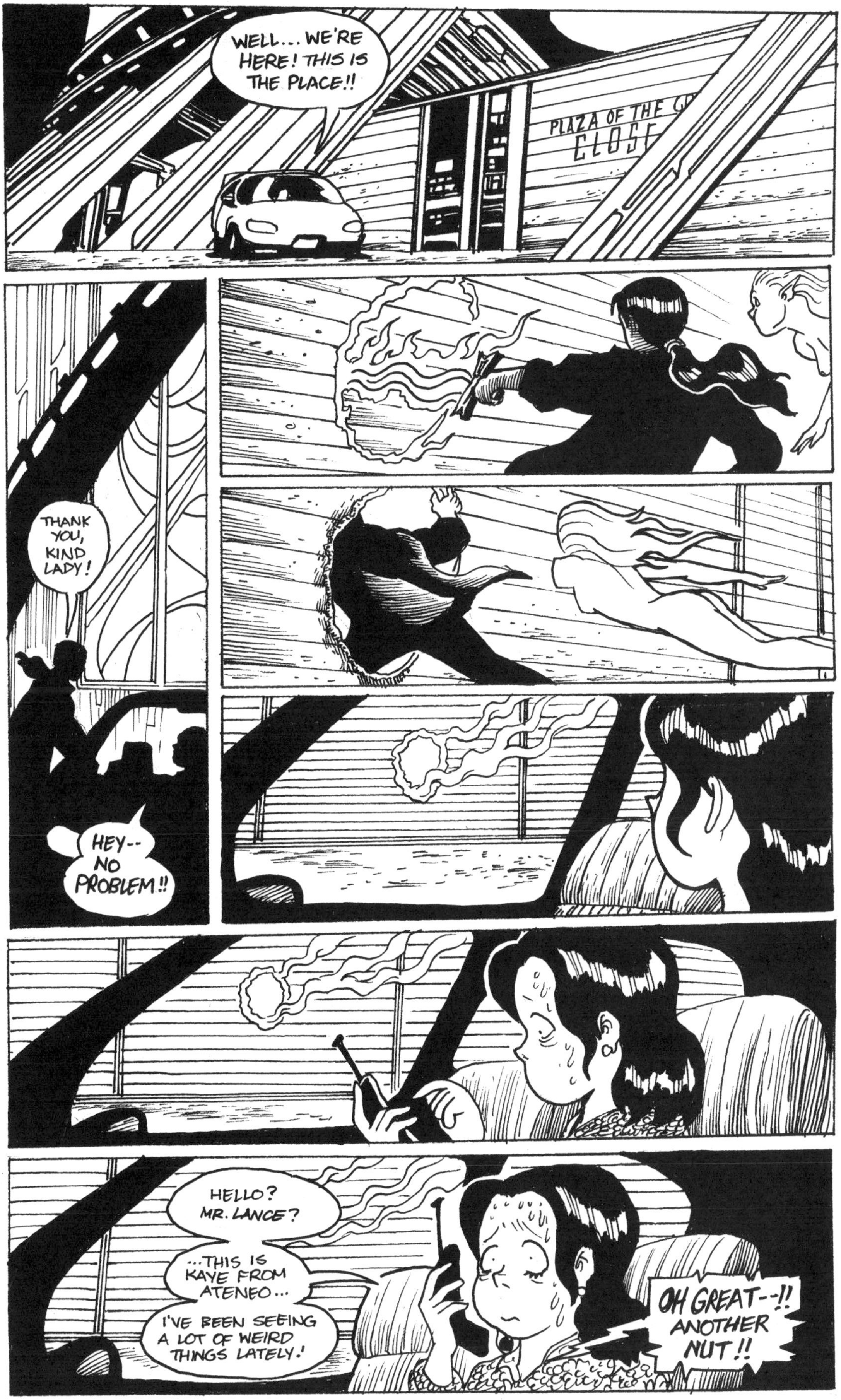
WELL... WE'RE HERE! THIS IS THE PLACE!!
PLAZA OF THE G
CLOSE
THANK YOU, KIND LADY!
HEY-- NO PROBLEM!!
HELLO? MR. LANCE?
...THIS IS KAYE FROM ATENEO...
I'VE BEEN SEEING A LOT OF WEIRD THINGS LATELY!
OH GREAT--!! ANOTHER NUT!!

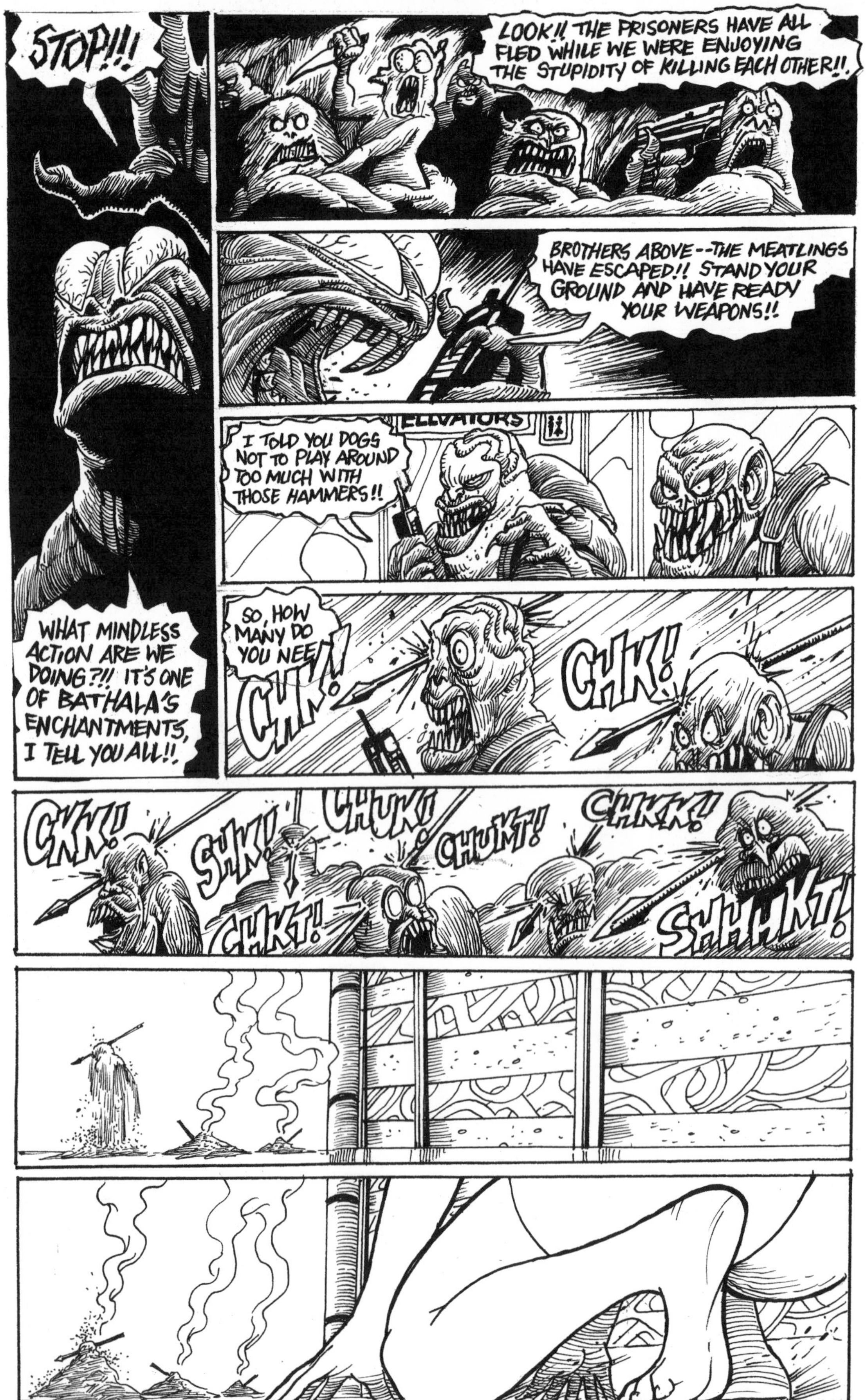
STOP!!!
LOOK!! THE PRISONERS HAVE ALL FLED WHILE WE WERE ENJOYING THE STUPIDITY OF KILLING EACH OTHER!!
BROTHERS ABOVE--THE MEATLINGS HAVE ESCAPED!! STAND YOUR GROUND AND HAVE READY YOUR WEAPONS!!
ELEVATORS
I TOLD YOU DOGS NOT TO PLAY AROUND TOO MUCH WITH THOSE HAMMERS!!
WHAT MINDLESS ACTION ARE WE DOING?!! IT'S ONE OF BATHALA'S ENCHANTMENTS, I TELL YOU ALL!!
SO, HOW MANY DO YOU NEE
CHK!
CHK!
CKK!
SHK!
CHUK!
CHUKT!
CHKK!
CHKT!
SHHHKT!

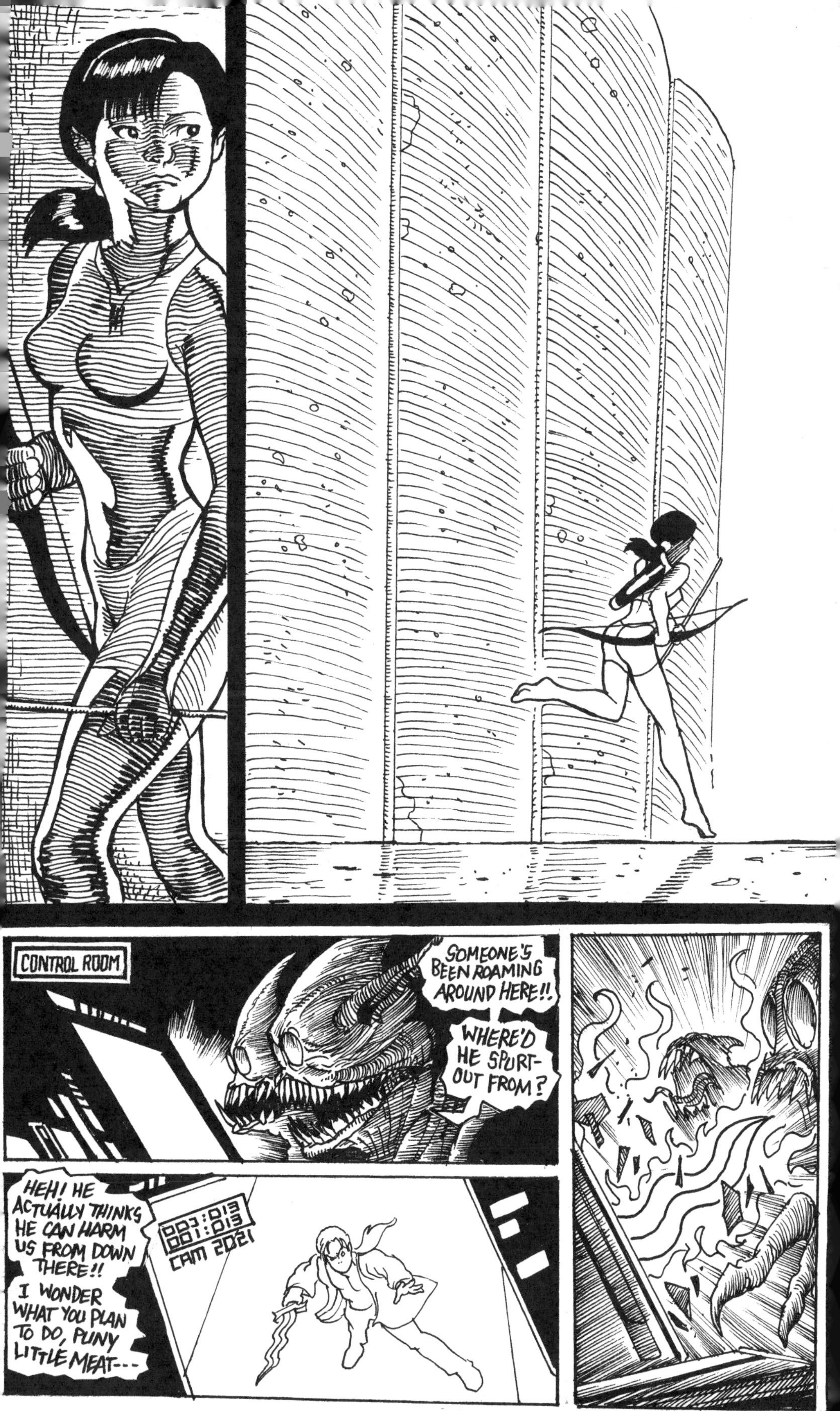
CONTROL ROOM
SOMEONE'S BEEN ROAMING AROUND HERE!!
WHERE'D HE SPURT-OUT FROM?
HEH! HE ACTUALLY THINKS HE CAN HARM US FROM DOWN THERE!!
I WONDER WHAT YOU PLAN TO DO, PUNY LITTLE MEAT---
003:013
001:013
CAM 2021

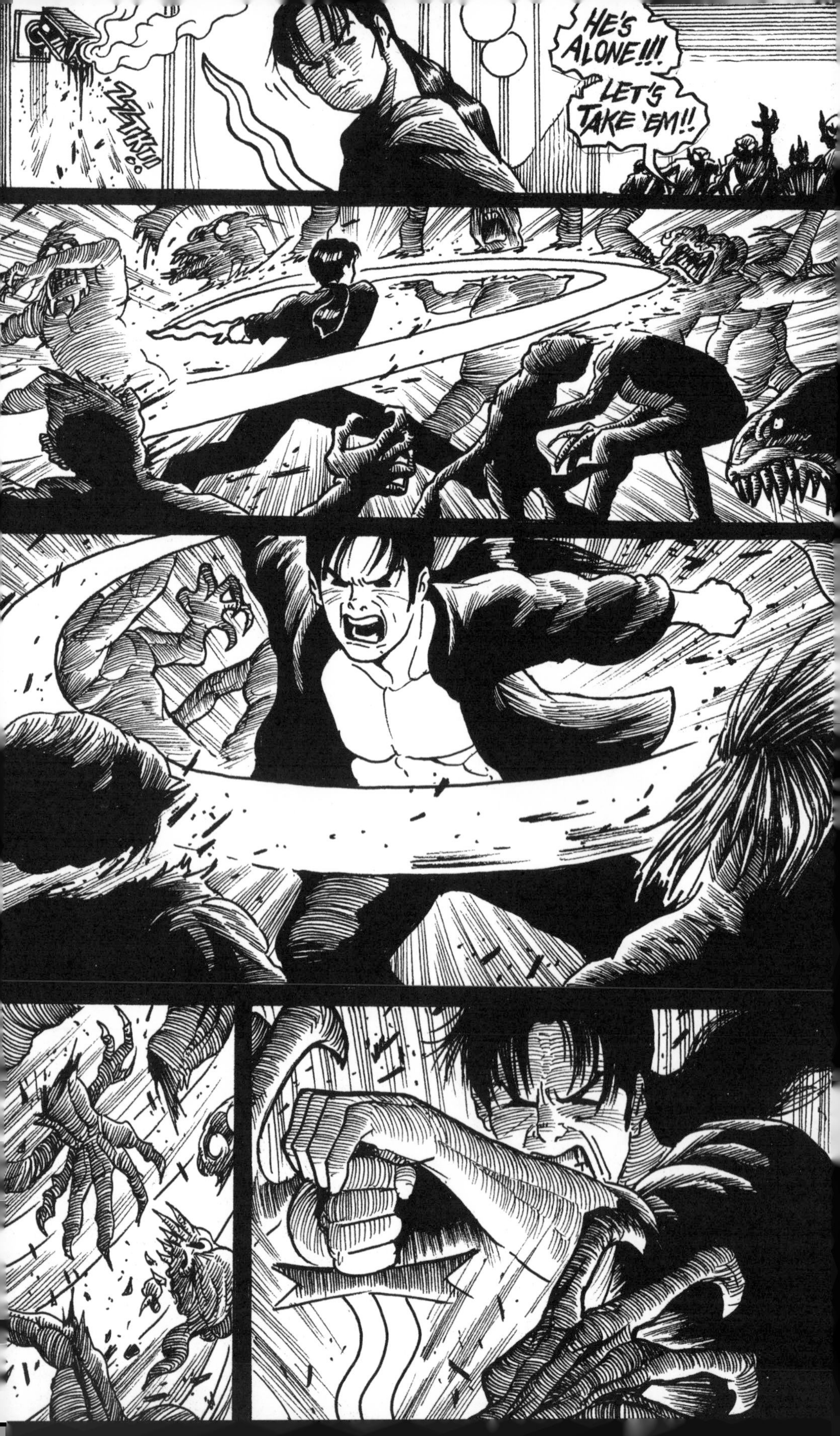
ZZZAT!!
HE'S ALONE!!!
LET'S TAKE 'EM!!

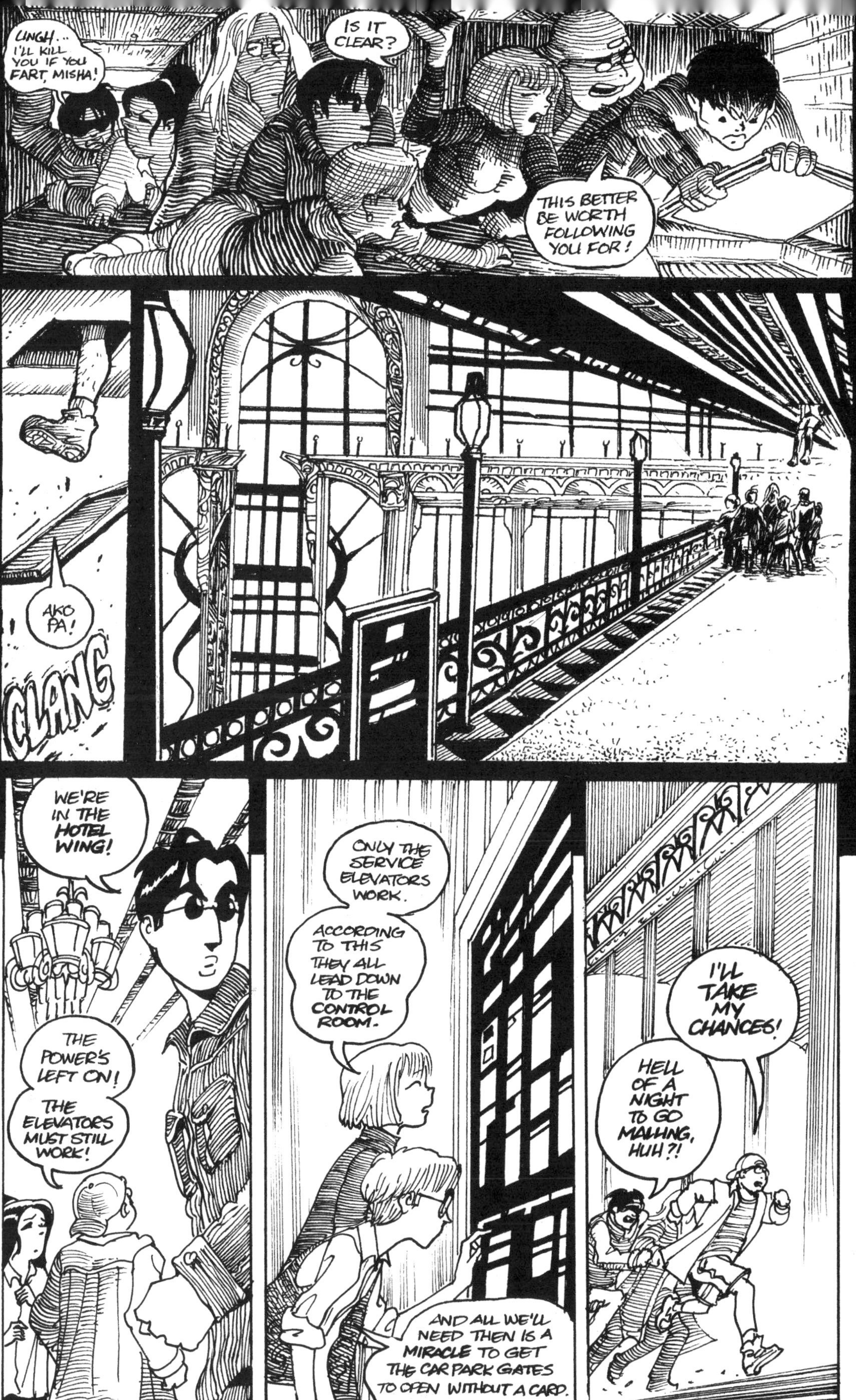
UNGH... I'LL KILL YOU IF YOU FART, MISHA!
IS IT CLEAR?
THIS BETTER BE WORTH FOLLOWING YOU FOR!
AKO PA!
CLANG
WE'RE IN THE HOTEL WING!
THE POWER'S LEFT ON!
THE ELEVATORS MUST STILL WORK!
ONLY THE SERVICE ELEVATORS WORK.
ACCORDING TO THIS THEY ALL LEAD DOWN TO THE CONTROL ROOM.
AND ALL WE'LL NEED THEN IS A MIRACLE TO GET THE CAR PARK GATES TO OPEN WITHOUT A CARD.
I'LL TAKE MY CHANCES!
HELL OF A NIGHT TO GO MALLING, HUH?!

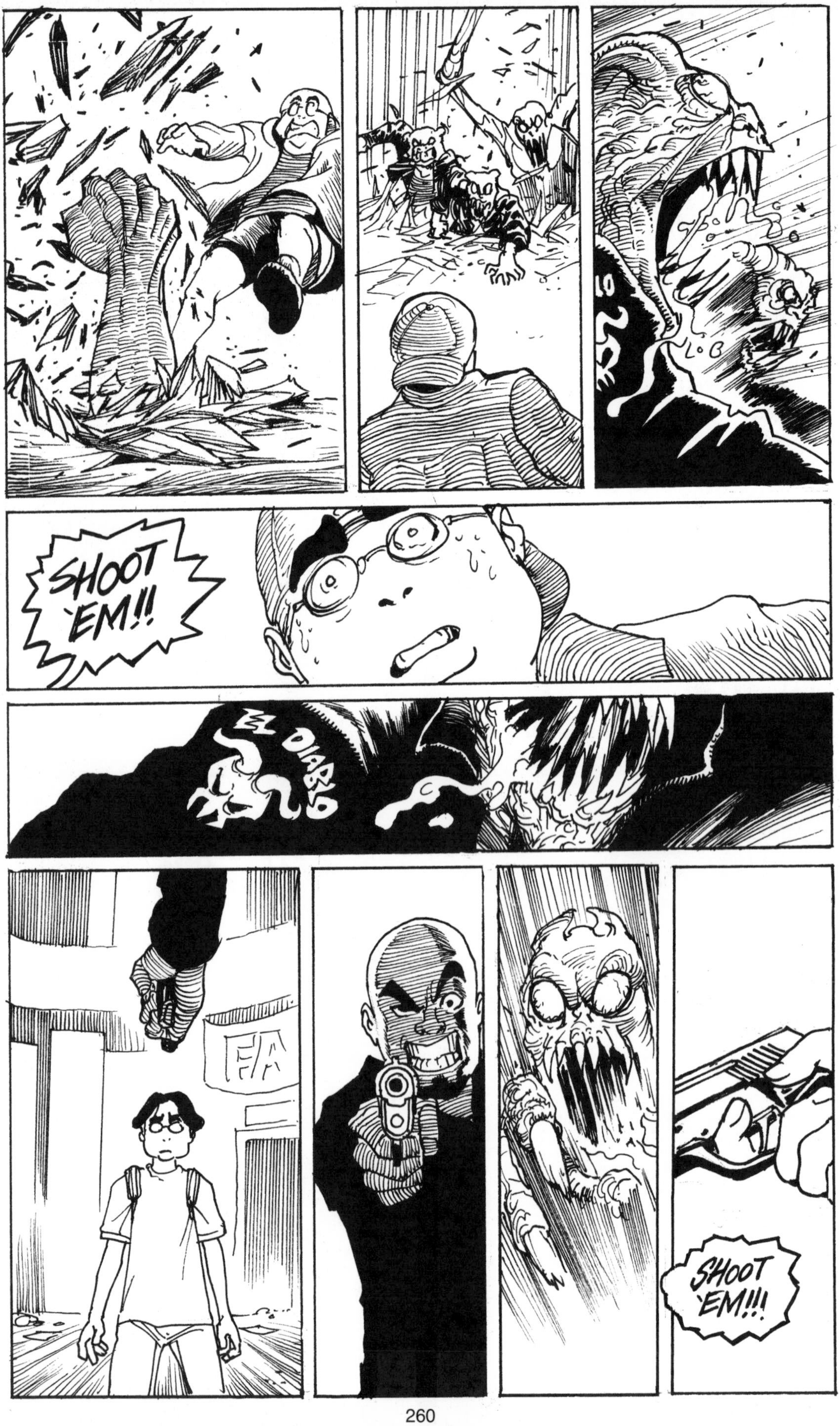

SHOOT 'EM!!
EL DIABLO
SHOOT 'EM!!!

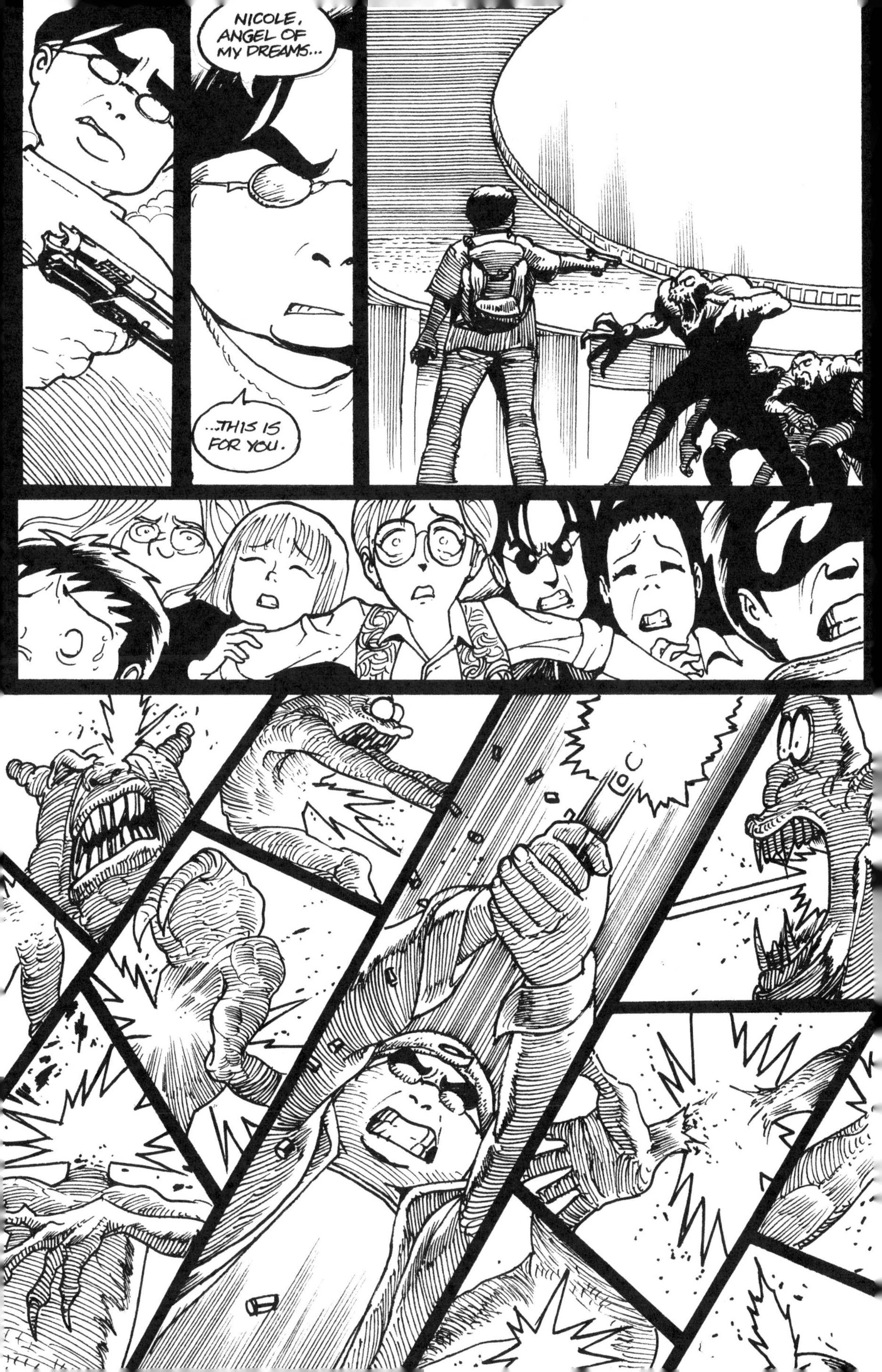
NICOLE, ANGEL OF MY DREAMS...
...THIS IS FOR YOU.

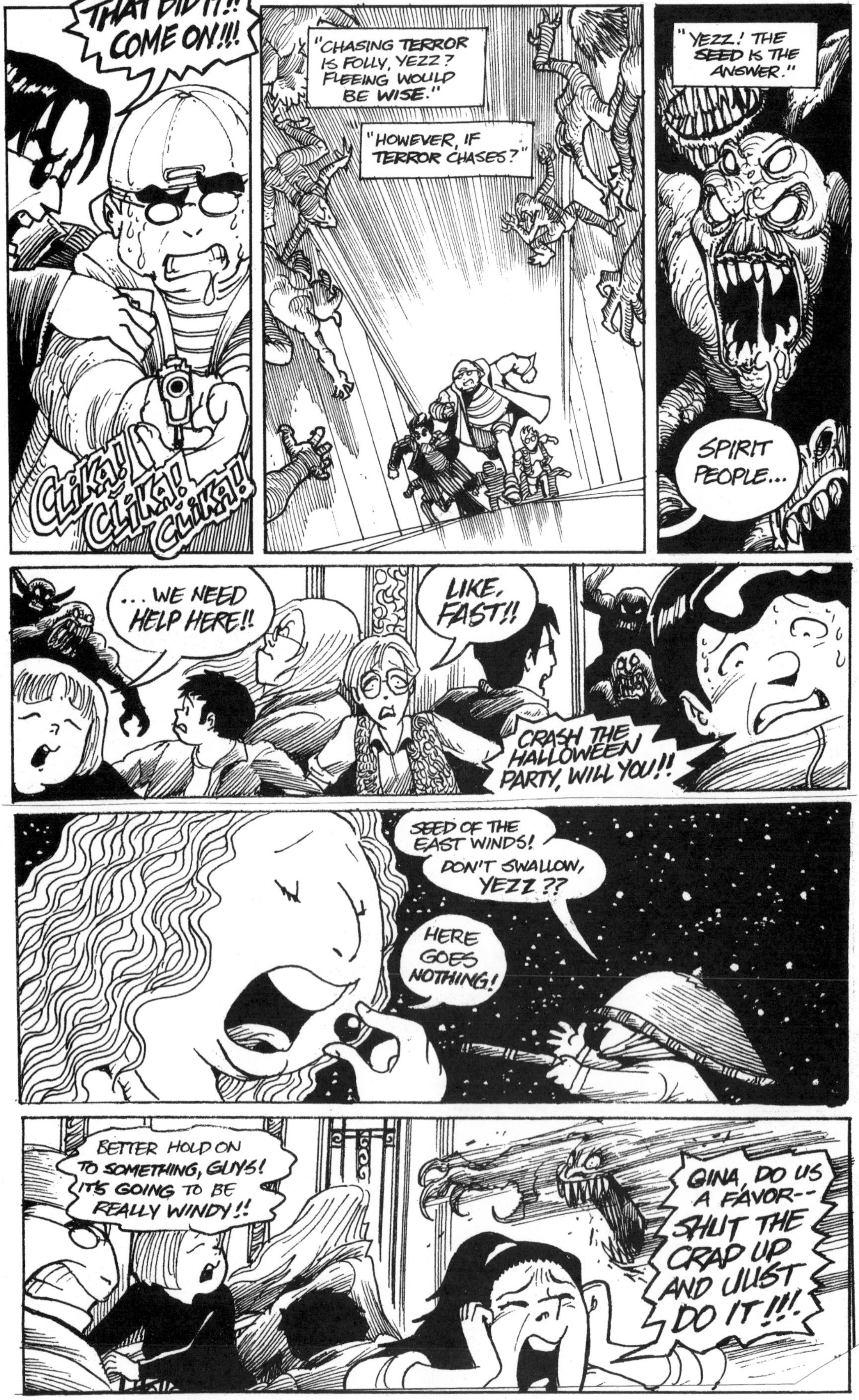
THAT DID IT!! COME ON!!!
CLIKA! CLIKA! CLIKA!
"CHASING TERROR IS FOLLY, YEZZ? FLEEING WOULD BE WISE."
"HOWEVER, IF TERROR CHASES?"
"YEZZ! THE SEED IS THE ANSWER."
SPIRIT PEOPLE...
...WE NEED HELP HERE!!
LIKE, FAST!!
CRASH THE HALLOWEEN PARTY, WILL YOU!!
SEED OF THE EAST WINDS! DON'T SWALLOW, YEZZ??
HERE GOES NOTHING!
BETTER HOLD ON TO SOMETHING, GUYS! IT'S GOING TO BE REALLY WINDY!!
QINA, DO US A FAVOR-- SHUT THE CRAP UP AND JUST DO IT!!!

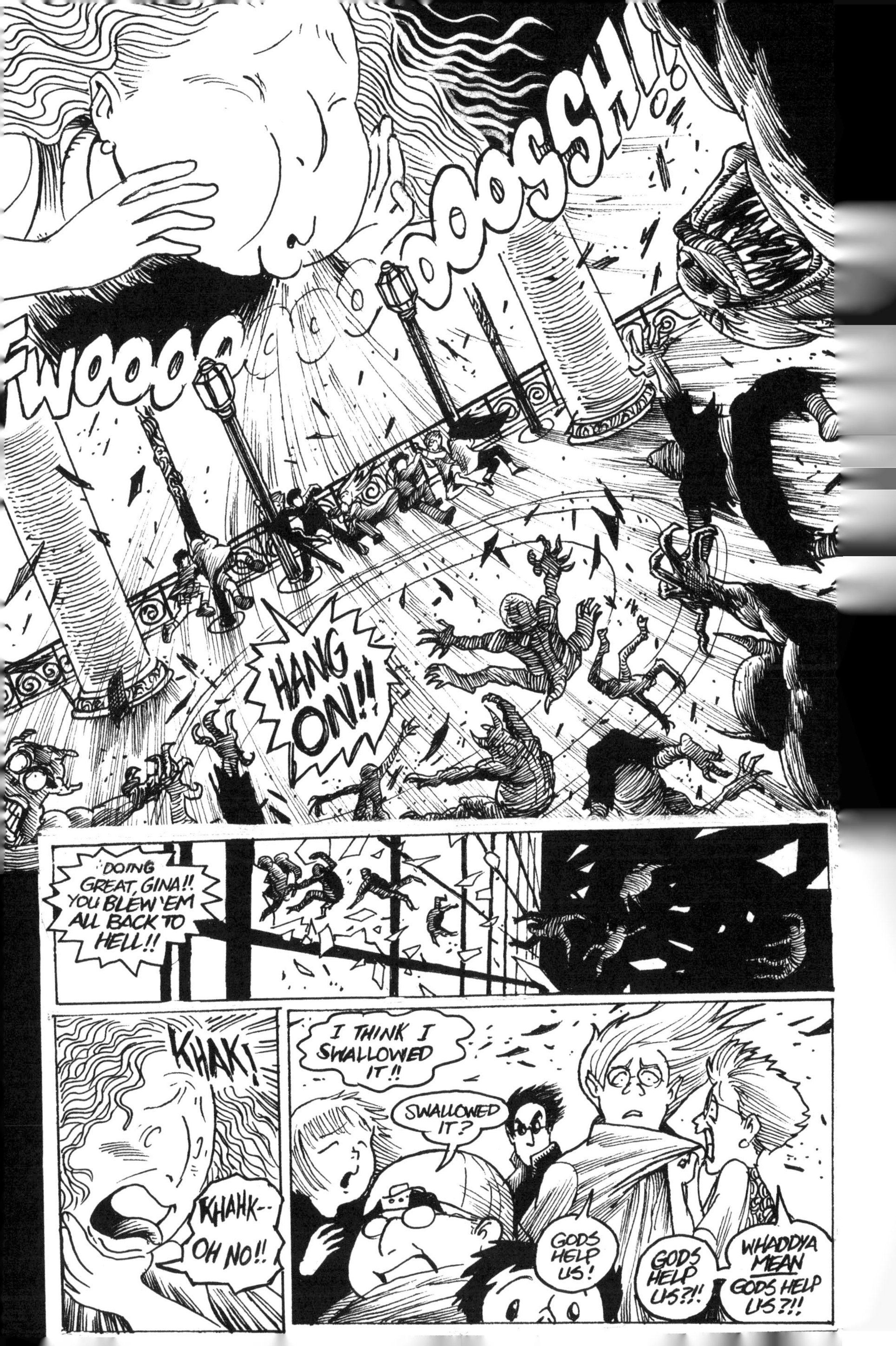
FWOOOOOOOOOSH!!
HANG ON!!
DOING GREAT, GINA!! YOU BLEW 'EM ALL BACK TO HELL!!
KHAK!
KHAHK--
OH NO!!
I THINK I SWALLOWED IT!!
SWALLOWED IT?
GODS HELP US!
GODS HELP US?!!
WHADDYA MEAN GODS HELP US?!!

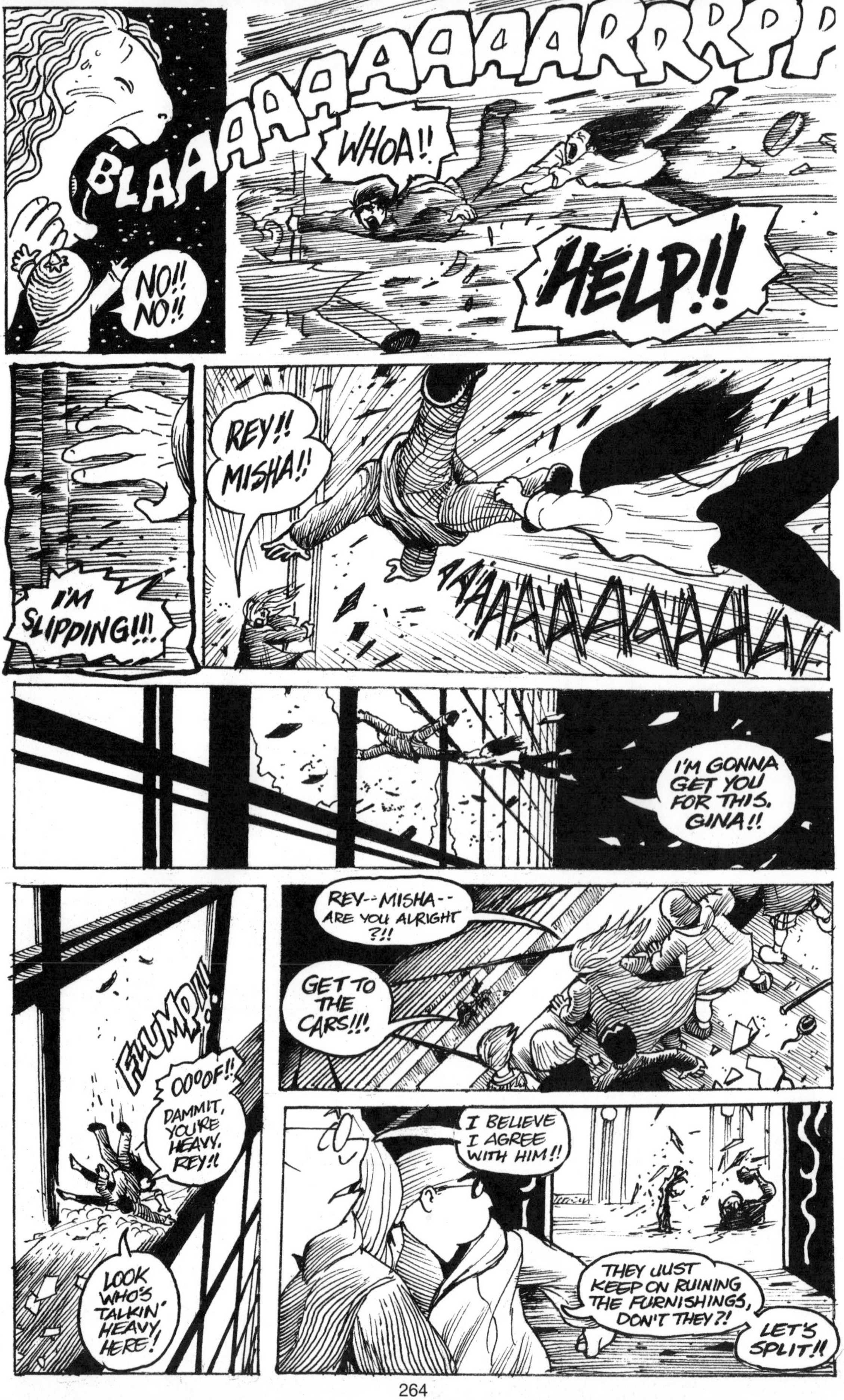
BLAAAAAAAAAAARRRPP
WHOA!!
NO!! NO!!
HELP!!
REY!! MISHA!!
I'M SLIPPING!!!
AAAAAAAAAAAAAAAAALLL
I'M GONNA GET YOU FOR THIS, GINA!!
FLUMP!!
OOOOF!!
DAMMIT, YOU'RE HEAVY, REY!!
LOOK WHO'S TALKIN' HEAVY HERE!
REY--MISHA-- ARE YOU ALRIGHT ?!!
GET TO THE CARS!!!
I BELIEVE I AGREE WITH HIM!!
THEY JUST KEEP ON RUINING THE FURNISHINGS, DON'T THEY?!
LET'S SPLIT!!

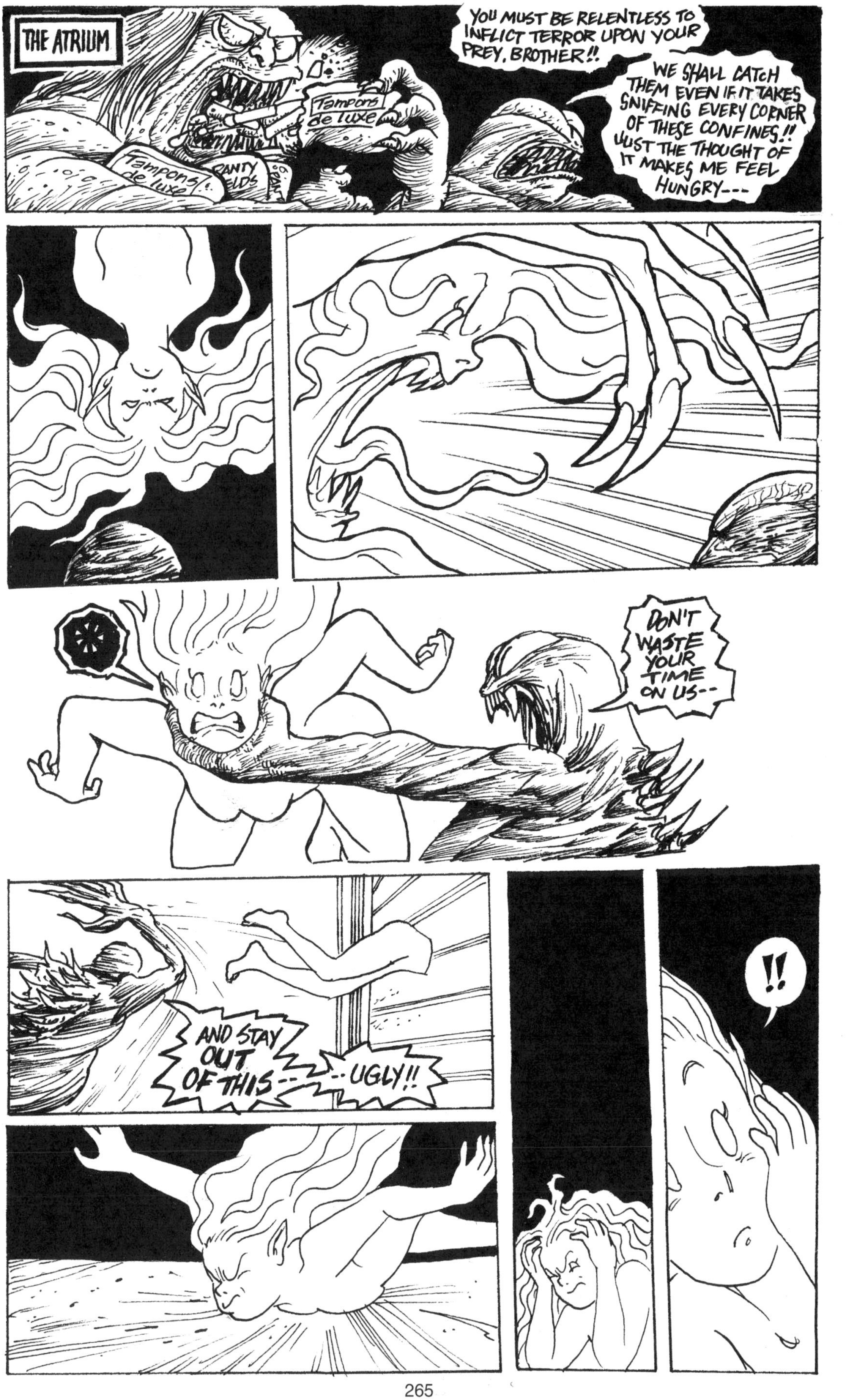
THE ATRIUM
Tampons de luxe
Tampons de luxe
PANTY SHIELDS
YOU MUST BE RELENTLESS TO INFLICT TERROR UPON YOUR PREY, BROTHER!!
WE SHALL CATCH THEM EVEN IF IT TAKES SNIFFING EVERY CORNER OF THESE CONFINES!! JUST THE THOUGHT OF IT MAKES ME FEEL HUNGRY---
DON'T WASTE YOUR TIME ON US--
AND STAY OUT OF THIS--
--UGLY!!
!!

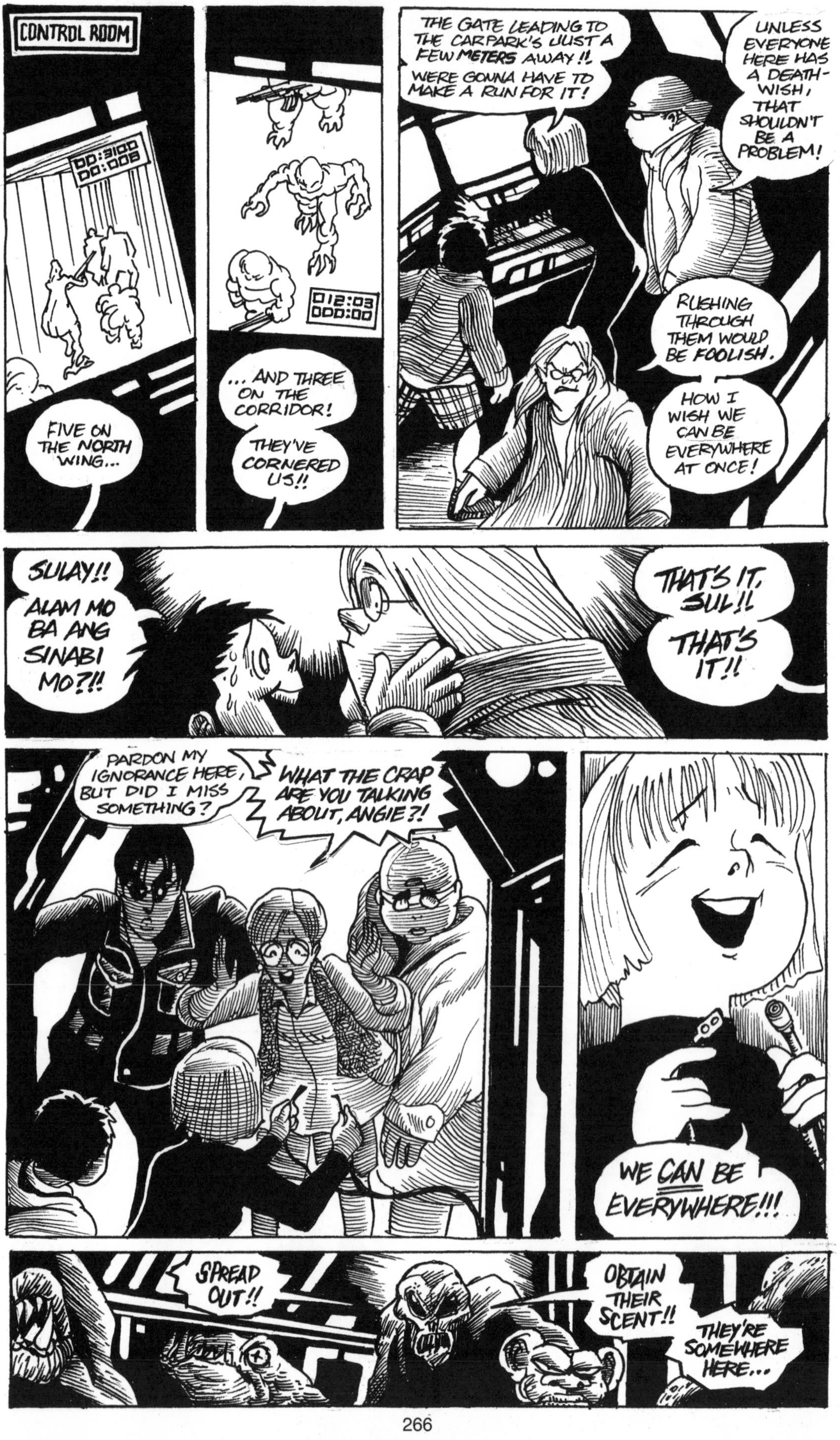
CONTROL ROOM
FIVE ON THE NORTH WING...
... AND THREE ON THE CORRIDOR!
THEY'VE CORNERED US!!
THE GATE LEADING TO THE CARPARK'S JUST A FEW METERS AWAY!!
WERE GONNA HAVE TO MAKE A RUN FOR IT!
UNLESS EVERYONE HERE HAS A DEATH-WISH, THAT SHOULDN'T BE A PROBLEM!
RUSHING THROUGH THEM WOULD BE FOOLISH.
HOW I WISH WE CAN BE EVERYWHERE AT ONCE!
SULAY!! ALAM MO BA ANG SINABI MO?!!
THAT'S IT, SUL!!
THAT'S IT!!
PARDON MY IGNORANCE HERE, BUT DID I MISS SOMETHING?
WHAT THE CRAP ARE YOU TALKING ABOUT, ANGIE?!
WE CAN BE EVERYWHERE!!!
SPREAD OUT!!
OBTAIN THEIR SCENT!!
THEY'RE SOMEWHERE HERE...

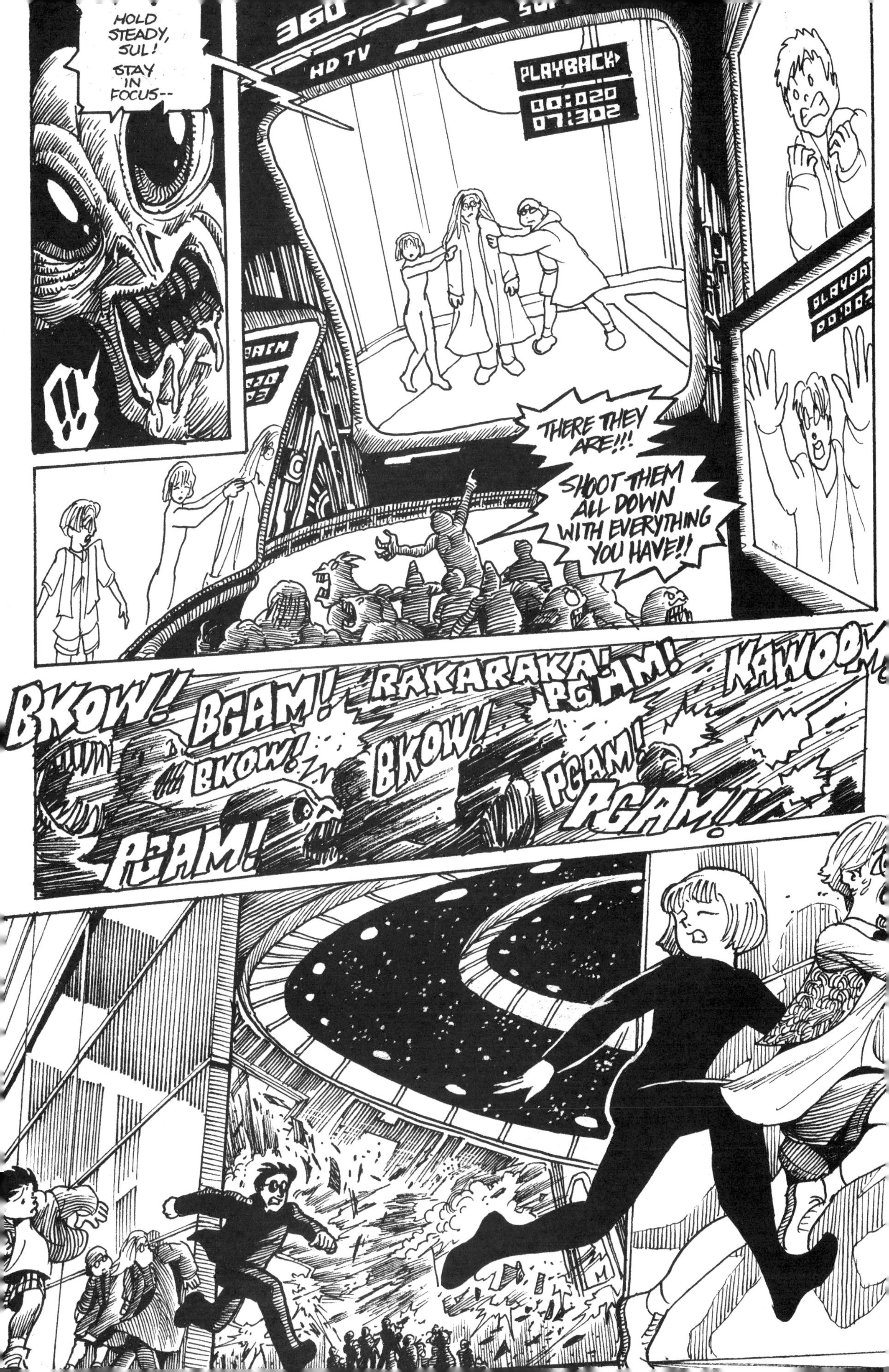

HOLD STEADY, SUL! STAY IN FOCUS--
HD TV
PLAYBACK
00:020
07:302
!!
THERE THEY ARE!!!
SHOOT THEM ALL DOWN WITH EVERYTHING YOU HAVE!!
BKOW!
BGAM!
RAKARAKA!
PGAM!
KAWOO
BKOW!
BKOW!
PGAM!
PGAM!
PGAM!

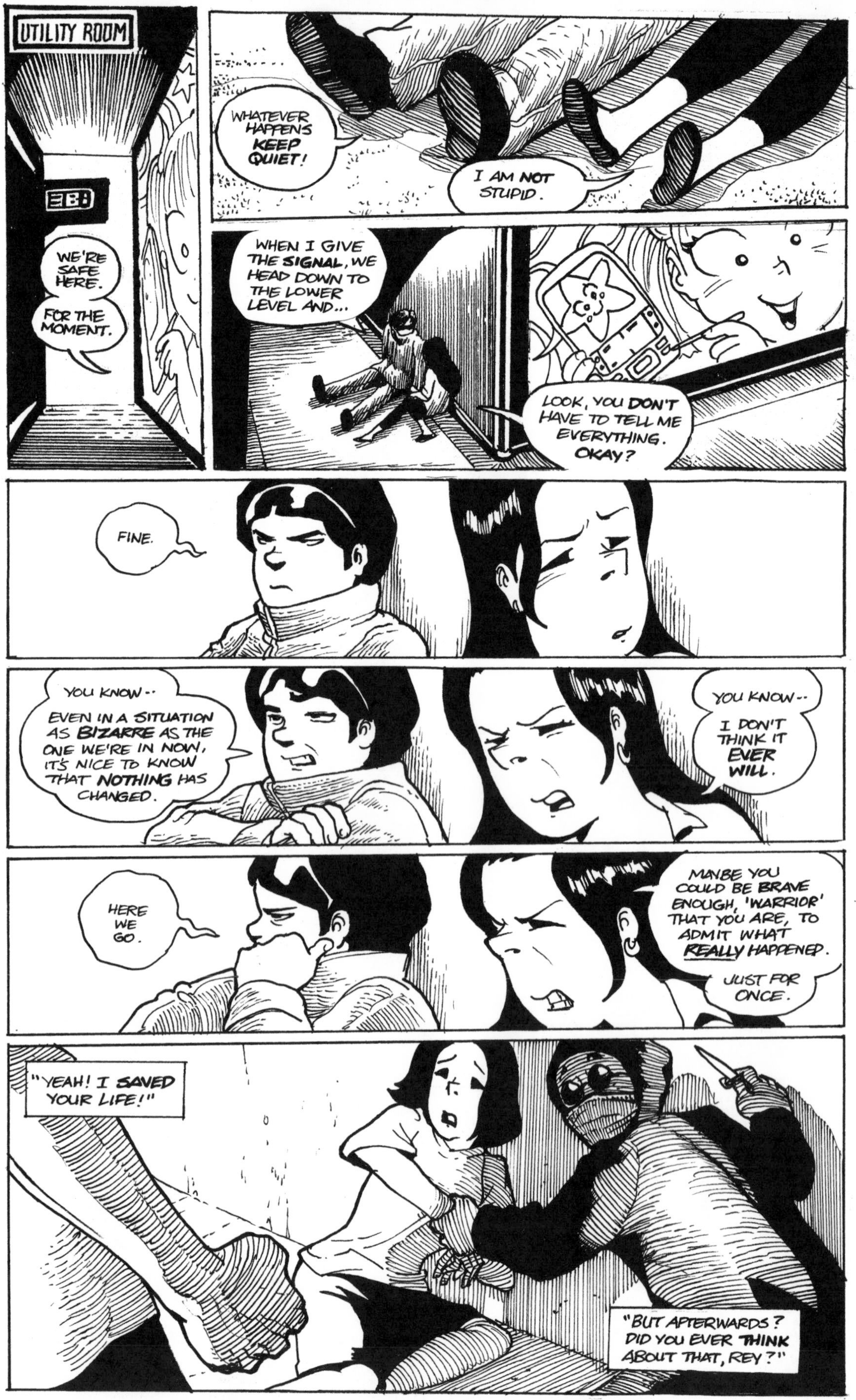
UTILITY ROOM
WHATEVER HAPPENS KEEP QUIET!
I AM NOT STUPID.
WE'RE SAFE HERE.
FOR THE MOMENT.
WHEN I GIVE THE SIGNAL, WE HEAD DOWN TO THE LOWER LEVEL AND...
LOOK, YOU DON'T HAVE TO TELL ME EVERYTHING. OKAY?
FINE.
YOU KNOW-- EVEN IN A SITUATION AS BIZARRE AS THE ONE WE'RE IN NOW, IT'S NICE TO KNOW THAT NOTHING HAS CHANGED.
YOU KNOW-- I DON'T THINK IT EVER WILL.
HERE WE GO.
MAYBE YOU COULD BE BRAVE ENOUGH, 'WARRIOR' THAT YOU ARE, TO ADMIT WHAT REALLY HAPPENED.
JUST FOR ONCE.
"YEAH! I SAVED YOUR LIFE!"
"BUT AFTERWARDS? DID YOU EVER THINK ABOUT THAT, REY?"

THANK YOU FOR SAVING ME.

YEAH. YOU SURELY DID. BUT YOU COULDN'T SAVE ME FROM YOURSELF.

YOU HELD ME UNDER LOCK AND KEY.

SO WHAT WAS I SUPPOSED TO DO...

...WHEN US BEING TOGETHER AND EVERYTHING ELSE...

...WAS JUST ONE BIG OBLIGATION AND NOTHING MORE?

BUT I DO APPRECIATE WHAT YOU'VE DONE FOR ME. I DO. I LEARNED A LOT THESE PAST FEW MONTHS AND YOU KNOW WHAT?

I'M THROUGH ARGUING. I'M TIRED OF IT.

SO I'VE BEEN DOING A LOT OF THINKING AND I KNOW WE CAN MAKE THIS WORK.

REY... WHAT I'M TRYING TO SAY IS...IS...

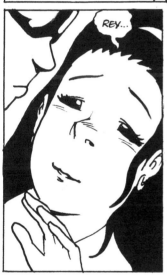
REY...

YEAH, I KNOW! IT'S NOT GONNA WORK, RIGHT?

WHAT?

SURE! I UNDERSTAND! HEY, I'M JUST THIS LOSER WHO'S BEEN IN LOVE WITH YOU FOREVER! WHY WOULD IT MATTER, RIGHT?!

WAIT! YOU DIDN'T LET ME FINISH--

WELL, I'VE PUT UP WITH YOU FAR TOO LONG. SO I'VE DONE MY OWN THINKING.

MISHA, IT IS OVER. I'M THROUGH WITH YOU. I WAS NEVER IN LOVE AND YOU NEVER MEANT ANYTHING TO ME.

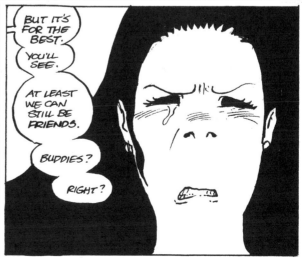
BUT IT'S FOR THE BEST. YOU'LL SEE.

AT LEAST WE CAN STILL BE FRIENDS.

BUDDIES?

RIGHT?

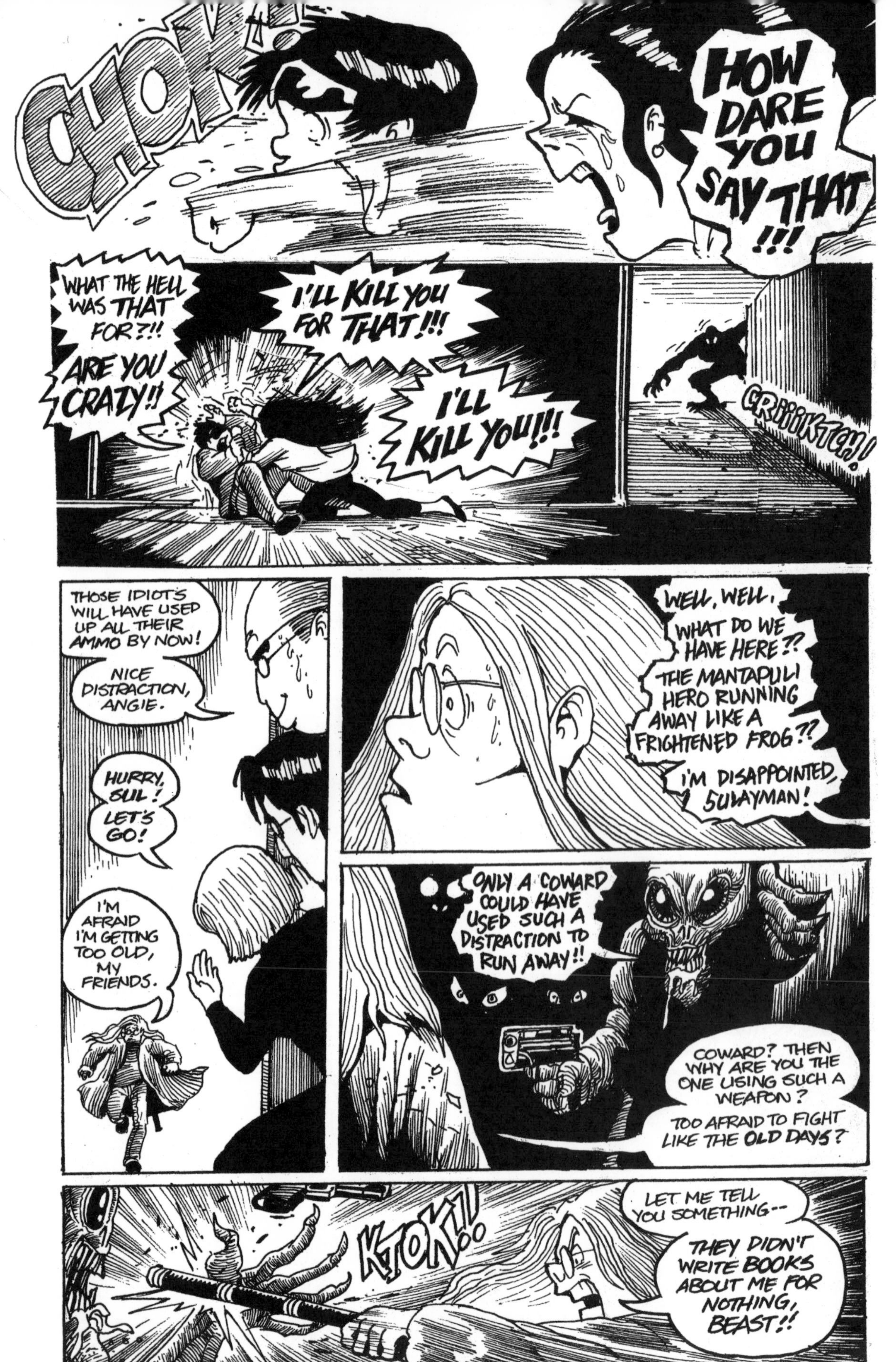
CHOK!!
HOW DARE YOU SAY THAT !!!
WHAT THE HELL WAS THAT FOR?!! ARE YOU CRAZY!!
I'LL KILL YOU FOR THAT!!!
I'LL KILL YOU!!!
CRIIIKTCH!!
THOSE IDIOTS WILL HAVE USED UP ALL THEIR AMMO BY NOW!
NICE DISTRACTION, ANGIE.
HURRY, SUL! LET'S GO!
I'M AFRAID I'M GETTING TOO OLD, MY FRIENDS.
WELL, WELL, WHAT DO WE HAVE HERE?? THE MANTAPULI HERO RUNNING AWAY LIKE A FRIGHTENED FROG??
I'M DISAPPOINTED, SULAYMAN!
ONLY A COWARD COULD HAVE USED SUCH A DISTRACTION TO RUN AWAY!!
COWARD? THEN WHY ARE YOU THE ONE USING SUCH A WEAPON?
TOO AFRAID TO FIGHT LIKE THE OLD DAYS?
KTOK!!
LET ME TELL YOU SOMETHING--
THEY DIDN'T WRITE BOOKS ABOUT ME FOR NOTHING, BEAST!!

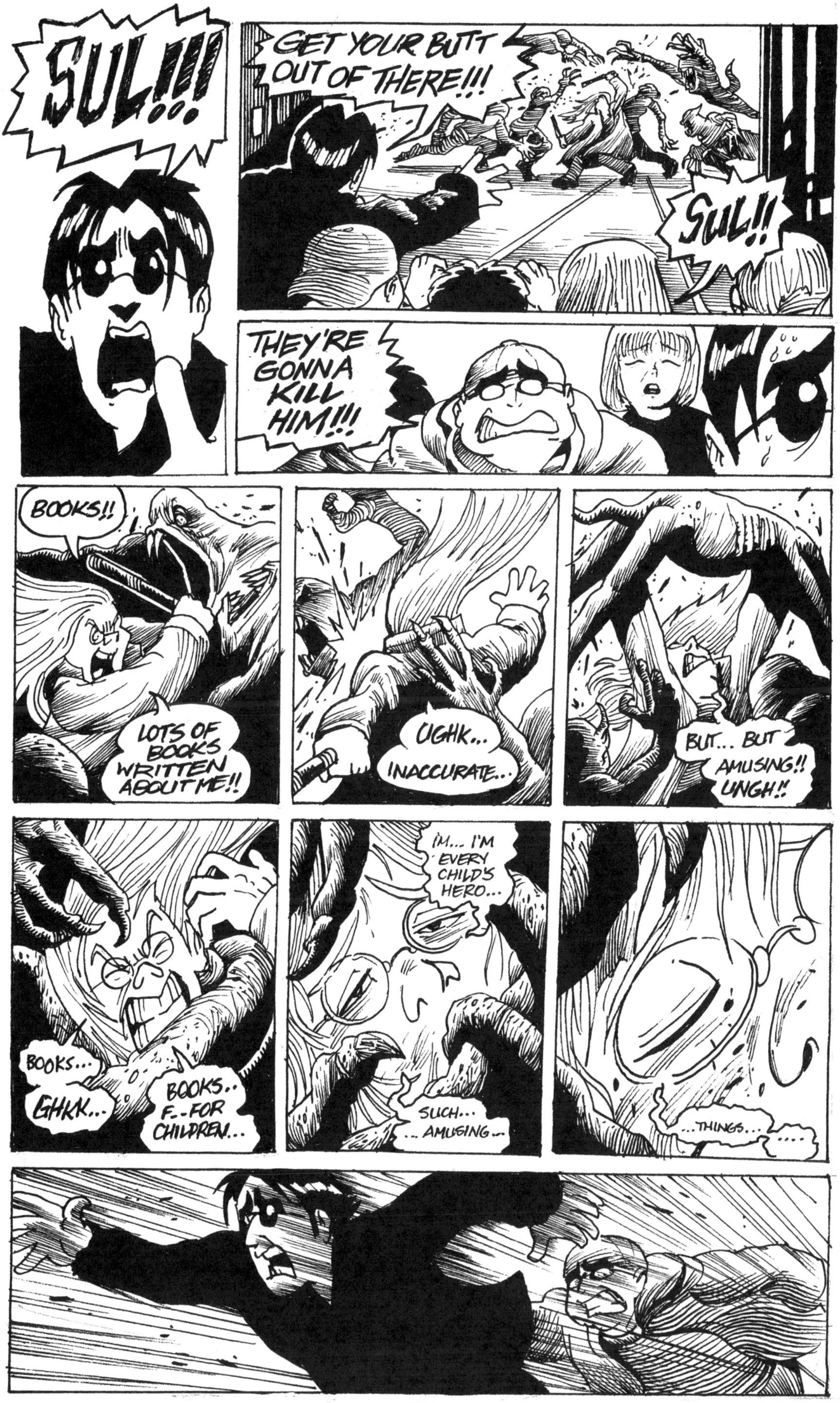
SUL!!!
GET YOUR BUTT OUT OF THERE!!!
SUL!!
THEY'RE GONNA KILL HIM!!!
BOOKS!!
LOTS OF BOOKS WRITTEN ABOUT ME!!
UGHK...
INACCURATE...
BUT... BUT
AMUSING!! UNGH!!
BOOKS...
GHKK...
BOOKS.. F..FOR CHILDREN...
I'M... I'M EVERY CHILD'S HERO...
SUCH...
...AMUSING...
...THINGS...
.....

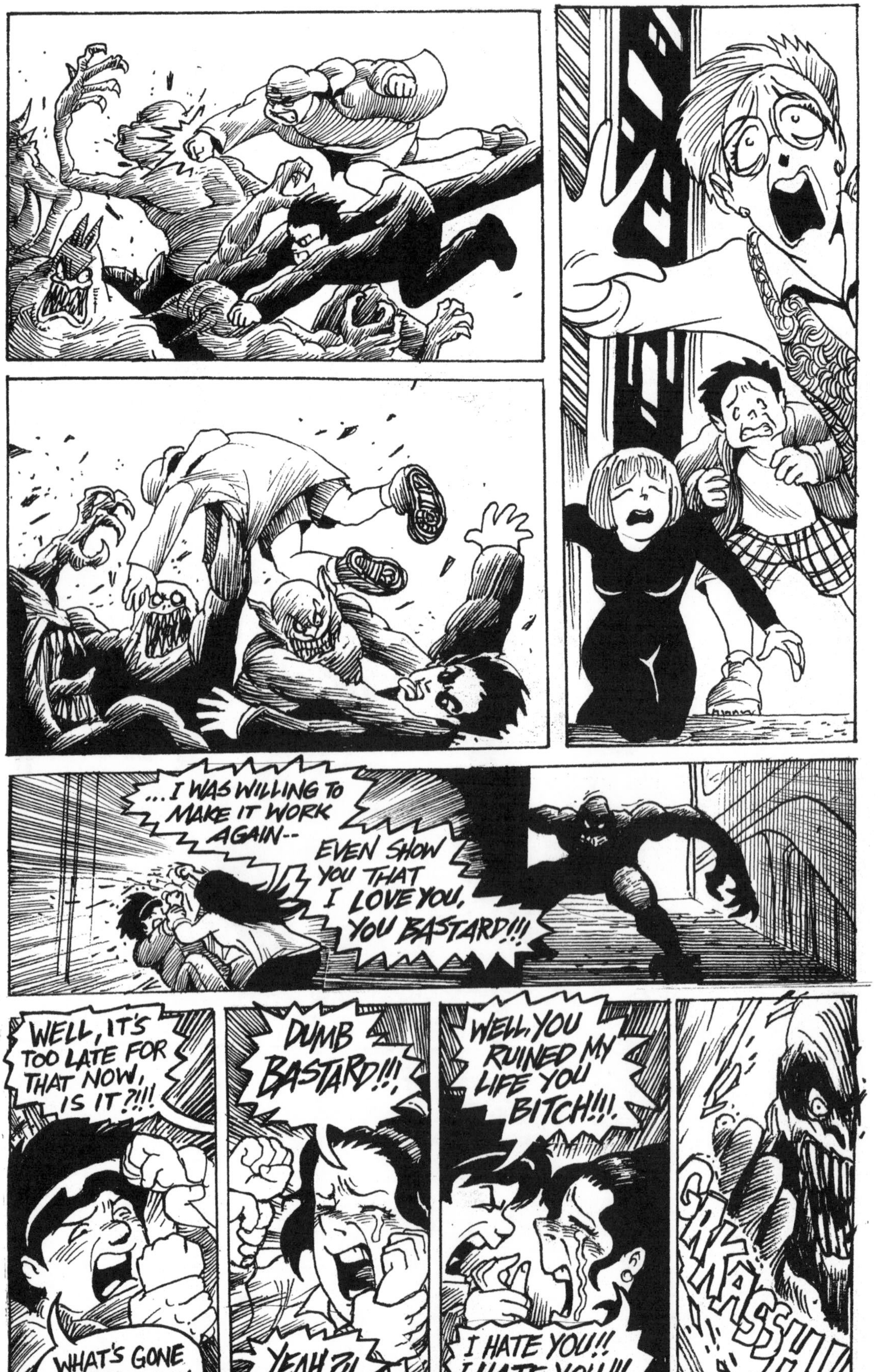
...I WAS WILLING TO MAKE IT WORK AGAIN--
EVEN SHOW YOU THAT I LOVE YOU, YOU BASTARD!!!
WELL, IT'S TOO LATE FOR THAT NOW, IS IT?!!!
WHAT'S GONE WRONG WITH YOU?!!
DUMB BASTARD!!!
YEAH?!!
WELL, YOU RUINED MY LIFE YOU BITCH!!!
I HATE YOU!! I HATE YOU!!! I HATE---
GRKASSH!!

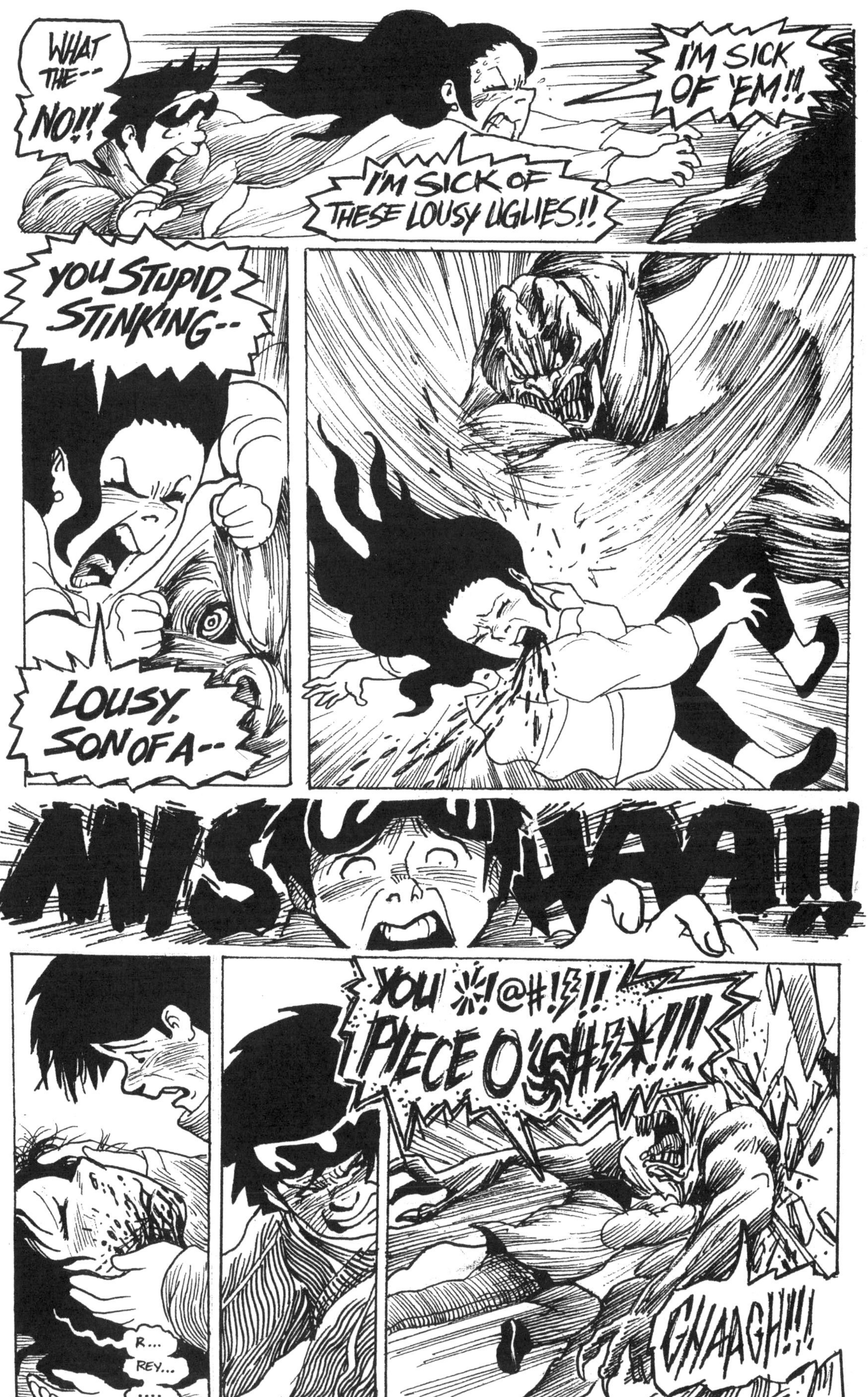

WHAT THE-- NO!!
I'M SICK OF 'EM!!
I'M SICK OF THESE LOUSY UGLIES!!
YOU STUPID, STINKING--
LOUSY, SON OF A--
YOU ※!@#!!! PIECE O' SH!*!!
R... REY... ....
GNAAGH!!!

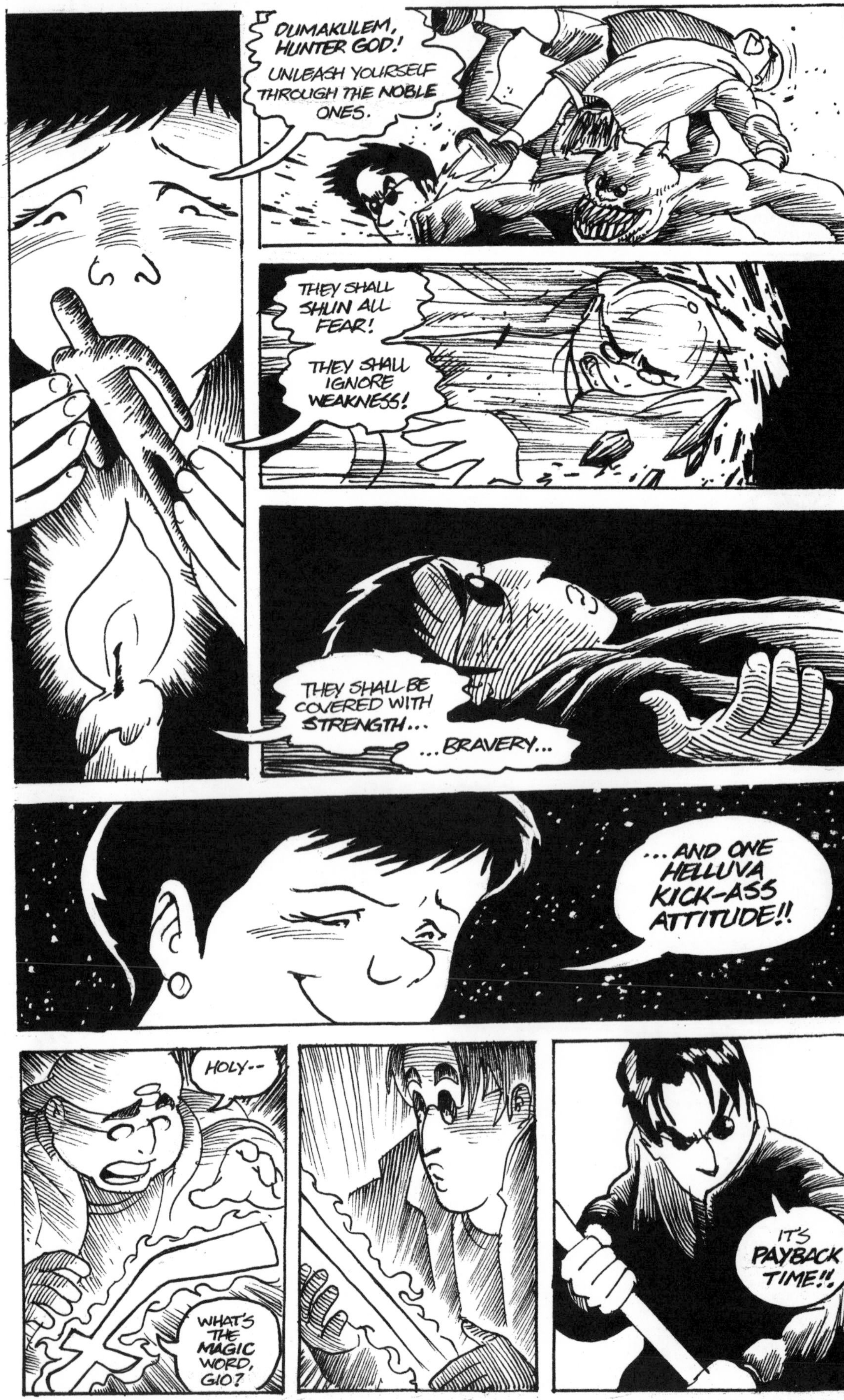
DUMAKULEM, HUNTER GOD!
UNLEASH YOURSELF THROUGH THE NOBLE ONES.
THEY SHALL SHUN ALL FEAR!
THEY SHALL IGNORE WEAKNESS!
THEY SHALL BE COVERED WITH STRENGTH...
...BRAVERY...
...AND ONE HELLUVA KICK-ASS ATTITUDE!!
HOLY--
WHAT'S THE MAGIC WORD, GIO?
IT'S PAYBACK TIME!!

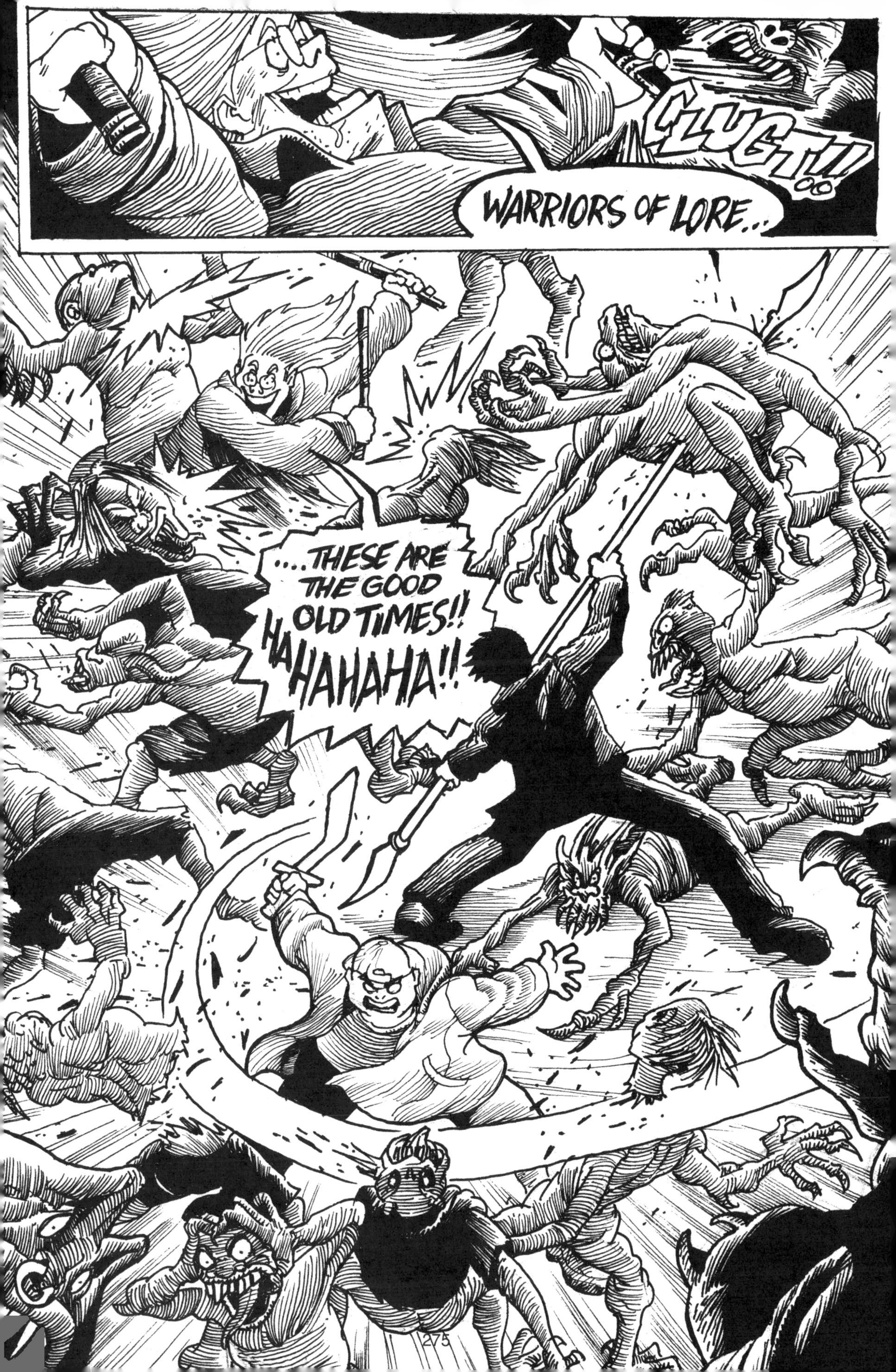

CLUG!!
WARRIORS OF LORE...
....THESE ARE THE GOOD OLD TIMES!!
HAHAHAHA!!

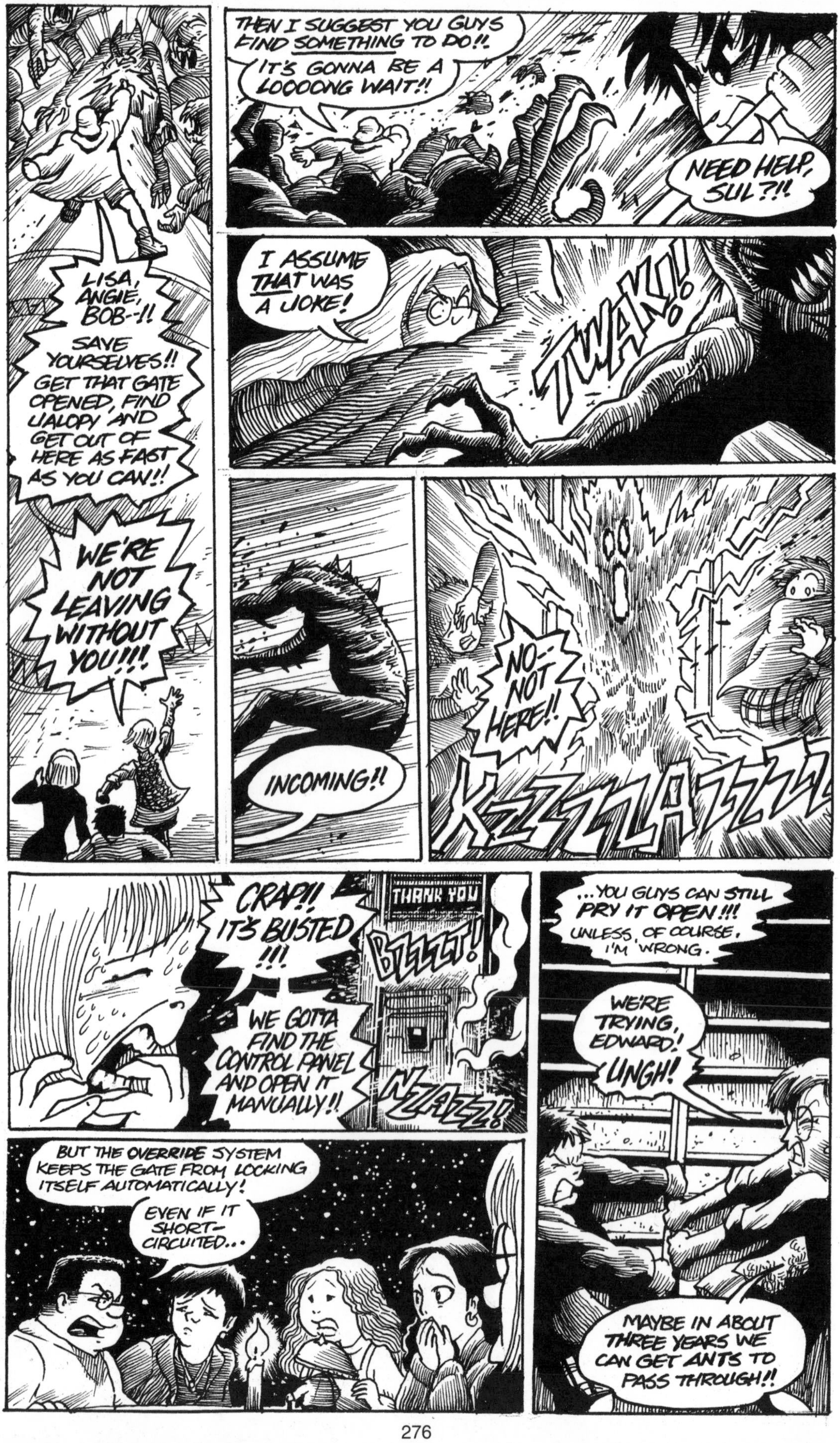
THEN I SUGGEST YOU GUYS FIND SOMETHING TO DO!!
IT'S GONNA BE A LOOOONG WAIT!!
NEED HELP, SUL?!!
LISA, ANGIE, BOB--!! SAVE YOURSELVES!! GET THAT GATE OPENED, FIND JALOPY AND GET OUT OF HERE AS FAST AS YOU CAN!!
I ASSUME THAT WAS A JOKE!
TWAK!
WE'RE NOT LEAVING WITHOUT YOU!!!
INCOMING!!
NO- NOT HERE!!
KZZZZAZZZ
CRAP!! IT'S BUSTED!!!
THANK YOU
BZZZT!
WE GOTTA FIND THE CONTROL PANEL AND OPEN IT MANUALLY!!
NZZZZ!
BUT THE OVERRIDE SYSTEM KEEPS THE GATE FROM LOCKING ITSELF AUTOMATICALLY!
EVEN IF IT SHORT-CIRCUITED...
...YOU GUYS CAN STILL PRY IT OPEN!!! UNLESS, OF COURSE, I'M WRONG.
WE'RE TRYING, EDWARD!
UNGH!
MAYBE IN ABOUT THREE YEARS WE CAN GET ANTS TO PASS THROUGH!!

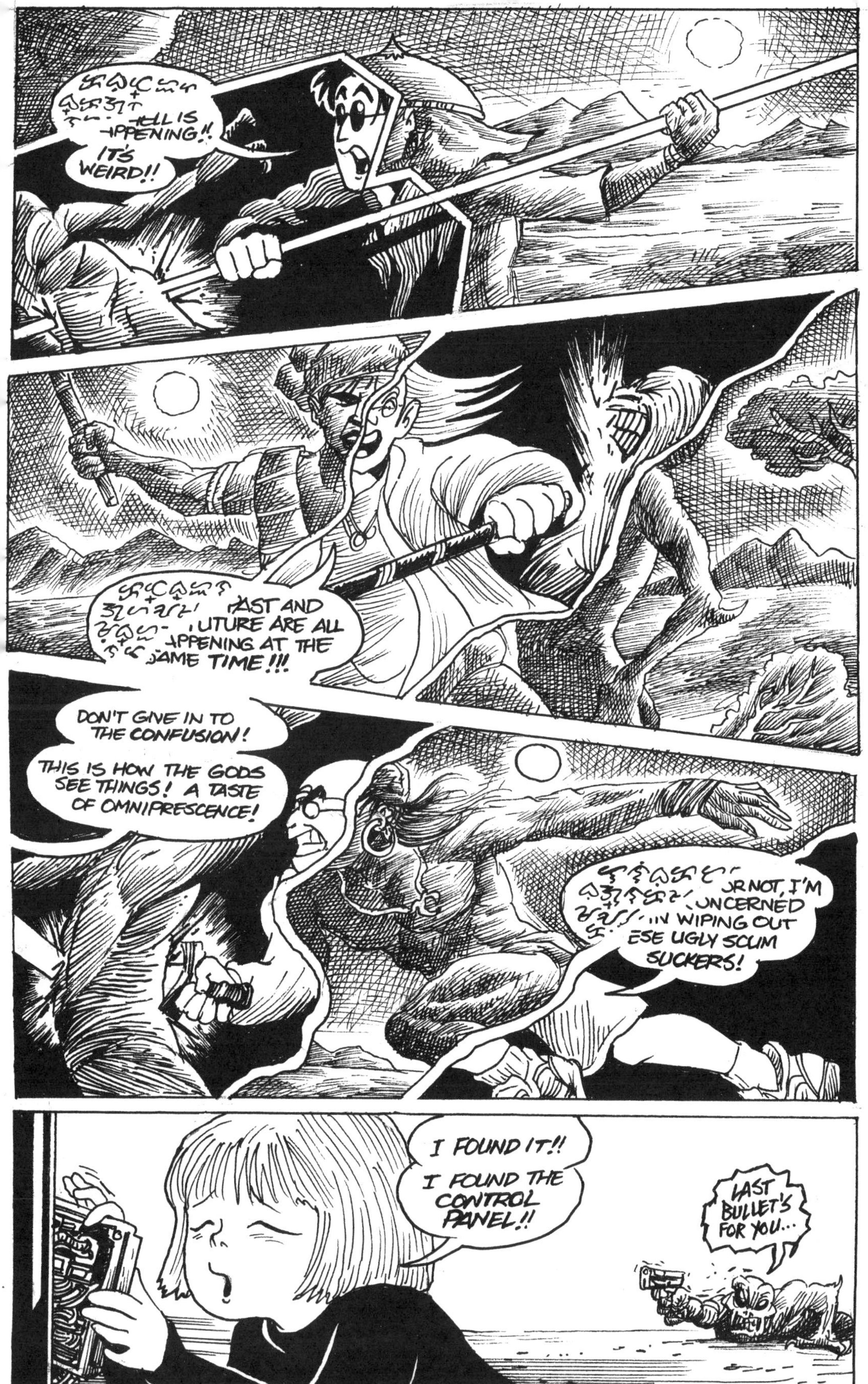

-HIS IS
-APPENING!!
IT'S WEIRD!!
-AST AND
-UTURE ARE ALL
-APPENING AT THE
-AME TIME!!!
DON'T GIVE IN TO THE CONFUSION!
THIS IS HOW THE GODS SEE THINGS! A TASTE OF OMNIPRESCENCE!
-R NOT, I'M
-UNCERNED
-N WIPING OUT
-ESE UGLY SCUM
SUCKERS!
I FOUND IT!!
I FOUND THE CONTROL PANEL!!
LAST BULLET'S FOR YOU...

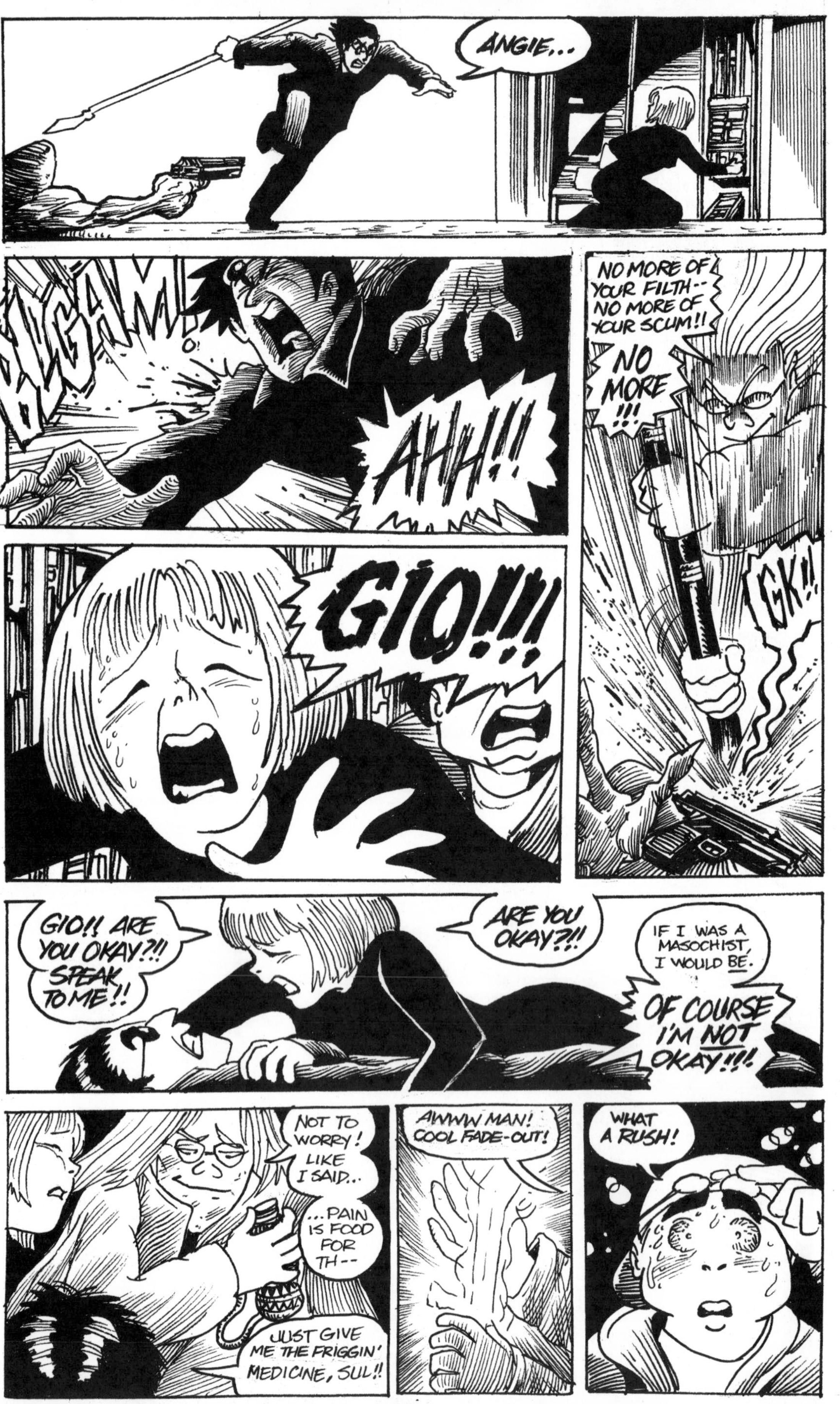
ANGIE...
BLGAM!
AHH!!
NO MORE OF YOUR FILTH-- NO MORE OF YOUR SCUM!!
NO MORE !!!
GK!!
GIO!!!
GIO!! ARE YOU OKAY?!! SPEAK TO ME!!
ARE YOU OKAY?!!
IF I WAS A MASOCHIST, I WOULD BE.
OF COURSE I'M NOT OKAY!!!
NOT TO WORRY! LIKE I SAID...
...PAIN IS FOOD FOR TH--
JUST GIVE ME THE FRIGGIN' MEDICINE, SUL!!
AWWW MAN! COOL FADE-OUT!
WHAT A RUSH!

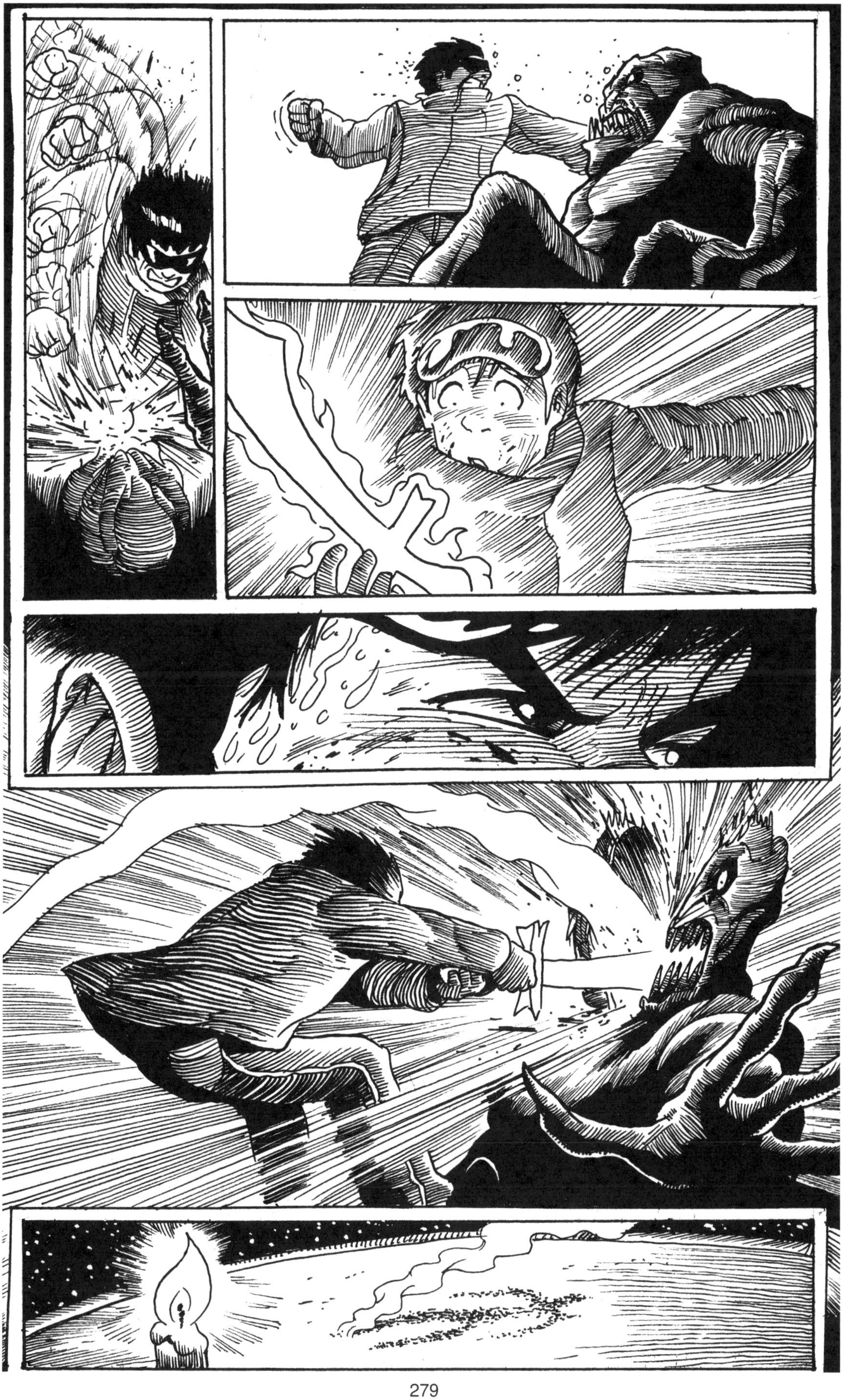

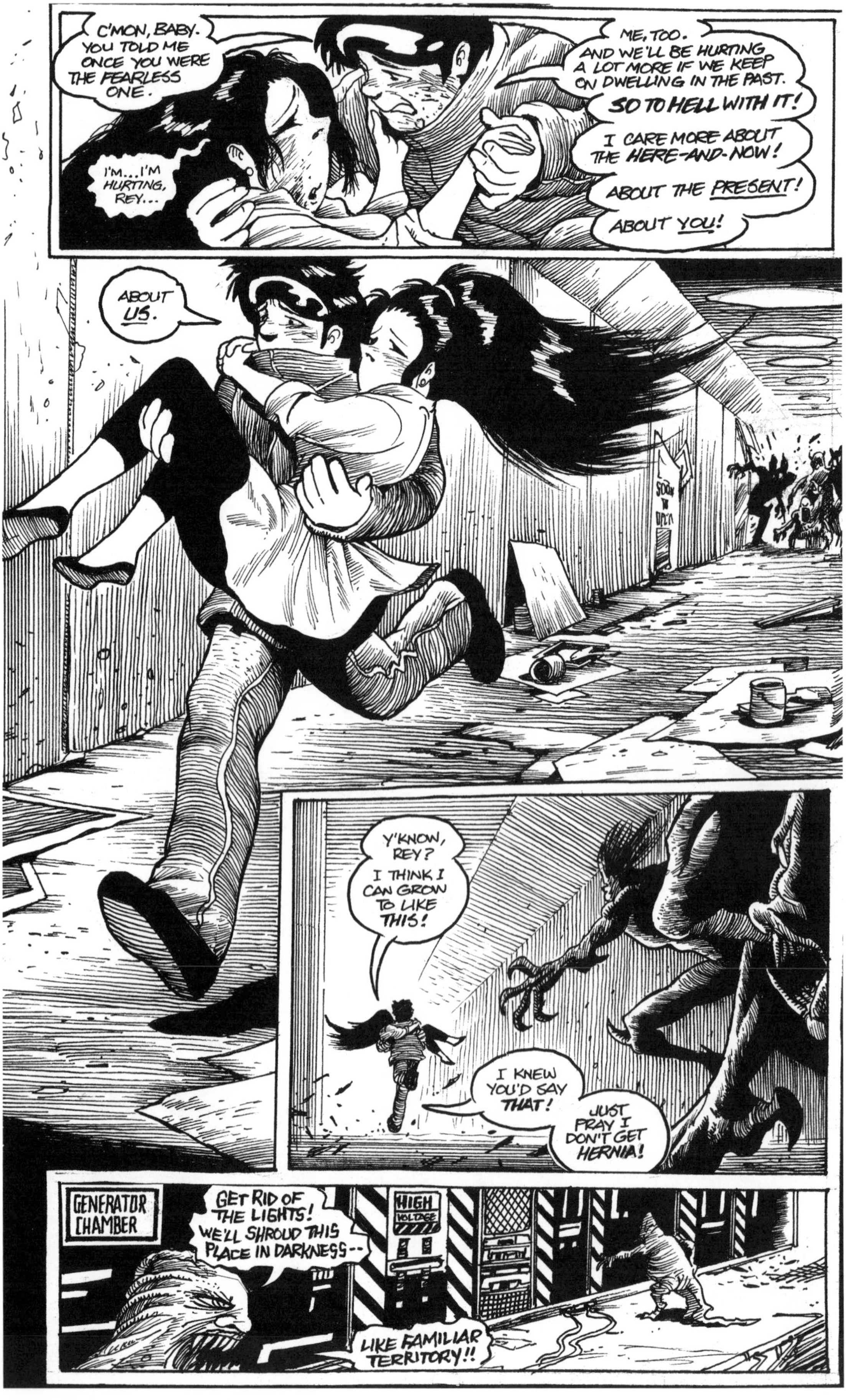

C'MON, BABY. YOU TOLD ME ONCE YOU WERE THE FEARLESS ONE.
I'M... I'M HURTING, REY...
ME, TOO. AND WE'LL BE HURTING A LOT MORE IF WE KEEP ON DWELLING IN THE PAST.
SO TO HELL WITH IT!
I CARE MORE ABOUT THE HERE-AND-NOW!
ABOUT THE PRESENT!
ABOUT YOU!
ABOUT US.
Y'KNOW, REY? I THINK I CAN GROW TO LIKE THIS!
I KNEW YOU'D SAY THAT!
JUST PRAY I DON'T GET HERNIA!
GENERATOR CHAMBER
HIGH VOLTAGE
GET RID OF THE LIGHTS! WE'LL SHROUD THIS PLACE IN DARKNESS--
LIKE FAMILIAR TERRITORY!!

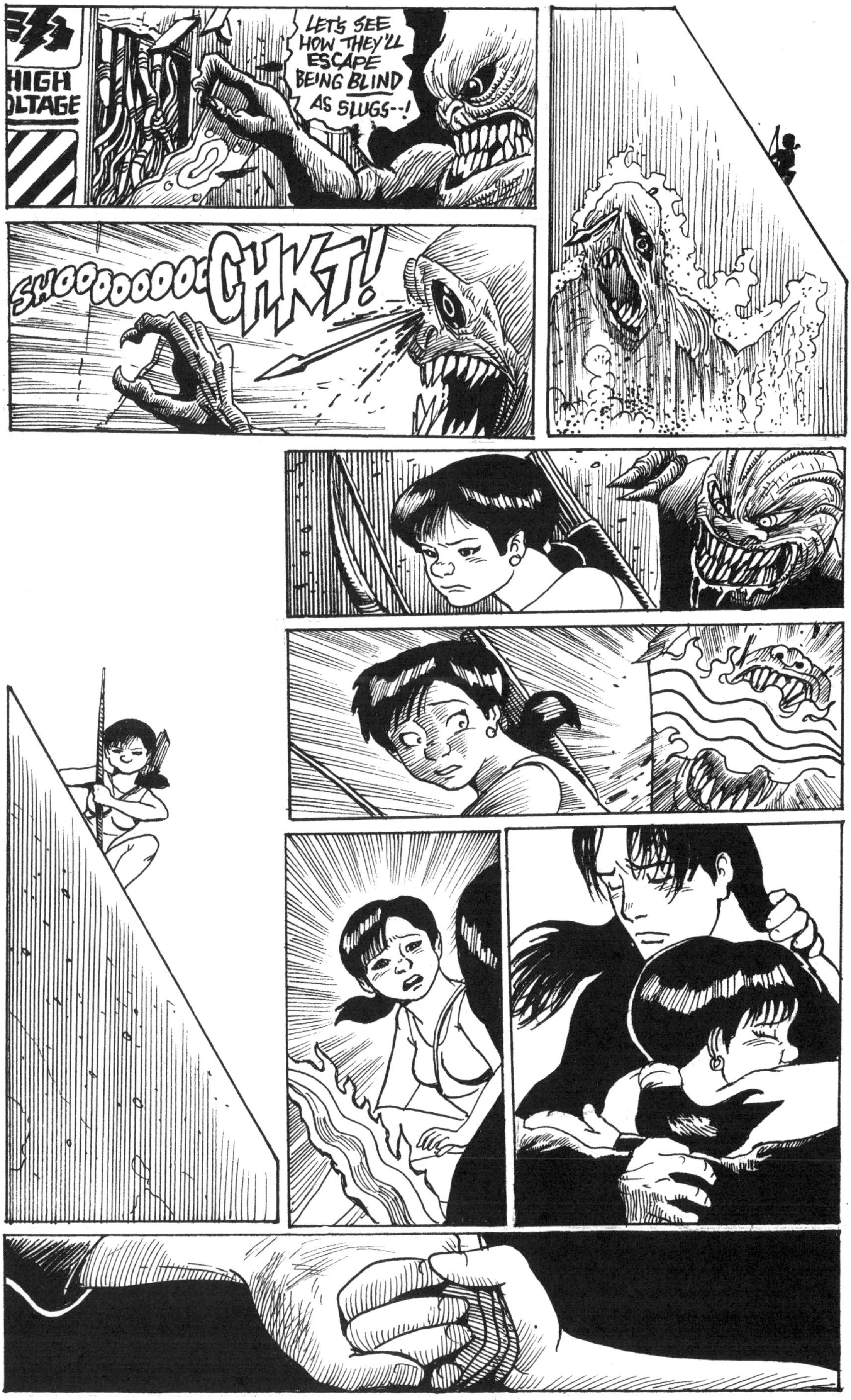
HIGH
OLTAGE
LET'S SEE HOW THEY'LL ESCAPE BEING BLIND AS SLUGS--!
SHOOOOOOOOCHKT!

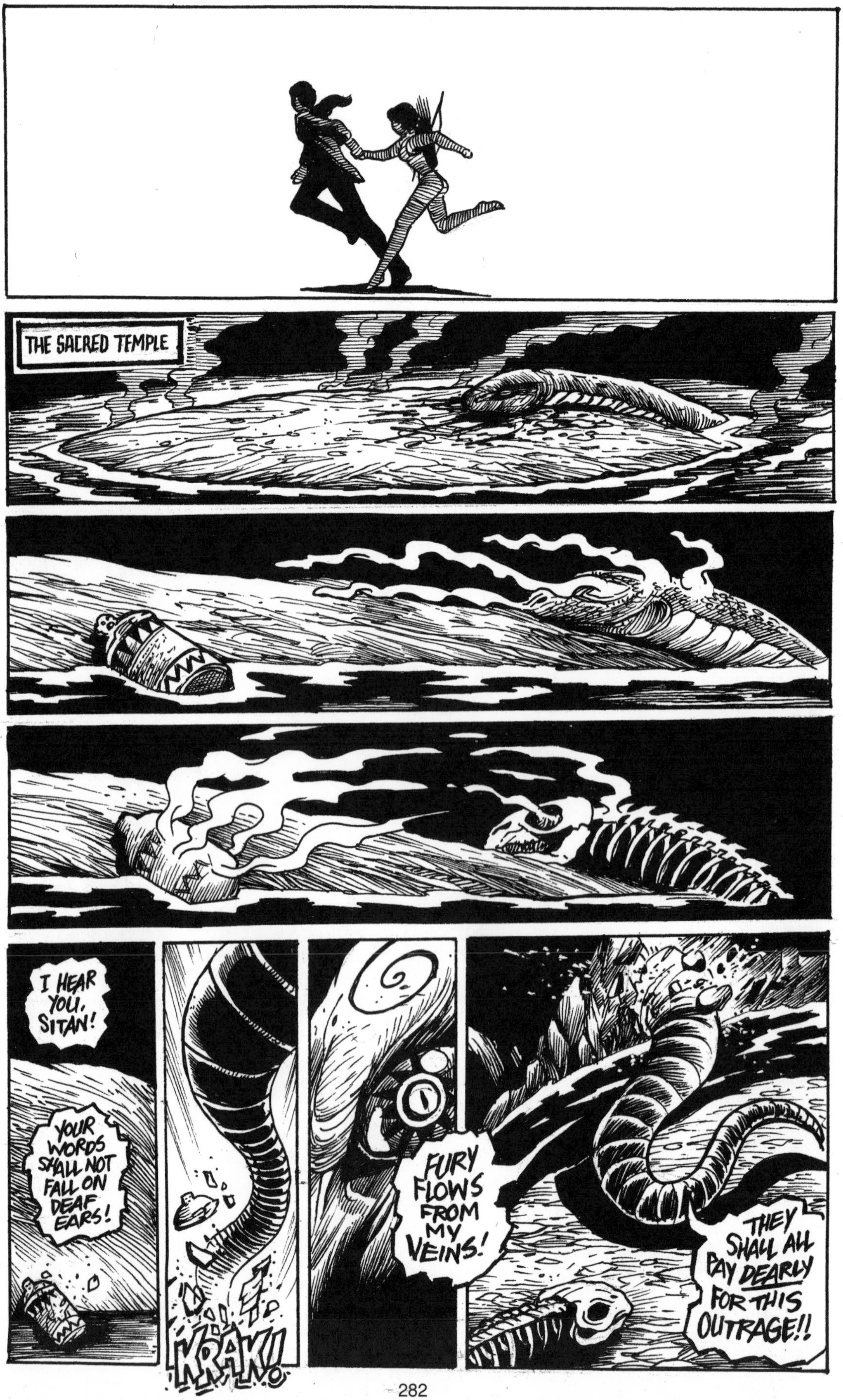
THE SACRED TEMPLE
I HEAR YOU, SITAN!
YOUR WORDS SHALL NOT FALL ON DEAF EARS!
KRAK!
FURY FLOWS FROM MY VEINS!
THEY SHALL ALL PAY DEARLY FOR THIS OUTRAGE!!

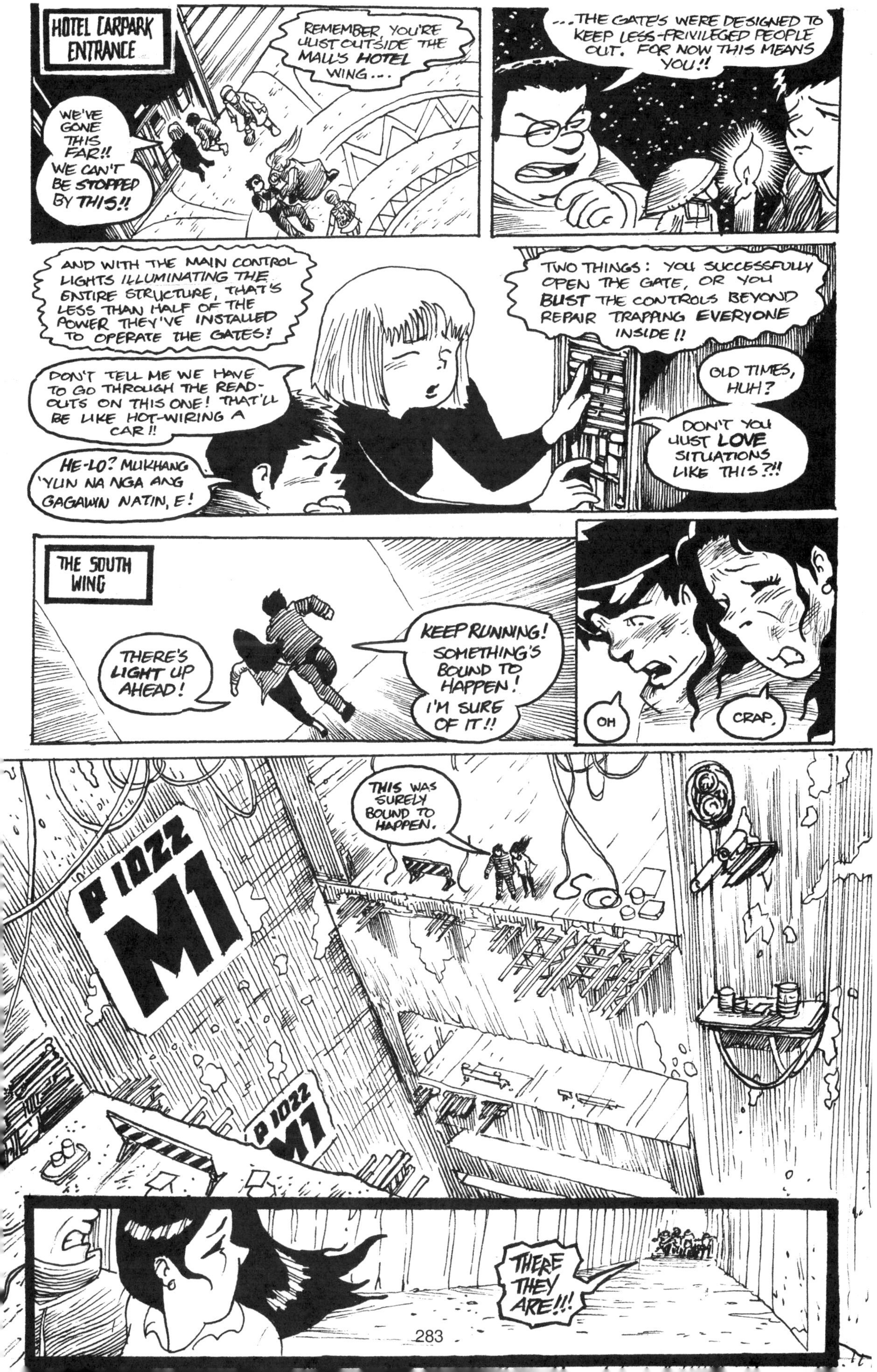
HOTEL CARPARK ENTRANCE
REMEMBER, YOU'RE JUST OUTSIDE THE MALL'S HOTEL WING...
WE'VE GONE THIS FAR!! WE CAN'T BE STOPPED BY THIS!!
...THE GATE'S WERE DESIGNED TO KEEP LESS-PRIVILEGED PEOPLE OUT. FOR NOW THIS MEANS YOU!!
AND WITH THE MAIN CONTROL LIGHTS ILLUMINATING THE ENTIRE STRUCTURE, THAT'S LESS THAN HALF OF THE POWER THEY'VE INSTALLED TO OPERATE THE GATES!
DON'T TELL ME WE HAVE TO GO THROUGH THE READ-OUTS ON THIS ONE! THAT'LL BE LIKE HOT-WIRING A CAR!!
HE-LO? MUKHANG 'YUN NA NGA ANG GAGAWIN NATIN, E!
TWO THINGS: YOU SUCCESSFULLY OPEN THE GATE, OR YOU BUST THE CONTROLS BEYOND REPAIR TRAPPING EVERYONE INSIDE!!
OLD TIMES, HUH?
DON'T YOU JUST LOVE SITUATIONS LIKE THIS?!!
THE SOUTH WING
THERE'S LIGHT UP AHEAD!
KEEP RUNNING! SOMETHING'S BOUND TO HAPPEN! I'M SURE OF IT!!
OH
CRAP.
THIS WAS SURELY BOUND TO HAPPEN.
P 1022 M1
P 1022 M1
THERE THEY ARE!!!

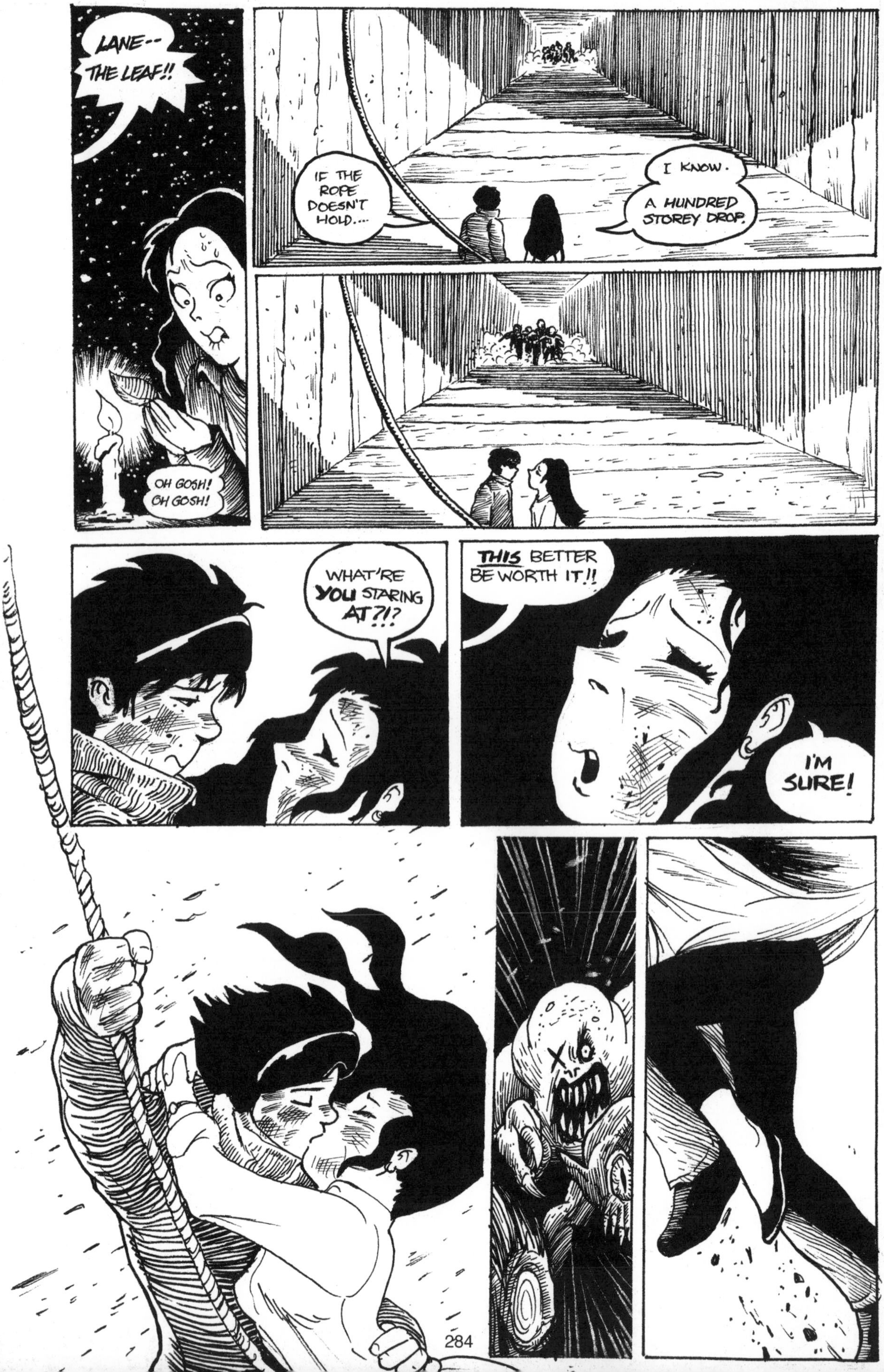
LANE-- THE LEAF!!
IF THE ROPE DOESN'T HOLD....
I KNOW.
A HUNDRED STOREY DROP.
OH GOSH! OH GOSH!
WHAT'RE YOU STARING AT?!?
THIS BETTER BE WORTH IT!!
I'M SURE!

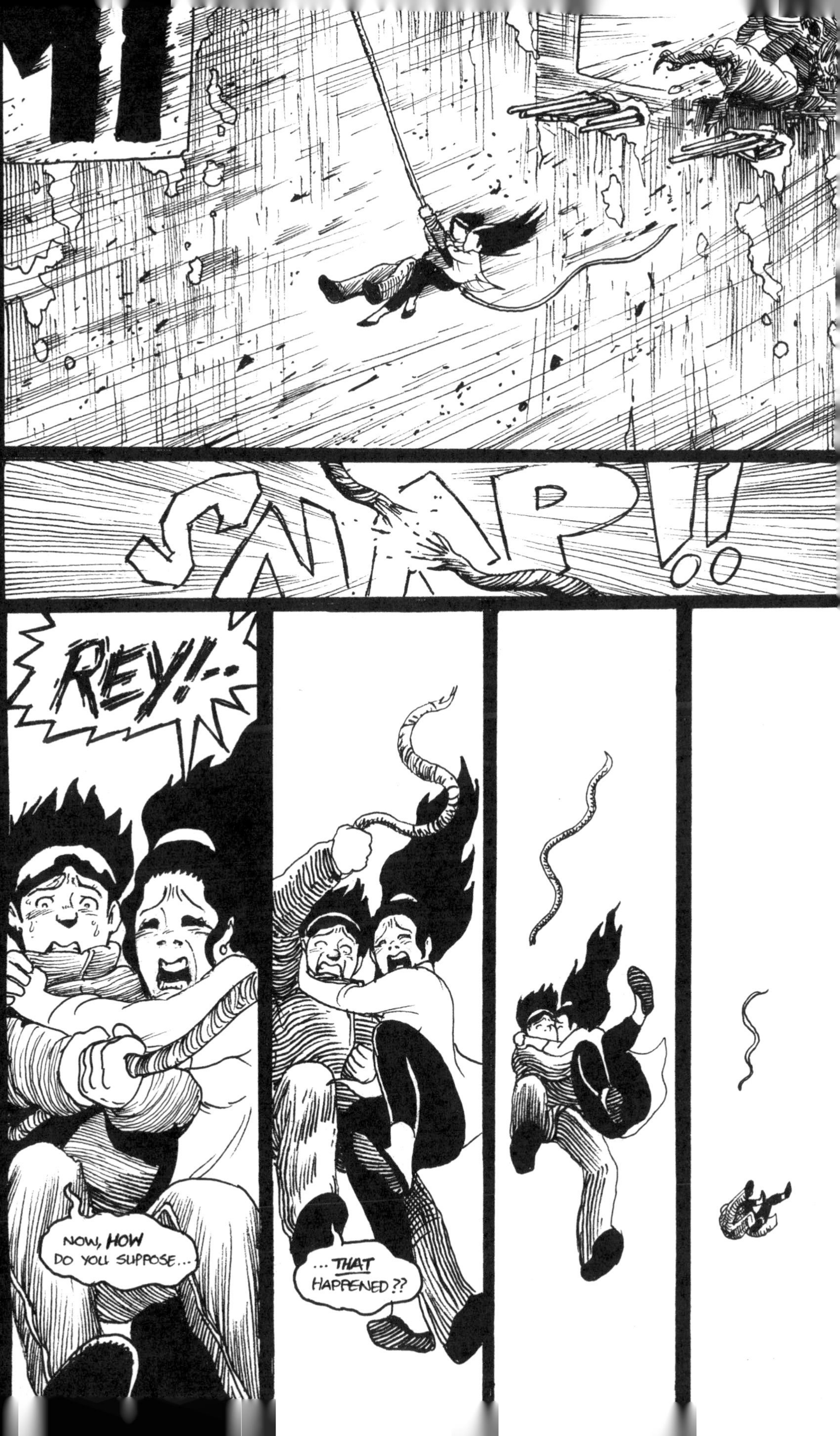
SNAP!!
REY!..
NOW, HOW DO YOU SUPPOSE...
...THAT HAPPENED??

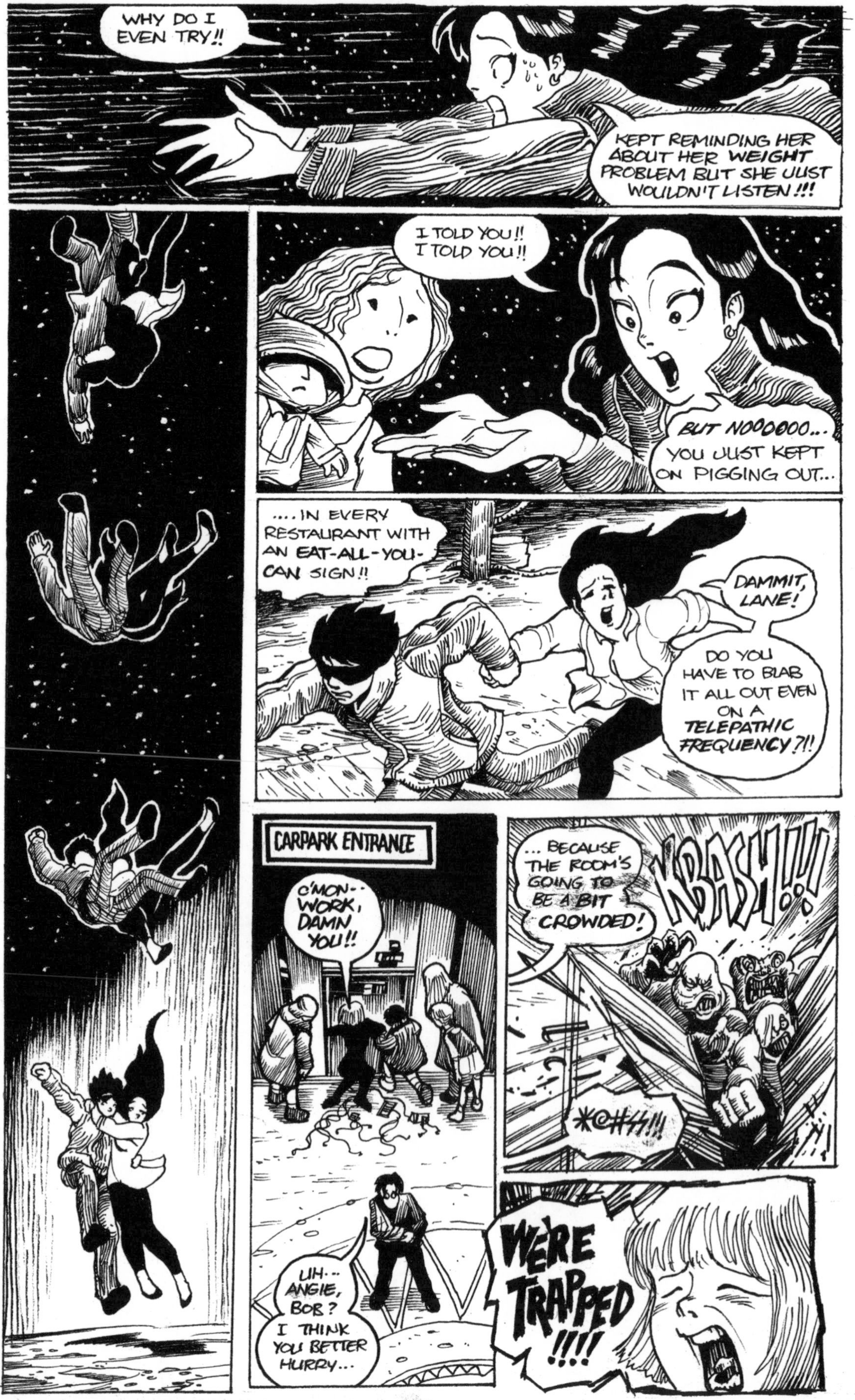
WHY DO I EVEN TRY!!
KEPT REMINDING HER ABOUT HER WEIGHT PROBLEM BUT SHE JUST WOULDN'T LISTEN!!!
I TOLD YOU!! I TOLD YOU!!
BUT NOOOOOO... YOU JUST KEPT ON PIGGING OUT...
....IN EVERY RESTAURANT WITH AN EAT-ALL-YOU-CAN SIGN!!
DAMMIT, LANE!
DO YOU HAVE TO BLAB IT ALL OUT EVEN ON A TELEPATHIC FREQUENCY?!!
CARPARK ENTRANCE
C'MON-- WORK, DAMN YOU!!
UH-- ANGIE, BOB? I THINK YOU BETTER HURRY...
... BECAUSE THE ROOM'S GOING TO BE A BIT CROWDED!
KBASH!!!
*@#$!!!
WE'RE TRAPPED!!!!

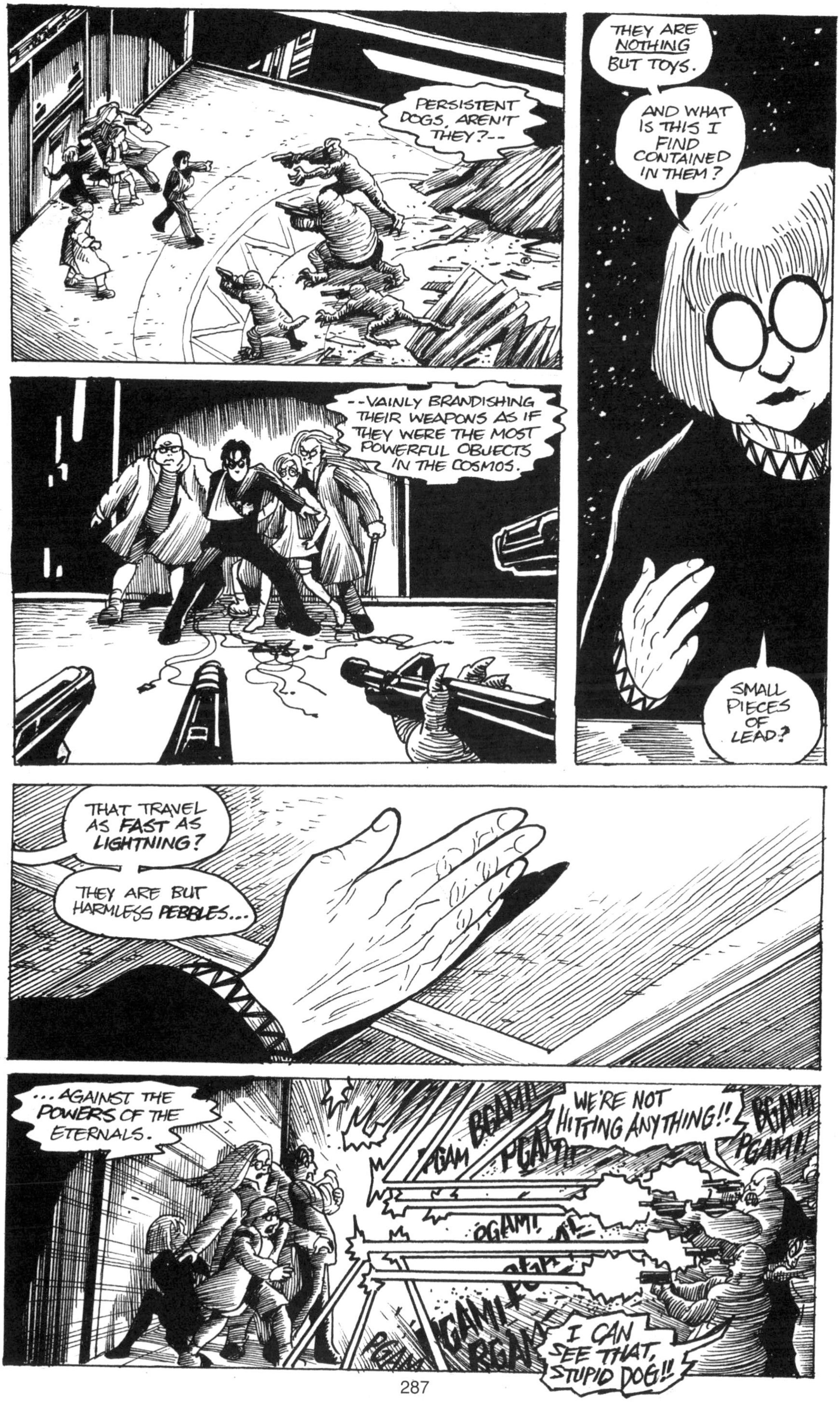
PERSISTENT DOGS, AREN'T THEY?--
THEY ARE NOTHING BUT TOYS.
AND WHAT IS THIS I FIND CONTAINED IN THEM?
--VAINLY BRANDISHING THEIR WEAPONS AS IF THEY WERE THE MOST POWERFUL OBJECTS IN THE COSMOS.
SMALL PIECES OF LEAD?
THAT TRAVEL AS FAST AS LIGHTNING?
THEY ARE BUT HARMLESS PEBBLES...
...AGAINST THE POWERS OF THE ETERNALS.
BGAM!!
WE'RE NOT HITTING ANYTHING!!
BGAM!!
PGAM
PGAM!!
PGAM!!
PGAM!
I CAN SEE THAT, STUPID DOG!!

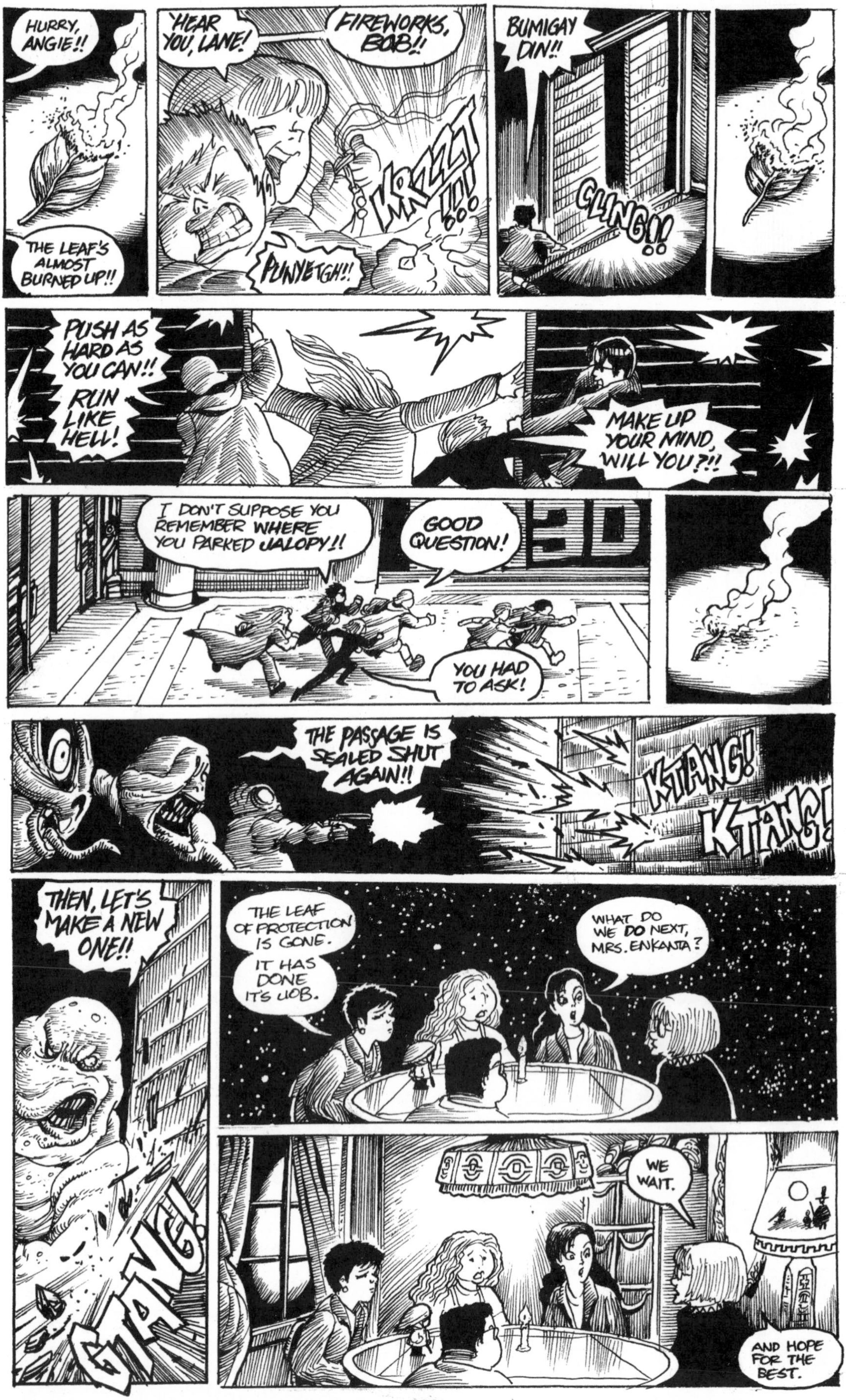
HURRY, ANGIE!!
THE LEAF'S ALMOST BURNED UP!!
'HEAR YOU, LANE!
FIREWORKS, BOB!!
KRZZZT!!
PUNYETGH!!
BUMIGAY DIN!!
CLING!!
PUSH AS HARD AS YOU CAN!! RUN LIKE HELL!
MAKE UP YOUR MIND, WILL YOU?!!
I DON'T SUPPOSE YOU REMEMBER WHERE YOU PARKED JALOPY!!
GOOD QUESTION!
YOU HAD TO ASK!
THE PASSAGE IS SEALED SHUT AGAIN!!
KTANG!
KTANG!
THEN, LET'S MAKE A NEW ONE!!
GTANG!
THE LEAF OF PROTECTION IS GONE.
IT HAS DONE IT'S JOB.
WHAT DO WE DO NEXT, MRS. ENKANTA?
WE WAIT.
AND HOPE FOR THE BEST.

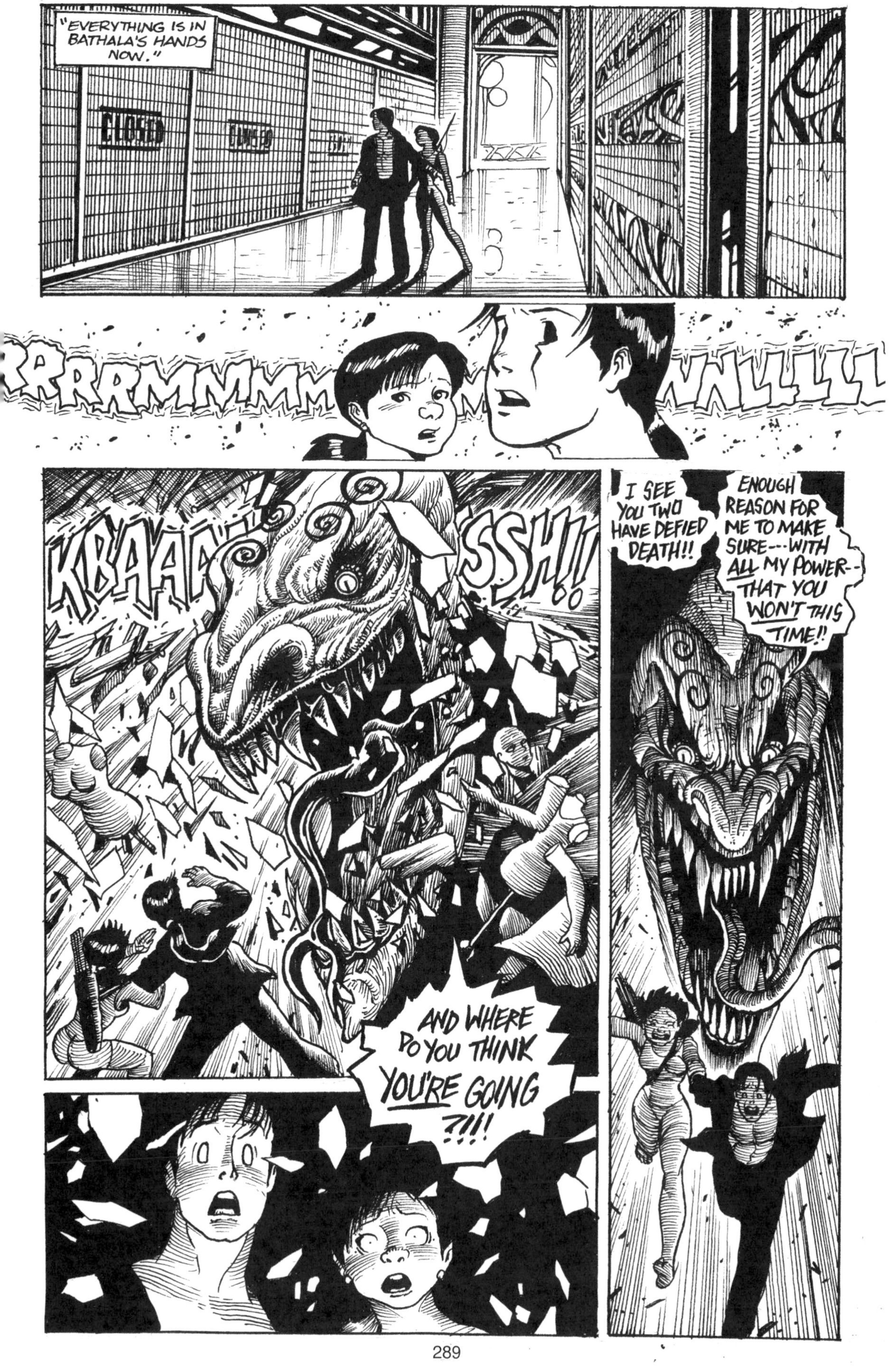
"EVERYTHING IS IN BATHALA'S HANDS NOW."
CLOSED
RRRMMMMMMMWWLLLLL
KBAAA...SSH!!
AND WHERE DO YOU THINK YOU'RE GOING ?!!!
I SEE YOU TWO HAVE DEFIED DEATH!!
ENOUGH REASON FOR ME TO MAKE SURE---WITH ALL MY POWER--THAT YOU WON'T THIS TIME!!

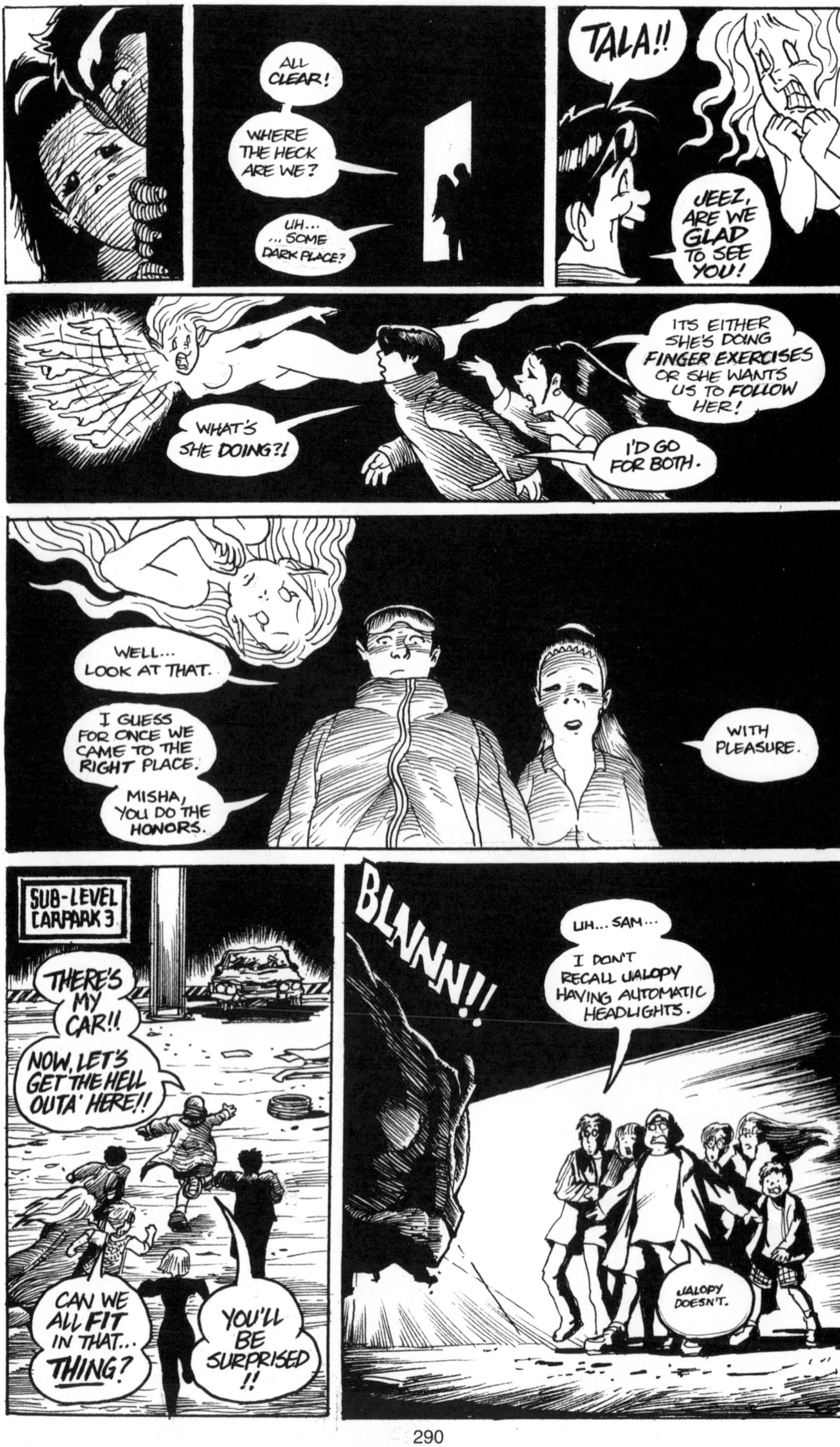
ALL CLEAR!
WHERE THE HECK ARE WE?
UH... ...SOME DARK PLACE?
TALA!!
JEEZ, ARE WE GLAD TO SEE YOU!
WHAT'S SHE DOING?!
ITS EITHER SHE'S DOING FINGER EXERCISES OR SHE WANTS US TO FOLLOW HER!
I'D GO FOR BOTH.
WELL... LOOK AT THAT.
I GUESS FOR ONCE WE CAME TO THE RIGHT PLACE.
MISHA, YOU DO THE HONORS.
WITH PLEASURE.
SUB-LEVEL CARPARK 3
THERE'S MY CAR!!
NOW, LET'S GET THE HELL OUTA' HERE!!
CAN WE ALL FIT IN THAT... THING?
YOU'LL BE SURPRISED!!
BLNNN!!
UH... SAM...
I DON'T RECALL JALOPY HAVING AUTOMATIC HEADLIGHTS.
JALOPY DOESN'T.

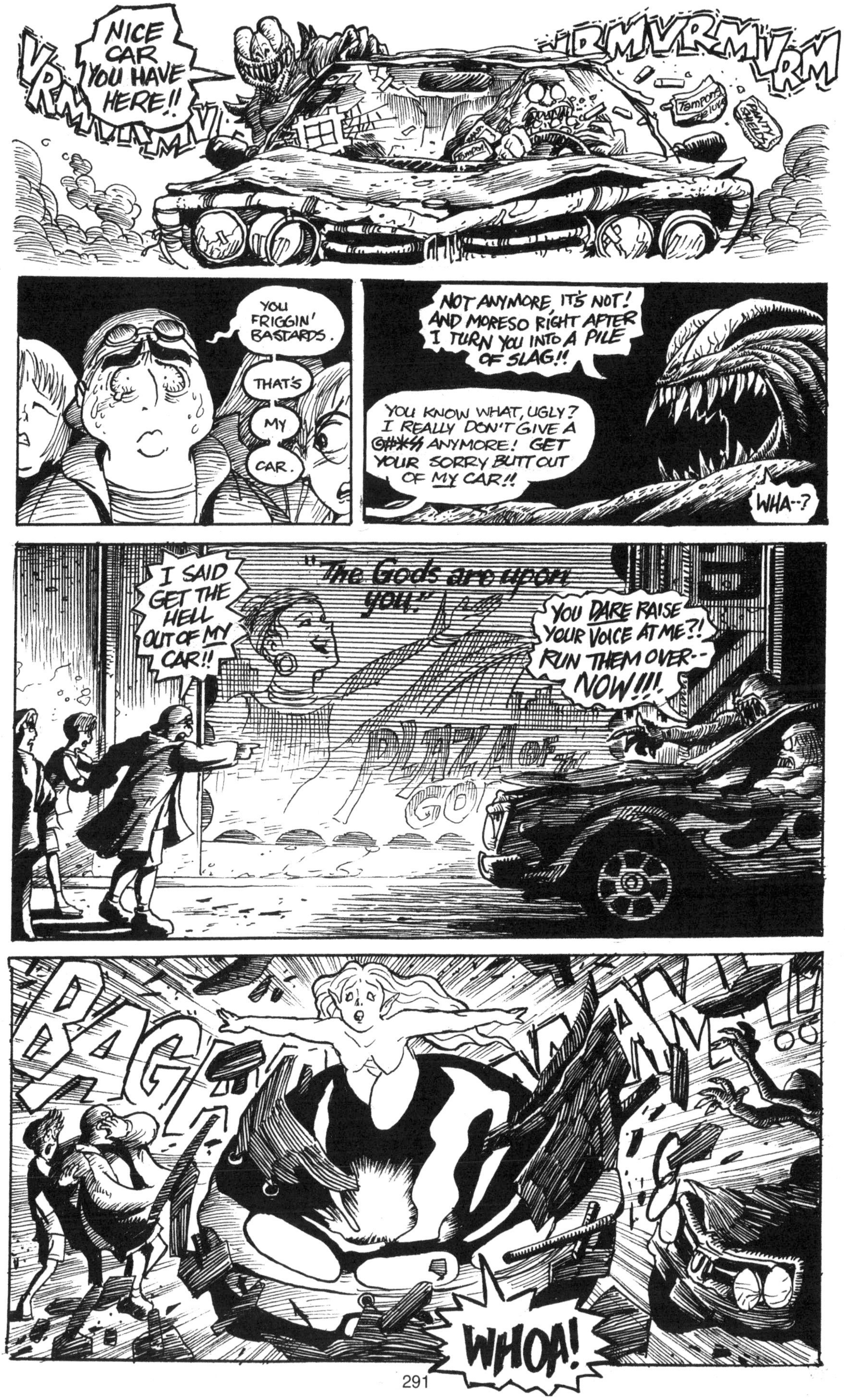
VRMMMMMV
NICE CAR YOU HAVE HERE!!
VRMVRMVRMVRM
YOU FRIGGIN' BASTARDS.
THAT'S
MY
CAR.
NOT ANYMORE, IT'S NOT! AND MORESO RIGHT AFTER I TURN YOU INTO A PILE OF SLAG!!
YOU KNOW WHAT, UGLY? I REALLY DON'T GIVE A @#*$ ANYMORE! GET YOUR SORRY BUTT OUT OF MY CAR!!
WHA--?
I SAID GET THE HELL OUT OF MY CAR!!
"The Gods are upon you."
YOU DARE RAISE YOUR VOICE AT ME?! RUN THEM OVER-- NOW!!!!
BAGAAM!!
WHOA!

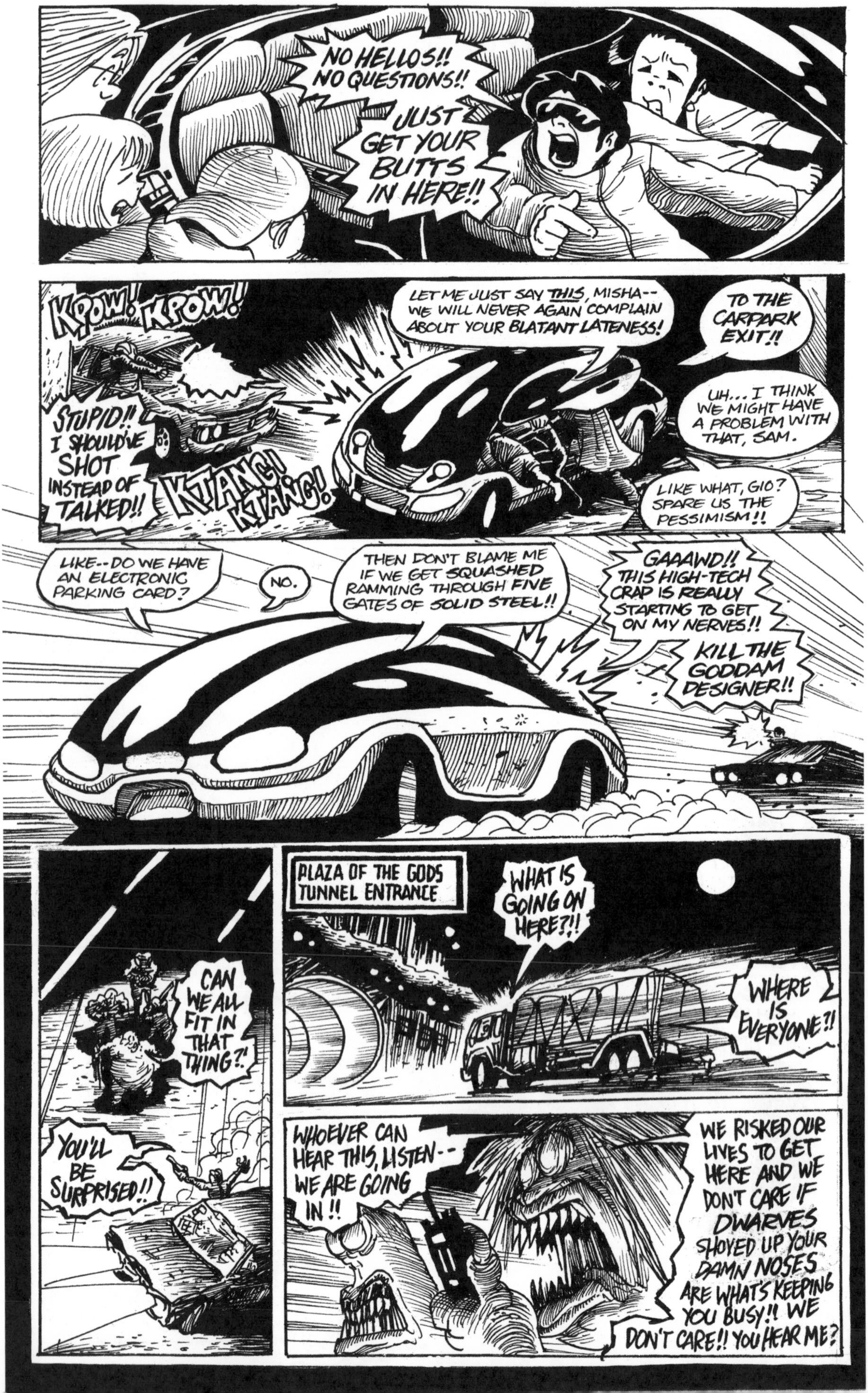
NO HELLOS!! NO QUESTIONS!!
JUST GET YOUR BUTTS IN HERE!!
KPOW! KPOW!
LET ME JUST SAY THIS, MISHA-- WE WILL NEVER AGAIN COMPLAIN ABOUT YOUR BLATANT LATENESS!
TO THE CARPARK EXIT!!
STUPID!! I SHOULD'VE SHOT INSTEAD OF TALKED!!
KTANG! KTANG!
UH... I THINK WE MIGHT HAVE A PROBLEM WITH THAT, SAM.
LIKE WHAT, GIO? SPARE US THE PESSIMISM!!
LIKE--DO WE HAVE AN ELECTRONIC PARKING CARD?
NO.
THEN DON'T BLAME ME IF WE GET SQUASHED RAMMING THROUGH FIVE GATES OF SOLID STEEL!!
GAAAWD!! THIS HIGH-TECH CRAP IS REALLY STARTING TO GET ON MY NERVES!!
KILL THE GODDAM DESIGNER!!
CAN WE ALL FIT IN THAT THING?!
YOU'LL BE SURPRISED!!
PLAZA OF THE GODS TUNNEL ENTRANCE
WHAT IS GOING ON HERE?!!
WHERE IS EVERYONE?!
WHOEVER CAN HEAR THIS, LISTEN-- WE ARE GOING IN!!
WE RISKED OUR LIVES TO GET HERE AND WE DON'T CARE IF DWARVES SHOVED UP YOUR DAMN NOSES ARE WHAT'S KEEPING YOU BUSY!! WE DON'T CARE!! YOU HEAR ME?

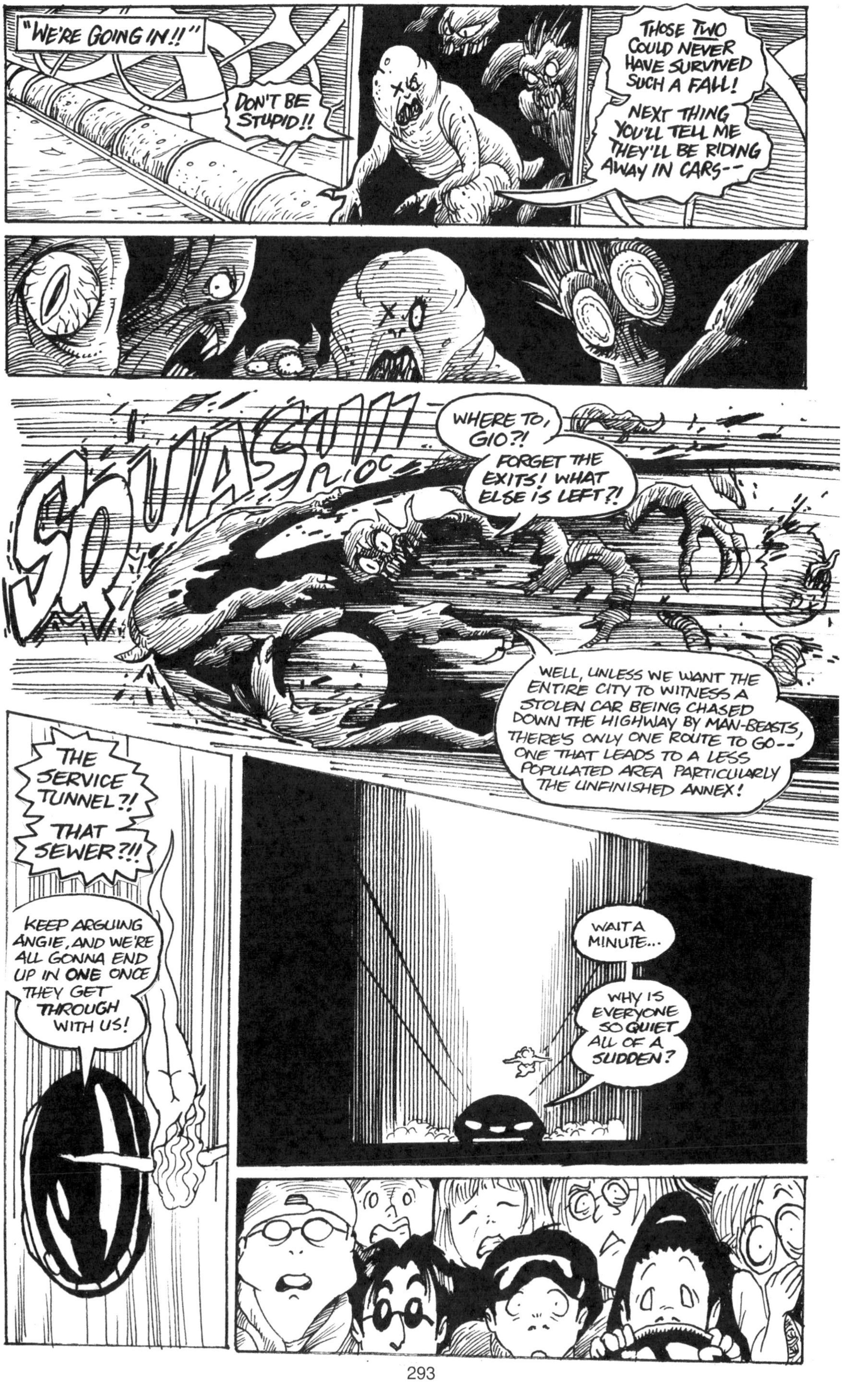
"WE'RE GOING IN!!"
DON'T BE STUPID!!
THOSE TWO COULD NEVER HAVE SURVIVED SUCH A FALL!
NEXT THING YOU'LL TELL ME THEY'LL BE RIDING AWAY IN CARS--
SQUASHHH
WHERE TO, GIO?!
FORGET THE EXITS! WHAT ELSE IS LEFT?!
WELL, UNLESS WE WANT THE ENTIRE CITY TO WITNESS A STOLEN CAR BEING CHASED DOWN THE HIGHWAY BY MAN-BEASTS, THERE'S ONLY ONE ROUTE TO GO-- ONE THAT LEADS TO A LESS POPULATED AREA PARTICULARLY THE UNFINISHED ANNEX!
THE SERVICE TUNNEL?! THAT SEWER?!!
KEEP ARGUING ANGIE, AND WE'RE ALL GONNA END UP IN ONE ONCE THEY GET THROUGH WITH US!
WAIT A MINUTE...
WHY IS EVERYONE SO QUIET ALL OF A SUDDEN?

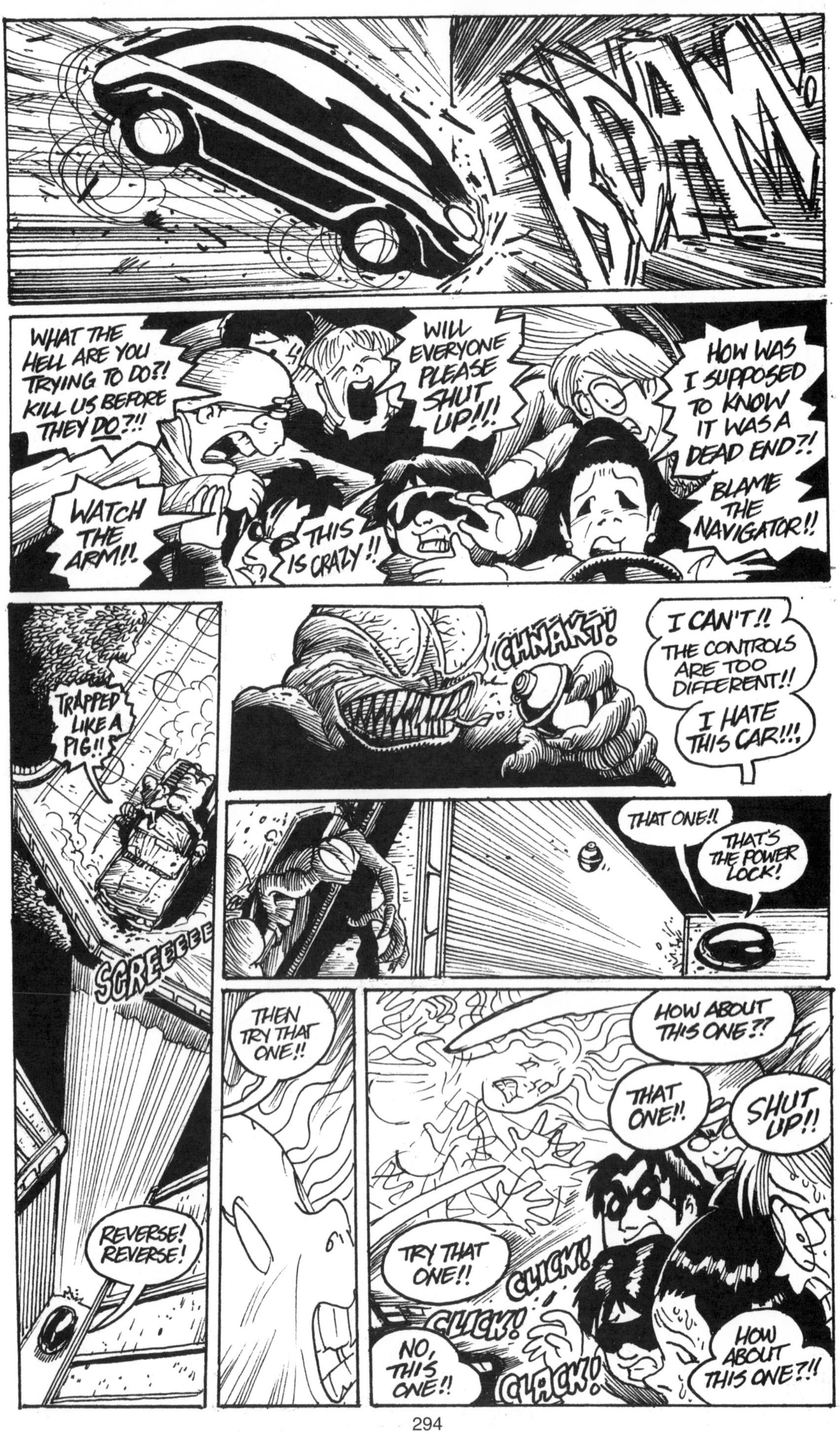
KRAM
WHAT THE HELL ARE YOU TRYING TO DO?! KILL US BEFORE THEY DO?!!
WILL EVERYONE PLEASE SHUT UP!!!
HOW WAS I SUPPOSED TO KNOW IT WAS A DEAD END?!
WATCH THE ARM!!
THIS IS CRAZY!!
BLAME THE NAVIGATOR!!
TRAPPED LIKE A PIG!!
SCREEEEEE
CHNAKT!
I CAN'T!! THE CONTROLS ARE TOO DIFFERENT!!
I HATE THIS CAR!!!
THAT ONE!!
THAT'S THE POWER LOCK!
REVERSE! REVERSE!
THEN TRY THAT ONE!!
HOW ABOUT THIS ONE??
THAT ONE!!
SHUT UP!!
TRY THAT ONE!!
CLICK!
CLICK!
NO, THIS ONE!!
CLACK!
HOW ABOUT THIS ONE?!!

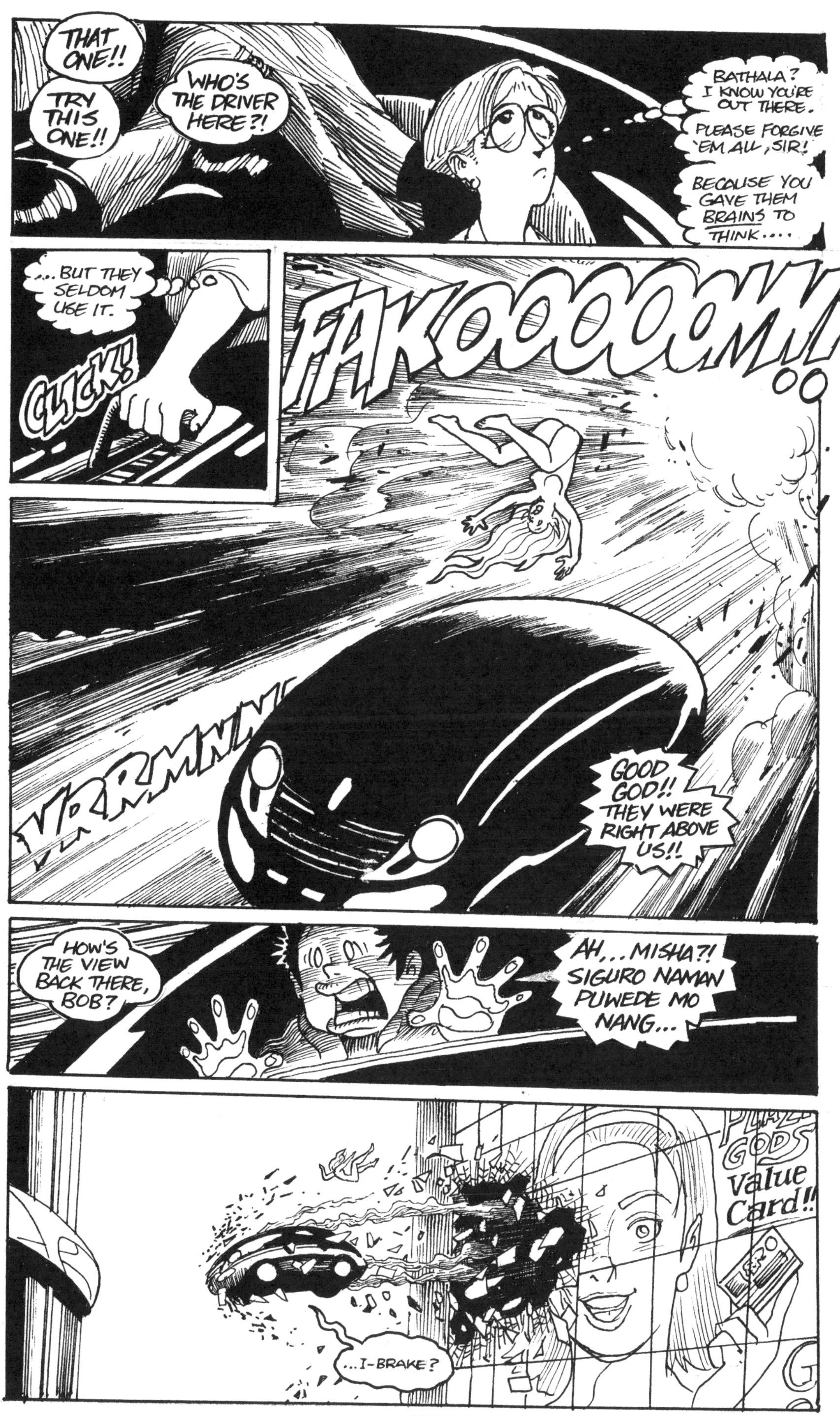
THAT ONE!!
TRY THIS ONE!!
WHO'S THE DRIVER HERE?!
BATHALA? I KNOW YOU'RE OUT THERE.
PLEASE FORGIVE 'EM ALL, SIR!
BECAUSE YOU GAVE THEM BRAINS TO THINK....
...BUT THEY SELDOM USE IT.
CLICK!
FAKOOOOOM!!
VRRMNN
GOOD GOD!! THEY WERE RIGHT ABOVE US!!
HOW'S THE VIEW BACK THERE, BOB?
AH,... MISHA?! SIGURO NAMAN PUWEDE MO NANG...
GODS
Value Card!!
...I-BRAKE?

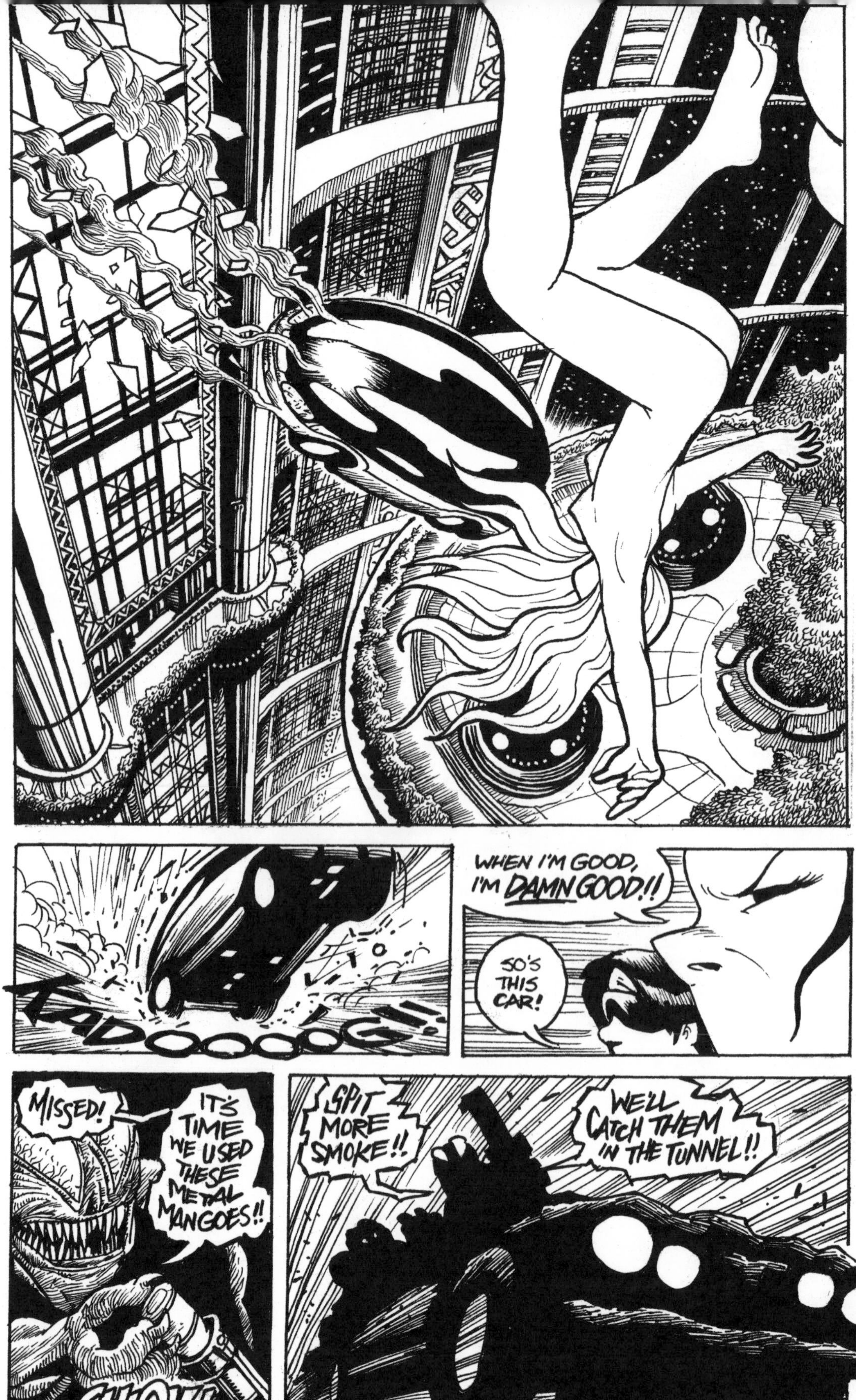
KADOOOOOG!!!
WHEN I'M GOOD, I'M DAMN GOOD!!
SO'S THIS CAR!
MISSED!
IT'S TIME WE USED THESE METAL MANGOES!!
CHLONK!
SPIT MORE SMOKE!!
WE'LL CATCH THEM IN THE TUNNEL!!

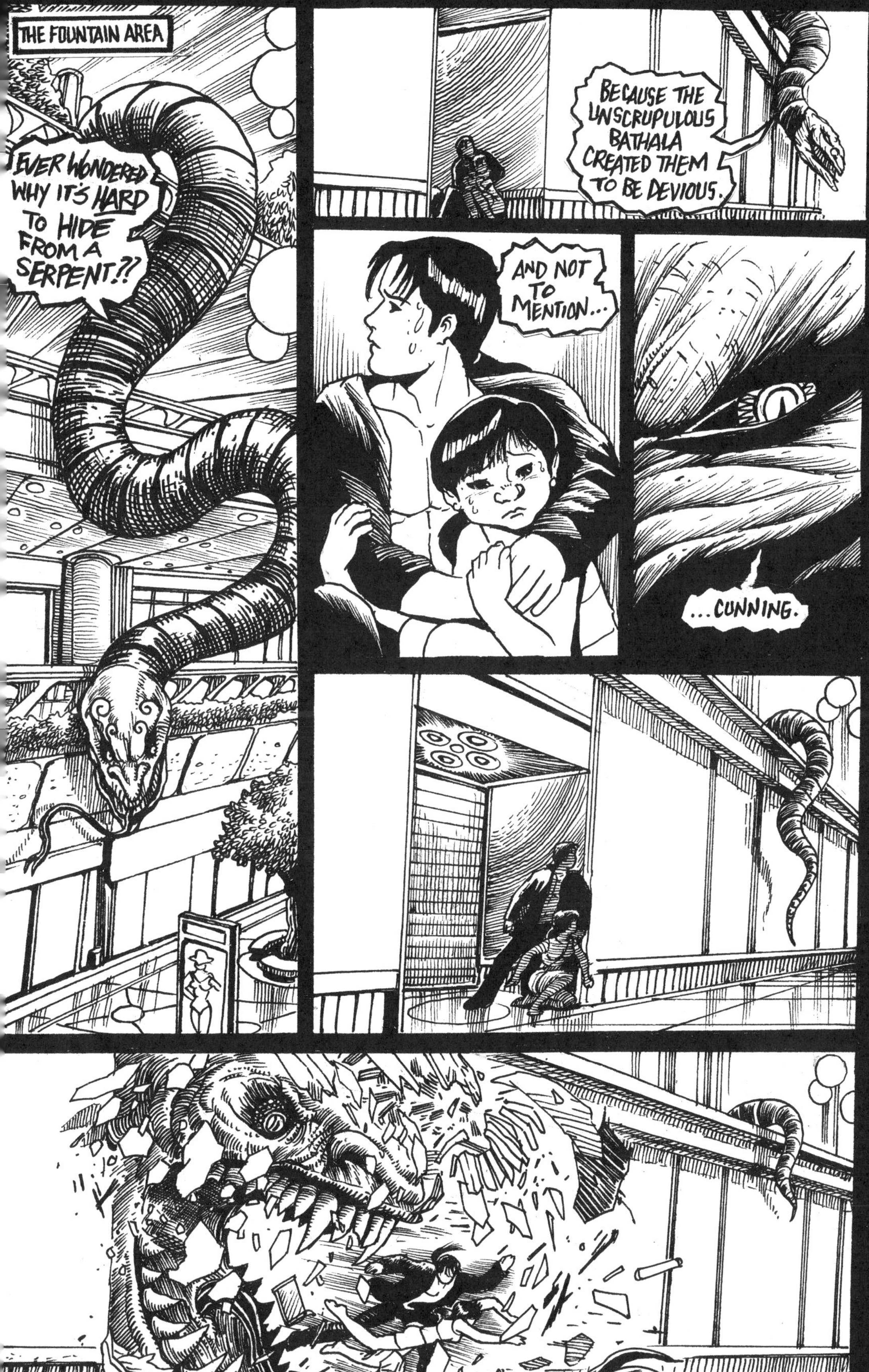
THE FOUNTAIN AREA
EVER WONDERED WHY IT'S HARD TO HIDE FROM A SERPENT??
BECAUSE THE UNSCRUPULOUS BATHALA CREATED THEM TO BE DEVIOUS.
AND NOT TO MENTION...
...CUNNING.

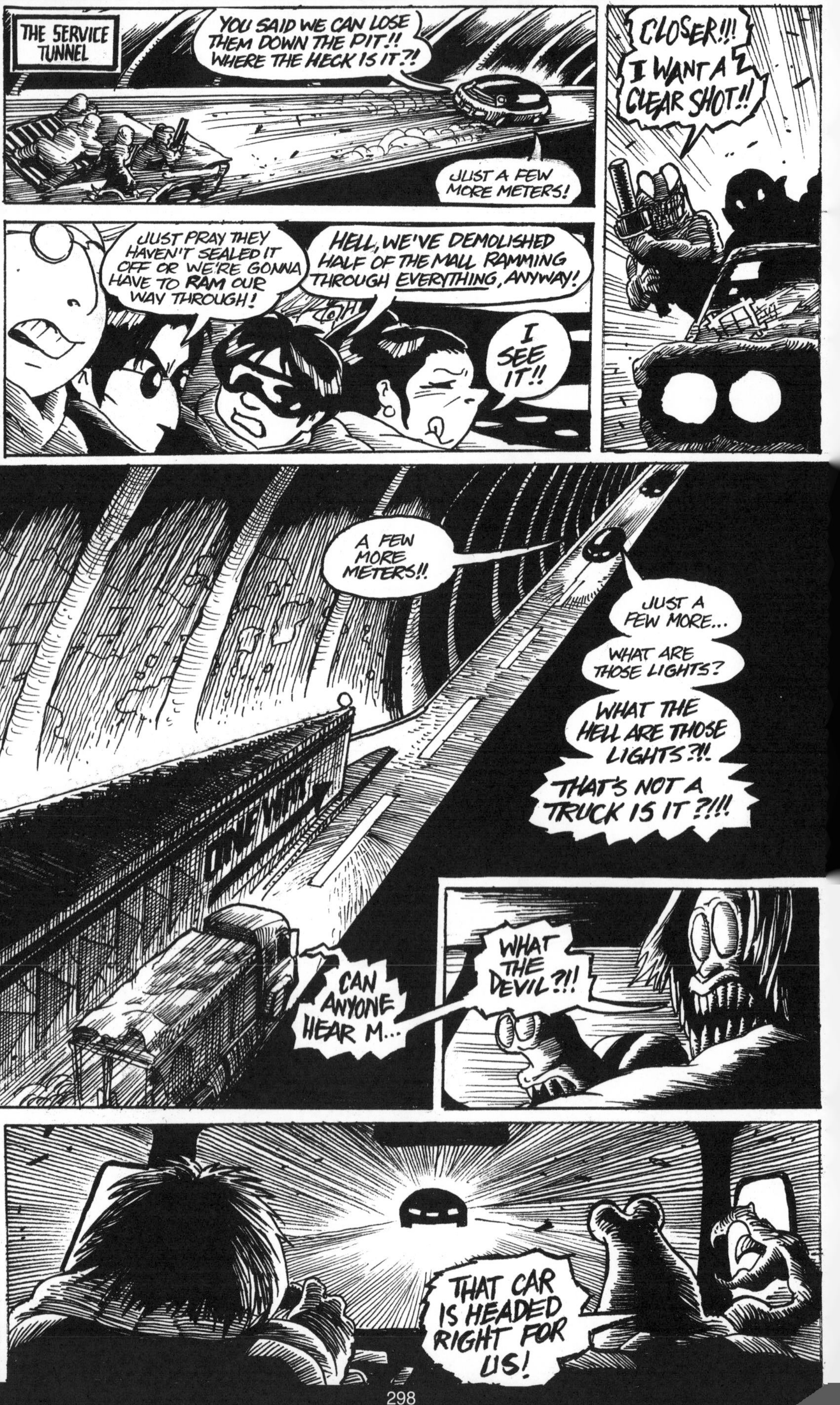
THE SERVICE TUNNEL
YOU SAID WE CAN LOSE THEM DOWN THE PIT!! WHERE THE HECK IS IT?!
JUST A FEW MORE METERS!
CLOSER!!! I WANT A CLEAR SHOT!!
JUST PRAY THEY HAVEN'T SEALED IT OFF OR WE'RE GONNA HAVE TO RAM OUR WAY THROUGH!
HELL, WE'VE DEMOLISHED HALF OF THE MALL RAMMING THROUGH EVERYTHING, ANYWAY!
I SEE IT!!
A FEW MORE METERS!!
JUST A FEW MORE...
WHAT ARE THOSE LIGHTS?
WHAT THE HELL ARE THOSE LIGHTS?!!
THAT'S NOT A TRUCK IS IT?!!!
ONE WAY
CAN ANYONE HEAR M...
WHAT THE DEVIL?!!
THAT CAR IS HEADED RIGHT FOR US!

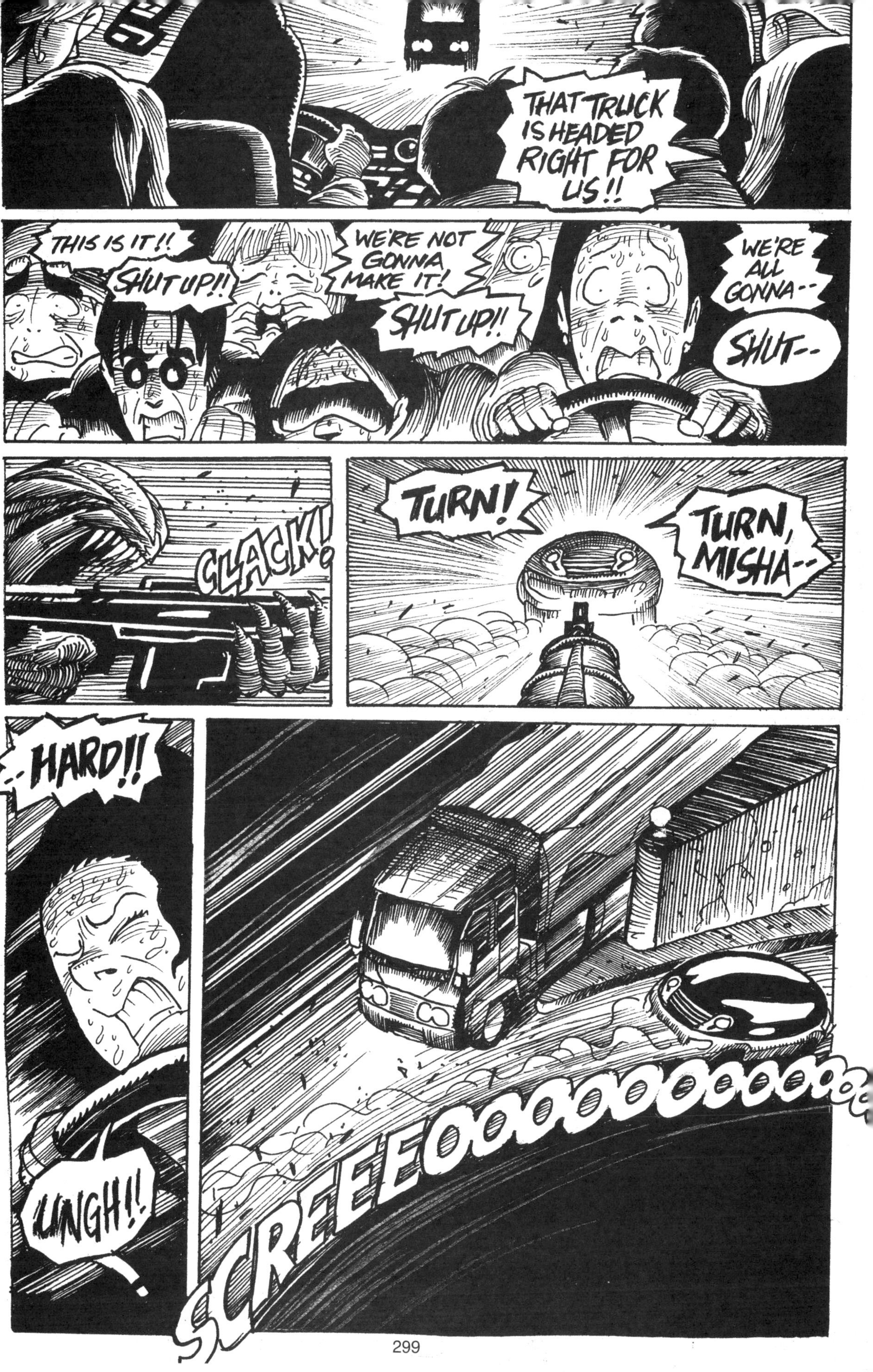
THAT TRUCK IS HEADED RIGHT FOR US!!
THIS IS IT!!
SHUT UP!!
WE'RE NOT GONNA MAKE IT!
SHUT UP!!
WE'RE ALL GONNA--
SHUT--
CLACK!
TURN!
TURN, MISHA--
--HARD!!
UNGH!!
SCREEEOOOOOOOOOOOOOOO

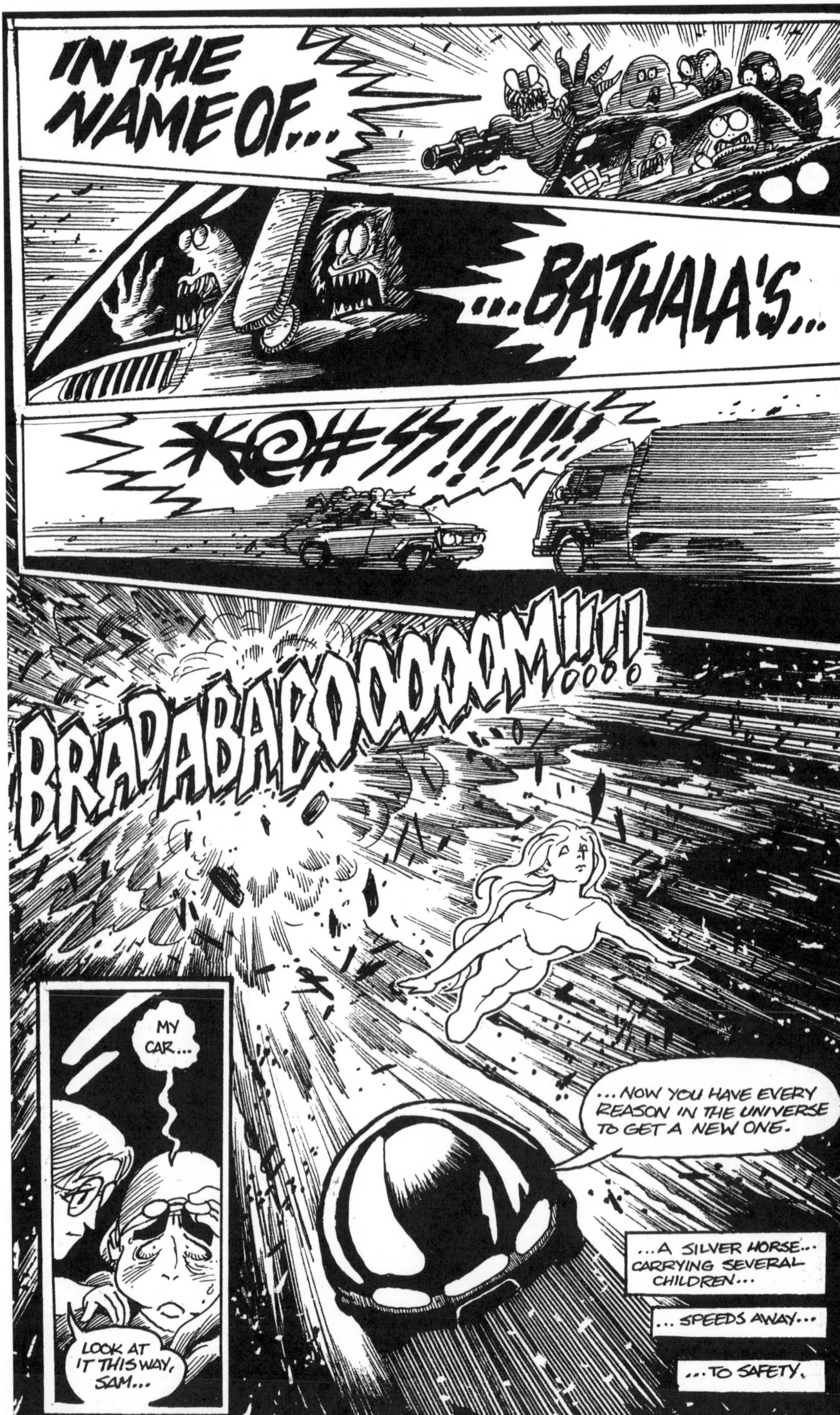

IN THE NAME OF...
...BATHALA'S...
*@#$!!!!!
BRADABABOOOOOM!!!!
MY CAR...
LOOK AT IT THIS WAY, SAM...
...NOW YOU HAVE EVERY REASON IN THE UNIVERSE TO GET A NEW ONE.
...A SILVER HORSE... CARRYING SEVERAL CHILDREN...
...SPEEDS AWAY...
...TO SAFETY.

SUCH COURAGE...

...YET ALL IN VAIN.

FOR COUNTLESS CENTURIES I HAVE WAITED TO SPREAD TERROR AMONG BATHALA'S CHILDREN.

AND TONIGHT...

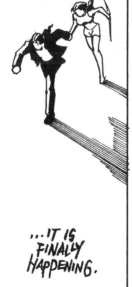

...IT IS FINALLY HAPPENING.

I SHALL DEVOUR YOUR MEMORIES.

YOUR DREAMS

YOUR HOPES.

I SHALL CONSUME THEM...

...AND SAVOUR IT FOR ALL TIME.

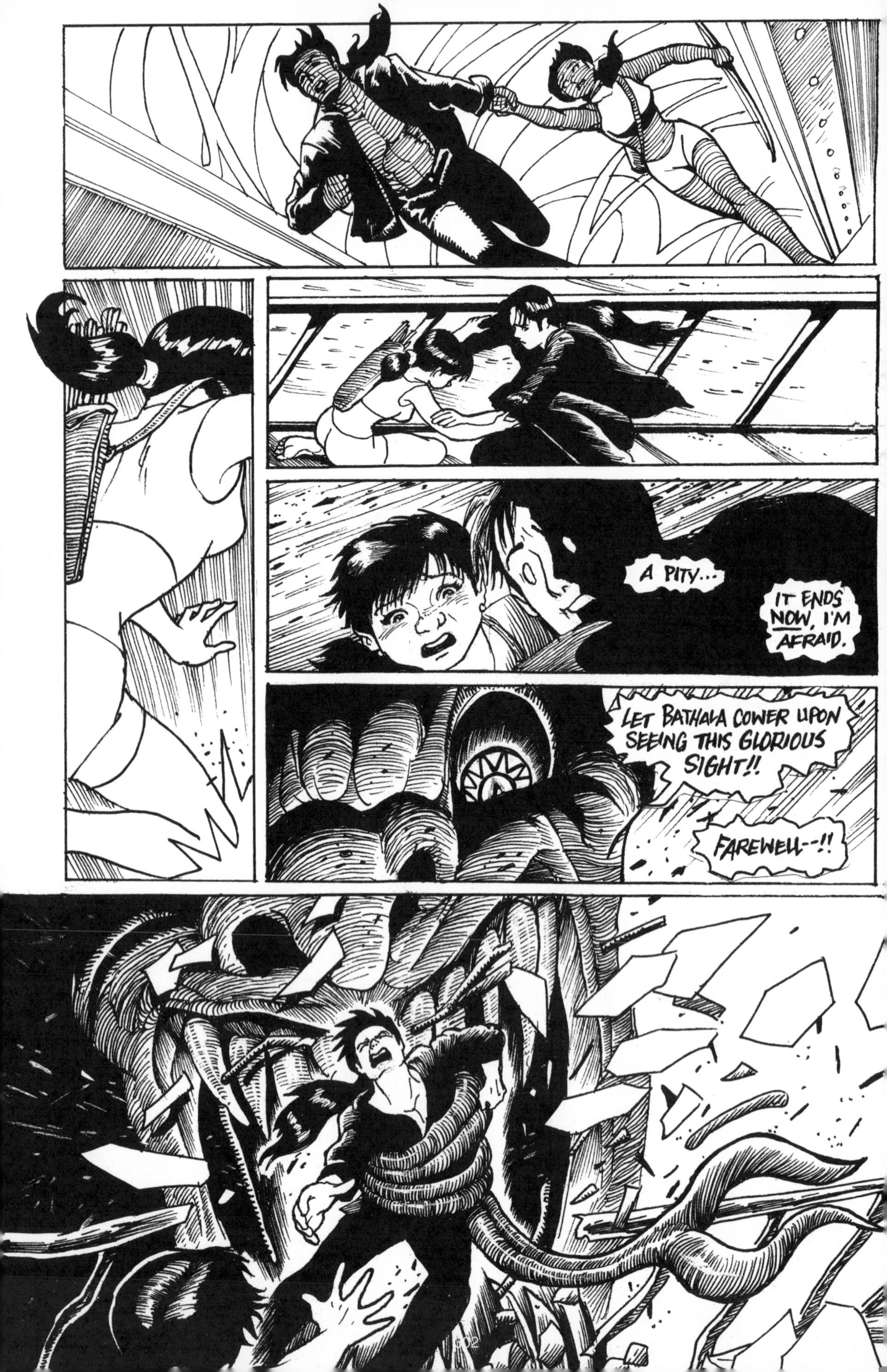
A PITY...
IT ENDS NOW, I'M AFRAID.
LET BATHALA COWER UPON SEEING THIS GLORIOUS SIGHT!!
FAREWELL--!!

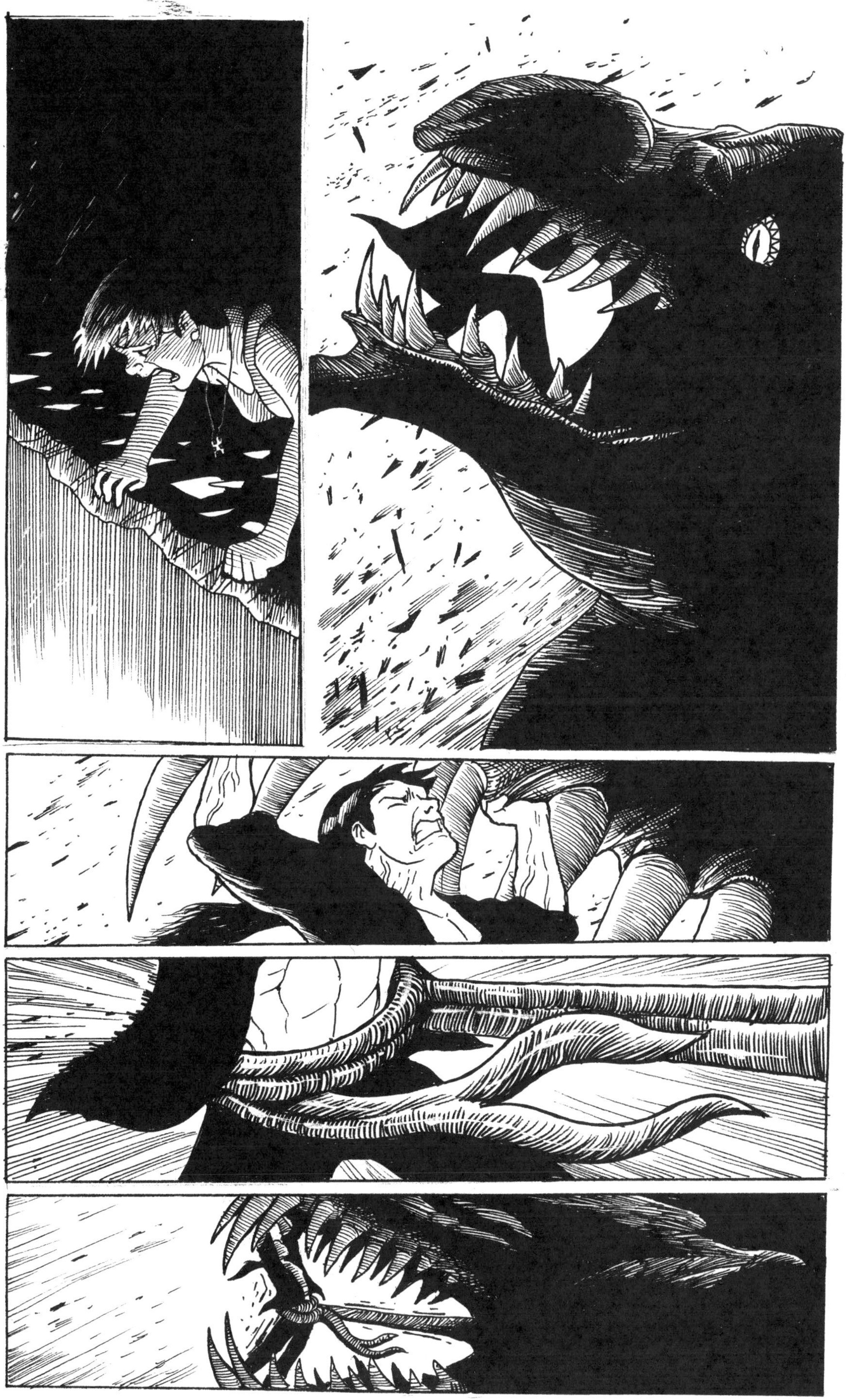

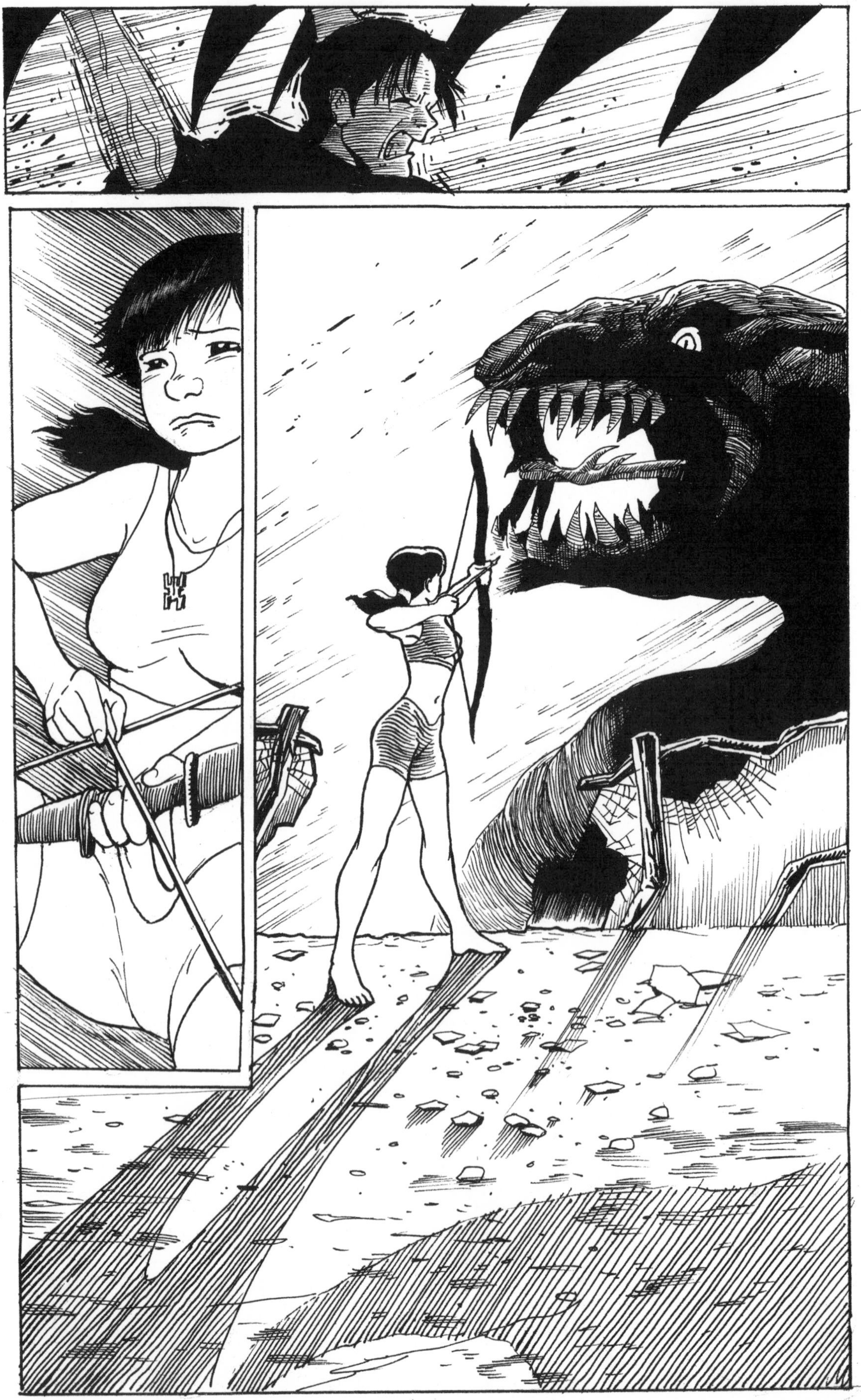

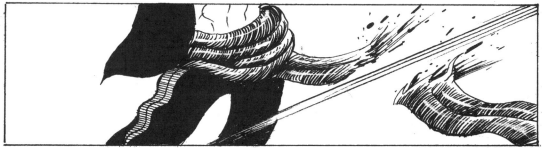

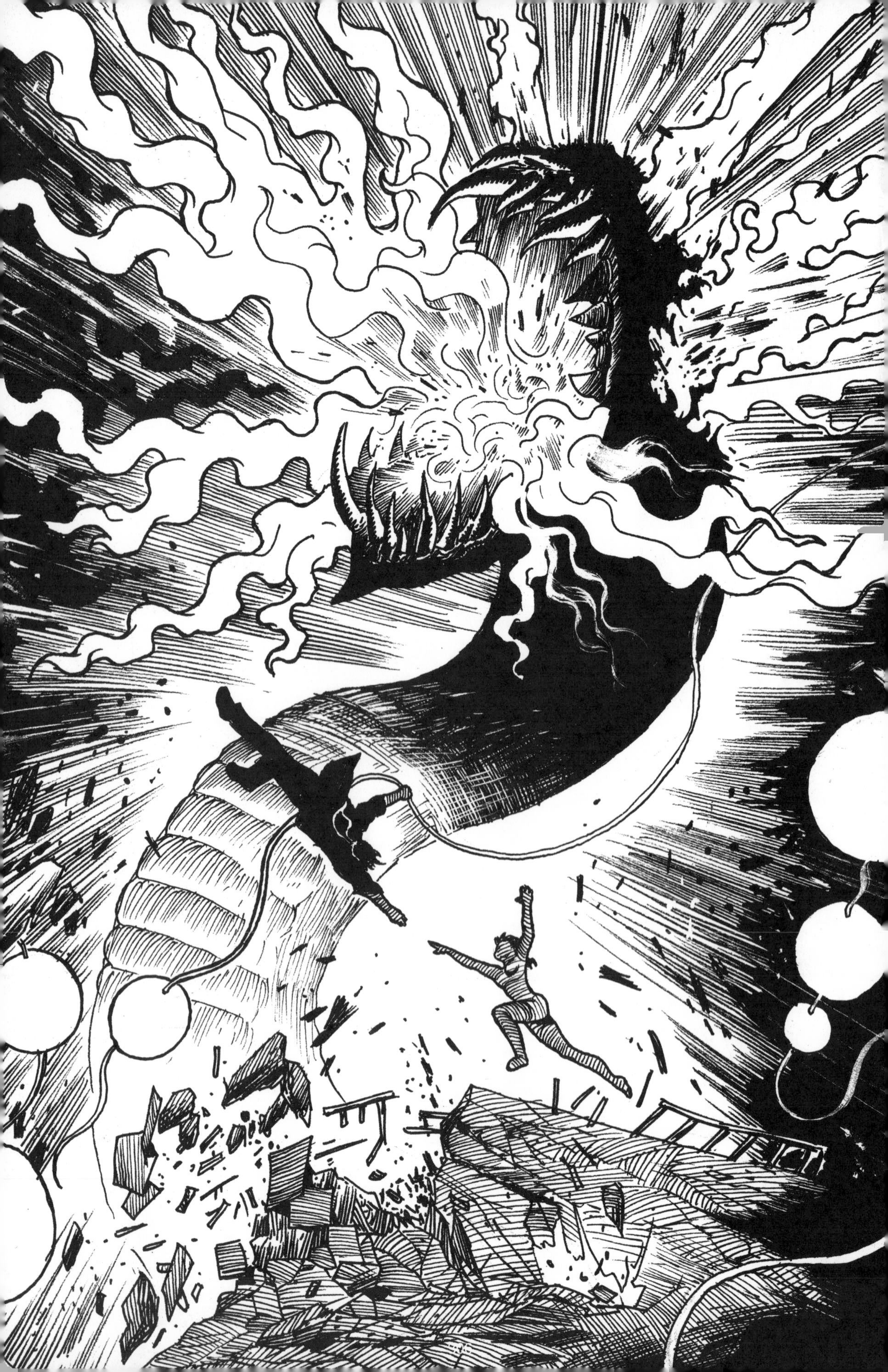

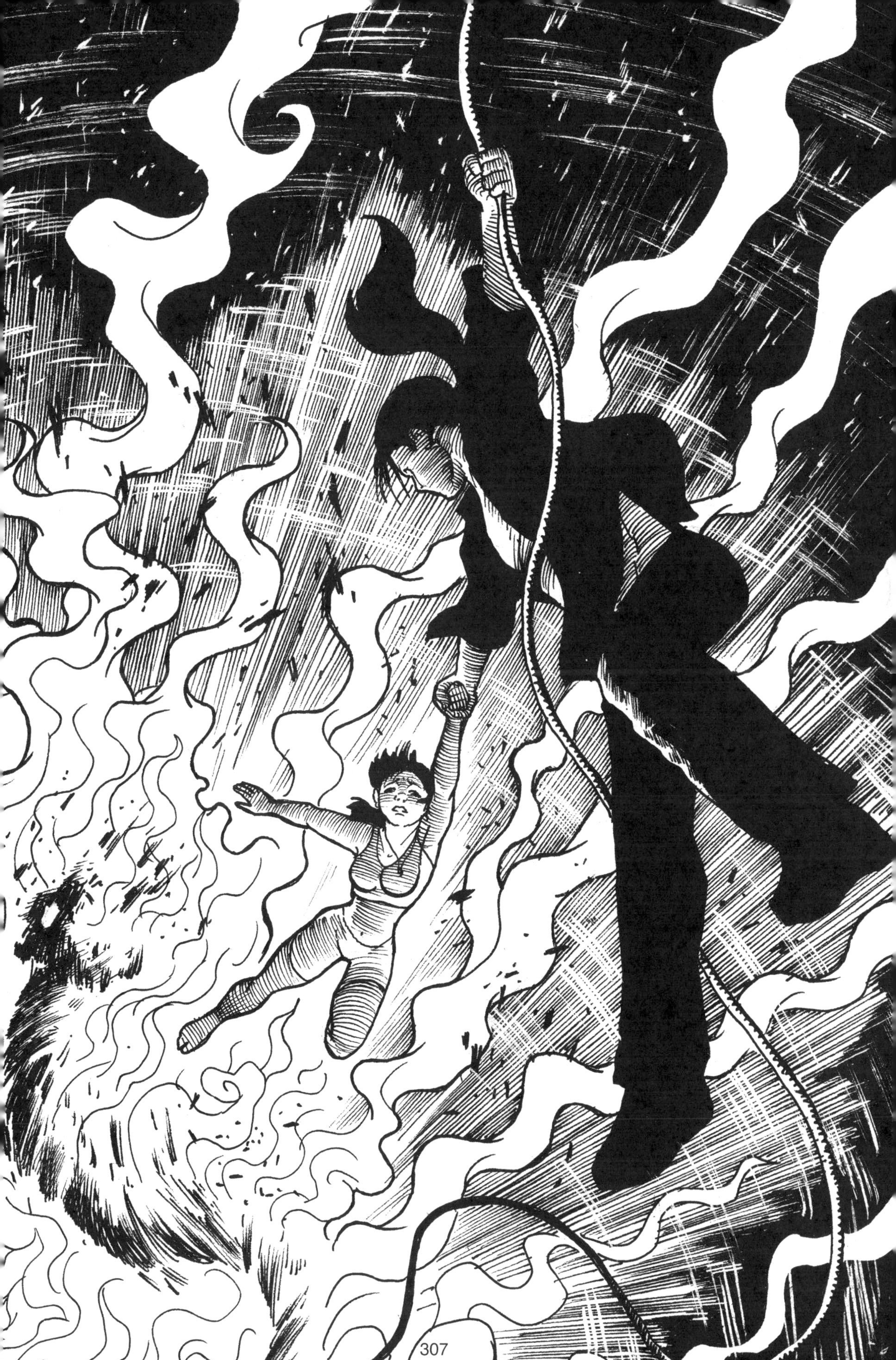

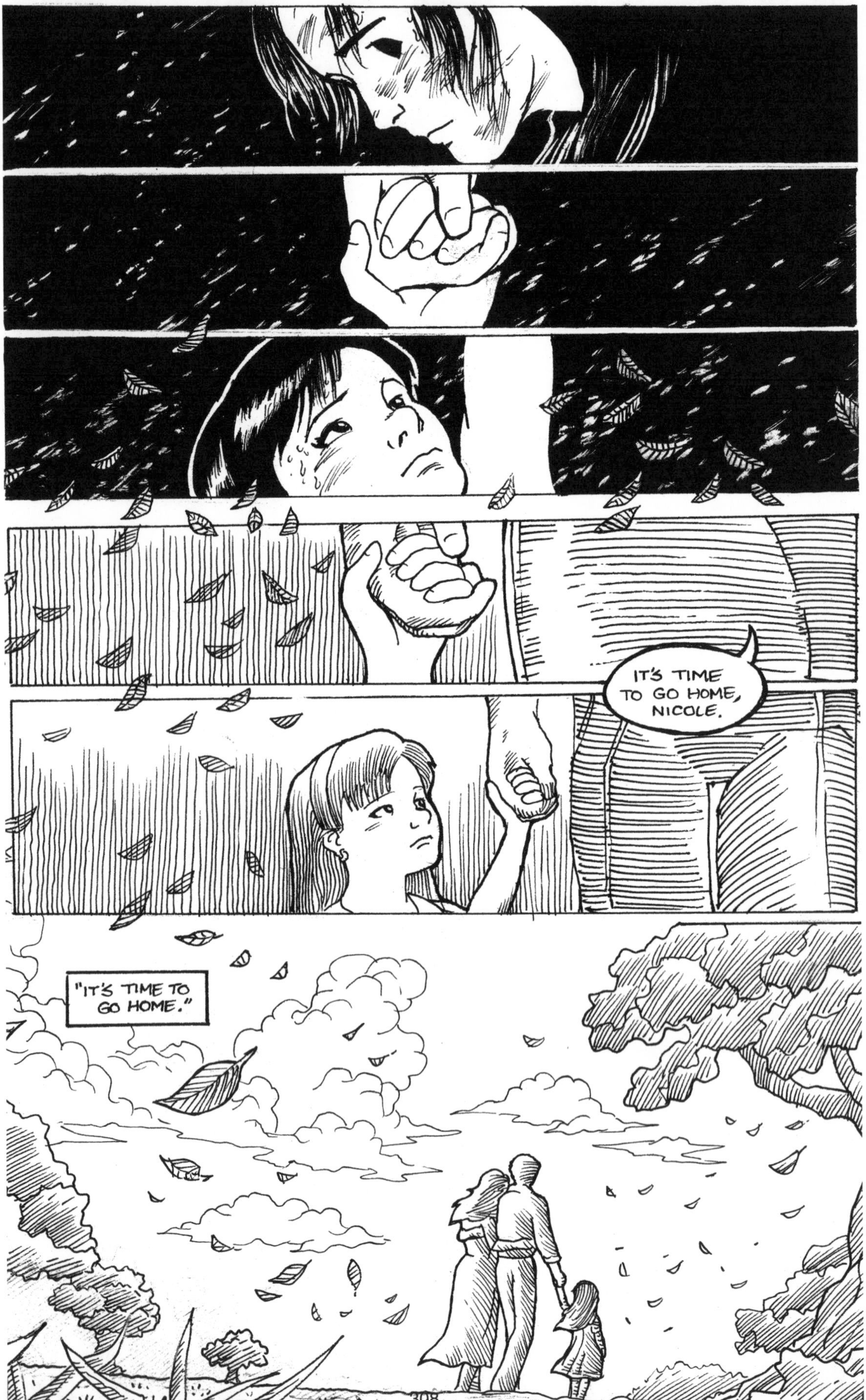
IT'S TIME TO GO HOME, NICOLE.
"IT'S TIME TO GO HOME."

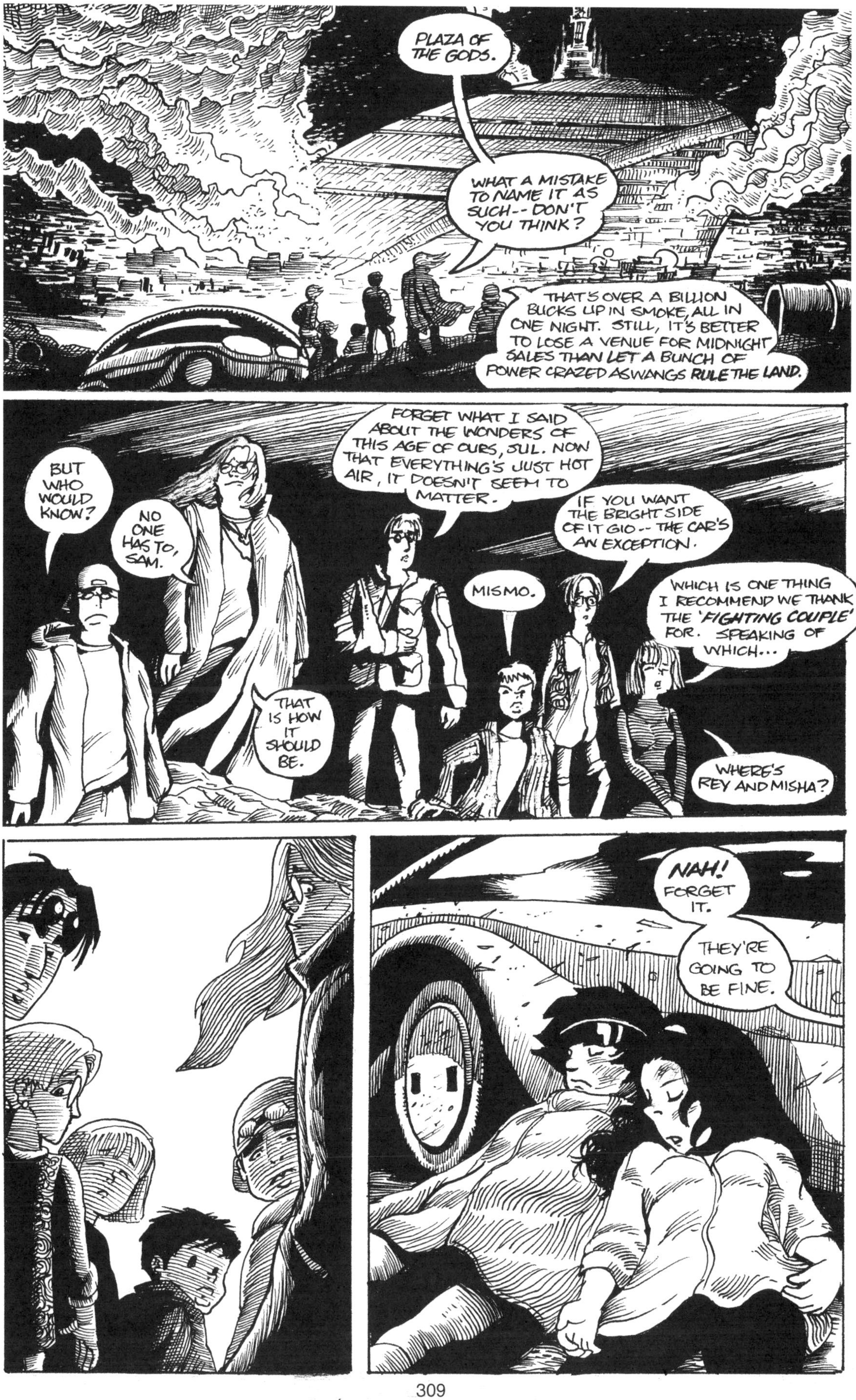
PLAZA OF THE GODS.
WHAT A MISTAKE TO NAME IT AS SUCH-- DON'T YOU THINK?
THAT'S OVER A BILLION BUCKS UP IN SMOKE, ALL IN ONE NIGHT. STILL, IT'S BETTER TO LOSE A VENUE FOR MIDNIGHT SALES THAN LET A BUNCH OF POWER CRAZED ASWANGS RULE THE LAND.
BUT WHO WOULD KNOW?
NO ONE HAS TO, SAM.
THAT IS HOW IT SHOULD BE.
FORGET WHAT I SAID ABOUT THE WONDERS OF THIS AGE OF OURS, SUL. NOW THAT EVERYTHING'S JUST HOT AIR, IT DOESN'T SEEM TO MATTER.
MISMO.
IF YOU WANT THE BRIGHT SIDE OF IT GIO -- THE CAR'S AN EXCEPTION.
WHICH IS ONE THING I RECOMMEND WE THANK THE 'FIGHTING COUPLE' FOR. SPEAKING OF WHICH...
WHERE'S REY AND MISHA?
NAH! FORGET IT.
THEY'RE GOING TO BE FINE.

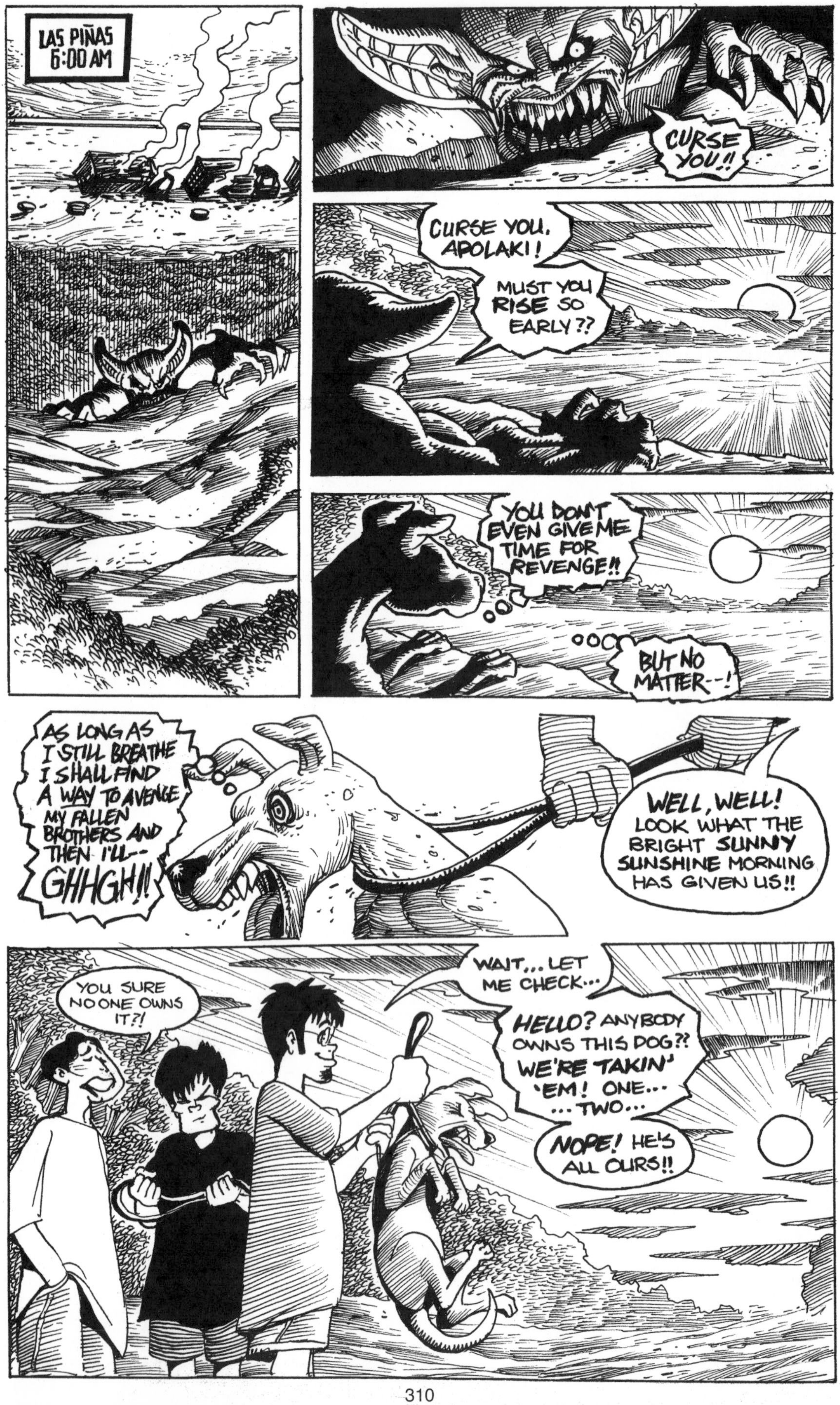
LAS PIÑAS
6:00 AM
CURSE YOU!!
CURSE YOU, APOLAKI!
MUST YOU RISE SO EARLY??
YOU DON'T EVEN GIVE ME TIME FOR REVENGE!!
BUT NO MATTER--!
AS LONG AS I STILL BREATHE I SHALL FIND A WAY TO AVENGE MY FALLEN BROTHERS AND THEN I'LL--
GHHGH!!
WELL, WELL! LOOK WHAT THE BRIGHT SUNNY SUNSHINE MORNING HAS GIVEN US!!
YOU SURE NO ONE OWNS IT?!
WAIT... LET ME CHECK...
HELLO? ANYBODY OWNS THIS DOG?? WE'RE TAKIN' 'EM! ONE... ...TWO...
NOPE! HE'S ALL OURS!!

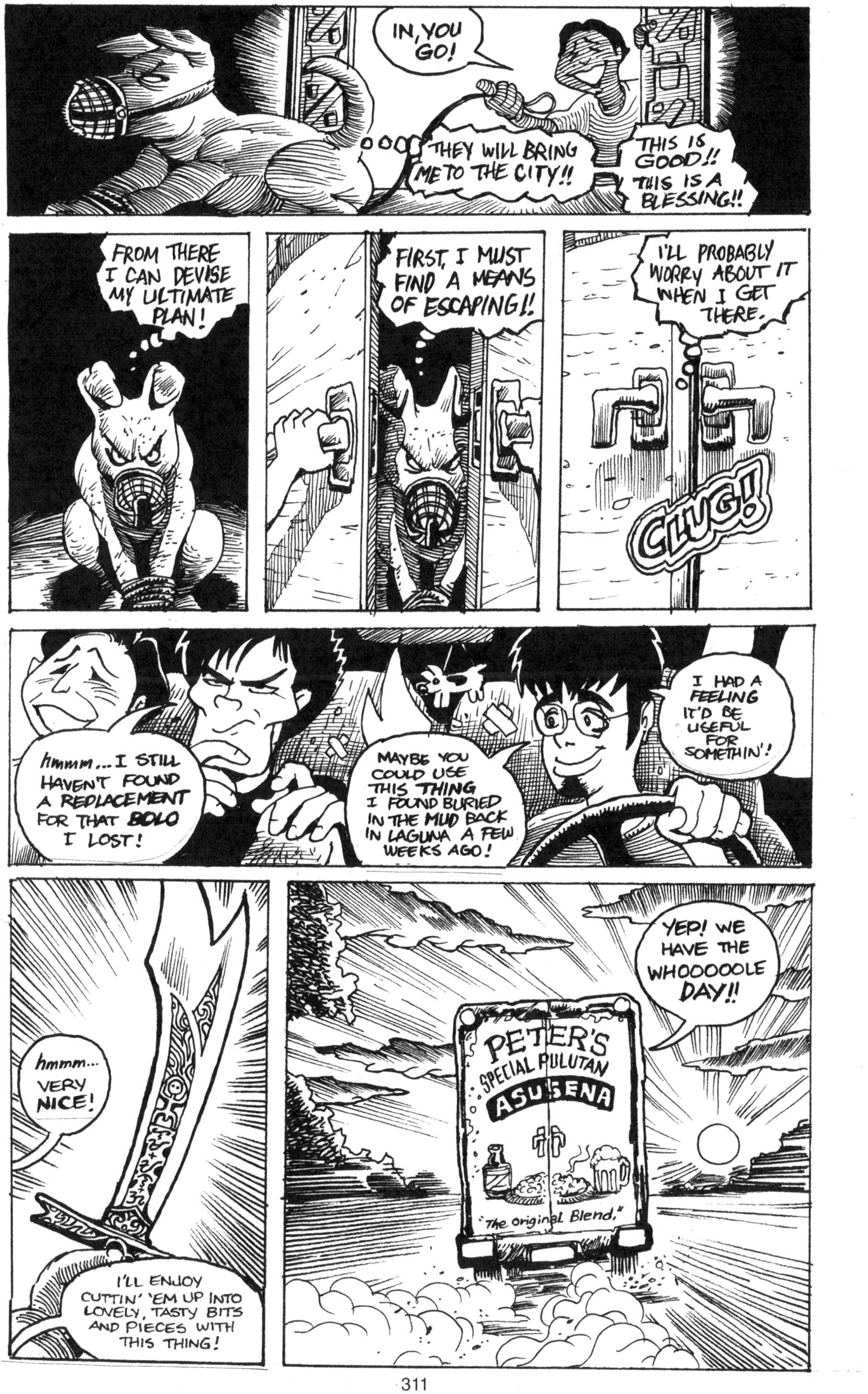
IN, YOU GO!
THEY WILL BRING ME TO THE CITY!!
THIS IS GOOD!! THIS IS A BLESSING!!
FROM THERE I CAN DEVISE MY ULTIMATE PLAN!
FIRST, I MUST FIND A MEANS OF ESCAPING!!
I'LL PROBABLY WORRY ABOUT IT WHEN I GET THERE.
CLUG!
hmmm... I STILL HAVEN'T FOUND A REPLACEMENT FOR THAT BOLO I LOST!
MAYBE YOU COULD USE THIS THING I FOUND BURIED IN THE MUD BACK IN LAGUNA A FEW WEEKS AGO!
I HAD A FEELING IT'D BE USEFUL FOR SOMETHIN'!
hmmm... VERY NICE!
I'LL ENJOY CUTTIN' 'EM UP INTO LOVELY, TASTY BITS AND PIECES WITH THIS THING!
PETER'S SPECIAL PULUTAN
ASUSENA
"The original Blend."
YEP! WE HAVE THE WHOOOOOLE DAY!!

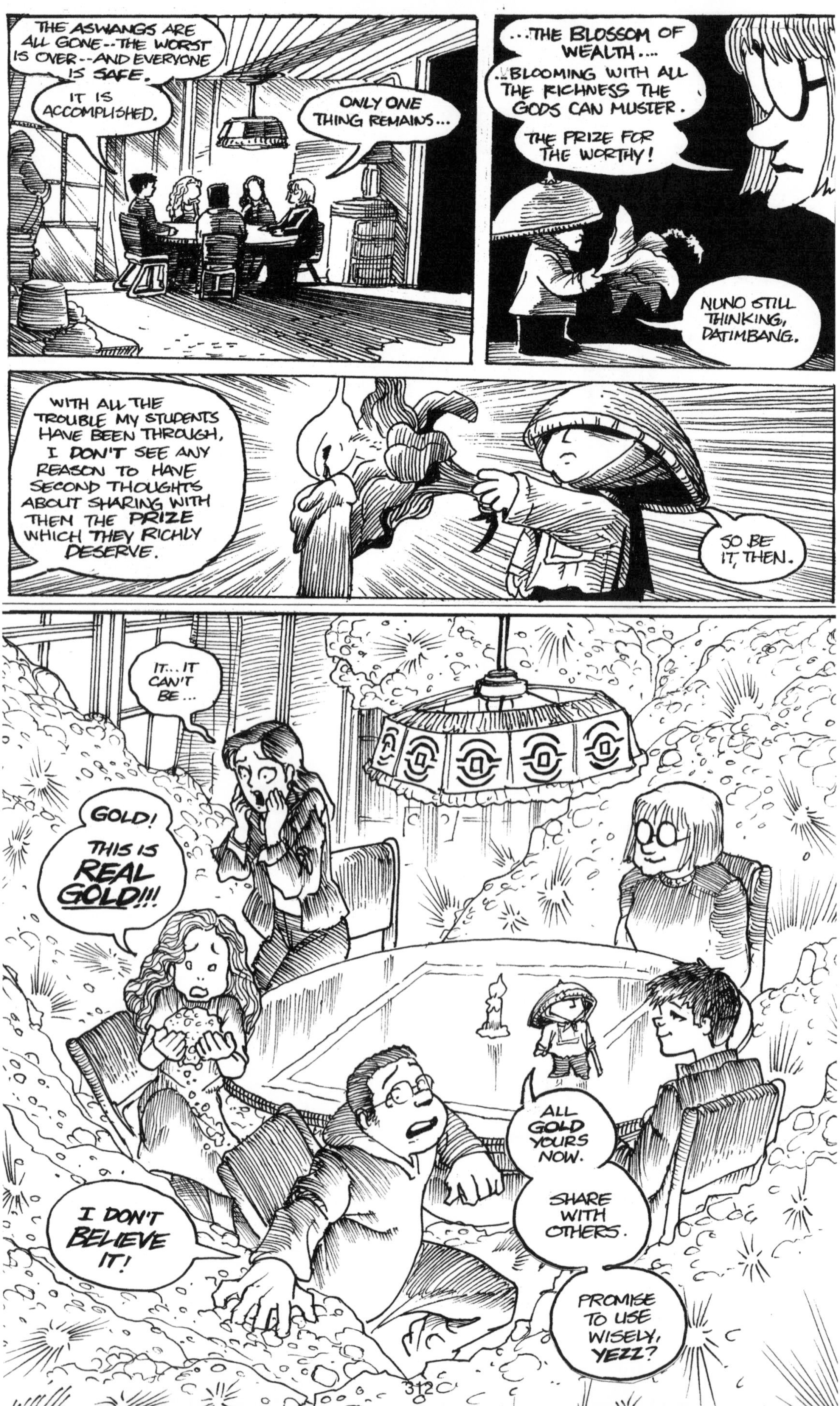

THE ASWANGS ARE ALL GONE--THE WORST IS OVER--AND EVERYONE IS SAFE.
IT IS ACCOMPLISHED.
ONLY ONE THING REMAINS...
...THE BLOSSOM OF WEALTH....
...BLOOMING WITH ALL THE RICHNESS THE GODS CAN MUSTER.
THE PRIZE FOR THE WORTHY!
NUNO STILL THINKING, DATIMBANG.
WITH ALL THE TROUBLE MY STUDENTS HAVE BEEN THROUGH, I DON'T SEE ANY REASON TO HAVE SECOND THOUGHTS ABOUT SHARING WITH THEN THE PRIZE WHICH THEY RICHLY DESERVE.
SO BE IT, THEN.
IT... IT CAN'T BE...
GOLD! THIS IS REAL GOLD!!!
I DON'T BELIEVE IT!
ALL GOLD YOURS NOW.
SHARE WITH OTHERS.
PROMISE TO USE WISELY, YEZZ?

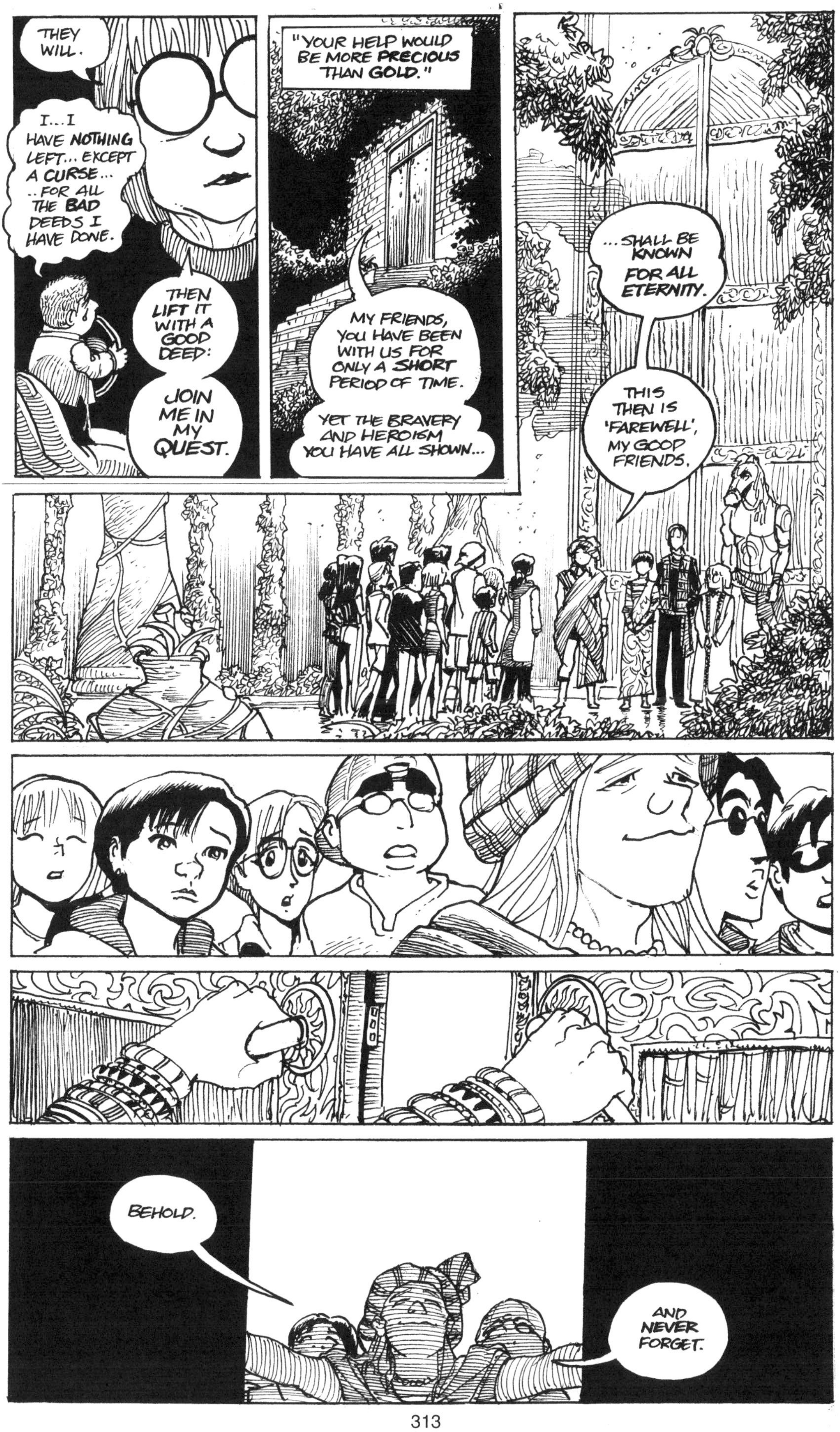
THEY WILL.
I... I HAVE NOTHING LEFT... EXCEPT A CURSE... ..FOR ALL THE BAD DEEDS I HAVE DONE.
THEN LIFT IT WITH A GOOD DEED:
JOIN ME IN MY QUEST.
"YOUR HELP WOULD BE MORE PRECIOUS THAN GOLD."
MY FRIENDS, YOU HAVE BEEN WITH US FOR ONLY A SHORT PERIOD OF TIME.
YET THE BRAVERY AND HEROISM YOU HAVE ALL SHOWN...
...SHALL BE KNOWN FOR ALL ETERNITY.
THIS THEN IS 'FAREWELL', MY GOOD FRIENDS.
BEHOLD.
AND NEVER FORGET.

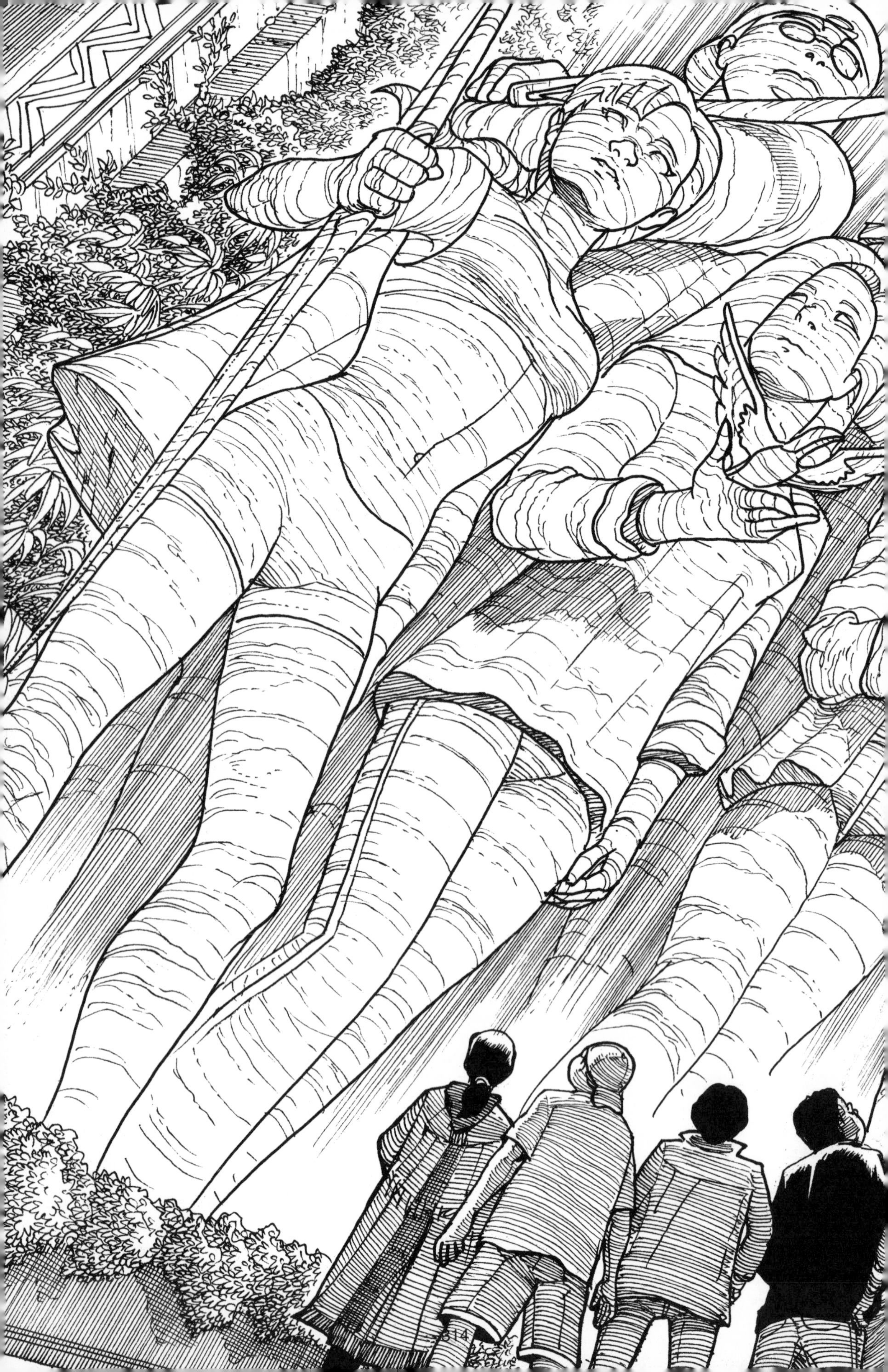

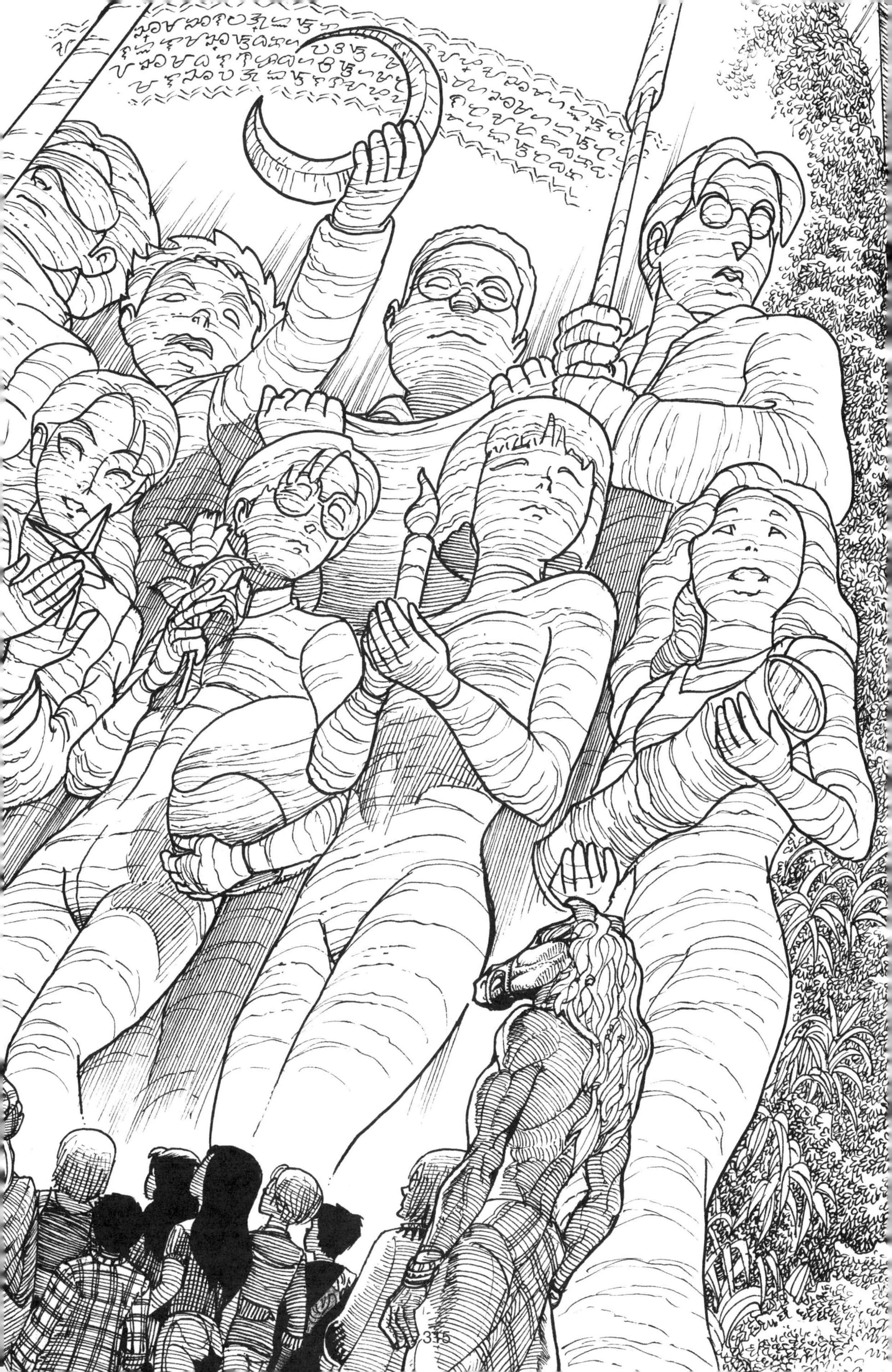

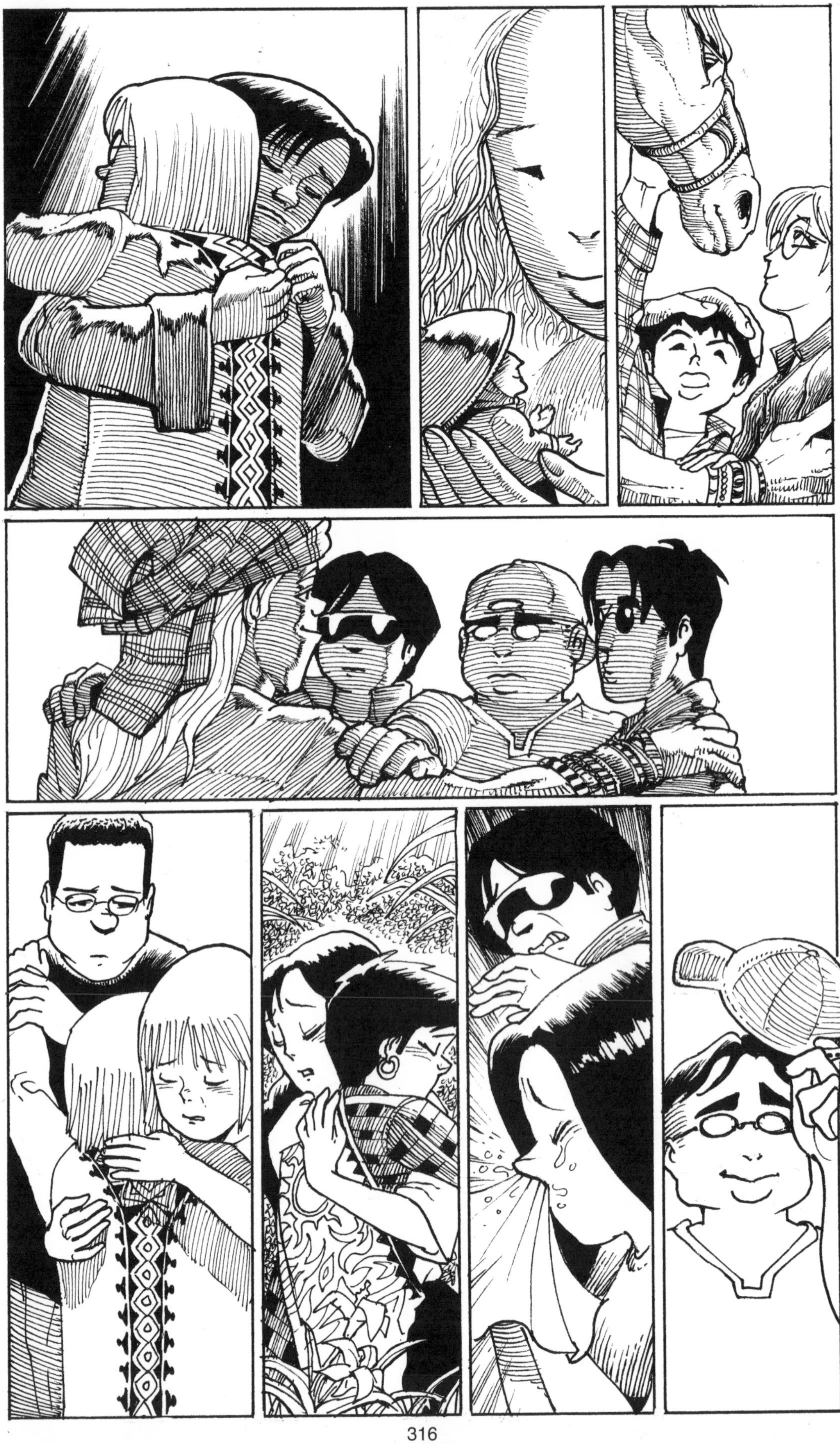

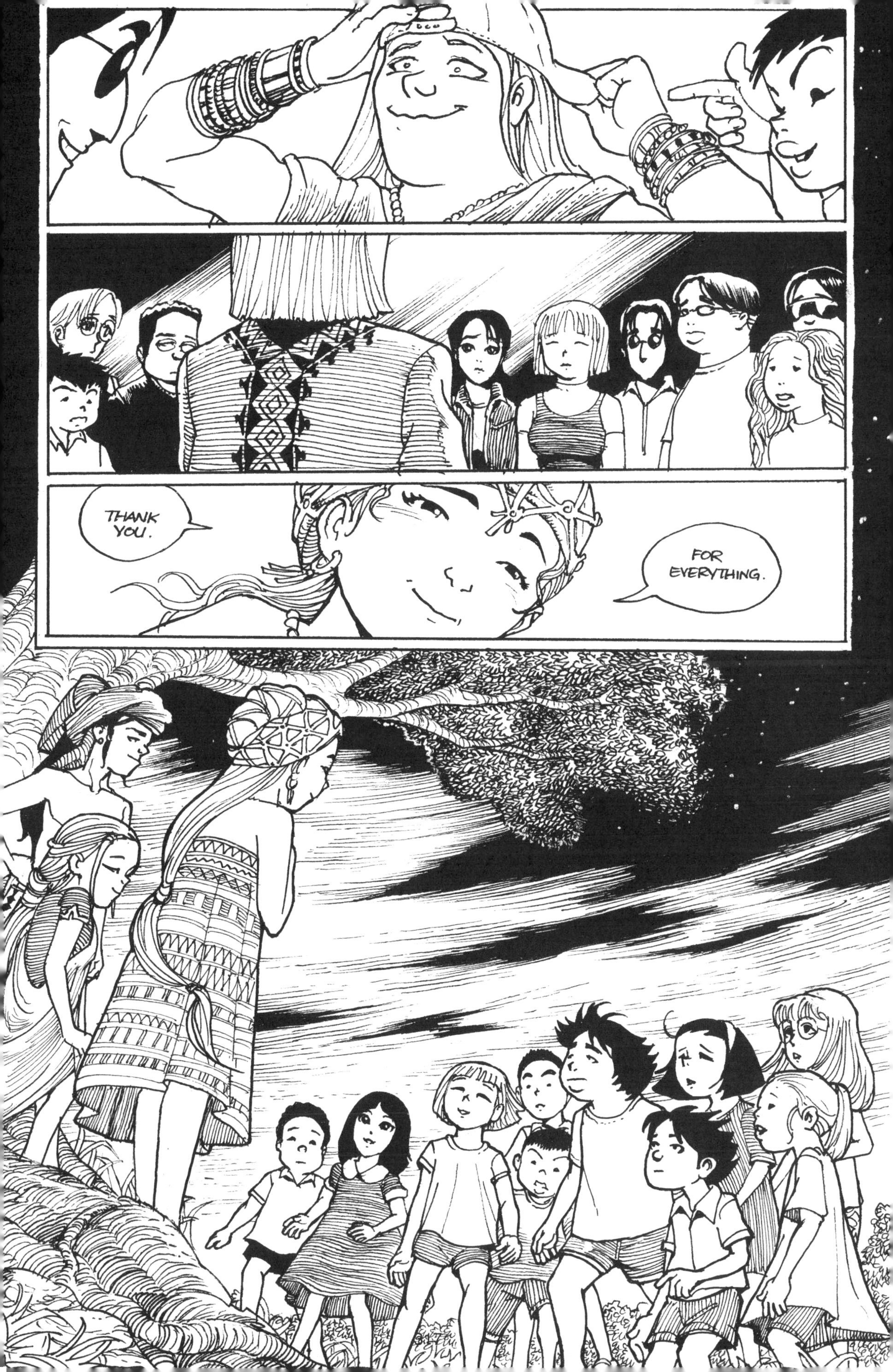
THANK YOU.
FOR EVERYTHING.

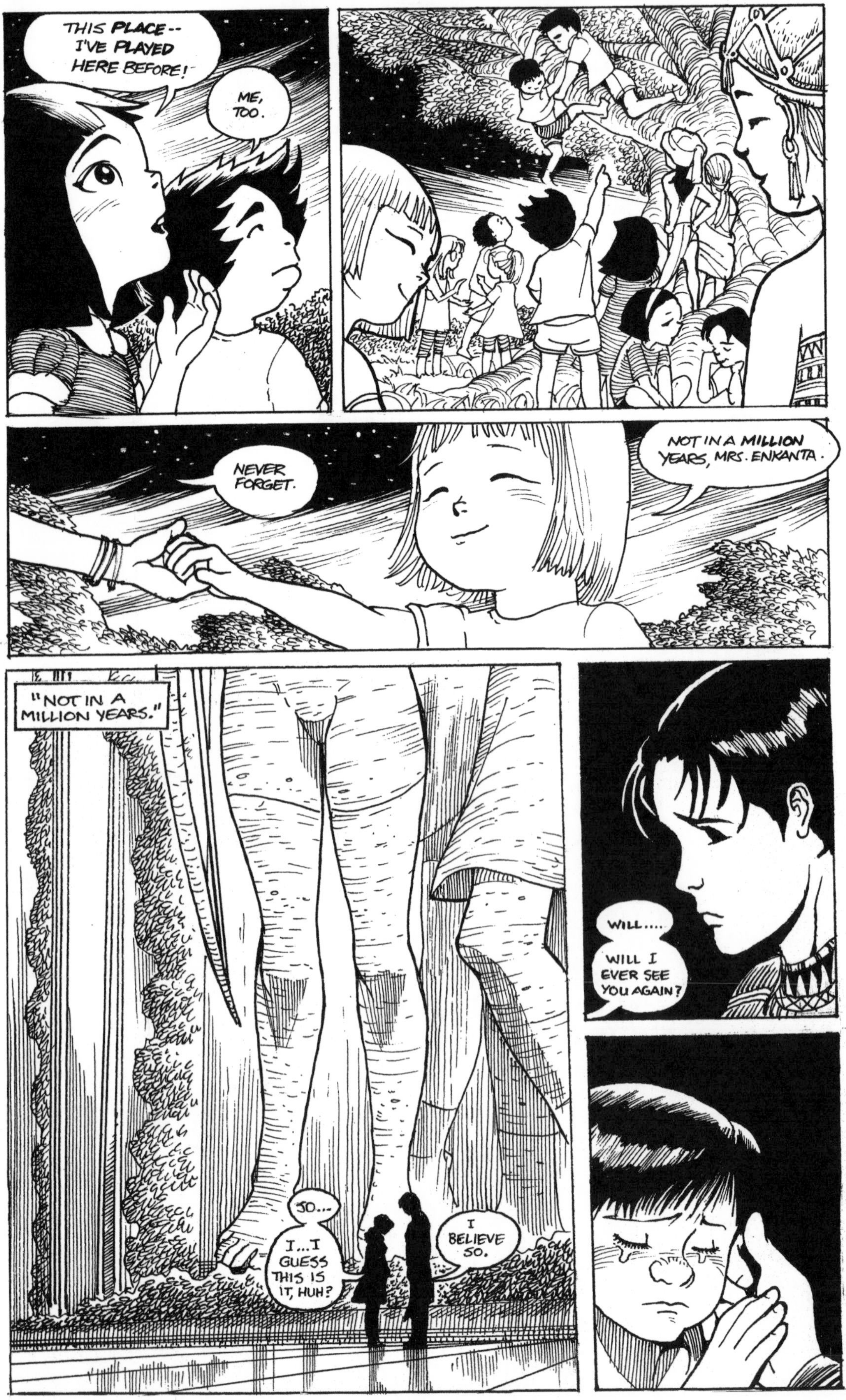
THIS PLACE-- I'VE PLAYED HERE BEFORE!
ME, TOO.
NEVER FORGET.
NOT IN A MILLION YEARS, MRS. ENKANTA.
"NOT IN A MILLION YEARS."
SO...
I...I GUESS THIS IS IT, HUH?
I BELIEVE SO.
WILL.....
WILL I EVER SEE YOU AGAIN?

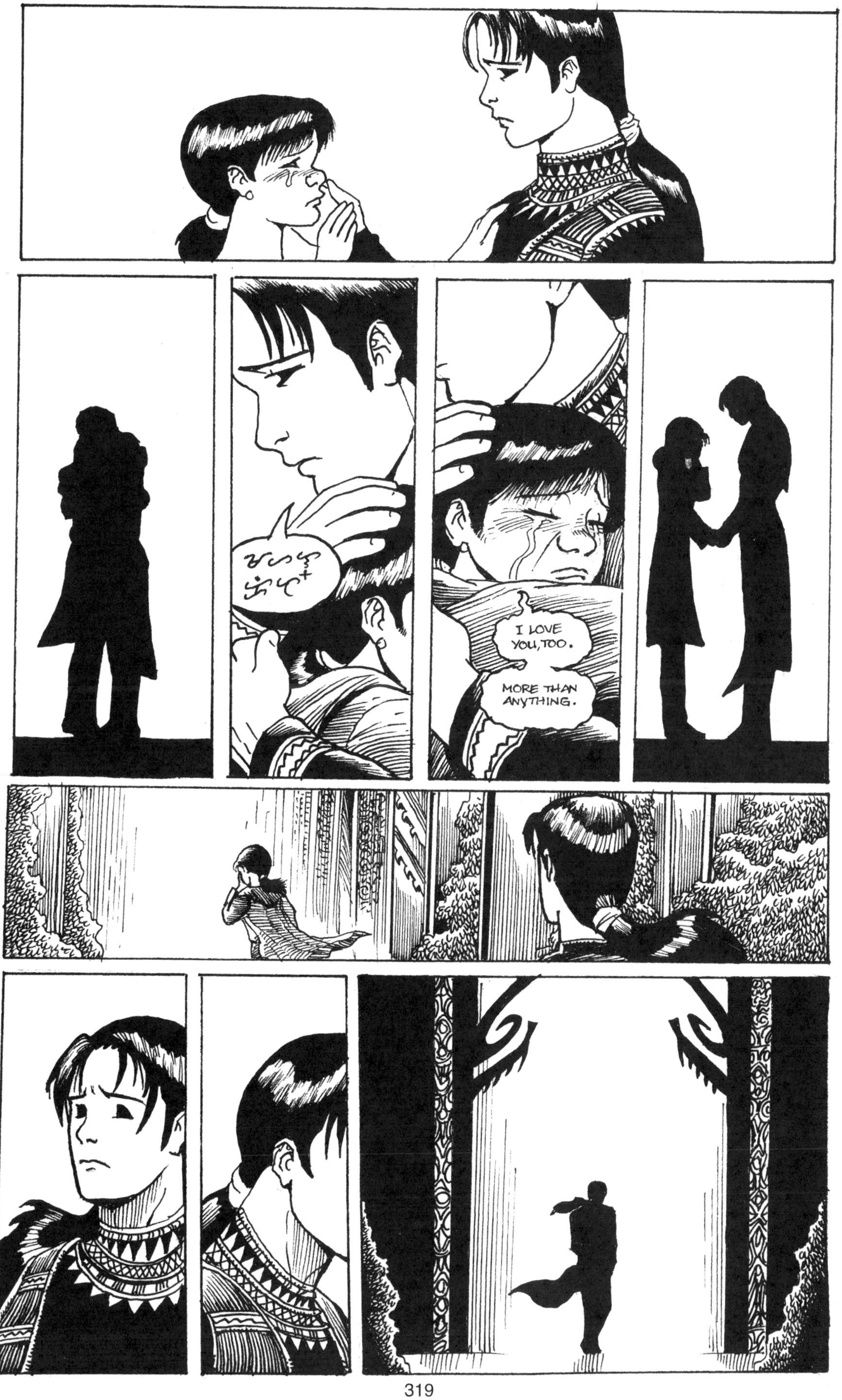
I LOVE YOU, TOO.
MORE THAN ANYTHING.

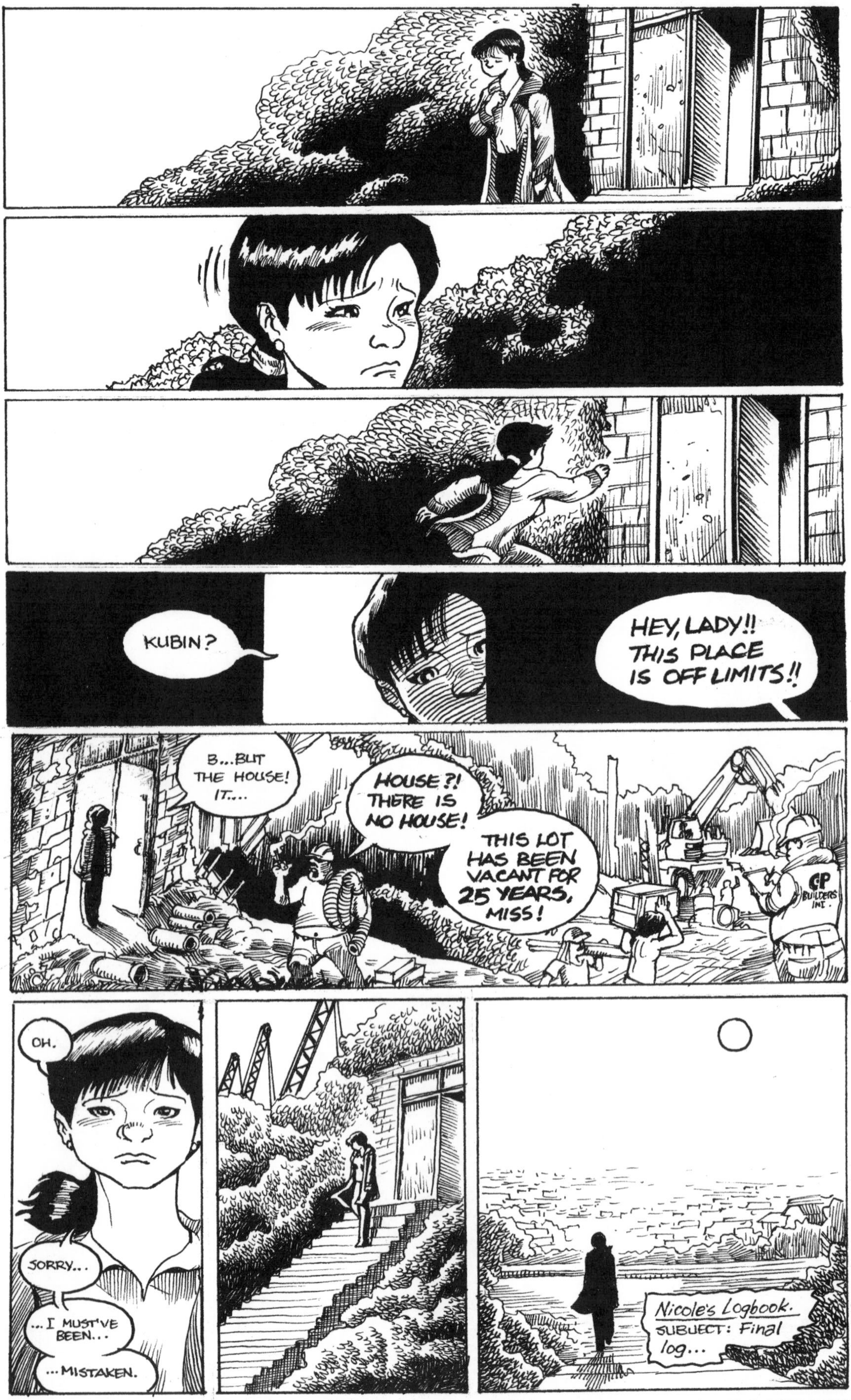
KUBIN?
HEY, LADY!! THIS PLACE IS OFF LIMITS!!
B...BUT THE HOUSE! IT...
HOUSE?! THERE IS NO HOUSE!
THIS LOT HAS BEEN VACANT FOR 25 YEARS, MISS!
CP BUILDERS INI.
OH.
SORRY...
...I MUST'VE BEEN...
...MISTAKEN.
Nicole's Logbook.
SUBJECT: Final log...

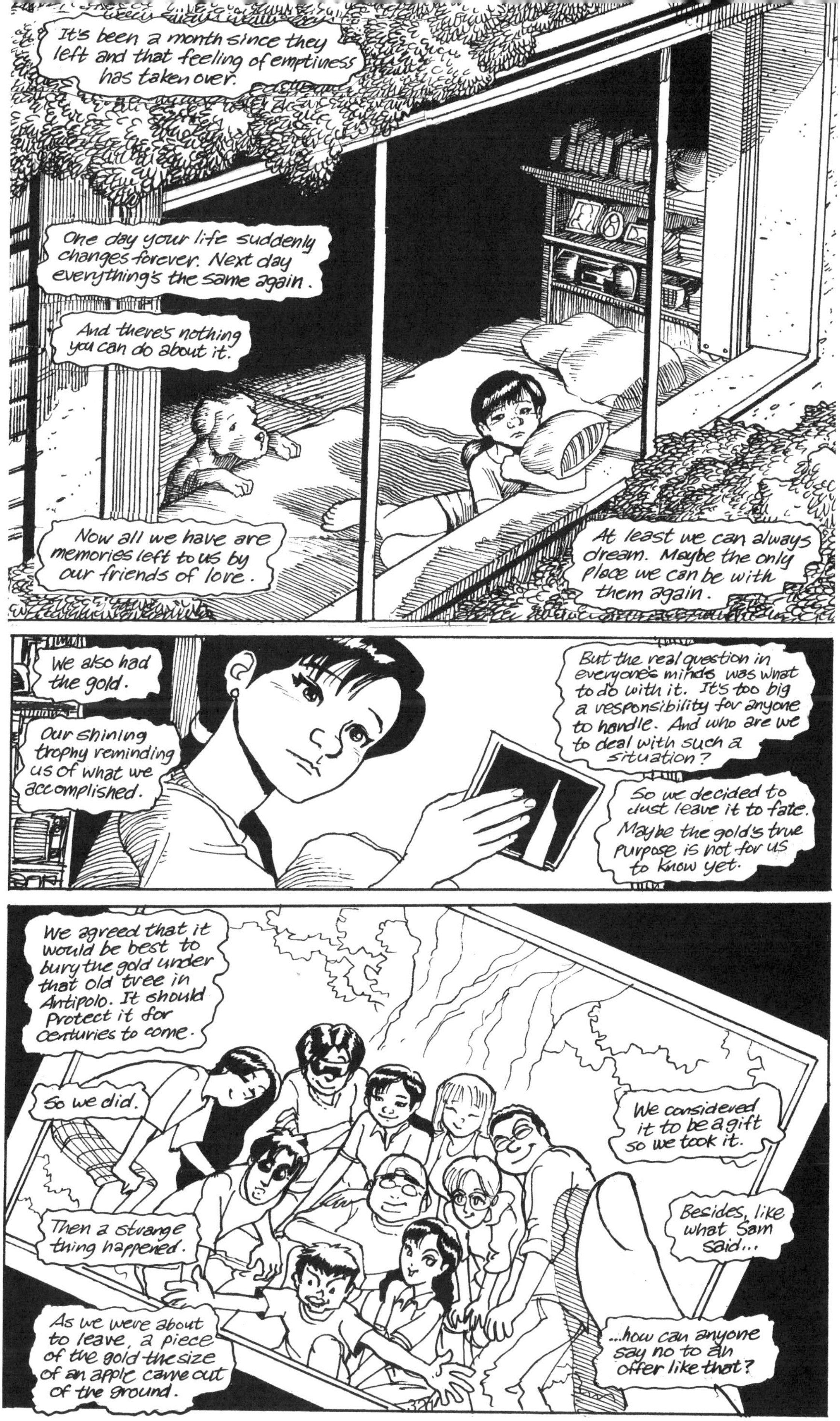
It's been a month since they left and that feeling of emptiness has taken over.
One day your life suddenly changes forever. Next day everything's the same again.
And there's nothing you can do about it.
Now all we have are memories left to us by our friends of love.
At least we can always dream. Maybe the only place we can be with them again.
We also had the gold.
Our shining trophy reminding us of what we accomplished.
But the real question in everyone's minds was what to do with it. It's too big a responsibility for anyone to handle. And who are we to deal with such a situation?
So we decided to just leave it to fate. Maybe the gold's true purpose is not for us to know yet.
We agreed that it would be best to bury the gold under that old tree in Antipolo. It should protect it for centuries to come.
So we did.
Then a strange thing happened.
As we were about to leave, a piece of the gold the size of an apple came out of the ground.
We considered it to be a gift so we took it.
Besides, like what Sam said...
...how can anyone say no to an offer like that?

But I still believe there's one thing far more precious than a piece of yellow rock.

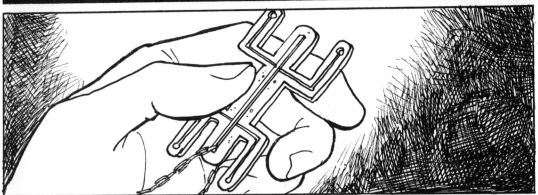

So it's time to move on.

Time to go out there and be amongst simple folk.

Time to be part of the regular world again.

But for me and my friends, the world will never be the same again.

And we wouldn't want to have that any other way for all the gold in the world.

I'M SO SORRY FOR KEEPING YOU WAITING, KAYE. CHARITY WORK'S BEEN KEEPING ME BUSY THESE PAST FEW DAYS. 'HOPE YOU'LL UNDERSTAND.

OH---HERE! I'M RETURNING ALL THE PSYCHOLOGY BOOKS YOU LENT ME ALL THESE YEARS.

I'M HAPPY TO SAY THAT I'VE BEGUN LIVING A WHOLE NEW LIFE NOW. I GUESS I WON'T BE NEEDING 'EM ANYMORE.

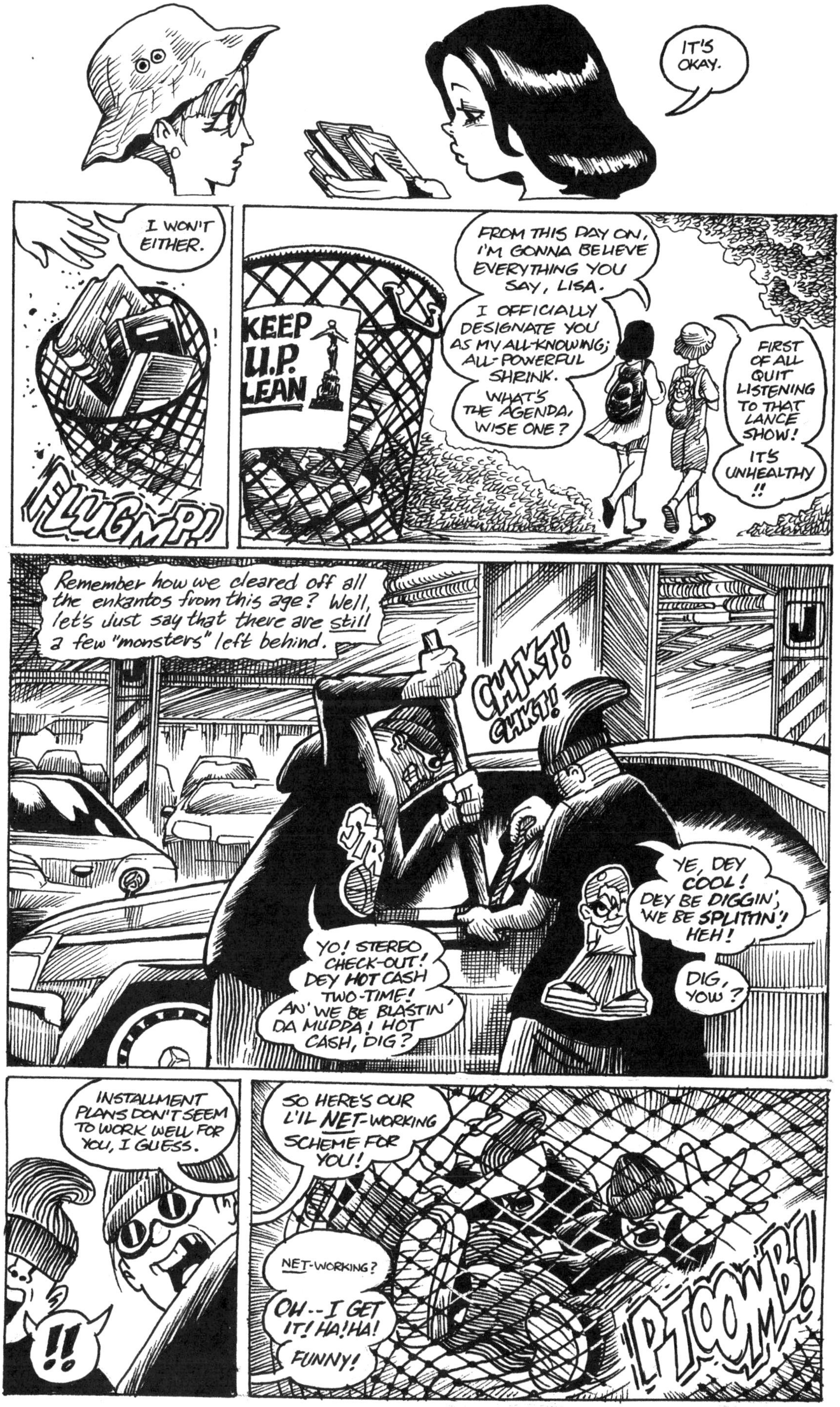
IT'S OKAY.
I WON'T EITHER.
FLUGMP!
KEEP U.P. CLEAN
FROM THIS DAY ON, I'M GONNA BELIEVE EVERYTHING YOU SAY, LISA.
I OFFICIALLY DESIGNATE YOU AS MY ALL-KNOWING; ALL-POWERFUL SHRINK.
WHAT'S THE AGENDA, WISE ONE?
FIRST OF ALL QUIT LISTENING TO THAT LANCE SHOW!
IT'S UNHEALTHY!!
Remember how we cleared off all the enkantos from this age? Well, let's just say that there are still a few "monsters" left behind.
CHKT! CHKT!
YE, DEY COOL! DEY BE DIGGIN', WE BE SPLITTIN'! HEH!
DIG, YOW?
YO! STEREO CHECK-OUT! DEY HOT CASH TWO-TIME! AN' WE BE BLASTIN' DA MUDDA! HOT CASH, DIG?
INSTALLMENT PLANS DON'T SEEM TO WORK WELL FOR YOU, I GUESS.
!!
SO HERE'S OUR L'IL NET-WORKING SCHEME FOR YOU!
NET-WORKING?
OH--I GET IT! HA! HA! FUNNY!
PTOOMB!

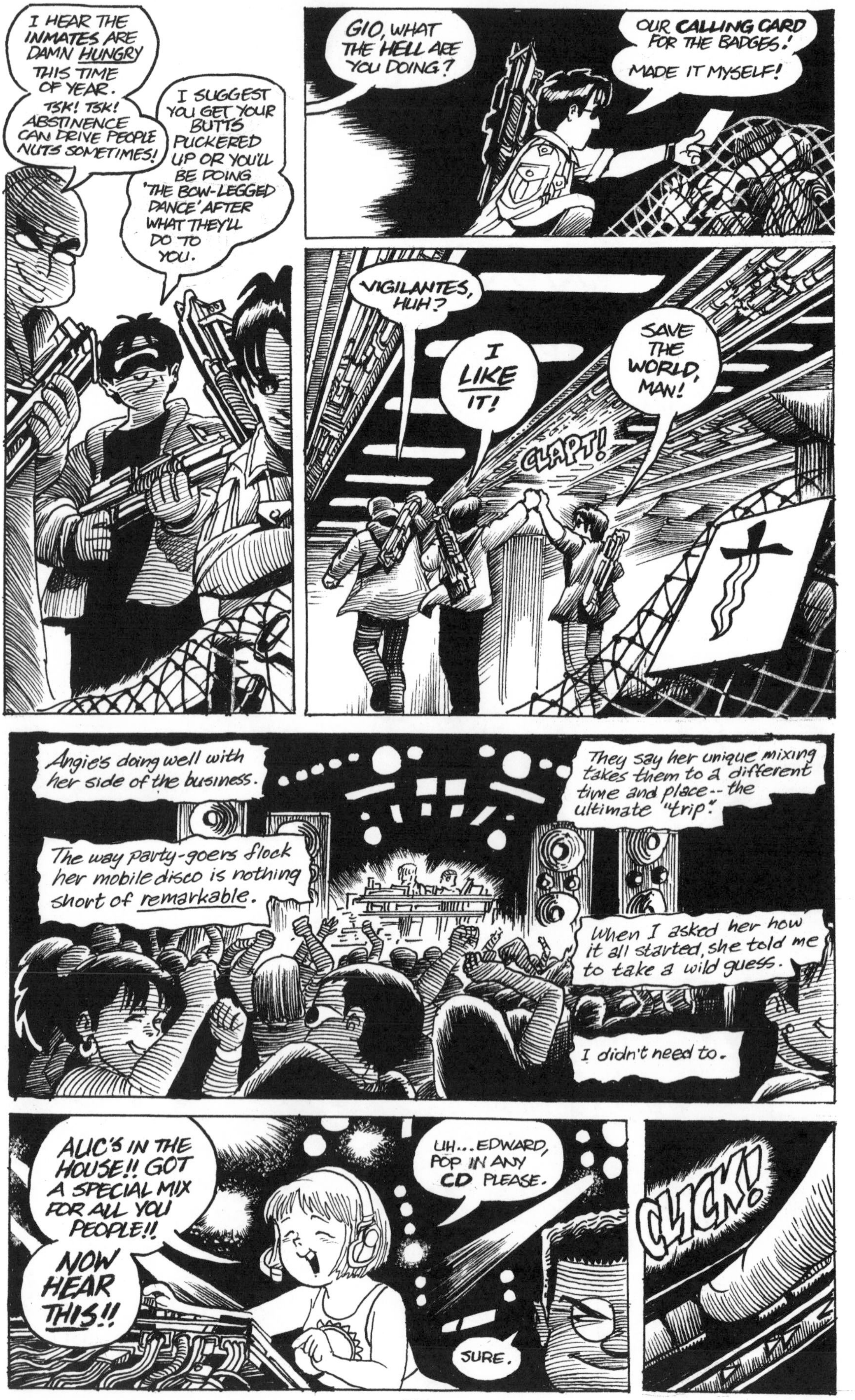
I HEAR THE INMATES ARE DAMN HUNGRY THIS TIME OF YEAR. TSK! TSK! ABSTINENCE CAN DRIVE PEOPLE NUTS SOMETIMES!
I SUGGEST YOU GET YOUR BUTTS PUCKERED UP OR YOU'LL BE DOING 'THE BOW-LEGGED DANCE' AFTER WHAT THEY'LL DO TO YOU.
GIO, WHAT THE HELL ARE YOU DOING?
OUR CALLING CARD FOR THE BADGES! MADE IT MYSELF!
VIGILANTES, HUH?
I LIKE IT!
SAVE THE WORLD, MAN!
CLAPT!
Angie's doing well with her side of the business.
They say her unique mixing takes them to a different time and place -- the ultimate "trip".
The way party-goers flock her mobile disco is nothing short of remarkable.
When I asked her how it all started, she told me to take a wild guess.
I didn't need to.
ALIC'S IN THE HOUSE!! GOT A SPECIAL MIX FOR ALL YOU PEOPLE!!
NOW HEAR THIS!!
UH... EDWARD, POP IN ANY CD PLEASE.
SURE.
CLICK!

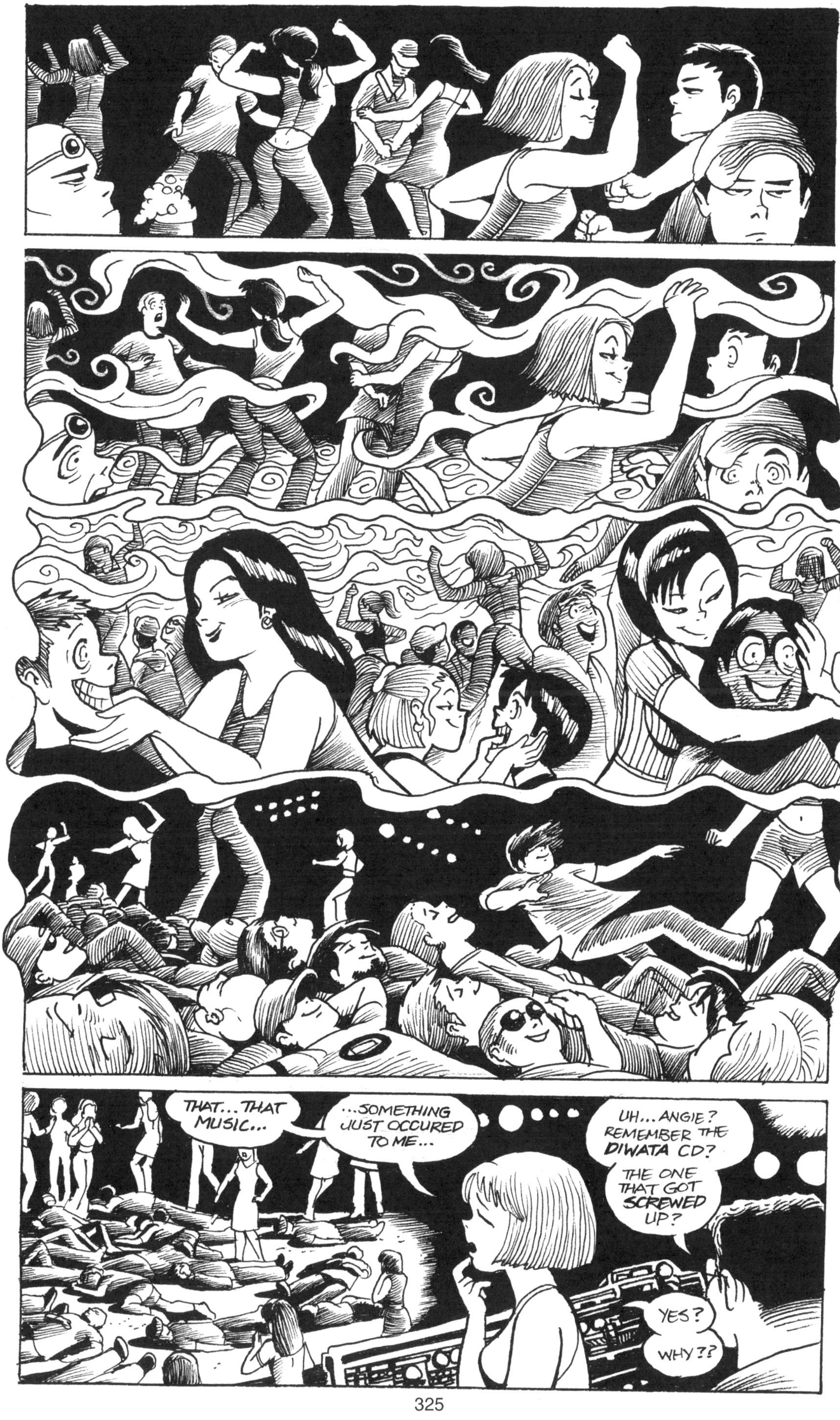
THAT... THAT MUSIC...
...SOMETHING JUST OCCURED TO ME...
UH... ANGIE? REMEMBER THE DIWATA CD?
THE ONE THAT GOT SCREWED UP?
YES?
WHY??

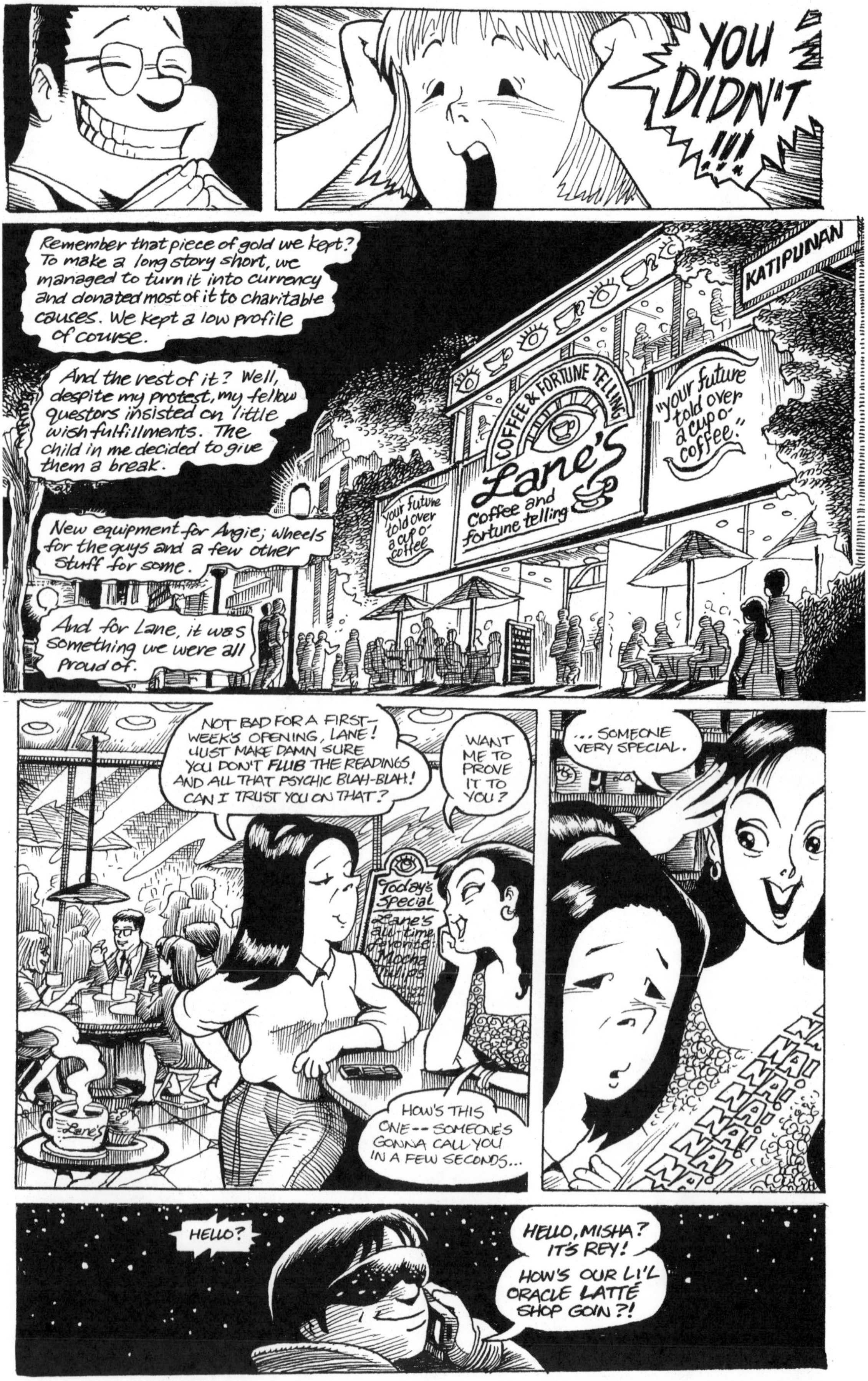
YOU DIDN'T !!!
Remember that piece of gold we kept? To make a long story short, we managed to turn it into currency and donated most of it to charitable causes. We kept a low profile of course.
And the rest of it? Well, despite my protest, my fellow questors insisted on little wish fulfillments. The child in me decided to give them a break.
New equipment for Angie; wheels for the guys and a few other stuff for some.
And for Lane, it was something we were all proud of.
KATIPUNAN
COFFEE & FORTUNE TELLING
Lane's
Coffee and fortune telling
"your future told over a cup o' coffee."
your future told over a cup o' coffee
NOT BAD FOR A FIRST-WEEK'S OPENING, LANE! JUST MAKE DAMN SURE YOU DON'T FLUB THE READINGS AND ALL THAT PSYCHIC BLAH-BLAH! CAN I TRUST YOU ON THAT?
WANT ME TO PROVE IT TO YOU?
Today's Special
Lane's
HOW'S THIS ONE-- SOMEONE'S GONNA CALL YOU IN A FEW SECONDS...
...SOMEONE VERY SPECIAL.
NA! NA! NA! NA! NA!
HELLO?
HELLO, MISHA? IT'S REY! HOW'S OUR LI'L ORACLE LATTE SHOP GOIN?!

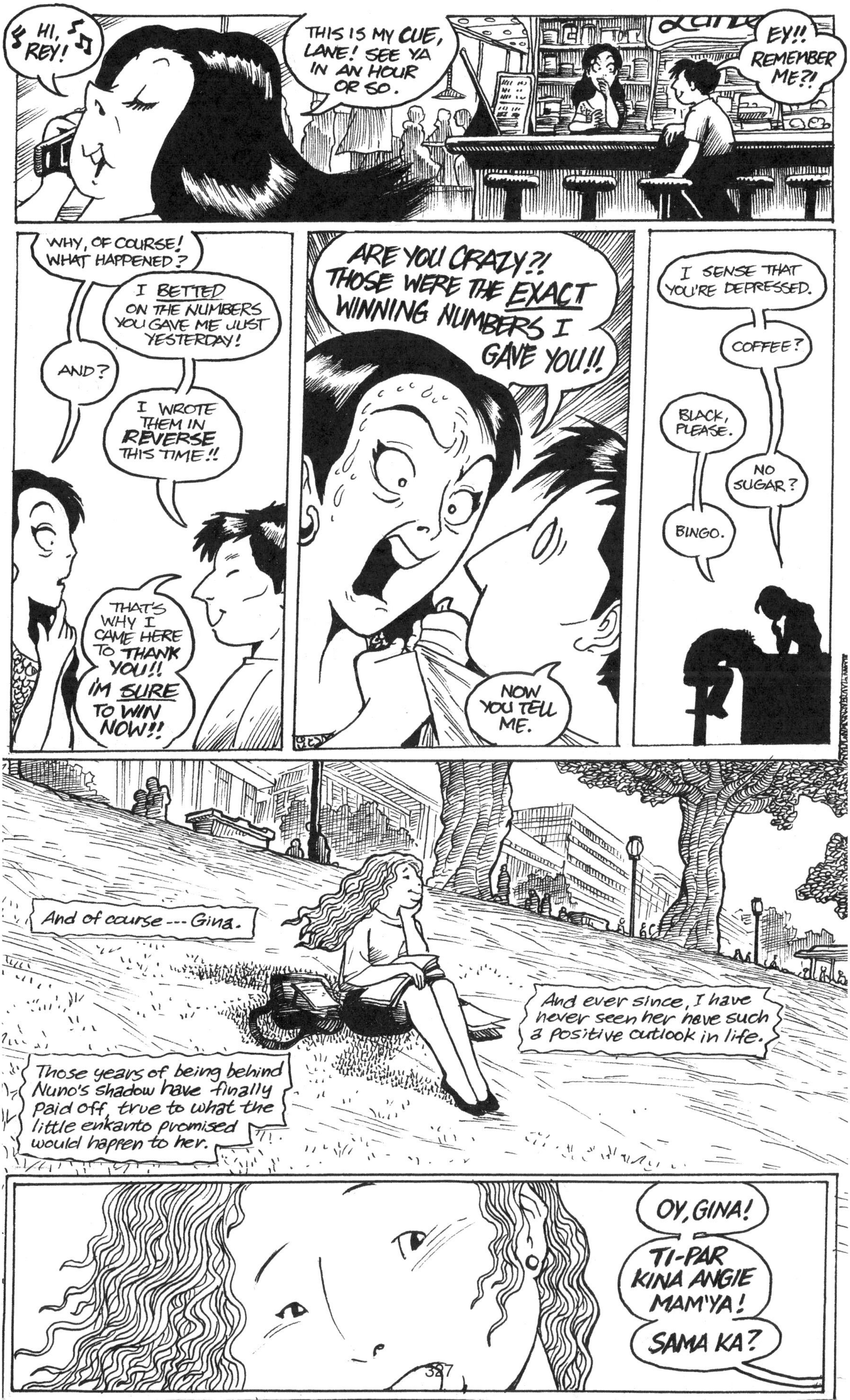
HI, REY!
THIS IS MY CUE, LANE! SEE YA IN AN HOUR OR SO.
EY!! REMEMBER ME?!
WHY, OF COURSE! WHAT HAPPENED?
I BETTED ON THE NUMBERS YOU GAVE ME JUST YESTERDAY!
AND?
I WROTE THEM IN REVERSE THIS TIME!!
THAT'S WHY I CAME HERE TO THANK YOU!! I'M SURE TO WIN NOW!!
ARE YOU CRAZY?! THOSE WERE THE EXACT WINNING NUMBERS I GAVE YOU!!
NOW YOU TELL ME.
I SENSE THAT YOU'RE DEPRESSED.
COFFEE?
BLACK, PLEASE.
NO SUGAR?
BINGO.
And of course --- Gina.
And ever since, I have never seen her have such a positive outlook in life.
Those years of being behind Nuno's shadow have finally paid off, true to what the little enkanto promised would happen to her.
OY, GINA!
TI-PAR KINA ANGIE MAM'YA!
SAMA KA?

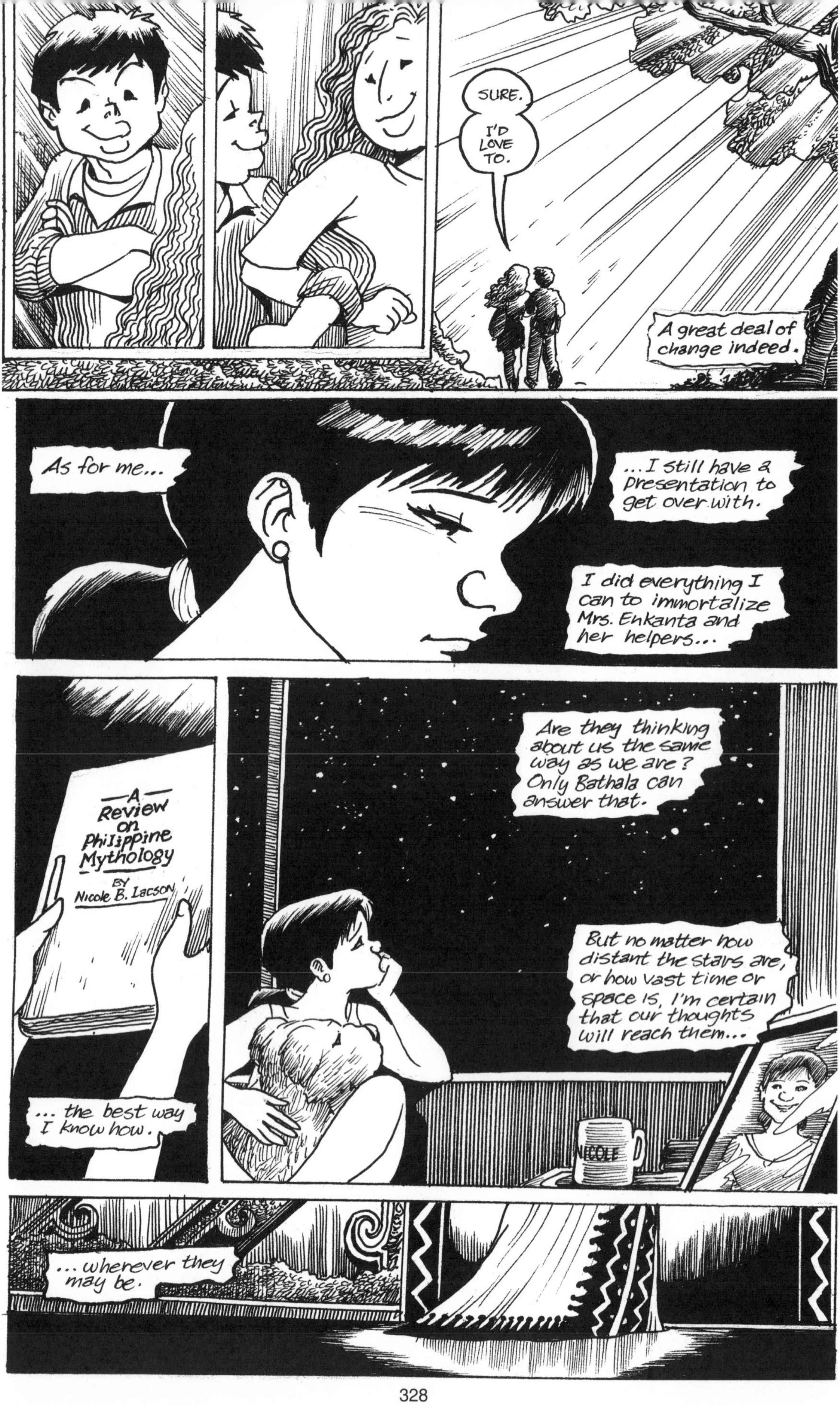
SURE.
I'D LOVE TO.
A great deal of change indeed.
As for me...
...I still have a presentation to get over with.
I did everything I can to immortalize Mrs. Enkanta and her helpers...
A Review on Philippine Mythology
BY Nicole B. Lacson
... the best way I know how.
Are they thinking about us the same way as we are? Only Bathala can answer that.
But no matter how distant the stars are, or how vast time or space is, I'm certain that our thoughts will reach them...
NICOLE
...wherever they may be.

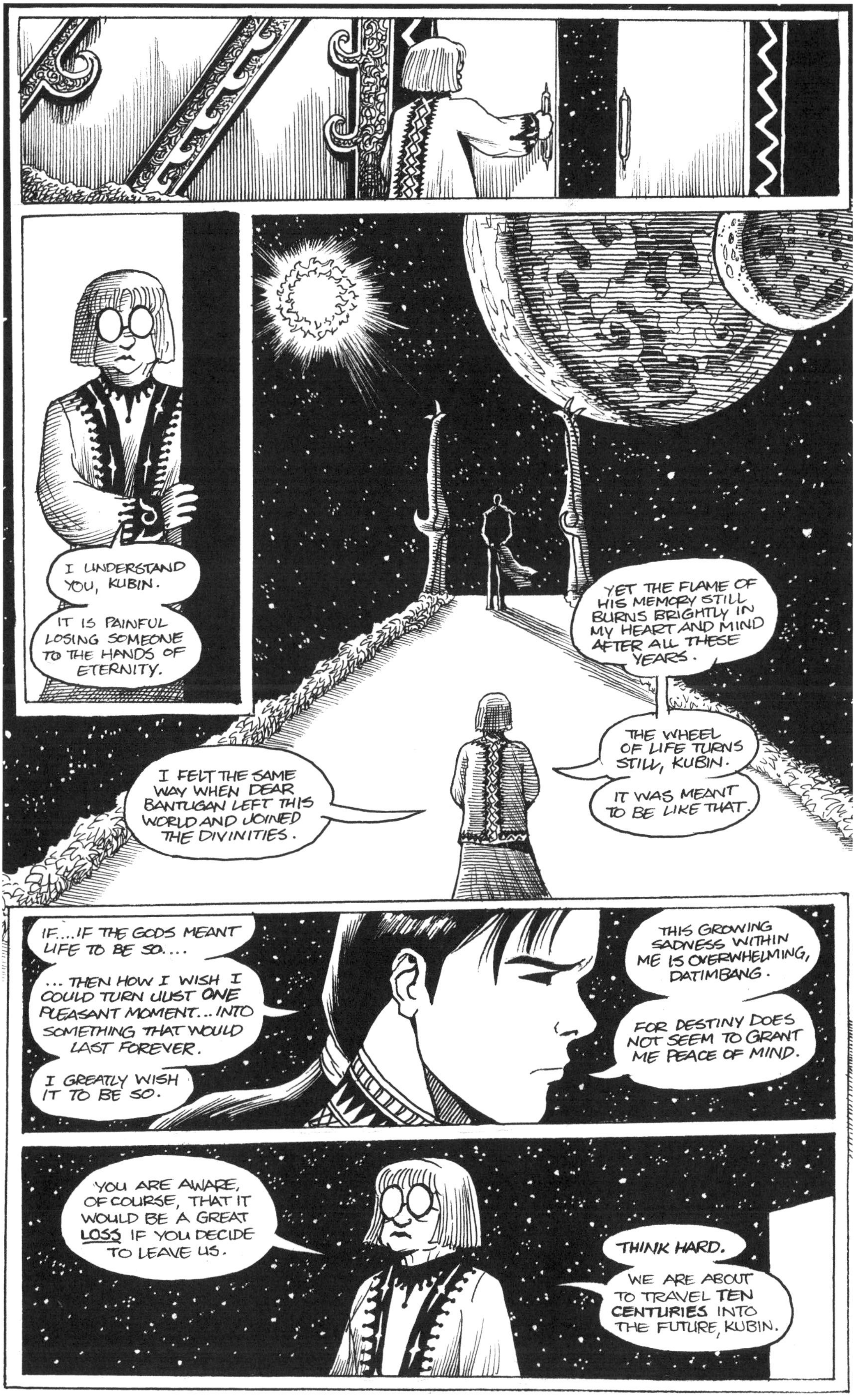

I UNDERSTAND YOU, KUBIN.
IT IS PAINFUL LOSING SOMEONE TO THE HANDS OF ETERNITY.
YET THE FLAME OF HIS MEMORY STILL BURNS BRIGHTLY IN MY HEART AND MIND AFTER ALL THESE YEARS.
THE WHEEL OF LIFE TURNS STILL, KUBIN.
IT WAS MEANT TO BE LIKE THAT.
I FELT THE SAME WAY WHEN DEAR BANTUGAN LEFT THIS WORLD AND JOINED THE DIVINITIES.
IF....IF THE GODS MEANT LIFE TO BE SO....
...THEN HOW I WISH I COULD TURN JUST ONE PLEASANT MOMENT...INTO SOMETHING THAT WOULD LAST FOREVER.
I GREATLY WISH IT TO BE SO.
THIS GROWING SADNESS WITHIN ME IS OVERWHELMING, DATIMBANG.
FOR DESTINY DOES NOT SEEM TO GRANT ME PEACE OF MIND.
YOU ARE AWARE, OF COURSE, THAT IT WOULD BE A GREAT LOSS IF YOU DECIDE TO LEAVE US.
THINK HARD.
WE ARE ABOUT TO TRAVEL TEN CENTURIES INTO THE FUTURE, KUBIN.

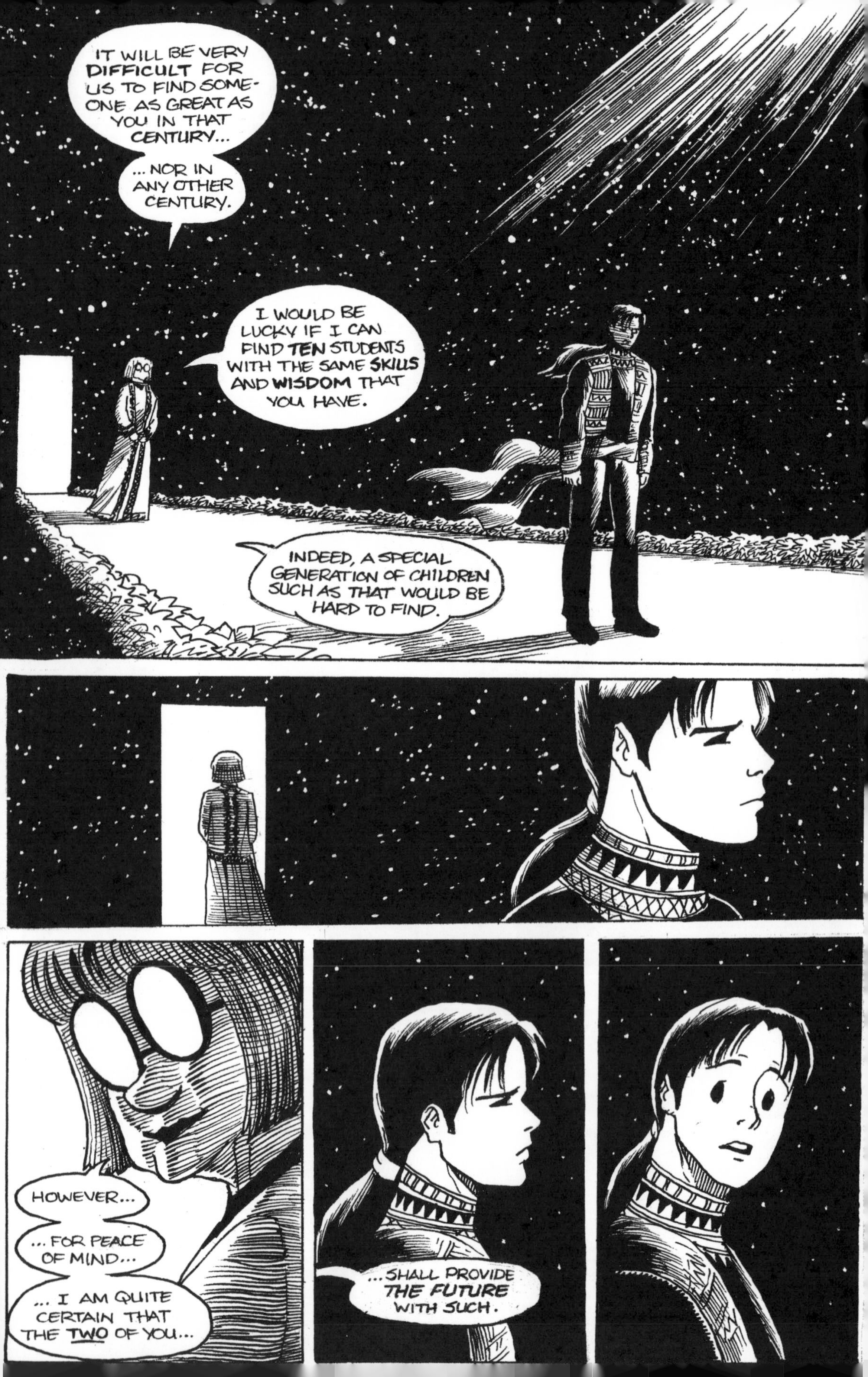

IT WILL BE VERY DIFFICULT FOR US TO FIND SOMEONE AS GREAT AS YOU IN THAT CENTURY...
...NOR IN ANY OTHER CENTURY.
I WOULD BE LUCKY IF I CAN FIND TEN STUDENTS WITH THE SAME SKILLS AND WISDOM THAT YOU HAVE.
INDEED, A SPECIAL GENERATION OF CHILDREN SUCH AS THAT WOULD BE HARD TO FIND.
HOWEVER...
...FOR PEACE OF MIND...
... I AM QUITE CERTAIN THAT THE TWO OF YOU...
...SHALL PROVIDE THE FUTURE WITH SUCH.

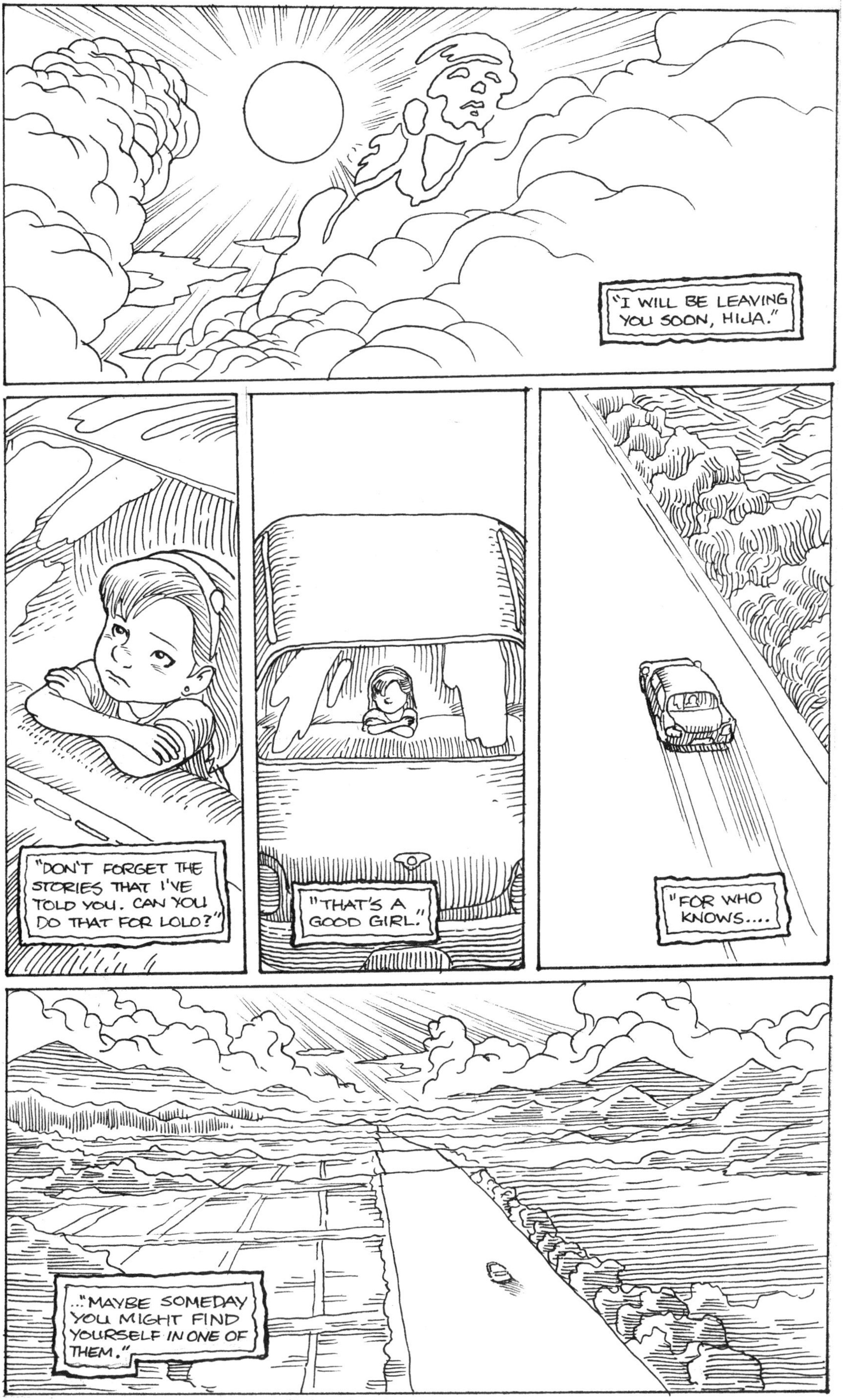
"I WILL BE LEAVING YOU SOON, HIJA."
"DON'T FORGET THE STORIES THAT I'VE TOLD YOU. CAN YOU DO THAT FOR LOLO?"
"THAT'S A GOOD GIRL."
"FOR WHO KNOWS....
..."MAYBE SOMEDAY YOU MIGHT FIND YOURSELF IN ONE OF THEM."

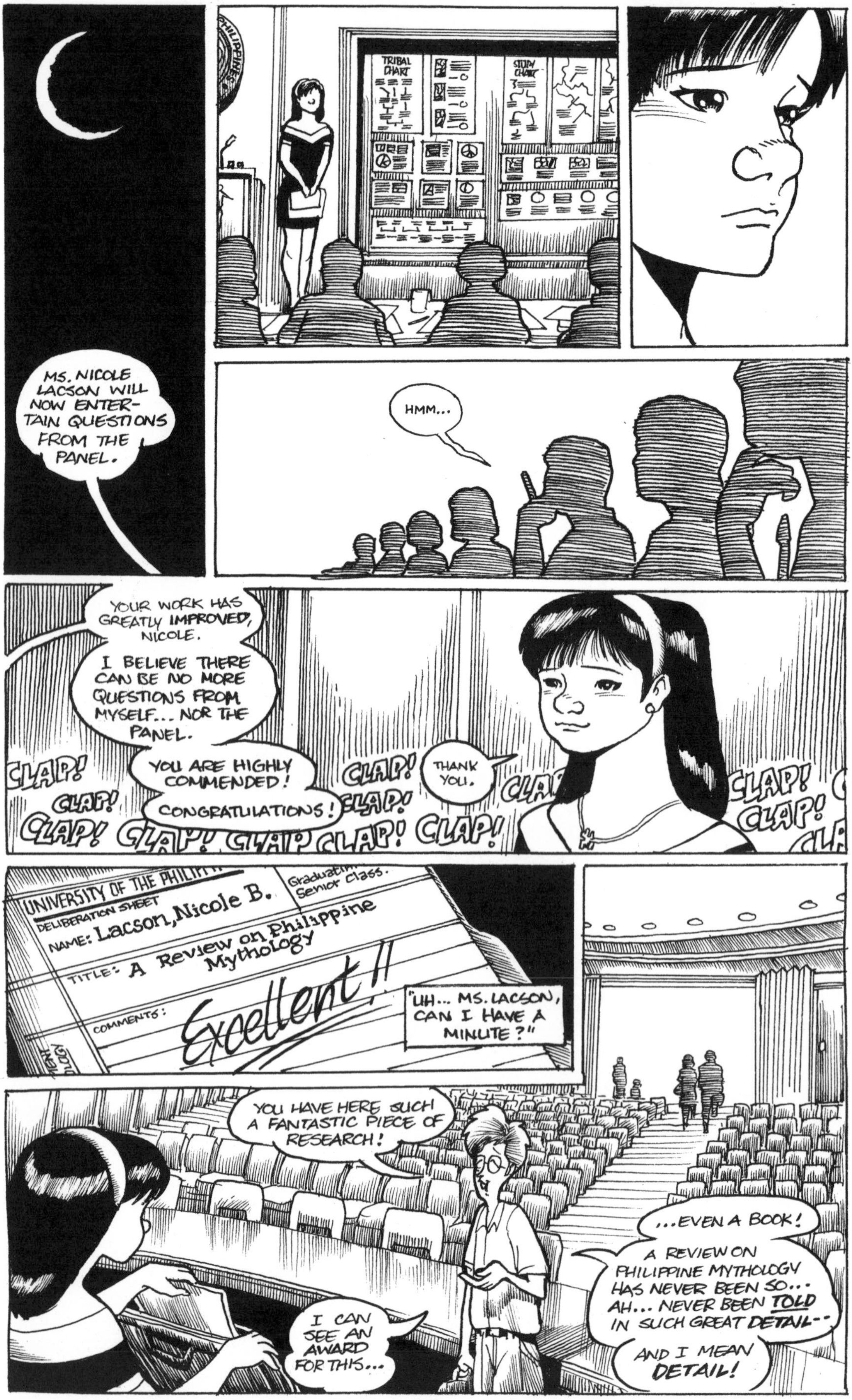
TRIBAL CHART
STORY CHART
MS. NICOLE LACSON WILL NOW ENTERTAIN QUESTIONS FROM THE PANEL.
HMM...
YOUR WORK HAS GREATLY IMPROVED, NICOLE.
I BELIEVE THERE CAN BE NO MORE QUESTIONS FROM MYSELF... NOR THE PANEL.
YOU ARE HIGHLY COMMENDED!
CONGRATULATIONS!
THANK YOU.
CLAP! CLAP! CLAP! CLAP! CLAP! CLAP! CLAP! CLAP! CLAP! CLAP! CLAP!
UNIVERSITY OF THE PHILI
DELIBERATION SHEET
Graduating Senior Class.
NAME: Lacson, Nicole B.
TITLE: A Review on Philippine Mythology
COMMENTS: Excellent!!
"UH... MS. LACSON, CAN I HAVE A MINUTE?"
YOU HAVE HERE SUCH A FANTASTIC PIECE OF RESEARCH!
I CAN SEE AN AWARD FOR THIS...
...EVEN A BOOK!
A REVIEW ON PHILIPPINE MYTHOLOGY HAS NEVER BEEN SO... AH... NEVER BEEN TOLD IN SUCH GREAT DETAIL--
AND I MEAN DETAIL!

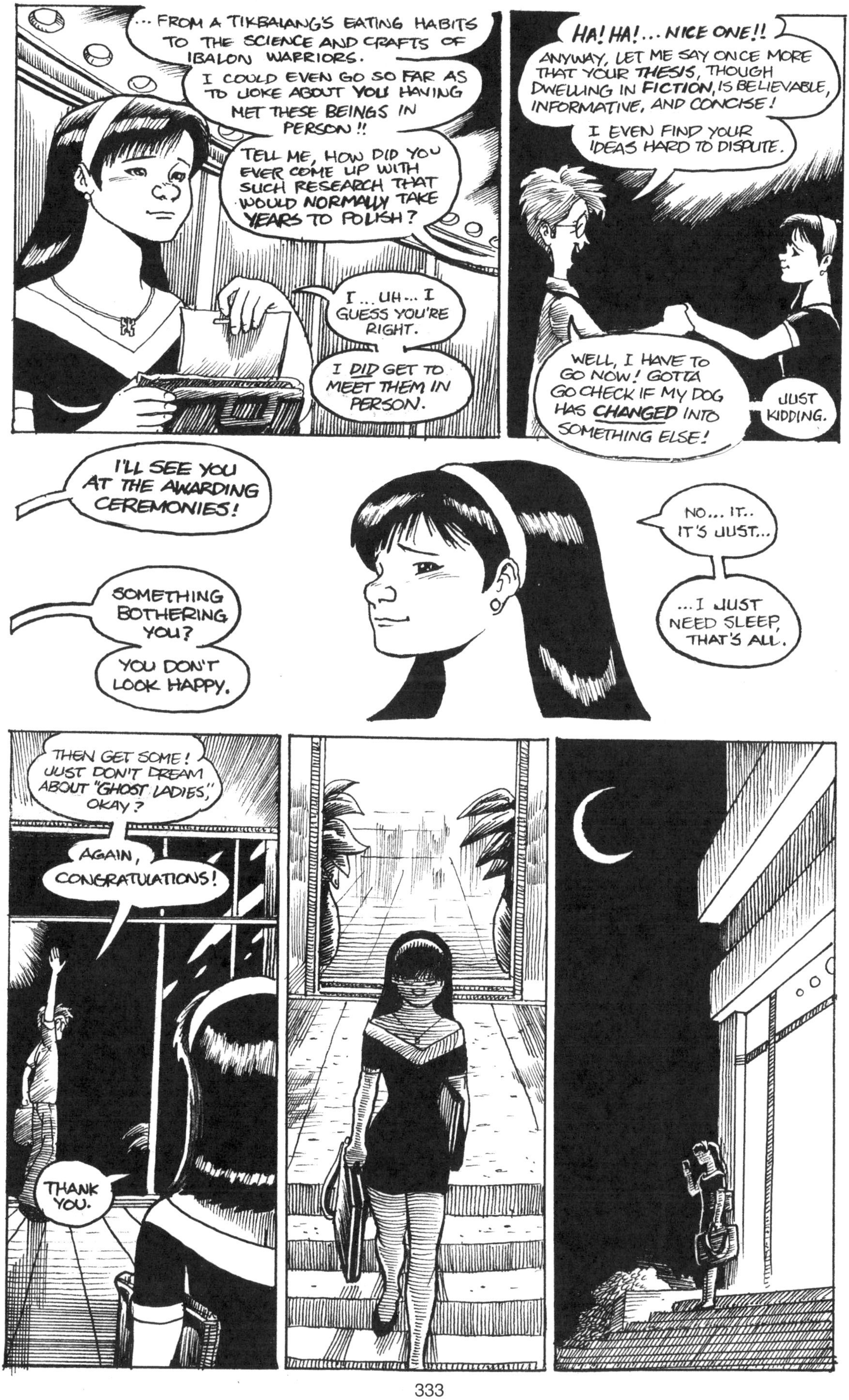
... FROM A TIKBALANG'S EATING HABITS TO THE SCIENCE AND CRAFTS OF IBALON WARRIORS.
I COULD EVEN GO SO FAR AS TO JOKE ABOUT YOU HAVING MET THESE BEINGS IN PERSON!!
TELL ME, HOW DID YOU EVER COME UP WITH SUCH RESEARCH THAT WOULD NORMALLY TAKE YEARS TO POLISH?
I... UH... I GUESS YOU'RE RIGHT.
I DID GET TO MEET THEM IN PERSON.
HA! HA!... NICE ONE!!
ANYWAY, LET ME SAY ONCE MORE THAT YOUR THESIS, THOUGH DWELLING IN FICTION, IS BELIEVABLE, INFORMATIVE, AND CONCISE!
I EVEN FIND YOUR IDEAS HARD TO DISPUTE.
WELL, I HAVE TO GO NOW! GOTTA GO CHECK IF MY DOG HAS CHANGED INTO SOMETHING ELSE!
JUST KIDDING.
I'LL SEE YOU AT THE AWARDING CEREMONIES!
SOMETHING BOTHERING YOU?
YOU DON'T LOOK HAPPY.
NO... IT.. IT'S JUST...
...I JUST NEED SLEEP, THAT'S ALL.
THEN GET SOME! JUST DON'T DREAM ABOUT "GHOST LADIES," OKAY?
AGAIN, CONGRATULATIONS!
THANK YOU.

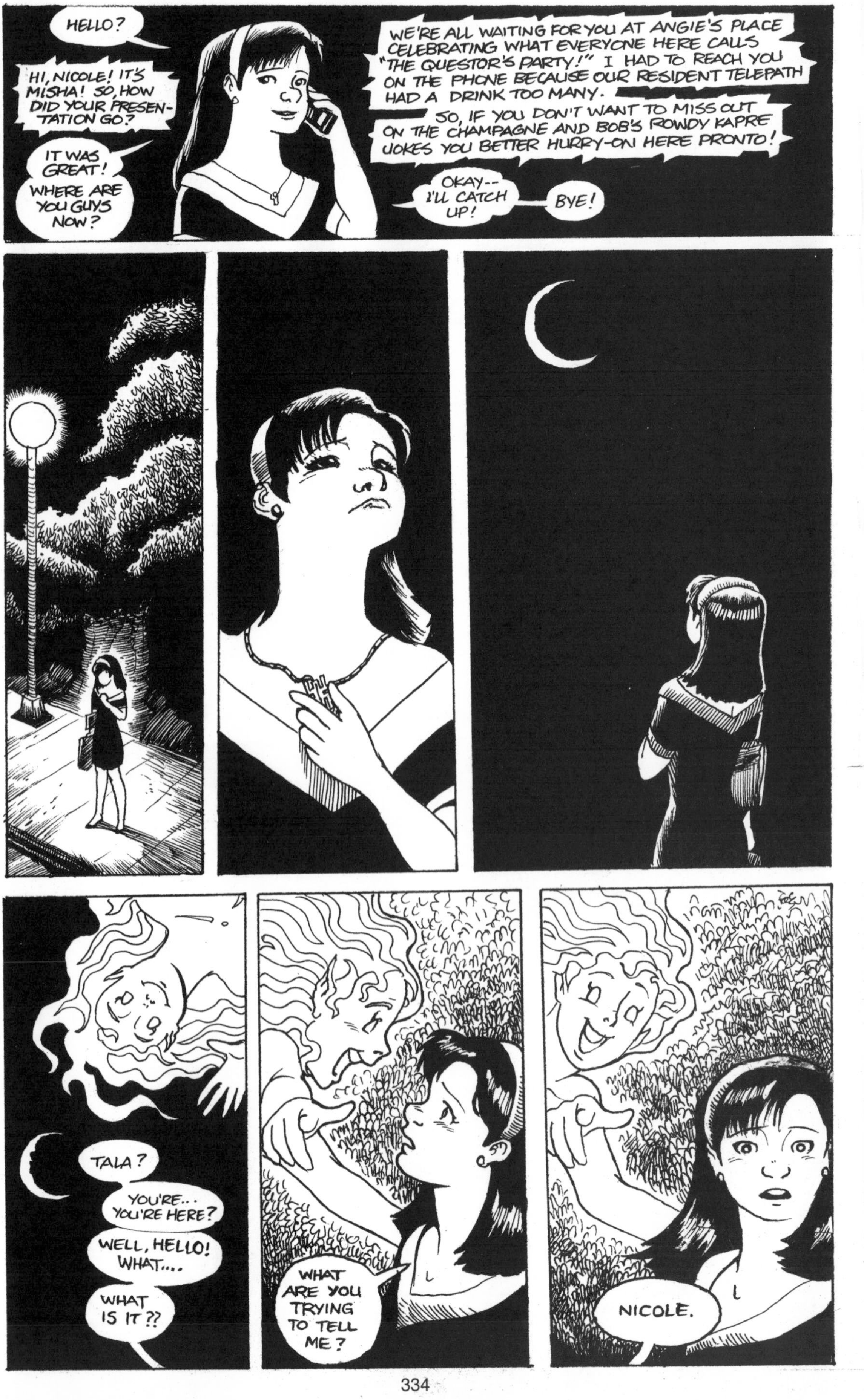
HELLO?
HI, NICOLE! IT'S MISHA! SO, HOW DID YOUR PRESENTATION GO?
IT WAS GREAT!
WHERE ARE YOU GUYS NOW?
WE'RE ALL WAITING FOR YOU AT ANGIE'S PLACE CELEBRATING WHAT EVERYONE HERE CALLS "THE QUESTOR'S PARTY!" I HAD TO REACH YOU ON THE PHONE BECAUSE OUR RESIDENT TELEPATH HAD A DRINK TOO MANY.
SO, IF YOU DON'T WANT TO MISS OUT ON THE CHAMPAGNE AND BOB'S ROWDY KAPRE JOKES YOU BETTER HURRY-ON HERE PRONTO!
OKAY-- I'LL CATCH UP!
BYE!
TALA?
YOU'RE... YOU'RE HERE?
WELL, HELLO! WHAT....
WHAT IS IT??
WHAT ARE YOU TRYING TO TELL ME?
NICOLE.

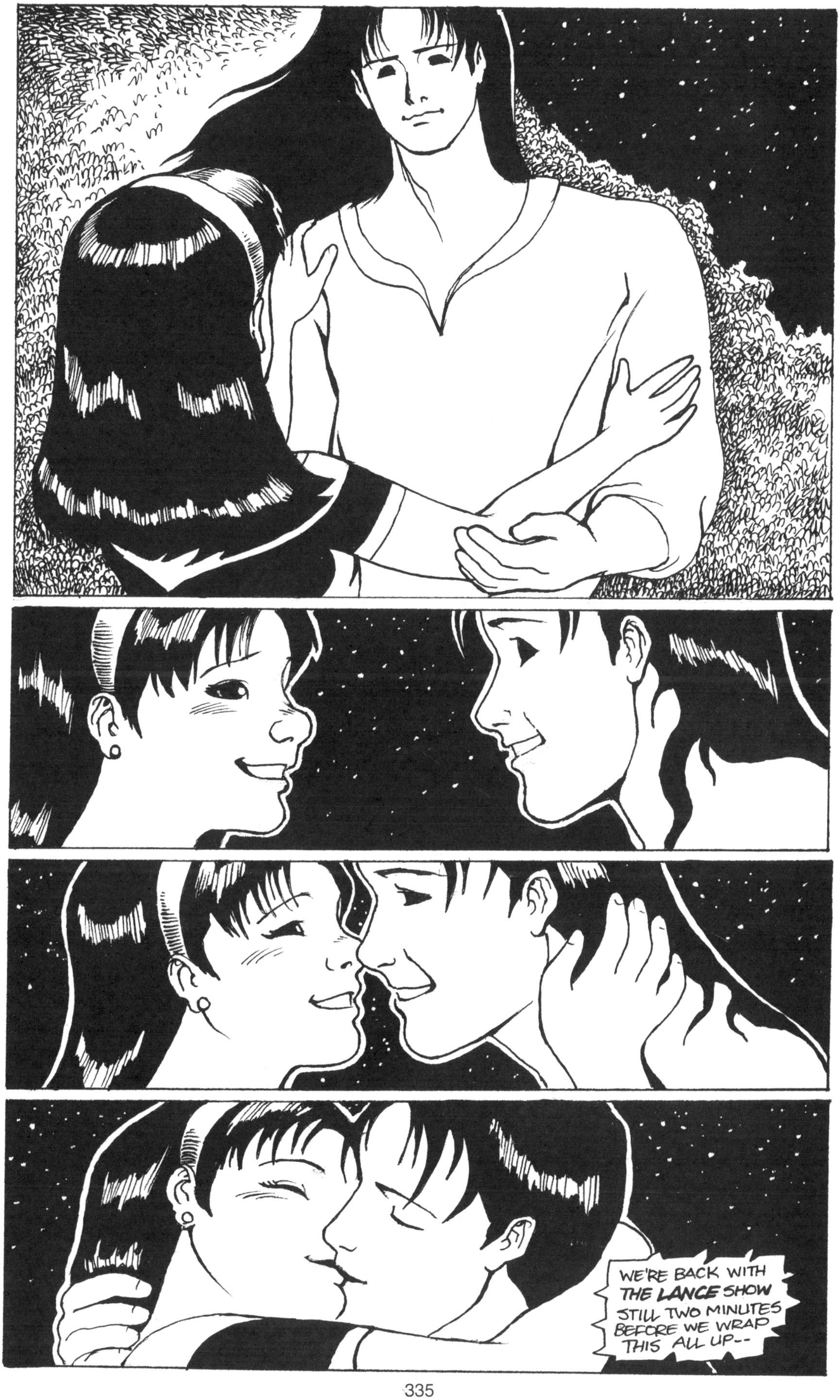
WE'RE BACK WITH THE LANCE SHOW STILL TWO MINUTES BEFORE WE WRAP THIS ALL UP--

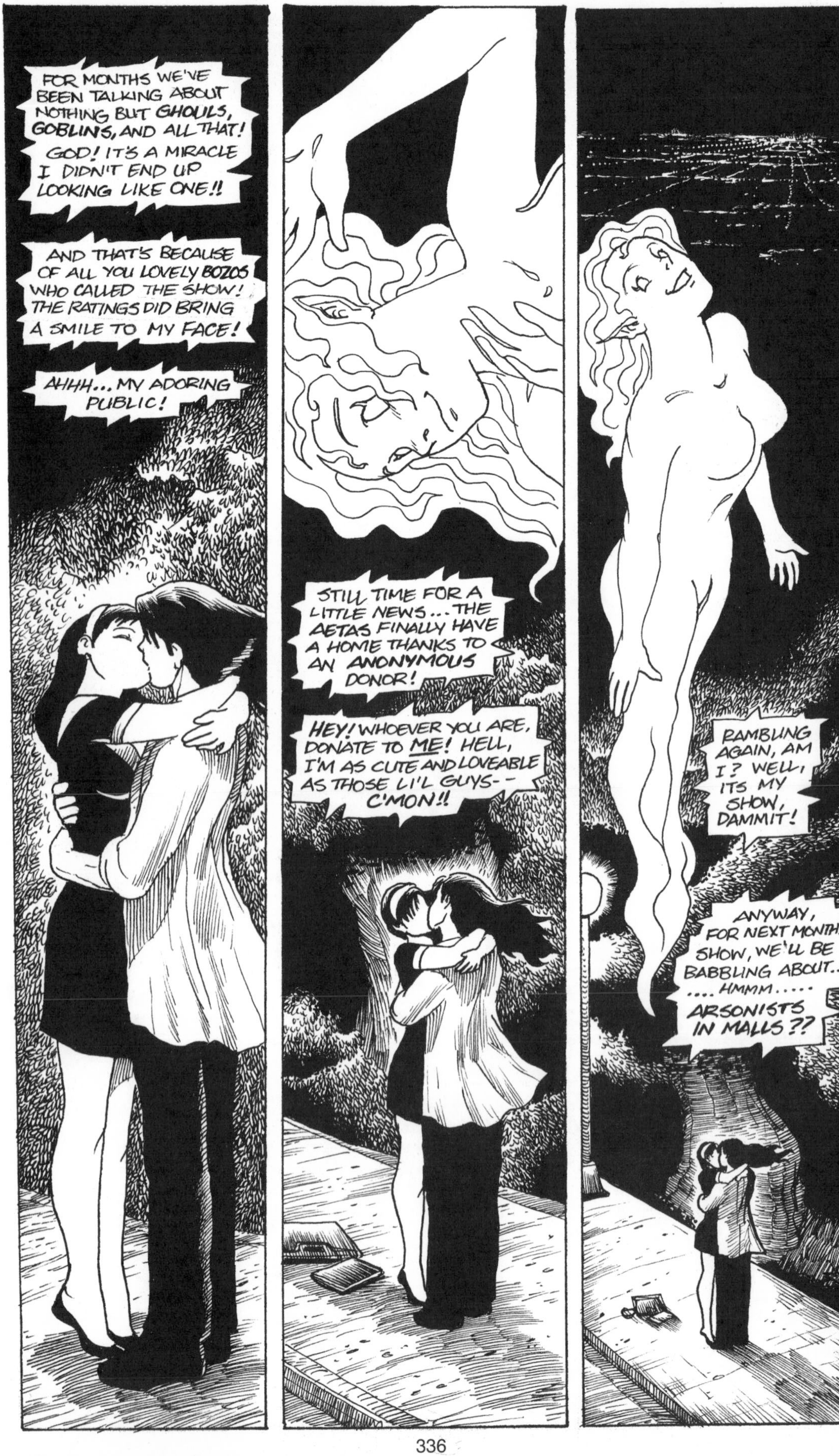
FOR MONTHS WE'VE BEEN TALKING ABOUT NOTHING BUT GHOULS, GOBLINS, AND ALL THAT!
GOD! IT'S A MIRACLE I DIDN'T END UP LOOKING LIKE ONE!!
AND THAT'S BECAUSE OF ALL YOU LOVELY BOZOS WHO CALLED THE SHOW! THE RATINGS DID BRING A SMILE TO MY FACE!
AHHH... MY ADORING PUBLIC!
STILL TIME FOR A LITTLE NEWS... THE AETAS FINALLY HAVE A HOME THANKS TO AN ANONYMOUS DONOR!
HEY! WHOEVER YOU ARE, DONATE TO ME! HELL, I'M AS CUTE AND LOVEABLE AS THOSE LI'L GUYS-- C'MON!!
RAMBLING AGAIN, AM I? WELL, ITS MY SHOW, DAMMIT!
ANYWAY, FOR NEXT MONTH'S SHOW, WE'LL BE BABBLING ABOUT... ....HMMM..... ARSONISTS IN MALLS??

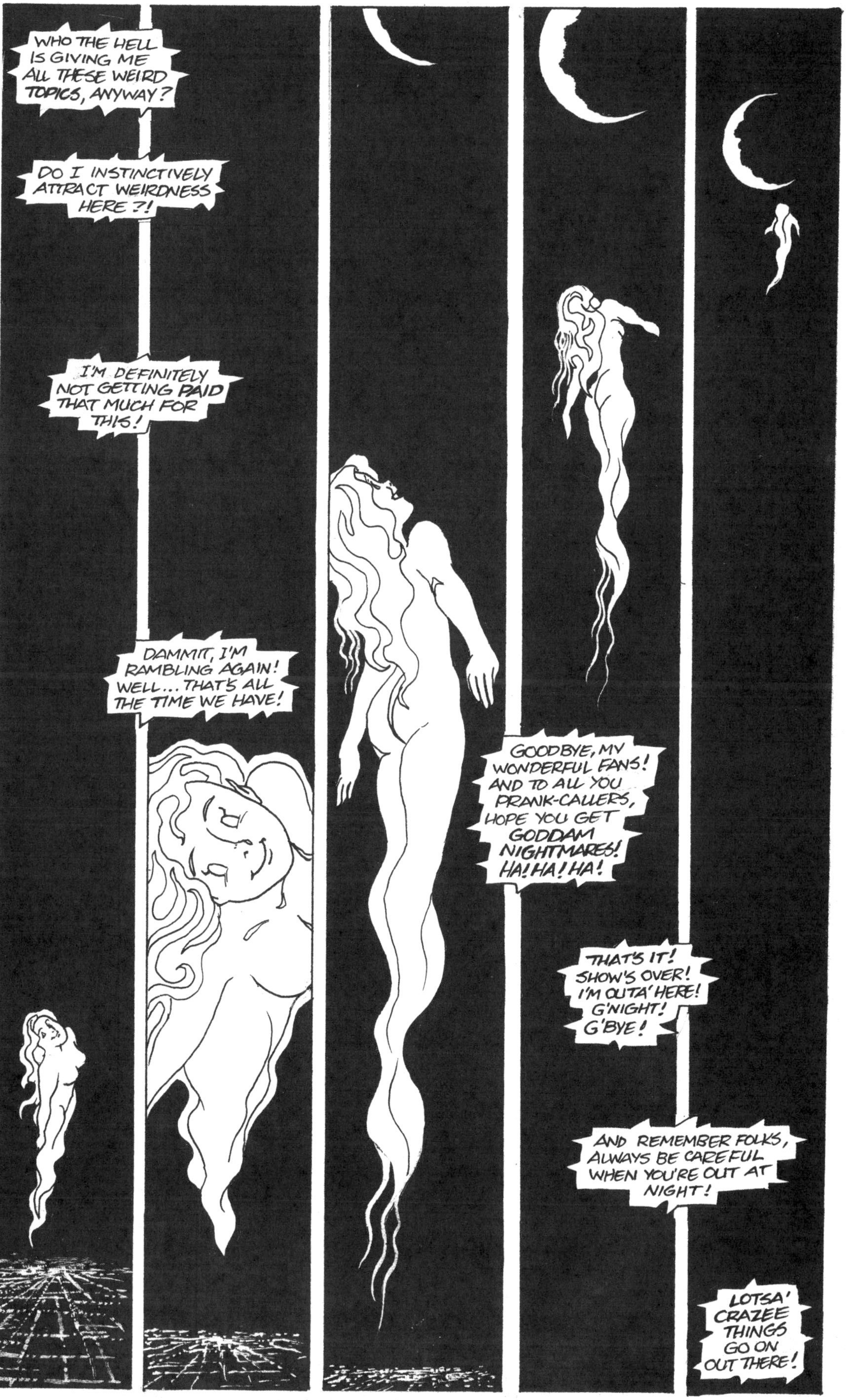
WHO THE HELL IS GIVING ME ALL THESE WEIRD TOPICS, ANYWAY?
DO I INSTINCTIVELY ATTRACT WEIRDNESS HERE?!
I'M DEFINITELY NOT GETTING PAID THAT MUCH FOR THIS!
DAMMIT, I'M RAMBLING AGAIN! WELL... THAT'S ALL THE TIME WE HAVE!
GOODBYE, MY WONDERFUL FANS! AND TO ALL YOU PRANK-CALLERS, HOPE YOU GET GODDAM NIGHTMARES! HA! HA! HA!
THAT'S IT! SHOW'S OVER! I'M OUTA' HERE! G'NIGHT! G'BYE!
AND REMEMBER FOLKS, ALWAYS BE CAREFUL WHEN YOU'RE OUT AT NIGHT!
LOTSA' CRAZEE THINGS GO ON OUT THERE!

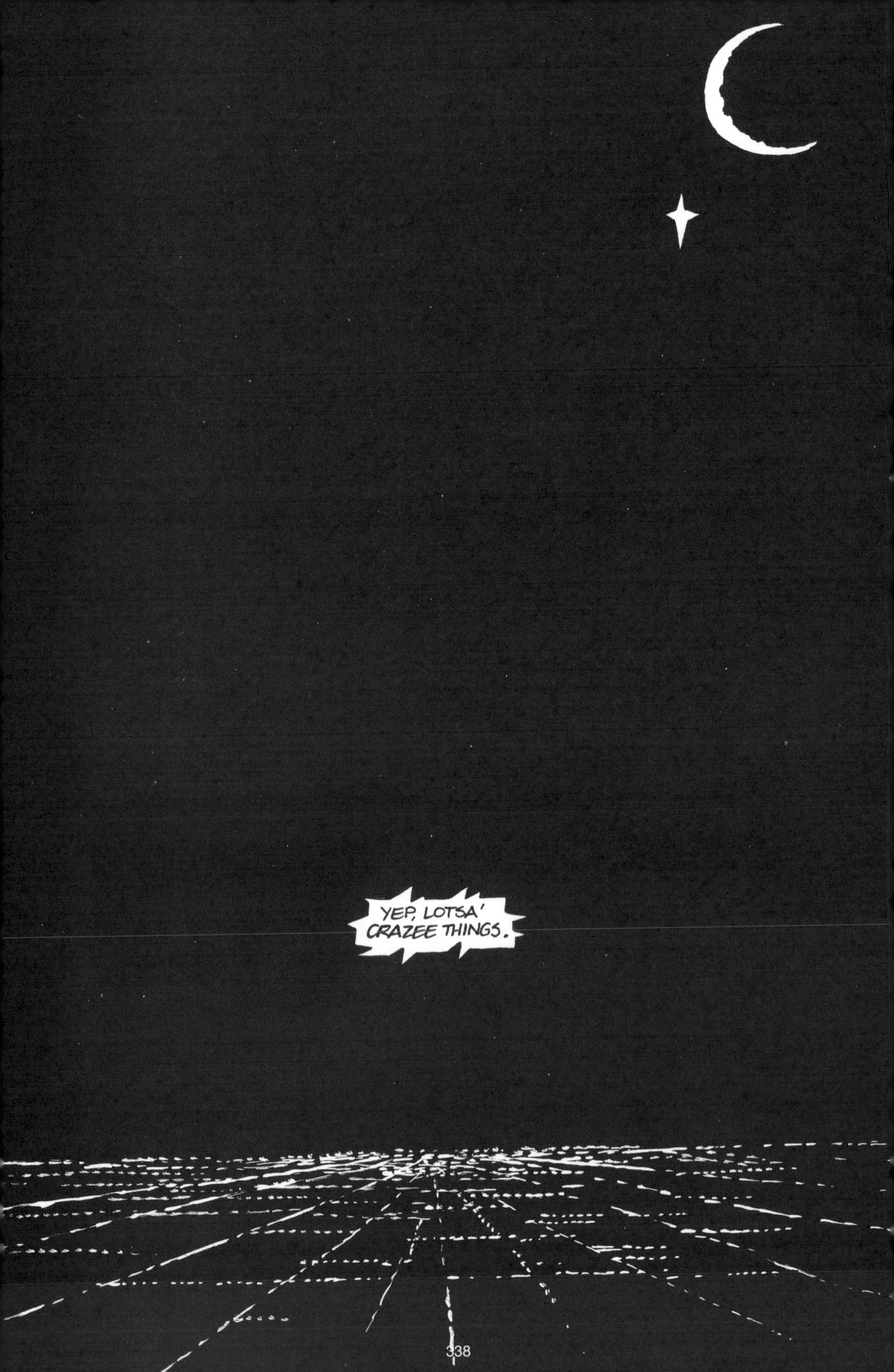
YEP, LOTSA' CRAZEE THINGS.

AFTERWORD

Since this is the afterword, you are probably on a pretty big high right now after just having finished reading (or re-reading, which wouldn't surprise me) The Mythology Class. I'll bet you feel a connection to these Philippine myths that you have either never felt before or has waned over the years. That is the magic of this modern classic that Arnold Arre has crafted. Just like the mythology it references, this wonderful graphic novel replaces the sense of dread our vast and mysterious world often instills in us with a feeling of wonder and awe. Not only that, like the best myths, it also inspires people to be better, to strive to do more, to believe that the unknown and the mysterious can not only be overcome, but harnessed for the benefit of all.

I think that it is no coincidence that many of the successful Philippine independent comics today mix in Philippine mythology with other genres like crime or sci-fi, the way American comics have superheros as the dominant genre, with other genres being fused to it to gain a foothold in the market. I believe that The Mythology Class, when it was first released at the start of the millennium, is the comic that inspired most of the major local comic creators today and opened the eyes of Filipino comic readers to the possibilities of Philippine mythology as a modern storytelling genre. This was the book that made many young aspiring artists and writers back in the day go, "Whoa! I wanna make comics as awesome as this!"

And yet, while he may have influenced a new generation of comic creators in a country that is known for its world-class comic artistry, for my money no other comic creator has come close to matching Arnold in pure skill, talent, and heart. In a way, Arnold is a legendary hero himself, especially to comic creators and fans. I have personally seen how inhumanly fast he is at drawing. He completed one of his 300-page graphic novels in just around three months. Another time, he drew a full issue for me in half the time it took a team of three artists to do the same. And yet, even with his speed, the quality of his work is unparalleled. Backgrounds are intricate when they need to be, the paneling and layout experimental when called for, but even close ups and simple facial expressions overflow with emotion with just a few simple lines. It is clear that no stroke is ever wasted with Arnold and every one serves the purpose of telling the story. As a writer, he has the same discipline, as he is able to balance epic plotting and sweeping action with sharp, natural sounding dialogue that fleshes out characters with just a line or two. This is why Arnold serves as a shining example of what all comic artists, both local and foreign, should strive to be.

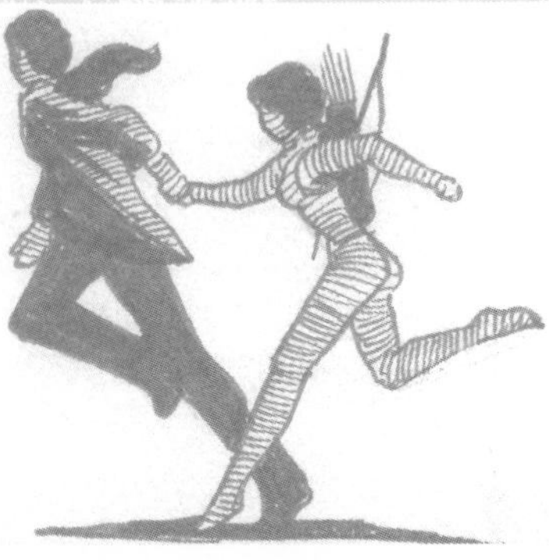

The Mythology Class was the first local comic I read after college. It was the comic that reignited my faith in the local comics industry, and made me believe that we could make great comics in the Philippines. So yes, I was one of those "I wanna make comics as awesome as this!" people.

I was lucky enough to meet Arnold in 2005 when we happened to be the only Filipinos at a Korean Comics convention. I was already a fan, but then we became friends. Shortly after, we became collaborators, and now I am also his publisher. But the reason I am all these things is because I was a fan first and still am. The reason I want to publish Arnold's books is because I personally just want Arnold to keep making comics and I want as many people as possible to read his works. That's what we do for legendary heroes, isn't it? We spread the word to make their legend grow. And it's an honor to be able to spread this particular legend far and wide.

The Mythology Class has shown us that epic stories are not only there to inspire us from afar, but they are something we can participate in and contribute to. Legendary heroes are not only pillars of virtue to model ourselves after, but mentors and friends who continue to work with new blood as their stories continue. So I hope reading The Mythology Class has inspired you to either read more local comics (especially more of Arnold's stuff, and I'm not just saying that because I'm his publisher) or to try to create comics of your own down the line. And remember that if you do take up the torch (or the kampilan, if you will), just like Nicole and her friends did to continue the legacy of the legendary heroes, Arnold will be right there with us, guiding us, and continuing to push boundaries, just as Kubin and Sulayman and the other heroes of old did for the class.

So are you ready to be part of this ongoing legend? I know I am.

JAMIE BAUTISTA
Alabang, October 31 2014

SINCEREST THANKS TO...

My family–Leonardo & Nancy Arre, Leslie & Aurora Bauzon,
Lenn, Ate Ruby, Gian, Jing, Gladys, Calvin, Inches,
Jamie & Iyay Bautista and Nautilus Comics, Gerry & Ilyn Alanguilan,
Karen Kunawicz, Marco Dimaano, Leinil & Yai Yu, Manix Abrera,
Erwin Romulo and Esquire Philippines, Jerrold Tarog, Marie Jamora,
Quark Henares, Yvette Tan, Ramon de Veyra, Buddy & Earnest Zabala,
Gang Badoy & Jay Capati of Rock Ed Philippines, Luis Katigbak, Emil and
Aimee Flores, Sherry Baet-Zamar, Ariel Atienza, Lyndon Gregorio, and
the entire KOMIKON Team, Ani Almario-David, friends, fellow artists...
and YOU for being part of the class.

ABOUT THE AUTHOR

 Arnold Arre lives in Quezon City with his wife, Cynthia, and their marmalade cat. He's been drawing & writing comics for more than 20 years and is also currently honing his skills as an animator.

Visit www.arnold-arre.com

Published by Tuttle Publishing, an imprint of Periplus Editions (HK) Ltd.

www.tuttlepublishing.com

Library of Congress Cataloging-in-Publication Data is in process.

ISBN: 978-0-8048-5542-6

Distributed by

North America, Latin America & Europe
Tuttle Publishing
364 Innovation Drive,
North Clarendon,
VT 05759-9436, USA
Tel: 1 (802) 773 8930;
Fax: 1 (802) 773 6993
info@tuttlepublishing.com
www.tuttlepublishing.com

Asia Pacific
Berkeley Books Pte. Ltd.
3 Kallang Sector #04-01
Singapore 349278
Tel: (65) 67412178
Fax: (65) 67412179
inquiries@periplus.com.sg
www.tuttlepublishing.com

First edition
25 24 23 22   5 4 3 2 1

Printed in Singapore   2203TP

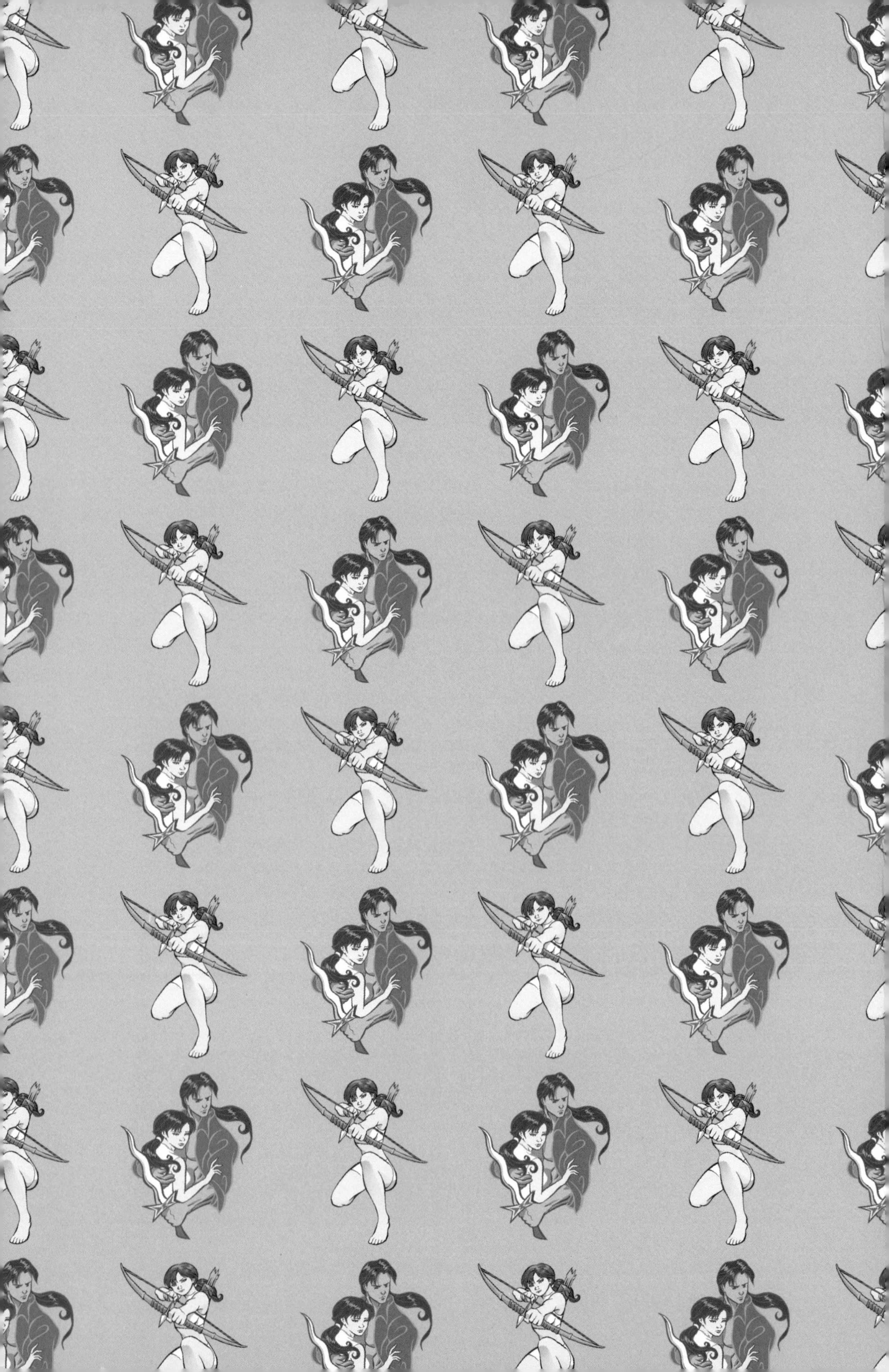